What every Doctor needs:

☑ *A great bedside manner!*

Temperature Rising

What every Doctor doesn't need:

☑ *The quintessential male chauvinist as a patient.*

☑ *A handsome malpractice lawyer with a personal grudge.*

☑ *A sexy male housekeeper with a private agenda.*

The *Doctors'* Temperatures are rising!

Relive the romance . . .

Three complete novels by your favorite authors!

About the Authors

JoAnn Ross—Author of forty-two novels, JoAnn wrote her first story—a romance about two star-crossed mallard ducks—when she was seven years old. Now, she has more than eight million copies of her books in print and her novels are favorites with readers around the world. JoAnn married her high school sweetheart—twice—and makes her home in Phoenix, Arizona.

Tess Gerritsen—A premier author of romantic and mainstream suspense novels, Tess is also a scriptwriter for network and cable television, as well as for feature films. A physician, she now writes full-time out of her home on the coast of Maine, where she lives with her husband and two sons.

Jacqueline Diamond—Author of a score of romance novels as well as two hardcover suspense titles. A news reporter and editor for over a decade, Jacqueline currently writes a weekly television column for Associated Press, interviewing such stars as Faye Dunaway, Billy Dee Williams and Raquel Welch. Jacqueline lives in California with her husband and son.

Temperature Rising

JoAnn Ross
Tess Gerritsen
Jacqueline Diamond

Harlequin Books

TORONTO • NEW YORK • LONDON
AMSTERDAM • PARIS • SYDNEY • HAMBURG
STOCKHOLM • ATHENS • TOKYO • MILAN
MADRID • WARSAW • BUDAPEST • AUCKLAND

HARLEQUIN BOOKS

by Request—Temperature Rising

Copyright © 1994 by Harlequin Enterprises B.V.

ISBN 0-373-20099-4

The publisher acknowledges the copyright holders of the individual works as follows:
LOVE THY NEIGHBOR
Copyright © 1985 by JoAnn Ross
UNDER THE KNIFE
Copyright © 1990 by Terry Gerritsen
AN UNEXPECTED MAN
Copyright © 1987 by Jackie Hyman

This edition published by arrangement with Harlequin Enterprises B. V.

® and TM are trademarks of the publisher. Trademarks indicated with ® are registered in the United States Patent and Trademark Office, the Canadian Trade Marks Office and in other countries.

Printed in U.S.A.

CONTENTS

What Dr. Laurel Britton doesn't need:

☑ *The quintessential male chauvinist as a patient.*

LOVE THY NEIGHBOR

JoAnn Ross

To Lori Copeland,
for always being there when I need her
and for making me laugh.
Here's lookin' at you, kid.

1

SHE'D DONE IT! Dr. Laurel Britton, the ex-Mrs. Geoffrey Britton, had successfully moved her household, consisting of one four-year-old Siamese cat, one seven-year-old boy and one thirty-year-old physician all the way from Seattle, Washington to Phoenix, Arizona, without a single mishap. Except for a burst radiator hose, and that could have happened to anyone. Even Geoffrey.

Unfortunately, the unscheduled stop in Indio, California was the reason for Laurel's arrival in a strange town, two days behind her furniture. The long Veterans Day holiday only complicated matters, but after a disgusting display of feminine wheedling, something she personally detested, as well as the promise of holiday overtime, she'd persuaded the moving company to deliver her furniture. Due to start first thing tomorrow as the newest physician at the Phoenix Sports Medicine Clinic, the last thing she needed was all her worldly possessions locked up in a warehouse somewhere across the sprawling desert city. The utility company, regrettably, had proved less helpful and so far no one had shown up to turn on her electricity or her water.

At least the movers were nearly finished. According to her checklist, the only piece of furniture left on the truck was her piano. She watched as the younger of the two men bent to check the canvas strap that held the ancient upright on the dolly.

"Is this an antique?"

Laurel smiled, remembering how long it had taken to refinish the two-hundred-dollar instrument. She and Geoffrey had bought it at a flea market, the expense far too extravagant for two medical students, but she'd fallen in love with it at first sight, and in those days Geoffrey had occasionally found her enthusiasm a delight and not an embarrassment.

"No," she murmured, "it's just very old."

"My gram has one kinda like this. She's got it covered with one of those lacy doily things and tons of pictures of all the relatives."

"I keep pictures on mine, too," she offered, thinking to herself that only photos of Danny remained these days.

"Yeah, I guess everyone does that with pianos all right," he agreed cheerfully, looking back over his shoulder. "Ready, Mike?"

The only response from the man at the other end of the piano was a grunt, which Laurel determined must be a yes since the piano started to make its way down the sloping ramp. She breathed a sigh of relief, drawing a firm, straight line through the listing on her inventory.

Just as she was congratulating herself on having passed her first test in desert survival, an apparition about four feet tall appeared around the corner of the orange-and-black moving van. In place of its face was the huge single eye of a blue swimming mask and a snorkel extended upward from where a mouth should have been. Long black rubber flippers flapped noisily against the sidewalk.

"I'm all ready to go swimming, Mom."

Laurel's eyes scanned the immediate vicinity. "Danny, where is Circe? Aren't you supposed to be watching her?"

No sooner had the question escaped her lips than she heard a strident yowl, the high sound peculiar to Siamese cats. That feline complaint was directly followed by a series of rumbling barks that undoubtedly registered on Richter scales all over the state.

"Danny, catch her!"

Laurel's warning came too late. A flash of creamy fur darted between her legs, followed immediately by one far larger, the color of dark golden caramel. The enormous animal pursuing her fleeing cat plowed into Laurel, knocking her off her feet, and as Circe made a beeline for the open moving van, Laurel opened her mouth to shout out a warning.

From that point, things appeared to happen in slow motion. Sprawled on the blistering hot sidewalk, Laurel watched helplessly as her frightened cat sprang through the air, landing with feline grace on all fours atop the upright piano. The dog was slower, but still swifter than the mover as he rammed into the back of the man's knees. With a colorful series of oaths, the young man fell off the ramp, and to Laurel's fascination her piano rolled down the ramp onto the sidewalk, continuing unrestrained down the hill, headed directly for a jet-black Ferrari parked at the curb. Circe was still riding shotgun, screaming bloody murder at the top of her lungs, her high Siamese yowls shattering the sultry morning air.

"Mom, it's going to hit that car!"

"Of course it's not," Laurel assured her son, jumping to her feet to chase down her runaway piano. "When it hits that speed bump, it'll have to stop."

The young mover was still cursing a blue streak, his epithets competing with Circe's wild howling and the huge furry dog's enthusiastic barking. Laurel had almost caught up with the dolly when it hit the bump in the asphalt, flinging Circe through the air in a long, high arc. The cat landed spread-eagle on the roof of the sports car, her long talons making a screeching sound against the metal top like fingernails on a chalkboard.

Laurel's prediction proved false as the speed bump only caused the dolly to slow on its inevitable collision with the Ferrari. She was a mere six inches away, her hands outstretched, when the sound of crunching metal blended with the shattering of wood. Laurel stopped in her tracks, staring at the pile of mahogany that was once her beloved piano.

"What in the hell is going on out here? World War III?"

The loud, masculine shout had her spinning around to view a man striding furiously toward her. He was clad simply in a pair of faded cutoffs, worn low on the hips. His sun-streaked blond hair was tousled, and from the blistering expression on his face, Laurel decided he probably wasn't from the local welcoming committee.

"What do you people think you're doing?"

Before Laurel could answer, his green eyes cut to the rumpled fender of the Ferrari.

"Damn."

He raked his fingers through his hair, ruffling it even further as he rolled his eyes toward the blue desert sky. "Wasn't yesterday's game enough? Do you have to add insult to injury?"

Dropping almost gingerly to his knees, he ran his fingertips over the crumpled metal. "Why me? Of all the houses on all the streets in Phoenix, why do I get Laurel and Hardy for neighbors?"

"Laurel and Danny," Laurel corrected with vastly more calm than she was feeling at the moment.

His expression, as he dragged his rueful gaze from his car, was blank. "What?"

"Laurel Britton," she offered, holding out her hand in what she hoped he'd take as a conciliatory gesture. "And my son's name is Danny."

"You have a son?"

For the first time since he'd come storming out there, the man's interest turned to Laurel. She was definitely not the teenager he'd taken her for at first glance, Nick McGraw determined. His appraising green gaze moved from the top of her head, tracing every curve and plane, down to her sneaker-clad feet, the journey taking far longer on the way back to her brown eyes. No, this pleasantly disheveled individual was definitely all woman, albeit too slender for his taste. Nick sought an appropriate word and came up with willowy. That fit, he decided, his expert eye taking another slow, leisurely tour of her body.

Laurel had had her share of professional athletes as patients—tennis, baseball, basketball players—all men in peak physical condition, their bodies hard and well toned. But this man, whose gaze seemed to be searing through the thin cotton of her T-shirt, was different. From his challenging stance, to the rock-hard strength of his coppery chest, to the muscled columns of his legs, he was almost too rawly masculine.

She wanted to push back the dark chestnut hair that was clinging in damp strands to her forehead, but withheld the impulse, finding it somehow too feminine a gesture to make before this stranger who was definitely all male.

His gaze slid to Danny, who'd managed to corral Circe and was holding the cat against his chest, his eyes wide blue saucers behind his swim mask.

"So the midget from the Black Lagoon is yours. You don't look that old. What were you, a child bride?" It wasn't meant as a compliment to her youthful looks. The mockery in his voice was unmistakable.

"The *midget* is a seven-year-old boy." Laurel laced her tone with acid sarcasm. "And I don't see that my age when I married is any of your business."

His answering smile was deliberately provocative, meant to annoy. "Sorry, it's just difficult to believe a grown woman could behave so irresponsibly. I hope for the safety of the neighborhood, your husband keeps you on a tight leash."

Laurel pulled herself up to her full height of five-foot-six. "I beg your pardon?"

"Of course you do," he countered. "And not only do you owe me an apology, don't you think it's time to let me in on what you're going to do about fixing my car?" He looked down at her, his crossed-arm pose exuding arrogance.

As furious as Laurel was becoming, knowing the horrible man was baiting her every step of the way, she also accepted the fact that her piano had careered into his car. Surely her insurance would cover the cost of repairs. She opened her mouth to tell him that when a huge golden ball of fur galloped up, the wide banner of his tail wagging happily, his long red tongue hanging out.

"That animal is yours?" She stared as the man absently patted the beast atop its massive head.

"This *animal* is a registered golden retriever," he corrected. "And yes, Rowdy belongs to me."

Laurel's gaze moved slowly from the dog to the pieces of wood and wire that had once been her beloved piano. Why should she pay anything to fix his car when his beast had caused all the problems in the first place?

"I'd say you're a little confused," she stated finally. "The question here is what are you going to do about my piano?"

One tawny blond brow climbed his forehead before crashing down to join the other. "Lady, you're not only a menace, you're downright certifiable! Why should I do anything about your piano? After all, my car was parked at the curb, minding its own business, when your battered old hunk of wood attacked it."

"After your monster attacked Circe!"

"Circe?"

"My cat." She jerked her head in the direction of the Siamese, whose creamy fur was still standing on end, bristling as if caught in an electric storm.

He ran an exploratory finger over the roof of his car. "That explains this bit of vandalism. Claws." His glance flicked rapierlike over Circe. "I don't like cats."

On cue, Circe hissed. "Then you're even," Laurel retorted, with a shake of her dark head, "because she doesn't like you."

She knew her behavior was infinitely childish. They were acting like two kindergartners fighting at opposite sides of the sandbox, and from the bright interest in Danny's eyes, Laurel realized her son was as amazed as she by her atypical behavior.

The glowering man flung his hand over his chest and Laurel attempted not to notice his skin was tanned to the color of teak. Just as she vowed not to be affected by how the blond arrowing of curly body hair disappearing below his belt gleamed gold in the desert sun.

"Come on, lady," he drawled sarcastically. "You're breaking my heart."

"Impossible. You don't have one."

As he returned her glare, the antagonistic mood was suddenly broken by the older of the two forgotten moving men. "Hey, I know you. Nick McGraw, right?"

"Right," her neighbor responded, not moving his gaze from Laurel's face.

"Saw the game yesterday and I can't figure out why the papers keep clamoring for Morgan. As far as I'm concerned, you *are* the Thunderbirds, Nick!"

To Laurel's amazement, Nick McGraw's face broke into a wide grin and he laughed, a deep hearty sound. "Now here's a man who knows his football."

"Gosh, we're sorry about the accident, Nick." The younger man joined his partner. "It just got away from us. But don't worry, our company will make things right."

Laurel's jaw dropped as Nick waved his hand uncaringly. "Hey, don't worry about it. Accidents happen. It's no big deal. I shouldn't have been parking on the street, but we had a party last night and I never got around to moving it back into the driveway."

Laurel furiously decided the truth was he wouldn't have been able to stand, let alone drive.

"I sure hope we didn't wake you up, Nick. We had to get started early because of this heat. Damn, but it's hard to believe it's November!" The man named Mike wiped his brow with a sweat-darkened handkerchief.

Nick turned a rueful glance to the Ferrari, realizing he'd yet to take the window sticker off the new car. However, these days he needed all the fans he could get. There sure wasn't any point in alienating these two.

"That's okay," he assured them with a wry grin. "I had to come out to move my car, anyway."

The static of a radio in the cab of the van filled the air as the men were instructed to return to the warehouse if finished.

"We'll have our boss call you about the car first thing tomorrow morning," Mike assured Nick once again.

"Fine."

"Well, little lady, if you'll just sign here, we'll be on our way."

Laurel tried not to visibly bristle at the chauvinistic term. "What about my piano?"

"Don't worry, it's insured. You paid for it when you signed the contract in Seattle."

Since all the king's horses and all the king's men would never be able to put her beloved instrument together again, Laurel neglected mentioning she'd rather have her piano than the money. She sighed as she signed the form.

"Sixty cents a pound." Mike threw the words back over his shoulder as he walked toward the truck.

"What?"

"Sixty cents a pound. That's what the insurance pays off. You'll probably be getting a check in six weeks or so. Enjoy your new house, lady."

"Sixty cents a pound?" She stared after them. "That's ridiculous!" But an answer wasn't forthcoming as the garish van drove off down the curving hillside. She turned on Nick McGraw, her exhaustion, frustration and the blazing Arizona sun making her words rash.

"How come your dog caused all this trouble, but they knock themselves out for you and all I get is sixty cents a pound?"

"Simple. I'm a star."

That much was true. Or at least it had been, Laurel admitted inwardly. Nick McGraw, quarterback for the Phoenix Thunderbirds football team, had been one of the golden men of the game. She'd read about the injury that had sidelined him most of last season and wondered if he was actually going to try to defy the medical experts and return to play another full season.

"I see. So that makes everything you do just wonderful, right?"

"Hey," he objected, "don't forget, I'm the innocent bystander here. After all, you did damage my brand-new car, which in some circles would be considered a hanging offense. Not to mention the fact that you single-handedly shattered the peace and quiet of the neighborhood. It is a holiday, you know."

"I know," Laurel said with heartfelt frustration. "The power company has made that perfectly clear." She eyed the huge adobe house next door, wondering how he'd been able to hear the commotion from indoors. "I was told these homes are virtually soundproof. The realtor assured me they were built that way for energy conservation."

Amazingly, Nick appeared honestly chagrined and shoved his hands into his back pockets. Laurel tried not to notice how the faded denim cutoffs hugged his flat stomach even more tightly.

"Yeah, they are," he surprised her by admitting. "But it doesn't do much good if you're sleeping outside now, does it?"

Laurel's judicious gaze swept over his rugged face, settling momentarily on those disconcerting green eyes. She imagined under normal conditions they'd be devastatingly gorgeous. But this morning the whites were veined with red lines, like a Rand McNally atlas. It must have been one heck of a party next door last night.

"Next time try crawling indoors," she counseled, turning back toward her own house.

"Next time be a little more considerate and I won't have to," he countered. "Besides, crawling is definitely out. Bad knees."

She turned back. This time her gaze was purely professional, dropping down to study the scars crisscrossing his legs. Whatever else he was—rude, unneighborly, arrogant—the man's legs were enough to make her cry.

"I've never seen legs in worse shape."

The resultant light in his eyes seemed oddly impersonal, giving Laurel the feeling the seductive gleam was more automatic than due to any fact he found her more appealing than he had a moment before.

"That's what they all say," he agreed cheerfully. "You've no idea how many women can't wait to take me home and play nurse."

At the same time Laurel resented Nick McGraw's masculine self-confidence, she didn't believe he was exaggerating. The man was, with the exception of those battered knees, a magnificent physical specimen. His *Playgirl* centerfold had adorned the wall of the women's lounge in her Seattle hospital, and she knew the average woman drooling over that physique had not been looking for scars.

"Nick? Could I have your autograph?" Danny was standing beside them, staring up with undisguised hero worship.

Nick surprised Laurel by remembering her son's name. "Sure, Danny. Are you a Thunderbirds fan?"

"Kinda. But I'm really a Seahawks fan. My dad took me to some of the games. I saw the Thunderbirds play last year in Seattle, but you were out and Morgan was the quarterback. He was pretty good. You guys beat us."

At the dark expression moving across Nick's face, Laurel realized the topic of his replacement was not a popular one, but she couldn't stop Danny's next words.

"Is Morgan taking your place as starting quarterback, Nick? Or is your knee all better?"

"No, to the first. Yes, to the second," he said in a grim tone that made Laurel wonder how much was determination and how much was medical fact.

"Golly, wait until the guys back home hear I live next door to Nick McGraw!"

Danny's young face wore an expression of absolute bliss, making Laurel realize her son had just found something positive about this hard-fought move to Phoenix. While she certainly didn't appreciate the way Nick had come storming over here like an ill-tempered Titan, she had to be thankful for his effect on Danny.

"Why don't you put Circe in the backyard?" she suggested, casting a wary eye at the squirming cat and the bright brown eyes of the dog as he looked ready to begin around two. "Then you can get your football for Mr. McGraw to autograph."

"Neat-o idea, Mom," Danny agreed instantly, heading in a trot toward the house. Both adults were silent, watching him leave.

"Mom," Nick murmured, rubbing his jaw. "That's still a bit hard to believe." His gaze cut quickly to her left hand. Laurel was faster, shoving it into her pocket. "Is there a dad?"

She gave him a saccharine smile. "Of course. Didn't your father ever tell you about the birds and the bees?"

"Nope. I learned all that mushy stuff from Mary Jane Marshall in the back of her father's pickup."

"And I'm certain you were a fast learner," she retorted, finding his teasing grin both irritating and boyishly attractive. "So you shouldn't have had to ask that question in the first place."

Nick wondered why it bothered him that Laurel Britton was married. After all, she definitely wasn't his type. She was too slender, her body lacking the voluptuous curves he normally admired in women. Her hair was neither tawny red nor shimmering blond nor gleaming jet. It was simply a nice glossy chestnut, and she'd tugged it back into a ponytail. Her eyes were rather nice, he decided—dark, like those of a gentle doe and sparked with an intelligence he was not used to viewing in his women. *Your women? Knock it off, McGraw, she's taken.*

The unfathomable emotion in Nick's eyes as they settled on Laurel's face made her distinctly uneasy, and she realized belatedly she was holding her breath. *This is ridiculous,* she chided herself mentally. The man was a womanizing jock whose IQ was probably a smaller number than his neck size. What did she care what he thought of her? He was definitely not her type.

"Mom?" Danny's reappearance shattered the oddly unnerving silence.

"What is it?"

"I can't find my football."

"Don't worry, Danny," Nick reassured him. "The Thunderbirds haven't put me on waivers yet. I'll be around at least until you get everything unpacked."

"Thanks, Nick." Danny's expression was beatific. "Mom, can I go swimming like you promised? I'm all ready."

"Not until tomorrow when the man shows up to test the water," she told him apologetically.

She'd used the pool as a bribe to make Danny feel more enthusiastic about leaving his friends, neighborhood and school. And although Laurel felt like the Wicked Witch of the West, she didn't know the first thing about taking care of a swimming pool.

"Ah gee, Mom. Nobody ever checks the water in the lake and I've never croaked of nothin' yet."

"Of anything, Danny," she corrected absently, feeling the brilliant green gaze still on her back. "Haven't croaked, er, died of anything yet."

"See?" He pressed on with childish logic. "The lake's filled with all sorts of slimy stuff—tadpoles, fish, water skippers. I didn't see noth—uh, anything like that in the pool."

"The slimy things in the pool are too small to be seen by the naked eye, Danny." Nick's deep voice backed Laurel up. "Want me to show your dad how to check that pool?"

There was a long, uncomfortable silence and Laurel cried inwardly as Danny's small face fell. *Damn,* she felt like screaming, *not now! Not when I'm hot and tired and sticky.*

In her attempt to shelter Danny from the fact that his father found him less than enjoyable as a full-time experience, Laurel had brushed over far too many missed weekends together. She'd thought it important for her son to believe he had two parents who loved him equally.

That mistake had come home to her when she'd been offered this opportunity in Phoenix. They'd gone through two months of temper tantrums and when she received a call from Danny's second grade teacher that the normally easygoing youngster was behaving no better at school, she'd blithely promised him he could spend Christmas with his father. And Geoffrey's *perfect* wife. With that promise, and the lure of a swimming pool in his own backyard, Danny had given in.

"My dad lives in Seattle."

So she was a free agent after all. Interesting. Nick's green eyes moved to Laurel and he nodded thoughtfully.

"Hey, the offer still stands; I'll teach you instead. This is a pretty big place for your mother to be handling all alone."

He looped his arm around Danny's shoulder and headed off in the direction of the backyard before Laurel had a chance to speak. Her irritation rose even further when she considered Nick's chauvinistic tone. As if she was some hothouse flower who couldn't function without a male. She'd done just fine for some time now and could certainly continue to survive without any assistance from a man who probably only saw women in one role—that of cheerleader.

"I've hired a pool service to do that," she pointed out coolly.

He shrugged wide shoulders. "Hey, don't sweat it. I'll be right back." As she watched, he strode off across the decking to a cedar gate in the six-foot-high adobe wall separating the two backyards.

"I didn't see that gate the first time I was here," she complained, unreasonably disturbed about Nick McGraw's having such easy access to her yard.

"The place belonged to a friend of mine. We built the gate to make things easier."

"I'll bet," she muttered, picturing romantic nocturnal visits.

"J.D. was a running back for the Thunderbirds. He had to sell the house when he was traded to San Diego," Nick enlightened Laurel, his dancing eyes letting her know he'd read her thoughts.

"J.D. Neeman? I'm living in J.D. Neeman's house?" Danny's eyes widened behind the ridiculous mask he'd been wearing almost the entire drive down from Washington.

"Yep," Nick called back over his shoulder.

"Wow, Mom. Think of that." He stared around the backyard, whispering as if in a shrine.

"Think of that," she echoed, not having the faintest idea who the man was, but happy that the idea of living in his house gave Danny inordinate pleasure.

Taking advantage of Nick's absence, Laurel escaped to the bathroom, trying to brush her shoulder-length hair into some semblance of order. The adolescent ponytail, while effectively getting her hair off the back of her neck, was less than appealing.

"Look at you," she criticized her reflection. "You're grimy, sweaty and those clothes should've been put in the rag bin months ago."

It was amazingly hot inside the house and she reached into the shower, twisting the knob as if perhaps the fates would smile on her and make water magically come out, despite the fact the man from the water company had yet to make an appearance.

"I've got water over at my place."

Laurel glanced back over her shoulder to view Nick leaning laconically against the doorframe to her bathroom. "Look, McGraw," she said tiredly, "I don't know what type of open-door relationship you had with your running-back friend, but consider things changed." She belatedly regretted her snippy tone, but not the words so she remained silent as his eyes darkened dangerously.

He lifted his hands in a gesture of self-defense. "Hey, lady, don't get so uptight, okay? Your son sent me to find you so you could learn how to test the chemicals, too. He says you're good at stuff like that." His voice held a question.

"If I can light a furnace without burning down the house, I suppose I can learn to detect algae in a swimming pool," she agreed, meeting his gaze with a challenging one of her own. "After all, how hard can it be? If a *football player* can do it?"

Nick crossed his arms over his bare chest, barring her way as effectively as if a mountain had suddenly sprung up in her doorway.

"I think this is where I let you know I'm not wild about dumb jock remarks."

"Then we're even. Because I'm not ecstatic about dumb, helpless women remarks, either."

The silence swirled about them in the stifling heat of the room. Finally, he rubbed his jaw thoughtfully. "I suppose, if we're going to be neighbors, we ought to forge some type of truce."

"Or we can just stay in our own yards," she suggested pointedly.

He ignored her words, wondering what it was about this woman that both annoyed and intrigued him all at the same time. "It's going to be hard for this old dog to learn a new trick, but I'll try if you will." His green eyes encouraged complaisance, while his lopsided grin was expertly disarming.

"For the sake of peace," she agreed, brushing her damp hair off her forehead. "Now, will you let me out of this blast-furnace before I faint."

"I thought I was supposed to think of you as a woman incapable of swooning."

Laurel knew he was laughing at her. "Move, McGraw, or I'll test out that new knee with the toe of my sneaker."

He let her by. "That wasn't funny, Laurel," he murmured in her ear as she moved passed him.

"Neither are you, McGraw. Neither are you."

The unseasonably hot November sun beat down on her head as Laurel dangled her bare feet in the cool water, knowing if Danny wasn't here she'd slide into the inviting turquoise depths, not worrying about algae and pH and all those other important items in Nick's portable test kit.

"It's okay," he announced, after making both Laurel and Danny do the tests three times in order to make certain they'd learned. Laurel thought about all the advanced chemistry classes she'd taken in medical school and almost laughed as Nick led her through the procedures at an excruciatingly slow speed. "The pH is a little high, but I've got some acid over at my place I can give you."

"Thanks, but I'll get my own."

"You don't believe in neighbors borrowing from one another?"

"Not really. It just makes for complications."

"And you're a lady who doesn't like complications."

She nodded firmly. "Right." It was a warning and they both knew it.

Laurel was surprised at the sudden flash of heat that seared through her as Nick's steady green eyes held hers. She tried to blame her increasing vertigo on the blazing ball of desert sun overhead but knew the source of warmth came from something much nearer. A dangerous man, she warned herself. Despite his display of boyish charm, Laurel knew Nick McGraw was nothing but trouble.

"Hey, Mom, Nick! Watch me go off the diving board!"

"It's Mr. McGraw," Laurel corrected automatically, her gaze moving to her son.

"Let him call me Nick. All the kids do."

"I don't believe in children calling adults by their first names," she countered.

"Then we shouldn't have any problem."

"Oh?" Her arched brow invited elaboration.

"Since I've the distinct impression you don't put athletes in the same category as adults. Can he swim?" Nick asked under his breath as Danny walked out onto the short fiberglass board.

"Like a fish. And you're wrong. I happen to like athletes." Professionally, she meant, but realized a moment later Nick was determined to take it the wrong way.

"Terrific. This might turn out to be a friendly neighborhood after all."

The leer was automatic. She knew it was. "You know, you're right," she surprised him by admitting freely.

"I am?"

"You *are* an overgrown adolescent. And if you don't quit drooling over me like I'm your own personal smorgasbord, I'm going to call your mother to take you home."

"You know something, Laurel?"

"What?"

"You get far too uptight about the little things. I think you need to cool off."

Before she could open her mouth, Nick's hands were on her shoulders, pushing her into the water. As Laurel bobbed to the surface, she bit back the stream of epithets that came to mind, none of them remotely appropriate to shout in front of her son. But she would have had to yell them at Nick's back because he was sauntering toward the gate in the shared wall, closing it with a decisive bang.

LAUREL PULLED HER CAR into the parking lot of the Phoenix Sports Medicine Clinic forty minutes late her first day on the job. So much for establishing a professional image right off the bat, she groaned inwardly. This was definitely not the recommended A.M.A. method to create a terrific first impression.

"I'm sorry," she apologized, rushing into Dr. Matthew Adams's office in a swirl of crisp linen skirt. "But it took longer to get Danny enrolled in school than I'd expected."

The older man's cool gray eyes observed her steadily. "That's quite all right, Dr. Britton. I understand."

While his words were studiously proper, Laurel recognized her superior's expression. And the tone. She knew that although he'd hired her for her skills, the jury was still out on whether a less-qualified male physician might not prove ultimately more suitable.

"It won't happen again," she assured him, feeling unreasonably like a first-year intern.

He nodded an iron-gray head. "I'm pleased to hear that. We need to know we can count on you to be both prompt and efficient, Dr. Britton." It was definitely an order, and while the commandment might not have come from above, Laurel had no doubt it was written in stone. "Now, Doctor, let's go over your schedule."

She'd toured the clinic two months previously, finding it exactly what she'd been seeking. The field of sports medicine was fairly new; her specialty had not yet been recognized as a standard residency program and the doctors practicing in the field were basically self-educated after first obtaining their medical degree and licenses. In Laurel's case, much of her ability to treat basic overuse injuries and odd ailments came from painful experience, a result of her own dedication to daily running. Additional knowledge was acquired through extensive reading and working in a clinical practice with otherwise healthy patients.

Despite the lack of attention given the specialty in general, this clinic boasted the latest in equipment and the staff were among the best in their field. Laurel knew she was fortunate to be in such company and wasn't about to let Dr. Adams's less than cordial attitude spoil her first day.

The morning went routinely as she treated a constant stream of minor injuries. Taking a breather between patients, she stepped into the doctors' lounge and poured herself a cup of coffee.

"Whew, is it always this busy?" she asked the other occupant of the room.

Dr. Tony Lee grinned sympathetically, his eyes sparkling behind the amber-tinted lenses of his glasses. "Heck no. We cleverly planned all this for your first day, Dr. Britton. Trial by fire—that's Adams's way."

"I wouldn't be at all surprised," she murmured, adding two lumps of sugar to the thick black liquid masquerading as coffee.

"He's not so bad once you get used to him."

"I hear that's what they say about the Ayatollah, too." Laurel took a tentative sip. Grimacing, she added yet another lump of sugar and a heaping teaspoon of powdered creamer.

"I can see nutrition wasn't your specialty." Laughing dark eyes were focused on her plastic cup.

"Did you make this coffee?"

He grinned. "Guilty as charged."

"Then you're in no position to criticize. This stuff would make mud taste great."

"Are you offering to become chief coffeemaker?" There was a laughing challenge in her colleague's tone.

Laurel considered. "If I do, it'll only be because I don't want to leave my child an orphan. Too much of this stuff has to be hazardous to a person's health. It won't be because I'm the only female doctor on staff. Agreed?"

"Agreed. I know I speak for the rest of the staff when I extend my heartfelt thanks, Doctor. They've never been wild about my coffee, either, but so far no one else has volunteered to take up the task." He grinned happily.

"What about you? You can't tell me you like this coffee?"

"I stick to tea bags," he explained, his black eyes twinkling as he lifted his cup to his lips. "It's safer that way."

Laurel laughed as she was supposed to, sinking down onto the soft leather couch. She kicked off her shoes, allowing her feet a few blissful moments of freedom. Wiggling her toes happily, she sipped her too-sweet coffee, priding herself on making it through an unusually hectic morning.

Forced to treat not only her scheduled patients but the emergency walk-ins as well, she had managed to attend to everyone without falling behind. That came as a relief, since she was aware of Dr. Adams's almost constant observation. Laurel had the odd feeling he was just waiting for her to make a mistake. She was scanning the patient list in her hands when one name jumped off the page.

"N. McGraw," she groaned. "Don't tell me."

"Nick McGraw," Dr. Lee agreed. "He was Ben Phillips's patient, before the old man retired. Since you're inheriting his clinic practice, McGraw comes with the territory."

"I'd assume the Thunderbirds have their own physicians."

"They do. But that injury last year seems to have McGraw spooked. He insists on using his own doctors, rather than trust the team physicians."

Laurel could understand that. She'd seen far too many cases of team physicians looking the other way while trainers shot up athletes with enough xylocaine to numb a bull elephant, so they could continue to play. If Nick's injury had been as bad as she'd heard, he was wise to seek outside medical advice. She did, however, hate to think about the possible fireworks when that quintessential male chauvinist discovered his new doctor was a woman.

Dr. Adams entered the lounge, as if conjured up by the hobgoblins of Laurel's darkening mood. Cold gray eyes raked over the two physicians, his expression definitely disapproving as he took in her stocking-clad feet.

"Dr. Britton, I hate to break up this little tête-à-tête, but you have a patient waiting." At Laurel's unconscious glance downward toward her paper, he stated briskly, "An unscheduled emergency. Another one of those three-day-weekend idiots."

As she reached down slipping on her shoes, Laurel wondered idly if there was anyone Dr. Adams *did* approve of. When she'd come to Phoenix to investigate this position, she'd met with the saturnine administrator only once, and that had been a brief, uneventful interview. She'd much preferred the idea of working with the chief of staff, Dr. Jeremy Parrish. Unfortunately, Dr. Parrish had taken a leave of absence to concentrate on new treatments for torn tendons and until a new chief of staff was appointed, Laurel would be working directly under Dr. Adams, a cold fish if she'd ever met one.

"I'll see the patient right away," she said quickly, rising to her feet, more than willing to escape the steady unblinking stare of her superior.

Matthew Adams won the last word. "That was the idea, Doctor."

A young woman was seated on the examining table, her tanned face displaying far more frustration than pain.

"Hi," she greeted Laurel glumly. "I sure hope you've got better news than my family doctor."

"Hi. Let's see what we've got here." Laurel skimmed the chart. "You jog?"

"I run," the woman corrected firmly. "Jogging is for faddists."

Laurel smiled, understanding completely. "I know. I run, too."

The woman's expression perked up and she appeared more hopeful. "You do? Then you'll understand why I can't stay off my foot for two months. I'll go stark raving bonkers!"

Laurel nodded, her fingers probing delicately at the woman's ankle. "How long ago did you get this sprain?"

The woman flinched as Laurel's fingers hit a sore spot. "A few months ago. Five or six," she added sullenly.

"And you didn't slow down your activities, right?"

"I was in training."

Laurel sighed. "I wish I had a nickel for every time I've heard that. I could have retired in luxury long ago."

"You're as bad as my family doctor. He says I've got to stay off it entirely," she complained.

Before Laurel could comment, a flurry of activity at the doorway caught her attention. Her patient's interested gaze followed hers to the tall man standing in a circle of ardent admirers.

"Oh, my God, is that who I think it is?" The young woman was practically swooning.

"It is if you think it's Nick McGraw," Laurel replied briskly, determined to ignore that odd twinge deep inside her that his appearance had triggered. "Now, about this ankle . . ."

"I can't believe it. Nick McGraw! Right here in person." She patted her hair into place and sat up a little straighter.

"In living color," Laurel agreed dryly. "Now, what you've done, Ms Dalton, is exacerbate your injury by excessive movement. You never allowed your sprain to heal in the first place. You should have—"

"He's coming over here," her patient hissed, obviously not hearing a word of Laurel's professional diagnosis.

Here we go, Laurel thought to herself, unconsciously holding her breath as she awaited Nick's reaction. She steeled herself for a display of wounded male pride.

As Nick moved toward Ben Phillips's old examining table, he thought the nurse-practitioner seated on the low stool looked oddly familiar. There was something about the slender line of her shoulder and the sleek curve to her chestnut hair. Laurel, he decided, she reminded him of Laurel. But that was ridiculous; he only made the connection because he'd been thinking about his new neighbor far too much during the past twenty-four hours. That prickly female had gotten under his skin and he was damned if he could figure out why.

"Excuse me, but I was told the doctor would see me next."

Laurel turned slowly, keeping her smile brightly professional. "I'll be with you as soon as I finish with this patient, Mr. McGraw."

Nick knew he was staring and struggled to keep his expression nonchalant. Images of his arrogantly male behavior with the pool-testing kit flew into his mind and he wondered if he was actually blushing. He must have looked like a first-class idiot teaching this woman how to read chlorine residuals.

"So it's *Dr.* Britton. This *is* a surprise."

"Isn't it?" she agreed hesitantly, her smile wobbling just a little. Was that dark red flush rising from his collar because he was angry? Laurel desperately hoped not.

She breathed a sigh of relief as he appeared disinclined to argue the point. "Go ahead, Doc." He nodded his blond head toward the young woman. "I'll just sit here quietly and watch you do your medical thing."

"If you'd prefer, you could wait out in the lobby," she suggested hopefully. "There are some magazines there. They're probably ancient, but . . ." Laurel knew she was rambling, but Nick's steady green gaze was definitely unnerving.

"I've read them all, Laurel," he stated smoothly. "Now, don't mind me. I promise to be so unobtrusive you won't even know I'm here."

Ha, Laurel considered grimly, feeling his gaze riveted on her as she turned back to Jenny Dalton, fat chance of that. She was all too aware of his presence, just as she hadn't missed the way he'd lingered a shade too long over her first name, caressing it in an oddly personal manner. Even her patient appeared to notice, her curious gaze flicking back and forth between Nick and Laurel.

Laurel forced her attention back to the woman's ankle. "You have to understand that doctors who aren't involved in sports themselves have a tendency to be ultracautious. The truth is most injuries will heal faster with sensible self-doctoring and moderate activity."

She pulled the woman's sports sock back up. "Next time you have an injury, treat yourself immediately with ice. Ice, compression and elevation. Then, as soon as possible, gently move the injured part to flush out the fluids and cell debris in the injured area. That'll also help restore normal range of movement."

"Okay," the woman replied in a miffed tone. "So that's what I should've done. Are you telling me it's too late? That I've got to stay off my ankle entirely?"

"Of course not," Laurel corrected briskly. "But you must utilize some common sense. How far do you usually run a day?"

"Ten miles."

Laurel chewed thoughtfully on the end of her pen, then began writing on a prescription pad. "Okay, here's what I'm going to suggest. I want you to begin with a three-mile walking and jogging workout. First walk briskly until you're no longer limping, then jog as long as you can without feeling the pain. When the pain starts again, walk until it disappears, then start in running again."

She tapped a stern warning on the pad with her ballpoint pen. "Now remember, the key is to build up cautiously. Try taping the ankle and see if that gives you additional support. And whatever you do, don't increase the stress load until the sprain is healed. Is that clear?"

The young woman nodded, her sulky expression replaced by a wide smile. "Sure, I can handle that. Thanks a lot, Dr. Britton, you've made my day."

"Make mine and allow time for that ankle to heal properly," Laurel cautioned with an answering smile.

"You've got it," the woman agreed, her attention returning to Nick McGraw. "Would you sign an autograph for my kids? They'd kill me if they knew I'd shared an examination table with you and didn't ask."

Nick's attention had been on Laurel. He'd been entranced by her full pink lips and strong white teeth as she'd chewed thoughtfully on that pen. He was going to have to taste those ridiculously sexy lips, he decided. Realizing belatedly that Laurel's patient had spoken to him, Nick forced his mind to her words.

"Kids?" he answered automatically, knowing exactly what the young woman wanted to hear. "You don't look old enough to have kids."

Laurel decided it must be a pat line with the man. Watching the woman's beaming response, she also realized it brought results.

"I've got two.... But, of course I got married right out of high school."

"You sure don't look any older than that now. Running obviously agrees with you."

Nick's expression was masculinely appreciative while unthreatening, and Laurel considered how easily these lines came to him. With those gorgeous green eyes and devastating smile, Nick McGraw must have women falling at his feet.

Taking the piece of paper the woman extended, he glanced over at Laurel, patting the pocketless chest of his polo shirt. "Ah, may I borrow your pen, Doctor?"

Laurel handed it over, jerking back from the odd shock as their fingers touched. Nick felt it, too; she knew from the bright light suddenly gleaming in his eyes.

"Static electricity," she murmured.

"Of course," he agreed instantly, returning his attention to Laurel's patient. "What are their names?"

Jenny Dalton had been staring, her eyes drinking in so much man only a few feet away. "Names?" she inquired blankly.

"Your kids," he reminded her.

"Oh! Ryan and Megan."

"Nice Irish names," he remarked. "Do they like football?"

"They *love* the Thunderbirds. And of course they think you're the best quarterback in the league."

"It's nice to know I've got a few fans left out there," he said, his words tinged with heavy irony.

"Oh, at least three. I think you're absolutely wonderful, too."

Laurel watched Nick's dispassionate answering smile, noting it didn't extend to his eyes, the way it had when the moving men had complimented his playing ability.

"Thanks." He handed the paper to the woman and the pen back to Laurel.

"Oh, thank you, Nick," Jenny Dalton breathed, eyeing the bold black script. Then her attention returned to Laurel. "Thank you, too, Dr. Britton." She grinned up at Nick. "You're real lucky. She's a great doctor."

"I've always been lucky," he murmured thoughtfully as Jenny floated away, still on cloud nine.

But Nick failed to watch her leave; his attention was drawn to Laurel's face. Her eyes were as wide and as velvety brown as he remembered, her lashes a thick, lush fringe. But why hadn't he noticed those high, delicate cheekbones yesterday? And her lips. No doctor had any business with lips like that. Lushly pink, and sensually full, they brought to mind physical images that were definitely not of a medical nature. Her rainwater-straight hair was the color of chestnuts, falling in a sleek curve to her shoulders, and he wondered why he'd ever thought redheads more interesting, blondes sexier.

In her own oddly jarring way, Laurel Britton was far more interesting and ultimately sexier than any woman of his past experience. His gaze moved over her white lab coat, as he remembered how firm her breasts had been under the damp cotton T-shirt.

"You'll have to take your pants off."

Considering the erotic train of his thoughts, Laurel's words brought Nick up sharply. "What?"

She nodded a glossy head toward his jeans. "Your pants. I can't examine your knee when you're dressed."

For the first time since adolescence, Nick worried about the control he had over his body. Laurel Britton might be a doctor, and from the way she handled that patient earlier, he knew she was probably a damn good one. But she was also a woman. And that was the problem.

"How come I don't rate a private room?" he asked.

Laurel's gaze swept the large room. "They're all being used at the moment."

He crossed his arms over his chest. "Ben Phillips always examined me in a private room."

"Perhaps you never showed up on a Tuesday after a three-day weekend," she countered. "Come on, McGraw, let's see a little cooperation here."

"I'm not used to taking off my clothes in front of strange women."

Laurel's judicious gaze moved over him, taking in his wide shoulders, broad chest and trim waist. Although he was reaching the end of his playing days, Nick's body was definitely not that of a man past his prime. He was in excellent shape, she noticed as a physician. The woman in her admitted he was also gorgeous.

She couldn't help smiling. "Oh, I think you're being overly modest, McGraw. I've the impression you've been known to do exactly that more times than either of us would care to count. Besides, any man who's willing to pose in the nude for *Playgirl* can't be all that shy... Now, do you take them off, or shall I?"

A thundercloud moved ominously across his dark face. "I wasn't nude."

She waved a dismissing hand. "Well, you certainly couldn't have told that from the photos. The pants?" she reminded him pointedly.

He glanced around the busy examining room. "Not until you put up a screen."

"Oh, for Pete's sake." Laurel expelled a sigh of exasperation, marching across the floor to retrieve the folding screen. She wondered how this man had survived all the years of public locker rooms if he was so blasted shy.

"There . . . Now will you cooperate?" She stuck the screen in front of her table, arranging the three sides to supply privacy, remaining outside to allow him to strip down to his underwear.

"Ready."

He was seated on the end of the table, his long legs dangling over the end, and once again she breathed in sharply as she viewed the crisscross scars violating the dark skin covering his knees. While Laurel had seen injuries just as critical, none had ever caused that odd stab of pain somewhere deep inside her.

"That bad?"

"They're not pretty." She shook her head. "Is it worth it?"

"What?"

She nodded in the direction of his legs. "The surgery, the pain, all that. Is it really worth it? Just so you can play one more season?"

"I could ask you how you feel about breathing," he answered simply. "And by the way, it wasn't my idea to pose for that layout. I fought it like hell for months."

Laurel had the odd impression that it was important to Nick that she know that. Why should he care what she thought? She shrugged.

"It really isn't any of my business; it was unprofessional of me to bring it up. I'm sorry."

He refused to let the issue drop. For some reason, he hated that look of disapproval that came into her eyes from time to time. Although he knew it would allow her unwelcome insight into his problems, he wanted to make her understand the desperation that had led to his behavior of the past year. The magazine layout, the parties, his admittedly wild life-style. But it was all so complicated. And he wasn't certain he understood himself.

Laurel's fingers pressed against his leg with gentle strength as she examined the injured knee. Nick reached out, cupping her chin in his fingers, lifting her gaze to his.

"My agent insisted that if I was going to be out of action for an entire season, we needed to keep my name out there in front of the public. At least it was better than all the portraits the sportswriters were painting of a washed-up, battered old wreck."

A little voice in the far reaches of Laurel's mind reminded her that this was hardly professional behavior. Her hands were trembling on the man's naked leg, as she drowned in the warm green pools of his eyes. His fingers were literally burning her skin, but she was in no hurry for him to take them away.

She made a weak attempt at levity. "That was not the body of a battered old wreck."

His gaze didn't move from hers. "Then you've seen it?"

"Hasn't everyone?"

"So my agent says," he muttered with self-deprecating humor. "Did you like it?"

"It'll do, McGraw, it'll do."

The smile lit up her face, making her extraordinarily attractive. Nick had a sudden urge to kiss her, and wondered what would happen to the briskly professional Dr. Britton if he pulled the lovely Laurel into his arms and covered those ridiculously sensuous lips with his own.

Laurel felt trapped as she stared into Nick's darkening eyes and every feminine instinct she possessed told her Nick McGraw was about to kiss her.

"Don't," she said softly.

His thumb played at the corner of her lips. "Why not?"

"I'm your doctor." Laurel was grateful she was sitting down as his tantalizing touch turned her bones to melted wax.

"You're also a beautiful woman."

She faltered for a moment, caught up in Nick's desirous gaze. Then her sense of humor saved her and she managed an honest grin.

"Thanks, McGraw. I think I'll take that as a compliment, without worrying about how many times you've already handed it out today."

"Laurel." His voice was husky, rough and soft at the same time, reminding Laurel of ebony velvet.

She shook her head. "Don't complicate things, Nick."

God, what he'd give for just one taste of those luscious ripe lips. "I believe it's a little late for that advice. You must realize I want you, lovely Laurel . . ."

Laurel's mouth went suddenly dry. "You may want me as a woman, but you *need* me as your doctor," she managed to say after a long silence.

Okay, Nick decided, they'd play the game her way. For now. He'd always enjoyed a challenge and something told him Laurel Britton was going to prove exactly that. But he was going to have her, of that Nick had not the slightest doubt.

He released his light hold on her chin, splaying his fingers on his dark thighs, the gesture intentionally provocative.

"Well then, as my doctor, what's your diagnosis?"

Laurel was shaken, but determined not to show it. "I've seen horses shot for less."

"I'm only planning to play a football game, Dr. Britton. Not run the Kentucky Derby."

She sighed. "Your records show you had your surgery less than a year ago, and unfortunately, tendon tears are the worst injuries an athlete can sustain. I know Dr. Phillips told you to give it at least a year—even eighteen months wouldn't be an unreasonable period of recovery time. Try a little patience," she counseled in her most professional tone.

"I don't have a year." At Laurel's dubious expression, Nick exhaled a frustrated breath. "Look, Laurel—" He hesitated. "May I call you Laurel? I feel a little funny calling you Dr. Britton after yesterday."

"Are you saying you don't normally push your physicians into the pool?"

"No."

"That's a relief." Laurel started making notations on his chart.

"But of course they usually don't ask for it, either."

Her pen stopped in midsentence as she glanced up at him. Nick's expression was bland, but his green eyes were smiling. She allowed herself a slight grin.

"You may have a point. I was tired, out of sorts and aggravated with the world in general. And you didn't exactly welcome me to the neighborhood."

"Hey, whose piano crashed into whose brand-new car?"

Laurel held her ground. "And whose dog attacked whose cat?"

Their eyes locked and finally Nick shrugged. "This argument sounds vaguely familiar."

She wondered what it was about Nick McGraw that had her veering from unwilling interest to infuriating aggravation, all in a span of a few seconds. The one thing he'd yet to do was bore her.

"You're right. Let's drop it. Why don't you spend a half hour or so in the whirlpool?" She nodded her head in the direction of the therapy room. "I'd like to put you on the Cybex and measure the strength of that leg, but there's a line for it a mile long, so I suppose we can save it until next time."

He slid off the table with an exaggerated groan. "I knew it— you're going to abuse my body for your own amusement. You women are all alike."

"If there's any abusing of your body going on, it's going to be in a strictly medical capacity, McGraw." Her words held a definite warning.

He studied her for one full minute, his fingers rubbing thoughtfully at his chin. The longer he was around this paradox of woman-doctor, the more she intrigued him. He found himself wanting to know everything about her.

"Is that a fact?"

Laurel nodded, holding his appraising gaze with a level one of her own. Even as she allowed herself a fleeting fantasy of how his hard male body would feel against hers, she forced herself to remember their positions.

"Fact."

His eyes held a faint light of amusement as they lingered on her face. "Are you so sure about that?"

Pretending disinterest, she turned away to remove the screen. "Positive."

Nick hated to lose the privacy the temporary wall allowed. He reached out to grasp her arm but common sense overruled more primitive urges. He withdrew his hand and forced a careless shrug.

"Hey, it's okay by me. I just didn't want you kicking yourself when you realized what you'd turned down."

Laurel eyed him curiously over her shoulder. Once again his masculine gaze was unnervingly impersonal.

"I'll survive," she muttered. "You know where the therapy room is; I'll catch up with you as soon as I call Danny's school."

"Is something wrong?" This time the interest in Nick's green eyes was genuine, she realized. As was his obvious concern.

"Not wrong. I'm going to be late picking him up. It's a private school and while it costs a bit more to have them keep him after class, it's worth it for my peace of mind. I don't like the idea of a child as young as Danny home by himself all afternoon."

"But he shouldn't have to stay *there* all day, either," he argued. "When I was Danny's age, I couldn't wait to get out of school."

"I take it your mother didn't work."

"Sure, she worked. At home. Taking care of us kids, cooking, you know—old-fashioned mom stuff."

Laurel detected a hint of sarcasm in his tone and crossed her arms militantly across her white lab jacket. What business did this man have criticizing her parenting? She'd been doing it alone for some time now and while she knew there was always room for improvement, she'd done her best to be both mother and father to Danny, as well as breadwinner for her family.

"I'm not wild about the setup, either, but right now it's the best I've found. So why don't you just mind your own business and spare me the assorted tales from 'Father Knows Best'?"

Nick was surprised by Laurel's unexpected vulnerability. She wasn't as tough as he'd thought. His expression immediately softened.

"You're right. It's none of my business. Although I'd venture a guess this isn't exactly an easy day for you—a new house, a new job, Danny in a new school. It's a lot for one lady to handle."

Laurel's answering laugh was tinged with faint bitterness. "It's a lot for one person—man or woman—to handle. But I haven't had a lot of volunteers lately." She began folding away the screen, but this time Nick gave into instinct, reaching out to forestall her progress.

"I'm volunteering, Laurel," he said simply.

She stared up at him, searching his face for the chauvinistic punch line she knew would be coming. "Volunteering? For what?" As soon as the question escaped her lips, Laurel cringed, knowing she'd handed him a perfect straight line. But Nick surprised her by not picking up on it.

"I've got a practice this afternoon after I leave here. Why don't I pick Danny up at school and take him out to the field with me?"

"You've got to be kidding!"

"Not at all. Don't you think he'd like it?"

"He'd love it and you know it. But I couldn't impose like that."

"Complications," he murmured softly, reminding her of their conversation by the pool. "You don't get involved with your neighbors."

Laurel simply nodded, not willing to trust her voice. She couldn't believe he was actually offering to help out of simple kindness. There had to be a catch, yet she certainly couldn't find proof of it in his expression.

"Would you agree if I assured you it would be a big help to me personally?"

"How?" she inquired suspiciously.

"I could use a little moral support today. Although Danny's a Seahawks fan, I'm betting he'll extend a little loyalty to a neighbor."

"It's that rough?" she asked softly. Laurel was honestly surprised to find this strong, rawly masculine man needing moral support from anyone.

"I could ask you the same question," he countered, his tone low enough to keep their conversation from being overheard by anyone else in the room. He expelled a harsh sigh. "Look, this is a year of changes for both of us, so let's just see what happens if we try being friends. I'd say you could probably use one about now and I know I'd feel better knowing someone was in my corner."

Nick knew Laurel was thrown by his suggestion. She dragged her eyes away from his.

"I'm not sure that's a good idea," she decided finally.

"Afraid?" he asked lazily.

The laughing tone in his voice only served to irritate her. "Of course not."

By the way her fingers trembled as she replaced the ballpoint pen in the breast pocket of her starched white lab jacket, Nick knew Laurel was growing angry at his persistence. But she was also affected more than she cared to admit. He pressed his advantage.

"If you're not afraid, what else could you have against a simple neighborly friendship?"

Laurel felt herself being maneuvered, even as she forced herself to study this situation with a somewhat detached eye. Every feminine instinct she possessed assured her there would be nothing simple about any relationship with Nick McGraw. An intimate relationship with the man would be bound to be short-lived, fiery and totally against her own best interests. However, there *was* an outside chance they could maintain some sort of casual friendship.

The mother in Laurel pointed out Nick could certainly help Danny overcome his resentment about leaving Seattle. What little boy wouldn't be in seventh heaven if allowed to spend time with a professional quarterback of Nick's fame and status?

She nodded slowly and they both knew a silent understanding had been achieved. "You've got yourself a deal," she agreed, holding out her hand. "And a weary mother's heartfelt thanks."

As Laurel's slim palm disappeared into his grip, Nick granted himself the pleasure of holding her hand longer than necessary for a casual handshake. Knowing it to be a risky gesture at this point, he couldn't resist lifting her wrist to his nose.

"Mmm, nice. Arpège? Chanel?"

Laurel tugged her hand free, deciding this had to be the shortest truce on record. "Phisohex. And we're talking just friends here, McGraw. So don't forget."

He grinned, a devastatingly attractive smile. "Just friends," he agreed cheerfully. Then, giving her a snappy salute, he turned in the direction of the therapy room, apparently oblivious of his underclad state. "Oh, and Laurel?"

On her way to phone the school about her change in plans, she stopped, eyeing him over her shoulder. As he stood so unselfconsciously in the center of the room, Laurel realized he'd only insisted on the screen to ensure a chance to speak with her privately. The man was definitely an expert in manipulation. She'd have to stay on her toes.

"Yes?"

Nick waggled his tawny blond eyebrows in an outrageously lustful manner. "I'll pick up something for dinner and when you come home, you're invited to be as friendly as you like."

He winked and was gone before she could destroy him with a few well-chosen words. The resultant roar of laughter from the examining room full of spectators demonstrated that everyone had enjoyed Nick's performance immensely. Everyone, that is, except Dr. Adams, who was eyeing Laurel with overtly cold disapproval.

Forcing herself to ignore the lingering chuckles, Laurel went to dial the telephone number of the school, receiving a maddening busy signal her first two tries. It had already been an incredibly long day and she had the uncomfortable feeling that with Nick determined to call the shots, the evening was bound to prove even more of a challenge.

3

LAUREL WORKED WITHOUT a break the rest of the afternoon, the unscheduled patients outnumbering the ones with appointments nearly two to one.

"I hate three-day weekends," she muttered, preparing an immobilizing cast for a teenager who'd pulled a ligament in his knee during a strenuous tennis match the previous day.

"They're the worst," Tony Lee agreed as he studied a set of X rays. "Tell me what you think of this."

Laurel glanced up at the backlit board. "A stress fracture," she diagnosed easily. "But why did you bother with an X ray? The treatment's the same as a bad sprain."

"It's her third this year."

Laurel stopped her work, stripping off her gloves. She moved across the room to stand beside him. "Is she a runner?"

"Long distance."

"Premenopausal amenorrheic?"

"She's thirty-two and hasn't had a normal menstrual cycle for three years," he answered, examining the X ray intently. "I'm thinking about scheduling a CT."

Laurel gave the idea brief consideration, hating to argue with a colleague her first day on the job. The computerized axial tomography scanner detected bone density and she was well aware of the recent findings that indicated women who were hard-training, long-distance runners might he inadvertently causing irreversible damage to their bones. As a runner herself, she'd studied all the data available thus far.

"Why don't you first check her calcium absorption?" she suggested carefully.

"If the woman is suffering form osteoporosis, due to athletic amenorrhea, Dr. Lee's suggested course of action is sound enough." Dr. Adams's voice entered the conversation as he came up behind the pair.

Laurel reminded herself that it would certainly not help anything to get fired by entering into a heated argument with her superior. Giving her words serious consideration, she answered slowly.

"From what I've read on the subject so far, the reports are interesting, but little more than a scare. There's no real factual data. They've lumped a few women runners with fertility problems together with women who have amenorrhea from totally different causes. It's as if we took a test group of individuals who all had broken legs and assumed they'd gotten them in the same way."

Matthew Adams's expression was inscrutable. "Are you saying Dr. Lee should simply ignore the problem?"

She felt Tony's encouraging dark eyes on her, realizing he'd never intended this to end up an inquisition. Drawing a deep breath, Laurel said a silent prayer that she wouldn't offend the younger doctor.

"Of course not. But I still suggest Dr. Lee first check his patient's calcium intake. Then instead of the CT, if he still feels a need to measure bone density, I'd recommend gaining access to a photon absorptiometer instead. Not only does it provide a more precise and accurate measurement, it's less expensive. Plus there's the matter of a much lower radiation exposure."

"The amount of radiation exposure required by the CT scanner isn't all that significant, Dr. Britton," Dr. Adams pointed out.

Laurel managed a slight smile, mustering up the courage to stick to her point. "That's true, of course. But it's still more than it needs to be. Less would be an advantage because Dr. Lee could test more frequently. With the photon absorptiometer, the patient would only be subjected to what she'd get from the normal background in two weeks. From the CT she'd receive the equivalent of a year and a half's natural radiation."

Laurel decided to jump in all the way. Her words came out in a slight rush. "I know Dr. Parrish applied for funds to purchase the machine. I'd like to second that motion."

Dr. Adams's gray eyes flicked over her face. "Are you always so opinionated, Dr. Britton?"

Laurel's cheeks grew warm at his icy insinuation. "I'm afraid so," she answered honestly. "But only when I have strong feelings about something. As well as the knowledge to back those feelings up."

"Yet you're willing to ignore the fact women runners are possibly in grave danger of risking permanent bone loss."

"I'm ignoring nothing," Laurel argued, her temper starting to flare at his demeaning tone. "I simply believe the findings are preliminary and have been blown all out of proportion by male sports journalists who want to force women off the athletic field and back into the kitchen."

He gave her a sharp glance. "I don't believe this is the place for women's liberation speeches, Doctor. But even if it were, you're a damn poor choice to talk women's equality."

Now Laurel was incensed. She rose up to her full height, forgetting her vow to discuss this issue calmly. "Exactly what do you mean by that?"

"I was referring to your display with that football player." He heaped an extra helping of scorn on the term, his prejudices blatantly obvious. "One day on the job and you're already arranging intimate little evenings at home with one of your patients."

Dr. Adams's eyes were steely little marbles. "Is that why you turned to *sports medicine* in the first place, Dr. Britton?" His tone, when stressing her specialty, was as acid as it had been earlier when stating Nick's.

"That question does not justify an answer."

"It was a rhetorical one, Doctor. After all, it's obvious you'll meet more eligible men in this field than you would in the more traditional women's roles of pediatrician or obstetrician." With that last verbal slap in the face, Dr. Adams turned on his heel and left the room.

"I can't believe that man," Laurel spluttered furiously.

"Neither can I," Tony seconded in amazement. "The man's never been Mr. Personality, but other than asking me the first week I was here why I hadn't gone into acupuncture, he's left me pretty much alone."

"He was probably afraid you'd poison the coffee and he'd never be able to tell until it was too late," Laurel shot back.

Tony laughed appreciatively. "You've got a point." Then his look changed to one of obvious interest. "Uh, I was going to try to figure out how to lead into this gracefully, but since our *führer* already brought the subject up, what's between you and Nick McGraw? This morning you were moaning about meeting the guy."

"I was moaning about *treating* him," Laurel corrected. "I met the man yesterday. Under less than optimum conditions."

"Anything juicy for the clinic's gossip line?"

"Not unless you're into stories from Ripley's Believe It or Not. My piano put a dent in his brand-new Ferrari."

"How in the world did that happen?"

Laurel grimaced. "Believe me, you had to have been there."

Tony rolled his eyes. "I'm glad I wasn't. The man must have hit the roof."

"Hey, what about my piano?" Laurel countered.

Instead of answering, her colleague crossed his arms and leaned back against a desk, eyeing her with renewed interest. "Did you argue like this with Nick McGraw?"

"Of course. Just because he's a famous football player and we happen to be neighbors, doesn't mean that—"

"You're neighbors?"

"Yes."

"How close?"

"Next door, but I don't see what that has to do with anything."

"Ah so, the plot thickens." He grinned as Laurel muttered a low oath and returned to her work. The plaster mix had hardened during the interim and she was forced to begin all over again.

"Don't start spreading tales," she warned. "There's absolutely nothing between us and I intend to keep it that way."

"Are you so sure about that?" He asked exactly the same question Nick had when he'd issued the challenge, Laurel realized. She wondered if men got together in locker rooms periodically to rehearse these pat little lines.

"Positive. Why?" she tacked on suspiciously when her colleague didn't answer.

He took the X ray down and slipped it into a wide white folder, which he tucked under his arm. "Because," he said as he left the room, "it doesn't exactly take much to see that Nick McGraw has an entirely different idea about that."

He only laughed as she threatened to throw the entire mess of soggy plaster at him.

LAUREL WAS EXHAUSTED when she pulled into her driveway much later that day. The November sun was low on the western horizon, but every bone in her body was insisting it was long past her bedtime. A quick glance next door showed that Nick's car must be in for repair. An older model Ferrari that was still a great deal more flamboyant than her American-built compact was parked in the driveway.

"What do you have against American industry?" she asked instantly as Nick opened her front door.

He braced an elbow on the doorframe, looking down at her with a puzzled expression on his face. "That's a new one. Whatever happened to 'hello dear, did you have a nice day at the office?'"

"I was referring to your choice in transportation. I've never known anyone who got an Italian sports car for a loaner."

Comprehension dawned and he grinned boyishly. "They agreed to make an exception in my case. This body would automatically reject a Plymouth."

She shook her head. "It must be nice to get everything you want out of life."

Nick neglected to tell her how far off base she was with that statement. "It's better than a jab in the eye with a sharp stick," he agreed cheerfully.

Laurel wondered why she even tried to relate to this obviously spoiled superstar. She ducked under his arm, entering her foyer.

"How's Danny?" she asked with inner trepidation. Laurel didn't know if she was up to handling tantrums and complaints this evening.

"Terrific," Nick related, following her into her living room. "He read the entire Nip the Bear book, impressing his teacher considerably, I was given to understand. Then he hit a double at recess, driving in the winning run, although he regrettably got left on third base when a less adept batter struck out. And his football has been autographed by the entire offensive line of the Phoenix Thunderbirds. As we speak I've got the kid setting the table out by the pool so we can have a picnic."

He grinned, his appraising gaze sweeping over her. "Your son, Dr. Britton, had a very good day. You, on the other hand, look about as beat up as I feel." Nick handed her a glass of chilled white wine.

"Thanks," she murmured, forgetting for the moment that she was furious with him for embarrassing her at the clinic. She took a sip of the smooth Chardonnay, finding it the perfect prescription. "Although I might point out you don't do a heck of a lot for a woman's ego, McGraw. Whatever happened to pretty compliments?"

Nick took her briefcase from her hand, tossing it down onto a pile of boxes. "I didn't think they'd work with you," he said simply.

A slight grin hovered at the corners of his mouth and Laurel noticed a scar curving up and outward from his top lip. A face mask, she decided, wondering what drove these professional athletes. It had to be more than money and fame. They suffered from their obsession far more than their fans would ever realize.

"Would they?" His deep voice broke into her thoughts.

"Would what?" she answered blankly, dragging her gaze from his firmly cut lips.

"Would pretty compliments work?"

Laurel took another sip of her wine, eyeing him silently over the rim of her glass. He'd located her dishes, she realized irrelevantly. That in itself must have been a major achievement, considering her rather haphazard packing method.

"I don't know," she answered finally. "Right now I'm so tired and discouraged that any kind word would probably seem like manna from heaven."

She was beat, Nick determined, reading the vulnerability in her eyes. Resisting the voice of conscience trying to make itself heard in the back of his mind, he closed the slight gap between them, coming to stand just inches away. Laurel drew in a breath as he reached out and tucked her dark hair behind her ear.

"I could try telling you that your hair reminds me of liquid silk. Would that appeal to your feminine ego, Laurel?"

Laurel wanted to close her eyes to the tantalizing gentle touch, but that would mean giving up viewing the bright green gaze warming her face with its darkening heat.

"It might," she murmured. "But not if you say it to every woman you meet."

"I don't. Usually the women I know have fat hair."

And they know how to play this game, he added silently, watching Laurel's brown eyes soften dangerously. Even with the fatigue lacing them, they were still the most alluring eyes he'd ever seen. Nick felt as if he was drowning in rich, melted chocolate.

Laurel knew encouraging such words from a man who probably considered seduction a national pastime was rash behavior. But she was powerless to move as she felt the slow, inexorable tightening of the silken web around them.

"Fat hair?"

Nick saw the movement in her throat as she swallowed. Like taking candy from a baby, he mused. She'd let her guard down and it would be so, so easy.

He lifted random strands of her glossy chestnut hair, running them through his fingers like sifting sand. "Fat hair," he repeated. "You know—three feet high, two feet wide and hard as concrete. That stuff can put a guy's eye out if he's not careful."

"Oh. Fat hair," she whispered.

The confusion in her eyes oddly failed to give him pleasure. Nick felt a flash of irritation at his uncharacteristic vacillation. This wasn't going as planned. He was creating havoc to her senses, but damn it, she wasn't supposed to be doing the same thing to him. Laurel Britton was a challenge—a lovely, desirable woman he intended to have simply because he wanted her. And Nick was used to getting everything he wanted, especially when it came to women. He frowned, annoyed by the way her liquid dark eyes created doubts that billowed in his mind like thick clouds of smoke from a prairie fire. He was frustrated, but secretly relieved as a crash from outside shattered the mood.

"Oh, my God, I completely forgot about Danny!"

"He's fine. Don't worry about him."

Laurel had broken free of the evocative mood, grateful for the flare of anger invoked by his off-handed tone. "Make up your mind, McGraw. This afternoon you questioned my mothering abilities and now you're telling me not to care when it sounds as if the house is falling down around my child's ears!"

Nick muttered a soft oath and followed her out to the brick terrace overlooking the rectangular, Grecian-style pool. Danny was fitfully sweeping up a pile of glass Laurel recognized as once having been a Waterford crystal pitcher. He paled as he looked up to see the two adults.

"Gee, Mom, it just slipped out of my hands. Nick and I made some lemonade and I wanted to put it in something real special. To celebrate your first day at work." Freckles stood out vividly on his ashen complexion. "I promise I'll buy you another pitcher. I'll get a job mowing lawns after school."

Laurel's heart turned over at her son's earnest expression. She gave him an encouraging smile as she hugged him. "It was only a pitcher. Besides, in case you haven't noticed, there're not a lot of lawns around here. Everyone has desert landscaping."

"Then I'll deliver papers," he vowed, breaking away to begin his furious sweeping once again. "Or wash cars, or something. Don't worry, I'll pay you back!"

Laurel firmly extracted the broom from his hands. "Hey, kiddo, I just realized you did me a big favor by getting rid of that old thing. I never should have brought it with me."

"But that was your extra best pitcher! You've had it forever. Longer than me even."

"It was a wedding present form Grandma Britton," Laurel informed her son dryly.

Danny grimaced at the idea of the Britton family's grim-faced matriarch. "Yuck."

Laurel chuckled as she ruffled her son's hair. "My sentiments exactly. Thinking about it, I should have just given it to Amanda as a wedding present. It's more her style."

As soon as the words escaped, Laurel knew she'd made a tactical error mentioning Geoffrey's second wife. "I like Amanda, Mom," Danny responded on cue.

Nick's steady green eyes were on her face as she forced a smile. "Hey, me too," she lied quickly, not about to force her child to choose sides. "It's just that since Amanda has more time to take care of things like silver and crystal, I should've given it to her in the first place."

Danny looked mollified. "I've got a great idea, Mom," he said, his voice alive with youthful enthusiasm. Laurel expelled a sigh of relief they'd gotten over that touchy subject once again.

Then, unwittingly, he managed to drive a stake into her heart. "When I go home for Christmas, you can send all the fancy stuff you don't want back with me."

Feeling Nick's curious study of her stricken expression, Laurel knelt, keeping her head down as she picked up the larger shards of crystal. Ever since discovering her own infertility, Amanda had been pressuring Geoffrey to talk Laurel into allowing Danny to live with them. Laurel knew her ex-husband had no real wish to have his son with him full time, but if it made his wife happy, he'd certainly give it his best shot. While he hadn't yet gone as far as suing for custody, Laurel suspected he and Amanda were planning to convince Danny during his Christmas visit that he'd be happier in Seattle.

She had to force her answer past the lump in her throat. "Good idea, Danny. Do you have any of that lemonade left?" When he nodded, she suggested with feigned brightness, "Why don't you go fill a plastic pitcher this time and bring it out?"

Her eyes were burning with unshed tears as she turned away from Nick's observant gaze. "Home," she murmured, as if to herself. "Of course he still thinks of Seattle as home."

Nick knew Laurel was hurting and wondered at the cause. It had to be more than the fact Danny was suffering from normal homesickness. He wondered how long Laurel had been divorced. Had her husband left her for this Amanda person? Was she still carrying a torch for him? Was she here in Phoenix because, unable to watch her ex-husband basking in connubial bliss with his new wife, she'd run away? That idea caused an oddly unpleasant feeling of jealousy that he forced away.

He came up behind her, cupping her slumped shoulders in his strong palms. "Hey, that's only natural. The kid's lived there all his life. Give it some time, Laurel."

She sniffed inelegantly, wiping at the traitorous tears with the back of her hand. "I know all that, intellectually. Damn. You must think I'm an absolute idiot."

Forgetting for the moment his desire to get her into his bed, Nick only wanted to comfort. "No, I think you're dead on your feet," he corrected calmly. "Just wait until you get Dr. McGraw's famous, fast-acting, pleasant-tasting, secret formula for weary bodies and aching bones. It's guaranteed to cure all ills that dare to plague beautiful, sexy women physicians."

Laurel managed a shaky laugh at his encouraging tone. "I'm afraid to ask."

"Do you like gourmet Italian fare, m'lady?"

"You're kidding!"

"Of course I'm not," he countered, an expression of mock affront on his tanned face. "In fact, even as we speak, the finest Italian chefs are working their fingers to the bone preparing a feast that'll make your lusciously attractive mouth water."

His eyes danced with a devilish gleam that reminded Laurel of Danny's, when he'd gotten into mischief.

"I think you've just slipped the bonds of maturity once again, McGraw," she accused lightly. "Why do I get the feeling there's more to this than meets the eye?"

At that moment, as if on cue, Danny reappeared, supplying her answer. "Hey, Nick, I need twenty dollars. The guy's here with the pizzas."

"Gourmet?" She arched a dark eyebrow.

Nick shrugged, digging into his back pocket for his wallet. "Hey, don't worry your pretty little head about it. I spare no expense when it comes to my friends."

He grinned, ruffling her hair with the same easy familiarity she had Danny's. "Take your shoes off and sit down, Dr. Britton," he prescribed over his shoulder as he left to pay the deliveryman. "Dinner is served."

Laurel was amazed they got through the meal without a single argument, or a repeat of that disturbing sensuality that settled over them from time to time. Danny talked a mile a minute, his words coming like machine-gun fire as he told her all about his day. It was easy to tell the high point had been the Thunderbirds' practice.

"Hey, Mom," he offered into a moment of comfortable silence. "You should've seen Nick! He got sacked on the last play and still ran wind sprints after scrimmage."

The wedge of gooey pizza had been on the way to her mouth but at Danny's admiring statement she slowly lowered it to her plate. Her gaze cut to Nick's impassive face.

"Since when is the quarterback fair game in scrimmages?"

He shrugged with exaggerated nonchalance. "Since Carr took over as coach. His feeling is that they hit quarterbacks in the game, why not in practice?"

Laurel stared at him, waiting to hear it was merely his idea of a bad joke. "You've got to be kidding."

He wished he was. "Nope. The day of putting a red jersey on a quarterback that says 'don't hit this poor bastard' is over, I guess. At least as far as the Thunderbirds go."

"That knee of yours can't take that many hits," she said sharply. "It's criminal that your own coach is allowing such behavior. Encouraging it, even."

He waved a dismissive hand, casting a quick glance toward Danny, who was watching the exchange with avid interest. "Hey, don't worry about it. I can still take a few hits, can't I, sport?"

Danny nodded vigorously, his mouth filled with pizza. His eyes were bright with obvious hero worship and Laurel knew that as his physician, she and Nick were going to have to discuss this seriously. But he was right. There was no point in worrying her son.

"Wind sprints?" she asked under her breath as Danny took off toward the gate, carrying a thick slice of pepperoni pizza to Rowdy, who'd been whining on his side of the fence.

"You'd better believe it," Nick groaned, dropping his macho pose for the moment. "Three-and-a-half miles of forty-yard dashes."

"I'm not allowing that!"

He managed a wry grin. "What am I supposed to do? Bring a note from my neighbor?"

She crossed her arms over her chest. "No—from your doctor. You're in danger of causing permanent injury to that knee, Nick McGraw. I can't believe you'd take a stupid risk like that."

"I've got to play, Laurel. And I'll put up with whatever Carr tries to force me off the team rather than quit." His expression grew momentarily fierce. "Hell, I know the message he's sending. He's letting me know that while I may admittedly be the star, he pulls the strings. It's just a power play with some guys."

Nick was amazed as Laurel cursed him fluently, her tone low in deference to her son, but her words extremely colorful and as imaginative as any he'd heard.

"Is that any way to talk to your poor wounded patient?" he objected. "Don't tell me they taught you that language in medical school, Dr. Britton."

She glared at him, finding the amusement in his green eyes even more maddening than his devil-may-care attitude about his safety.

"This isn't funny," she snapped.

His gaze turned solemn. "I never said it was."

Nick sighed, rising from his chair to pace back and forth in silent aggravation. Laurel couldn't help noticing the pronounced limp that hadn't been there earlier that day when she'd examined him.

Her tone was measurably softer, coaxing compliance this time, rather than demanding obedience. "At least sit down."

He did as requested, flinging his body onto a lounge chair. Linking his fingers together behind his head, he closed his eyes for a long, thoughtful time.

Free to study him openly, Laurel detected definite signs of fatigue she'd not noticed earlier. Weary from the unexpected patient load, trying to learn unfamiliar office procedures and putting up with Dr. Adams's uncordial attitude, she hadn't considered the possibility that Nick would be every bit as exhausted as she. More so, she amended, considering the outrageous practice he'd undergone.

She rose slowly, moving to sit on the edge of the lounge. "I've an idea," she suggested softly. "Why don't I give you a massage and you can get to bed? I've been a selfish rat letting you take care of Danny and provide dinner, too.... See what happens to people who volunteer? They get taken advantage of."

His eyes remained shut. "It was only pizza."

She smiled and Nick could hear it in her voice. "It sure tasted like gourmet Italian cooking to me, McGraw. I was so starved I would've settled for the box it came in."

He opened his eyes at that, sharing the smile with her. As their gazes locked, he found his exhaustion being rapidly replaced by a familiar, escalating desire.

"Who's suggesting that message? Dr. Britton, or her lovely alter ego, Laurel?"

The message in Nick's deep velvety voice was unmistakable and Laurel had to fight against every rebellious atom in her body as she forced a casual tone. "Sorry, Mr. Football Star, but that offer came from Dr. Britton."

He trailed a finger up her arm. "I know why you're doing this, Laurel."

"Doing what?"

"Taking care of me like this."

"I'm your doctor," she reminded him, as well as herself.

His gaze was bright with insinuation. "True, but there's another reason you're not being honest enough to admit."

"Oh, really?" Her voice was unsteady as the treacherous finger traced a line along her collarbone. Dear God, it was happening again.

He winked a brilliant emerald eye. "Of course. You need help unpacking all those crates and I wouldn't be of much use hobbling around on a pair of crutches, now would I?"

Laurel didn't return his teasing smile this time. "If you're not careful, you'll end up in far worse shape than that."

He shook his blond head. "Laurel, Laurel," he said on a deep sigh. "Didn't I tell you not to sweat the little stuff?"

"Nick—"

"Now hush, woman. I don't want to disillusion what may be my last remaining fan."

He looked over her shoulder at Danny, who was returning from feeding the dog. Laurel bit off her frustrated response, forced to save her argument for later.

Danny's broad grin claimed his freckled face. "Rowdy's a great dog, Nick."

"I've always thought so. But he gets awfully lonely now that I'm back at work. I don't suppose you'd be willing to help me out with that little problem?" he asked casually.

Laurel watched her son's eyes light with hopeful anticipation. "Sure. But how?"

Nick sat up, swinging his feet to the ground. "This battered old body isn't as spry as it used to be. Especially after daily practice. Rowdy needs someone younger to play fetch, swim with him, spend a little time with him each evening. You wouldn't know anyone willing to do that, would you?"

"I would!"

"And of course I'll pay you," Nick tacked on.

"Wow! Did you hear that, Mom?"

"I heard it, but you certainly can't take any money for playing with Nick's dog, Daniel Britton, so get that gleam of avarice out of your eyes."

"He wouldn't be playing, Laurel," Nick argued smoothly. "He'd be exercising Rowdy for me." His eyes shone devilishly. "Unless you think a nightly jog with my dog would be good for my knees."

"Of course not," she snapped, wishing he'd take his situation more seriously.

Nick rubbed his hands together, grinning with obvious satisfaction. "Then it's a deal. A dollar a day, and all the lemonade you can drink."

Danny looked as if he'd just been given the assignment to search for the Holy Grail. "Wow," he repeated once again. "It's a deal. And I promise never to miss a day!"

Nick laughed and Laurel managed a tentative smile as Danny began talking about the practice once again. The conversation turned to anecdotes about games played during Nick's long professional career, and as the last faint color of day tinged the sky a brilliant scarlet and gold, Danny's lashes began to drift closed.

"He's had an exciting day," she murmured. "I think it's time for him to go to bed."

"Need some help?" he inquired as Danny's head settled into the curve of her shoulder.

"No, I can handle it. Why don't you pour us some more wine and I'll be back out to give you that massage I promised."

He sighed happily. "Wine, a lovely lady and a massage, all in one night. I'm not certain I can handle that much happiness, Laurel."

"You're tough, McGraw. Believe me, you'll survive."

The answering smile faded from Nick's face as he watched her leave. He lay back on the lounge, attempting to sort out these inexplicable feelings for Laurel he kept experiencing.

He couldn't say he'd been instantly drawn to her. That would be a lie. Yet, from the moment she'd begun arguing about that ridiculous excuse for a piano, he'd felt a certain unwilling admiration for her behavior. Good old-fashioned spunk was what his father would call it, he knew.

He empathized with the way her life had suddenly altered and knew how wearisome and oftentimes frightening it was to adapt to change. He hadn't handled his own life well this past year. Nick hoped he could salvage the situation by regaining his ranking as one of the top three quarterbacks in the country. Although he was no longer capable of scrambling the intricate patterns that had earned the Thunderbirds three trips to the Super Bowl and two national titles, he could still pass. And if he had to put up with all Carr's marine-sergeant drills to get back on top, then so be it.

He liked the way Laurel seemed honestly concerned about him and sensed her worry came as much from the woman as the doctor. He certainly wasn't used to genuine concern. Most women gushed over him when he'd first been injured, but he'd always known that the first Sunday he couldn't drag himself out onto the field, the crowd of willing admiring females would disappear. They were along for the ride, and it was understood they wouldn't be expected to tag along if it took a downhill turn anywhere along the way.

Laurel was the flip side of that coin. Nick expected one hell of an argument about his practice routines. He could practically see her storming onto the field, giving Coach Ward Carr a piece of her mind. That was something he was going to have to make certain didn't happen, if he had to tie her up and sit on her.

"Something funny?"

She'd returned and was standing over him, a puzzled expression on her face. Nick realized he'd been smiling at the thought of holding the feisty Dr. Britton down anywhere against her will.

"I was considering the logistics of holding you down when you'd made up your mind to do something," he admitted.

Laurel didn't mince words. "Like telling that idiot who's masquerading as a football coach what I think of live hitting in his damn scrimmages?"

Nick knew the anger flashing in her dark eyes was not meant for him. He patted the lounge, inviting her to sit down. "That was one of the more unwelcome scenarios."

"I don't know if you understand how important it is for you to go slowly, Nick."

His level gaze held hers. "And I'm not certain you understand how important it is for me to make a full comeback this season."

She realized he was actually going to jeopardize his knee in order to continue playing. It was times like this she wanted to pick up the nearest thing and knock some sense into these obsessive athletes. Laurel ran—every day as a rule—but she'd never behaved as if it was the only thing in her life.

She rose from the lounge in an abrupt, jerky movement, wrapping her arms about herself as she walked to the edge of the pool. They'd turned on the underwater light earlier in the evening, making the water gleam a bright, welcoming aquamarine. But her mind was not on the inviting depths. Instead she was seeing Nick's torn and battered knee.

"If you're insisting on miracle cures, you've got the wrong doctor, McGraw. Try signing on a faith healer instead. Because I don't have anything to offer."

Oh yes, you do, lovely Laurel, he could have answered. He still wanted her. His fingertips tingled with the need to experience the satin of her skin and he knew he'd go crazy if he couldn't taste those luscious ripe lips soon. Nick tilted back his head, tossing off the rest of his wine. He couldn't remember when he'd wanted—needed—a woman more.

Although he was vaguely disturbed by the fact Laurel had already affected him more deeply than other women of his experience, Nick refused to allow himself to worry. If things became too difficult, he could always solve this dilemma by getting up, walking through that gate and remaining forever on his own side of the fence. He knew that with an ironclad certainty. Just as he knew he wasn't going to do it.

4

"I THOUGHT WE'D agreed to be friends," Nick said simply.

Laurel didn't turn around. "We agreed to try being friends. But it isn't going to work; you're too hardheaded."

"And you're not?"

Laurel sighed, slowly turning toward him. Her distress was written all over her face. "Of course I am. But I'm your doctor and you refuse to listen to me!"

He rose, gingerly favoring his right leg as he came to stand in front of her. Only a few inches separated them as he gazed down, his eyes caressing her face.

"You're also an attractive woman, Laurel. And I've listened to every word you've said."

His thumb moved lightly up her throat, tracing the line of her slender jaw, coming to rest at the corner of her lips.

"You have such a beautiful mouth," he murmured, his square-cut thumbnail following the full upper arch of her top lip. "It just begs to be kissed."

"Now you're being fanciful," she whispered, trembling slightly at the feathery touch against her skin.

"No, I'm not," he corrected firmly but gently. "Tell me the truth, haven't you been wondering all day what this kiss would be like?"

To her dismay, Laurel found herself incapable of denying his words. "It's only a natural curiosity," she finally said softly, trying to explain away these sensations. Every time she considered the idea of Nick McGraw's firm lips pressing against hers, she felt as if she'd been buffeted by a brisk autumn wind.

"Only natural," he agreed. "And since we're both adults, there's really no harm in satisfying a totally normal curiosity."

"So long as it's only a kiss, I suppose no harm could come of it. Since we're both adults," she echoed on a whisper.

His eyes moved across her face with the intensity of a physical caress as his thumb toyed at the corner of her lips. Laurel felt her mouth go suddenly dry and as she nervously licked her lips, Nick stifled a deep masculine groan.

"I'm going to kiss you now, Laurel," he warned her with great gravity.

Her softly-lit dark eyes gave him her answer as Laurel swallowed again, watching Nick's sun-streaked head come closer. She closed her eyes, breathing in the enticing scent of his aftershave. Green, she decided, like a forest, but not a brisk pine. It was warm and primeval. Blending with Nick's own masculine scent, the aroma was of moist dark earth—pungent, heady and so very, very right for him.

As his mouth touched hers lightly, she thought, *I shouldn't be doing this.* Not with this man. Definitely not with this man, she repeated even while delighting in the mint-sprigged taste of his breath.

Nick's fingers cupped her jaw, not moving to explore her body as they experienced how thrilling a mere kiss can be when two people come together at that perfect moment in time. His lips plucked at hers, tenderly, teasingly, and as they blazed a trail over her uptilted face, leaving sparks on every inch of heated skin—her eyelids, her cheeks, her temple, her chin—Laurel knew this kiss surpassed any that might have come before it.

"Nice," he murmured, his teeth nibbling with gentle beguilement on her earlobe.

"Very nice," she agreed on a soft sound of pleasure.

"Shall we try again?"

She knew she was playing with fire, but like a moth drawn to a flame, she couldn't resist the gleaming warmth in his eyes.

"I still have a little bit of curiosity left," she admitted, her melted-chocolate gaze handing him a clear invitation.

"I'm giving you fair warning, sweetheart. All this is piquing mine even more." His voice was gruff, unmistakably laced with bridled passion.

Laurel couldn't remember moving, but a moment later she was folded in his arms. "This is madness," she murmured, a faint tinge of regret in her tone.

"Mmm," he said. "Let's hear it for the loonies. They really know how to live."

A slow kindling longing was building up inside Laurel as her breasts yielded softly to the strength of his chest and she gave herself up to the absolute glory of his kiss, knowing that if this was indeed madness, she didn't know why sanity had always been held up as the ideal.

Degree by glorious degree he deepened the kiss, and Laurel willingly responded, her lips hungry under his. The rest of the world slipped away as her attention centered solely on Nick's lips. Lips that were continually changing, first hard and strong, then soft and gentle. And sweet, so wonderfully, dazzlingly sweet. It was as if he meant to kiss her endlessly, and as his lips became the center of her universe, the sun of her existence, Laurel prayed he'd never stop.

"Well?"

His deep voice sliced through the sensual fog of her thoughts and Laurel's eyes flew open to view Nick observing her with an inordinate amount of outward calm.

She did her best to match it, not wanting him to know she had been taken to the very edge of reason with a mere kiss.

"I'd say my curiosity has been satisfied. You're a very good kisser, Nick. But I suppose it's like everything else—practice makes perfect."

Nick forced his attention away from the fire surging through his veins. He wanted to be alone with Laurel; he wanted to explore her satiny skin at his leisure, to taste and touch and experience every inch of her slender, perfect body. Need vibrated through him even as his mind attempted to make sense of the fact this woman had succeeded in turning his world upside down with only a kiss.

"It helps," he agreed cheerfully. Lord, he didn't want to ever let her go. "Want to practice together?"

Laurel knew if she allowed an encore of that performance, she'd be an absolute goner. Besides, a faint little voice of reason was trying to make itself heard in the distant pockets of her mind. It was telling her this was a far cry from a professional patient-doctor relationship.

She pressed against the rock-hard strength of his shoulders. "I'd say we've satisfied our curiosity, Nick. Let's leave it at that."

At her crisp, professional tone, Nick wondered if Dr. Laurel Britton was actually capable of such iron-clad control. Impossible. She was, however, a hell of an actress. He struggled to maintain an appearance of nonchalance, deciding to allow her this retreat for the time being.

While he was definitely not a patient man, Nick knew that by not forcing the issue, his eventual victory would be even sweeter. She wanted him; everything from her softly glazed dark eyes to her trembling as she'd pressed her willowy body against his gave her away. It was only a matter of time.

"It's probably just as well," he said lightly. "You'd just let slip what a magnificent lover I was to one of your girlfriends, and I'd have to sell my house, change my name and move to another town in order to get any rest."

"Your ego is as fat as your medical chart, McGraw," Laurel said with a laugh, relieved by his easy acceptance and enjoying his good humor.

She'd been afraid she was going to have a fight on her hands and cool waves of relief rushed over her as she slipped out of the circle of his arms and began gathering up paper plates and glasses.

"Hey, what are you doing?"

"Cleaning up so I can get to sleep. I work, remember?"

"What about my massage?"

Laurel recognized determination when she saw it, possessing a fair share of that personality trait herself. Nick McGraw wanted her, and if she was to be perfectly honest, she'd have to admit he wasn't alone in his desire. But Laurel also knew their mutual attraction was far too dangerous. To get involved with this man would be like strapping sticks of TNT to her body and walking into a roomful of pyromaniacs armed with matches. It was only a passing infatuation, she assured herself. Just avoid temptation and it would run its natural course.

"I've already massaged that oversize male ego by admitting you're a pretty fair kisser, Nick. Let's save the body for some other night."

She was definitely shaken. Nick gave himself points as he stood his ground, his grin surprisingly boyish. "Promise?"

Laurel sought refuge in her profession. "Do you promise to take it easy during practice?" she countered.

"I promise to hit the deck every time I see a human mountain heading my way."

Her expression was one of genuine concern. "Do you swear? No heroics?"

He lifted a palm in the gesture of a pledge. "No unnecessary heroics," he agreed.

Laurel's breath escaped on a rippling sigh. It was impossible not to catch his alteration of her request. "Go home, McGraw. I've had about as much of you as I can take for one day."

Nick was not used to receiving such dismissal from anyone, let alone a woman. He'd discovered at the early age of twelve his extraordinary talent with a football caused people to cater to him, granting his every wish. Fawning females had never irritated him; on the contrary, he'd taken their presence as his natural right. He was a star, and it only made sense that as such, he received preferential treatment.

But if Laurel was the type of woman to pay homage to any man, he'd yet to see any indication of such forthcoming behavior. She'd teased him, argued with him and steadfastly refused him. She'd also intrigued him. Even as badly as he wanted her body, Nick found himself wanting to know this woman better. He was determined to stay close to her until all his curiosity about the lovely Dr. Laurel Britton was finally satisfied.

"May I pick Danny up from school again tomorrow?"

Laurel shook her head slowly. *Keep him at a distance*, she warned herself firmly. "I don't think so. I don't want him to get used to spending every evening with you."

"Hey, I didn't say anything about the evening." His crooked grin was mildly apologetic as he glibly thought up the lie. "As it happens, I've got a date tomorrow night. I was going to suggest you could pick him up at the field after you finish at the clinic. Practice won't be over until about six."

Laurel fought against revealing the disappointment his words caused. Of course there would be a plethora of women in this man's life, what did she expect?

"Oh. Then I suppose it's all right. If you're certain he's no bother."

"None at all. I like kids, believe it or not. Even ones who root for the Seahawks." His smile extended to his eyes. "Good night, Laurel."

"Good night, Nick," she murmured, lifting her hand in farewell as he disappeared through the gate.

She finished cleaning up, then undressed, flinging her clothing in a careless trail behind her as she made her way through the maze of unpacked cartons to the master bedroom. As she slid beneath the sheet emblazoned with rainbows, it crossed Laurel's mind that not in the three years since her divorce, had this king-size bed ever seemed so lonely. Then, exhausted, she gave herself up to a much needed sleep.

LAUREL'S SECOND DAY at the clinic proved less stressful than the first. Now that the rash of holiday injuries had passed, her patient load was far more manageable, and she found herself falling into the routine as if she'd been there for months, and not just two days. The only fly in the ointment, she considered with wry resignation, was Dr. Adams. Continually during the day she felt those steely gray eyes watching her, observing her silently, as if waiting for a misstep. He did, however, refrain from entering into direct confrontation.

"Hey, you look great," Tony Lee complimented her as she exited the women's lounge after freshening up at the end of the day. "Hot date tonight?"

Laurel self-consciously smoothed nonexistent wrinkles from her cream linen skirt. "Not at all. In fact, I'm unpacking tonight."

Her colleague's dark eyes danced devilishly. "I see. And you always dress up like that for manual labor."

"I'm not dressed up. For heaven's sake, it's the same outfit I've worn all day."

His observant gaze moved judiciously from the top of her head, taking in her freshly brushed dark hair, down to her toes. "You weren't wearing high heels," he pointed out.

She shrugged. "Flats are more practical for work."

He nodded solemnly. "Of course. Just like heels are more practical for unpacking moving crates." A teasing grin quirked at the corner of his lips. "You've also unfastened an additional button on that enticing silk blouse you kept unkindly covered by a starched lab coat all day. And the seductive cloud of fragrance hovering about you is definitely not antiseptic, Dr. Britton."

Before she could come up with an appropriate answer to Tony's all-too-accurate observation, Dr. Adams stopped by on his way to the parking lot.

"Doing a little trolling this evening, Dr. Britton?"

"Excuse me?"

For an instant, Laurel thought she detected a glimmer of interest in the man's cold eyes as they flicked over her. "Bait, Dr. Britton, obviously bait. If that football player responds to White Shoulders, I'd say you're going to land a big one tonight." With that, he walked away.

Laurel watched him go, shaking her head in genuine confusion. "I cannot figure that man out." She turned toward Tony. "Did you get the odd impression that . . . Oh, skip it, that's ridiculous."

"That our illustrious administrator displayed a moment of honest masculine appreciation before slipping back behind his carp mask?"

Laurel was sorry she'd brought it up. She was not one to dig for masculine compliments, nor was it usual behavior to go out of her way to appear attractive to one certain man as she admittedly had this evening.

"I told you it was ridiculous."

"Of course it's not," Tony countered swiftly. "If I wasn't happily married, I'd be hoping you'd gone to that much trouble for me." His teasing grin appeared playfully expectant. "You didn't, did you?"

"Do you want to lock up or shall I?" she countered abruptly, changing the subject.

Tony shoved his hands into his pockets, knowing when to give up. "You go on ahead, Laurel. I'll take care of things. And hey, have a nice evening." When she looked at him sharply, he gave her an expression of sheer innocence. "With your unpacking."

Laurel's nervousness increased as she drove to the Phoenix Thunderbirds' practice field. Would Nick notice she'd gone out of her way to appear feminine and appealing? Would he realize that although she disliked admitting it, even to herself, she'd dressed with him in mind?

"Of course he will, dummy," she muttered as she idled her compact car at a red light. "Even Adams noticed. And I'll bet my little black bag it's been years since any life stirred in that man's icy blue blood."

The thought of her acrimonious superior made her scowl at the same time her attention shifted toward the car next to her. The middle-aged man had been eyeing her with friendly interest, but at her blistering gaze, a dark red flush rose from his collar and he quickly swivelled his head toward the windshield. Laurel sighed, shifting gears as the light changed and she made her way through the intersection.

She spotted Danny right away at the field, and as she walked along the sidelines to where he waited behind the Thunderbirds' bench, her appearance drew a few admiring whistles. While she managed to keep her head high and her eyes straight ahead, Laurel secretly admitted the attention was rather nice.

A roar rose from the spectators and she stopped momentarily to watch the action on the field. Although it was November and early evening, the unseasonable temperature was in the high nineties. She was surprised to see the players practicing in full gear.

Nick took the snap from the center, dropped back and scanned the coverage. She cringed, hoping he wouldn't swivel too abruptly and put to much pressure on his damaged knee, but as it turned out, he didn't have time. A linebacker the size of an enormous sequoia broke through the offensive line and Nick vanished under an avalanche of bodies. The watching fans breathed the united sound a crowd makes while watching Fourth of July fireworks. Then to Laurel's amazement, they began to applaud.

It was all she could do to keep from running out on the field, both the doctor and the woman in her aghast at the intensity of the hit. She pressed her fingers against her lips, forcing herself to wait.

A murmur ran through the ranks as Nick rose to his feet, apparently unharmed. But Laurel knew that if practices continued at this level, it would be a miracle if he made it all the way through the season.

"Isn't that a pretty hard tackle for a scrimmage, coach?"

She turned in the direction of the question, observing the television camera on the sidelines focused on the short, stocky coach.

Ward Carr pushed his Thunderbirds cap back on his head. "Hell, football is a tough game. A violent game. No cream puffs need apply," he replied in a gravelly, rough voice.

"Are you calling Nick McGraw a cream puff?" the sportscaster asked on a note of disbelief.

"Look, in this sport pain is just a state of mind. I'm no doctor— if McGraw says he's ready to play, then he damn well better be ready to get hit. Every player knows he's going to get hurt, and the chances are he could get hurt bad. If a guy can't take it, let him get the hell out of the game. That's football. We intend to make winners out of these guys if we have to do it over their dead bodies."

His tone was casual, even flippant, and Laurel felt her temper escalating to dangerous proportions. The man was an absolute menace. She was on the verge of telling him exactly that, on television if possible, when she felt a hand tugging at the sleeve of her blouse.

"Hi, Mom. Isn't it nifty?"

"It's criminal," she answered, raising her voice to a level she hoped would be picked up by the microphone. Her furious gaze held Ward Carr's as well at that of the surprised sportscaster, who glanced back over his shoulder to see who was interfering with his taped interview. "This kind of rough practice is ridiculous at the professional level."

She heard Carr mumble something under his breath, earning an appreciative laugh from the sportscaster as they returned their attention to the subject at hand. Laurel fumed silently, glancing toward the field just in time to see Nick complete a short, hard pass.

"Can we stay a little longer, Mom? They're almost finished."

She knew watching the vicious scrimmage would only aggravate her further. But the sight of Nick, clad in a red-and-gold jersey, held an unwilling fascination.

"Just a bit," she agreed. "We've a lot to do at home, though. We can't keep living like Gypsies."

"Gee, thanks Mom. You're the greatest!" His freckled face was wreathed in a smile and Laurel said a silent prayer Danny would remember that at Christmas, when he was back with his father in Seattle.

She agonized during the next half hour as the practice became even more vicious and the pileups deepened. The assistant coaches had obviously been instructed to hold their whistle-blowing to a minimum, and fistfights were becoming almost routine after every play. One particularly savage hit drove Nick into a group of players watching from behind the line of scrimmage, stretching him out flat on the turf. She was distressed but not surprised when he came up swinging at the offending linebacker, and the players had to separate these opposing members of the same team.

That was fortunately the last play of the day, and after an incredible series of wind sprints, the players were allowed to limp their way to the showers. Instead of leaving the field immediately, Nick came toward her, waving his gold helmet in his hand.

"Are you all right?" Her worried brown eyes skimmed his body, as if searching for injuries before focusing on his face.

He shrugged, reaching out to tousle Danny's hair. "Just a nice, light workout for an autumn evening. You look terrific, by the way, Dr. Britton. And don't tell me that's Phisohex."

Laurel smiled. "No," she admitted. "White Shoulders."

"My favorite kind."

"Perfume?"

"That, too."

He grinned, his teasing gaze moving over her amber silk blouse, as he envisioned her pearly skin underneath. She'd gone out of her way to leave Dr. Britton back at the clinic, he determined. This luscious lady was definitely the lovely Laurel. Oh no, they weren't finished. Not by a long shot.

Laurel could feel the silken web settling over them once again and was relieved when Danny broke the evocative silence.

"Can I come again tomorrow, Mom?"

She looked from her son to Nick. "I don't know."

Nick shrugged, his shoulders appearing even more massive in the wide shoulder pads. "It's okay with me, Laurel."

"We'll talk about it when we get home, Danny," she hedged, taking his hand as she nodded to Nick. "I think you'd better put some ice on that elbow, Nick. It looked as if you jarred it when you were hit that last time."

His eyes were glued to her mouth. "Yeah, I did," he answered absently. As she appeared ready to leave, he had to fight back the urge to reach out and touch her. "Hey, want me to walk you and Danny out to your car?"

Laurel shook her head, keeping her regret from showing on her face. "No. You'd better get showered and changed. You'll be late for your date."

As Nick watched Laurel walk away, her back straight, her stride long and purposeful, he had an overwhelming urge to shout out for her to stop.

5

LAUREL TRIED HER BEST to stop her imagination from conjuring up such vivid pictures of what Nick was doing on his date while the evening progressed. She threw herself into her work, determined to make some inroads into the herculean task before her. Making her way through the kitchen boxes first, she vowed to go shopping during her lunch break tomorrow and buy some nutritious food. While she knew Danny would happily continue eating takeout for the rest of his life, she felt guilty about not providing him with home-cooked, well-balanced meals.

By midnight she'd emptied all the crates in the kitchen, dining room and living room. Danny had been sound asleep for hours, and she went upstairs to take a shower, scrubbing at the newsprint stains on her skin. As she rubbed herself dry with a soft terry towel, Laurel couldn't help fantasizing the touch of Nick's wide, strong hands.

What was he doing now, she wondered, clutching the towel to her breasts. Was he lying with some voluptuous blonde, his lips and fingertips caressing every lush curve? She allowed the towel to drop unheeded to the floor, her judicious gaze taking in her reflection in the full-length mirror.

"You're too skinny for a man like him," she murmured, knowing while her uptilted breasts were firm, she'd never have a photographer from *Playboy* banging on her door. She splayed her fingers on her waist, giving herself credit for its narrow span. However, as her hands traced her hips, Laurel admitted that while she could be considered boyishly attractive in jeans, her curves would never inspire erotic fantasies in a man with the ready-made harem Nick McGraw probably possessed.

Her legs were long, her thighs firm from running, the well-defined curve of her calves leading to trim ankles. "Maybe he's an ankle man," she mused, wondering if she had the nerve to go out and buy one of those slim gold chains to see if it would garner Nick's attention.

She shook herself firmly back to reality, pulling her short blue robe from a hook on the back of the bathroom door. "That idea is ridiculous for a woman of your age," she scolded herself firmly. "Next you'll be thinking of putting a ruby in your navel and wearing crimson harem pants. Physicians do not dress like belly dancers." She marched out of the bathroom, flicking off the light behind her. "And they definitely don't fantasize about making love with their patients!"

Still irritatingly wide-awake, Laurel wandered into the kitchen to make herself a cup of hot chocolate, hoping it would help her sleep. She couldn't keep herself from glancing out the window. It had began to rain, and through the slanting drops she saw a few random lights on in Nick's house. Was he home? Was he in one of those darkened rooms, lying in a passionate embrace, his masculine appetites temporarily satiated?

Laurel groaned, unwilling to submit herself to any further mental torture. She dragged her gaze downward to the pan of milk, determinedly watching for the little ring of bubbles. Moments later, a knock at the kitchen door startled her.

"Nick!" She stared up at him as he opened the door.

"Hi. I saw your light and thought you might not mind some company." He leaned against her doorframe, smiling down at her as if he saw nothing unusual about dropping in at this late hour.

In truth, he'd had to force himself to wait this long. Now, in retrospect, he was glad he'd waited. Her flushed, freshly bathed skin exuded a faint, intoxicating fragrance that weakened his knees. Then Nick belatedly realized he hadn't come up with an excuse for coming over here. He couldn't allow her to think his only motive had been the simple need to see her again.

"I thought you might like a little help with your unpacking," he ad-libbed the lie.

This can't become a habit, she told herself firmly. *If you let him come over here after dates like this, you're only going to end up getting hurt.*

"I was just going to bed," she lied badly, her fingers gripping the edges of her short satin robe a little closer together. From the gleam that suddenly lit his eyes, Laurel knew he'd perceived she was wearing nothing under the robe.

Nick feigned absolute innocence, directing his gaze past her shoulder. "Your milk's burning."

"Oh damn!" Laurel spun around, taking the pan from the heat and dumping the caramelized remains down the drain.

"Let me," he suggested. "I make a hell of a cup of cocoa."

"You?" She arched a challenging eyebrow. "I find that extremely difficult to believe."

"Why?"

"I just can't imagine you being handy in the kitchen."

His green eyes gleamed with a provocative message. "Oh, I don't know, I've been assured that I'm pretty handy all over the house." He allowed a long, wicked pause. "Want me to audition?"

Her gaze narrowed as she held the lapels of her robe more tightly together. The increased beat of her heart thumped wildly in her ears and Laurel irrationally worried Nick could hear it as well.

"We're talking cocoa here, right?"

"Of course. From scratch, actually," he stated calmly, eyeing her instant hot chocolate mix with a frown. He dug around in her cupboard, pulling things out and lining them up on the counter. "Let's see, cocoa, sugar, salt, a little vanilla, cinnamon. You're going to love this."

Unfortunately, Laurel believed him. She tried to find something about the man she didn't like. "What happened to your date?" she asked caustically. "Did the great Nick McGraw strike out?"

"That's baseball. And I never kiss and tell."

"A casanova with principles. Will wonders never cease."

He grinned as he observed her over his shoulder. "Ouch. 'They have sharpened their tongues like a snake.'"

"Is that Shakespeare?" she inquired, wishing her premed studies had allowed more of an acquaintance with liberal arts.

Laurel always felt uneasy with people who could spout clever quotations. It was certainly not that she was undereducated; she'd just never found any way to fit the structure of the DNA molecule into casual conversation.

"Nope. The Bible. Psalms." He was stirring the mixture and missed her incredulous gaze.

"A casanova who quotes Psalms? Now that is unique."

"I'm one in a million," he agreed cheerfully, reaching into a cupboard and taking down two handcrafted ceramic mugs. Laurel watched the little spiral of steam rise as he poured the dark chocolate mixture.

"Here, try this."

She lifted the bright, flowered mug to her lips, taking a tentative sip. It was rich, sweet and a definite improvement over the uninspired drink she'd been going to make.

"You're hired," she said immediately.

Nick chuckled, pulling up a chair and straddling it, folding his arms along the top. "Why do I have a feeling that while you are probably one terrific Dr. Frankenstein in the laboratory, you're not that comfortable in the kitchen?"

"I've been known to burn water," she admitted. "Fortunately Danny has simple tastes. His father finally gave up on my culinary efforts and ate at the hospital." She managed a wry grin. "If you've ever tasted institutional food, that gives you some indication of my questionable abilities in the kitchen."

Nick's gaze was as warm as Laurel's cocoa. "I think you're underestimating yourself," he murmured, his eyes moving over her face with the impact of a physical caress. "I'm sure you're marvelous in the kitchen. In the bathroom. In the bedroom, and—"

"Nick." She cut him off with a shaky note of warning.

"Spoilsport."

His smile was masculinely challenging as he eyed her over the top of his mug. When he patted his lips with a paper napkin, Laurel wondered why she should find that simple gesture so provocative. She focused on those firmly cut lips and her blood warmed at the memory of the feel of them against her own.

Nick didn't miss the rosy flush under her skin, but he forced himself to keep the conversation casual. For now.

"Danny's father is a doctor, too?"

Laurel nodded.

"Sports?"

That earned a bitter laugh. "Hardly."

"Something less than honorable in treating jocks?" he asked curiously.

Nick had to fight to keep his eyes on her face. Her robe had parted just enough to allow an entrancing view of silky skin and he longed for the opportunity to view Laurel's slender body at his leisure. White Shoulders fit her perfectly, he decided, stealing a surreptitious glance at her creamy flesh.

"No, it's just that Geoffrey chose a specialty more suited to his image of himself as a healer. He's a cardiovascular surgeon. He feels it inspires more awe than general practitioners taking care of runny noses, or sports specialists taping up swollen ankles."

"I suppose I can understand that. But I for one am glad you chose your particular specialty, Dr. Britton." His eyes were gleaming emeralds, filled with insinuation, and as they dropped to the open folds of her robe flames suddenly rose in their depths, like sparks escaping an untended fire.

"How are you feeling?" She drew the edges of her robe back together, forcing her voice into a professional tone.

"Laurel—"

"I do hope you weren't too vigorous on your date," she said swiftly, not willing to accept the way his lush voice embraced her name. "I probably should have warned you to stay away from positions number forty-nine and eighty-seven with that knee....

"After all, McGraw, it may be my job to glue you back together after a game, but any injuries you get on your own time are your responsibility." Laurel knew she'd begun to babble but was helpless to stop.

"Dammit, Laurel, I didn't come over here for a round of verbal sparring."

"Why did you come over?" she asked, honestly curious.

He shrugged. "I don't know."

Nick stared down into the dark chocolate depths of his mug, as if the swirling liquid held some special meaning for him. When he slowly lifted his gaze to her face, his expression was unnervingly solemn.

"I think I wanted to explain about this evening."

"Your date?"

He nodded.

Laurel rose immediately, taking her empty mug to the sink and rinsing it before putting it into the dishwasher. She kept her back to Nick the entire time.

"Don't worry about it, Nick. I never expected anything because of last night. Good heavens, who was it who said 'one swallow doesn't make a summer'?"

"Aristotle." He amazed Laurel by answering her rhetorical question.

She turned around and stared at him, wishing she could understand this man who had more facets to his personality than a well-cut diamond.

"Aristotle," she repeated slowly. Then, gathering her scattered thoughts, she nodded firmly. "Well, just as one swallow doesn't make a summer, one kiss certainly doesn't make a love affair. So don't worry about me misunderstanding, Nick."

He was standing over her in two long strides. "We shared two kisses last night, Laurel. Not one. I'm hurt you could forget so easily."

She was suddenly drowning in the warm green pools of his eyes and Laurel knew Nick could read the answering spark in her own gaze.

"I didn't forget."

Nick reminded himself that while Laurel was attractive and definitely appealing, especially wearing this silky robe that displayed her long slender legs, his telephone directory was filled with women who were just as attractive, just as appealing, and didn't expect anything but a good time.

That was a lie, he admitted inwardly. He knew of no woman as appealing as Laurel Britton. Why hadn't he met her two years ago? Before his perfect life had begun unraveling at the seams.

"I didn't forget, either," he muttered, pulling her against him.

His mouth suddenly ground on hers in a bruising kiss that threatened to take her breath away. Nick's frustration with his situation made him rash; there was none of the tenderness he'd displayed with those experimental kisses of last night. He was all primitive male as he wanted and he took, his burning need spiraling out of control. His tongue stabbed its way between her shocked lips and his mouth crushed hers in an electric, endless demand.

At the first startling impact, a kaleidoscope of swirling colors exploded behind Laurel's eyes, releasing the desire that had been building up for this man all night. Her fingers moved up his arms, digging into his broad shoulders as she clung to his strength. She gave herself up entirely to his raw masculine demands, wanting his superior power, in truth, needing it. Nick's overwhelming physical force and brutal aggression was allowing her to fling aside her rigid mental restraints, meeting him with an equal passion of her own.

Nick groaned his approval as Laurel's tongue slipped between his harsh male lips, sweeping the dark cavern of his mouth, gathering in the moisture from every secret corner. She dragged her fingers through his wheat-blond hair, holding his head in her palms as she deepened the kiss, her own need no gentler than his, her own demands no less desperate.

His arms tightened about her, and as she rose up on her toes, he could feel her warm, pliant female shape fitting itself to him from her breasts to her thighs. He was standing on the very brink of sanity and as he tugged on the sash of the blue satin robe, opening it to allow his palms to skim her body, Nick knew there would be no turning back.

Laurel closed her eyes to the erotic torment of Nick's hands roving her body at will. Reason was scattered to the four winds as she allowed him forbidden intimacies, encouraged him with her breathless cries of pleasure. As Nick's fingers grasped her buttocks, the soft swell of her breasts, the satiny skin of her inner thighs, his touch was everything she'd imagined and more. So much more. His hands were everywhere, leaving a warmth that engulfed her in a cresting tide of desire. When her own fingers began to tear at the buttons of his dress shirt, Nick covered her hand with his own, lifting her wrist to his lips for a brief kiss. His eyes flamed as they burned into hers, holding her gaze as she deftly opened his shirt with one hand. His skin burned with the need for her touch and as Laurel's palms pressed against his chest, Nick sucked in a deep harsh breath.

In a slower, sensual response, his hands traced her slender curves, like conquerors mapping out an exotic, foreign territory. She was so incredibly soft; her skin seemed to flow warmly under his touch, like liquid satin. Nick dragged his mouth from

Laurel's, pressing his cheek against the silky strands of her hair, breathing in the lushly fragrant scent of floral shampoo. Her arms wrapped around him and her hands splayed over his back as she arched her body against his in a spiraling feminine need.

He was unable to stifle the groan as he sucked the air into his lungs on a harsh breath. Laurel suddenly froze.

"You're hurt!" Her wide brown eyes searched his face, seeking the truth there first.

Damn! He shrugged in a dismissing gesture. "Football players are always hurt." His palms shaped her shoulders, encouraging her to forget the untimely interruption. "And just in case you've any questions along those lines, let me assure you all the important parts are in full working order."

But Laurel backed away a few inches, her eyes narrowing. "Don't joke about this, Nick. I probed all around that knee yesterday without you flinching, and it had to have been tender. You've a very high tolerance for pain, so for you to moan like that, something's definitely wrong."

Her fingers began to move over him, their intent more precise, more determined than the graceful fluttering pattern they'd danced on his skin a moment earlier.

"That was merely a moan of passion," he tried, knowing that the mood had been shattered for tonight.

Laurel didn't answer, intent upon her examination. When she pressed against his rib cage, Nick drew in an involuntary breath.

"Lift up your arms," she instructed.

"Not until you answer a question for me."

Her fingers were carefully tracing a line from his side to the center of his chest. Laurel was furious, but certainly not at Nick, and she tried to keep the anger from her voice. But her words came out short and crisp.

"What now, McGraw?"

"Are we finished with the passionate part of this evening?" The sight of her forbidden pearly skin was making concentration difficult. He forced his gaze to a point somewhere beyond Laurel's left shoulder.

She looked up, finding his face an inscrutable mask. "Yes," she acknowledged with a sigh. "It was a bad idea in the first place."

"I don't know, I kind of enjoyed it," he argued, gritting his teeth as her fingers probed deeper into his flesh. "Very much, actually."

"So did I," she admitted. "But we've satisfied as much curiosity as I'm going to allow." Laurel didn't miss Nick's short intake of breath as her fingers hit home.

"Ow!"

"That's what I thought. You've cracked a rib." She shook her head. "You're lucky that's all that happened, the way you were throwing yourself under those linebackers during practice. I thought you weren't going to try to be a hero."

"Believe me, Laurel, I didn't try to get in those guys' way. It certainly isn't my idea of fun being run over by 225 pounds of human mountain."

"I don't understand why they were hitting you like that," she complained. Nick read the distress in her soft brown eyes and wondered how it could affect him so deeply. Everything about Laurel Britton hit like a jolt of lightning from a clear blue sky. Nick wasn't certain he liked the feeling.

"They want to play," he said simply, grimacing as he tried a careless shrug. "If they don't play by Carr's rules, they'll be warming the bench Sunday. It's his way or the highway, that's what he's fond of quoting to the press."

"Sometimes I think you're all crazy." She sighed with heartfelt exasperation. "At least promise me you'll wear your flak jacket Sunday."

He was relieved they weren't going to get into an argument, not being in the mood to explain how important this upcoming game was. How vital this season was. He was Nick McGraw, star quarterback. That's who he'd been for as long as he could remember, and Nick didn't know how to separate the man from the football player, even if he'd wanted to. Which he damn well didn't.

"Cross my heart and hope to die," he pledged, making a corresponding sign over his bare chest. A wicked light danced in his green eyes. "Uh, Laurel, are you sure you're not interested in indulging in a little heavy breathing?"

Her soft, caring gaze hardened. "I hate it when you slip into that automatic seduction routine."

A smile played on his lips. "That's a nope, right?"

"Right."

"Then could you do me a favor, Dr. Britton?"

She eyed him suspiciously. "What kind of favor?"

Nick rubbed his palm over his face, shaking his head with regret. "Could you please tie the sash on that robe? It's awfully hard to behave with temptation so deliciously near."

She glanced down, realizing in her concern for Nick she'd forgotten all about her state of undress. She wrapped the material about herself, yanking the sash tight.

"You should have said something."

He arched an incredulous eyebrow. "Hey, I thought we'd at least determined I'm not a dumb jock. Why should I give up such delectable scenery?"

Her eyes flashed dangerously. "You're incorrigible McGraw."

"I honestly tried to tell you, Laurel. But Dr. Britton was too busy sadistically poking her lovely fingers into my battered old flesh."

Laurel's anger dissolved as rapidly as it had flared and her brow furrowed with concern. "It's far from old, Nick. And it would be in perfect condition if you'd just quit playing football."

His face turned to stone. "Don't even suggest that," he warned in a cold, remote tone. "Because it isn't going to happen."

He was kidding again. He had to be. "Sure," she shot back flippantly. "You're going to be playing until they carry you off the field at the ripe old age of ninety-nine. And I'll be submitting all your doctor bills to Medicare."

He raked his fingers through his sun-streaked hair and from the way they were trembling with restrained fury, Laurel realized Nick found nothing humorous about the turn their conversation had taken.

"You and Carr should get together and take that act on the road." His tone was harsh as he turned on his heel and marched out the door, slamming it thunderously behind him.

Laurel was left to stare out into the dark, stunned by this newest aspect of Nick McGraw's frustratingly complex personality.

AT LEAST THE RAIN had cooled things off, Laurel considered, breathing in the fresh desert air as she drove to the clinic the next morning with the car windows down. Her uplifted spirits plummeted as she reached her office, finding it occupied by two burly workmen.

"Roof leaked last night," one of them explained, pointing to the gaping hole above her desk.

She grimaced at the stack of damp papers on her desk. "Is my office the only one affected?"

"Nope. The private treatment rooms are going to be out of commission for a while, too. The tar paper pulled loose on this part of the building." He shook his head. "Can't trust these flat roofs in the rain," he advised, returning to his work.

Laurel wasn't looking forward to working another day in the fishbowl atmosphere of the common treatment room, under the intense scrutiny of Dr. Adams, but realized pragmatically she had no choice. Stifling a sigh, she went to work.

"Dr. Britton, there's a call for you on line five."

Laurel glanced up sometime later from the pulled hamstring she'd been examining. "Can you get a number and I'll return the call?"

"Sure." The receptionist was back a moment later. "Mr. McGraw says he'll hold."

Laurel didn't miss Tony Lee's smug smile. "All right," she said, picking up the receiver of the wall phone. "Hello."

"I just called to tell you I'll pick Danny up today," Nick began without preamble.

"That's not necessary."

"But I want to."

This was definitely no place for a personal conversation. Tony was displaying unabashed interest as he rummaged through a stack of wrist splints and Laurel could feel Dr. Adams's gray eyes directed at her back.

"Thank you anyway," she replied briskly, "but I'd really prefer you didn't."

"Would it help if I apologized?" Nick asked, his voice deep and beguiling.

"No."

"I am sorry, you know."

"Well, thank you for calling," Laurel said lightly, wanting to end this conversation before it became so personal every interested bystander in the treatment room would know the intimate details of her life.

Nick instantly perceived her intention. "If you hang up, Laurel, you're only going to have to continue this conversation in person. Because I'll be down at the clinic in a half hour."

"You're not on my schedule," she complained.

"Pencil me in as an emergency," he instructed, his firm tone indicating he expected nothing less.

Laurel experienced a momentary stab of concern. "Are you all right? Is it your knee?"

"My knee's fine," he assured her instantly. "It's my ribs. I need them taped before practice."

"That's what the team has trainers for, Nick."

"I'd rather have you do it. See you in a while, Dr. Britton." He hung up the phone.

"That will be fine then, Mr. McGraw," Laurel said into the disconnected telephone, unwilling to let the others know he'd hung up on her. "I'll be expecting you."

"More trouble with that knee?" Tony asked.

"No. He cracked a rib and needs it taped up."

"I thought trainers usually did that," he offered guilelessly.

Laurel shot him a mock glare. "Don't push it, Lee. Or you'll be back on coffee duty."

"Please spare us that unspeakable indignity, Dr. Britton," Dr. Adams murmured as he left the room. "Yours, while definitely not gourmet, is at least drinkable."

Laurel watched him go, then shrugged, unable to tell whether the man had made a joke or not. She didn't know who had ever stated women were the complicated sex; men easily won that title, hands down.

She didn't even need to glance toward the door; the flurry of activity twenty minutes later could only mean one thing. Nick had arrived. Refusing to be part of the crowd of females surrounding him, she leaned against her treatment table, watching as he made his way across the room.

"Like Moses parting the Red Sea," she murmured.

"I'm afraid that reference escapes me," he admitted with a smile.

Laurel shrugged. "I was just observing the way you forged your way through that sea of admirers." She turned her back, pulling out a roll of wide tape. "Sit up and take your shirt off, McGraw."

He didn't move. "Is it that you don't like athletes in general? Or is it me in particular?"

Laurel's back was still to him. "I told you, I like athletes. Professionally," she tacked on with pointed emphasis.

"But not personally."

She turned around, her expression firmly set into one of brisk impatience. "Are you going to take your shirt off so I can tape up that rib? You *are* cutting into my schedule, you know. The least you can do is to be cooperative."

The soft violet shadows under her eyes were mute testimony to the fact she hadn't managed any more sleep last night than he had. Encouraged, Nick held his ground.

"Answer my question first."

"Look, McGraw, I've already spent four long years with one man who wanted to be treated like God. If I was masochistic enough to get involved with another, I'd simply go somewhere they practice self-flagellation."

His green eyes narrowed dangerously, and she was intrigued by the muscle jerking along his thrusting jawline. Before she could utter a word of complaint, his hand was cupping her elbow.

"You're coming with me."

"The hell I am," Laurel retorted in a low harsh whisper, her dark eyes darting around the room to see if they were being observed.

It didn't help to discover she and Nick were the center of attention. The usually bustling atmosphere had suddenly become as quiet as a tomb, the spectators' attention all directed toward the drama being played out before them.

Nick's gaze followed hers. "Damn." Then, to her utter amazement, his fingers tightened on her arm and he started walking across the floor.

"Nick, let go of me!" It was still a whisper, but easily heard in the swirling silence of the room.

"You can come along with me to your office peacefully, or I'll carry you screaming and kicking over my shoulder," he replied with amazing calm. One look upward into those glittering green eyes assured Laurel he meant every word.

"My office has people working in it," she argued. At his dubious expression, she elaborated. "The roof leaked last night."

"Then we'll go somewhere else," he countered immediately.

"I have other patients."

"This will only take a minute." He continued walking, stopping only momentarily at Tony Lee's treatment table. "Is there someplace private around here?"

Tony nodded in the direction of the hallway. "Third door on your left. It's the doctors' lounge," he stated helpfully.

"Thanks." Nick didn't release Laurel as he continued toward the door.

"Thanks a lot," she ground out over her shoulder at Tony.

He grinned unrepentantly. "My pleasure."

Nick didn't mince words. "All right," he said, the moment they were alone, "you have every right to be angry with me. I behaved like a bastard last night and took out my trouble on you. So, I'm sorry."

"Apology accepted," she said in a tight voice. "Now may I return to my work?"

"This is more important than your work, Laurel!"

She lifted her chin, meeting his furious gaze with a challenging one of her own. "Oh? And what would you do if I marched out onto your precious football field and hauled you off into the showers for a personal conversation?"

A wide smile suddenly lit his face. "Why, I'd offer to wash your back, of course."

"Cute, McGraw. Real cute."

Nick sighed, shaking his head. Laurel tried not to be affected by the way a sun-streaked blond lock fell across his brow, contrasting so vividly with his dark tan.

"I really don't want to fight with you, Laurel. I understand how important your work is. I just want to explain that my behavior last night was due to a personal problem I'm trying to work out. It had nothing to do with you. With us."

"There is no *us*, Nick. Get that through your head right now," she warned.

Even as she said it, Laurel realized it was a lie. She had grown incredibly close to this man in a few short days, but she knew it was only a sexual attraction. He was handsome, famous and actually very nice, when he wasn't coming on like a storm trooper. Any woman would be infatuated. It was nothing more than that, she assured herself—a chemical brain bath.

At this moment, frustrated by Laurel's continued intransigence, Nick could have cheerfully strangled her. "But there is," he argued, hitting one strong fist into his palm. "Number one, we're neighbors—"

"I've read somewhere that the majority of Americans don't know their neighbors' first names," she interrupted.

"Number two, we're friends."

"That's debatable."

He pretended not to hear that one. "And reason number three is that you're going to hurt Danny if you suddenly cut off the practices without a good explanation."

She slumped down into a chair at the table, cupping her chin in her palm as she looked up at him. "If you're honestly concerned about Danny, let's talk about what's going to happen if I let you infiltrate yourself into his life and then you lose interest. That would hurt him a great deal more, Nick."

He had the feeling there was more to Laurel's objection than met the eye, but decided not to press her for the moment. Instead, he sat down next to her, his gaze unbearably serious. "I wouldn't do that, Laurel. You have to believe that."

"I believe you wouldn't mean to; but soon you'd have a lot better ways to spend your time than with a seven-year-old boy. The end result would be the same."

Laurel's expression was intent as she tried to make Nick understand. "Danny's having enough trouble getting over leaving his father. I don't want him to have the same problem with you."

"I'm not going anywhere," he said simply. "Look, we'll stick to being just friends, if that makes you feel any better about the arrangement. And if you want, I'll begin letting Danny down easily, but for now, I think it's helping him adjust to the move."

Laurel sighed a deep, surrendering breath. "All right. But no more late-night visits. It's strictly a good neighbor policy where you and I are concerned, McGraw."

Nick gave her a crooked smile. "You're probably right," he agreed on an answering sigh. "One thing neither of us needs right now is more complications." That much was true, but even as Nick agreed he knew he'd never be able to keep his word.

His eyes darkened dangerously. "But it would've been good, Laurel. Very good." He observed her for a long, silent moment. "Danny can come to practice, then?"

She nodded, unable to force an answer past the lump in her throat.

"I can bring him home," Nick offered. "Save you a trip downtown."

Laurel asked herself if she could honestly bar Nick McGraw from her house if he showed up at her door. Especially since Danny would undoubtedly ask Nick to stay for dinner. It would be inviting disaster, she decided.

"Don't bother. I'll pick him up at the field."

"Promise not to get into any brawls with Coach Carr?" A familiar, dancing light reappeared in his eyes.

Laurel managed a shaky smile. "I promise to be on my best behavior."

"Good." His answering grin grew a little wider. "It would play havoc with my tough-guy image if a woman started fighting my battles for me."

"Your doctor's supposed to watch out for your welfare, Nick," she reminded him softly.

"And such a lovely doctor you are, Laurel Britton," he murmured, his eyes softening as he gazed down at her thoughtfully. Laurel was certain she'd stopped breathing when he reached out and lightly brushed his knuckles along her cheek. "Absolutely lovely." Then he opened the door, preparing to leave.

"Your rib." Laurel belatedly recalled Nick's purpose in coming to the clinic in the first place.

He winked a bright emerald eye. "Hey, lady—what do you think they have trainers for?"

6

LAUREL FELL INTO a familiar pattern of working at the clinic, then stopping by the Thunderbirds' practice field to pick up Danny. Nick kept his distance, and although it admittedly bothered her, she knew she'd made the right decision.

She'd planned a private party at home to celebrate completing her first week at her new job and had picked up the makings for spaghetti and meatballs—Danny's favorite.

"Look what Nick gave me," he greeted her, waving his prize over his head like a banner as he ran up to her. "They're tickets for Sunday's game. On the fifty-yard line!"

Laurel had known she wouldn't be able to ignore the upcoming game. She'd told herself it was only because she was concerned about Nick's knee. It was a professional interest, nothing more. She'd told herself that over and over again, but at no time had it sounded the least bit convincing, even to her own ears.

She forced a smile. "That's terrific. I hope you thanked him."

As he climbed into the car, Danny gave her a severe look that reminded her uncomfortably of Geoffrey. "Of course I did. What do you think I am, a dope?"

Laurel shook her head. "Certainly not. How could such an intelligent woman as myself have a less than brilliant son?" Then she delicately attempted to minimize the bond that was developing between Nick and her son. "You know, honey, I wouldn't expect Nick to give us tickets to all his home games."

Bright blue eyes observed her questioningly. "Why not? He's my best friend. And I'm taking great care of Rowdy."

He had certainly done that, Laurel admitted. She'd grown used to having the huge animal underfoot. On the first visit she'd locked Circe in the bedroom, but the Siamese's strident complaints had only increased the animosity between the two animals. Finally, she'd given up and to her amazement, after an initial few moments of mistrust, the two had settled into a truce. At times, watching her cat bat playfully at the wide sweeping golden tail, Laurel could almost imagine they'd begun to like each other.

"It's possible he might want to give his tickets to someone else," she suggested carefully. "We don't want to take up too much of Nick's time."

"I don't take up too much of his time. Besides, he likes kids. He's got loads of brothers and sisters."

"Really?" Laurel wasn't particularly surprised. Nick's behavior with Danny had seemed almost too easy, too casual for a single man.

"Yeah. Eight of them."

"Eight?"

Danny nodded. "He's the oldest."

Laurel wondered how her son had discovered this amazing fact. "When did he tell you that?"

He shrugged, looking out the car window, his attention on the palm trees flanking the roadway. "I dunno. We just talk." He turned toward her, looking somewhat guilty. "I guess I was kinda telling him how it got lonely around here sometimes."

Laurel managed to keep her expression nonchalant. "I suppose it does. But you'll be making friends soon and then it'll get better."

"Friends aren't brothers and sisters," he pointed out with the straightforward logic of a seven-year-old. "How come I don't have any brothers or sisters?"

Because your father was upset enough about me getting pregnant with you, Laurel thought. "We've discussed this before, Danny," she replied calmly. "Your father and I were both in medical school when you were born. Then he had his internship and his residency, and I went back to school. . . . We just didn't think we could give enough time to two children."

"I would have helped."

She smiled, reaching over to pat his knee. He was wearing shorts and she smiled at how tanned he'd already become in less than a week. He had skin like Geoffrey's. It wasn't dark, but it tanned easily, despite his reddish hair and freckles. She, on the other hand, could probably live in Phoenix her entire life and still have milky-white skin. Laurel sighed, certain the women Nick dated probably sported tans the color of dark, golden honey. She couldn't compete, even if she wanted to. *Which I don't*, Laurel reminded herself firmly.

She returned to the conversation. "I know you'd be a big help, Danny. But it's a moot point. I'm not married any longer, so you're going to have to settle for Circe and me."

"You could always marry Nick."

"What?"

From the earnest expression on her son's face, Laurel realized Danny had been giving the matter a great deal of thought. He had a logical mind that went directly to the heart of a problem, quickly and incisively. Another thing he had in common with his father. Sometimes she wondered if Danny had inherited any of her attributes.

The idea of Danny's genetic similarity to Geoffrey caused an all-too-familiar little spiral of fear to crawl up Laurel's spine. *I won't think about that*, she vowed. *Not tonight. In fact, if the phone rings, I won't even answer it.*

Danny's voice broke into her troubled thoughts. "It's simple, Mom," he explained patiently, as if instructing a rather dense kindergartner. "Look, you like kids, right?"

"I like you."

"And Nick likes kids. But neither one of you are married. So if you married each other, your problems would be solved." He nodded, pleased with his reasoning. "You'd have a husband, I'd have a live-in dad, Nick would have a son and then I could have some brothers and sisters."

Then he added what he obviously considered the clincher. "And think of the money you'd both save, only needing one house. We could sell ours and move in with Nick."

"I like our house, Danny," Laurel pointed out. "I thought you did, too."

He rushed in to reassure her. "Hey, it's a great house, Mom. But it has stairs."

"May I point out that was one of the things you requested?" she inquired dryly, remembering how long fulfilling that particular request had taken, especially when combined with a pool, walking distance to a good school and a tree in the backyard big enough for a tree house. She'd found everything but the tree. "I seem to recall something about Circe being able to chase her ball down them."

"Yeah, well, that was okay just for us. But stairs would be hard on Nick's bad knee," he pointed out. "I think we should move into his house, instead."

Laurel shook her head. "Danny," she said with a certain amount of alarm, "you haven't discussed this idea with Nick, have you?"

"Not yet," he admitted. "I wanted him to get used to the idea of having me around first."

"Don't," she warned.

"But, Mom—"

Laurel's expression was firm as she pulled the car into the driveway. She turned off the engine and took the keys from the ignition. Resting her forearms on tip of the steering wheel for a moment, she lowered her forehead to them, garnering strength.

Then giving Danny her sternest look, she said, "If you so much as mention a word of this conversation to Nick, Daniel Patrick Britton, today will be the last practice you ever attend. Is that clear?"

He paled visibly, his freckles darker for the contrast. "Okay, Mom," he agreed in a small voice. "It was just an idea."

"Not one word," she repeated, wagging her finger.

He made the gesture he'd learned last year in school, zipping his mouth, locking it and throwing away the key.

Laurel managed a laugh. "That's better. Now, help me carry in the groceries. We're having your favorite dinner."

"Pasghetti?"

"With hot fudge sundaes for dessert."

Danny hurried to help, the subject mercifully dropped. But Laurel knew her son well. He had a habit of worrying a problem to death, if it interested him. She had the uneasy feeling she hadn't heard the last on this particular matter.

LAUREL HAD NEVER BEEN to a professional football game and was stunned at the noise level the crowd made in the bowl-shaped stadium. Danny's hand trembled with excitement as she held it on the way to their seats, but as soon as the team came onto the field, he tugged free. He didn't want Nick to think of him as a child, she realized, watching him straighten to attention. She felt like assuring her son that Nick would be far too busy to spare even a glance in their direction, when Danny started jumping up and down, waving his red-and-gold pennant wildly.

"There he is, Mom! Nick! Hey, Nick!"

His high, young voice was drowned out by the volume of the crowd, but to Laurel's amazement, Nick turned, looking directly at them. He grinned—a broad, marvelously attractive smile—and waved his helmet in greeting. For a brief moment his gaze locked with Laurel's and the pleasure in his green eyes at seeing her made her heart turn a series of out-of-control somersaults. Then he lifted his hand, his fingers spread in a V sign, before turning his attention back to the coaches.

"He saw us!"

Laurel nodded. "He certainly did. Now stop waving that thing around before you put someone's eye out." Her voice was firm but the smile on her face belied her tone, and Danny grinned, shoving the pennant under his seat, his enthusiasm not in the least bit dampened.

The game got off to a less than impressive start as the opposing Raiders displayed a brutal ground offense, marching continuously through the Thunderbirds' defensive line for a hard-fought touchdown. Laurel's eyes were on Nick as he paced the sidelines in obvious frustration. A conversion put the Raiders ahead by seven, and as the offensive team took to the field, there were a few scattered shouts for Morgan to go in as quarterback.

Nick caught the snap and went back for a pass, but it was blocked by the Raiders' defensive end. The calls for Morgan increased. A second pass was blocked the same way, this time sent back at Nick as if he'd thrown it into a brick wall. The fans were building up steam, the atmosphere reminding Laurel of the Christians and the lions. She decided if an opinion poll was taken for Nick's survival chances, over half the people in the stadium would put thumbs down.

She saw him shout something at the player who'd blocked the shots, watched that player shout something back, but the roar of the crowd made it impossible to know what had been said.

"Mom!" Danny objected, his eyes wide as he stared at the red-faced fans, all on their feet, shouting for Carr to pull Nick from the game.

"Ignore them, Danny. Nick'll do just fine." She only wished her voice held more conviction.

As they lined up for the third down, Laurel crossed her fingers behind her back, resting her other hand on her son's shoulder. Nick dropped back to pass, scanned the field for a fraction of a second, then tucked the ball and galloped away for the necessary ten yards.

All objections melted away as the fans roared their approval. When three plays later the Thunderbirds were on the scoreboard, opposition to Nick seemed to have become ancient history. After that less than spectacular start the Thunderbirds' defense shut down the Raiders' running attack, and Laurel was relieved as Nick stuck to a passing game the remainder of the afternoon. When the game ended, Nick and his Thunderbirds had won, 31-7.

If Danny was ecstatic, Laurel was no less so, her voice hoarse, her throat sore from screaming. She felt like a child herself as they jumped up and down, hugging each other wildly. When Nick looked up at where they were celebrating, she waved Danny's banner, her smile reaching from ear to ear.

It took the rest of the evening to get Danny calmed down enough to go to sleep. He'd begged to go over and congratulate Nick, but judging by the continuous stream of sports cars roaring up to the house next door, Laurel decided it was certainly no place for an idealistic young boy. Assuring her son he'd see Nick tomorrow, she put him to bed, smiling as he fell promptly asleep, running down abruptly like a spring-wound clock.

She sat alone out by the pool, listening to the music and the cacophonous sounds from the wild party going on next door. No wonder the real estate agent had neglected to mention Nick McGraw was her neighbor. If it was going to be like this every Sunday night, she'd be a wreck on Monday mornings. Laurel glared in the direction of the gate in the shared wall, wishing she had the nerve to march over there right now and tell him to quiet things down. Tomorrow, she vowed, tomorrow she'd confront him after practice and insist he behave with more consideration for his neighbors.

She'd just gone in to pour herself another cup of coffee when the phone rang.

"Hello?"

"Laurel?" She wasn't surprised he couldn't hear her. The music in the background was deafening.

"Nick? Turn down the music."

"What?"

"I said, turn down the music!" she shouted.

"I still can't hear you, Laurel. Can you hear me?"

"Barely," she shouted a little louder, wondering why she was even trying. She should just hang up. "What do you want?"

"I need you over here, Laurel," he yelled. A female giggle came over the wires.

"It sounds like you're doing just fine without me, McGraw," she said, furious he had the nerve to invite her to his damn party this late. Not that she would have gone if he'd suggested it earlier. She slammed the receiver down, deciding he could undoubtedly hear that well enough.

Seconds later her phone rang again. "Look, not that anyone could get any sleep around here, but I'd like to try. So knock it off," she shouted.

There was dead silence on the other end. "I really do need you, Laurel," he said finally. She could still hear the party noise in his backyard and wondered where he'd gone that it was suddenly so quiet.

"Where are you?"

"In my bedroom. Alone."

"That shouldn't prove an unsolvable problem. Just open the door and you'll have to fight the women away with a stick."

"I don't know if I can make it to the door."

His low, pained tone caused ice water to run through her veins. "Is it your knee?" she whispered, clutching the receiver with suddenly moist hands.

"That's right. My knee." She heard a muffled groan. "I really do need you, Laurel."

"Give me two minutes to dress and I'll be right there." Laurel hung up the phone, flinging off her robe and nightgown as she ran up the stairs to her bedroom. She pulled a pair of jeans and a T-shirt out of her closet, throwing them on her body, not taking time for anything else. Soon she was through the gate and pushing her way through the throng, desperate to get to him.

"Are you the doc?" A huge man with a neck the circumference of a tree trunk came up to her, eyeing her bag.

"That's right. I'm Dr. Britton."

"Tom Shaw," he introduced himself, sticking out an enormous hand. "I'm the one who's supposed to keep Nick from getting that pretty face bashed in.... He's in the house. I'll show you the way," he offered.

"Is he hurt badly?" she asked as he led her down a long hallway.

Tom answered with an enigmatic smile. "I think he'll be fine now." He opened the door. "Good luck, Nick. I think you're going to need it," he called before making a hasty retreat.

Nick was seated on the end of a wide bed, his forearms on his thighs, his hands clasped loosely together between his knees. Laurel rushed to kneel beside him.

"Can you take those jeans off by yourself, or do you need some help?"

He slowly lifted his head, his green eyes brightening considerably. "Now that is, without a doubt, the most inviting offer I've had all evening."

Laurel studied Nick suspiciously, not seeing the expected shadowing of pain in his eyes. "Your knee," she reminded him.

He gave her a tentative smile. "My knee is fine, Laurel."

She was on her feet instantly. "You lied to me, Nick McGraw! You said you needed me."

"I didn't lie. I do need you." He lifted his palms in a helpless gesture. "I'll admit I stretched the truth about my leg a little in order to get you over here. I didn't think you'd come otherwise." He looked at her curiously. "Would you have?"

As his gaze settled disconcertingly on her breasts, Laurel remembered she'd neglected to put on a bra. She crossed her arms over her chest.

"Of course not. I'm not into orgies."

He sighed, raking his fingers through his hair as he rose to stand over her. "It's only a party."

Laurel turned away, preparing to leave. "Sure, try telling that to the vice squad when they raid the place. Do you usually have an entire line of nearly naked cheerleaders dancing on your kitchen counter?"

"Laurel . . ."

She stopped, unable to walk away from the request in his low voice. But she refused to turn around, knowing she'd never survive the expression he was probably directing her way.

"What it it?"

"I'm lonely, Laurel. That's why I called you."

"Lonely?" She managed a brittle laugh. "Take a look out there, Nick," she advised, waving her hand in the direction of his backyard. "Between the house and the yard there must be two hundred people roaming around this place. Two hundred very noisy people," she tacked on pointedly.

He came up behind her. Although he hadn't yet touched her, Laurel could feel the heat of his body unnervingly near her back. He bent his head, his words a mint-sprigged summer breeze in her ear.

"Haven't you ever been lonely in the middle of a crowd?" he asked softly.

Of course she had. Innumerable times when she'd attended parties with Geoffrey. But that had never seemed so unusual. She'd been lonely at home with her ex-husband, too.

"That's the worst kind of lonely, Laurel." He pressed his case. "Because you realize that you need something more than mere bodies. You need one special person to make everything all right again."

Even as he uttered the seductive words, Nick realized they were true. Unwilling to try to decode why these atypical emotions kept surfacing whenever he was around Laurel, he forced his mind to focus on the obvious. Like the soft scent of wildflowers wafting from her skin. The glossy sheen of her nut-dark hair. And the way her body was trembling of its own volition. Nick knew she was afraid, just as he knew every nerve in her body mirrored his own overwhelming need.

"I'm not that person," she protested in a whisper, wrapping her arms about herself in an unconsciously protective gesture. *Don't listen to this,* she instructed her mind. But she was fast discovering a rosy cloud had settled over her brain and she was left with only her feelings.

"Yes, you are. And I know I'm a rat to take advantage of you like this, but I managed to win a very important game today. A game that meant a lot more to me than the final score would indicate. I want to share that victory with one very special person."

He hesitated, his hands going lightly around her waist as he drew her back against him. "I want . . . no, I need to share these feelings with you, lovely Laurel. Please don't turn me down."

Oh dear Lord, how could she refuse a request like that? "I can't stay here, Nick," she said slowly, turning in his arms to look up at him. "Danny's asleep alone. I only left him because I thought it was an emergency."

Their eyes held and there was a moment of heat as Nick appeared on the brink of kissing her. But he refrained, shaking his head with a soft sigh.

"It *was* an emergency. I had to see you, Laurel. I had to hold you like this. I had to feel how perfectly you fit into my arms."

"Nick—"

"We'll go over to your house," he said simply. "Then Danny won't be alone."

Laurel knew she was playing with a fire that was on the verge of blazing wildly out of control. But it felt so good to have Nick's arms around her, it felt so wonderfully right to have him looking at her, his green eyes smoldering with undisguised desire.

She fought for a lifeline of sanity, forcing herself to throw away the blinders and face his reputation straight on. "I don't know how you usually celebrate a victory, Nick. But as marvelous as today's was, it isn't going to end with you in my bed."

He nodded. "Fair enough." He ran his hand down her side, tracing her slender curves. "I'm not going to lie and say I don't want to make love to you, Laurel. But I'm willing to respect your ground rules. If all we do is talk, that'll be okay, too."

Her soft brown eyes mirrored her vacillation. "Promise?"

"Scout's honor."

That earned a light laugh. "I find it hard to believe the host of that party out there was ever a Boy Scout."

"Eagle Scout. My dad was scoutmaster, actually."

For some odd reason, it was a surprise to think of Nick with a family. Laurel decided perhaps if they got to know each other better, grew more comfortable with each other, this constant attraction would fade. She seriously doubted that, but she wanted to come up with some excuse for allowing Nick to return to her house with her.

"How can you leave your own party?"

He shrugged. "Don't worry about it. No one will notice I'm gone except Tom, and he'll figure out where I am easily enough."

Laurel wondered what kind of friends these were that they were supposed to be here celebrating Nick's victory and wouldn't even care enough to notice he'd disappeared. She and Nick McGraw obviously moved in different circles. They were light-years apart and no amount of sexual chemistry was ever going to change that.

"Just for a while," she warned.

He smiled, brushing a kiss as light as a snowflake against her lips. "Just for a while," he agreed. "Thank you, Laurel."

She gave a brief nod, finding his grave note of sincere appreciation did nothing to instill calm.

7

"AH, PEACE." Nick sighed happily as he sank down onto Laurel's living-room sofa. He linked his fingers behind his head, resting it against the muted striped material as he closed his eyes.

"If peace and quiet were what you were seeking tonight, you've got an awfully funny way of showing it," Laurel pointed out.

He opened one eye. "You sure know how to get to the heart of the matter, don't you, Dr. Britton?"

Then he surprised her by suddenly sitting up straight and looking at her with a certain amount of censure. "Don't you ever have any self-doubts? Or are you so confident about your abilities you can't imagine being like the rest of us poor slobs?"

Laurel stared down at him, wondering where he'd gotten that mistaken impression. Could she possibly come off so cold, so unfeeling? Self-doubts? Good Lord, her life was filled with them. But they were too personal, went too deep and hurt too painfully to share them with anyone. Especially Nick, who had demonstrated all too clearly that depth wasn't what he looked for in a woman.

He gave a sigh, but this time it lacked the pleased note it had a moment earlier. "Do you have anything to drink around here?"

"I've got some coffee," she offered. "Or if you'd like something a little stronger, I think there's a bottle of brandy that managed to arrive down here unbroken."

"Brandy would be terrific," he agreed. "The adrenaline from the game is starting to wear off and I think I need an analgesic."

She gave him a concerned look. "Is your knee hurting?"

Nick smiled, shaking his head. "Honey, my entire body feels like it's been run over by a steamroller."

Laurel opened her mouth to tell him that perhaps he should consider quitting, if this was all the reward he received. But she held her tongue, knowing that when they had that conversation, she'd stand a better chance of making Nick listen to reason when he wasn't so tired. Lines she'd never noticed before were etched into his tanned face and she experienced an inexplicable urge to reach out and stroke them away with her fingertips.

"I'll get the brandy," she told him instead.

He nodded, closing his eyes once more as he leaned his head against the back of the sofa. Sweet. Despite her often irritatingly professional demeanor, the woman was undeniably sweet. And soft. God, how incredibly soft. As he fantasized holding Laurel in his arms, making love to her with uninhibited abandon, Nick drifted off into oblivion.

"Here you are."

His eyes flew open as Laurel sat down beside him and she had the feeling he'd been asleep. "You should be in bed," she scolded.

The heat was still surging through his veins. "I agree. *We* should be in bed."

Laurel fought the response his deeply crooned suggestion created deep within her. "You promised, Nick," she reminded him firmly.

Give it time, he warned himself. Just a little more time. Her pupils were wide and dark, her brown eyes giving away her deepest secrets as they gleamed with an alien heat. Nick managed a casual, yet admittedly regretful tone.

"So I did, Laurel. So I did." He nodded reluctantly, taking the glass from her hand. "Thank you."

As he lifted the glass to his lips, Laurel received a definite jolt. Did everything about this man have to affect her so erotically? It was absolute folly to be sitting here, so close to him, the lights low, the stillness of her home, in direct contrast to the bedlam next door, making the mood seem all the more intimate.

As the bracing liquor cleared his mind, Nick tried to remind himself he was a civilized man. He could not give in to instinct and ravish Laurel right there and then. He damned that pledge he'd made, although he knew that if he hadn't, she wouldn't have allowed him to be sitting there at the moment. He wanted her—Lord, how he wanted her—more than he'd ever wanted a woman in his life. He tried to tell himself it was only to cap off the day in style, to achieve a victory on all fronts, but something in that explanation rang false.

She'd been driving him crazy since the beginning, infiltrating his thoughts, disturbing his sleep. He saw her in his mind's eye when he was supposed to be concentrating on plays—she appeared to him in a myriad of ways and images, constantly changing, like the facets of a child's kaleidoscope. Who the hell was the lovely Dr. Laurel Britton, he wondered. And what was she doing to his mind? To his life?

"I enjoyed the game today," she murmured into the deep silence, running her fingernail along the rim of the glass.

"I'm glad. I'm also glad you came."

"I couldn't very well let Danny down," she replied, struggling to school her voice to a calm nonchalance.

How could she tell him that it would have been impossible to stay away from the game because she'd already discovered it was an impossibility to stay away from him?

"Of course not," he agreed brusquely. "We have to let him down gently."

So that's all it was. A maternal duty. The very idea made Nick feel like a fool for the rush of pleasure he'd experienced when he'd seen her in the stands.

"That's the kindest way."

"I suppose you know best."

"I do." Her firm expression included more than her decision about her son's relationship with Nick McGraw. Even more important was the fact that she was not going to become involved with the man.

Sure, taunted the little voice of reason deep inside her. *That's why you're sitting inches apart in a dimly lit room, sipping brandy with him.*

Nick could no longer be this near Laurel without touching her; every atom in his body was screaming with anticipation. Feeling like a teenager on his first date, he carefully slid his arm around her shoulders. He didn't miss her quick little intake of breath as his fingers curved lightly about her upper arm, but she didn't protest.

"What did you yell at that player today?" she asked blankly, trying to concentrate on something—anything—besides the warmth of his touch on her bare skin.

He took a drink, eyeing her curiously. "Which one?"

"The big one," she managed to answer as his long fingers created havoc with their gentle strokes.

That earned a smile. "Laurel, football players are all big. Could you be a little more specific?"

God, he agonized, her skin was so fragrant, so silky. How could she expect him to keep his mind on football? For the first time in his life, Nick wished he'd never heard of the game.

As the dangerous hand moved down her arm, Laurel felt as if he'd taken a sparkler to her skin. She drew in a deep breath, attempting to focus on this conversation.

"The one who blocked your first two passes."

Nick watched her breasts rise and fall with her breathing under the scant covering of blue cotton and had to grip the stem of his glass to keep his other hand from reaching out and touching her.

His eyes flamed with emerald fire as their gazes met and held. "Oh, him. I told him to stay down."

"Oh," she whispered, engulfed by the warmth directed her way. "But I saw him yell back. What did he say?"

"You have the loveliest mouth, Laurel. It reminds me of an old-fashioned Gibson girl. What do they call it, a Cupid's bow?"

"Something like that," she stammered softly. "What did he say?"

"It just begs to be kissed." His head moved a little closer, his fingers tightening perceptibly on her arm.

"I don't believe he said that," she argued, entranced as his blond head drew nearer. Her lips parted slightly in anticipation as he took her glass from her hand and laid it down with his onto the table in front of them with a slow, deliberate motion. At no time did his eyes leave her mouth.

"You're right. That's not what he said. He warned me that the next one would be an interception. So I surprised the hell out of everyone who thought I couldn't move with this knee and ran the play instead.... Would I be breaking the rules if I kissed you?"

"Yes." It was a not very assertive whisper.

"Then you're going to be forced to call a penalty, sweetheart. Because I'm about to break the rules."

Nick groaned a gentle oath and with that his lips finally bridged the distance, his satisfied sigh filling her mouth. There was no hint of urgency in his manner; it was as if they both surpassed the ordinary realm of time and space as he tasted of Laurel's sweet lips at his leisure.

How amazing that this man who earned his living in such a brutal fashion could be so gentle, so tender, she thought through the rosy fog clouding her mind. His lips were plucking gently at hers, teasing, coaxing, warming her skin with heat that spread through her body in escalating waves.

Laurel told herself this was madness, insanity. The Nick McGraw who had led his team to victory this afternoon had undoubtedly celebrated this way after winning games since high school. By allowing this behavior, she was permitting herself to be nothing but a long-established tradition. A reward for a game well played. Even as she told herself that, the persuasive, wonderful kiss was sending a delicious whisper of pleasure up and down the delicate bones of her spine. Soon, she promised her practical self. Soon she would end this glorious embrace. But, dear Lord, how she wanted it to go on for just a little longer.

The tip of his tongue brushed along the full upper curve of her lip, stroking with little intoxicating movements, bringing every inch of the soft pink flesh to tingling awareness. When his teeth captured the thrusting curve of her lower lip, Laurel tried to remember that what was sheer ecstasy for her was only a victory ritual for Nick.

"Nick, please," she whispered against his lips.

His tongue soothed where his teeth had darkened her skin. "Please, yes?" he inquired on a husky, uneven note. "Or please, no?"

Unable to answer, Laurel closed her eyes, as well as her mind to the tormenting voice of reason as his tongue insinuated itself between her ravished lips, flicking like a finger of flame against the sensitized skin within.

Their bodies pressed together as their mouths met in desperate hunger. Laurel was shocked by the extent of her passion—her skin came alive wherever his roaming hand touched, the blood beneath infused with a thick warmth like heated honey. Her lips moved under his, murmuring inarticulate words that caused Nick's own passion to escalate to a point just short of explosion.

He felt her shudder as his hands slipped under the cotton T-shirt to cup her breasts. She felt so good, so right. Her firm breasts swelled at his touch, her nipples tightening as his palms teased their sensitive nerve endings.

It suddenly flashed through Nick's mind that today he'd proved to everyone that they'd written Nick McGraw's obituary prematurely. There'd been no sign of his injury when he surprised the defensive linemen and ran for that first down. The fans had dropped their objections, lining up behind him once again because they could recognize a winner. He had his life back on track. Everything was as it once was, as it should be, including a beautiful willing woman to make his victory taste even sweeter.

Even as he thought all that, Nick realized his hands were shaking. He was in danger of losing control, which made no sense to his beleaguered mind. He'd had every intention of ending up this evening in Laurel's bed, yet he was stunned by the fact that merely kissing her, simply touching her, was driving him to the ragged edge of sanity.

Nick McGraw made love as he played football—with a practiced skill that made every movement seem inordinately natural. Yet as his fingers fumbled desperately with the zipper on Laurel's jeans, the reason why this physical act, which he had performed so many times before in his lifetime, should suddenly seem so new, so different, eluded his understanding. Before he could dwell on that thought any further, Laurel caught his searching hand.

"Nick, I can't." Part of her was crying out for Nick's exquisite lovemaking. But something equally as strong counseled caution. Laurel had no idea what was happening, but instinct told her they were plunging into something far more entangling than a casual affair. And it was all happening too fast.

"Of course you can." His mouth swallowed her weak protest as his teasing touch created havoc within every fiber of her being. "You can't deny you want me as badly as I want you."

Her palms framed his face: her smoky dark eyes spoke volumes. "Of course I want you," she admitted on a soft sigh. "But we can't always have everything we want."

Nick was appalled by the flash of desperation that seared through him as Laurel began to straighten her clothing, covering up that lustrous creamy skin.

"We can damn well try."

"We can try a little patience, too," she argued, moving away to the other end of the couch.

Laurel knew her behavior could easily be considered irrational and dangerous. She was a grown woman, she knew better than to allow things to get out of control like this. Nick was so much stronger than she, and at the moment his blistering expression was anything but encouraging. If he chose to finish what they'd both begun, Laurel knew she'd be powerless to stop him.

Laurel's obvious trepidation only served to irritate Nick further. While he hated to let her go, he'd never used force on a woman yet and he wasn't about to begin with this one.

"Patience is an overrated virtue . . . Dammit, Laurel, this is ridiculous! I want you. You want me. We're both adults, so what is the matter?"

Laurel desperately wished she knew. "I never meant for this to happen," she said softly. "Not tonight."

"I did," he admitted, rising from the couch in an abrupt movement. He retrieved his glass of brandy, downing the amber liquid in long, thirsty swallows.

"But you promised," she reminded him softly.

He shrugged, trying for a nonchalant attitude. "I lied."

"Oh."

Laurel reached out with trembling hands, picking up her own glass from the table. She eyed him thoughtfully as she sipped the comforting brandy, taking in his rigid stance. Every muscle in the man's body looked horribly tense.

"You do that very well," she murmured finally.

"Which are you talking about? Making love? Or lying?"

"Both, I suppose."

He turned abruptly, walking over to the desk where she'd left the bottle of brandy. "I've had a lot of practice," he said, refilling his glass. He turned back to her, his green eyes glittering masculine warning. "I'm not giving up, you know."

She met his frank gaze with assumed tranquillity, but an inward tremor. "Hasn't a woman ever turned you down, McGraw?"

He leaned his hips against the desk, crossing his legs at the ankles. "What do you think?"

"I think this just may be a first for the infamous star quarterback."

He shook his head. "You've got it all wrong, Laurel. All you've done tonight is postpone the inevitable."

"With delusions of grandeur like that, I think you need a psychiatrist a lot more than you do a sports doctor," she shot back.

Nick enjoyed watching the spark of fury darken her eyes. God, she was a passionate woman! Making love to her was going to be like trying to tame an erupting volcano.

"Wrong." He grinned maddeningly. "I know one particular sports doctor I need a great deal." He came toward her slowly, his desirous gaze riveted to her face. Their eyes warred for a long, silent moment. Hers were dark and stormy, his glittered with dangerous, masculine purpose.

"Someone really ought to tell you that you're not irresistible," she said in a low voice.

Nick maintained his bland smile. "Don't you find me even moderately irresistible?"

"Hardly." Laurel waited irrationally for the bolt of lightning to strike her for telling such an outrageous lie.

Her haughty tone caused his own temper to flare, but Nick fought to control it. He did, however, give in to a primitive instinct as he pulled her abruptly off the couch and into his arms. "Prove it."

She tried to jerk away, but his palm cupped the back of her head. "Nick," she protested, her palms pressing against his shirt.

"Prove it," he repeated once again, his fingers tightening in her hair.

Laurel read the anger in his eyes and fought against the thrill of excitement created by his hard, tense body pressed so intimately against hers. Nick felt her slight tremor, and guided by some inner compulsion, he found his world centered for a dangerous, suspended time on this one woman. As they stared at each other, both Nick and Laurel were overwhelmingly shaken. But neither wanted to be the one to admit it.

Nick spoke first. "Next time you won't say no."

"There won't be a next time," she protested softly.

He traced the bow-shaped curve of her mouth with his fingertip. "Oh yes, lovely Laurel, there will definitely be a next time, as well as several after that. I fully intend to make love to you every time those ridiculously seductive lips get within kissing distance." Then, he added silently, having satisfied his curiosity and desire he could get on with rebuilding his life.

He stepped back, eyeing her thoughtfully. "Later," he said, before turning to walk back to his own house and a party that had been a lousy idea to begin with.

Laurel's discerning eyes had not missed his pronounced limp. The physician in her surfaced coming to the rescue of the bewildered woman.

"Would you like that massage I promised you the other night?" she inquired calmly.

Nick looked back over his shoulder, his answering expression incredulous. "Are you serious?"

"Absolutely."

His gaze narrowed. "What kind of massage are we talking about here?"

Laurel had to smile at that. "Don't worry, McGraw, I'm not going to attack you. We've got Dr. Britton back now, and she's the take-charge lady, remember?"

Nick did not mention that he'd been having trouble with that one, too. In fact, he hadn't found one aspect of this woman that didn't intrigue him, make him want to know her better.

"Well?" She was waiting for his answer.

Nick weighed his options. There were any number of beautiful, willing women next door. The night wouldn't have to be a total loss. He frowned as he realized he only wanted Laurel. He didn't want to dilute her taste, diminish the feel of her firm, slender curves with any other companion.

Damn her, he considered with a fresh burst of irritation. She'd infiltrated his system like a drug and as much as he wanted to walk away, he found that he couldn't.

"I think maybe I would like that massage," he answered finally. "After all these years I thought I was well acquainted with every bone in my body. But I discovered a few new ones today."

"I'll get the lotion." She turned away.

"Laurel?"

"Yes, Nick?"

"Are you sure?"

She met his questioning gaze with a level one of her own. "Don't worry, I've yet to rape one of my patients." Her tone was dry and Nick didn't know whether to be irritated or impressed by the way she appeared to have recovered her composure. "You're safe enough."

She escaped the room and as Nick stripped to his shorts he realized Laurel couldn't begin to understand how false a statement that was. He was fast discovering her to be the most dangerous woman he'd ever met.

Laurel leaned against the sink as she splashed cold water over her face, gathering up her scattered senses. Then she tried a variety of expressions in the bathroom mirror until she found one to her liking. There. That looked far more self-confident than she felt.

"My God," she breathed softly as she returned. "You look absolutely terrible."

"Now I know why you're not worried about a near-naked man lying on your couch. A couple more of those ego boosters and I wouldn't be able to do anything, anyway," he grumbled.

Laurel eyed the darkening bruises with deep concern. "This isn't funny; you look like a side of beef."

He glanced down indifferently at his body. "Hey, they'll fade. They always do."

She reached up, tracing the scar that extended outward from his top lip. "Always?" she inquired, arching an argumentative brow.

"Usually. That's just a reminder of what happens when you don't move fast enough to avoid a blitz."

Her worried gaze dropped to his knee. "You don't have that much mobility these days," she argued. "How are you going to avoid those blitzes the rest of the season?"

He shrugged, disliking this subject intensely. "One game at a time, I suppose. The same way I always have."

Laurel spread a towel out on the coach, motioning for him to lie down. "I see. And after the season's over?"

Nick expelled a deep sigh of relief as he stretched out on his stomach, his hands under his chin. "Then I spend the summer working out. Building up the knee some more."

"If it isn't completely destroyed," she muttered under her breath, rubbing some lotion between her hands.

"I didn't quite catch that," he invited.

As Laurel's palms spread over his broad back, she could feel the tension in every muscle. Nick was sore, tired and had ridden an emotional roller coaster all day. This was definitely not the time to bring it up.

"And after the summer?" she forced herself to ask casually.

"Then there's next season," he stated simply.

"I see. And you plan to play next season?"

He looked up over his shoulder at her. "Of course."

"Of course," she repeated softly, having suspected his answer before she'd asked the question. Laurel moved her palms in long, flowing strokes over his back.

"You have nice hands," he murmured, his mind beginning to float comfortably.

"Thank you. And you have very tense muscles."

"That's the name of the game."

"If you're going to be football's old man, McGraw, you're going to have to learn to take better care of your body."

"Hey," he complained as she began kneading the swollen muscle tissue. "I'm in pretty good shape. Better than some of the rookies. I'll have you know, the opening day of training camp I had a 3.25 body-fat ratio. Lowest on the team."

Laurel had no doubt. He was all lean muscle and strong sinew. But he was not a machine. She wondered sadly when he'd realize that fact for himself.

"You should have had this massage hours ago, instead of letting your muscles swell up like this," she scolded, wringing out his tense muscles with a kneading, rolling motion.

"Ah, but I couldn't find anyone at the party who had such great hands."

Laurel couldn't help herself. She pinched him. Hard.

"Ow!"

"Excuse me," she said sweetly. "Speaking of that party, is it going to be a weekly occurrence? I'd like to book Danny's and my hotel room in advance next time."

"Would you believe that's the last one of the year?"

Laurel's fingertips were moving in a deep, slow circular movement, as she sought to break up the muscle knots constricting Nick's blood vessels. "Really?"

He turned his head, looking up at her, his expression serious. "Really. I've always hated them, which is why I quit going to them years ago. Until . . ." His voice dropped off and Laurel felt his shrug under her fingertips.

"Until your knee injury," she guessed correctly.

He nodded. "It was as if I started acting like a rookie again, then I could play like one." He shot her a warning glance. "Don't you dare laugh. I've spent the past year of my life going crazy."

"I can understand that." Laurel began a vibrating massage along both sides of his spine, encouraging relaxation. "It must have been a shock to have to face a premature end to your career. I can see how regression would be a likely stage."

"Now you sound just like a doctor," he complained.

"I *am* a doctor," she shot back. "And if you want to keep playing, McGraw, you'd better begin treating this body with more respect. I'm prescribing a daily massage and expect your trainer to do it after each practice."

"I don't like his as well as yours," Nick grumbled. "He does all that hitting with the side of his hand. Not to mention his fist. I think the man's a closet sadist."

"Hey, we're getting to that part next," she warned. "Look, Nick—" Laurel's voice turned deadly serious "—this is important. Especially with the practices Carr is giving you. You must feel the difference to your body."

He could definitely feel the change Laurel's wonderful touch was having on him. Not wanting to give up the pleasure, he refrained from the seductive answer that came to mind.

"I know I hurt like hell from all those live hits during practice."

Laurel fought down her temper at the reminder of the Thunderbird coach's obvious strategy to force Nick off the team. "It's more than that. With all the sustained activity you're putting in during practice, you're forcing your blood vessels into a restricted state."

She sought to come up with an example. "Have you ever seen pictures of the New York marathon?"

"I think so," he muttered sleepily. Laurel smiled as she realized the massage was beginning to take.

"Can you recall the runners on the Verrazano-Narrows Bridge?"

"The one where they're all crowded together from one end of it to the other?"

Laurel nodded. "That's it. Think of that bridge as your blood vessels after practice. The millions of blood cells carrying nutrients and waste are all jammed together, and the intake of oxygen and removal of lactic acid become insufficient for the needs of your muscles. So their ability to contract or relax deteriorates. The muscles tighten, your coordination and power diminishes and bang—you're just asking for an injury. I want you to promise you'll have a massage every day, at least during the season."

"I promise, Doc," he agreed.

Laurel smiled, pleased with herself for getting her point across. As a long-distance runner herself, she knew massage could even have a curative effect. She considered it vital to good training, and with the way Nick had accepted her medical advice so easily, she wondered if she might not convince him to see the light and quit altogether, before he was critically injured.

Then he proved once again that he was one step ahead of her. "I suppose, as my physician, you'd like me most likely to come to you for my daily treatment."

"I already suggested the team trainer," she reminded him, finishing up with a variety of light percussion movements up and down his back.

"I want you."

"Even a famous football star doesn't get everything he wants in life, Nick. It's probably time you learned that little lesson." She increased the strength of her touch considerably.

"Hey, take it easy. Now you're starting to feel like Louie," he complained as her hands tapped vigorously against his back. Then he returned his attention to their argument. "If you refuse to treat me, Laurel, I'll complain to the A.M.A. and they'll take away your license," he warned.

"That's ridiculous," she snapped.

"Really? Haven't you ever heard of the Hippocratic oath? I think you're stuck with me, Dr. Britton."

As Laurel opened her mouth to issue a scathing comment, she realized Nick had drifted off to sleep. Her heart went out to him as she observed his bruised body and wondered what it was inside Nick McGraw that drove him to play football week after week, year after year, despite the constant pain and chronic injuries that were part and parcel of his chosen sport.

There was far more to this man than met the eye, which was intriguing, because what was visible was undeniably gorgeous. Except for the dark bruises and random scars.

With a slight sigh, Laurel retrieved a pillow and blanket from the linen closet. As she covered his nearly nude body, the feelings washing over her in warm waves were definitely those of a woman rather than physician. She bent down, brushing a kiss against his temple. Then, with one last glare in the direction of the ruckus still going on next door, she wearily climbed the stairs to bed.

NICK WAS STILL sound asleep when Laurel tiptoed by him on her way outside the next morning. A slight smile curved her lips even as she expelled a soft sigh. Nick McGraw was a paradox. How was it she could go from wanting to bat the man over the head with the nearest object to caring for him so deeply all in a span of a few brief seconds?

As she began her daily run through the deserted early-morning streets, Laurel allowed her mind to wander the complicated maze of her feelings for him. She was used to handling men, both professionally and personally. The one thing she'd always prided herself on was her inner strength. Her slender, feminine body housed a core of steel that had enabled her to survive medical school, her internship, residency and a loveless marriage.

However, she was the first to admit she was also a creature of impulsive decisions, most of which had turned out just fine. The reckless lovemaking that had resulted in Danny might not have been a firm foundation for a marriage, but it had given Laurel her son—whom she would not trade for all the wealth in the world. After she'd taken up running to rid herself of the combined stresses of a home, child and medical school, Laurel had impulsively switched specialties from family medicine to sports medicine. And look how that had turned out.

That change had brought her to the sports medicine clinic, and that in turn, had brought her Nick. She grinned to herself as she waved good-morning to an elderly neighbor who'd come out to retrieve his newspaper. Even her piano, another impulsive decision, had led her to Nick. Or at least to his car. Her smile widened as she recalled how furious he'd appeared, storming out of his yard like a wounded lion. Sparks had flown between them from the beginning.

And that was why, she decided, she was so drawn to him. Their relationship had started out as a contest of wills. Although her feminist nature hated to admit it, Laurel decided there was something undeniably exciting about being pursued by a man who didn't know the meaning of retreat.

As she did a series of cool-down exercises outside her kitchen door, Laurel reviewed Nick's other attributes. He was handsome, intelligent, and although she had a feeling it was a side of Nick McGraw he preferred to keep hidden from women, he was actually a caring, gentle man. If things were different, if she wasn't his doctor. . . .

Laurel shook her head, disallowing that rogue thought. She'd never been one for wishful thinking and this was definitely no time to start.

"Good morning." The object of Laurel's soul-searching was seated at her kitchen table, sharing breakfast with Danny.

"Hey Mom, did you know Nick slept here last night?"

"I knew," she replied somewhat breathlessly, still slightly winded from her run. "It was too noisy over at his house. . . . Hi. How are you feeling this morning?"

He took a bite of toast, observing her while he chewed. His bright green eyes took a slow tour of her slender body, clad in a

T-shirt and running shorts, and Nick was reminded of the first time he'd met her, only a week ago. Seven short days and he felt as though his life would never be the same again.

He shrugged, answering her question. "Sore. But I'll spend some time in the whirlpool this morning, and that'll help."

"You don't have practice today?"

"Nope. Generally we have the day after a game off. Then we used to begin with a light workout and work our way up to game day. Although who knows what Carr will think up before the season's over."

"I want to check that knee over before you have another scrimmage," she instructed, picking up a piece of crisp bacon from Danny's plate. "This is good, but you certainly didn't have to cook breakfast, Nick."

He smiled, getting her a cup of coffee. "It wasn't any problem since I would've cooked something, anyway. I was going to fix you a plate and keep it warm, but Danny said you don't eat breakfast."

Laurel took a bite of her son's toast. "I don't usually."

He gave her a stern look. "Didn't they teach nutrition in medical school, Dr. Britton? Breakfast is the most important meal of the day."

Laurel sighed, smiling her thanks as she took the cup of coffee he offered. She sat down in a chair at the table. "I know that. I just picked up atrocious eating habits while I was an intern, and I'm afraid they stuck. Thirty-six hours on, then ten off, then another thirty-six on do strange things to your inner clock."

He rested his elbows on the table, holding his cup between his palms as he observed her thoughtfully. "Were you married in those days?"

Laurel nodded. "Married and a mother."

Something flickered in the dark green depths of his eyes, but Laurel could not discern its meaning. "That must've been tough."

She smiled toward Danny. "It was worth it." Then, swallowing her coffee quickly, she rose. "Danny, make yourself a peanut butter and jelly sandwich and wrap up an apple and some of those cookies we bought yesterday for your lunch. I'm going to take a shower and get ready for work."

"Sure, Mom." He drank the rest of his milk in long, thirsty swallows, wiping away the creamy mustache with the back of his hand.

"Oh, and don't forget to put the dishes in the dishwasher," she called over her shoulder.

"I never do," he countered with an aggravated tone. "I do my share around here."

She gave him a smile. "I apologize. You always have and I appreciate it, too."

Danny nodded, carrying his plate to the sink. "I know you do, Mom. Like you always say, the two of us make a great team."

Laurel held her breath, hoping Danny wouldn't choose this morning to bring up his idea of inviting Nick into their small family. Her luck held as her son remained blessedly silent.

8

WHEN LAUREL REENTERED the kitchen fifteen minutes later, Danny was sitting at the table reading a book while Nick spread a thick layer of strawberry jelly onto a piece of bread.

"What are you doing?" She stood in the doorway, staring at the unfamiliar scene.

Danny's head shot up and a guilty expression flashed across his face before he buried it back into the book. Nick, however, gave her a devastating grin.

"I told Danny I'd make his lunch," he volunteered.

Laurel crossed her arms over her chest. "Why?"

He tore a long sheet of plastic off the roll, put the two pieces of bread together into a thick sandwich and wrapped it. Then he moved to the refrigerator. "Where are the apples?"

"In the vegetable crisper," she answered absently. "I'd like an answer, Nick."

He located the fruit and tossed it into Danny's Mr. T lunchbox, along with the sandwich. He seemed oblivious of her irritation.

"Are the cookies in here?" he asked, reaching for a ceramic container on the counter.

"No. They're in the cupboard to the left of the stove," she snapped.

Nick looked at her curiously. "Hey, you don't have to bite my head off. That is a cookie jar, Laurel. The logical assumption would have been—"

"Don't assume anything, Nick," she shot back, her tone letting him know this conversation went far beyond that of Oreos.

There was a long, uncomfortable silence. Out of the corner of her eye, Laurel saw Danny peeking over the top of his book.

"Come on, Danny, I'll walk you to school," Laurel said briskly.

His eyes widened. "But Mom, I can walk by myself. I've been doing it all week." He looked back and forth between the two of them. "I told you she wouldn't like it," he said to Nick.

"So I've discovered," he agreed. "Now what'll I do to get back in her good graces?"

Danny's young brow furrowed thoughtfully. "Whenever she gets mad at me, I usually draw her a picture. She puts it on the refrigerator and I know everything's okay."

Nick cast a wary eye at Laurel. "I'm not certain crayons will cut this one, sport. I think we need something stronger."

"When I was five, I painted Circe yellow to match my room," Danny volunteered. "Mom was looking at me a lot like she is at you right now."

"Terrific. What happened to get you and your mother back on speaking terms?"

"That was the only time she ever spanked me," he recalled. "Then, afterward she cried and said she was sorry."

Nick's green eyes were bright with insinuation as they turned from her son to Laurel. "Interesting idea," he murmured.

Laurel would have had to be blind to miss the sexual invitation in his teasing gaze. "That's enough, you two. Danny, you're right. You can walk yourself to school. I need to talk to Nick."

"Are you going to fight?" he asked with interest, taking his lunchbox from Laurel's hand.

"Of course not," she reassured him. "We're simply going to discuss a few important matters."

"Oh." His small face seemed to actually fall at that and he turned toward the door. Even Laurel's farewell hug and kiss didn't bring a smile to his face.

"Hey, Danny?"

"Yeah, Nick?"

"I think it's going to be a knock-down-and-drag-out brawl."

His face lit up like a Christmas tree. "See ya, Mom. See ya later, Nick. Good luck today." He waved goodbye as he escaped out the door.

Laurel turned on Nick as soon as he was gone. "What do you mean by telling my son that we're going to have a fight?"

He leaned against the counter, crossing his long legs at the ankles. "Aren't we?"

"Of course we are, dammit! But I don't want to concern Danny with things that are none of his business."

Nick gave her a long, level glance. "Since I've the distinct impression all this began because I was making the kid a peanut butter and jelly sandwich, I'd say it very much concerns Danny. And if you think he didn't realize that himself, then you're not giving your son very much credit, Laurel."

She pushed her hair off her forehead with a furious gesture, her dark eyes blazing. "Forgive me if I'm not real keen about taking parenting advice from rank amateurs," she forced out between clenched teeth. "Unless you're applying for permanent father status, I suggest you stay out of my son's life!"

"And what if I am?" he roared back.

That question caught them both by surprise. The silence swirled about them, a living breathing thing until Laurel broke it first, sinking down into a chair at the table and looking up at him.

"What did that mean?"

He rubbed his hand over his face, shaking his head. "I don't know," he admitted. "You just got me mad and I said the first thing that popped into my mind."

"I wasn't proposing, Nick," she said sternly.

He gave her a slanted smile. "I never thought you were, Laurel." He straddled a chair, leaning his forearms along the top and resting his chin on them. "Want to talk?"

She glanced down at her watch. "I've got to get to work."

"Call in and say you'll be a little late. I think this is more important."

Laurel couldn't escape the somber green gaze, and even though she knew Dr. Adams would suspect the worst, she nodded.

"I'll be right back," she said, not wanting to use the kitchen phone. She needed some time to gather her scattered thoughts and she certainly couldn't do it in the same room with Nick.

"Fine. I'll make us some fresh coffee."

She managed a weak smile. "I'll say this for you, McGraw—you sure are handy to have around a kitchen."

He returned the smile and feeling a little more optimistic, Laurel left the room. When she returned, not only had he made coffee, but a stack of fragrant cinnamon toast rested in the center of the table.

"You really should eat something," he explained at her questioning gaze.

"I thought *I* was supposed to be taking care of *you*," she reminded him. "After all, I am your doctor."

"And I'm your friend," he countered easily. "I've always thought that's what friends did. Watched out for one another. Made each other feel good."

Laurel sat down and took a sip of coffee, eyeing Nick thoughtfully. They were adults, she told herself firmly. Surely they could discuss sex without things getting out of hand.

"Is that what you call what we were doing last night?"

Nick was standing over her, his expression an inscrutable mask. His eyes were green shields, and it was impossible for Laurel to discern what the man was thinking.

"What do you call it?" he answered her question with one of his own.

Laurel shrugged with feigned casualness. "Foolishness, I suppose." Her hand shook as she lowered her cup to its saucer, the rattling sound unnaturally loud in the morning stillness of the kitchen.

Nick reached out, taking her hand in his, linking their fingers together. His expression had softened. "There was nothing wrong in what we were doing, Laurel. It was natural and right. Which is why we're going to end up making love sooner or later, so you may as well get used to the idea."

He couldn't stop himself from staring at her mouth, remembering the petaled softness of her lips, the incredibly sweet taste. He could feel his body filling with that now-familiar ache.

Laurel found it impossible to think with his gleaming eyes focused on her lips. "You really do take too much for granted, Nick," she protested softly.

He arched a challenging brow. "Kiss me and tell me that."

"Not on your life." She managed to refuse with a light laugh. "I may be reckless, McGraw. But I'm not a complete fool."

Even as her continued resistance made him want to wring her lovely neck, Nick found her valiant effort admirable. He wasn't used to such strength in a woman. It frustrated him, admittedly.

But at the same time it also intrigued him. Nick knew the little feminine game of two steps forward and one step back could add spice to the chase. But Laurel was definitely taking things to the extreme; if this was how she usually responded to a man's pursuit, he'd be willing to bet not a lot had managed to catch her.

Nick's expression turned momentarily stormy at the idea of Laurel lying in bed with any other man. He sighed, raking his long fingers through his hair with obvious frustration. This wasn't going well. Not well at all. *Keep it loose, McGraw,* he'd counseled himself, *let the lady know you're not in the market for anything but fun and games.*

"Laurel, how many men have you been to bed with?"

She stared at him. "That's a very personal question, Nick."

He shrugged. "It doesn't matter. I'm willing to bet not a hell of a lot. Like I'm also willing to bet you were a virgin bride."

Laurel rose abruptly from the table, turning her back on him as she poured herself another cup of coffee. "Don't bet the farm, Nick," she counseled grimly, "because that remark just proves how little you know about me. I was a pregnant bride, actually."

His cup was halfway to his lips when she bit out the circumstances of her marriage in a short, gritty tone. Lowering it slowly to the saucer, Nick studied her intently, the lines in his forehead deepening.

"Were you in medical school when you got pregnant?"

She gave him a crooked, self-deprecating smile. "You know, your shocked expression is the same one all our friends gave us when they heard the news. It is, I'll admit, a nice little bit of irony. Geoffrey later used that as an example of one more thing I hadn't managed to do right."

"The man sounds more and more like a jerk." Nick dismissed Laurel's ex-husband with a careless wave of his hand. "Why didn't you do something about it?" he wondered aloud.

She sat down again, sipping her coffee thoughtfully, remembering Geoffrey's insistence along those very lines. "You mean an abortion. . . . You can say the word in front of me, Nick. After all, I'm a doctor. We don't embarrass easily."

And you don't love lightly, he thought. Vaguely disturbed, he dismissed the idea to return to the subject of Laurel's son.

"All right, as terrific a kid as Danny is, the news must not have come as a welcome surprise. Most people wouldn't have wanted the inconvenience. Abortion *was* the logical choice."

Laurel frowned into the depths of her coffee. "Love isn't always logical," she said after a pause. "Besides, it's not that I don't accept the idea of abortion in theory, under the right circumstances. But I never felt it was right for me."

Nick reached across the table, taking both her hands in his. Laurel tried not to be affected by the warmth his thumbs were creating as they traced little circles on her palms.

"You can be a very nice women, Dr. Laurel Britton, when you're not trying to destroy a man's delicate ego."

"Delicate?" she countered with a slight smile. "Your ego, McGraw, is anything but delicate. In fact, if you ever figure out how to bottle it, I want to buy in. We'll rule the world."

He threw back his head and laughed. As Nick relaxed, he decided Laurel's reason for resisting was probably due to a desire to avoid any entanglements right now. Her life was filled with enough complications as it was. A new city, a new job, a new home. And something else he still couldn't quite put his finger on.

"May I ask one question?"

Laurel nodded, tugging her hands free as she put her elbows on the table. Lacing her fingers together, she rested her chin on them, meeting his curious gaze.

"I suppose that's safe enough," she allowed.

"What started all this? Why did you get angry just because I was making Danny a sandwich?"

Laurel rubbed her forehead wearily with her fingertip. "It's a little complicated," she admitted. "I'm just a bit touchy these days about my mothering techniques. I've always felt having Danny help out with things around the house taught him independence. When I saw you fixing his lunch, I thought you were criticizing me for not taking better care of him."

Nick's eyes widened, displaying genuine surprise. "I'd never do that. Anyone can see you're a good mother, Laurel. Danny's a great kid; you've obviously done a terrific job."

She managed a weak smile, not knowing how to explain Amanda's theory that a child deserved a full-time mother. She'd been hearing that argument at least once a week from Geoffrey for months. He'd even gone so far as to hint that her career would benefit, as if she'd willingly sacrifice her son for her work. Laurel shrugged inwardly. Why wouldn't her ex-husband think that way? He'd never shown any interest in his son until Amanda had come into the picture.

She realized Nick was watching her with unnerving intensity and forced her mind back to this conversation. "Thank you," she murmured. "Then, there's the fact I'm still worried you and Danny are getting too close. If we were to have an affair, then you disappeared from his life, he'd be badly hurt. He's just adjusting to the idea of being away from his father, although he certainly never saw that much of him when he lived in Seattle."

"Danny said you've been divorced quite a few years."

"Three. But, quite honestly, our marriage never really took." She laughed, no longer finding the memories painful. "Morning sickness did it in."

Nick couldn't imagine not loving a woman who was willing to put up with those mysterious changes in her body in order to carry his child. Geoffrey was not only a jerk, he decided, the man was a fool.

"But why—"

"Why did we stay married all those years?" Laurel shook her head. "I don't know, exactly. I suppose I was far too busy to worry about whether or not I was happy. I had Danny, school, work. Considering the juggling act I was doing with my life, I probably could've signed on with Ringling Brothers."

"And Geoffrey?" Even as he said the name aloud for the first time, Nick hated the guy who'd lived with Laurel. Loved with her. Made a baby with her.

She exhaled a small sigh of regret. "He had his work. You have to understand that no Britton, in the history of a very illustrious family tree, had ever gotten a divorce. Geoffrey's mother threatened to disinherit him if he sued, and quite honestly, I didn't really care one way or another in those days. He was never home, anyway."

"What made you finally decide?" Nick regretted asking the question when her eyes shadowed to a lusterless ebony. The man had hurt her badly. Busy framing her answer to Nick's question, Laurel missed the frown darkening Nick's eyes at the thought.

"Geoffrey fell in love. Amanda's a very well-brought-up lady, a member of the Junior League and all that—definitely not the type to carry on a tawdry little affair with a married man. Besides—" she managed a grim smile "—her father coincidentally happens to be a cardiologist himself, who's built his heart institute to worldwide prominence."

"And who just happened to be near retirement?" Nick asked dryly.

Laurel gave him a faint, rewarding smile. "My goodness, you *are* pretty smart for a jock."

"I like to think so," he replied cheerfully. "Is this fight over now?"

"Why?" she shot back. "Are you suggesting we kiss and make up?" As soon as she issued the challenge, Laurel knew it was a mistake.

Sparks danced in his green eyes as he observed her with unmistakable desire. "I'm game if you are," he agreed. "Just a friendly kiss, of course. Nothing the slightest bit passionate."

"I think I'll pass," she decided, not trusting herself any more than she did Nick. She was an adult, she reminded herself firmly. She could certainly control her body's rebellious urges. It was just going to be a little more difficult than she ever would have thought possible.

"I really have to get to work," she said, picking her purse up from the counter and heading toward the door. "I think Dr. Adams would love an excuse to send me packing back to Seattle."

"Fair enough," Nick said. Laurel enjoyed the light touch of his hand on her back as he walked her to her car. "Will you let Danny spend this afternoon with me?" he asked as he opened the door for her. "He's got some crazy idea we should sign Rowdy up for obedience training at the park."

His grin was boyishly attractive. "Do you know, sometimes I feel like that kid's the real adult around here? He definitely seems to have all the answers."

For a moment Laurel was afraid Danny had discussed marriage with Nick, but his friendly open gaze seemed to discount that fear. "He's seven going on thirty-five," she agreed. "Believe it or not, he was actually born that way."

"Then you'll let us try to turn Rowdy into a responsible member of society?"

"If it'll protect the rest of my furniture, I'm all for it. You and Rowdy are spending more time with Danny lately than I am. I'm beginning to suspect you're only putting up with me to get to my son."

Her accusation was leveled at Nick in a light tone, but his answering expression was unnervingly grave. "You know better than that, Laurel. If I'd met you two years ago . . . Oh, hell," he muttered. "Forget it."

Nick reminded himself that neither of them was looking for a relationship with any strings. Both their lives were too unsettled for muddying the waters with any type of commitment. She had her work at the clinic and he had a career to salvage. Even as he repeated those facts to himself, the need to touch her grew almost unbearable. Nick shoved his hands into his pockets.

Laurel managed a slight, agreeing smile but found the effort more difficult than it should have been. "It's forgotten," she said. Then she remembered something that had been tugging at her mind ever since Danny had left the house.

"Do you know why Danny looked like he'd just gotten his Christmas present early when you told him we were going to have a fight?"

To her amazement, Nick appeared chagrined and somewhat embarrassed. "I might," he admitted.

She arched an inquiring dark brow, inviting elaboration.

One hand left his pocket to rake through his hair. "All right. He asked me why you and I argued so much and I told him if people really care about one another, little spats don't mean anything. That if we always saw eye to eye, we'd bore each other silly."

He resisted the impulse to kiss her but was not strong enough to avoid the silken pull of Laurel's velvety brown eyes. Reaching out, he stroked his palm down her hair instead. As his fingers grazed her shoulders, she couldn't hide her slight tremor.

Nick took a deep breath, as if gathering strength. "The one thing you'll never do, Dr. Britton," he promised, "is bore me."

Laurel slid into her bucket seat, escaping the warmth of his hand and the provocative gleam in his green eyes. "I know the feeling," she admitted. Then, turning the key in the ignition she looked up at him, her own eyes displaying her concern.

"I want you to stop by the clinic today so I can examine that knee before tomorrow's practice," she instructed.

"I've got a busy day planned," he protested. "Why don't you just make it a house call this evening?"

"I don't make house calls, Nick. That's one reason I chose this specialty. So I wouldn't have to race off and leave Danny at all hours of the night."

"You made one last night," he reminded her with a wicked, teasing grin.

"Don't look so smug, McGraw," she threatened on a light laugh, shifting the car into gear. "Just wait until you see my bill."

As she pulled away, Laurel caught a glimpse of Nick in her rearview mirror, his hands thrust into the back pockets of his jeans, a thoughtful expression on his face.

"YOU'VE LOST NEARLY eight percent of your strength in that knee," Laurel scolded, after testing Nick's leg strength on the clinic's Cybex machine.

"I prefer to think of it as still having ninety-two percent of my strength," he countered calmly.

Laurel fought down the unprofessional display of anger his stubborn words provoked. She knew that as his doctor she had every right to be concerned about his cavalier attitude. The problem was, the level of her caring went far beyond that.

She crossed her arms over the chest of her lab coat. "Terrific, using that theory, by the end of the season you'll be crawling off the field."

"Don't push it, Laurel," he warned in a low tone. "You've no proof I'm going to continue losing strength at that rate. Hell, the way I've been working out, I'll probably be stronger than ever by the play-offs."

"And don't you talk to me that way, Nick McGraw," she snapped. "I'm your doctor and I think I know more about your body than you do!"

"Not as much as I'd like you to," he retorted. Then, as they glared at each other, a slow smile chased away Nick's aggravated glower. "If you want me to think of you as a physician, Dr. Britton, you should stop looking so enticing."

Laurel didn't answer as she met his unmistakably appreciative gaze. She had met and overcome a great many challenges in her life. But this was proving to be her toughest.

"I think perhaps I ought to transfer you to Dr. Lee," she murmured as she tapped her pen thoughtfully on his file. "I don't believe I can be properly objective in your treatment."

Nick shook his head. "You're my doctor, Laurel. I won't accept any other."

"But Nick . . ."

He sighed, rising slowly—gingerly, she noted with concern—from the chair. Placing his broad palms on the glossy patina of her desktop, he leaned toward her.

"Speaking as my physician now, just tell me one thing."

"I'll try."

"Do you have any concrete proof that if I continue to play, I'll end up permanently disabled?"

"Of course not. I don't own a crystal ball."

He nodded, his eyes gleaming with a victorious light. "There, you see. There isn't any reason for me not to play."

Laurel knew all too well the athletic mind. The average patient was a consumate expert at hearing exactly what he or she wanted to hear and no more. She wasn't going to allow Nick to twist her answer that way.

"As I said, I don't have a crystal ball. But I do have a file filled with examinations and X rays, and test results that show you're taking a risk every time you walk out onto that field."

Swearing violently under his breath he gave her a fulminating glare. "I'm taking a risk every time I walk across the street, Laurel. That's the way life is. You can't cower behind the curtains in your house and hide from it."

She half rose from her chair, her dark eyes flashing dangerously. "You're far too intelligent to use that old argument! When are you going to quit acting like a spoiled child?"

"And what, exactly, does that mean?" His tone was razor-sharp and electricity arced between them as he held her gaze with the sheer strength of his will.

She refused to back down. "You're behaving like a four-year-old who's afraid someone's going to take away his favorite toy. You're a grown man, Nick, so why don't you just hang up your helmet and allow yourself the satisfaction of having been one of the best quarterbacks to play the game?"

She belatedly realized she'd gone too far as a muscle jerked dangerously along his rigid jawline. Reaching across the desk, Laurel placed her hand on his arm, her expression earnest.

"I know you don't want to give it up, Nick. It's the rare athlete who knows exactly when to quit. Most of you have a tendency to let your minds set dates your bodies can't keep." She took a deep breath, garnering strength. "When are you going to admit that your playing days are over?" she asked softly.

Nick jerked his arm away as if she'd burned it, and Laurel recognized the look in his eyes as they hardened to green crystal.

"When I retire," he grated through tight lips, "it'll be because I want to. Because I no longer enjoy the sport, or because I can't win any longer. But get this one thing through your head, Laurel—no sportswriter, coach or even a doctor, no matter how lovely she may be, is going to make that decision for me."

His harsh expression could have been carved onto the side of Mount Rushmore and his eyes gave her an unmistakable warning. "Is that clear?"

"Perfectly."

"Good." He turned toward the door. "I'll see you this evening," he said as he left. Before Laurel could object, he was gone.

"Burning the candle at both ends, Dr. Britton?" Dr. Adams was standing in the open doorway, his gray gaze inscrutable.

She sighed, deciding it was time to get this out into the open. She had far too many problem males in her life right now; something had to give.

"Dr. Adams, may we talk frankly?"

He entered the room, taking the chair Nick had just vacated. Crossing his arms over the gray pin-striped vest, he nodded. "Talk away, Dr. Britton."

"Do you object to the way I conduct my practice?"

"If I had any objections, you wouldn't be here," he replied with the air of a man perfectly used to getting his own way.

Laurel admitted to herself that much was probably true. "If you're worried about my professional behavior, you should know that while I consider him a friend, I won't allow anything to happen between Nick McGraw and myself."

"That sounds like quite a challenge, since the man is obviously very taken with you. And you're neighbors," he added smoothly.

Her eyes widened. "How in the world did you know that?"

An expression suspiciously like a smile passed over his face. "Never discount the clinic grapevine, Dr. Britton." Then he surprised her by appearing almost sympathetic. "I know this must be a difficult time for you. Men like Nick McGraw are hard to deal with, even discounting a personal involvement."

"You know what I'm up against, then?"

"The fact that he refuses to accept the idea that his athlete's body may be more fragile than his determination?"

"He refuses to think about retiring. I've tried to point out to him that he's taking a risk every time he walks out onto that football field." Her hands were shaking as she toyed with her pen, displaying all too well her dismay with Nick's attitude.

Matthew Adams's steady gaze held her attention, but there was a warmth in his eyes Laurel had never before witnessed. "It's always upsetting when a patient won't listen to reason, but aren't you taking too much of this onto your own shoulders? Nick McGraw is not your only patient."

He was right. Laurel knew several of her patients would continue the same behavior that had earned them their injuries. Yet she didn't spend all her waking hours and far too many sleepless nights worrying about them.

"I think you should assign another physician to him."

He shook his head, rising to leave. "I'm not going to do that for a number of reasons, Dr. Britton. In the first place, if anyone can get the man to listen to reason, it's probably you. In the second place, you're unquestionably the most qualified doctor on staff to treat an injury of that magnitude. In the third place, as a runner yourself, you can at least empathize with the athlete who doesn't want to suddenly find himself inactive."

"But he's going to end up permanently inactive if he doesn't stop," Laurel pointed out, her dark eyes mirroring her distress.

Her superior shrugged his gray-suited shoulders. "Then I'd suggest you accept that possibility and be prepared to deal with it when the time comes."

This time she knew his expression was honestly sympathetic. "I don't envy you these next few months. However, if you were in another specialty, you'd already have dealt with the reality of losing a patient. While our losses aren't as life threatening as say, cardiology, if you want a medical practice with no risk involved, Dr. Britton, I'd suggest you consider dermatology. To my knowledge, no one has ever succumbed to acne."

He gave her a wry smile that this time actually reached his eyes. "If it's any consolation, Laurel, I feel privileged to have you on staff here. Seattle's loss has definitely been Phoenix's gain."

The smile grew warmer as his gaze swept over her in a far from professional manner. "And I'd still say that, even if I wasn't particularly fond of White Shoulders." With that surprising remark he turned on his heel and left the room, leaving Laurel to stare after him.

9

ALTHOUGH IT WAS NEVER spoken of directly, a silent truce was forged between Laurel and Nick. In the almost balmy autumn days that followed, she found herself looking forward to sharing her evenings with Nick and Danny. Practices remained as brutal as ever, and although Laurel could see they were having a detrimental effect on Nick's injury, she forced herself to remain silent.

She had finally come to realize that Nick couldn't conceive of a life without playing this game, even as everything and everyone seemed against him making it through the season. She wished she could help him come to terms with his dilemma, but for the time being, all she could do was tape him up and try to keep him healthy enough to play, while hoping he came to view things more realistically. She didn't want to mar their time together with fruitless arguments.

She gave him daily massages, treated his various sprains and waited for the inevitable. As the Thunderbirds climbed to second place in their division, a play-off spot was clinched.

Laurel amazed herself on Thanksgiving by cooking a superb dinner. The turkey, she thought proudly, looked like something out of a cookbook.

"Wow, Mom," Danny exclaimed as he sat down to eat. "This stuff looks really good."

"I had help," she admitted, smiling over the top of her son's head at Nick, who was busily carving the huge bird.

He returned the smile, shrugging his wide shoulders. "It's not that I'm particularly talented. It's just that everyone in my family was assigned various jobs. I usually ended up with kitchen duty."

"Was it neat having loads of brothers and sisters, Nick?" Danny asked. Laurel shot her son a warning glance, but he only smiled innocently in return.

"Most of the time. Although there were admittedly occasions I wished I'd been born a little lower in the rotation. Even after my mom quit work to stay home, I still ended up with a lot of the responsibility."

"Your mother worked?"

Nick laughed, putting some slices of turkey breast onto her plate. "Laurel, any mother with nine children works."

"You know what I meant," she protested. "You told me once she stayed home and did all that mom stuff."

"She worked until I was around Danny's age. By then the McGraw clan was too big to find sitters willing to take us on."

"What did she do?" Laurel inquired, ignoring Danny's expression of protest as she passed him the bowl of sweet green peas. Her firm nod indicated he was expected to take some and with a grimace of distaste, he complied.

"She was an English professor at Columbia," Nick stated, pacifying Danny by handing him an enormous drumstick. "After she quit, she still kept her hand in, working as a free-lance editor for several publishing houses."

"That explains why quotations come so trippingly off your tongue," she commented. "Was your father a professor, too?"

Nick took a Parker House roll from the basket Laurel handed him, smiling his thanks as she refilled his wineglass with crisp Chablis from the chilled bottle.

"No. He was a Presbyterian minister."

"Psalms," she guessed.

He grinned. "You've got it. Between the two of them, I can probably come up with something to fit almost every occasion."

"Amazing," Laurel murmured.

"What's the matter, Dr. Britton, are you surprised a football player can read something besides his playbook?" There was a teasing challenge in his tone.

"No. I'm just moderately impressed. What did you do, spend your infancy teething on a copy of Bartlett's?"

Nick threw back his head and laughed, trying to recall the last time he'd felt this relaxed. "Almost. I can't remember our house not being filled with books." He smiled into the golden depths of his wine. "We kids used to play a game to see if we could find a saying that'd stump our folks. We kept a pool going for years, the winner taking all the pennies. Although it wasn't that often that anyone was paid off, I guess the hours spent looking up obscure quotations obviously stuck."

"What did they think about you wanting to be a football player?" she asked curiously.

Nick watched Danny hiding the hated peas in his mashed potatoes and had to stifle a grin of remembrance of his own stubborn youth. Laurel followed his gaze and as Nick's eyes caught hers, they shared a companionable smile. Then he answered her question.

"For their day, I think they were really ahead of the times. While neither of them knew a touchdown from a home run, they wanted me to do whatever would make me happy."

His expression softened and his eyes stared off into space, as if looking back in time. "They were so proud when I got a scholarship to play for USC. Dad flew the entire family out to Los Angeles from New York for my first game . . . I still think about how much everyone sacrificed to pay for that trip."

His gaze returned to Laurel. "I've got a nice family. You'll like them."

She smiled, wondering if he'd meant to put it quite that way. There was a formality about meeting a man's parents that signified a certain commitment and the one thing they'd both agreed on was this was a friendship without ties. It had been a casual statement, nothing more, she decided, not wanting to search for hidden meanings in Nick's words.

"I hope you won," she said.

Danny stopped gnawing on the gargantuan drumstick long enough to protest. "Mom! Of course he did. . . . Didn't you, Nick?"

Nick winked an emerald eye. "I sure did. You know, even with the Super Bowl rings, I sometimes think that was the best game I've ever played."

"Your parents must have been thrilled," Laurel murmured, feeling an adolescent thrill at Nick's dazzling smile.

She loved the way his face lit up when he talked about playing, and hated it, all at the same time. How was he ever going to give it up? The game obviously flowed in his veins right along with his blood. It was as much a part of Nick McGraw as his thick, sun-gilded hair and gorgeous green eyes.

Nick viewed the look of sadness momentarily taking possession of Laurel's face and sought a way to banish it.

"There's a funny story about that," he said, smiling at her. "I'd just passed for a touchdown and the defensive team was on the field when I felt someone tapping me on the shoulder. It was Dad."

He took a sip of wine, his expression reminiscent. "I asked him what he was doing down there and he said that I'd made Mom and him real proud."

"That's nice," Laurel murmured.

Nick's grin widened. "That's not the funny part," he protested. "All of a sudden I looked around and there I was, standing on the sidelines all by myself. The defensive team had come off the field and everyone was out there waiting for the quarterback."

"Oh, no!"

"Gee Nick, what did you do then? Did you get in trouble?"

Nick's gaze toward Danny was undeniably fond. "Well, I didn't exactly get the medal for brilliance that day, but I didn't get in trouble, either. Which was amazing, because as I started running out onto the field, trying to cram my helmet onto my head, I realized someone was running right along beside me."

"Your father," Laurel guessed, her eyes filling with bright tears of laughter.

Nick nodded. "Picture it: my first game as quarterback of a nationally ranked college team, standing in a huddle, in the middle of the USC Coliseum, with my dad standing there right beside me. I told him he wasn't allowed on the field, that we were supposed to be playing a football game."

Danny's eyes were wide, his drumstick long forgotten. "What happened next?"

"Well, when you meet my dad, Danny, you'll discover his most amazing trait is his unflappability. He simply glanced around at the other players, looked up at the clock, and said, 'Oh. I thought you were all finished and had just come out here to shake hands with the other fellows.'"

Sharing in Nick's enjoyment of the story, Laurel couldn't remember a more marvelous day. The only thing that would have made the day even more perfect, she considered as she went to bed that night, was if Nick was lying here beside her. The attraction that had sparked between them from the beginning was steadily increasing day by day and she was admittedly surprised Nick had not made a renewed effort to seduce her.

Laurel had no way of knowing that Nick was as confused as she by his inexplicable hesitation. More than once during the past weeks, he'd picked up the phone to call a woman. Any woman. Just to prove to himself that this yearning he felt for Laurel was merely a simple biological attraction easily satiated by any warm and willing woman. But each time he replaced the receiver to its cradle without dialing. There was only one woman he wanted.

This evening was proving no different, and struggling against an almost overwhelming torrent of need, Nick reached out and dialed the number indelibly etched in his memory.

"Hello?" Her voice sounded hesitant, almost afraid.

"Laurel, are you all right?"

He could hear her expelled sigh of relief. "Oh, Nick. Hi. I'm fine." Her throaty voice curled over him, warm and inviting.

"You sounded upset," he probed.

"I thought it might be Geoffrey. He promised to call Danny today."

Nick glanced at the clock beside the telephone. "With the time difference it's nearly midnight in Seattle."

"I know. He and Amanda probably got stuck at a party, which is just as well. I honestly hoped he wouldn't call." Even as Laurel said her wish aloud, she felt a stab of guilt. She'd watched Danny disappointedly eyeing the silent telephone all afternoon and evening.

"He hurt you that badly?"

She shook her head, the gesture ineffectual over the telephone lines. How could she explain the pressure Geoffrey had been exerting, without giving Nick a far too intimate picture of her life?

"Laurel?"

"No . . . I just didn't want any clouds hanging over a perfect day," she answered finally.

"It was nice, wasn't it?"

"Lovely. The sunshine, the dinner and especially the company," she agreed, holding the receiver nearer to her ear, as if she could bring Nick closer with the effort.

Nick didn't want to be alone tonight. Although he'd grown accustomed to spending holidays by himself, today had reminded him of the pleasures a family held on these special days.

"Want to help me build a couple of turkey sandwiches?"

His husky deep tone invited far more than cold turkey and Laurel closed her eyes, fighting off a rebellious wave of desire.

"I don't think so." She turned him down gently. "I have to get up early tomorrow morning." She cast a glance down at the anniversary clock on her bedside table. "This morning," she corrected.

"Hey," he said quickly, casually, "it's okay. It was just an idea."

"A nice idea." Her voice held a soft regret.

"Yeah. Well, I'll see you tomorrow then. Good night, Laurel."

"Good night," she whispered, her lips pressed against the cold ivory plastic.

Nick hung up and walked over to the window, looking up for a long, frustrating time at Laurel's bedroom. Cursing her heatedly and wanting her outrageously, he flung open the liquor cabinet, seeking the numbing effects of Jack Daniel's.

THE THUNDERBIRDS PLAYED their final game of the regular season out of town, and as Laurel and Danny watched on television, she was distressed to see Nick's passing game slowly deteriorate. He had five blocked passes, three interceptions and was given no room to move. Neither did he receive any help from a running game that was shut down with only seventeen yards for the entire afternoon. The Thunderbirds lost to the Miami

Dolphins, 16-0, but it could have been 100-0 for all the chance they had.

For Laurel, however, the game resulted in a victory of sorts. Because as the beleaguered offense finally escaped, Nick had been able to walk off, instead of being carried off the field on a stretcher.

Watching the ten o'clock news, she was not surprised to find Coach Carr less than pleased. "I want to apologize to the fans," he declared during the after-game interview. "That team fumbling around out there today was not only an embarrassment to Phoenix and the entire state of Arizona, it was an embarrassment to the game of football."

As he glowered into the camera, Laurel glared back. "But I'm going to change all that. We're having a scrimmage tomorrow at 8.00 a.m. sharp. With full pads."

"In the morning?" the sportscaster asked incredulously. "But you're going to have to fly all night just to get back to Phoenix by 8.00 a.m. Is that really fair?"

"Look," Carr growled, "I'm the one who makes the decisions, and it's fair to me."

Laurel pointed her remote control at the bulldoglike coach, wishing it was something far more lethal as she pushed the button, darkening the screen.

"HI, GOT SOME TIME for a battle-weary old quarterback?" Nick asked with false enthusiasm as he limped into the treatment room.

Laurel forced her face into a mask of professional composure. "I believe we can fit you in, McGraw. How's the knee?"

"Like all those buildings in Venice." At Laurel's questioning glance, he elaborated. "Ancient and crumbling steadily, day by day."

She opened her mouth to answer and promptly shut it, knowing that after that game yesterday and another brutal practice this morning, he was probably in no mood to rehash old arguments. "Let's take a look," she suggested instead.

It took every ounce of her inner strength not to gasp as she proceeded through the examination. "What happened to this thumb?" she inquired calmly, observing it was swollen to three times its normal size.

"Collision with a helmet," he mumbled. "Played havoc with my passing game."

So that explained yesterday's dismal performance. "It's going to take at least three weeks to heal properly."

Nick shrugged. "It usually does," he agreed.

Laurel ran her palm down his side where Nick's skin was turning an unappealing shade of yellow and purple. "And this?"

"Clothesline shot."

"Terrific, McGraw."

"Isn't it?"

She moved to his knee, probing carefully, surprised when Nick didn't flinch. Even he couldn't be that much in control, she thought suspiciously.

"Look over at the wall," she instructed.

"Why?"

"Because your doctor just told you to."

A wary expression moved across his face, but Nick did as he was told. Laurel pulled a long needle from the tray beside her, inserting it into the bruised flesh surrounding his knee. There was no response and Laurel had to restrain herself from screaming.

"You damn idiot," she said in a furious whisper. "You let them shoot you up with xylocaine, didn't you?"

Nick's answering expression was guileless. "Of course I didn't."

She was trembling with rage, at the coaches who encouraged such behavior, the trainers who were all too willing to risk a player's entire future, and mostly, at this moment, Laurel felt like killing Nick.

"Is that so?" she tossed back in exasperation. "Then would you like to explain why you can't feel that needle?"

He glanced down. "You cheated, Laurel."

"No," she retorted firmly, "you cheated, Nick. You cheated yourself when you pulled that stunt. Don't you realize that with your knee deadened like that, you'd have no way of knowing if you were placing too much stress on it until it was too late?"

Nick dragged a hand through his hair and swore. "Look," he argued, "I sure as hell wasn't wild about the idea, myself. But I was in constant pain during the entire last half. I couldn't concentrate, Laurel. I had to do something. It was that or throw the game away completely." His broad shoulders slumped. "So, I agreed to shoot up. It won't happen again."

Laurel was tempted to send one sharp kick at that battered knee right then and end all this nerve-racking waiting. Nick was an intelligent man and he'd been around the game too long not to realize this could easily become a disabling habit. Damn him, she fumed.

"I suppose it would be foolish of me to point out that you didn't win yesterday," she observed, not bothering to hide her annoyance.

"Not only foolish," he agreed, "but impolite as well."

With an unfeminine snort of impatience, Laurel withdrew the needle, tossing it uncaringly toward the tray. It skittered across the metal surface with a force born of her anger, falling onto the floor. Neither Nick nor Laurel noticed.

"You could have taken yourself out of the game."

His green gaze turned definitely challenging. "Sure, and let Morgan go in and pull my fat out of the fire?"

For a moment they measured each other in silence. Finally Laurel spoke. "Are you honestly interested in the Thunderbirds winning? Or are you more concerned about the great Nick McGraw regaining his fame and fortune?"

He slid off the examining table, buttoning his shirt as he glared down at her. "That was a cheap shot, Dr. Britton, even for a lady with the fastest mouth in the West. Are you implying I'd risk the team losing rather than take myself out of the game?"

"I don't know what you'd do, Nick. Up until today, I thought you were an intelligent man. That little stunt with the painkiller makes me realize I don't know you at all."

"Do *you* think Morgan could've won that game?

Laurel shrugged. "How should I know? I'm certainly no expert. I've never even seen the man play."

"He wouldn't have," Nick bit out, "so just get that idea out of your head." A grimace of pain crossed his face as he bent down to tie his running shoes and Laurel's heart went out to him.

"Nick," she said softly. "Let's not fight like this."

He slowly straightened, staring down at her for a long, silent moment. When he spoke, his voice was unusually husky. "You're right. We've made it this far, let's not toss it all away now. Just a few more weeks and I'll have everything under control."

"No more xylocaine?"

He raised his hand in a pledge. "I swear, Dr. Britton, if I see anyone coming at me with a needle, I'll take off running."

"Considering your knee, that doesn't give me a lot of hope."

He bent his head, giving her a quick hard kiss on the lips that sent a flash of lightning sparking through her entire body. Nick felt it, too. He lifted his head, gazing down at her in obvious wonder.

"Wow," he murmured, his finger tracing the line of her upper lip.

"Wow," she agreed breathlessly.

"For a doctor," he observed in a voice that was far from steady, "you sure as hell don't know much about chemistry, Dr. Britton. I thought you've been assuring me this attraction would pass."

Laurel had recently come to her own conclusions about that. And knowing Nick's propensity for uninvolvement, her thoughts had been anything but encouraging. She lifted her shoulders in a careless shrug.

"I may have made a misdiagnosis. Are you planning to sue?"

He glanced around the treatment room, grinning wickedly as he found it momentarily deserted. "No, I've got a much better idea."

Laurel's arms went around his neck, her mouth yielding deliciously as they shared a kiss that seemed to go on forever. *Don't think,* she warned herself. *Don't ruin this by analyzing it. Just feel. And enjoy.*

"When I win the Super Bowl," he murmured against her lips, "will you come to New Orleans and celebrate with me?"

Her answer was immediate, honest. "I'd go to Timbuktu to celebrate with you, McGraw," she said punctuating her words with brief, feathery kisses.

"Oh, excuse me." Tony Lee's smooth apology interrupted them before Nick could renew the blissful kiss. "But you've got an emergency, Dr. Britton. An overenthusiastic volleyball player."

"I'll see you later," Nick said, releasing Laurel slowly, regretfully. "I wanted to go with you when you took Danny to the airport, but Carr's called a team meeting this evening."

"That's okay, I understand." No strings, she reminded herself. No obligations.

"May I drop his present by the house?"

Laurel nodded. "He'd love it." Then she looked at him suspiciously. "I never did ask. It isn't anything that eats Puppy Chow, is it?"

He laughed, a rich, happy sound that banished the last of Laurel's irritation. "Of course not." Then his grin grew absolutely wicked. "You do know a place around here where we can get some oats and hay, don't you?"

"Nick McGraw, you didn't get him a pony?" Danny had been hinting for one, but surely Nick wouldn't be so foolish?

He shook his head. "You know, lady, you sure do get uptight about the little stuff. See you later." He winked and as he sauntered from the room, Nick felt ten years younger.

All the aches and pains he'd brought into the clinic with him seemed to have been cured by Laurel's very special magic. She was an extraordinary woman, he mused, piloting the Ferrari almost automatically through the streets crowded with last-minute Christmas shoppers.

A man would have to be crazy not to be attracted to her. She was beautiful, strong, intelligent and independent. She was also gentle, loving and so damn sexy that the fantasies she inspired in a man's mind created havoc in his body. Nick grasped hold of that idea, like a drowning man reaching for a length of rope. There had been too many times lately he'd experienced an unnamed twinge of emotion—a feeling toward Laurel that defied description.

It was simply the way she'd forced him to wait, he assured himself, as he pulled the sleek sports car into his driveway. She'd become an obsession and so long as he recognized it for what it was, he could keep his feelings for her in perspective.

The problem solved, he began to whistle "Jingle Bells" as he crossed the yards to Laurel's house, intent on giving Danny his present before he left for Seattle. But the usually jaunty holiday tune sounded hollow, even to his own ears.

THE HOUSE SEEMED so empty. Laurel wandered through the rooms, knowing as she did so she was being foolish. Danny was only visiting his father for the holidays, as promised. Yet here she was, acting as if he'd died. Even as Laurel knew she was over-reacting, she couldn't help the depression that settled over her in a black, suffocating cloud.

"Anybody home?" Nick's deep voice broke into her thoughts, but she couldn't find the words to answer.

"Laurel? Did you get Danny off okay?"

Nick was struck by the eerie silence and the total absence of light. She never did lock her doors. What if something had happened to her? That idea made his blood run a little colder and he took the stairs two at a time, oblivious of his bad knee. He held his breath as he opened her bedroom door, expelling it in a frustrated cloud as that room proved as quiet and as empty as the rest of the house.

Danny's room was next, and now that his eyes had adapted to the darkness he could see her, sitting stiffly on the end of her son's bed.

"Laurel? What are you doing sitting alone in the dark like this?" The mattress sank under his weight as he sat down beside her, taking her ice-cold hands in his.

Laurel surprised him with her next action, as she flung her arms around him and pressed her cheek against his shirt. "Oh Nick," she whispered. "Please hold me. I'm so frightened. I'm so horribly afraid."

He could feel her trembling, and as his arms tightened about her, Nick knew he'd give up everything he'd ever worked for if he could banish whatever was causing Laurel this pain.

"Hey—" he lifted her chin, smiling encouragingly "—airplanes are safer than bathtubs. Danny will be fine, believe me."

She shook her head, taking a deep tortured breath. "That's not it."

He tucked her hair behind her ears, the gesture soothingly gentle. Her eyes were as dark and bleak as tombs and Nick felt his heart ripping in two. What was the matter with her?

"But it does have something to do with Danny?" he probed delicately.

Laurel nodded as her shoulders slumped defeatedly. "He's going to stay in Seattle, Nick." Tears sprang to her eyes and Nick watched in admiration as she fought to control them.

He tried to understand. "Danny's staying in Seattle? With his father?"

Laurel nodded again. Slowly, painfully.

"But when was that decided? I thought you had permanent custody of him."

"I do," she said flatly. "But Geoffrey and Amanda want him."

Nick wanted to break in and ask what that had to do with anything. Especially since the stories he'd heard about Geoffrey Britton were anything but complimentary. So the guy wanted his son after all this time. Tough. Nick forced himself to wait, allowing Laurel to tell the story at her own pace.

"Amanda discovered six months ago that she's sterile," she said after a long pause. Her tone was flat, her eyes expressionless as they stared out into the darkness. "They'd been trying to have a child for the past three years and she finally went to a specialist who diagnosed her condition."

"There's always adoption," Nick pointed out.

Laurel nodded. "You'd think that would be the logical answer, wouldn't you? But Amanda feels Geoffrey deserves to have his own flesh and blood."

Suddenly Nick caught the gist of this conversation. He had a sudden urge to put his fist through the nearest wall in lieu of the illustrious cardiologist's face.

"Danny."

Laurel drew a long, shaky breath. "Danny," she agreed in a whisper.

It still didn't make any sense. Why should Laurel be anything but annoyed by the entire suggestion? He probed delicately, not wanting to rush in and cause her unnecessary pain.

"Honey, just because your ex-husband and his wife get the idea in their heads that they'd like your son to live with them full time doesn't mean that it's going to happen. You've got custody of Danny. He loves you; you're a terrific mother.... I still don't understand."

She dashed at the fresh moisture stinging her eyes, shaking her head in a violent gesture. Laurel was more upset at her atypical lack of control, he realized, than anything he'd said.

"Amanda is perfect," she mumbled. "She's exactly what a mother is supposed to be."

Suddenly Nick fully understood that ridiculous argument they'd had over Danny's peanut butter sandwich. "She's the charmingly competent, domestic type?"

Laurel nodded, giving him a weary look. "Amanda could give Donna Reed lessons."

"So?"

"So, while he's at home, she and Geoffrey will gang up on him and make life so wonderfully perfect, he won't want to come back to me. Nick, he didn't want to come here in the first place, he's bound to want to stay with them."

It took every ounce of control Nick possessed not to tell Laurel that was the most ridiculous thing he'd ever heard. From the bleak expression shadowing her brown eyes, he could tell she fully believed that garbage. What kind of line had that bastard been feeding her for the past six months?

"*This* is his home, Laurel," he said matter-of-factly.

She clung to him, unnaturally cold. "You don't understand." She sobbed into the firm line of his shoulder. "The woman bakes chocolate chip cookies. From scratch."

If Laurel hadn't been so honestly distressed, Nick would have burst out laughing. Instead, he rocked her in his arms, engulfed by a tenderness he'd never before experienced. Staggered by the intimacy of this moment, her grief became his. It tore through him, and as she sobbed harshly Nick's own eyes grew suspiciously moist.

He felt her tears dampening the material of his shirt, and as he remained silent, wanting Laurel to cry out the pain she was obviously feeling, he realized she'd been secretly fearing this all along, keeping it inside, struggling to deal with it in her own stubbornly independent way. She was too damn close to the problem; if only she'd told him sooner.

Laurel gave in to her grief and fear, loving the strength of Nick's arms about her, the tenderness in his touch, the softly crooning words of comfort he was murmuring in her ear. Not for the first time, she considered how wonderfully gentle he could be, despite his obvious strength. Nick was strong enough to be tender, something Geoffrey had never been. Something Geoffrey could never be.

Laurel slowly felt her will returning. She'd be damned if she was going to allow her son to grow up in the vast wasteland of Amanda's and Geoffrey's marriage. Both of them were too selfish to know how to love.

"She isn't going to have him."

"Of course not," Nick agreed instantly, feeling the change in Laurel immediately. She was going to be all right, not that he'd possessed a moment's doubt.

"I'm not going to allow them to turn his head with all sorts of promises."

"Not to mention chocolate chip cookies," he added with a slight smile that encouraged an answering one.

Laurel tried. "It sounds pretty silly when you say it out loud, doesn't it?"

He took both her hands in his. "A little," he admitted. "But I think your former spouse has been waging a tough campaign lately, sending you on one hell of a guilt trip. On top of all the other changes in your life, it would make sense you'd be a little vulnerable right now."

"You know I worry about Danny," she admitted.

"I know. Just as I know you're a wonderful mother. And he adores you."

Laurel met his gaze bravely. "But he's only seven, Nick. His head can be turned by promises."

Nick's green eyes observed her with gentle censure. "Do you honestly believe Danny is so shallow that he'd trade the love you two share for a couple of cookies?"

"When you put it that way, I guess not."

He kissed the top of her head. "You're damn right he wouldn't. Besides, you've got an ace in the hole, Laurel."

"And what's that?"

He winked. "If you'd told me all about this earlier, I could've told you—I bake one terrific chocolate chip cookie."

Laurel had to share in his laughter, and as she did, the chains that had been gripping her heart during the past six months of

Geoffrey's battle to win Danny broke away. The mood suddenly changed as their eyes met, the desire sparking higher than it ever had before.

"Would you do something for me?"

"Anything."

She traced the thin white scar away from his firmly cut upper lip, brushing her trembling fingertips lightly over the chiseled lines of his handsome face.

"Make love with me, Nick," she whispered.

10

NICK NEEDED no second invitation. Rising slowly from the bed, he gathered her into his arms, carrying her down the hall to her own room.

The doctor in Laurel tried to make herself heard. "Your knee," she whispered.

He covered her mouth instantly with his own, disallowing another word of protest. When he reached her bedroom, he laid her with an almost reverent care on the bed, staring down at her with unmasked emotion.

Laurel was shaken by the extent of feeling in his flaming green eyes. They warmed her everywhere they touched, from her forehead, across her face, through her plum silk blouse and heather slacks, right down to her toes. She felt the icy chill of her unreasonable dread melting, and with it went any last lingering vestige of reserve.

Nick knelt beside the bed, not feeling the broken pieces of cartilage that usually made such movement painful. His mind was on Laurel as he slowly unfastened the pearl buttons of her blouse, folding back the material with extreme care, as if unwrapping the most precious of Christmas presents. His lips greeted each new bit of creamy skin, and as he blazed a trail of kisses along the scalloped edge of her bra, Laurel shivered deliciously.

"You are so incredibly soft," he murmured, moving over her heated flesh. When his tongue dampened the filmy material covering her breasts, Laurel bit her bottom lip to keep from crying out.

Nick lifted his head, his gaze locked to hers as his tongue soothed the skin her teeth had reddened. "Don't do that," he whispered. "Don't hold anything back from me, Laurel. I want to know what gives you pleasure."

Her liquid dark gaze was filled with desire. "You pleasure me, Nick."

He groaned, reminding himself that they had waited a long time for this and it must be done right. He forced himself to go slowly.

"God, you're so incredibly perfect." He tugged the lace down a bit to allow himself a taste of her fragrant skin. "Do you have any idea how wild I am about your creamy flesh? How wild I am about all of you?"

Laurel's skin warmed and the blood hummed in her veins like a live wire as Nick's lips and hands moved over her, learning her body's intimate secrets. Her blouse seemed to dissolve away, followed by her bra and in short order her light wool slacks, as Nick undressed her with an agonizing leisure. Each new discovery was treated to the same extended exploration, his lips tasting every inch of bared skin as he drew out each exquisite sensation until she felt certain she could take no more of his tender torture.

When his fingers slid under the waistband of her silky bikini briefs, Laurel lifted her hips off the mattress, pressing against his hand.

"Nick, please," she whispered, her voice a ragged little thread of sound.

"Not yet." His warm breath fanned the satin skin of her abdomen, moving downward, following the path his fingers blazed as they rid her of the final barrier. His tongue played with agonizing abandon and as his fingers teased her, Laurel reached out, her palm coming in contact with his shirt.

"Let me," she complained, realizing through this dizzying golden mist surrounding them that Nick was still fully dressed. She was doing all the taking, not giving anything in return.

But Nick caught her hand in his, lifting it to his lips, where he pressed an evocative kiss deep into the center of her palm. Laurel was stunned as the innocent gesture caused a respondent quickening in the most feminine core of her body.

"We've all night," he whispered, shaking his head with a slow, deliberate gesture as he leaned her back against the pillows, encouraging her to enjoy what he was offering.

"Look at this," he murmured on a low groan. "Didn't I tell you your flesh is exactly like gleaming pearls?"

Laurel risked a glance downward, her blood heating to volcanic temperatures as she viewed his wide dark hand on the pale expanse of her stomach. The contrast was jolting, and as she dared to look into the boiling green pools of his eyes, she knew Nick was affected as potently as she.

His stroking touch became more demanding, his lips firmer as they traveled on her body, only to return again and again to savor the sweetness of her mouth. He couldn't get enough of the feel of her, her taste, her scent that swirled in his mind like an inhaled drug, serving to drive him mad.

Laurel's pliant body moved fluidly under Nick's passionate embrace, and if she was capable of speech, she knew she would be begging him to take her now. But as he discovered points of pleasure she had never even known existed, she could only close her eyes and ride the spiraling passion that carried her higher and higher.

When Nick's roving tongue slid up the sensitive skin of the inside of her thighs, Laurel quivered in response, and her breathing quickened as she moaned his name. His stabbing tongue grew greedy, causing Laurel to turn to quicksilver in his hands. She trembled under his touch, crying out as she came to a dizzying, shuddering release.

Nick left her only long enough to strip off his own clothes before returning to the bed, overcome with an attack of pure insanity. His lips roved over every inch of her body, tasting every feminine pore as passion too long suppressed exploded.

Caught up in the escalating energy surrounding them, Laurel discovered her own needs once again as great, her own passion soaring as high and as strong as Nick's. Together they brought each other to the very heights, riding a spiral that carried them beyond anything they'd ever known, out into a universe of their own making where the air grew thin and their minds whirled with a dizzying speed. Just when Laurel thought they'd gone too high, too far to survive, she was flung to a place where the sun exploded into golden shards of light, blinding in its brilliance.

Laurel was unaware of how long they lay there; it could have been minutes, or hours. She was stunned by the intensity of the feelings Nick had unleashed. But even more astounding was the realization that she loved him. Laurel Britton, pragmatic physician, had fallen in love with a man unable, or unwilling, to enter into a commitment. That thought was too depressing to consider and she forced it away, choosing instead to bathe in the warm afterglow of their lovemaking.

As Nick gradually became aware of his surroundings, he attempted to move away.

"Don't," she whispered, her fingers running light trails over the rippling muscles of his back. "I love the feel of you inside me. Stay a little longer."

"I'll crush you," he said, not in any honest hurry to move.

She laughed, a rich musical sound. "That's all right. I know a great sports doctor who's terrific at healing any little sprains or bruises."

His palm ran down her side, delighting even now in the feel of her satiny skin. Nick had believed once he'd made love to Laurel, he'd be over his obsessive passion. But now, sheathed in her velvet warmth, he knew he'd never get enough of her.

"I never knew it could be like that," Laurel murmured, pressing a series of kisses along the bumpy line of a shoulder that had seen more than its share of injuries.

Nick reluctantly left the soft cushion of her body, rolling onto his side, pulling Laurel with him. His hands followed her slender curves, and he smiled down at her. "You're a remarkable woman, Dr. Britton."

She slid her palm down his body, loving the feel of Nick's hard, toned muscles under her fingertips. "You're not so bad yourself, Mr. Football Hero."

Nick felt renewed desire stirring in his loins as Laurel's hand rested idly on his thigh. He hated to ask, but he had to know.

"Any regrets?"

"Not a one," Laurel answered honestly.

He leaned forward, capturing her mouth in a deep kiss. Laurel met the kiss ardently, her lips greedy as she wrapped her arms about him, willing her mind to go blank. Stunned by her desperate response, Nick felt the earth slipping away.

"Wow," he said as they came up for air. "If that's your latest tactic for keeping me off the football field, I may just end up spending the rest of my days right here in your bed."

"If I believed you meant that, I'd take you up on it," Laurel said softly. *Don't push,* she warned herself, concentrating instead on the magic of Nick's caressing hands.

"We could always give it a try," he suggested, his eyes gleaming with renewed desire.

She smiled. "That's what I like about you, McGraw," she said on a throaty laugh. "You're always open to suggestion."

Nick covered her lips with his own, their lovemaking this time gentler and more leisurely but no less satisfying, as Laurel's worries disintegrated like a misty fog under a desert sun.

CHRISTMAS EVE MORNING dawned bright and sunny, a far cry from holidays Laurel had experienced in the Northwest. Nick surprised her by serving breakfast in bed, but she was unaware of what she was eating as her gaze surreptitiously swept over him, loving every rugged feature.

Reminding Laurel more of Danny than an adult who'd already seen thirty-five Christmas Eves come and go, Nick radiated more and more excitement as the day wore on. They spent the day at his house, hanging an eclectic assortment of ornaments he'd collected since childhood on the tall tree he'd saved for them to decorate together. While the three of them had spent hours two weeks ago decorating the massive blue spruce in Laurel's living room, he'd kept this white pine bare, instinctively knowing she'd need something to keep her from dwelling on Danny's absence.

"Where's the angel?" she asked, digging through the discarded boxes.

Nick's eyes were drawn to the rounded curve of her derriere, enhanced by her snug corduroy jeans. She was dressed all in red—a scarlet sweater and crimson jeans—reminding him of a bright, vibrant flame. Her cheeks were flushed, her eyes still glowing from their night of lovemaking. The dark smudges under her eyes added a softness to her appearance, making her appear infinitely delicate and extremely vulnerable. Nick knew that he would remember the way she looked right now for the rest of his life. Years down the road, the image of her so lovely, so desirable, would remain indelibly etched onto his mind.

Laurel was suddenly aware of Nick's intense gaze. She straightened slowly, her eyes searching his face.

"Nick?" she inquired softly, amazed by the warm desire rekindling in her nether regions. How could it be possible to spend all night making glorious, passionate love and still want more? To still be instantly aroused by a darkening glow in those beautiful jade eyes?

She tried again. "The angel?"

He drew her into his arms for a long, lingering kiss. "Right here," he murmured, taking little bites of her rosy lips.

"Ah, McGraw," she said, sighing happily. "You always know exactly the right thing to say. I suppose there are a few definite advantages to having an affair with a man who's had so much practice."

Nick searched for a hidden meaning in her words, looking for some resentment of his admittedly less than noble past. Or a hint that Laurel had changed her mind and now wanted more. But all he received in response was a dazzling smile as she reached up, playing with the errant blond wave dipping across his forehead.

"Back to work," she said firmly. "The tree looks positively naked without an angel on top."

"I don't have an angel. It's a star."

Laurel shook her head on a sigh. "It figures. As long as I can remember, I've always had a fat angel with fluffy yellow hair atop my Christmas tree."

"And I've always had a silver star with twinkling lights," he argued lightly. "Want to fight it out somewhere a little more comfortable? How are you at wrestling?"

"Mats or mud?" she asked, her eyes gleaming as they danced with the provocative idea.

His brilliant green gaze moved slowly down her body. "Actually, I had a bed in mind, but mud does offer a realm of intriguing possibilities."

"Yeah, like who's going to clean the mess up afterward," she pointed out.

"Wise lady. Since it's unlikely we'd find a janitorial service willing to come out on a holiday, we'd better stick to mattresses. Two out of three pins?"

Laurel reached up to press a kiss against his smiling mouth. "At least. But later. The way you keep wanting to play, Mc-Graw, it's going to take us until Easter to decorate this thing."

As they continued working, she and Nick carefully avoided the topics of football or his knee, managing to keep the mood light. Despite their efforts to remain carefree, Laurel couldn't help noticing Nick grew decidedly nervous as the day wore on.

"If you're looking for Santa Claus," she offered dryly, after he'd gone to the window for the third time, "he never comes until all good little boys and girls are in bed."

Nick turned from the large bay window facing the street, his smile devilishly provocative. "That's undoubtedly the most ingenious idea I've ever heard. Want to give it a shot?"

Laurel answered his smile with a warm, womanly one of her own that reminded Nick of the look Eve must have given Adam. She came across the room, standing on her toes to brush a light kiss against his lips. Her fingers began to unbutton his shirt with a tantalizing deliberation.

"I'd say it's definitely worth a try, darling." Linking her fingers in his, she led him down the hall to his bedroom.

Standing beside the wide water bed covered by a dark caramel spread, Laurel resumed her task of unbuttoning Nick's shirt. Tugging it free of his belt, she ran her hands around to his back, pressing into his flesh, delighting in the steely strength of the muscles she found there.

"Laurel," he groaned, attempting to capture her lips.

"Not yet," she murmured, her hands roaming down his sides, and around to his chest.

He repeated her name on a deep moan of male need that Laurel could feel echoed in the galloping of his heartbeat under her fingertips. But she was intoxicated with the effect she was having on him and longed to draw these marvelous sensations out to the fullest. Between each freed button she allowed a long lingering kiss, her tongue slipping between his lips to explore the dark secrets of his mouth. When she finally pushed the shirt off his shoulders, and allowed it to drop to the floor, her hands splayed over his bare chest, her kiss growing more wanton. She twined her tongue around his, playing a little game of thrust and parry until he fell backward onto the bed, pulling her with him.

"Lord, how I want you," he said, pressing his palms on the rounded curves of her derriere as she lay atop him. He moved her against his arousal, and Laurel's breath caught in her throat at the thought she could cause such a fiery response.

"I know," she murmured against his lips, "but it's too soon. Much too soon."

She laughed softly, sliding down his body, her lips and tongue sampling the mysterious male taste of his skin. Her tongue flicked at the pulse throbbing in his throat, and she could feel its thundering beat treble under her sensuous stroking.

Laurel grew dizzy with an overwhelming sense of feminine power as she rained a stinging trail of kisses over Nick's hard chest and down his firm, flat stomach. She followed the arrowing of golden hair with her lips, exalting in the dark musky taste of his skin, until forced to stop, cruelly impeded by his belt.

Laurel knew this man's body intimately; she'd been tending to it for weeks, she'd lain pressed against it all last night. Yet it had suddenly become unknown, foreign territory she longed to explore. Nick murmured her name with a ragged groan as Laurel unfastened his jeans, pulling them slowly over his hips and down his legs. The palms that delighted in the hard corded muscles of his thighs were not those of a physician, but of a woman, reveling in the inherent differences between the sexes.

He was so strong, so hard; the sinews straining down the columns of his legs were so taut they took her breath away. When her lips replaced her exploring fingers at the inside of his thighs, Nick bucked upward, his masculine body eloquently stating its need.

Even as Laurel's head spun with a heady sense of power, she discovered she indeed was going mad herself. For the more she stoked Nick's flames of passion the more her own blazed a little higher. Her clothes were discarded in a mindless flurry and as she fit her slender body to lie full-length atop him, Laurel was overcome with a devastating need to possess—to be possessed. Desire for him vibrated through her, made her reckless as she pressed her body hard against him, the tips of her breasts stabbing into his chest, her long satiny legs tangling with his rougher, hairy ones.

Nick heard the roaring in his ears and shuddered without being aware of it. Her movements against him were driving him insane; he wanted her to stop before she drove him over the edge . . . he wanted her to never stop.

"My God, Laurel," he muttered, his tongue stabbing into her ear, his hands burning a trail from her shoulders to the backs of her thighs. "You're going to set this bed on fire."

"You can't burn up a water bed." She gave a laugh, a silvery musical sound.

"Want to bet? As his hand slid between their moist bodies, pressing against her molten core, Laurel gasped. As exquisite as his touch was, she needed more; she needed all of him. Sensing his need and sharing it, he rolled her over, his deep thrusts driving her into the fluid softness of the bed.

Sanity shattered, taking them beyond the realm of thought and reason. Laurel's cries were muffled into the hard line of his shoulder as she crested with an explosive force. Nick shuddered, closing his eyes to the forceful release, feeling his strength ebbing away as he held Laurel close, murmuring inarticulate words of love that neither heard nor understood.

"You have one terrific bedside manner, Dr. Britton," Nick murmured much later.

His teasing words hit too close to home, and as much as she'd prefer putting it off Laurel knew the time had come to broach the subject of Nick's future treatment.

"Thank you, Nick. But I don't suppose you'd make this easier on me and accept Dr. Lee as your physician?"

"Not on your lovely life. I'm a guy who likes to travel first class, sweetheart. I only settle for the best. In women and in doctors."

Her fingers toyed in the soft blond curls covering his chest. "I can't be sleeping with you and treating you at the same time," she argued softly. "It's unethical."

Covering her hand, Nick linked their fingers together. "Don't tell me I'm going to have to choose between being treated by Dr. Britton, or making love to her charming alter ego."

She closed her eyes to the liquid warmth created by his lips as he pressed a kiss against the sensitive skin of her inner wrist. "Those were the rules from the beginning," she reminded him.

"Ah, but in the beginning you didn't realize what you were turning down," he argued, feeling more anxiety than he was willing to let on. If he had to give her up now . . .

Laurel was actually relieved to see the old Nick reasserting himself. She could deal with this arrogant football star much more easily than with the tender man who'd not only claimed her body, but her heart as well.

"Won't you just talk with Tony? Do you have to be so stubborn?"

Growing frustrated, Nick hitched himself up in bed, dragging Laurel with him. "I've a right to be stubborn when It's my knee we're talking about. I'll be damned if I turn it over to some quack just because of your ridiculous ideas about who you should and shouldn't be sleeping with."

She shook free, meeting his angry gaze squarely. "Tony Lee is no quack. And I find it fascinating that after maintaining an irresponsibly cavalier attitude all season, you're suddenly concerned about your knee."

His only answer was harsh, rude and brief. As they remained at a standoff, Nick told himself his anger was due to her intransigence and not a result of any despair on his own part about their situation. He'd finally made love to a woman he'd been wanting for weeks. So why did he feel so miserable?

"Look, honey," he said, trying to find a middle ground, "let's just let things ride the way they are."

Her dark eyes were eloquent in their distress. "But—"

He placed a firm finger against her lips. "It doesn't make any sense for me to change doctors now. There's only a few short weeks left in the season, anyway."

He leaned his cheek against the top of her head, inhaling the wildflower fragrance of her shampoo, determined to remember it always.

Laurel was relieved Nick couldn't see the inner gloom she knew was mirrored in her eyes. She wanted to ask about next season. But that would be presupposing a relationship she had insisted she didn't want. *You went into this with your eyes wide open, kiddo,* she told herself. *So don't muddy the waters by looking for feelings that don't exist.*

"Okay, Nick," she agreed softly. "After all, you're right about it only being a few weeks."

"It's a good thing we're not the type of people to want complications," he said, frowning up at the ceiling.

Laurel closed her eyes. "A very good thing. Someone could end up getting hurt, otherwise."

"But we've managed to avoid that. I think even Danny will be able to accept my leaving."

The pain jolted through her, hot and unrestrained. "You're leaving?" she murmured, more to herself than to him.

It was a rhetorical question, but Nick answered anyway, forcing his tone to remain matter-of-fact.

"This is the last year of a five-year contract for me. Does that make things any clearer?"

It did. Horribly clear. "You don't think the Thunderbirds are going to renew?"

Nick shrugged, wondering why, as many times as he'd been forced to face the prospect of a career move, it had never seemed so bleak as now.

"Sometimes on my good days I convince myself that if I'm indispensable to the team and take us all the way, they'll have to. But speaking as my doctor, would you sign this body to a long-term contract?"

Yes, she cried out inwardly. "I can see their point." Her sigh echoed his.

"Hell, I could spend the next five years in five different towns." He looked down at her and his eyes mirrored the hopelessness in her heart. "All the more reason for us to live for the moment, wouldn't you say?" His mouth sought hers, craving release from thoughts he had no business thinking.

No regrets, she reminded herself, flinging her arms about his neck, determined to make the most of the short time they had left.

11

"CLOSE YOUR EYES," Nick instructed some time later as they walked across the yards to Laurel's house.

"If I close my eyes, I won't be able to see where I'm going," she pointed out. "I'll probably fall into the pool."

"That's okay, sweetheart, I've always found wet women extremely sexy."

"I'll just bet," she muttered, unreasonably jealous of any women who'd passed through Nick's life before she'd met him. She forced the feeling away, refusing to allow the negative emotion to destroy the happiness she was feeling. *If this is all I'm going to have,* she told herself, *I want it to be as perfect as possible.*

"The pool heater isn't on; do you find women with hypothermia sexy?"

"I always find you sexy," he answered immediately. "But don't worry, I'll hold your hand."

Laurel allowed him to lead her through the kitchen and into the living room. The piquant scent of blue spruce heightened her anticipation of Christmas.

"Okay, you can open your eyes now."

She blinked, her gaze immediately focusing on the most incredible instrument she'd ever seen. "What is that?"

"If you don't recognize a piano when you see one, honey, I think we're in trouble."

Laurel moved as if in a trance, running her fingers over the glossy sheen of the ebony cabinet. "This isn't just a piano," she whispered. "It's a concert grand."

"I tried to find a twin to the one that shattered, but they don't make ancient old uprights like that anymore," he apologized. "I didn't think you'd have time to refinish any of the relics I did manage to find." He came up behind her, wrapping his arm about her waist. "I was hoping you'd accept this as a substitute."

Laurel shook her head. "I can't let you do this. It's far too extravagant."

"Hey, it was my dog," Nick reminded her. "You were quick enough to point that out to me while surrounded by pieces of mahogany and piano wire."

"But the other was insured. I was going to buy a new one when I got the check from the moving company."

"Lovely, Laurel," Nick said, sighing. "Do you have any idea how much piano one can buy for sixty cents a pound?"

"I can't let you do this," she repeated weakly, her fingers running over the ebony and ivory keys. It had a beautiful tone.

"It's only money, Laurel," he argued softly. "Let me do this for you."

"Nick, I—"

"Try it out," he instructed, pulling out the bench. "I'm told you can't properly judge a piano by its case."

Drawn by the beauty of the instrument, Laurel succumbed, sitting down, executing a graceful glissando up and down the keys. Almost against her will, she began playing a part of Bach's *The Well Tempered Clavier,* forgetting Nick as she lost herself to the rich, perfect sounds. After she'd finished the brief piece, her hands fell to her lap, her eyes guarded as she looked up at him.

"I won't take it back," he warned her. "I like giving people presents, Laurel."

"My mother always said there were certain gifts a woman could accept from a man."

"I see." His green eyes were bright with laughter. "And what, pray tell, did those gifts include?"

Laurel couldn't help herself, drawn irresistibly to the keys, her fingers played a few random chords as she answered. "You know, the usual things. Flowers, candy . . ."

"Did she ever specifically say a piano was against the rules?" He pressed his point.

Laurel had to laugh at that. "Of course not."

"Then, we're okay. Please keep it, Laurel, it's no use to me. I can't even pound out a bad rendition of 'Chopsticks.'" He bent down, brushing a snowflake-soft kiss against her lips.

"I still don't approve," she murmured, knowing Nick had no intention of taking the gift back. She managed a teasing smile. "Well, now we definitely have to see you through the upcoming play-offs."

"How come?"

"Because if you don't sign a big contract, you might fall behind on the payments and cause the store to come and repossess it. I'd hate that."

He laughed, as he was supposed to, wondering why giving Laurel the piano didn't make him feel as good as he'd anticipated. The salesman had assured him the Steinway was the most exquisite instrument to be found anywhere in the city. He enjoyed giving expensive presents. One of the nicest things he'd found about money was the pleasure it could give.

He'd also discovered long ago that women were quick to display amazing gratitude for something as easily obtained as a fur coat or a diamond bracelet. That had admittedly been part of the appeal. In fact, he'd planned for this piano to be the instrument of Laurel's capitulation. But after all they'd shared last night, it suddenly seemed superfluous.

"I suppose you come from one of those families who always open presents on Christmas Eve," she said, smiling up at him.

Nick's gaze was unexpectedly solemn. "Only Mom and Dad got away with that. They said Christmas Day was for the kids and Christmas Eve was for lovers."

"Oh." Their gazed held and once again there was that flash of heat. "I'll get yours," she said on a whisper.

He smiled. "I've got some champagne chilling next door. I'll be right back, okay?"

Laurel nodded, turning away before Nick could view the unexpected tears that suddenly brightened her eyes. What in heaven's name was the matter with her? Laurel told herself it was just the holidays. Any normal woman who was spending her first Christmas in seven years without her son, in a new town, would get a little weepy. Then, with a deep-seated sense of honesty, she admitted that it was the idea of losing Nick that was causing these atypical feelings of depression. She forced a smile as he returned and she handed him his gift.

"I love it!" Nick's face lit with a huge smile as he sat leafing through the leather-bound set of Shakespeare's plays. He'd told Laurel about coveting his mother's set for years, and she'd been pleased with her purchase.

At first, Laurel felt a little distressed her present couldn't begin to equal his. Then she reminded herself that while her salary was certainly more than adequate, Nick's was in the millions. If he never worked another day in his life, he'd never have to worry about money. Yet she knew that wasn't what was driving him to return to the football field Sunday after Sunday.

"It's a wonderful present, Laurel. Thank you."

"It's not as extravagant as yours," she protested softly.

He drew her into the circle of his arms, punctuating his words with hard little kisses that tasted like champagne. "You've already given me the most wonderful present any man could wish for. I'll always remember these days as the best of my life."

The tenderly issued words brought with them an unexpected flood of anguish. Laurel rested her forehead against Nick's shoulder, absorbing the pain fully, allowing it to course through her, infiltrating her every cell.

This was how she'd feel after he'd gone, she realized with a detached sense of fatalism. Oh, the pain would lessen, but she'd never be free of the dull, aching sense of loss. It had taken root in her heart like a native weed, and she realized that despite all her best intentions Laurel Britton M.D., an intelligent woman with no desire for unnecessary attachments, had fallen desperately in love with a man who definitely shared her independent view of life. It was so ironic she'd have to laugh. Once she got over the pain.

Nick was aware of Laurel's sudden change in mood and realized he'd come dangerously close to telling her exactly how much she'd come to mean to him. *Don't complicate things, McGraw,* he reminded himself. *You were attracted to this woman because she's strong and independent. Don't expect her to change, just because you're having second thoughts.*

"You never did ask me what I got Danny," he remembered aloud.

Laurel's hand flew to her mouth. "I completely forgot." Her eyes circled the room. "I don't see any hay, so it can't be anything too bad." As his eyes lit devilishly, Laurel observed him with genuine alarm. "You didn't get him that pony did you?"

When he didn't answer, Laurel stood up, her hands on her hips. "Really, Nick McGraw, I'm not about to allow you to—"

He silenced her with a hard kiss. "Hey, I know how you felt about that, Laurel. Besides, a horse would make it too crowded around here."

"What did you get him, then?"

Nick frowned abstractly, thinking this was another idea that had seemed perfect at the time but was going to fall flat.

"Rowdy."

A puzzled frown skittered across her brow as her gaze slid to the huge ball of fur snoring happily as he stretched out under the piano. Circe was curled up in a tight ball next to him, her charcoal-colored paw resting on his back.

"Rowdy? You gave Danny your dog?"

"Hell, Laurel—" he defended his present with undue emotion "—he spends more time over here than he does at my place."

"I know that, but—"

He shrugged. "I figured when I moved on, the two of them would miss each other. Besides, I'll probably just rent apartments since I don't expect to settle down for the next few years. That's no life for a dog."

Nor a man, she argued silently. Laurel knew Nick's intentions had been good. "I suppose you're right, but why didn't Danny tell me about it when I drove him to the airport?"

He gave her a guilty grin. "I warned him it might be better if I broke the news. I didn't know how you'd take it. I suppose I should have discussed it with you ahead of time, but it seemed like such a great idea . . ."

"It was a nice thought, Nick," she murmured. "Don't worry about it. Danny must have been thrilled."

"He was."

They fell silent, both unexpectedly depressed.

"Have you ever made love on the top of a grand piano?" he asked suddenly, trying to break the gloomy mood.

Laurel's dark brown eyes widened. "Of course not."

Nick regarded her silently for a full ten seconds. "I'll be right back," he said, turning as if to leave the room.

"Wait a minute." She reached out to pull him back to her. "Where are you going?"

"To get a blanket. That wood looks a little hard."

"I'm not making love with you on top of my brand-new Christmas piano," she insisted, even as her heartbeat speeded up in response to the seductive gleam in his eyes.

"Oh no?" he mused. "Are you so certain about that?"

She laughed. "I'm certain."

"You know, Laurel, sometimes you can be a very hard woman." He put his hand on her back, bringing her body against his with gentle pressure. His other hand moved between them, delving under the red cashmere until his fingers found her breast.

"But most of the time you're soft, lovely Laurel." He pulled the sweater over her head in a flash, lowering his head to flick the rosy peaks with the tip of his tongue. "So, so soft."

Laurel's protest turned into a moan of desire as Nick's tongue moved from one breast to the other, drawing wide wet circles on her flaming skin until she thought she'd explode from sheer want of him. When he took her fully in his mouth and suckled ravenously, she felt something shatter deep within her.

"Come to bed," he groaned, his lips recapturing hers. Nick's mind was aflame, reason disintegrating. The last coherent thought he managed was the wonder that every time he made love to Laurel, it only served to make him need her more. He was insatiable, unquenchable.

"No," she whispered. "Here. Now." With a strength born of passion, Laurel pulled Nick with her to the plush expanse of blue carpeting. Carried beyond the realm of ordinary time and space, they lost themselves in a December storm that belied the desert sunshine outdoors.

Laurel and Nick remained in a rose-colored world of their own making for the remainder of Danny's time in Seattle. They took long walks in the mellow winter sunshine, holding hands with a comfortable ease that suggested they'd been together for years. Nick took on the herculean project of teaching Laurel to cook, but more often than not the prepared meal would burn, or turn cold on the table as they succumbed to shared desire.

As if by unspoken agreement, they no longer discussed the future, settling for the pleasure they were receiving by living for each golden moment. Laurel couldn't remember laughing or loving so much, and she'd never received such exquisite pleasure from one man's company. Yet despite their carefree attitude, she still backed away from professing her love, afraid such an admission would only revive that uneasy tension between them.

She was admittedly relieved as her son's phone calls became more and more frequent, his homesickness evident.

"I don't think Dad and Amanda are very used to kids," Danny stated as she drove home from the airport.

"Oh?" *Don't pry,* she scolded herself. *Just thank your lucky stars he came home without a fuss.*

"Yeah. I made them a little uptight." A guilty expression crossed his young face. "Especially when I broke the window."

Laurel took her attention from the freeway driving for a moment, sending a quick glance her son's way. "You broke a window? Surely it was an accident."

He colored vividly. "Of course it was. What do you think I am? Some J.D. or something?"

Laurel laughed, reaching out to ruffle her son's hair. "Of course I don't think you're a juvenile delinquent," she responded instantly. "I was just surprised they'd get upset about a little thing like that."

"Well," he replied slowly, "it was a little more than that."

Laurel lifted an inquiring brow.

"I wanted to practice spotting my target when I passed, like Nick taught me. I was throwing the football at this tree next to the house."

"And you missed and it went through the window?"

"Right. It landed on the kitchen table, right in the middle of a tray of those smelly fish-egg things."

"Fish-egg things?"

He shrugged. "Yeah, you know. Caviar. Yuck."

"Oh no. Amanda was having a party?"

"A New Year's Eve party. Gosh, Mom, you should've seen it— there must've been four hundred people there. Anyway, this was about an hour before the party started and Amanda got really mad because the gloppy old stuff slid right off the tray down the front of her party dress."

Laurel had to bite her lip to keep from laughing out loud. "I can see where that might make Amanda a bit unhappy, Danny," she responded in a voice choked with restrained mirth.

"Yeah.... Well, then she and Dad got in a big fight. She accused him of having a holy terror for a son." He looked at her, his smooth brow furrowed. "Am I a holy terror, Mom?"

She reached out, sliding her arm around his shoulders. "Not in the least, sport. I think you're pretty terrific, actually. I'm sure your father told Amanda the same thing."

A flush darkened his face and Danny suddenly displayed an avid interest in the billboards lining the Black Canyon Highway.

"Danny?"

"Yeah, Mom?" he answered with what Laurel recognized to be feigned casualness.

"Since you brought this subject up, may I ask what Geoffrey did have to say?"

"He said since the accident was just like some crazy stunt you'd pull, I obviously took after you." The words fell out pell-mell, and Danny looked decidedly uncomfortable.

"Then Amanda yelled back that if he thought she was going to try to undo the damage that had already been done, he had another think coming. I decided about then it would be a good idea to go upstairs, so I didn't hear any more. Besides, the party started soon and everything settled down."

"I'm glad," Laurel murmured.

"You know something?"

"What, honey?"

"They don't fight like you and Nick. It's kinda scary with them."

Laurel shook her head. "Well, it's none of our business. I'm just glad to have you home."

He exhaled a long sigh. "Boy, am I glad to be home." As Danny carried his suitcases into his bedroom, he asked, "Are you going to Cleveland with Nick?"

"No. I don't think so."

Once again she was reminded of Danny's astuteness. "It's because of me you're not going to his play-off game, huh?"

Laurel knew better than to lie to her son. "Hey, kiddo, you just got home."

"I want you to go, Mom. I can always stay over at Billy's house for the weekend."

He named one of his new friends. Laurel hesitated. She'd met Nora Bradley at the school open house and knew her to be a friendly, responsible woman with a nice family. But it was not in Laurel's nature to ask favors from anyone.

"I don't know," she mused.

"I'll call him right now," Danny offered.

She caught his arm, making her decision. "No, you unpack and put your dirty clothes in the hamper. I'll call Mrs. Bradley."

"Way to go!" he yelled after her as Laurel left the room.

"DR. ADAMS? May I talk with you a moment?"

Her superior looked up from the medical journal he'd been perusing. "Dr. Britton, your timing is superb. I was just going to send for you."

She entered the office, taking a chair across from him. "Is something wrong?"

He shook his silvery head. "Nothing at all. In fact, I believe you'll find this good news."

Laurel smiled to herself, wondering how anything could possibly make her feel better than she had the past ten days. "I'd like you to consider taking on some additional responsibility," he stated.

Laurel couldn't understand how that was exactly good news, but she kept the expectant smile on her face.

He folded his hands in front of him. "I'm offering you the position of chief of staff, Dr. Britton."

Her head spun as his words sunk in. "Chief of staff? But I'm so new here."

"Length of employment isn't a criterion for selecting a qualified physician," he returned instantly. "Your athletic pursuits have obviously piqued your interest in your field far beyond that of simple professional curiosity. I've yet to meet a doctor with more knowledge of sports medicine than you, Dr. Britton. Now all you have to do is continue putting this knowledge to work in a clinical situation."

"But surely the others wouldn't want me as their superior," she argued. "After all, I am the new kid on the block."

He sighed, meeting her distressed gaze with a level one of his own. "Would it ease your fears in that regard to know that to a man, every doctor at this clinic offered your name to succeed Dr. Parrish?"

Laurel was amazed. "That's another point. I'm the only woman on staff. Doesn't that bother you?"

He arched a pewter eyebrow. "No, why should it?"

Laurel's fingers twisted together in her lap. "Well, I got the impression that you didn't appreciate women doctors in the sports medicine field."

His lips quirked. "Just testing your mettle a bit, Dr. Britton. I had to make certain you wouldn't fold under pressure."

"Are you telling me that I've been under consideration for the top spot since the day I walked in here?"

"Of course," he responded simply. "Dr. Parrish recommended you very highly, and after watching you work I concur with his opinion. You're a fine physician, Dr. Britton. You combine textbook knowledge with a human touch that's needed when dealing with the ego problems of athletes. You're perfect in every possible way. Now, will you accept, or do you need time to think about it?"

Laurel's impulse was to cry out an unqualified yes. But even though they'd avoided any discussion of a future together, she wanted to talk about the offer with Nick.

"I'd like a few days to think it over," she said slowly. "May I give you your answer on Monday?"

"After the Thunderbirds' play-off game," he said with uncanny insight.

She nodded, feeling the blush darken her skin.

"Of course that's satisfactory, Dr. Britton. I assume you're taking the weekend off?"

She hoped he wouldn't think she was already taking advantage of her offered position. "That's what I came to talk to you about, Dr. Adams. You see, I hadn't really planned until last night to go, and—"

He waved a dismissing hand. "Don't give it another thought. You go to Cleveland, and I'll cover you here."

"You?" She couldn't help staring.

"I *am* a licensed physician, Dr. Britton," her superior reminded her pointedly.

"Uh, of course, sir, it's just that I didn't realize you, that is, I didn't believe—"

"That I enjoyed treating patients? That I much preferred sitting behind this vast expanse of executive desk, wielding the reins of power over one and all?" he inquired dryly.

"I suppose that's pretty much it," she agreed quietly.

"When I accepted this position, I believed it to be exactly what I wanted," he stated. "Power, prestige and a six-figure income. But like everything else in life, Dr. Britton, there were trade-offs. I found, to my later regret, I rather miss the direct contact with patients."

He smiled encouragingly. "Fortunately for you, the chief of staff still maintains a patient load, although it's admittedly less than you have now. I assure you, however, the cases will be far more challenging and your surgery schedule will definitely increase. You're much too talented to be putting ice on minor sprains."

He rose, holding out his hand, indicating to Laurel their meeting was over. "I'm looking forward to returning to the treatment room this weekend, Doctor. And give my best wishes to Mr. McGraw. If the weather forecast is accurate, he'll need all the help he can get."

12

"MY GOD," Laurel gasped, rubbing her gloved hands together, "how cold is it out here?"

"Officially one degree below zero," the fan wearing a bright, knitted scarf and cap next to her ground out. "But with this wind, I'd guess the windchill factor is probably somewhere around a million below."

She shivered, glancing around the stadium at the crowd of over 77,000 intrepid sports fans wrapped in a variety of outer garments. When a tractor came out onto the field, scraping away a sheeting of ice and snow, Laurel's heart froze along with the rest of her body. It would be an absolute miracle if Nick's knee survived playing on that icy field.

Making a decision, she marched down the concrete steps, coming up behind the short, stocky Coach Carr. He turned as she tapped him on the shoulder.

"Hey, lady, no broads allowed on the bench."

"I am not a broad, Mr. Carr," she said, her voice coated with icicles. "I'm a sports physician. Dr. Laurel Britton."

"Good for you," he grunted. "Now you'd better get off the field before I call security."

"Hey, I know her." An assistant coach suddenly made the connection. "This is McGraw's doctor. The one from the clinic."

Coach Carr's eyes were beady little marbles as they raked over Laurel's face. "You're kidding."

Laurel fought down the anger created by his derisive tone. "I'm Nick McGraw's physician," she stated firmly. "And since there's a distinct possibility of his being injured today, I'm staying here on the sidelines."

"We don't allow girlfriends on the sidelines." He turned away. "As for medical treatment, we've got trainers here."

Laurel grabbed his arm, jerking him about to face her with a force that would amaze her later. "Trainers that'll shoot him full of xylocaine. On that icy field, with a numb leg, he'd be bound to lose his footing," she retorted furiously.

"McGraw's a big boy. If he wants a shot, we're not going to go to his mama for permission. Or his girlfriend."

Laurel felt like slapping his face, but restrained the impulse, knowing it would do no good. She put her hands on her hips and looked the man directly in the eye.

"Look, I'm his doctor, and I'm staying. If you don't like that, Coach Carr, then you're going to have to have me arrested and hauled from the field, because that's the only way I'm leaving."

Her dark eyes flashed dangerously, boring like lasers into his face. Obviously deciding he'd met his match, the coach shrugged uncaringly. "Hey, if you want to give up a good seat, it's your business." Then he waved an ungloved finger in her face. "But if you say one word to any of my players I'll take you up on that offer. Understand?"

Laurel nodded.

He shook his head, turning away. "Broads. Who can figure them?"

The game was a comedy of errors from the start. In the course of the first nineteen plays, there were seven turnovers, as player after player fumbled the ice-coated pigskin.

"Watching these guys is like going to the dentist," mumbled a television cameraman standing next to Laurel.

"It's not pretty," she agreed, cringing as Nick disappeared under a pile of Cleveland players.

"Hell, it's downright ugly," he protested, focusing on the play. "This is not the way the game was meant to be played."

The ball popped loose, Cleveland recovered and as Nick limped slowly off the field, Laurel noted he had snow for hair and ice for eyes. As the fumbles and miscues became commonplace, the intensity on the field increased. Frustration and cold were making tempers short as the ball continued to bounce off numbed fingers. Laurel had to cover her mouth with her hand to keep from crying out as Nick was hit again.

"If Cleveland wins, they're going to call that the blitz that killed Phoenix," the cameraman said, wincing as the mountain of bodies on top of Nick increased.

"This is the worst thing I've ever seen," she objected. "Why doesn't someone do something?"

The man shrugged. "Hey, that's what the Browns have been saying they were going to do all week. Their entire game plan was to worry McGraw with an exotic set of blitzes. They know his knee can't take much abuse, especially on that frozen surface."

"They're purposefully trying to injure him?" Laurel wondered who'd misnamed this sport a game. What was happening out on the field was definitely a war.

The cameraman gave her a strange look. "Sure. With the defense aimed at McGraw, he won't be around by the end of the game. Morgan hasn't had much playing time all season, so he'll be cold.... Well, that's the half," he said as the buzzer sounded.

Laurel knew there was no believably professional reason for her to invade the locker room. She crossed her frozen fingers, said any number of small prayers and paced the sidelines, wishing for the game to be over.

Cleveland came out in the second half more determined than ever to put pressure on Nick. "The Thunderbirds have been pulling weird stuff out of their bag of tricks all season," the opinionated cameraman muttered as he followed the play downfield. There was a resounding crash of helmets as Nick went down again. "Looks like they emptied their bag to get here."

"If you're such an expert," Laurel snapped, tired of his constant sarcasm, "then why don't you just put that camera down and go out there and try it for a few minutes?"

He stared at her, his frost-tinged lashes blinking his surprise. "Hey, lady, don't get uptight. I didn't mean anything."

But Laurel failed to hear his apology, her attention directed once again to Nick. Amazingly, he completed two short passes, and handed off twice more, moving the ball down the field in a series of successful plays. Calling time, he jogged to the sidelines, where Ward Carr was waiting.

"Okay, McGraw, here's your chance to redeem yourself," the coach said. "I want to hit Richardson in the end zone."

Laurel could hear the exchange and didn't miss the surprise in Nick's voice. "You're going with the pass?"

"Hell yes, we're going for all the marbles on this play."

"It's only the third quarter," Nick argued.

"Look, McGraw, if you don't want to be pulled right now, execute the play I've just called. You may be the guy making the big bucks, but I'm the coach. Understand? Now get out there, and if nobody's open, throw the damn ball into Lake Erie."

When several heads bobbed up out of the huddle a minute later to look incredulously at the sidelines, Laurel realized Nick was not alone in thinking the play risky. Not expecting it, Cleveland wasn't prepared and Nick's receiver was able to catch the ball in the end zone. He took several steps with it before a Cleveland player came in from behind and chopped it out of his hands.

When the official ruled "no catch," the fans in the stadium went wild, but Laurel didn't notice. Her attention was riveted on Nick, who'd gone down on a late hit. He wasn't getting up, and the team trainer had run out onto the field.

"Well, looks like the miracle comeback quarterback just flat ran out of miracles," the cameraman observed, directing his lens toward the action.

"Is he moving his leg?" she asked, wanting to hit the man for his heartless remark, but realizing he was able to see far more with his telephoto lens than she could.

"Nope. They just tried bending it, and he looked like he was going to pass out," he related. "He's out for the day."

"If it's what I think it is," she said with a sigh, fighting back unprofessional tears, "he's out, period."

She followed the stretcher out onto the field. Nick was propped up on his elbows, eyeing the scoreboard incredulously. "What in the hell's going on here? What do they mean no catch?" As he attempted to struggle to his feet, both the trainer and Laurel pushed him back down.

"Nick, you can't put any weight on that knee until I have a chance to examine it," she protested.

"That's a fair catch, dammit!"

"That's not the point right now."

He turned his blazing glare directly on her. "The hell it isn't!"

He was still blustering about the injustice of it all as they wheeled him into the emergency room of a nearby hospital and continued until the painkiller she prescribed finally knocked him out.

It was dark when Nick woke up much later. He looked around, trying to remember where he was. Oh God, he thought. The memory of the game was coming back.

"Laurel?"

She rose from the chair beside his bed, bending down to press a light kiss against his temple. "I'm right here."

"Did we lose?"

Dear Lord, she wondered, how could he care right now? She nodded. "I'm afraid so. It was a ridiculous day for football. The Thunderbirds couldn't help losing."

"It was a ridiculous day for the Browns, too. And they won," he reminded her. He linked his fingers behind his head. "Well, I suppose that's that. At least now we don't have to get me back on my feet for the Super Bowl. We've got the whole off-season to build my knee back up."

Laurel said nothing, knowing denial was often the first response of anyone facing an unpleasant medical fact.

Nick's head felt surrounded by a dense fog and his mouth was dry. He reached out for the glass of water beside the bed, thanking Laurel with his eyes as she held it for him.

"I'm glad you came," he murmured. "I wouldn't have wanted to entrust my body to just any old quack."

Laurel managed a smile. "I'm not wild about you entrusting that body to anyone other than me, McGraw. I've got first dibs."

Nick returned the smile with a weak one of his own. "What did you prescribe down in that emergency room, anyway? I feel like I'm floating somewhere out in space."

"Close your eyes and you won't be so dizzy," she instructed.

He did as she said. "Hey, this is kinda nice. If you're into flying merry-go-rounds."

Laurel bent down to kiss him. "Go to sleep, darling. I'll be here when you wake up."

Laurel called Danny, assuring him Nick would be just fine. Nora Bradley got on the line to say Danny was no trouble, and was welcome to stay as long as he wished. Her next call was to the clinic.

"Is it what we feared?" Matthew Adams asked.

"Yes, the damage to the tendons is extensive, and the cartilage is just lying in ruins." Tears welled up in her eyes and Laurel sniffled inelegantly, blowing her nose.

"Well, that's that," he replied after a long silence.

"That's that," she agreed flatly. "I'm bringing Nick back to Phoenix the day after tomorrow."

"Does he know?"

Laurel sighed. "I'm sure he must. I haven't said anything, but the man's been an athlete long enough to be well acquainted with what his body can and cannot do. Besides, he's always known the risk."

"That he has," the older man agreed. "Have a safe flight back, Dr. Britton."

"Thank you," she murmured. She went downstairs once again to X ray, studying the films carefully, determined to be able to give Nick as much encouragement about his prognosis as possible. It didn't look at all good, she decided. But it could have been a lot worse. And that was what she was going to have to make him understand.

"Hi," Nick greeted her as she entered the room before noon. "You're just in time for the news. Want to watch the report of yesterday's debacle?"

Laurel shook her head. "Not really. But I don't suppose we have any choice?"

"Nope. I never did get to see that touchdown pass they stole from me." He managed a smile. "I knew I was in trouble when I looked up and saw that monster blocking out the sun."

They viewed what the sportscaster was calling highlights of the game, although Laurel considered them badly labeled. Neither team had distinguished itself, the weather proving a much tougher opponent.

"Hell yes, I have to blame McGraw." Coach Carr came onto the screen, his face set in a scowl.

"It was a team loss," the sportscaster pointed out. "McGraw actually played quite well, considering the circumstances."

"McGraw makes the most money; he's well paid to perform."

"Is it true that last hit ended his playing days?"

As Laurel sat on the edge of his hospital bed beside him, she felt Nick tense, but he remained silent.

"That's what they say."

"What does that mean to next year's Thunderbirds?"

"I don't believe the myth about needing a veteran quarterback."

Nick only grunted as they wrapped up the interview. Then Laurel's clinic came onto the screen.

"We're here with Dr. Matthew Adams, administrator for the Phoenix Sports Medicine Clinic, where Nick McGraw has been receiving daily therapy for an injury suffered last season," the reporter announced. "Dr. Adams, is it true that Nick's physician is in Cleveland with him at the moment?"

"That's right. Our chief of staff, Dr. Britton, has examined Mr. McGraw and will be returning to Phoenix with him tomorrow."

"Chief of staff?" Nick asked, looking at Laurel with obvious surprise. "When did that happen?"

"It's a long story," she murmured, reaching for the remote control before Adams could continue. "And the announcement is definitely premature. I haven't accepted it yet."

He held the control out of her reach. "But you've been offered the post."

Laurel nodded. "A couple of days ago. Let's turn it off."

"Wait a minute, they're talking about you, Dr. Britton."

"And Dr. Britton's prognosis about his future?" the reporter asked.

"I'm afraid Nick McGraw's playing days are over."

Nick froze and Laurel risked a tentative glance in his direction. "Nick," she began softly.

The television screen darkened as he pointed the control in its direction. "Is that what you told him?" His voice was under tight control.

"Let me explain."

As he flung her hand off his arm, his eyes were expressionless. "I asked you a question, Laurel. Is that what you told him?"

"Yes." It was a whisper, but Nick had trouble hearing it in the swirling silence of the room.

"I see. Is that your best guess? Or are you positive?"

"Positive. But you'll be able to walk, Nick," she rushed to add.

"Walk. But no football."

She shook her head. "No, no football."

"They told me that last year," he reminded her.

"That was different. Dr. Phillips only said he wouldn't recommend it. He didn't say it was a total impossibility. Believe me, there's no way your knee will be able to sustain any more hits. And it isn't flexible enough to allow you the mobility you need out on the playing field."

"That's your opinion."

"That's my opinion," she agreed.

"I'm requesting a consultation with another specialist," he stated firmly, crossing his arms over his chest.

Laurel understood his reasoning and welcomed it. She didn't want him to ever wonder if she'd lied, in order to get him to stop playing.

"I think that's a good idea. Anyone in particular?"

He shook his head. "No. I'll let you choose. So long as you promise not to stack the deck against me."

Laurel bent down, kissing Nick with all the love she held for him in her heart. "I promise," she pledged.

She arranged for the extensive examination the day after they returned to Phoenix. She wanted Nick to accept the full extent of his injury as soon as possible, so he could get on with his life.

"Well, I guess that's about it," he commented flatly, alone with Laurel after the famed sports physician she had brought in from Boston had confirmed her diagnosis.

"I'm afraid so," she agreed softly. "Nick, I'm truly sorry."

"Not as sorry as I am." He laughed hollowly. "I should've known it would never work out."

"You managed to play the entire season," she pointed out. "Against incredible odds."

"Believe it or not, I wasn't talking about football, Laurel. I was talking about us."

"Us?"

"The chief of staff and the washed-up jock."

The finality in his low tone frightened Laurel. "What do you mean? Why should this change anything between us?"

"You're the lady who didn't want complications."

"So I've changed my mind." She decided to take a chance. "And I think you have, too."

His gaze swept over her. In the dark, linen shirtwaist dress and pumps she looked every inch the successful professional woman. The hoops in her ears as well as her watch and stickpin were simply fashioned in gold, but expensive. This was a woman with her life on track. She'd faced odds that had equaled his own right now and succeeded. Admirably. And more important, she'd done it on her own. The one thing Laurel Britton didn't need was to be saddled with his problems. For a time their lives had run a parallel course, but now hers was rocketing skyward, while his had fizzled and was crashing down toward earth.

"Look, Laurel, you've got the world in the palm of your hand right now. Chief of staff—"

"I haven't accepted that," she interrupted.

"You will," he overrode her firmly. "Your career is booming, and now that Geoffrey and Amanda have changed their mind about wanting to share their perfect home with a spirited young boy, you don't have any more worries about Danny.

"You're intelligent, lovely and, quite honestly, the most lovable as well as loving woman I've ever met. You're going to have the guys lining up outside your door in droves, sweetheart. The last thing you need is an aging, battered old has-been."

"Don't you dare talk that way about the man I love," she protested heatedly. It was the first time the word had been spoken aloud and its importance reverberated around the room as Nick and Laurel observed each other for a full minute. Nick finally broke the heavy silence.

"You don't love me." He groaned unconsciously as he slowly slid off the examining table, accepting the cane she offered him with a grim expression. "You're just confusing love with pity, Doctor. You're going to have to learn to maintain a more professional attitude."

"Nick . . ." Laurel reached out, but he shook free of her arm.

"Let it go, Laurel," he pleaded. "I'm just not any good for

anyone right now. Don't you see, I'm not in any position to be making any decisions."

"Don't you understand?" Tears ran unchecked down her cheeks as she remained unaware she was weeping. "I fell in love with you in spite of the fact that you played football. Not because you did."

"It's who I am," he objected firmly. "All my life, I've thought of myself as a football player. My entire life. I can't separate the two, Laurel, and I've never wanted to."

He drew a long, painful breath. "I'm intelligent enough to realize there's no way in hell I'm ever going to play the game again. So obviously I can't offer you anything."

He reached out his free hand, brushing her hair from her face, tucking it behind her ear in a heartbreakingly familiar gesture.

"Laurel, do me a favor."

"Anything."

"Don't love me. I really can't handle that right now, and it's definitely not fair to you."

Laurel was angry and desperate as she saw their life together slipping away like grains of sand through open fingers. "Don't tell me what's fair and not fair. And you've no right to tell me who I can and cannot love."

As she lifted a tear-stained face to his, Nick's fingers moved over her delicate features, as if the memory of her would have to last him a lifetime.

"Be good to yourself," he said gruffly, turning away, his own eyes unnaturally moist.

Laurel couldn't believe he was actually going to go until she watched the black Ferrari pull out of the parking lot and disappear around the corner. He was gone, her brain echoed hollowly. Just like that, he'd driven out of her clinic and out of her life.

13

LAUREL KEPT ABREAST of Nick's progress for the next two weeks through Danny, as her son visited his house every day. She waited for a message that he asked about her, wanted her, anything. But he seemed determined to make their break permanent, only keeping his promise not to hurt her son.

She was also hurt, but not surprised, when the consulting physician she'd brought in from Boston telephoned, letting her know he'd scheduled Nick for some minor-repair surgery. Nick didn't even want her as a doctor any longer. Laurel knew he was purposely remaining as cold and distant as possible, in an attempt to persuade her not to love him. But he might as well have attempted to stop the sun from rising every morning.

On Super Bowl Sunday, Laurel watched two teams, neither of which she cared anything about, battle throughout the afternoon. Knowing how much this game had meant to Nick, she was unable to expunge the mental image of him watching the game in his self-imposed isolation. It had to be extremely painful for him, knowing that he'd never again play the game that his entire life had revolved around.

She rose from her chair, going over to the window, staring at his house for a long, silent time. The man was so damnably frustrating, she seethed inwardly, thinking back over Nick's behavior. He was arrogant, stubborn and incredibly shortsighted. And stupid. Because he hadn't understood how much he meant to her; how deeply she loved him.

Suddenly, Laurel knew what she had to do. The answer hit her with all the crystal clarity of a spring-fed mountain stream.

"I'm going next door," she said to her son, who was still engrossed in the action taking place on the television screen.

Danny turned his attention from the game momentarily. "It's about time," he said simply. As Laurel pulled the bottle of champagne she'd been saving out of the refrigerator, Danny called out from the family room. "Hey, have fun. And don't worry about me. I'll microwave something for dinner."

She looked around the doorframe. "Am I ever glad your father never realized what a prize you are, kiddo."

He grinned a little self-consciously, a blush spreading out under the freckles. "Ah gee, Mom, you know I'd never live with him and Amanda. They don't love each other like you and Nick. We're going to have a neat-o family, huh?"

From the mouths of babes. "Absolutely neat-o," she agreed.

She walked across their backyards, making her way to Nick's back door. "Hi Rowdy," she whispered, as the huge golden retriever came bounding into the kitchen, sliding on the rug, his feet almost going out from under him in his eagerness to greet Laurel.

Danny had returned the dog to Nick, insisting Nick needed company, and Laurel had been surprised to find she actually missed the friendly beast constantly underfoot. She held the bottle high above her head as he placed his huge paws on her shoulders and vigorously began washing her face.

"Rowdy?" Nick called out. "What's going on in there?"

Laurel pushed the dog down, smoothed the front of her sweater and took a deep calming breath. Then she made her way bravely toward Nick's den.

"He was saying hello to a neighbor," she said simply.

Nick's eyes widened and he felt as if his heartbeat had suddenly trebled its rate. "Laurel, what are you doing here?" He quickly got up out of his chair.

She reached down and flicked off the television. "I've come to seduce you, Nick."

"Laurel—"

She wasn't about to give him an opportunity to object. "See, I've even brought champagne." She gave him a breathtakingly beautiful smile as she handed him one of the stemmed crystal glasses. "I've never been terribly good at this, but I think it's about…ah, there it goes." She nodded her approval as the cork popped with the retort of a rifle shot.

Ignoring Nick's questioning gaze, she poured some effervescent champagne into both glasses, lifting hers in the gesture of a toast.

"To strings," she murmured. "And celebrations."

Nick stared down into her shining face. Lord, she was so beautiful. "May I ask what we're celebrating?"

"Why, our upcoming marriage," she answered, her eyes guileless. "I lied, Nick. I want a lifetime of loving, glorious complications." She dipped her finger into the champagne, lifting it to the harshly cut line of his lips, wetting them with the icy liquid.

"Laurel," he protested on a weak ragged note, attempting to maintain a semblance of sanity as her finger worked its way between his lips. Her eyes were dark black pools, drawing him deeper and deeper into their depths, and suddenly Nick realized what it must feel like to be drowning in quicksand. He put his glass down slowly onto the table.

Moaning a soft oath, he lowered his head, his mouth capturing hers. His fingers thrust through her hair, holding her to a suddenly savage kiss that was naked in its need. Laurel was staggered by the intensity of his lips but even more stunned by her own, as they moved desperately under his. Neither noticed as her glass dropped to the carpet, spilling a trail of golden liquid that Rowdy happily lapped up.

"I'm not leaving here until you make love to me, Nick Mc-Graw," Laurel said, her lips plucking at his as she punctuated her words with hard little kisses. "Then I dare you to tell me that you don't want to spend the rest of our lives together."

Nick wanted to take her to bed right then. But there was something he had to take care of first. He forced his mind to the words he'd been rehearsing all morning.

"There's nothing I'd like better than spending the rest of our life in carefree decadence," he began, his hand moving over one cashmere-clad breast.

Laurel felt that familiar stirring as his fingers plucked idly at the hardening tip. "Mmm. I think that sounds like a perfect idea."

"Unfortunately, I do have other obligations." The roving hand slid under her sweater, and his palm cupped intimately.

Laurel was finding words more and more difficult. "Why do I have the feeling you're trying to tell me something?"

"I don't know. What could I possibly have to tell you except that I've got a new job?" He lowered his head, his breath warming her skin through the wispy material of her bra.

Laurel pulled his head up by his blond hair. "A job? What job? When? Where? Not in football? Did you take it?"

He laughed. "Hey, slow down. Which of those questions do you want answered first?"

"When? And why didn't you tell me?"

"I accepted it this morning and have been working up my nerve all day to make that long trek next door. I suddenly realized I didn't know what I'd do if you told me to get lost."

There were little seeds of worry in his green eyes that Laurel hastened to dispel. "Never," she said instantly, pressing a hard kiss on his lips. "Where?" She held her breath.

"Phoenix."

So far so good. "In football?"

He shrugged. "In a way. I'll be directing a YMCA winter youth league. My main responsibility will be training the volunteer coaches to make certain the boys have fun. Everyone gets to play, and there's less emphasis on winning at all costs compared to some of the other programs available."

His expression grew earnest. "Despite my reluctance to retire, I've been giving the whole thing a lot of thought the past few months. I didn't want to sell cars, or open a restaurant or even try sportscasting like so many other ex-jocks. I've no inclination to go to Hollywood, and I hate the idea of people using me to push deodorants and shaving cream. . . .

"But I like the idea of this, Laurel. And I think I can do a good job."

"I know you can," she said with heartfelt conviction. "You'll be wonderful. Terrific. In fact, you'll be the best coach those kids will ever have and someday we'll be watching your players in the Super Bowl." Her enthusiasm for the idea escalated. "Isn't that an incredible thought? Just think of it—"

She was just getting wound up when Nick pressed his fingers against her lips. "Laurel?"

"Yes?"

"I thought you'd come here to seduce me," he reminded her on a deep, husky note. The lambent heat in his darkening jade eyes told its own story.

"Oh yes," she whispered, going up on her toes to press her lips against his. "And don't you dare try to argue with me, McGraw, because I'm not taking no for an answer."

"Lovely Laurel," Nick groaned as she fit her curves to his body. His lips met hers in a heated demand, rekindling the fires he'd tried to keep safely banked these long and lonely days.

Every vestige of restraint fled as Laurel gave herself fully to Nick's ravenous kiss, her fingers desperately at the buttons of his shirt. She had to touch him, had to know that his skin flamed for her, just as hers was on fire for him.

"Oh yes," he encouraged, closing his eyes to the feel of her fingertips against his moist skin. He moaned his pleasure as she dragged her lips from his to taste of his tangy flesh.

The taste, that marvelous male taste of his hard chest that she'd not been able to exorcise from her memory, only had her wanting more. His belt. It had to go, she couldn't bear it any longer. She had to reestablish her claim over all of this man who'd scorched away reason and made her a prisoner of her own blazing need.

She lifted her arms in mute assistance as he tugged her red sweater over her dark head. The wispy scarlet bra followed and his mouth moved hungrily to her breast, his teeth tugging at a rosy erect nipple, causing Laurel to cry out.

"I want to be gentle with you, to go slowly," he groaned, burying his head in her yielding softness.

Laurel clung to him, her hips moving against his, kindling fires that were raging wildly out of control. "Don't think," she advised in a throaty voice far removed from her usual clear tone. Her hand moved between them, stroking his hard flesh through the worn denim of his jeans. "Just feel, my darling."

Taking his hand, Laurel gave him a seductive, womanly smile as she led him down the hallway to his bedroom. She lay on the vast expanse of water bed, holding her arms out to him, inviting him to join her. Nick needed no further encouragement, gathering her to him for a long, deliriously wonderful kiss. Their clothing was rapidly dispatched, as if burned away by a wildfire, flung to the farthest corners of the room.

The drapes were drawn to the late-afternoon sun, but the darkness in the room seemed to lighten and glow with a fire of its own. As Nick's hands and lips and tongue moved over Laurel's body, he was stunned at the heat of her flesh.

"You're on fire," he murmured, thrilled by her response. "God, how I love it when you burn for me, lovely Laurel."

His hand moved down her body, scorching the flesh of her stomach, trailing sparks down the insides of her thighs and back up again. Laurel gave a little cry of delight.

When his lips moved where his fingers had teased, strange heats burst inside her, little fires that spiraled outward from her innermost core. His tongue became a sensual weapon, probing into the warm satin of her body, and Laurel knew that at any moment she was going to be flung into the reaches of the universe, beyond anything she'd ever experienced, even with Nick. The idea was thrilling, but frightening in its intensity, and she didn't want to go there alone.

"Please, Nick, I need you." Her fingers tangled in his hair as she pulled him up to cover her.

Nick had never known this potential for heat and passion. His body burned, sought, and so did hers. She opened for him and when he plunged into her, it was as if a thousand blazing stars exploded behind his eyes. Laurel responded with a rhythm and ferocity that matched his own, her fingernails raking primitive paths down the moist, rippling muscles of his back.

She wondered how this man could cause every atom in her body to flame; how was it that Nick McGraw could make her toss away every vestige of self-restraint for the sheer, overwhelming feel of his lips against hers, his flesh against her flesh. She wanted to understand—to know what magic this man possessed to make her world continually spin out of control, to make everything and everyone before him commonplace.

But then she was beyond all thought, beyond reason, as their heat exploded into a gigantic white fireball, sending them spinning outward into a world of their own making, a place of blinding lights and vivid colors that swirled about them, enveloping them in the dazzling glow.

Afraid of crushing her, Nick carefully rolled over, still holding her, not yet willing to give up the pleasures of her velvet warmth. The heat gradually faded as they lay together for a long, silent time in the slowly cooling aftermath of passion, her dark hair scented webbing against his chest.

"Laurel?"

"Mmm?" She'd never known such contentment.

"I love you."

She opened her eyes, lifting them to his cautious gaze. "I know," she said simply.

"Any regrets?"

Her smile was beatific. "Regrets? How could I have any regrets? I was just thinking how it would be impossible to be any happier than I am at this moment."

"Are you sure about that?"

"Very sure." She pressed a kiss against his chest.

Nick's hands moved enticingly over the pink-tipped hills of her breasts. "What would you say if I told you I wanted you again?"

Her eyes gleamed a deep ebony as she nodded slowly. "I'd say that I may have been a bit hasty in that assessment."

"Shall we put it to the test?"

Laurel reached up, pulling his head down to her kiss. "Most definitely."

"I'M GOING TO NEED a doctor if you keep up that wanton behavior," Nick complained a long time later. "I don't think I'll ever move again." He lay beside Laurel, his lashes a golden fringe against his tanned cheeks.

Laurel sighed contentedly. "I know what you mean."

He reached out, his hand unerringly finding her breast. "Happy?"

"I couldn't be happier," she answered honestly.

"How do you really feel about the job?" he asked with a casualness she suspected was feigned. She turned her head, finding him watching her carefully.

Tapping a thoughtful fingernail against her front tooth, Laurel chose her words carefully. "You'd do a wonderful job, Nick. You're terrific with kids."

"I like kids."

She nodded as she considered Nick in that role. He'd be perfect, but would it be enough? "I know," she murmured, lost in thought. "And they all like you."

"Why am I hearing a *but* in that less than enthusiastic response?"

"There's not much fame in youth sports, Nick," she felt obliged to point out. She hadn't come this far to stop being honest with him now.

"I've had enough fame to last me a lifetime, Laurel. Believe me, I'm looking forward to a life of blissful anonymity."

"And fortune. You didn't say what they're paying, but it can't be that generous."

He chuckled. "Now that you're a big shot chief of staff, can't you support a loving husband and a couple of kids?"

Laurel felt herself melting as a light gleamed in his emerald eyes. "A couple?" she whispered.

"Didn't Danny tell you about his master plan? About you and me and a brother or sister?"

"Oh, my God," Laurel groaned. "When did he tell you about that?"

"The first week. It seems like a reasonable enough request to me. In fact, the poor kid's been waiting such a long time, we should probably get started on that little project as soon as possible." He gave her a long, lingering kiss.

"The game," she remembered belatedly. "It's probably still on."

"Forget the game," he murmured, his lips nuzzling at her ear. "I can think of a much better way to spend the day."

"My goodness," she teased, "could this possibly be the same fellow who professed he couldn't separate the man from the football player?"

His teeth bit down lightly on her tender lobe. "It is. But a certain sexy sports doctor once suggested there was more to life than football. Although that idea bordered on heresy, since I didn't have anything better to do, I thought I might as well check it out."

Her fingers played with the thick blond waves curling against the back of his neck. "And what did you find?"

Nick's laugh was deep and filled with satisfaction as he pulled Laurel into his arms. "I found," he said, his kiss pledging a future filled with love, "that there's a lot to be said for indoor sports."

What Dr. Kate Chesne doesn't need:

☑ *A handsome malpractice lawyer with a personal grudge.*

UNDER THE KNIFE

Tess Gerritsen

To my mother and father

Prologue

Dear God, how the past comes back to haunt us.

From his office window, Dr. Henry Tanaka stared out at the rain battering the parking lot and wondered why, after all these years, the death of one poor soul had come back to destroy him.

Outside, a nurse, her uniform spotty with rain, dashed to her car. Another one caught without an umbrella, he thought. That morning, like most Honolulu mornings, had dawned bright and sunny. But at three o'clock the clouds had slithered over the Koolau range and now, as the last clinic employees headed for home, the rain became a torrent, flooding the streets with a river of dirty water.

Tanaka turned and stared down at the letter on his desk. It had been mailed a week ago; but like so much of his correspondence, it had been lost in the piles of obstetrical journals and supply catalogs that always littered his office. When his receptionist had finally called it to his attention this morning, he'd been alarmed by the name on the return address: Joseph Kahanu, Attorney at Law.

He had opened it immediately.

Now he sank into his chair and read the letter once again.

Dear Dr. Tanaka,

As the attorney representing Mr. Charles Decker, I hereby request any and all medical records pertaining to the obstetrical care of Ms. Jennifer Brook, who was your patient at the time of her death....

Jennifer Brook. A name he'd hoped to forget.

A profound weariness came over him—the exhaustion of a man who has discovered he cannot outrun his own shadow. He tried to muster the energy to go home, to slog outside and climb into his car, but he could only sit and stare at the four walls of his office. His sanctuary. His gaze traveled past the framed diplomas, the medical certificates, the photographs. Everywhere there were snapshots of wrinkled newborns, of beaming mothers and fathers. How many babies had he brought into the world? He'd lost count years ago....

It was a sound in the outer office that finally drew him out of his chair: the click of a door shutting. He rose and went to peer out at the reception area. "Peggy? Are you still here?"

The waiting room was deserted. Slowly his gaze moved past the flowered couch and chairs, past the magazines neatly stacked on the coffee table, and finally settled on the outer door. It was unlocked.

Through the silence, he heard the muted clang of metal. It came from one of the exam rooms.

"Peggy?" Tanaka moved down the hall and glanced into the first room. Flicking on the light, he saw the hard gleam of the stainless-steel sink, the gynecologic table, the supply cabinet. He turned off the light and went to the next room. Again, everything was as it should be: the instruments lined up neatly on the counter, the sink wiped dry, the table stirrups folded up for the night.

Crossing the hall, he moved toward the third and last exam room. But just as he reached for the light switch, some instinct made him freeze: a sudden awareness of a presence—something malevolent—waiting for him in the darkness.

In terror, he backed out of the room. Only as he spun around to flee did he realize that the intruder was standing behind him.

A blade slashed across his neck.

Tanaka staggered backward into the exam room and toppled an instrument stand. Stumbling to the floor, he found the linoleum was already slick with his blood. Even as he felt his life drain away, a coldly rational pocket of his brain forced him to assess his own wound, to analyze his own chances. *Severed artery. Exsanguination within minutes. Have to stop the bleeding.* . . . Numbness was already creeping up his legs.

So little time. On his hands and knees, he crawled toward the cabinet where the gauze was stored. To his half-senseless mind, the feeble light reflecting off those glass doors became his guiding beacon, his only hope of survival.

A shadow blotted out the glow from the hall. He knew the intruder was standing in the doorway, watching him. Still he kept moving.

In his last seconds of consciousness, Tanaka managed to drag himself to his feet and wrench open the cabinet door. Sterile packets rained down from the shelf. Blindly he ripped one apart, withdrew a wad of gauze and clamped it against his neck.

He didn't see the attacker's blade trace its final arc.

As it plunged deep into his back, Tanaka tried to scream but the only sound that issued from his throat was a sigh. It was the last breath he took before he slid quietly to the floor.

CHARLIE DECKER lay naked in his small hard bed and he was afraid.

Through the window he saw the blood-red glow of a neon sign: *The Victory Hotel.* Except the *t* was missing from *Hotel*. And what was left made him think of *Hole*, which is what the place really was: *The Victory Hole*, where every triumph, every joy, sank into some dark pit of no return.

He shut his eyes but the neon seemed to burrow its way through his lids. He turned away from the window and pulled the pillow over his head. The smell of the filthy linen was suffocating. Tossing the pillow aside, he rose and paced over to the window. There he stared down at the street. On the sidewalk below, a stringy-haired blonde in a miniskirt was dickering with a man in a Chevy. Somewhere in the night people laughed and a jukebox was playing "It Don't Matter Anymore." A stench rose from the alley, a peculiar mingling of rotting trash and frangipani: the smell of the back streets of paradise. It made him nauseated. But it was too hot to close the window, too hot to sleep, too hot even to breathe.

He went over to the card table and switched on the lamp. The same newspaper headline stared up at him.

Honolulu Physician Found Slain.

He felt the sweat trickle down his chest. He threw the newspaper on the floor. Then he sat down and let his head fall into his hands.

The music from the distant jukebox faded; the next song started, a thrusting of guitars and drums. A singer growled out: "I want it bad, oh yeah, baby, so bad, so bad. . . ."

Slowly he raised his head and his gaze settled on the photograph of Jenny. She was smiling; as always, she was smiling. He touched the picture, trying to remember how her face had felt; but the years had dimmed his memory.

At last he opened his notebook. He turned to a blank page. He began to write.

This is what they told me:
"It takes time . . .
Time to heal, time to forget."
This is what I told them:
That healing lies not in forgetfulness
But in remembrance
Of you.
The smell of the sea on your skin;
The small and perfect footprints you leave in the sand.
In remembrance there are no endings.
And so you lie there, now and always, by the sea.
You open your eyes. You touch me.
The sun is in your fingertips.
And I am healed.
I am healed.

Chapter One

With a steady hand, Dr. Kate Chesne injected two hundred milligrams of sodium Pentothal into her patient's intravenous line. As the column of pale yellow liquid drifted lazily through the plastic tubing, Kate murmured, "You should start to feel sleepy soon, Ellen. Close your eyes. Let go...."

"I don't feel anything yet."

"It will take a minute or so." Kate squeezed Ellen's shoulder in a silent gesture of reassurance. The small things were what made a patient feel safe. A touch. A quiet voice. "Let yourself float," Kate whispered. "Think of the sky... clouds...."

Ellen gave her a calm and drowsy smile. Beneath the harsh operating-room lights, every freckle, every flaw stood out cruelly on her face. No one, not even Ellen O'Brien, was beautiful on the operating table. "Funny," she murmured. "I'm not afraid. Not in the least...."

"You don't have to be. I'll take care of everything."

"I know. I know you will." Ellen reached out for Kate's hand. It was only a touch, a brief mingling of fingers. The warmth of Ellen's skin against hers was one more reminder that not just a body, but a woman, a friend, was lying on this table.

The door swung open and the surgeon walked in. Dr. Guy Santini was as big as a bear and he looked faintly ridiculous in his flowered paper cap. "How we doing in here, Kate?"

"Pentothal's going in now."

Guy moved to the table and squeezed the patient's hand. "Still with us, Ellen?"

She smiled. "For better or worse. But on the whole, I'd rather be in Philadelphia."

Guy laughed. "You'll get there. But minus your gallbladder."

"I don't know.... I was getting kinda...fond of the thing...." Ellen's eyelids sagged. "Remember, Guy," she whispered. "You promised. No scar...."

"Did I?"

"Yes...you did....."

Guy winked at Kate. "Didn't I tell you? Nurses make the worst patients. Demanding broads!"

"Watch it, Doc!" one of the O.R. nurses snapped. "One of these days we'll get *you* up on that table."

"Now *that's* a terrifying thought," remarked Guy.

Kate watched as her patient's jaw at last fell slack. She called softly: "Ellen?" She brushed her finger across Ellen's eyelashes. There was no response. Kate nodded at Guy. "She's under."

"Ah, Katie, my darlin'," he said, "you do such good work for a—"

"For a *girl*. Yeah, yeah. I know."

"Well, let's get this show on the road," he said, heading out to scrub. "All her labs look okay?"

"Blood work's perfect."

"EKG?"

"I ran it last night. Normal."

Guy gave her an admiring salute from the doorway. "With you around, Kate, a man doesn't even have to think. Oh, and ladies?" He called to the two O.R. nurses who were laying out the instruments. "A word of warning. Our intern's a lefty."

The scrub nurse glanced up with sudden interest. "Is he cute?"

Guy winked. "A real dreamboat, Cindy. I'll tell him you asked." Laughing, he vanished out the door.

Cindy sighed. "How does his wife stand him, anyway?"

For the next ten minutes, everything proceeded like clockwork. Kate went about her tasks with her usual efficiency. She inserted the endotracheal tube and connected the respirator. She adjusted the flow of oxygen and added the proper proportions of forane and nitrous oxide. She was Ellen's lifeline. Each step, though automatic, required double-checking, even triple-checking. When the patient was someone she knew and liked, being sure of all her moves took on even more urgency. An anesthesiologist's job is often called ninety-nine percent boredom and one percent sheer terror; it was that one percent that Kate was always anticipating, always guarding against. When complications arose, they could happen in the blink of an eye.

But today she fully expected everything to go smoothly. Ellen O'Brien was only forty-one. Except for a gallstone, she was in perfect health.

Guy returned to the O.R., his freshly scrubbed arms dripping wet. He was followed by the "dreamboat" lefty intern, who appeared to be a staggering five-feet-six in his elevator shoes. They proceeded on to the ritual donning of sterile gowns and gloves, a ceremony punctuated by the brisk snap of latex.

As the team took its place around the operating table, Kate's gaze traveled the circle of masked faces. Except for the intern, they were all comfortably familiar. There was the circulating nurse, Ann Richter, with her ash blond hair tucked neatly beneath a blue surgical cap. She was a coolheaded professional who never mixed business with pleasure. Crack a joke in the O.R. and she was likely to flash you a look of disapproval.

Next there was Guy, homely and affable, his brown eyes distorted by thick bottle-lens glasses. It was hard to believe anyone so clumsy could be a surgeon. But put a scalpel in his hand and he could work miracles.

Opposite Guy stood the intern with the woeful misfortune of having been born left-handed.

And last there was Cindy, the scrub nurse, a dark-eyed nymph with an easy laugh. Today she was sporting a brilliant new eye shadow called Oriental Malachite, which gave her a look reminiscent of a tropical fish.

"Nice eye shadow, Cindy," noted Guy as he held his hand out for a scalpel.

"Why thank you, Dr. Santini," she replied, slapping the instrument into his palm.

"I like it a lot better than that other one, Spanish Slime."

"Spanish *Moss*."

"This one's really, really striking, don't you think?" he asked the intern who, wisely, said nothing. "Yeah," Guy continued. "Reminds me of my favorite color. I think it's called Comet cleanser."

The intern giggled. Cindy flashed him a dirty look. So much for the dreamboat's chances.

Guy made the first incision. As a line of scarlet oozed to the surface of the abdominal wall, the intern automatically dabbed away the blood with a sponge. Their hands worked automatically and in concert, like pianists playing a duet.

From her position at the patient's head, Kate followed their progress, her ear tuned the whole time to Ellen's heart rhythm. Everything was going well, with no crises on the horizon. This was when she enjoyed her work most—when she knew she had everything under control. In the midst of all this stainless steel, she felt right at home. For her, the whooshes of the ventilator and the beeps of the cardiac monitor were soothing background music to the performance now unfolding on the table.

Guy made a deeper incision, exposing the glistening layer of fat. "Muscles seem a little tight, Kate," he observed. "We're going to have trouble retracting."

"I'll see what I can do." Turning to her medication cart, she reached for the tiny drawer labeled Succinylcholine. Given intravenously, the drug would relax the muscles, allowing Guy easier access to the abdominal cavity. Glancing in the drawer, she frowned. "Ann? I'm down to one vial of Succinylcholine. Hunt me down some more, will you?"

"That's funny," said Cindy. "I'm sure I stocked that cart yesterday afternoon."

"Well, there's only one vial left." Kate drew up 5 cc's of the crystal-clear solution and injected it into Ellen's IV line. It would take a minute to work. She sat back and waited.

Guy's scalpel cleared the fat layer and he began to expose the abdominal muscle sheath. "Still pretty tight, Kate," he remarked.

She glanced up at the wall clock. "It's been three minutes. You should notice some effect by now."

"Not a thing."

"Okay. I'll push a little more." Kate drew up another 3 cc's and injected it into the IV line. "I'll need another vial soon, Ann," she warned. "This one's just about—"

A buzzer went off on the cardiac monitor. Kate glanced up sharply. What she saw on the screen made her jump to her feet in horror.

Ellen O'Brien's heart had stopped.

In the next instant the room was in a frenzy. Orders were shouted out, instrument trays shoved aside. The intern clambered onto a footstool and thrust his weight again and again on Ellen's chest.

This was the proverbial one percent, the moment of terror every anesthesiologist dreads.

It was also the worst moment in Kate Chesne's life.

As panic swirled around her, she fought to stay in control. She injected vial after vial of adrenaline, first into the IV lines and then directly into Ellen's heart. *I'm losing her,* she thought. *Dear God, I'm losing her.* Then she saw one brief fluttering across the oscilloscope. It was the only hint that some trace of life lingered.

"Let's cardiovert!" she called out. She glanced at Ann, who was standing by the defibrillator. "Two hundred watt seconds!"

Ann didn't move. She remained frozen, her face as white as alabaster.

"Ann?" Kate yelled. *"Two hundred watt seconds!"*

It was Cindy who darted around to the machine and hit the charge button. The needle shot up to two hundred. Guy grabbed the defibrillator paddles, slapped them on Ellen's chest and released the electrical charge.

Ellen's body jerked like a puppet whose strings have all been tugged at once.

The fluttering slowed to a ripple. It was the pattern of a dying heart.

Kate tried another drug, then still another in a desperate attempt to flog some life back into the heart. Nothing worked. Through a film of tears, she watched the tracing fade to a line meandering aimlessly across the oscilloscope.

"That's it," Guy said softly. He gave the signal to stop cardiac massage. The intern, his face dripping with sweat, backed away from the table.

"*No,*" Kate insisted, planting her hands on Ellen's chest. "It's not over." She began to pump—fiercely, desperately. "*It's not over.*" She threw herself against Ellen, pitting her weight against the stubborn shield of rib and muscles. The heart had to be massaged, the brain nourished. She had to keep Ellen alive. Again and again she pumped, until her arms were weak and trembling. *Live, Ellen,* she commanded silently. *You have to live....*

"Kate." Guy touched her arm.

"We're not giving up. Not yet...."

"Kate." Gently, Guy tugged her away from the table. "It's over," he whispered.

Someone turned off the sound on the heart monitor. The whine of the alarm gave way to an eerie silence. Slowly, Kate turned and saw that everyone was watching her. She looked up at the oscilloscope.

The line was flat.

KATE FLINCHED as an orderly zipped the shroud over Ellen O'Brien's body. There was a cruel finality to that sound; it struck her as obscene, this convenient packaging of what had once been a living, breathing woman. As the body was wheeled off to the morgue, Kate turned away. Long after the squeak of the gurney wheels had faded down the hall, she was still standing there, alone in the O.R.

Fighting tears, she gazed around at the bloodied gauze and empty vials littering the floor. It was the same sad debris that lingered after every hospital death. Soon it would be swept up and incinerated and there'd be no clue to the tragedy that had just been played out. Nothing except a body in the morgue.

And questions. Oh, yes, there'd be questions. From Ellen's parents. From the hospital. Questions Kate didn't know how to answer.

Wearily she tugged off her surgical cap and felt a vague sense of relief as her brown hair tumbled free to her shoulders. She needed time alone—to think, to understand. She turned to leave.

Guy was standing in the doorway. The instant she saw his face, Kate knew something was wrong.

Silently he handed her Ellen O'Brien's chart.

"The electrocardiogram," he said. "You told me it was normal."

"It was."

"You'd better take another look."

Puzzled, she opened the chart to the EKG, the electrical tracing of Ellen's heart. The first detail she noted was her own initials, written at the top, signifying that she'd seen the page. Next she scanned the tracing. For a solid minute she stared at the series of twelve black squiggles, unable to believe what she was seeing. The pattern was unmistakable. Even a third-year medical student could have made the diagnosis.

"That's why she died, Kate," Guy said.

"But— This is impossible!" she blurted. "I couldn't have made a mistake like this!"

Guy didn't answer. He simply looked away—an act more telling than anything he could have said.

"Guy, you *know* me," she protested. "You know I wouldn't miss something like—"

"It's right there in black and white. For God's sake, your *initials* are on the damn thing!"

They stared at each other, both of them shocked by the harshness of his voice.

"I'm sorry," he apologized at last. Suddenly agitated, he turned and clawed his fingers through his hair. "Dear God. She'd had a heart attack. A *heart attack*. And we took her to surgery." He gave Kate a look of utter misery. "I guess that means we killed her."

"IT'S AN OBVIOUS CASE of malpractice."

Attorney David Ransom closed the file labeled O'Brien, Ellen, and looked across the broad teak desk at his clients. If he had to choose one word to describe Patrick and Mary O'Brien, it would be *gray*. Gray hair, gray faces, gray clothes. Patrick was wearing a dull tweed jacket that had long ago sagged into shapelessness. Mary wore a dress in a black-and-white print that seemed to blend together into a drab monochrome.

Patrick kept shaking his head. "She was our only girl, Mr. Ransom. Our only child. She was always so good, you know? Never complained. Even when she was a baby. She'd just lie there in her crib and smile. Like a little angel. Just like a darling little—" He suddenly stopped, his face crumpling.

"Mr. O'Brien," David said gently, "I know it's not much of a comfort to you now, but I promise you, I'll do everything I can."

Patrick shook his head. "It's not the money we're after. Sure, I can't work. My back, you know. But Ellie, she had a life insurance policy, and—"

"How much was the policy?"

"Fifty thousand," answered Mary. "That's the kind of girl she was. Always thinking of us." Her profile, caught in the window's light, had an edge of steel. Unlike her husband, Mary O'Brien was done with her crying. She sat very straight, her whole body a rigid testament to grief. David knew exactly what she was feeling. The pain. The anger. Especially the anger. It was there, burning coldly in her eyes.

Patrick was sniffling.

David took a box of tissues from his drawer and quietly placed it in front of his client. "Perhaps we should discuss the case some other time," he suggested. "When you both feel ready...."

Mary's chin lifted sharply. "We're ready, Mr. Ransom. Ask your questions."

David glanced at Patrick, who managed a feeble nod. "I'm afraid this may strike you as...cold-blooded, the things I have to ask. I'm sorry."

"Go on," prompted Mary.

"I'll proceed immediately to filing suit. But I'll need more information before we can make an estimate of damages. Part of that is lost wages—what your daughter would have earned had she lived. You say she was a nurse?"

"In obstetrics. Labor and delivery."

"Do you know her salary?"

"I'll have to check her pay stubs."

"What about dependants? Did she have any?"

"None."

"She was never married?"

Mary shook her head and sighed. "She was the perfect daughter, Mr. Ransom, in almost every way. Beautiful. And brilliant. But when it came to men, she made . . . mistakes."

He frowned. "Mistakes?"

Mary shrugged. "Oh, I suppose it's just the way things are these days. And when a woman gets to be a—a certain age, she feels, well, *lucky* to have any man at all. . . ." She looked down at her tightly knotted hands and fell silent.

David sensed they'd strayed into hazardous waters. He wasn't interested in Ellen O'Brien's love life, anyway. It was irrelevant to the case.

"Let's turn to your daughter's medical history," he said smoothly, opening the medical chart. "The record states she was forty-one years old and in excellent health. To your knowledge, did she ever have any problems with her heart?"

"Never."

"She never complained of chest pain? Shortness of breath?"

"Ellie was a long-distance swimmer, Mr. Ransom. She could go all day and never get out of breath. That's why I don't believe this story about a—a heart attack."

"But the EKG was strongly diagnostic, Mrs. O'Brien. If there'd been an autopsy, we could have proved it. But I guess it's a bit late for that."

Mary glanced at her husband. "It's Patrick. He just couldn't stand the idea—"

"Haven't they cut her up enough already?" Patrick blurted out.

There was a long silence. Mary said softly, "We'll be taking her ashes out to sea. She loved the sea. Ever since she was a baby . . ."

It was a solemn parting. A few last words of condolence, and then the handshakes, the sealing of a pact. The O'Briens turned to leave. But in the doorway, Mary stopped.

"I want you to know it's not the money," she declared. "The truth is, I don't care if we see a dime. But they've ruined our lives, Mr. Ransom. They've taken our only baby away. And I hope to God they never forget it."

David nodded. "I'll see they never do."

After his clients had left, David turned to the window. He took a deep breath and slowly let it out, willing the emotions to drain from his body. But a hard knot seemed to linger in his stomach. All that sadness, all that rage; it clouded his thinking.

Six days ago, a doctor had made a terrible mistake. Now, at the age of forty-one, Ellen O'Brien was dead.

She was only three years older than me.

He sat down at his desk and opened the O'Brien file. Skipping past the hospital record, he turned to the curricula vitae of the two physicians.

Dr. Guy Santini's record was outstanding. Forty-eight years old, a Harvard-trained surgeon, he was at the peak of his career. His list of publications went on for five pages. Most of his research dealt with hepatic physiology. He'd been sued once, eight years ago; he'd won. Bully for him. Santini wasn't the target anyway. David had his cross hairs on the anesthesiologist.

He flipped to the three-page summary of Dr. Katharine Chesne's career.

Her background was impressive. A B.Sc in chemistry from U.C., Berkeley, an M.D. from Johns Hopkins, anesthesia residency and intensive-care fellowship at U.C., San Francisco. Now only thirty years old, she'd already compiled a respectable list of published articles. She'd joined Mid Pac Hospital as a staff anesthesiologist less than a year ago. There was no photograph, but he had no trouble conjuring up a mental picture of the stereotypical female physician: frumpy hair, no figure, and a face like a horse—albeit an extremely intelligent horse.

David sat back, frowning. This was too good a record; it didn't match the profile of an incompetent physician. How could she have made such an elementary mistake?

He closed the file. Whatever her excuses, the facts were indisputable: Dr. Katharine Chesne had condemned her patient to die under the surgeon's knife. Now she'd have to face the consequences.

He'd make damn sure she did.

GEORGE BETTENCOURT despised doctors. It was a personal opinion that made his job as CEO of Mid Pac Hospital all the more difficult, since he had to work so closely with the medical staff. He had both an M.B.A. and a Masters in public health. In his ten years as CEO, he'd achieved what the old doctor-led administration had been unable to do: he'd turned Mid Pac from a comatose institution into a profitable business. Yet all he ever heard from those stupid little surrogate gods in their white coats was criticism. They turned their superior noses up at the very idea that their saintly work could be dictated by profit-and-loss graphs. The cold reality was that saving lives, like selling linoleum, was a business. Bettencourt knew it. The doctors didn't. They were fools, and fools gave him headaches.

And the two sitting across from him now were giving him a migraine headache the likes of which he hadn't felt in years.

Dr. Clarence Avery, the white-haired chief of anesthesia, wasn't the problem. The old man was too timid to stand up to his own shadow, much less to a controversial issue. Ever since his wife's stroke, Avery had shuffled through his duties like a sleepwalker. Yes, he could be persuaded to cooperate. Especially when the hospital's reputation was at stake.

No, it was the other one who worried Bettencourt: the woman. She was new to the staff and he didn't know her very well. But the minute she'd walked into his office, he'd smelled trouble. She had that look in her eye, that crusader's set of the jaw. She was a pretty enough woman, though her brown hair was in a wild state of anarchy and she probably hadn't held a tube of lipstick in months. But those intense green eyes of hers were enough to make a man overlook all the flaws of that face. She was, in fact, quite attractive.

Too bad she'd blown it. Now she was a liability. He hoped she wouldn't make things worse by being a bitch, as well.

KATE FLINCHED AS Bettencourt dropped the papers on the desk in front of her. "The letter arrived in our attorney's office this morning, Dr. Chesne," he said. "Hand delivered by personal messenger. I think you'd better read it."

She took one look at the letterhead and felt her stomach drop away: *Uehara and Ransom, Attorneys at Law*.

"One of the best firms in town," explained Bettencourt. Seeing her stunned expression, he went on impatiently, "You and the hospital are being sued, Dr. Chesne. For malpractice. And David Ransom is personally taking on the case."

Her throat had gone dry. Slowly she looked up. "But how—how can they—"

"All it takes is a lawyer. And a dead patient."

"I've explained what happened!" She turned to Avery. "Remember last week—I told you—"

"Clarence has gone over it with me," cut in Bettencourt. "That isn't the issue we're discussing here."

"What *is* the issue?"

He seemed startled by her directness. He let out a sharp breath. "The issue is this: we have what looks like a million-dollar lawsuit on our hands. As your employer, we're responsible for the damages. But it's not just the money that concerns us." He paused. "There's our reputation."

The tone of his voice struck her as ominous. She knew what was coming and found herself utterly voiceless. She could only sit there, her stomach roiling, her hands clenched in her lap, and wait for the blow to fall.

"This lawsuit reflects badly on the whole hospital," he said. "If the case goes to trial, there'll be publicity. People—patients—will read those newspapers and it'll scare them." He looked down at his desk. "I realize your record up till now has been acceptable—"

Her chin shot up. "Acceptable?" she repeated incredulously. She glanced at Avery. The chief of anesthesia knew her record. And it was flawless.

Avery squirmed in his chair, his watery blue eyes avoiding hers. "Well, actually," he mumbled, "Dr. Chesne's record has been—up till now, anyway—uh, more than acceptable. That is . . ."

For God's sake, man! she wanted to scream. *Stand up for me!*

"There've never been any complaints," Avery finished lamely.

"Nevertheless," continued Bettencourt, "you've put us in a touchy situation, Dr. Chesne. That's why we think it'd be best if your name was no longer associated with the hospital."

There was a long silence, punctuated only by the sound of Dr. Avery's nervous cough.

"We're asking for your resignation," stated Bettencourt.

So there it was. The blow. It washed over her like a giant wave, leaving her limp and exhausted. Quietly she asked, "And if I refuse to resign?"

"Believe me, Doctor, a resignation will look a lot better on your record than a—"

"Dismissal?"

He cocked his head. "We understand each other."

"No." She raised her head. Something about his eyes, their cold self-assurance, made her stiffen. She'd never liked Bettencourt. She liked him even less now. "You don't understand me at all."

"You're a bright woman. You can see the options. In any event, we can't let you back in the O.R."

"It's not right," Avery objected.

"Excuse me?" Bettencourt frowned at the old man.

"You can't just fire her. She's a physician. There are channels you have to go through. Committees—"

"I'm well acquainted with the proper channels, Clarence! I was hoping Dr. Chesne would grasp the situation and act appropriately." He looked at her. "It really is easier, you know. There'd be no blot on your record. Just a notation that you resigned. I can have a letter typed up within the hour. All it takes is your..." His voice trailed off as he saw the look in her eyes.

Kate seldom got angry. She usually managed to keep her emotions under tight control. So the fury she now felt churning to the surface was something new and unfamiliar and almost frightening. With deadly calm she said, "Save yourself the paper, Mr. Bettencourt."

His jaw clicked shut. "If that's your decision..." He glanced at Avery. "When is the next Quality Assurance meeting?"

"It's—uh, next Tuesday, but—"

"Put the O'Brien case on the agenda. We'll let Dr. Chesne present her record to committee." He looked at Kate. "A judgment by your peers. I'd say that's fair. Wouldn't you?"

She managed to swallow her retort. If she said anything else, if she let fly what she really thought of George Bettencourt, she'd ruin her chances of ever again working at Mid Pac. Or anywhere else, for that matter. All he had to do was slap her with the label Troublemaker; it would blacken her record for the rest of her life.

They parted civilly. For a woman who'd just had her career ripped to shreds, she managed a grand performance. She gave Bettencourt a level look, a cool handshake. She kept her composure all the way out the door and on the long walk down the carpeted hall. But as she rode the elevator down, something inside her seemed to snap. By the time the doors slid open again, she was shaking violently. As she walked blindly through the noise and bustle of the lobby, the realization hit her full force.

Dear God, I'm being sued. Less than a year in practice and I'm being sued....

She'd always thought that lawsuits, like all life's catastrophes, happened to other people. She'd never dreamed she'd be the one charged with incompetence. *Incompetence.*

Suddenly feeling sick, she swayed against the lobby telephones. As she struggled to calm her stomach, her gaze fell on the local directory, hanging by a chain from the shelf. *If only they knew the facts,* she thought. *If I could explain to them...*

It took only seconds to find the listing: *Uehara and Ransom, Attorneys at Law.* Their office was on Bishop Street.

She wrenched out the page. Then, driven by a new and desperate hope, she hurried out the door.

Chapter Two

"Mr. Ransom is unavailable."

The gray-haired receptionist had eyes of pure cast iron and a face straight out of *American Gothic*. All she needed was the pitchfork. Crossing her arms, she silently dared the intruder to try—just try—to talk her way in.

"But I have to see him!" Kate insisted. "It's about the case—"

"Of course it is," the woman said dryly.

"I only want to explain to him—"

"I've just told you, Doctor. He's in a meeting with the associates. He can't see you."

Kate's impatience was simmering close to the danger point. She leaned forward on the woman's desk and managed to say with polite fury, "Meetings don't last forever."

The receptionist smiled. "This one will."

Kate smiled back. "Then so can I."

"Doctor, you're wasting your time! Mr. Ransom *never* meets with defendants. Now, if you need an escort to find your way out, I'll be happy to—" She glanced around in annoyance as the telephone rang. Grabbing the receiver, she snapped, "Uehara and Ransom! Yes? Oh, yes, Mr. Matheson!" She pointedly turned her back on Kate. "Let's see, I have those files right here . . ."

In frustration, Kate glanced around at the waiting room, noting the leather couch, the Ikebana of willow and proteus, the Murashige print hanging on the wall. All exquisitely tasteful and undoubtedly expensive. Obviously, Uehara and Ransom was doing a booming business. All off the blood and sweat of doctors, she thought in disgust.

The sound of voices suddenly drew Kate's attention. She turned and saw, just down the hall, a small army of young men and women emerging from a conference room. Which one was Ransom? She scanned the faces but none of the men looked old enough to be a senior partner in the firm. She glanced back at the desk and saw that the receptionist still had her back turned. It was now or never.

It took Kate only a split-second to make her decision. Swiftly, deliberately, she moved toward the conference room. But in the doorway she came to a halt, her eyes suddenly dazzled by the light.

A long teak table stretched out before her. Along either side, a row of leather chairs stood like soldiers at attention. Blinding sunshine poured in through the southerly windows, spilling across the head and shoulders of a lone man seated at the far end of the table. The light streaked his fair hair with gold. He didn't notice her; all his attention was focused on a sheaf of papers lying in front of him. Except for the rustle of a page being turned, the room was absolutely silent.

Kate swallowed hard and drew herself up straight. "Mr. Ransom?"

The man looked up and regarded her with a neutral expression. "Yes? Who are you?"

"I'm—"

"I'm so sorry, Mr. Ransom!" cut in the receptionist's outraged voice. Hauling Kate by the arm, the woman muttered through her teeth, "I *told* you he was unavailable. Now if you'll come with me—"

"I only want to talk to him!"

"Do you want me to call security and have you thrown out?"

Kate wrenched her arm free. "Go ahead."

"Don't tempt me, you—"

"What the hell is going on here?" The roar of Ransom's voice echoed in the vast room, shocking both women into silence. He aimed a long and withering look at Kate. "Just who *are* you?"

"Kate—" She paused and dropped her voice to what she hoped was a more dignified tone. "*Doctor* Kate Chesne."

A pause. "I see." he looked right back down at his papers and said flatly, "Show her out, Mrs. Pierce."

"I just want to tell you the facts!" Kate persisted. She tried to hold her ground but the receptionist herded her toward the door with all the skill of a sheepdog. "Or would you rather *not* hear the facts, is that it? Is that how you lawyers operate?" He studiously ignored her. "You don't give a damn about the truth, do you? You don't want to hear what really happened to Ellen O'Brien!"

That made him look up sharply. His gaze fastened long and hard on her face. "Hold on, Mrs. Pierce. I've just changed my mind. Let Dr. Chesne stay."

Mrs. Pierce was incredulous. "But—she could be violent!"

David's gaze lingered a moment longer on Kate's flushed face. "I think I can handle her. You can leave us, Mrs. Pierce."

Mrs. Pierce muttered as she walked out. The door closed behind her. There was a very long silence.

"Well, Dr. Chesne," David said. "Now that you've managed the rather miraculous feat of getting past Mrs. Pierce, are you just going to stand there?" He gestured to a chair. "Have a seat. Unless you'd rather scream at me from across the room."

His cold flippancy, rather than easing her tension, made him seem all the more unapproachable. She forced herself to move toward him, feeling his gaze every step of the way. For a man with his highly regarded reputation, he was younger than she'd expected, not yet in his forties. *Establishment* was stamped all over his clothes, from his gray pinstripe suit to his Yale tie clip. But a tan that deep and hair that sun-streaked didn't go along with an Ivy League type. *He's just a surfer boy, grown up*, she thought derisively. He certainly had a surfer's build, with those long, ropy limbs and shoulders that were just broad enough to be called impressive. A slab of a nose and a blunt chin saved him from being pretty. But it was his eyes she found herself focusing on. They were a frigid, penetrating blue; the sort of eyes that missed absolutely nothing. Right now those eyes were boring straight through her and she felt an almost irresistible urge to cross her arms protectively across her chest.

"I'm here to tell you the facts, Mr. Ransom," she said.

"The facts as you see them?"

"The facts as they *are*."

"Don't bother." Reaching into his briefcase, he pulled out Ellen O'Brien's file and slapped it down conclusively on the table. "I have all the facts right here. Everything I need." *Everything I need to hang you,* was what he meant.

"Not everything."

"And now *you're* going to supply me with the missing details. Right?" He smiled and she recognized immediately the unmistakable threat in his expression. He had such perfect, sharp white teeth. She had the distinct feeling she was staring into the jaws of a shark.

She leaned forward, planting her hands squarely on the table. "What I'm going to supply you with is the truth."

"Oh, naturally." He slouched back in his chair and regarded her with a look of terminal boredom. "Tell me something," he asked offhandedly. "Does your attorney know you're here?"

"Attorney? I—I haven't talked to any attorney—"

"Then you'd better get one on the phone. Fast. Because, Doctor, you're damn well going to need one."

"Not necessarily. This is nothing but a big misunderstanding, Mr. Ransom. If you'll just listen to the facts, I'm sure—"

"Hold on." He reached into his briefcase and pulled out a cassette recorder.

"Just what do you think you're doing?" she demanded.

He turned on the recorder and slid it in front of her. "I wouldn't want to miss some vital detail. Go on with your story. I'm all ears."

Furious, she reached over and flicked the Off button. "This isn't a deposition! Put the damn thing away!"

For a few tense seconds they sized each other up. She felt a distinct sense of triumph when he put the recorder back in his briefcase.

"Now, where were we?" he asked with extravagant politeness. "Oh, yes. You were about to tell me what *really* happened.'' He settled back, obviously expecting some grand entertainment.

She hesitated. Now that she finally had his full attention, she didn't know quite how to start.

"I'm a very...careful person, Mr. Ransom," she said at last. "I take my time with things. I may not be brilliant, but I'm thorough. And I don't make stupid mistakes."

His raised eyebrow told her exactly what he thought of that statement. She ignored his look and went on.

"The night Ellen O'Brien came into the hospital, Guy Santini admitted her. But I wrote the anesthesia orders. I checked the lab results. And I read her EKG. It was a Sunday night and the technician was busy somewhere so I even ran the strip myself. I wasn't rushed. I took all the time I needed. In fact, more than I needed, because Ellen was a member of our staff. She was one of *us*. She was also a friend. I remember sitting in her room, going over her lab tests. She wanted to know if everything was normal."

"And you told her everything was."

"Yes. Including the EKG."

"Then you obviously made a mistake."

"I just told you, Mr. Ransom. I don't make stupid mistakes. And I didn't make one that night."

"But the record shows—"

"The record's wrong."

"I have the tracing right here in black and white. And it plainly shows a heart attack."

"That's *not* the EKG I saw!"

He looked as if he hadn't heard her quite right.

"The EKG I saw that night was normal," she insisted.

"Then how did this abnormal one pop into the chart?"

"Someone put it there, of course."

"Who?"

"I don't know."

"I see." Turning away, he said under his breath: "I can't wait to see how this plays in court."

"Mr. Ransom, if I made a mistake, I'd be the first to admit it!"

"Then you'd be amazingly honest."

"Do you really think I'd make up a story as—as *stupid* as this?"

His response was an immediate burst of laughter that left her cheeks burning. "No," he answered. "I'm sure you'd come up with something much more believable." He gave her an inviting nod. In a voice thick with sarcasm, he jeered, "Please, I'm *dying* to know how this extraordinary mix-up happened. How did the wrong EKG get in the chart?"

"How should I know?"

"You must have a theory."

"I don't."

"Come on, Doctor, don't disappoint me."

"I said I don't."

"Then make a guess!"

"Maybe someone beamed it there from the *Starship Enterprise*!" she yelled in frustration.

"Nice theory," he said, deadpan. "But let's get back to reality. Which, in this case, happens to be a particular sheet of wood by-product, otherwise known as paper." He flipped the chart open to the damning EKG. "Explain *that* away."

"I told you, I can't! I've gone crazy trying to figure it out! We do dozens of EKGs every day at Mid Pac. It could have been a clerical error. A mislabeled tracing. Somehow, that page was filed in the wrong chart."

"But you've written your initials on this page."

"No, I didn't."

"Is there some other K.C., M.D.?"

"Those are my initials. But I didn't write them."

"What are you saying? That this is a forgery?"

"It—it has to be. I mean, yes, I guess it is...." Suddenly confused, she shoved back a rebellious strand of hair off her face. His utterly calm expression rattled her. Why didn't the man react, for God's sake? Why did he just sit there, regarding her with that infuriatingly bland expression?

"Well," he said at last.

"Well what?"

"How long have you had this little problem with people forging your name?"

"Don't make me sound paranoid!"

"I don't have to. You're doing fine on your own."

Now he was silently laughing at her; she could see it in his eyes. The worst part was that she couldn't blame him. Her story *did* sound like a lunatic's ravings.

"All right," he relented. "Let's assume for the moment you're telling the truth."

"Yes!" she snapped. "Please do!"

"I can think of only two explanations for why the EKG would be intentionally switched. Either someone's trying to destroy your career—"

"That's absurd. I don't have any enemies."

"Or someone's trying to cover up a murder."

At her stunned expression, he gave her a maddeningly superior smile. "Since the second explanation obviously strikes both of us as equally absurd, I have no choice but to conclude you're lying." He leaned forward and his voice was suddenly soft, almost intimate. The shark was getting chummy; that had to be dangerous. "Come on, Doctor," he prodded. "Level with me. Tell me what really happened in the O.R. Was there a slip of the knife? A mistake in anesthesia?"

"There was nothing of the kind!"

"Too much laughing gas and not enough oxygen?"

"I told you, there were *no* mistakes!"

"Then why is Ellen O'Brien dead?"

She stared at him, stunned by the violence in his voice. And the blueness of his eyes. A spark seemed to fly between them, ignited by something entirely unexpected. With a shock, she realized he was an attractive man. Too attractive. And that her response to him was dangerous. She could already feel the blush creeping into her face, could feel a flood of heat rising inside her.

"No answer?" he challenged smoothly. He settled back, obviously enjoying the advantage he held over her. "Then why don't I tell *you* what happened? On April 2, a Sunday night, Ellen O'Brien checked into Mid Pac Hospital for routine gallbladder surgery. As her anesthesiologist, you ordered routine pre-op tests, including an EKG, which you checked before leaving the hospital that night. Maybe you were rushed. Maybe you had a hot date waiting. Whatever the reason, you got careless and you made a fatal error. You missed those vital clues in the EKG: the elevated ST waves, the inverted T waves. You pronounced it normal and signed your initials. Then you left for the night—never realizing your patient had just had a heart attack.''

"She never had any symptoms! No chest pain—"

"But it says right here in the nurses' notes—let me quote—" he flipped through the chart ''—'Patient complaining of abdominal discomfort.' ''

"That was her gallstone—"

"Or was it her heart? Anyway, the next events are indisputable. You and Dr. Santini took Ms. O'Brien to surgery. A few whiffs of anesthesia and the stress was too much for her weakened heart. So it stopped. And you couldn't restart it.'' He paused dramatically, his eyes as hard as diamonds. "There, Dr. Chesne. You've just lost your patient.''

"That's not how it happened! I remember that EKG. It was *normal*!''

"Maybe you'd better review your textbook on EKGs.''

"I don't need a textbook. I *know* what's normal!'' She scarcely recognized her own voice, echoing shrilly through the vast room.

He looked unimpressed. Bored, even. "Really—'' he sighed ''—wouldn't it be easier just to admit you made a mistake?''

"Easier for whom?''

"For everyone involved. Consider an out-of-court settlement. It'd be fast, easy, and relatively painless.''

"A settlement? But that's admitting a mistake I never made!''

What little patience he had left finally snapped. "You want to go to trial?'' he shot back. "Fine. But let me tell you something about the way I work. When I try a case, I don't do it halfway. If I have to tear you apart in court, I'll do it. And when I'm finished, you'll wish you'd never turned this into some ridiculous fight for your honor. Because let's face it, Doctor. You don't have a snowball's chance in hell.''

She wanted to grab him by those pinstriped lapels. She wanted to scream out that in all this talk about settlements and courtrooms, her own anguish over Ellen O'Brien's death had been ignored. But suddenly all her rage, all her strength, seemed to drain away, leaving her exhausted. Wearily she slumped back in her chair. "I wish I *could* admit I made a mistake," she said quietly. "I wish I could just say, 'I know I'm guilty and I'll pay for it.' I wish to God I could say that. I've spent the last week wondering about my memory. Wondering how this could have happened. Ellen trusted me and I let her die. It makes me wish I'd never become a doctor, that I'd been a clerk or a waitress—anything else. I love my work. You have no idea how hard it's been—how much I've given up—just to get to where I am. And now it looks as if I'll lose my job...." She swallowed and her head drooped in defeat. "And I wonder if I'll ever be able to work again...."

David regarded her bowed head in silence and fought to ignore the emotions stirring inside him. He'd always considered himself a good judge of character. He could usually look a man in the eyes and tell if he was lying. All during Kate Chesne's little speech, he'd been watching her eyes, searching for some inconsistent blip, some betraying flicker that would tell him she was lying through her teeth.

But her eyes had been absolutely steady and forthright and as beautiful as a pair of emeralds.

The last thought startled him, popping out as it did, almost against his will. As much as he might try to suppress it, he was all at once aware that she *was* a beautiful woman. She was wearing a simple green dress, gathered loosely at the waist, and it took just one glance to see that there were feminine curves beneath that silky fabric. The face that went along with those very nice curves had its flaws. She had a prizefighter's square jaw. Her shoulder-length mahogany hair was a riot of waves, obviously untamable. The curly bangs softened a forehead that was far too prominent. No, it wasn't a classically beautiful face. But then he'd never been attracted to classically beautiful women.

Suddenly he was annoyed not only at himself but at her, at her effect on him. He wasn't a dumb kid fresh out of law school. He was too old and too smart to be entertaining the peculiarly male thoughts now dancing in his head.

In a deliberately rude gesture, he looked down at his watch. Then, snapping his briefcase shut, he stood up. "I have a deposition to take and I'm already late. So if you'll excuse me..."

He was halfway across the room when her voice called out to him softly: "Mr. Ransom?"

He glanced back at her in irritation. "What?"

"I know my story sounds crazy. And I guess there's no reason on earth you should believe me. But I swear to you: it's the truth."

He sensed her desperate need for validation. She was searching for a sign that she'd gotten through to him; that she'd penetrated his hard shell of skepticism. The fact was, he didn't *know* if he believed her, and it bothered the hell out of him that his usual instinct for the truth had gone haywire, and all because of a pair of emerald-green eyes.

"Whether I believe you or not is irrelevant," he said. "So don't waste your time on me, Doctor. Save it for the jury." The words came out colder than he'd intended and he saw, from the quick flinch of her head, that she'd been stung.

"Then there's nothing I can do, nothing I can say—"

"Not a thing."

"I thought you'd listen. I thought somehow I could change your mind—"

"Then you've got a lot to learn about lawyers. Good-day, Dr. Chesne." Turning, he headed briskly for the door. "I'll see you in court."

Chapter Three

You don't have a snowball's chance in hell.

That was the phrase Kate kept hearing over and over as she sat alone at a table in the hospital cafeteria. And just how long did it take for a snowball to melt, anyway? Or would it simply disintegrate in the heat of the flames?

How much heat could she take before she fell apart on the witness stand?

She'd always been so adept at dealing with matters of life and death. When a medical crisis arose, she didn't wring her hands over what needed to be done; she just did it, automatically. Inside the safe and sterile walls of the operating room, she was in control.

But a courtroom was a different world entirely. That was David Ransom's territory. He'd be the one in control; she'd be as vulnerable as a patient on the operating table. How could she possibly fend off an attack by the very man who'd built his reputation on the scorched careers of doctors?

She'd never felt threatened by men before. After all, she'd trained with them, worked with them. David Ransom was the first man who'd ever intimidated her, and he'd done it effortlessly. If only he was short or fat or bald. If only she could think of him as human and therefore vulnerable. But just the thought of facing those cold blue eyes in court made her stomach do a panicky flip-flop.

"Looks like you could use some company," said a familiar voice.

Glancing up, she saw Guy Santini, rumpled as always, peering down at her through those ridiculously thick glasses.

She gave him a listless nod. "Hi."

Clucking, he pulled up a chair and sat down. "How're you doing, Kate?"

"You mean except for being unemployed?" She managed a sour laugh. "Just terrific."

"I heard the old man pulled you out of the O.R. I'm sorry."

"I can't really blame it on old Avery. He was just following orders."

"Bettencourt's?"

"Who else? He's labeled me a financial *liability*."

Guy snorted. "That's what happens when the damned M.B.A.'s take over. All they can talk about is profits and losses! I swear, if George Bettencourt could make a buck selling the gold out of patients' teeth, he'd be roaming the wards with pliers."

"And then he'd send them a bill for oral surgery," Kate added morosely.

Neither of them laughed. The joke was too close to the truth to be funny.

"If it makes you feel any better, Kate, you'll have some company in the courtroom. I've been named, too."

She looked up sharply. "Oh, Guy! I'm sorry. . . ."

He shrugged. "It's no big deal. I've been sued before. Believe me, it's that first time that really hurts."

"What happened?"

"Trauma case. Man came in with a ruptured spleen and I couldn't save him." He shook his head. "When I saw that letter from the attorney, I was so depressed I wanted to leap out the nearest window. Susan was ready to drag me off to the psych ward. But you know what? I survived. So will you, as long as you remember they're not attacking *you*. They're attacking the job you did."

"I don't see the difference."

"And *that's* your problem, Kate. You haven't learned to separate yourself from the job. We both know the hours you put in. Hell, sometimes I think you practically live here. I'm not saying dedication's a character flaw. But you can overdo it."

What really hurt was that she knew it was true. She did work long hours. Maybe she needed to; it kept her mind off the wasteland of her personal life.

"I'm not completely buried in my job," she said. "I've started dating again."

"It's about time. Who's the man?"

"Last week I went out with Elliot."

"That guy from computer programming?" He sighed. Elliot was six-foot-two and one hundred and twenty pounds, and he bore a distinct resemblance to Pee-Wee Herman. "I bet that was a barrel of laughs."

"Well it was sort of . . . fun. He asked me up to his apartment."

"He did?"

"So I went."

"You *did*?"

"He wanted to show me his latest electronic gear."

Guy leaned forward eagerly. "What happened?"

"We listened to his new CDs. Played a few computer games."

"And?"

She sighed. "After eight rounds of Zork I went home."

Groaning, Guy sank back in his chair. "Elliot Lafferty, last of the red-hot lovers. Kate, what you need is one of these dating services. Hey, I'll even write the ad for you. 'Bright, attractive female seeks—'"

"*Daddy!*" The happy squeal cut straight through the cafeteria's hubbub.

Guy turned as running feet pattered toward him. "There's my Will!" Laughing, he rose to his feet and scooped up his son. It took only a sweep of his arms to send the spindly five-year-old boy flying into the air. Little Will was so light he seemed to float for a moment like a frail bird. He fell to a very soft, very safe landing in his father's arms. "I've been waiting for you, kid," Guy said. "What took you so long?"

"Mommy came home late."

"Again?"

Will leaned forward and whispered confidentially. "Adele was *really* mad. Her boyfriend was s'posed to take her to the movies."

"Uh-oh. We *certainly* don't want Adele to be mad at us, do we?" Guy flashed an inquiring look at his wife Susan, who was threading her way toward them. "Hey, are we wearing out the nanny already?"

"I swear, it's that full moon!" Susan laughed and shoved back a frizzy strand of red hair. "All my patients have gone absolutely loony. I couldn't get them out of my office."

Guy muttered grumpily to Kate, "And she swore it'd be a part-time practice. Ha! Guess who gets called to the E.R. practically every night?"

"Oh, you just miss having your shirts ironed!" Susan reached up and gave her husband an affectionate pat on the cheek. It was the sort of maternal gesture one expected of Susan Santini. "My mother hen," Guy had once called his wife. He'd meant it as a term of endearment and it had fit. Susan's beauty wasn't in her face, which was plain and freckled, or in her figure, which was as stout as a farm wife's. Her beauty lay in that serenely patient smile that she was now beaming at her son.

"Daddy!" William was prancing like an elf around Guy's legs. "Make me fly again!"

"What am I, a launching pad?"

"Up! One more time!"

"Later, Will," said Susan. "We have to pick up Daddy's car before the garage closes."

"Please!"

"Did you hear that?" Guy gasped. "He said the magic word." With a lion's roar, Guy pounced on the shrieking boy and threw him into the air.

Susan gave Kate a long-suffering look. "Two children. That's what I have. And one of them weighs two hundred and forty pounds."

"I heard that." Guy reached over and slung a possessive arm around his wife. "Just for that, lady, you have to drive me home."

"Big bully. Feel like McDonald's?"

"Humph. I know someone who doesn't want to cook tonight."

Guy gave Kate a wave as he nudged his family toward the door. "So what'll it be, kid?" Kate heard him say to William. "Cheeseburger?"

"Ice cream."

"Ice cream. Now that's an alternative I hadn't thought of...."

Wistfully Kate watched the Santinis make their way across the cafeteria. She could picture how the rest of their evening would go. She imagined them sitting in McDonald's, the two parents teasing, coaxing another bite of food into Will's reluctant mouth. Then there'd be the drive home, the pajamas, the bedtime story. And finally, there'd be those skinny arms, curling around Daddy's neck for a kiss.

What do I have to go home to? she thought.

Guy turned and gave her one last wave. Then he and his family vanished out the door. Kate sighed enviously. *Lucky man.*

AFTER HE LEFT his office that afternoon, David drove up Nuuanu Avenue and turned onto the dirt lane that wound through the old cemetery. He parked his car in the shade of a banyan tree and walked across the freshly mown lawn, past the marble headstones with their grotesque angels, past the final resting places of the Doles and the Binghams and the Cookes. He came to a section where there were only bronze plaques set flush in the ground, a sad concession to modern graveskeeping. Beneath a monkeypod tree, he stopped and gazed down at the marker by his feet.

Noah Ransom
Seven Years Old

It was a fine spot, gently sloping, with a view of the city. Here a breeze was always blowing, sometimes from the sea, sometimes from the valley. If he closed his eyes, he could tell where the wind was coming from, just by its smell.

David hadn't chosen this spot. He couldn't remember who had decided the grave should be here. Perhaps it had simply been a matter of which plot was available at the time. When your only child dies, who cares about views or breezes or monkeypod trees?

Bending down, he gently brushed the leaves that had fallen on the plaque. Then, slowly, he rose to his feet and stood in silence beside his son. He scarcely registered the rustle of the long skirt or the sound of the cane thumping across the grass.

"So here you are, David," called a voice.

Turning, he saw the tall, silver-haired woman hobbling toward him. "You shouldn't be out here, Mother. Not with that sprained foot."

She pointed her cane at the white clapboard house sitting near the edge of the cemetery. "I saw you through my kitchen window. Thought I'd better come out and say hello. Can't wait around forever for you to come visit me."

He kissed her on the cheek. "Sorry. I've been busy. But I really *was* on my way to see you."

"Oh, naturally." Her blue eyes shifted and focused on the grave. It was one of the many things Jinx Ransom shared with her son, that peculiar shade of blue of her eyes. Even at sixty-eight, her gaze was piercing. "Some anniversaries are better left forgotten," she said softly.

He didn't answer.

"You know, David, Noah always wanted a brother. Maybe it's time you gave him one."

David smiled faintly. "What are you suggesting, Mother?"

"Only what comes naturally to us all."

"Maybe I should get married first?"

"Oh, of course, of course." She paused, then asked hopefully: "Anyone in mind?"

"Not a soul."

Sighing, she laced her arm through his. "That's what I thought. Well, come along. Since there's no gorgeous female waiting for you, you might as well have a cup of coffee with your old mother."

Together they crossed the lawn toward the house. The grass was uneven and Jinx moved slowly, stubbornly refusing to lean on her son's shoulder. She wasn't supposed to be on her feet at all, but she'd never been one to follow doctors' orders. A woman who'd sprained her ankle in a savage game of tennis certainly wouldn't sit around twiddling her thumbs.

They passed through a gap in the mock-orange hedge and climbed the steps to the kitchen porch. Gracie, Jinx's middle-aged companion, met them at the screen door.

"There you are!" Gracie sighed. She turned her mouse-brown eyes to David. "I have absolutely *no* control over this woman. None at all."

He shrugged. "Who does?"

Jinx and David settled down at the breakfast table. The kitchen was a dense jungle of hanging plants: asparagus fern and baby's tears and wandering Jew. Valley breezes swept in from the porch, and through the large window, there was a view of the cemetery.

"What a shame they've trimmed back the monkeypod," Jinx remarked, gazing out.

"They had to," said Gracie as she poured coffee. "Grass can't grow right in the shade."

"But the view's just not the same."

David batted away a stray fern. "I never cared for that view anyway. I don't see how you can look at a cemetery all day."

"I like my view," Jinx declared. "When I look out, I see my old friends. Mrs. Goto, buried there by the hedge. Mr. Carvalho, by the shower tree. And on the slope, there's our Noah. I think of them all as sleeping."

"Good Lord, Mother."

"Your problem, David, is that you haven't resolved your fear of death. Until you do, you'll never come to terms with life."

"What do you suggest?"

"Take another stab at immortality. Have another child."

"I'm not getting married again, Mother. So let's just drop the subject."

Jinx responded as she always did when her son made a ridiculous request. She ignored it. "There was that young woman you met in Maui last year. Whatever happened to her?"

"She got married. To someone else."

"What a shame."

"Yeah, the poor guy."

"Oh, David!" cried Jinx, exasperated. "When are you going to grow up?"

David smiled and took a sip of Gracie's tar-black coffee, on which he promptly gagged. Another reason he avoided these visits to his mother. Not only did Jinx stir up a lot of bad memories, she also forced him to drink Gracie's god-awful coffee.

"So how was *your* day, Mother?" he asked politely.

"Getting worse by the minute."

"More coffee, David?" urged Gracie, tipping the pot threateningly toward his cup.

"No!" David gasped, clapping his hand protectively over the cup. The women stared at him in surprise. "I mean, er, no, thank you, Gracie."

"So touchy," observed Jinx. "Is something wrong? I mean, besides your sex life."

"I'm just a little busier than usual. Hiro's still laid up with that bad back."

"Humph. Well, you don't seem to like your work much anymore. I think you were much happier in the prosecutor's office. Now you take the job so damned seriously."

"It's a serious business."

"Suing doctors? Ha! It's just another way to make a fast buck."

"My doctor was sued once," Gracie remarked. "I thought it was terrible, all those things they said about him. Such a saint..."

"Nobody's a saint, Gracie," David said darkly. "Least of all, doctors." His gaze wandered out the window and he suddenly thought of the O'Brien case. It had been on his mind all afternoon. Or rather, *she'd* been on his mind, that green-eyed, perjuring Kate Chesne. He'd finally decided she was lying. This case was going to be even easier than he'd thought. She'd be a sitting duck on that witness stand and he knew just how he'd handle her in court. First the easy questions: name, education, postgraduate training. He had a habit of pacing in the courtroom, stalking circles around the defendant. The tougher the questions, the tighter the circles. By the time he came in for the kill, they'd be face-to-face. He felt an unexpected thump of dread in his chest, knowing what he'd have to do to finish it. Expose her. Destroy her. That was his job, and he'd always prided himself on a job well done.

He forced down a last sip of coffee and rose to his feet. "I have to be going," he announced, ducking past a lethally placed hanging fern. "I'll call you later, Mother."

Jinx snorted. "When? Next year?"

He gave Gracie a sympathetic pat on the shoulder and muttered in her ear, "Good luck. Don't let her drive you nuts."

"*I?* Drive *her* nuts?" Jinx snorted. "Ha!"

Gracie followed him to the porch door where she stood and waved. "Goodbye, David!" she called sweetly.

FOR A MOMENT, Gracie paused in the doorway and watched David walk through the cemetery to his car. Then she turned sadly to Jinx.

"He's *so* unhappy!" she said. "If only he could forget."

"He won't forget." Jinx sighed. "David's just like his father that way. He'll carry it around inside him till the day he dies."

Chapter Four

Ten-knot winds were blowing in from the northeast as the launch bearing Ellen O'Brien's last remains headed out to sea. It was such a clean, such a natural resolution to life: the strewing of ashes into the sunset waters, the rejoining of flesh and blood with their elements. The minister tossed a lei of yellow flowers off the old pier. The blossoms drifted away on the current, a slow and symbolic parting that brought Patrick O'Brien to tears.

The sound of his crying floated on the wind, over the crowded dock, to the distant spot where Kate was standing. Alone and ignored, she lingered by the row of tethered fishing boats and wondered why she was here. Was it some cruel and self-imposed form of penance? A feeble attempt to tell the world she was sorry? She only knew that some inner voice, begging for forgiveness, had compelled her to come.

There were others here from the hospital: a group of nurses, huddled in a quiet sisterhood of mourning; a pair of obstetricians, looking stiffly uneasy in their street clothes; Clarence Avery, his white hair blowing like dandelion fuzz in the wind. Even George Bettencourt had made an appearance. He stood apart, his face arranged in an impenetrable mask. For these people, a hospital was more than just a place of work; it was another home, another family. Doctors and nurses delivered each other's babies, presided over each other's deaths. Ellen O'Brien had helped bring many of their children into the world; now they were here to usher her out of it.

The far-off glint of sunlight on fair hair made Kate focus on the end of the pier where David Ransom stood, towering above the others. Carelessly he pushed a lock of windblown hair into place. He was dressed in appropriately mournful attire—a charcoal suit, a somber tie—but in the midst of all this grief, he displayed the emotions of a stone wall. She wondered if there was anything human about him. *Do you ever laugh or cry? Do you ever hurt? Do you ever make love?*

That last thought had careened into her mind without warning. Love? Yes, she could imagine how it would be to make love with David Ransom: not a sharing but a claiming. He'd demand total surrender, the way he demanded surrender in the courtroom. The fading sunlight seemed to knight him with a mantle of unconquerability. What chance did she stand against such a man?

Wind gusted in from the sea, whipping sailboat halyards against masts, drowning out the minister's final words. When at last it was over, Kate found she didn't have the strength to move. She watched the other mourners pass by. Clarence Avery stopped, started to say something, then awkwardly moved on. Mary and Patrick O'Brien didn't even look at her. As David approached, his eyes registered a flicker of recognition, which was just as quickly suppressed. Without breaking stride, he continued past her. She might have been invisible.

By the time she finally found the energy to move, the pier was empty. Sailboat masts stood out like a row of dead trees against the sunset. Her foosteps sounded hollow against the wooden planks. When she finally reached her car, she felt utterly weary, as though her legs had carried her for miles. She fumbled for her keys and felt a strange sense of inevitability as her purse slipped out of her grasp, scattering its contents across the pavement. She could only stand there, paralyzed by defeat, as the wind blew her tissues across the ground. She had the absurd image of herself standing here all night, all week, frozen to this spot. She wondered if anyone would notice.

David noticed. Even as he waved goodbye and watched his clients drive away, he was intensely aware that Kate Chesne was somewhere on the pier behind him. He'd been startled to see her here. He'd thought it a rather clever move on her part, this public display of penitence, obviously designed to impress the O'Briens. But as he turned and watched her solitary walk along the pier, he noticed the droop of her shoulders, the downcast face, and he realized how much courage it had taken for her to show up today.

Then he reminded himself that some doctors would do anything to head off a lawsuit.

Suddenly disinterested, he started toward his car. Halfway across the parking lot, he heard something clatter against the pavement and he saw that Kate had dropped her purse. For what seemed like forever, she just stood there, the car keys dangling from her hand, looking for all the world like a bewildered child. Then, slowly, wearily, she bent down and began to gather her belongings.

Almost against his will, he was drawn toward her. She didn't notice his approach. He crouched beside her, scooped a few errant pennies from the ground, and held them out to her. Suddenly she focused on his face and then froze.

"Looks like you need some help," he said.

"Oh."

"I think you've got everything now."

They both rose to their feet. He was still holding out the loose change, of which she seemed oblivious. Only after he'd deposited the money in her hand did she finally manage a weak "Thank you."

For a moment they stared at each other.

"I didn't expect to see you here," he remarked. "Why did you come?"

"It was—" she shrugged "—a mistake, I think."

"Did your lawyer suggest it?"

She looked puzzled. "Why would he?"

"To show the O'Briens you care."

Her cheeks suddenly flushed with anger. "Is that what you think? That this is some sort of—of *strategy*?"

"It's not unheard of."

"Why are *you* here, Mr. Ransom? Is this part of *your* strategy? To prove to your clients you care?"

"I do care."

"And you think I don't."

"I didn't say that."

"You implied it."

"Don't take everything I say personally."

"I take everything you say personally."

"You shouldn't. It's just a job to me."

Angrily, she shoved back a tangled lock of hair. "And what *is* your job? Hatchet man?"

"I don't attack people. I attack their mistakes. And even the best doctors make mistakes."

"You don't need to tell me that!" Turning, she looked off to sea, where Ellen O'Brien's ashes were newly drifting. "I live with it, Mr. Ransom. Every day in that O.R. I know that if I reach for the wrong vial or flip the wrong lever, it's someone's life. Oh, we find ways to deal with it. We have our black jokes, our gallows humor. It's terrible, the things we laugh about, and all in the name of survival. Emotional survival. You have no idea, you lawyers. You and your whole damned profession. You don't know what it's like when everything goes wrong. When we lose someone."

"I know what it's like for the family. Every time you make a mistake, someone suffers."

"I suppose *you* never make mistakes."

"Everyone does. The difference is, you bury yours."

"You'll never let me forget it, will you?"

She turned to him. Sunset had painted the sky orange, and the glow seemed to burn in her hair and in her cheeks. Suddenly he wondered how it would feel to run his fingers through those wind-tumbled strands, wondered what that face would feel like against his lips. The thought had popped out of nowhere and now that it was out, he couldn't get rid of it. Certainly it was the last thing he ought to be thinking. But she was standing so dangerously close that he'd either have to back away or kiss her.

He managed to hold his ground. Barely. "As I said, Dr. Chesne, I'm only doing my job."

She shook her head and her hair, that sun-streaked, mahogany hair, flew violently in the wind. "No, it's more than that. I think you have some sort of vendetta. You're out to hang the whole medical profession. Aren't you?"

David was taken aback by her accusation. Even as he started to deny it, he knew she'd hit too close to home. Somehow she'd found his old wound, had reopened it with the verbal equivalent of a surgeon's scalpel. "Out to hang the whole profession, am I?" he managed to say. "Well, let me tell you something, Doctor. It's incompetents like you that make my job so easy."

Rage flared in her eyes, as sudden and brilliant as two coals igniting. For an instant he thought she was going to slap him. Instead she whirled around, slid into her car and slammed the door. The Audi screeched out of the stall so sharply he had to flinch aside.

As he watched her car roar away, he couldn't help regretting those unnecessarily brutal words. But he'd said them in self-defense. That perverse attraction he'd felt to her had grown too compelling; he knew it had to be severed, right there and then.

As he turned to leave, something caught his eye, a thin shaft of reflected light. Glittering on the pavement was a silver pen; it had rolled under her car when she'd dropped her purse. He picked it up and studied the engraved name: Katharine Chesne, M.D.

For a moment he stood there, weighing the pen, thinking about its owner. Wondering if she, too, had no one to go home to. And it suddenly struck him, as he stood alone on the windy pier, just how empty he felt.

Once, he'd been grateful for the emptiness. It had meant the blessed absence of pain. Now he longed to feel something—anything—if only to reassure himself that he was alive. He knew the emotions were still there, locked up somewhere inside him. He'd felt them stirring faintly when he'd looked into Kate Chesne's burning eyes. Not a full-blown emotion, perhaps, but a flicker. A blip on the tracing of a terminally ill heart.

The patient wasn't dead. Not yet.

He felt himself smiling. He tossed the pen up in the air and caught it smartly. Then he slipped it into his breast pocket and walked to his car.

THE DOG WAS deeply anesthetized, its legs spread-eagled, its belly shaved and prepped with iodine. It was a German shepherd, obviously well-bred and just as obviously unloved.

Guy Santini hated to see such a handsome creature end up on his research table, but lab animals were scarce these days and he had to use whatever the supplier sent him. He consoled himself with the knowledge that the animals suffered no pain. They slept blissfully through the entire surgical procedure and when it was over, the ventilator was turned off and they were injected with a lethal dose of Pentothal. Death came peacefully; it was a far better end than the animals would have faced on the streets. And each sacrifice yielded data for his research, a few more dots on a graph, a few more clues to the mysteries of hepatic physiology.

He glanced at the instruments neatly laid out on the tray: the scalpel, the clamps, the catheters. Above the table, a pressure monitor awaited final hookup. Everything was ready. He reached for the scalpel.

The whine of the door swinging closed made him pause. Footsteps clipped toward him across the polished lab floor. Glancing across the table, he saw Ann Richter standing there. They looked at each other in silence.

"I see you didn't go to Ellen's services, either," he said.

"I wanted to. But I was afraid."

"Afraid?" He frowned. "Of what?"

"I'm sorry, Guy. I no longer have a choice." Silently, she held out a letter. "It's from Charlie Decker's lawyer. They're asking questions about Jenny Brook."

"What?" Guy stripped off his gloves and snatched the paper from her hand. What he read there made him look up at her in alarm. "You're not going to tell them, are you? Ann, you can't—"

"It's a subpoena, Guy."

"Lie to them, for God's sake!"

"Decker's out, Guy. You didn't know that, did you? He was released from the state hospital a month ago. He's been calling me. Leaving little notes at my apartment. Sometimes I even think he's following me. . . ."

"He can't hurt you."

"Can't he?" She nodded at the paper he was holding. "Henry got one, just like it. So did Ellen. Just before she..." Ann stopped, as if voicing her worst fears somehow would turn them to reality. Only now did Guy notice how haggard she was. Dark circles shadowed her eyes, and the ash-blond hair, of which she'd always been so proud, looked as if it hadn't been combed in days. "It has to end, Guy," she said softly. "I can't spend the rest of my life looking over my shoulder for Charlie Decker."

He crumpled the paper in his fist. He began to pace back and forth, his agitation escalating to panic. "You could leave the islands—you could go away for a while—"

"How long, Guy? A month? A year?"

"As long as it takes for this to settle down. Look, I'll give you the money—" He fumbled for his wallet and took out fifty dollars, all the cash he had. "Here. I promise I'll send you more—"

"I'm not asking for your money."

"Go on, take it."

"I told you, I—"

"For God's sake, *take it*!" His voice, harsh with desperation, echoed off the stark white walls. "Please, Ann," he urged quietly. "I'm asking you, as a friend. Please."

She looked down at the money he was holding. Slowly, she reached out and took it. As her fingers closed around the bills she announced, "I'm leaving tonight. For San Francisco. I have a brother—"

"Call me when you get there. I'll send you all the money you need." She didn't seem to hear him. "Ann? You'll do this for me. Won't you?"

She looked off blankly at the far wall. He longed to reassure her, to tell her that nothing could possibly go wrong; but they'd both know it was a lie. He watched as she walked slowly to the door. Just before she left, he said, "Thank you, Ann."

She didn't turn around. She simply paused in the doorway. Then she gave a little shrug, just before she vanished out the door.

As Ann headed for the bus stop, she was still clutching the money Guy had given her. Fifty dollars! As if that was enough! A thousand, a million dollars wouldn't be enough.

She boarded the bus for Waikiki. From her window seat she stared out at a numbing succession of city blocks. At Kalakaua, she got off and began to walk quickly toward her apartment building. Buses roared past, choking her with fumes. Her hands turned clammy in the heat. Concrete buildings seemed to press in on all sides and tourists clotted the sidewalks. As she wove her way through them, she felt a growing sense of uneasiness.

She began to walk faster.

Two blocks north of Kalakaua, the crowd thinned out and she found herself at a corner, waiting for a stoplight to change. In that instant, as she stood alone and exposed in the fading sunlight, the feeling suddenly seized her: *someone is following me.*

She swung around and scanned the street behind her. An old man was shuffling down the sidewalk. A couple was pushing a baby in a stroller. Gaudy shirts fluttered on an outdoor clothing rack. Nothing out of the ordinary. Or so it seemed. . . .

The light changed to green. She dashed across the street and didn't stop running until she'd reached her apartment.

She began to pack. As she threw her belongings into a suitcase, she was still debating her next move. The plane to San Francisco would take off at midnight; her brother would put her up for a while, no questions asked. He was good that way. He understood that everyone had a secret, everyone was running away from something.

It doesn't have to be this way, a stray voice whispered in her head. *You could go to the police. . . .*

And tell them what? The truth about Jenny Brook? Do I tear apart an innocent life?

She began to pace the apartment, thinking, fretting. As she walked past the living-room mirror, she caught sight of her own reflection, her blond hair in disarray, her eyes smudged with mascara. She hardly recognized herself; fear had transformed her face into a stranger's.

It only takes a single phone call, a confession. A secret, once revealed, is no longer dangerous....

She reached for the telephone. With unsteady hands she dialed Kate Chesne's home phone number. Her heart sank when, after four rings, a recording answered, followed by the message beep.

She cleared the fear from her throat. "This is Ann Richter," she said. "Please, I have to talk to you. It's about Ellen. I know why she died."

Then she hung up and waited for the phone to ring.

IT WAS HOURS before Kate heard the message.

After she left the pier that afternoon, she drove aimlessly for a while, avoiding the inevitable return to her empty house. It was Friday night. T.G.I.F. She decided to treat herself to an evening out. So she had supper alone at a trendy little seaside grill where everyone but her seemed to be having a grand old time. The steak she ordered was utterly tasteless and the chocolate mousse so cloying she could barely force it down her throat. She left an extravagant tip, almost as an apology for her lack of appetite.

Next she tried a movie. She found herself wedged between a fidgety eight-year-old boy on one side and a young couple passionately making out on the other.

She walked out halfway through the film. She never did remember the title—only that it was a comedy, and she hadn't laughed once.

By the time she got home, it was ten o'clock. She was half undressed and sitting listlessly on her bed when she noticed that the telephone message light was blinking. She let the messages play back as she wandered over to the closet.

"Hello, Dr. Chesne, this is Four East calling to tell you Mr. Berg's blood sugar is ninety-eight.... Hello, this is June from Dr. Avery's office. Don't forget the Quality Assurance meeting on Tuesday at four.... Hi, this is Windward Realty. Give us a call back. We have a listing we think you'd like to see...."

She was hanging up her skirt when the last message played back.

"This is Ann Richter. Please, I have to talk to you. It's about Ellen. I know why she died...."

There was the click of the phone hanging up, and then a soft whir as the tape automatically rewound. Kate scrambled back to the recorder and pressed the replay button. Her heart was racing as she listened again to the agonizingly slow sequence of messages.

"It's about Ellen. I know why she died...."

Kate grabbed the phone book from her nightstand. Ann's address and phone number were listed; her line was busy. Again and again Kate dialed but she heard only the drone of the busy signal.

She slammed down the receiver and knew immediately what she had to do next.

She hurried back to the closet and yanked the skirt from its hanger. Quickly, feverishly, she began to dress.

THE TRAFFIC HEADING into Waikiki was bumper-to-bumper.

As usual, the streets were crowded with a bizarre mix of tourists and off-duty soldiers and street people, all of them moving in the surreal glow of city lights. Palm trees cast their spindly shadows against the buildings. An otherwise distinguished-looking gentleman was flaunting his white legs and Bermuda shorts. Waikiki was where one came to see the ridiculous, the outrageous. But tonight, Kate found the view through her car window frightening—all those faces, drained of color under the glow of streetlamps, and the soldiers, lounging drunkenly in nightclub doorways. A wild-eyed evangelist stood on the corner, waving a Bible as he shouted "The end of the world is near!"

As she pulled up at a red light, he turned and stared at her and for an instant she thought she saw, in his burning eyes, a message meant only for her. The light turned green. She sent the car lurching through the intersection. His shout faded away.

She was still jittery ten minutes later when she climbed the steps to Ann's apartment building. As she reached the door, a young couple exited, allowing Kate to slip into the lobby.

It took a moment for the elevator to arrive. Leaning back against the wall, she forced herself to breathe deeply and let the silence of the building calm her nerves. By the time she finally stepped into the elevator, her heart had stopped its wild hammering. The doors slid closed. The elevator whined upward. She felt a strange sense of unreality as she watched the lights flash in succession: three, four, five. Except for a faint hydraulic hum, the ride was silent.

On the seventh floor, the doors slid open.

The corridor was deserted. A dull green carpet stretched out before her. As she walked toward number 710, she had the strange sensation that she was moving in a dream, that none of this was real—not the flocked wallpaper or the door looming at the end of the corridor. Only as she reached it did she see it was slightly ajar. "Ann?" she called out.

There was no answer.

She gave the door a little shove. Slowly it swung open and she froze, taking in, but not immediately comprehending, the scene before her: the toppled chair, the scattered magazines, the bright red splatters on the wall. Then her gaze followed the trail of crimson as it zigzagged across the beige carpet, leading inexorably toward its source: Ann's body, lying facedown in a lake of blood.

Beeps issued faintly from a telephone receiver dangling off an end table. The cold, electronic tone was like an alarm, screaming at her to move, to take action. But she remained paralyzed; her whole body seemed stricken by some merciful numbness.

The first wave of dizziness swept over her. She crouched down, clutching the doorframe for support. All her medical training, all those years of working around blood, couldn't prevent this totally visceral response. Through the drumbeat of her own heart she became aware of another sound, harsh and irregular. Breathing. But it wasn't hers.

Someone else was in the room.

A flicker of movement drew her gaze across to the living room mirror. Only then did she see the man's reflection. He was cowering behind a cabinet, not ten feet away.

They spotted each other in the mirror at the same instant. In that split second, as the reflection of his eyes met hers, she imagined she saw, in those hollows, the darkness beckoning to her. An abyss from which there was no escape.

He opened his mouth as if to speak but no words came out, only an unearthly hiss, like a viper's warning just before it strikes.

She lurched wildly to her feet. The room spun past her eyes with excruciating slowness as she turned to flee. The corridor stretched out endlessly before her. She heard her own scream echo off the walls; the sound was as unreal as the image of the hallway flying past.

The stairwell door lay at the other end. It was her only feasible escape route. There was no time to wait for elevators.

She hit the opening bar at a run and shoved the door into the concrete stairwell. One flight into her descent, she heard the door above spring open again and slam against the wall. Again she heard the hiss, as terrifying as a demon's whisper in her ear.

She stumbled to the sixth-floor landing and grappled at the door. It was locked tight. She screamed and pounded. Surely someone would hear her! Someone would answer her cry for help!

Footsteps thudded relentlessly down the stairs. She couldn't wait; she had to keep running.

She dashed down the next flight and hit the fifth floor landing too hard. Pain shot through her ankle. In tears, she wrenched and pounded at the door. It was locked.

He was right behind her.

She flew down the next flight and the next. Her purse flew off her shoulder but she couldn't stop to retrieve it. Her ankle was screaming with pain as she hurtled toward the third-floor landing. Was it locked, as well? Were they all locked? Her mind flew ahead to the ground floor, to what lay outside. A parking lot? An alley? Is that where they'd find her body in the morning?

Sheer panic made her wrench with superhuman strength at the next door. To her disbelief, it was unlocked. Stumbling through, she found herself in the parking garage. There was no time to think about her next move; she tore off blindly into the shadows. Just as the stairwell door flew open again, she ducked behind a van.

Crouching by the front wheel, she listened for footsteps but heard nothing except the torrent of her own blood racing in her ears. Seconds passed, then minutes. Where was he? Had he abandoned the chase? Her body was pressed so tightly against the van, the steel bit into her thigh. She felt no pain; every ounce of concentration was focused on survival.

A pebble clattered across the ground, echoing like a pistol shot in the concrete garage.

She tried in vain to locate the source but the explosions seemed to come from a dozen different directions at once. *Go away!* she wanted to scream. *Dear God, make him go away....*

The echoes faded, leaving total silence. But she sensed his presence, closing in. She could almost hear his voice whispering to her *I'm coming for you. I'm coming....*

She had to know where he was, if he was drawing close.

Clinging to the tire, she slowly inched her head around and peered beneath the van. What she saw made her reel back in horror.

He was on the other side of the van and moving toward the rear. Toward her.

She sprang to her feet and took off like a rabbit. Parked cars melted into one continuous blur. She plunged toward the exit ramp. Her legs, stiff from crouching, refused to move fast enough. She could hear the man right behind her. The ramp seemed endless, spiraling around and around, every curve threatening to send her sprawling to the pavement. His footsteps were gaining. Air rushed in and out of her lungs, burning her throat.

In a last, desperate burst of speed, she tore around the final curve. Too late, she saw the headlights of a car coming up the ramp toward her.

She caught a glimpse of two faces behind the windshield, a man and a woman, their mouths open wide. As she slammed into the hood, there was a brilliant flash of light, like stars exploding in her eyes. Then the light vanished and she saw nothing at all. Not even darkness.

Chapter Five

"Mango season," Sergeant Brophy said as he sneezed into a soggy handkerchief. "Worst time of year for my allergies." He blew his nose, then sniffed experimentally, as if checking for some new, as yet undetected obstruction to his nasal passages. He seemed completely unaware of his gruesome surroundings, as though dead bodies and blood-spattered walls and an army of crime-lab techs were always hanging about. When Brophy got into one of his sneezing jags, he was oblivious of everything but the sad state of his sinuses.

Lieutenant Francis "Pokie" Ah Ching had grown used to hearing the sniffles of his junior partner. At times, the habit was useful. He could always tell which room Brophy was in; all he had to do was follow the man's nose.

That nose, still bundled in a handkerchief, vanished into the dead woman's bedroom. Pokie refocused his attention on his spiral notebook, in which he was recording the data. He wrote quickly, in the peculiar shorthand he'd evolved over his twenty-six years as a cop, seventeen of them with homicide. Eight pages were filled with sketches of the various rooms in the apartment, four pages of the living room alone. His art was crude but to the point. Body there. Toppled furniture here. Blood all over.

The medical examiner, a boyish, freckle-faced woman known to everyone simply as M.J., was making her walkaround before she examined the body. She was wearing her usual blue jeans and tennis shoes—sloppy dress for a doctor, but in her specialty, the patients never complained. As she circled the room, she dictated into a cassette recorder.

"Arterial spray on three walls, pattern height about four to five feet.... Heavy pooling at east end of living room where body is located.... Victim is female, blond, age thirty to forty, found in prone position, right arm flexed under head, left arm extended.... No hand or arm lacerations noted." M.J. crouched down. "Marked dependent mottling. Hmm." Frowning, she touched the victim's bare arm. "Significant body cooling. Time is now 12:15 a.m." She flicked off the cassette and was silent for a moment.

"Somethin' wrong, M.J.?" Pokie asked.

"What?" She looked up. "Oh, just thinking."

"What's your prelim?"

"Let's see. Looks like a single deep slash to the left carotid, very sharp blade. And very fast work. The victim never got a chance to raise her arms in defense. I'll get a better look when we wash her down at the morgue." She stood up and Pokie saw her tennis shoes were smeared with blood. How many crime scenes had those shoes tramped through?

Not as many as mine, he thought.

"Slashed carotid," he said thoughtfully. "Does that remind you of somethin'?"

"First thing I thought of. What was that guy's name a few weeks back?"

"Tanaka. He had a slash to the left carotid."

"That's him. Just as bloody a mess as this one, too."

Pokie thought a moment. "Tanaka was a doctor," he remarked. "And this one..." He glanced down at the body. "This one's a nurse."

"Was a nurse."

"Makes you wonder."

M.J. snapped her lab kit closed. "There's lots of doctors and nurses in this town. Just because these two end up on my slab doesn't mean they knew each other."

A loud sneeze announced Brophy's emergence from the bedroom. "Found a plane ticket to San Francisco on her dresser. Midnight flight." He glanced at his watch. "Which she just missed."

A plane ticket. A packed suitcase. So Ann Richter was about to skip town. Why?

Mulling over that question, Pokie made another circuit of the apartment, going through the rooms one by one. In the bathroom, he found a lab tech microscopically peering down at the sink.

"Traces of blood in here, sir. Looks like your killer washed his hands."

"Yeah? Cool cat. Any prints?"

"A few here and there. Most of 'em old, probably the victim's. Plus one fresh set off the front doorknob. Could belong to your witness."

Pokie nodded and went back to the living room. That was their ace in the hole. The witness. Though dazed and in pain, she'd managed to alert the ambulance crew to the horrifying scene in apartment 710.

Thereby ruining a good night's sleep for Pokie.

He glanced at Brophy. "Have you found Dr. Chesne's purse yet?"

"It's not in the stairwell where she dropped it. Someone must've picked it up."

Pokie was silent a moment. He thought of all the things women carried in their purses: wallets, driver's licenses, house keys.

He slapped his notebook closed. "Sergeant?"

"Sir?"

"I want a twenty-four-hour guard placed on Dr. Chesne's hospital room. Effective immediately. I want a man in the lobby. And I want you to trace every call that comes in asking about her."

Brophy looked dubious. "All that? For how long?"

"Just as long as she's in the hospital. Right now she's a sitting duck."

"You really think this guy'd go after her in the hospital?"

"I don't know." Pokie sighed. "I don't know what we're dealing with. But I've got two identical murders." Grimly he slid the notebook into his pocket. "And she's our only witness."

PHIL GLICKMAN was making a pest of himself as usual.

It was Saturday morning, the one day of the week David could work undisturbed, the one day he could catch up on all the paperwork that perpetually threatened to bury his desk. But today, instead of solitude, he'd found Glickman. While his young associate was smart, aggressive and witty, he was also utterly incapable of silence. David suspected the man talked in his sleep.

"So I said, 'Doctor, do you mean to tell me the posterior auricular artery comes off *before* the superficial temporal?' And the guy gets all flustered and says, 'Oh, did I say that? No, of course it's the other way around.' Which blew it right there for him." Glickman slammed his fist triumphantly into his palm. "Wham! He's dead meat and he knows it. We just got the offer to settle. Not bad, huh?" At David's lackluster nod, Glickman looked profoundly disappointed. Then he brightened and asked, "How's it going with the O'Brien case? They ready to yell uncle?"

David shook his head. "Not if I know Kate Chesne."

"What, is she dumb?"

"Stubborn. Self-righteous."

"So it goes with the white coat."

David tiredly dragged his fingers through his hair. "I hope this doesn't go to trial."

"It'll be like shooting rabbits in a cage. Easy."

"Too easy."

Glickman laughed as he turned to leave. "Never seemed to bother you before."

Why the hell does it bother me now? David wondered.

The O'Brien case was like an apple falling into his lap. All he had to do was file a few papers, issue a few threatening statements, and hold his hand out for the check. He should be breaking out the champagne. Instead, he was moping around on a gorgeous Saturday morning, feeling sleazy about the whole affair.

Yawning, he leaned back and rubbed his eyes. It'd been a lousy night, spent tossing and turning in bed. He'd been plagued by dreams—disturbing dreams; the kind he hadn't had in years.

There had been a woman. She'd stood very still, very quiet in the shadows, her face silhouetted against a window of hazy light. At first he'd thought she was his ex-wife, Linda. But there were things about her that weren't right, things that confused him. She'd stood motionless, like a deer pausing in the forest. Eagerly he'd reached out to undress her, but his hands had been impossibly clumsy and in his haste, he'd torn off one of her buttons. She had laughed, a deliciously throaty sound that reminded him of brandy.

That's when he knew she wasn't Linda. Looking up, he'd stared into the green eyes of Kate Chesne.

There were no words between them, only a look. And a touch: her fingers, sliding gently down his face.

He'd awakened, sweating with desire. He'd tried to fall back to sleep. Again and again the dream had returned. Even now, as he sank back in his chair and closed his eyes, he saw her face again and he felt that familiar ache.

Brutally wrenching his thoughts back to reality, he dragged himself over to the window. He was too old for this nonsense. Too old and too smart to even fantasize about an affair with the opposition.

Hell, attractive women walked into his office all the time. And every so often, one of them would give off the sort of signals any red-blooded man could recognize. It took only a certain tilt of the head, a provocative flash of thigh. He'd always been amused but never tempted; bedding down clients wasn't included in his list of services.

Kate Chesne had sent out no such signals. In fact she plainly despised lawyers as much as he despised doctors. So why, of all the women who'd walked through his door, was she the one he couldn't stop thinking about?

He reached into his breast pocket and pulled out the silver pen. It suddenly occurred to him that this wasn't the sort of item a woman would buy for herself. Was it a gift from a boyfriend? he wondered, and was startled by his instant twinge of jealousy.

He should return it.

The thought set his mind off and racing. Mid Pac Hospital was only a few blocks away. He could drop off the pen on his way home. Most doctors made Saturday-morning rounds, so there was a good chance she'd be there. At the prospect of seeing her again, he felt a strange mixture of anticipation and dread, the same churning in his stomach he used to feel as a teenager scrounging up the courage to ask a girl for a date. It was a very bad sign.

But he couldn't get the idea out of his mind.

The pen felt like a live wire. He shoved it back in his pocket and quickly began to stuff his papers into the briefcase.

Fifteen minutes later he walked into the hospital lobby and went to a house telephone. The operator answered.

"I'm trying to reach Dr. Kate Chesne," David said. "Is she in the building?"

"Dr. Chesne?" There was a pause. "Yes, I believe she's in the hospital. Who's calling?"

He started to give his name, then thought better of it. If Kate knew it was his page, she'd never answer it. "I'm a friend," he replied lamely.

"Please hold."

A recording of some insipid melody came on, the sort of music they probably played on elevators in hell. He caught himself drumming the booth impatiently. That's when it struck him just how eager he was to see her again.

I must be nuts, he thought, abruptly hanging up the phone. Or desperate for female companionship. Maybe both.

Disgusted with himself, he turned to leave, only to find that his exit was blocked by two very impressive-looking cops.

"Mind coming with us?" one of them asked.

"Actually," responded David, "I would."

"Then lemme put it a different way," said the cop, his meaning absolutely clear.

David couldn't help an incredulous laugh. "What did I do, guys? Double-park? Insult your mothers?"

He was grasped firmly by both arms and directed across the lobby, into the administrative wing.

"Is this an arrest or what?" he demanded. They didn't answer. "Hey, I think you're supposed to inform me of my rights." They didn't. "Okay," he amended. "Then maybe it's time *I* informed *you* of my rights." Still no answer. He shot out his weapon of last resort. "I'm an attorney!"

"Goody for you" was the dry response as he was led toward a conference room.

"You know damn well you can't arrest me without charges!"

They threw open the door. "We're just following orders."

"*Whose* orders?"

The answer was boomed out in a familiar voice. "*My* orders."

David turned and confronted a face he hadn't seen since his days with the prosecutor's office. Homicide Detective Pokie Ah Ching's features reflected a typical island mix of bloods: a hint of Chinese around the eyes, some Portuguese in the heavy jowls, a strong dose of dusky Polynesian coloring. Except for a hefty increase in girth, he had changed little in the eight years since they'd last worked together. He was even wearing the same old off-the-rack polyester suit, though it was obvious those front buttons hadn't closed in quite some time.

"If it isn't Davy Ransom," Pokie grunted. "I lay out my nets, and look what comes swimming in."

"Yeah," David muttered, jerking his arm free. "The wrong fish."

Pokie nodded at the two policemen. "This one's okay."

The officers retreated. The instant the door closed, David barked out: "What the hell's going on?"

In answer, Pokie moved forward and gave David a long, appraising look. "Private practice must be bringin' in the bucks. Got yourself a nice new suit. Expensive shoes. Humph. Italian. Doing well, huh, Davy?"

"I can't complain."

Pokie settled down on the edge of the table and crossed his arms. "So how's it, workin' out of a nice new office? Miss the ol' cockroaches?"

"Oh, sure."

"I made lieutenant a month after you left."

"Congratulations."

"But I'm still wearin' the same old suit. Driving the same old car. And the shoes?" He stuck out a foot. "Taiwan."

David's patience was just about shredded. "Are you going to tell me what's going on? Or am I supposed to guess?"

Pokie reached in his jacket for a cigarette, the same cheap brand he'd always smoked, and lit up. "You a friend of Kate Chesne's?"

David was startled by the abrupt shift of subject. "I know her."

"How well?"

"We've spoken a few times. I came to return her pen."

"So you didn't know she was brought to the E.R. last night? Trauma service."

"*What?*"

"Nothing serious," Pokie said quickly. "Mild concussion. Few bruises. She'll be discharged today."

David's throat had suddenly tightened beyond all hope of speech. He watched, stunned, as Pokie took a long, blissful drag on his cigarette.

"It's a funny thing," Pokie remarked, "how a case'll just sit around forever, picking up dust. No clues. No way of closing the file. Then, pow! We get lucky."

"What happened to her?" David asked in a hoarse voice.

"She was in the wrong place at the wrong time." He blew out a lungful of smoke. "Last night she walked in on a very bad scene."

"You mean . . . she's a witness? To what?"

Pokie's face was impassive through the haze drifting between them. "Murder."

THROUGH THE CLOSED DOOR of her hospital room, Kate could hear the sounds of a busy hospital: the paging system, crackling with static, the ringing telephones. All night long she'd strained to hear those sounds; they had reminded her she wasn't alone. Only now, as the sun spilled in across her bed and a profound exhaustion settled over her, did she finally drift toward sleep. She didn't hear the first knock, or the voice calling to her through the door. It was the gust of air sweeping into the room that warned her the door had swung open. She was vaguely aware that someone was approaching her bed. It took all her strength just to open her eyes. Through a blur of sleep, she saw David's face.

She felt a feeble sense of outrage struggle to the surface. He had no right to invade her privacy when she was so weak, so exposed. She knew what she *ought* to say to him, but exhaustion had sapped her last reserves of emotion and she couldn't dredge up a single word.

Neither could he. It seemed they'd both lost their voices.

"No fair, Mr. Ransom," she whispered. "Kicking a girl when she's down..." Turning away, she gazed down dully at the sheets. "You seem to have forgotten your handy tape recorder. Can't take a deposition without a tape recorder. Or are you hiding it in one of your—"

"Stop it, Kate. Please."

She fell instantly still. He'd called her by her first name. Some unspoken barrier between them had just fallen, and she didn't know why. What she did know was that he was here, that he was standing so close she could smell the scent of his aftershave, could almost feel the heat of his gaze.

"I'm not here to... kick you while you're down." Sighing, he added, "I guess I shouldn't be here at all. But when I heard what happened, all I could think of was..."

She looked up and found him staring at her mutely. For the first time, he didn't seem so forbidding. She had to remind herself that he *was* the enemy; that this visit, whatever its purpose, had changed nothing between them. But at that moment, what she felt wasn't threatened but protected. It was more than just his commanding physical presence, though she was very aware of that, too; he had a quiet aura of strength. Competence. If only he'd been *her* attorney; if only he'd been hired to defend, not prosecute her. She couldn't imagine losing any battle with David Ransom at her side.

"All you could think of was what?" she asked softly.

Shifting, he turned awkwardly toward the door. "I'm sorry. I should let you sleep."

"Why did you come?"

He halted and gave a sheepish laugh. "I almost forgot. I came to return this. You dropped it at the pier."

He placed the pen in her hand. She stared down in wonder, not at the pen, but at his hands. Large, strong hands. How would it feel, to have those fingers tangled in her hair?

"Thank you," she whispered.

"Sentimental value?"

"It was a gift. From a man I used to—" Clearing her throat, she looked away and repeated, "Thank you."

David knew this was his cue to walk out. He'd done his good deed for the day; now he should cut whatever threads of conversation were being spun between them. But some hidden force seemed to guide his hand toward a chair and he pulled it over to the bed and sat down.

Her hair lay tangled on the pillow and a bruise had turned one cheek an ugly shade of blue. He felt an instinctive flood of rage against the man who'd tried to hurt her. The emotion was entirely unexpected; it surprised him by its ferocity.

"How are you feeling?" he asked, for want of anything else to say.

She gave a feeble shrug. "Tired. Sore." She paused and added with a weak laugh, "Lucky to be alive."

His gaze shifted to the bruise on her cheek and she automatically reached up to hide what stood out so plainly on her face. Slowly she let her hand fall back to the bed. He found it a very sad gesture, as if she was ashamed of being the victim, of bearing that brutal mark of violence.

"I'm not exactly at my most stunning today," she said.

"You look fine, Kate. You really do." It was a stupid thing to say but he meant it. She looked beautiful; she was alive. "The bruise will fade. What matters is that you're safe."

"Am I?" She looked at the door. "There's been a guard sitting out there all night. I heard him, laughing with the nurses. I keep wondering why they put him there. . . ."

"I'm sure it's just a precaution. So no one bothers you."

She frowned at him, suddenly puzzled. "How did *you* get past him?"

"I know Lt. Ah Ching. We worked together, years ago. When I was with the prosecutor's office."

"You?"

He smiled. "Yeah. I've done my civic duty. Got my education in sleaze. At slave wages."

"Then you've talked to Ah Ching? About what happened?"

"He said you're a witness. That your testimony's vital to his case."

"Did he tell you Ann Richter tried to call me? Just before she was killed. She left a message on my recorder."

"About what?"

"Ellen O'Brien."

He paused. "I didn't hear about this."

"She *knew* something, Mr. Ransom. Something about Ellen's death. Only she never got a chance to tell me."

"What was the message?"

"'I know why she died.' Those were her exact words."

David stared at her. Slowly, reluctantly, he found himself drawn deeper and deeper into the spell of those green eyes. "It may not mean anything. Maybe she just figured out what went wrong in surgery—"

"The word she used was *why.* 'I know *why* she died.' That implies there was a reason, a—a *purpose* for Ellen's death."

"Murder on the operating table?" He shook his head. "Come on."

She turned away. "I should have known you'd be skeptical. It would ruin your precious lawsuit, wouldn't it? To find out the patient was murdered."

"What do the police think?"

"How would I know?" she shot back in frustration. Then, in a tired voice, she said, "Your friend Ah Ching never says much of anything. All he does is scribble in that notebook of his. Maybe he thinks it's irrelevant. Maybe he doesn't want to hear any confusing facts." Her gaze shifted to the door. "But then I think about that guard. And I wonder if there's something else going on. Something he won't tell me . . ."

There was a knock on the door. A nurse came in with the discharge papers. David watched as Kate sat up and obediently signed each one. The pen trembled in her hand. He could hardly believe this was the same woman who'd stormed into his

Under the Knife

office. That day he'd been impressed by her iron will, her determination.

Now he was just as impressed by her vulnerability.

The nurse left and Kate sank back against the pillows.

"Do you have somewhere to go?" he asked. "After you leave here?"

"My friends . . . they have this cottage they hardly ever use. I hear it's on the beach." She sighed and looked wistfully out the window. "I could use a beach right now."

"You'll be staying there alone? Is that safe?"

She didn't answer. She just kept looking out the window. It made him uneasy, thinking of her in that cottage, alone, unprotected. He had to remind himself that she wasn't his concern. That he'd be crazy to get involved with this woman. Let the police take care of her; after all, she was their responsibility.

He stood up to leave. She just sat there, huddled in the bed, her arms crossed over her chest in a pitiful gesture of self-protection. As he walked out of the room, he heard her say, softly, "I don't think I'll ever feel safe again."

Chapter Six

"It's just a little place," explained Susan Santini as she and Kate drove along the winding North Shore highway. "Nothing fancy. Just a couple of bedrooms. An absolutely ancient kitchen. Prehistoric, really. But it's cozy. And it's so nice to hear the waves...." She turned off the highway onto a dirt road carved through the dense shrubbery of halekoa. Their tires threw up a cloud of rich red dust as they bounced toward the sea. "Seems like we hardly use the place these days, what with one of us always being on call. Sometimes Guy talks about selling. But I'd never dream of it. You just don't find bits of paradise like this anymore."

The tires crunched onto the gravel driveway. Beneath a towering stand of ironwood trees, the small plantation-era cottage looked like nothing more than a neglected dollhouse. Years of sun and wind had faded the planks to a weathered green. The roof seemed to sag beneath its burden of brown ironwood needles.

Kate got out and stood for a moment beneath the trees, listening to the waves hiss onto the sand. Under the midday sun, the sea shone a bright and startling blue.

"There they are," said Susan, pointing down the beach at her son William, who was dancing a joyous little jig in the sand. He moved like an elf, his long arms weaving delicately, his head bobbing back and forth as he laughed. The baggy swim trunks barely clung to his scrawny hips. Framed against the brilliance of the sky, he seemed like nothing more than a collection of twigs among the trees, a mythical creature who might vanish in the blink of an eye. Nearby, a young woman with a sparrow-like face was sitting on a towel and flipping listlessly through a magazine.

"That's Adele," Susan whispered. "It took us half a dozen ads and twenty-one interviews to find her. But I just don't think she's going to work out. What worries me is William's already getting attached to her."

William suddenly spotted them. He stopped in his tracks and waved. "Hi, Mommy!"

"Hello, darling!" Susan called. Then she touched Kate's arm. "We've aired out the cottage for you. And there should be a pot of coffee waiting."

They climbed the wooden steps to the kitchen porch. The screen door squealed open. Inside hung the musty smell of age. Sunlight slanted in through the window and gleamed dully on the yellowed linoleum floor. A small pot of African violets sat on the blue-tiled countertop. Taped haphazardly to the walls was a whimsical collection of drawings: blue and green dinosaurs, red stick men, animals of various colors and unidentifiable species, each labeled with the artist's name: William.

"We keep the line hooked up for emergencies," Susan informed her, pointing to the wall telephone. "I've already stocked the refrigerator. Just the basics, really. Guy said we can pick up your car tomorrow. That'll give you a chance to do some decent grocery shopping." She made a quick circuit of the kitchen, pointing out various cabinets, the pots and pans, the dishes. Then, beckoning to Kate, she led the way to the bedroom. There she went to the window and spread apart the white lace curtains. Her red hair glittered in the stream of sunlight. "Look, Kate. Here's that view I promised you." She gazed out lovingly at the sea. "You know, people wouldn't need psychiatrists if they just had this to look at every day. If they could lie in the sun, hear the waves, the birds." She turned and smiled at Kate. "What do you think?"

"I think..." Kate gazed around at the polished wood floor, the filmy curtains, the dusty gold light shimmering through the window. "I think I never want to leave," she replied with a smile.

Footsteps pattered on the porch. Susan looked around as the screen door slammed. "So endeth the peace and quiet." She sighed.

They returned to the kitchen and found little William singing tunelessly as he laid out a collection of twigs on the kitchen table. Adele, her bare shoulders glistening with suntan oil, was pouring him a cup of apple juice. On the counter lay a copy of *Vogue*, dusty with sand.

"Look, Mommy!" exclaimed William, pointing proudly to his newly gathered treasure.

"My goodness, what a collection," said Susan, appropriately awed. "What are you going to do with all those sticks?"

"They're not sticks. They're swords. To kill monsters."

"Monsters? But, darling, I've told you. There aren't any monsters."

"Yes, there are."

"Daddy put them all in jail, remember?"

"Not all of them." Meticulously, he lay another twig down on the table. "They're hiding in the bushes. I heard one last night."

"William," Susan said quietly. "What monsters?"

"In the bushes. I told you, last night."

"Oh." Susan flashed Kate a knowing smile. "That's why he crawled into our bed at two in the morning."

Adele placed the cup of juice beside the boy. "Here, William. Your . . ." She frowned. "What's that in your pocket?"

"Nothing."

"I saw it move."

William ignored her and took a slurp of juice. His pocket twitched.

"William Santini, give it to me." Adele held out her hand.

William turned his pleading eyes to the court of last appeals: his mother. She shook her head sadly. Sighing, he reached into his pocket, scooped out the source of the twitching, and dropped it in Adele's hand.

Her shriek was startling, most of all to the lizard, which promptly flung itself to freedom, but only after dropping its writhing tail in Adele's hand.

"He's getting away!" wailed William.

There followed a mad scrambling on hands and knees by everyone in the room. By the time the hapless lizard had been recaptured and jailed in a teacup, they were all breathless and weak from laughter. Susan, her red hair in wild disarray, collapsed onto the kitchen floor, her legs sprawled out in front of her.

"I can't *believe* it," she gasped, falling back against the refigerator. "Three grown women against one itty-bitty lizard. Are we helpless or what?"

William wandered over to his mother and stared at the sunlight sparkling in her red hair. In silent fascination, he reached for a loose strand and watched it glide sensuously across his fingers. "My mommy," he whispered.

She smiled. Taking his face in her hands, she kissed him tenderly on the mouth. "My baby."

"YOU HAVEN'T TOLD ME the whole story," said David. "Now I want to know what you've left out."

Pokie Ah Ching took a mammoth bite of his Big Mac and chewed with the fierce concentration of a man too long denied his lunch. Swiping a glob of sauce from his chin, he grunted, "What makes you think I left something out?"

"You've thrown some heavy-duty manpower into this case. That guard outside her room. The lobby stakeout. You're fishing for something big."

"Yeah. A murderer." Pokie took a pickle slice out of his sandwich and tossed it disgustedly on a mound of napkins. "What's with all the questions, anyway? I thought you left the prosecutor's office."

"I didn't leave behind my curiosity."

"Curiosity? Is that all it is?"

"Kate happens to be a friend of mine—"

"Hogwash!" Pokie shot him an accusing look. "You think I don't ask questions? I'm a detective, Davy. And I happen to know she's no friend of yours. She's the defendant in one of your lawsuits." He snorted. "Since when're you getting chummy with the opposition?"

"Since I started believing her story about Ellen O'Brien. Two days ago, she came to me with a story so ridiculous I laughed

her out of my office. She had no facts at all, nothing but a dis-
jointed tale that sounded flat-out paranoid. Then this nurse,
Ann Richter, gets her throat slashed. Now *I'm* beginning to
wonder. Was Ellen O'Brien's death malpractice? Or murder?''

"Murder, huh?" Pokie shrugged and took another bite.
"That'd make it my business, not yours."

"Look, I've filed a lawsuit that claims it was malpractice. It's
going to be pretty damned embarrassing—not to mention a
waste of my time—if this turns out to be murder. So before I get
up in front of a jury and make a fool of myself, I want to hear
the facts. Level with me, Pokie. For old times' sake."

"Don't pile on the sentimental garbage, Davy. You're the one
who walked away from the job. Guess that fat paycheck was
too hard to resist. Me? I'm still here." He shoved a drawer
closed. "Along with this crap they call furniture."

"Let's get one thing straight. My leaving the job had nothing to do with money."

"So why did you leave?"

"It was personal."

"Yeah. With you it's always *personal*. Still tight as a clam,
aren't you?"

"We were talking about the case."

Pokie sat back and studied him for a moment. Through the
open door of his office came the sound of bedlam—loud voices
and ringing telephones and clattering typewriters. A normal
afternoon in the downtown police station. In disgust, Pokie got
up and shoved his office door closed. "Okay." He sighed, returning to his chair. "What do you want to know?"

"Details."

"Gotta be specific."

"What's so important about Ann Richter's murder?"

Pokie answered by grabbing a folder from the chaotic pile of
papers on his desk. He tossed it to David. "M.J.'s preliminary
autopsy report. Take a look."

The report was three pages long and cold-bloodedly graphic.
Even though David had served five years as deputy prosecutor, had read dozens of such reports, he couldn't help shuddering at the clinical details of the woman's death.

Left carotid artery severed cleanly...razor-sharp instrument.... Laceration on right temple probably due to incidental impact against coffee table.... Pattern of blood spatter on wall consistent with arterial spray....

"I see M.J. hasn't lost her touch for turning stomachs," David said, flipping to the second page. What he read there made him frown. "Now, this finding doesn't make sense. Is M.J. sure about the time of death?"

"You know M.J. She's always sure. She's backed up by mottling and core body temp."

"Why the hell would the killer cut the woman's throat and then hang around for three hours? To enjoy the scenery?"

"To clean up. To case the apartment."

"Was anything missing?"

Pokie sighed. "No. That's the problem. Money and jewelry were lying right out in the open. Killer didn't touch any of it."

"Sexual assault?"

"No sign of it. Victim's clothes were intact. And the killing was too efficient. If he was out for thrills, you'd think he would've taken his time. Gotten a few more screams out of her."

"So you've got a brutal murder and no motive. What else is new?"

"Take another look at that autopsy report. Read me what M.J. wrote about the wound."

"'Severed left carotid artery. Razor-sharp instrument.'" He looked up. "So?"

"So those are the same words she used in another autopsy report two weeks ago. Except that victim was a man. An obstetrician named Henry Tanaka."

"Ann Richter was a nurse."

"Right. And here's the interesting part. Before she joined the O.R. staff, she used to moonlight in obstetrics. Chances are, she knew Henry Tanaka."

David suddenly went very, very still. He thought of another nurse who'd worked in obstetrics. A nurse who, like Ann Richter, was now dead. "Tell me more about that obstetrician," he said.

Pokie fished out a pack of cigarettes and an ashtray. "Mind?"

"Not if you keep talking."

"Been dying for one all morning," Pokie grunted. "Can't light up when Brophy's around, whining about his damned sinuses." He flicked off the lighter. "Okay." He sighed, gratefully expelling a cloud of smoke. "Here's the story. Henry Tanaka's office was over on Liliha. You know, that god-awful concrete building. Two weeks ago, after the rest of his staff had left, he stayed behind in the office. Said he had to catch up on some paperwork. His wife says he always got home late. But she implied it wasn't paperwork that was keeping him out at night."

"Girlfriend?"

"What else?"

"Wife know any names?"

"No. She figured it was one of the nurses over at the hospital. Anyway, about seven o'clock that night, couple of janitors found the body in one of the exam rooms. At the time we thought it was just a case of some junkie after a fix. There were drugs missing from the cabinet."

"Narcotics?"

"Naw, the good stuff was locked up in a back room. The killer went after worthless stuff, drugs that wouldn't bring you a dime on the streets. We figured he was either stoned or dumb. But he was smart enough not to leave prints. Anyway, with no other evidence, the case sort of hit a wall. The only lead we had was something one of the janitors saw. As he was coming into the building, he spotted a woman running across the parking lot. It was drizzling and almost dark, so he didn't get a good look. But he says she was definitely a blonde."

"Was he positive it was a woman?"

"What, as opposed to a man in a wig?" Pokie laughed. "That's one I didn't think of. I guess it's possible."

"So what came of your lead?"

"Nothing much. We asked around, didn't come up with any names. We were starting to think that mysterious blonde was a red herring. Then Ann Richter got killed." He paused. "She was blond." He snuffed out his cigarette. "Kate Chesne's our first big break. Now at least we know what our man looks like. The artist's sketch'll hit the papers Monday. Maybe we'll start pulling in some names."

"What kind of protection are you giving Kate?"

"She's tucked away on the North Shore. I got a patrol car passing by every few hours."

"That's all?"

"No one'll find her up there."

"A professional could."

"What am I supposed to do? Slap on a permanent guard?" He nodded at the stack of papers on his desk. "Look at those files, Davy! I'm up to my neck in stiffs. I call myself lucky if a night goes by without a corpse rolling in the door."

"Professionals don't leave witnesses."

"I'm not convinced he *is* a pro. Besides, you know how tight things are around here. Look at this junk." He kicked the desk. "Twenty years old and full of termites. Don't even mention that screwy computer. I still gotta send fingerprints to California to get a fast ID!" Frustrated, he flopped back in his twenty-year-old chair. "Look, Davy. I'm reasonably sure she'll be okay. I'd like to guarantee it. But you know how it is."

Yeah, David thought. *I know how it is.* Some things about police work never changed. Too many demands and not enough money in the budget. He tried to tell himself that his only interest in this case was as the plaintiff's attorney; it was his job to ask all these questions. He had to be certain his case wouldn't crumble in the light of new facts. But his thoughts kept returning to Kate, sitting so alone, so vulnerable, in that hospital bed.

David wanted to trust the man's judgment. He'd worked with Pokie Ah Ching long enough to know the man was, for the most part, a competent cop. But he also knew that even the best cops made mistakes. Unfortunately cops and doctors had something in common: they both buried their mistakes.

THE SUN SLANTED DOWN on Kate's back, its warmth lulling her into an uneasy sleep. She lay with her face nestled in her arms as the waves lapped at her feet and the wind riffled the pages of her paperback book. On this lonely stretch of beach, where the only disturbance was the birds bickering and thrashing in the trees, she had found the perfect place to hide away from the world. To be healed.

She sighed and the scent of coconut oil stirred in her nostrils. Little by little, she was tugged awake by the wind in her hair, by a vague hunger for food. She hadn't eaten since breakfast and already the afternoon had slipped toward evening.

Then another sensation wrenched her fully awake. It was the feeling that she was no longer alone. That she was being watched. It was so definite that when she rolled over and looked up she was not at all surprised to see David standing there.

He was wearing jeans and an old cotton shirt, the sleeves rolled up in the heat. His hair danced in the wind, sparkling like bits of fire in the late-afternoon sunlight. He didn't say a thing; he simply stood there, his hands thrust in his pockets, his gaze slowly taking her in. Though her swimsuit wasn't particularly revealing, something about his eyes—their boldness, their directness—seemed to strip her against the sand. Sudden warmth flooded her skin, a flush deeper and hotter than any the sun could ever produce.

"You're a hard lady to track down," he said.

"That's the whole idea of going into hiding. People aren't supposed to find you."

He glanced around, his gaze quickly surveying the lonely surroundings. "Doesn't seem like such a bright idea, lying out in the open."

"You're right." Grabbing her towel and book, she rose to her feet. "You never know who might be hanging around out here. Thieves. Murderers." Tossing the towel smartly over her shoulder, she turned and walked away. "Maybe even a lawyer or two."

"I have to talk to you, Kate."

"I have a lawyer. Why don't you talk to him?"

"It's about the O'Brien case—"

"Save it for the courtroom," she snapped over her shoulder. She stalked away, leaving him standing alone on the beach.

"I may not be seeing you in the courtroom," he yelled.

"What a pity."

He caught up to her as she reached the cottage, and was right on her heels as she skipped up the steps. She let the screen door swing shut in his face.

"Did you hear what I said?" he shouted from the porch.

In the middle of the kitchen she halted, suddenly struck by the implication of his words. Slowly she turned and stared at him through the screen. He'd planted his hands on either side of the doorframe and was watching her intently. "I may not be in court," he said.

"What does that mean?"

"I'm thinking of dropping out."

"Why?"

"Let me in and I'll tell you."

Still staring at him, she pushed the screen door open. "Come inside, Mr. Ransom. I think it's time we talked."

Silently he followed her into the kitchen and stood by the breakfast table, watching her. The fact that she was barefoot only emphasized the difference in their heights. She'd forgotten how tall he was, and how lanky, with legs that seemed to stretch out forever. She'd never seen him out of a suit before. She decided she definitely liked him better in blue jeans. All at once she was acutely aware of her own state of undress. It was unsettling, the way his gaze followed her around the kitchen. Unsettling, and at the same time, undeniably exciting. The way lighting a match next to a powder keg was exciting. Was David Ransom just as explosive?

She swallowed nervously. "I—I have to dress. Excuse me."

She fled into the bedroom and grabbed the first clean dress within reach, a flimsy white import from India. She almost ripped it in her haste to pull it on. Pausing by the door, she forced herself to count to ten but found her hands were still unsteady.

When she finally ventured back into the kitchen, she found him still standing by the table, idly thumbing through her book.

"A war novel," she explained. "It's not very good. But it kills the time. Which I seem to have a lot of these days." She waved vaguely toward a chair. "Sit down, Mr. Ransom. I—I'll make some coffee." It took all her concentration just to fill the kettle and set it on the stove. She found she was having trouble with even the simplest task. First she knocked the box of paper filters into the sink. Then she managed to dump coffee grounds all over the counter.

"Let me take care of that," he said, gently nudging her aside.

She watched, voiceless, as he wiped up the spilled coffee. Her awareness of his body, of its closeness, its strength, was suddenly overwhelming. Just as overwhelming was the unexpected wave of sexual longing. On unsteady legs, she moved to the table and sank into a chair.

"By the way," he asked over his shoulder, "can we cut out the 'Mr. Ransom' bit? My name's David."

"Oh. Yes. I know." She winced, hating the breathless sound of her own voice.

He settled into a chair across from her and their eyes met levelly over the kitchen table.

"Yesterday you wanted to hang me," she stated. "What made you change your mind?"

In answer, he pulled a piece of paper out of his shirt pocket. It was a photocopy of a local news article. "That story appeared about two weeks ago in the *Star-Bulletin*."

She frowned at the headline: Honolulu Physician Found Slashed To Death. "What does this have to do with anything?"

"Did you know the victim, Henry Tanaka?"

"He was on our O.B. staff. But I never worked with him."

"Look at the newspaper's description of his wounds."

Kate focused again on the article. "It says he died of wounds to the neck and back."

"Right. Wounds made by a very sharp instrument. The neck was slashed only once, severing the left carotid artery. Very efficient. Very fatal."

Kate tried to swallow and found her throat was parched. "That's how Ann—"

He nodded. "Same method. Identical results."

"How do you know all this?"

"Lt. Ah Ching saw the parallels almost immediately. That's why he slapped a guard on your hospital room. If these murders are connected, there's something systematic about all this, something rational—"

"*Rational?* The killing of a doctor? A nurse? If anything, it sounds more like the work of a psychotic!"

"It's a strange thing, murder. Sometimes it has no rhyme or reason to it. Sometimes the act makes perfect sense."

"There's no such thing as a *sensible* reason to kill someone!"

"It's done every day, by supposedly sane people. And all for the most mundane of reasons. Money. Power." He paused. "Then again," he said softly, "there's the crime of passion. It seems Henry Tanaka was having an affair with one of the nurses."

"Lots of doctors have affairs."

"So do lots of nurses."

"Which nurse are we talking about?"

"I was hoping you could tell me."

"I'm sorry, but I'm not up on the latest hospital gossip."

"Even if it involves your patients?"

"You mean Ellen? I—I wouldn't know. I don't usually delve into my patients' personal lives. Not unless it's relevant to their health."

"Ellen's personal life may have been very relevant to her health."

"Well, she was a beautiful woman. I'm sure there were . . . men in her life." Kate's gaze fell once again to the article. "What does this have to do with Ann Richter?"

"Maybe nothing. Maybe everything. In the last two weeks, three people on Mid Pac's staff have died. Two were murdered. One had an unexpected cardiac arrest on the operating table. Coincidence?"

"It's a big hospital. A big staff."

"But those three particular people knew each other. They even worked together."

"But Ann was a surgical nurse—"

"Who used to work in obstetrics."

"What?"

"Eight years ago, Ann Richter went through a very messy divorce. She ended up with a mile-high stack of credit-card bills. She needed extra cash, fast. So she did some moonlighting as an O.B. nurse. The night shift. That's the same shift Ellen O'Brien worked. They knew each other, all right. Tanaka, Richter, O'Brien. And now they're all dead.''

The scream of the boiling kettle tore through the silence but she was too numb to move. David rose and took the kettle off the stove. She heard him set out the cups and pour the water. The smell of coffee wafted into her awareness.

"It's strange," she remarked. "I saw Ann almost every day in that O.R. We'd talk about books we'd read or movies we'd seen. But we never really talked about *ourselves*. And she was always so private. Almost unapproachable."

"How did she react to Ellen's death?"

Kate was silent for a moment, remembering how, when everything had gone wrong, when Ellen's life had hung in the balance, Ann had stood white-faced and frozen. "She seemed...paralyzed. But we were all upset. Afterward she went home sick. She didn't come back to work. That was the last time I saw her. Alive, I mean...." She looked down, dazed, as he slid a cup of coffee in front of her.

"You said it before. She must have known something. Something dangerous. Maybe they all did."

"But, David, they were just ordinary people who worked in a hospital—"

"All kinds of things can go on in hospitals. Narcotics theft. Insurance fraud. Illicit love affairs. Maybe even murder."

"If Ann knew something dangerous, why didn't she go to the police?"

"Maybe she couldn't. Maybe she was afraid of self-incrimination. Or she was protecting someone else."

A deadly secret, Kate thought. Had all three victims shared it? Softly she ventured, "Then you think Ellen was murdered."

"That's why I'm here. I want you to tell *me*."

She shook her head in bewilderment. "How can I?"

"You have the medical expertise. You were there in the O.R. when it happened. How could it be done?"

"I've already gone over it a thousand times—"

"Then do it again. Come on, Kate, *think*. Convince me it was murder. Convince me I *should* drop out of this case."

His blunt command seemed to leave her no alternative. She felt his eyes goading her to recall every detail, every event leading up to those frantic moments in the O.R. She remembered how everything had gone so smoothly, the induction of anesthesia, the placement of the endotracheal tube. She'd double-checked the tanks and the lines; she knew the oxygen had been properly hooked up.

"Well?" he prodded.

"I can't think of anything."

"Yes, you can."

"It was a completely routine case!"

"What about the surgery itself?"

"Faultless. Guy's the best surgeon on the staff. Anyway, he'd just started the operation. He was barely through the muscle layer when—" She stopped.

"When what?"

"He—he complained about the abdominal muscles being too tight. He was having trouble retracting them."

"So?"

"So I injected a dose of succinylcholine."

"That's pretty routine, isn't it?"

She nodded. "I give it all the time. But in Ellen, it didn't seem to work. I had to draw up a second dose. I remember asking Ann to fetch me another vial."

"You had only one vial?"

"I usually keep a few in my cart. But that morning there was only one in the drawer."

"What happened after you gave the second dose of succinylcholine?"

"A few seconds went by. Maybe it was ten. Fifteen. And then—" Slowly she looked up at him. "Her heart stopped."

They stared at each other. Through the window, the last light of day slanted in, knifelike, across the kitchen. He leaned forward, his eyes hard on hers. "If you could prove it—"

"But I can't! That empty vial went straight to the incinerator, with all the rest of the trash. And there's not even a body left to autopsy." She looked away, miserable. "Oh, he was smart, David. Whoever the killer was, he knew exactly what he was doing."

"Maybe he's too smart for his own good."

"What do you mean?"

"He's obviously sophisticated. He knew exactly which drugs you'd be likely to give in the O.R. And he managed to slip something deadly into one of those vials. Who has access to the anesthesia carts?"

"They're left in the operating rooms. I suppose anyone on the hospital staff could get to them. Doctors. Nurses. Maybe even the janitors. But there were always people around."

"What about nights? Weekends?"

"If there's no surgery scheduled, I guess they just close the suite down. But there's always a surgical nurse on duty for emergencies."

"Does she stay in the O.R. area?"

She shrugged helplessly. "I'm only there if we have a case. I have no idea what happens on a quiet night."

"If the suite's left unguarded, then anyone on the staff could've slipped in."

"It's not someone on the staff. I *saw* the killer, David! That man in Ann's apartment was a stranger."

"Who could have an associate. Someone in the hospital. Maybe even someone you know."

"A conspiracy?"

"Look at the systematic way these murders are being carried out. As if our killer—or killers—has some sort of list. My question is: Who's next?"

The clatter of her cup dropping against the saucer made Kate jump. Glancing down, she saw that her hands were shaking. *I saw his face,* she thought. *If he has a list, then my name's on it.*

The afternoon had slid into dusk. Agitated, she rose and paced to the open doorway. There she stood, staring out at the sea. The wind, so steady just moments before, had died. There was a stillness in the air, as if evening were holding its breath.

"He's out there," she whispered. "Looking for me. And I don't even know his name." The touch of David's hand on her shoulder made her tremble. He was standing behind her, so close she could feel his breath in her hair. "I keep seeing his eyes, staring at me in the mirror. Black and sunken. Like one of those posters of starving children . . ."

"He can't hurt you, Kate. Not here." David's breath seared her neck. A shudder ran through her body—not one of fear but of arousal. Even without looking at him, she could sense his need, simmering to the surface.

Suddenly it was more than his breath scorching her flesh; it was his lips. His face burrowed through the thick strands of her hair to press hungrily against her neck. His fingers gripped her shoulders, as if he was afraid she'd pull away. But she didn't. She couldn't. Her whole body was aching for him.

His lips left a warm, moist trail as they glided to her shoulder, and then she felt the rasp of his jaw.

He swung her around to face him. The instant she turned, his mouth was on hers.

She felt herself falling under the force of his kiss, falling into some deep and bottomless well, until her back suddenly collided with the kitchen wall. With the whole hard length of his body he pinned her there, belly against belly, thigh against thigh. Her lips parted and his tongue raged in, claiming her mouth as his. There was no doubt in her mind he intended to claim the rest of her, as well.

The match had been struck; the powder keg was about to explode, and her with it. She willingly flung herself into the conflagration.

No words were spoken; there were only the low, aching moans of need. They were both breathing so hard, so fast, that her ears were filled with the sound. She scarcely heard the telephone ringing. Only when it had rung again and again did her feverish brain finally register what it was.

It took all her willpower to swim against the flood of desire. She struggled to pull away. "The—the telephone—"

"Let it ring." His mouth slid down to her throat.

But the sound continued, grating and relentless, nagging her with its sense of urgency.

"David. Please . . ."

Groaning, he wrenched away and she saw the astonishment in his eyes. For a moment they stared at each other, neither of them able to believe what had just happened between them. The phone rang again. Jarred to her senses at last, she forced herself across the kitchen and picked up the reciever. Clearing her throat, she managed a hoarse "Hello?"

She was so dazed it took her a few seconds to register the silence on the line. "Hello?" she repeated.

"Dr. Chesne?" a voice whispered, barely audible.

"Yes?"

"Are you alone?"

"No, I— Who is this?" Her voice suddenly froze as the first fingers of terror gripped her throat.

There was a pause, so long and empty she could hear her own heart pounding in her ears. *"Hello?"* she screamed. *"Who is this?"*

"Be careful, Kate Chesne. For death is all around us."

Chapter Seven

The receiver slipped from her grasp and clattered on the linoleum floor. She reeled back in terror against the counter. "It's him," she whispered. Then, in a voice tinged with hysteria she cried out: *"It's him!"*

David instantly scrabbled on the floor for the receiver. "Who is this? Hello? *Hello?*" Cursing, he slammed the receiver back in the cradle and turned to her. "What did he say? Kate!" He took her by the shoulders and gave her a shake. "What did he say?"

"He—he said to be careful—that death was all around...."

"Where's your suitcase?" he snapped.

"What?"

"Your suitcase!"

"In—in the bedroom closet."

He stalked into the bedroom. Automatically she followed him and watched as he dragged her Samsonite down from the shelf. "Get your things together. You can't stay here."

She didn't ask where they were going. She only knew that she had to escape; that every minute she remained in this place just added to the danger.

Suddenly driven by the need to get away, she began to pack. By the time they were ready to leave, her compulsion to escape was so strong she practically flew down the porch steps to his car.

As he thrust the key in the ignition, she was seized by a wild terror that the car wouldn't start; that like some unfortunate victim in a horror movie, she would be stranded here, doomed to meet her death.

But at the first turn of the key, the engine started. The iron-wood trees lunged at them as David sent the BMW wheeling around. Branches slashed the windshield. She felt another stab of panic as their tires spun uselessly in the sand. Then the car leaped free. The headlights trembled as they bounced up the dirt lane.

"How did he find me?" she sobbed.

"That's what I'm wondering." David hit the gas pedal as the car swung onto paved road. The BMW responded instantly with a burst of power that sent them hurtling down the highway.

"No one knew I was here. Only the police."

"Then there's been a leak of information. Or—" he shot a quick look at the rearview mirror "—you were followed."

"Followed?" She whipped her head around but saw only a deserted highway, shimmering under the dim glow of street lamps.

"Who took you to the cottage?" he asked.

She turned and focused on his profile, gleaming faintly in the darkness. "My—my friend Susan drove me."

"Did you stop at your house?"

"No. We went straight to the cottage."

"What about your clothes? How'd you get them?"

"My landlady packed a suitcase and brought it to the hospital."

"He might have been watching the lobby entrance. Waiting for you to be discharged."

"But we didn't see anyone follow us."

"Of course you didn't. People almost never do. We normally focus our attention on what's ahead, on where we're going. As for your phone number, he could've looked it up in the book. The Santinis have their name on the mailbox."

"But it doesn't make sense," she cried. "If he wants to kill me, why not just do it and get it over with? Why threaten me with phone calls?"

"Who knows how he thinks? Maybe he gets a thrill out of scaring his victims. Maybe he just wants to keep you from co-operating with the police."

"I was alone. He could have done it right there...on the beach...." She tried desperately not to think of what could have happened, but she couldn't shut out the image of her own blood seeping into the sand.

High on the hillside, the lights of houses flashed by, each one an unreachable haven of safety. In all that darkness, was there a haven for her? She huddled against the car seat, wishing she never had to leave this small cocoon of safety.

Closing her eyes, she forced herself to concentrate on the hum of the engine, on the rhythm of the highway passing beneath their wheels—anything to banish the bloodstained image. BMW. The ultimate driving machine, she thought inanely. Wasn't that what the ads said? High-tech German engineering. Cool, crisp performance. Just the kind of car she'd expect David to own.

"...and there's plenty of room. So you can stay as long as you need to."

"What?" Bewildered, she turned and looked at him. His profile was a hard, clean shadow against the passing street-lights.

"I said you can stay as long as you need to. It's not the Ritz, but it'll be safer than a hotel."

She shook her head. "I don't understand. Where are we going?"

He glanced at her and the tone of his voice was strangely unemotional. "My house."

"HOME," SAID DAVID, pushing open the front door. It was dark inside. Through the huge living-room windows, moon-light spilled in, faintly illuminating a polished wood floor, the dark and hulking silhouettes of furniture. David guided her to a couch and gently sat her down. Then, sensing her desperate need for light, for warmth, he quickly walked around the room, turning on all the lamps. She was vaguely aware of the muted clink of a bottle, the sound of something being poured. Then he returned and put a glass in her hand.

"Drink it," he said.

"What—what is it?"

"Whiskey. Go on. I think you could use a stiff one."

She took a deep and automatic gulp; the fiery sting instantly brought tears to her eyes. "Wonderful stuff." She coughed.

"Yeah. Isn't it?" He turned to leave the room and she felt a sudden, irrational burst of panic that he was abandoning her.

"David?" she called.

He immediately sensed the terror in her voice. Turning back, he spoke quietly: "It's all right, Kate. I won't leave you. I'll be right next door, in the kitchen." He smiled and touched her face. "Finish that drink."

Fearfully she watched him vanish through the doorway. Then she heard his voice, talking to someone on the phone. The police. As if there was anything they could do now. Clutching the glass in both hands, she forced down another sip of whiskey. The room seemed to swim as her eyes flooded with tears. She blinked them away and slowly focused on her surroundings.

It was, somehow, every inch a man's house. The furniture was plain and practical, the oak floor unadorned by even a single throw rug. Huge windows were framed by stark white curtains and she could hear, just outside, waves crashing against the seawall. Nature's violence, so close, so frightening.

But not nearly as frightening as the violence of man.

AFTER DAVID HUNG UP, he paused in the kitchen, trying to scrape together some semblance of composure. The woman was already frightened enough; seeing his agitation would only make things worse. He quickly ran his fingers through his ruffled hair. Then, taking a deep breath, he pushed open the kitchen door and walked back into the living room.

She was still huddled pitifully on the couch, her hands clenched around the half-empty glass of whiskey. At least a trace of color had returned to her face, but it was barely enough to remind him of a frost-covered rose petal. A little more whiskey was what she needed. He took the glass, filled it to the brim and placed it back in her hands. Her skin was icy. She looked so stunned, so vulnerable. If he could just take her hands in his, if he could warm her in his arms, maybe he could coax some life back into those frozen limbs. But he was afraid to give in to the impulse; he knew it could lead to far more compelling urges.

He turned and poured himself a tall one. What she needed from him right now was protection. Reassurance. She needed to know that she would be taken care of and that things were still right with the world, though the truth of the matter was, her world had just gone to hell in a hand basket.

He took a deep gulp of whiskey, then set it down. What she really needed was a sober host.

"I've called the police," he said over his shoulder.

Her response was almost toneless. "What did they say?"

He shrugged. "What could they say? Stay where you are. Don't go out alone." Frowning at his glass, he thought, What the hell, and recklessly downed the rest of the whiskey. Bottle in hand, he returned to the couch and set the whiskey down on the coffee table. They were sitting only a few feet apart but it felt like miles of emptiness between them.

She stirred and looked toward the kitchen. "My—my friends—they won't know where I am. I should call them."

"Don't worry about it. Pokie'll let them know you're safe." He watched her sink back listlessly on the couch. "You should eat something," he said.

"I'm not hungry."

"My housekeeper makes great spaghetti sauce."

She lifted one shoulder—only one, as if she hadn't the energy for a full-blown shrug.

"Yep," he continued with sudden enthusiasm. "Once a week Mrs. Feldman takes pity on a poor starving bachelor and she leaves me a pot of sauce. It's loaded with garlic. Fresh basil. Plus a healthy slug of wine."

There was no response.

"Every woman I've ever served it to swears it's a powerful aphrodisiac."

At last there was a smile, albeit a very small one. "How helpful of Mrs. Feldman," she remarked.

"She thinks I'm not eating right. Though I don't know why. Maybe it's all those frozen-dinner trays she finds in my trash can."

There was another smile. If he kept this up, he just might coax a laugh out of her by next week. Too bad he was such a lousy comedian. Anyway, the situation was too damned grim for jokes.

The clock on the bookshelf ticked loudly—a nagging reminder of how much silence had passed between them. Kate suddenly stiffened as a gust rattled the windows.

"It's just the wind," he said. "You'll get used to it. Sometimes, in a storm, the whole house shudders and it feels like the roof will blow off." He gazed up affectionately at the beams. "It's thirty years old. Probably should have been torn down years ago. But when we bought it, all we could see were the possibilities."

"We?" she asked dully.

"I was married then."

"Oh." She stirred a little, as though trying to show some semblance of interest. "You're divorced."

He nodded. "We lasted a little over seven years—not bad, in this day and age." He gave a short, joyless laugh. "Contrary to the old cliché, it wasn't an itch that finished us. It was more like a . . . fading out. But—" he sighed "—Linda and I are still friendly. Which is more than most divorced couples can say. I even like her new husband. Great guy. Very devoted, caring. Something I guess I wasn't. . . ." He looked away, uncomfortable. He hated talking about himself. It made him feel exposed. But at least all this small talk was doing the trick. It was bringing her back to life, nudging the fear from her mind. "Linda's in Portland now," he went on quickly. "I hear they've got a baby on the way."

"You didn't have any children?" It was a perfectly natural question. He wished she hadn't asked it.

He nodded shortly. "A son."

"Oh. How old is he?"

"He's dead." How flat his voice sounded. As if Noah's death were as casual a topic as the weather. He could already see the questions forming on her lips. And the words of sympathy. That was the last thing he wanted from her. He'd heard enough well-meaning words of sympathy to last him the rest of his life.

"So anyway," he said, shifting the subject, "I'm what you'd call a born-again bachelor. But I like it this way. Some men just aren't meant to be married, I guess. And it's great for my career. Nothing to distract me from the practice, which seems to be going big guns these days."

Damn. She was still looking at him with those questions in her eyes. He headed them off with another change of topic.

"What about you?" he asked quickly. "Were you ever married?"

"No." She looked down, as if contemplating the benefits of another slug of whiskey. "I lived with a man for a while. In fact, he's the reason I came to Honolulu. To be near him." She gave a bitter laugh. "Guess that'll teach me."

"What?"

"Not to go chasing after some stupid man."

"Sounds like a nasty breakup."

She hiccuped. "It was very . . . civil, actually. I'm not saying it didn't hurt. Because it did." Shrugging, she surrendered to another gulp of whiskey. "It's hard, you know. Trying to be everything at once. I guess I couldn't give him what he needed: dinner waiting on the table, my undivided attention."

"Is that what he expected?"

"Isn't that what every man expects?" she snorted angrily. "Well, I didn't need all that—that male crap. I had a job that required me to jump at every phone call. Rush in for every emergency. He didn't understand."

"Was it worth it?"

"Was what worth it?"

"Sacrificing your love life for your career?"

She didn't answer for a while. Then her head drooped. "I used to think so," she said quietly. "Now I think of all those hours I put in. All those ruined weekends. I thought I was indispensable to the hospital. And then I find out I'm just as dispensable as anyone else. All it took was a lawsuit. Hell of an eye-opener." She tipped her glass at him bitterly. "Thanks for the revelation, counselor."

"Why blame me? I was just hired to do a job."

"For a nice fat fee, I imagine."

"I took the case on contingency. I won't be seeing a cent."

"You gave up all that money? Just because you think I'm telling the truth?" She shook her head in amazement. "I'm surprised the truth means so much to you."

"You have a nice way of making me sound like scum. But yes, the truth does matter to me. A great deal, in fact."

"A lawyer with principles? I didn't know there was such a thing."

"We're a recognized subspecies." His gaze inadvertently slid to the neckline of her gauze dress. The memory of how that silky skin had felt under his exploring fingers suddenly hit him with such force that he quickly turned and reached for the whiskey. There was no glass handy so he took a swig straight from the bottle. *Right,* he thought. *Get yourself drunk. See how many stupid things you can say before morning.*

Actually, they were both getting thoroughly soused. But he figured she needed it. Twenty minutes ago she'd been in a state of shock. Now, at least, she was talking. In fact she'd just managed to insult him. That had to be a good sign.

She gazed fervently into her glass. "God, I hate whiskey!" she said with sudden passion and gulped down the rest of the drink.

"I can tell. Have some more."

She eyed him suspiciously. "I think you're trying to get me drunk."

"Whatever gave you that idea?" He laughed, shoving the bottle toward her.

She regarded it for a moment. Then, with a look of utter disgust, she refilled her glass. "Good old Jack Daniel's," she sighed. Her hand was unsteady as she recapped the bottle. "What a laugh."

"What's so funny?"

"It was Dad's favorite brand. He used to swear this stuff was medicinal. Absolutely *hated* all my hair-of-the-dog lectures. Boy, would he get a kick out of seeing me now." She took a swallow and winced. "Maybe he's right. Anything that tastes this awful *has* to be medicinal."

"I take it your father wasn't a doctor."

"He wanted to be." She stared down moodily at her drink. "Yeah, that was his dream. He planned on being a country doctor. You know, the kind of guy who'd deliver a baby in exchange for a few dozen eggs. But I guess things didn't work out. I came along and then they needed money and..." She sighed. "He had a repair shop in Sacramento. Oh, he was handy! I used to watch him putter around in that basement. Dad could fix anything you put in his hands. TVs. Washing machines. He even held seventeen patents, none of them worth a damn cent. Except maybe the Handy Dandy apple slicer." She glanced at him hopefully. "Ever heard of it?"

"Sorry. No."

She shrugged. "Neither has anyone else."

"What does it do, exactly?"

"One flick of the wrist and whack! Six perfect slices." At his silence she gave him a rueful smile. "I can see you're terribly impressed."

"But I am. I'm impressed that your father managed to invent you. He must've been happy you became a doctor."

"He was. When I graduated from med school, he told me it was the very best day of his life." She stopped, her smile suddenly fading. "I think that's sad, don't you? That out of all the years of his life, that was the one single day he was happiest...." She cleared her throat. "After he died, Mom sold the shop. She got married to some high-powered banker in San Francisco. What a snooty guy. We can't stand each other." She looked down at her glass and her voice dropped. "I still think about that shop sometimes. I miss the old basement. I miss all those dumb, useless gadgets of his. I miss—"

He saw her lower lip tremble and he thought with sudden panic: *Oh, no. Now she's going to cry.* He could deal with sobbing clients. He knew exactly how to respond to their tears. Pull out the box of Kleenex. Pat them on the back. Tell them he'd do everything he could.

But this was different. This wasn't his office but his living room. And the woman on the verge of tears wasn't a client but someone he happened to like very much.

Just as he thought the dam would burst, she managed to drag herself together. He saw only the briefest glitter of tears in her eyes, then she blinked and they were gone. Thank God. If she started bawling now, he'd be utterly useless.

He took her glass and deliberately set it down on the table. "I think you've had enough for tonight. Come on, doctor lady. It's time for bed. I'll show you the way." He reached for her hand but she reflexively pulled back. "Something wrong?"

"No. It's just..."

"Don't tell me you're worried about how it looks? Your staying here, I mean."

"A little. Not much, actually. I mean, not under the circumstances." She gave an awkward laugh. "Fear does strange things to one's sense of propriety."

"Not to mention one's sense of legal ethics." At her puzzled look, he said, "I've never done this before."

"What? Brought a woman home for the night?"

"Well, I haven't done *that* in a while, either. What I meant was, I make it a point never to get involved with any of my clients. And certainly never with the opposition."

"Then I'm the exception?"

"Yes. You are definitely the exception. Believe it or not, I don't normally paw every female who walks into my office."

"Which ones do you paw?" she asked, a faint smile suddenly tracing her lips.

He moved toward her, drawn by invisible threads of desire. "Only the green-eyed ones," he murmured. Gently he touched her cheek. "Who happen to have a bruise here and there."

"That last part sounds suspiciously kinky," she whispered.

"No, it's not." The intimate tone of his voice made Kate suddenly fall very still. His finger left a scorching trail as it stroked down her face.

She knew the danger of this moment. This was the man who'd once vowed to ruin her. He could still ruin her. *Consorting with the enemy,* she thought in sudden panic as his face drew closer. But she couldn't seem to move. A sense of unreality swept over her; a feeling that none of this could be happening, that it was only some hot, drunken fantasy. Here she was, sharing a couch with the very man she'd once despised, and all she could think of was how much she wanted him to haul her into his arms and kiss her.

His lips were gentle. It was no more than a brushing of mouths, a cautious savoring of what they both knew might follow, but it was enough to touch off a thousand flames inside her. Jack Daniel's had never tasted so good!

"And what will the bar association say to that?" she murmured.

"They'll call it outrageous. . . ."

"Unethical."

"And absolutely insane. Which it is." Drawing away, he studied her for a moment; and his struggle for control showed plainly in his face. To her disappointment, common sense won out. He rose from the couch and tugged her to her feet. "When you file your complaint with the state bar, don't forget to mention how apologetic I was."

"Will it make a difference?"

"Not to them. But I hope it does to you."

They stood before the window, staring at each other. The wind lashed the panes, a sound as relentless as the pounding of her own heartbeat in her ears.

"I think it's time to go to bed," he said hoarsely.

"What?"

He cleared his throat. "I mean it's time you went to your bed. And I went to mine."

"Oh."

"Unless . . ."

"Unless?"

"You don't want to."

"Want to what?"

"Go to bed."

They looked at each other uneasily. She swallowed. "I think maybe I'd better."

"Yeah." He turned away and agitatedly plowed his fingers through his hair. "I think so, too."

"David?"

He glanced over his shoulder. "Yes?"

"Is it really a violation of legal ethics? Letting me stay here?"

"Under the circumstances?" He shrugged. "I think I'm still on safe ground. Barely. As long as nothing happens between us." He scooped up the whiskey bottle. Matter-of-factly he slid it into the liquor cabinet and shut the door. "And nothing will."

"Of course not," she responded quickly. "I mean, I don't need that kind of complication in my life. Certainly not now."

"Neither do I. But for the moment, we seem to need each other. So I'll provide you with a safe place to stay. And you can help me figure out what really happened in that O.R. A convenient arrangement. I ask only one thing."

"What's that?"

"We keep this discreet. Not just now but also after you leave. This sort of thing can only hurt both our reputations."

"I understand. Perfectly."

They both took a simultaneous breath.

"So... I think I'll say good-night," she said. Turning, she started across the living room. Her whole body felt like rubber. She only prayed she wouldn't fall flat on her face.

"Kate?"

Her heart did a quick somersault as she spun around to face him. "Yes?"

"Your room's the second door on the right."

"Oh. Thanks." Her flip-flopping heart seemed to sink like a stone as she left him standing there in the living room. Her only consolation was that he looked every bit as miserable as she felt.

LONG AFTER KATE had gone to her room, David sat in the living room, thinking. Remembering how she had tasted, how she had trembled in his arms. And wondering how he'd gotten himself into this mess. It was bad enough, letting the woman sleep under his roof, but to practically seduce her on his couch—that was sheer stupidity. Though he'd wanted to. God, how he'd wanted to.

He could tell by the way she'd melted against him that she hadn't been kissed in a very long time. Terrific. Here they were, two normal, healthy, *deprived* adults, sleeping within ten feet of each other. You couldn't ask for a more explosive situation.

He didn't want to think about what his old ethics professor would say to this. Strictly speaking, he couldn't consider himself off the O'Brien case yet. Until he actually handed the file over to another firm, he still had to behave as their attorney and was bound by legal ethics to protect their interests. To think how scrupulous he'd always been about separating his personal from his professional life!

If he'd had his head screwed on straight, he would have avoided the whole mess by taking Kate to a hotel or a friend's house. Anywhere but here. The problem was, he'd been having trouble thinking straight since the day he met her. Tonight, after that phone call, he'd had only one thought in mind: to keep her safe and warm and protected. It was a fiercely primitive instinct over which he had no control; and he resented it. He also resented her for stirring up all these inconvenient male responses.

Annoyed at himself, he rose from the couch and circled the living room, turning off lights. He decided he wasn't interested in being any woman's white knight. Besides, Kate Chesne wasn't the kind of woman who needed a hero. Or any man, for that matter. Not that he didn't like independent women. He did like them.

He also liked *her*. A lot.

Maybe too much.

KATE LAY CURLED UP in bed, listening to David's restless pacing in the living room. She held her breath as his footsteps creaked up the hall past her door. Was it her imagination or did he pause there for a moment before continuing on to the next room? She could hear him moving around, opening and closing drawers, rattling hangers in the closet. *My God*, she thought. *He's sleeping right next door.*

Now the shower was running. She wondered if it was a cold shower. She tried not to think about what he'd look like, standing under the stream of water, but the image had already formed in her head, the soapsuds sliding down his shoulders, the gold hairs matted and damp on his chest.

Now stop it. Right now.

She bit her lip—bit it so hard the image wavered a little. Damn. So this was lust, pure and unadulterated. Well, maybe slightly adulterated—by whiskey. Here she was, thirty years old, and she'd never wanted any man so badly. She wanted him on a level that was raw and wild and elemental.

She'd certainly never felt this way about Eric. Her relationship with Eric had been excruciatingly civilized; nothing as primitive as this—this animal heat. Even their parting had been civilized. They'd discussed their differences, decided they were irreconcilable, and had gone their separate ways. At the time she'd thought it devastating, but now she realized what had been hurt most by the breakup was her pride. All these months, she'd nursed the faint hope that Eric would come back to her. Now she could barely conjure up a picture of his face. It kept blurring into the image of a man in a shower.

She buried her head in the pillow, an act that made her feel about as brilliant as an ostrich. And she was supposed to be so bright, so levelheaded. Why, it was even official, having been stated in her performance evaluation as a resident: *Dr. Chesne is a superbly competent, levelheaded physician.* Ha! Levelheaded? Try dim-witted. Besotted. Or just plain dumb—for lusting after the man who'd once threatened to ruin her in court.

She had so many important things to worry about; matters, literally, of life and death. She was losing her job. Her career was on the skids. A killer was searching for her.

And she was wondering how much hair David Ransom had on his chest.

SHE WAS RUNNING down hundreds of steps, plunging deeper and deeper into a pit of darkness. She didn't know what lay at the end; all she knew was that something was right behind her, something terrible; she didn't dare look back to see its face. There were no doors, no windows, no other avenue of escape. Her flight was noiseless, like the flickering reel of a movie with no sound. In this silence lay the worst terror of all: no one would hear her scream.

With a sob, Kate wrenched herself awake and found herself staring up wildly at an unfamiliar ceiling. Somewhere a telephone was ringing. Daylight glowed in the window and she heard waves lapping the seawall. The ringing telephone suddenly stopped; David's voice murmured in another room.

I'm safe, she told herself. *No one can hurt me. Not here. Not in this house.*

The knock on the door made her sit up sharply.

"Kate?" David called through the closed door.

"Yes?"

"You'd better get dressed. Pokie wants us down at the station."

"Right now?"

"Right now."

It was his low tone of urgency that alarmed her. She scrambled out of bed and opened the door. "Why? What is it?"

His gaze slid briefly to her nightgown, then focused, utterly neutral, on her face. "The killer. They know his name."

Chapter Eight

Pokie slid the book of mug shots toward Kate. "See anyone you know, Dr. Chesne?"

Kate scanned the photographs and immediately focused on one face. It was a cruel portrait; every wrinkle, every hollow had been brought into harsh clarity by the camera lights. Yet the man didn't squint. He gazed straight ahead with wide eyes. It was the look of a lost soul. Softly she said, "That's him."

"You positive?"

"I—I remember his eyes." Swallowing hard, she turned away. Both men were watching her intently. They were probably worried she'd faint or get hysterical or do something equally ridiculous. But she wasn't feeling much of anything. It was as if she were detached from her body and were floating somewhere near the ceiling, watching a stock scene from a police procedural: the witness unerringly pointing out the face of the killer.

"That's our man," Pokie said with grim satisfaction.

A wan sergeant in plainclothes brought her a cup of hot coffee. He seemed to have a cold; he was sniffling. Through the glass partition, she saw him return to his desk and take out a bottle of nose spray.

Her gaze returned to the photo. "Who is he?" she asked.

"A nut case," replied Pokie. "The name's Charles Decker. That photo was taken five years ago, right after his arrest."

"On what charge?"

"Assault and battery. He kicked down the door of a medical office. Tried to strangle the doctor right there in front of the whole staff."

"A doctor?" David's head came up. "Which one?"

Pokie sat back, his weight eliciting a squeal of protest from the old chair. "Guess."

"Henry Tanaka."

Pokie's answer was a satisfied display of nicotine-stained teeth. "One and the same. It took us a while, but the name finally popped up on a computer search."

"Arrest records?"

"Yeah. We should've picked it up earlier, but it kind of slipped by during the initial investigation. See, we asked Mrs. Tanaka if her husband had any enemies. You know, routine question. She gave us some names. We followed up on 'em but they all came up clean. Then she mentioned that five years back, some nut had attacked her husband. She didn't remember his name and as far as she knew, the man was still in the state hospital. We went to the files and finally pulled out an arrest report. It was Charlie Decker's. And this morning I got word from the lab. Remember that set of fingerprints on the Richter woman's doorknob?"

"Charlie Decker's?"

Pokie nodded. "And now—" he glanced at Kate "—our witness gives us a positive ID. I'd say we got our man."

"What was his motive?"

"I told you. He's crazy."

"So are thousands of other people. Why did this one turn killer?"

"Hey, I'm not the guy's shrink."

"But you have an answer, don't you?"

Pokie shrugged. "All I got is a theory."

"That man threatened my life, Lieutenant," said Kate. "I think I have the right to know more than just his name."

"She does, Pokie," agreed David quietly. "You won't find it in any of your police manuals. But I think she has the right to know who this Charles Decker is."

Sighing, Pokie fished a spiral notebook out of his desk. "Okay," he grunted, flipping through the pages. "Here's what

I got so far. Understand, it's still gotta be confirmed. Decker, Charles Louis, white male born Cleveland thirty-nine years ago. Parents divorced. Brother killed in a gang fight at age fifteen. Great start. One married sister, living in Florida."

"You talked to her?"

"She's the one who gave us most of this info. Let's see. Joined the navy at twenty-two. Based in various ports. San Diego. Bremerton. Got shipped here to Pearl six years ago. Served as corpsman aboard the USS *Cimarron*—"

"Corpsman?" Kate questioned.

"Assistant to the ship's surgeon. According to his superior officers, Decker was kind of a loner. Pretty much kept to himself. No history of emotional problems." Here he let out a snort. "So much for the accuracy of military files." He flipped to the next page. "Had a decent service record, couple of commendations. Seemed to be moving up the ranks okay. And then, five years ago, it seems something snapped."

"Nervous breakdown?" asked David.

"Lot more than that. He went berserk. And it all had to do with a woman."

"You mean a girlfriend?"

"Yeah. Some gal he'd met here in the Islands. He put in for permission to get married. It was granted. But then he and his ship sailed for six months of classified maneuvers off Subic Bay. Sailor in the next bunk remembers Decker spent every spare minute writing poems for that girlfriend. Must've been nuts about her. Just nuts." Pokie shook his head and sighed. "Anyway, when the *Cimarron* returned to Pearl, the girlfriend wasn't waiting on the pier with all the other honeys. Here's the part where things get a little confused. All we know is Decker jumped ship without permission. Guess it didn't take long for him to find out what'd happened."

"She found another guy?" David guessed.

"No. She was dead."

There was a long silence. In the next office, a telephone was ringing and typewriters clattered incessantly.

Kate asked softly, "What happened to her?"

"Complications of childbirth," explained Pokie. "She had some kind of stroke in the delivery room. The baby girl died, too. Decker never even knew she was pregnant."

Slowly, Kate's gaze fell to the photograph of Charlie Decker. She thought of what he must have gone through, that day in Pearl Harbor. The ship pulling into the crowded dock. The smiling families. *How long did he search for her face?* she wondered. *How long before he realized she wasn't there? That she'd never be there?*

"That's when the man lost it," continued Pokie. "Somehow he found out Tanaka was his girlfriend's doctor. The arrest record says he showed up at the clinic and just about strangled the doctor on the spot. After a scuffle, the police were called. A day later, Decker got out on bail. He went and bought himself a Saturday-night special. But he didn't use it on the doctor. He put the barrel in his own mouth. Pulled the trigger." Pokie closed the notebook.

The ultimate act, thought Kate. *Buy a gun and blow your own head off.* He must have loved that woman. And what better way to prove it than to sacrifice himself on her altar?

But he wasn't dead. He was alive. And he was killing people.

Pokie saw her questioning look. "It was a very cheap gun. It misfired. Turned his mouth into bloody pulp. But he survived. After a few months in a rehab facility, he was transferred to the state hospital. The nuthouse. Their records show he regained function of just about everything but his speech."

"He's mute?" asked David.

"Not exactly. Vocal cords were ripped to shreds during the resuscitation. He can mouth words, but his voice is more like a—a hiss."

A hiss, thought Kate. The memory of that unearthly sound, echoing in Ann's stairwell, seemed to reach out from her worst nightmares. *The sound of a viper about to strike.*

Pokie continued. "About a month ago, Decker was discharged from the state hospital. He was supposed to be seeing some shrink by the name of Nemechek. But Decker never showed up for the first appointment."

"Have you talked to Nemechek?" asked Kate.

"Only on the phone. He's at a conference in L.A. Should be back on Tuesday. Swears up and down that his patient was harmless. But he's covering his butt. Looks pretty bad when the patient you just let out starts slashing throats."

"So that's the motive," said David. "Revenge. For a dead woman."

"That's the theory."

"Why was Ann Richter killed?"

"Remember that blond woman the janitors saw running through the parking lot?"

"You think that was her?"

"It seems she and Tanaka were—how do I put it?—very well acquainted."

"Does that mean what I think it means?"

"Let's just say Ann Richter's neighbors had no trouble recognizing Tanaka's photo. He was seen at her apartment more than once. The night he was killed, I think she went to pay her favorite doctor a little social call. Instead she found something that scared the hell out of her. Maybe she saw Decker. And he saw her."

"Then why didn't she go to the police?" asked Kate.

"Maybe she didn't want the world to know she was having an affair with a married man. Or maybe she was afraid she'd be accused of killing her lover. Who knows?"

"So she was just a witness," said Kate. "Like me."

Pokie looked at her. "There's one big difference between you and her. Decker can't get to *you*. Right now no one outside this office knows where you're staying. Let's keep it that way." He glanced at David. "There's no problem, keeping her at your house?"

David's face was unreadable. "She can stay."

"Good. And it's better if she doesn't use her own car."

"My car?" Kate frowned. "Why not?"

"Decker has your purse. And a set of your car keys. So he knows you drive an Audi. He'll be watching for one."

Watching for me, she thought with a shudder. "For how long?" she whispered.

"What?"

"How long before it's all over? Before I have my life back?"

Pokie sighed. "It might take a while to find him. But hang in there, Doc. The man can't hide forever."

Can't he? wondered Kate. She thought of all the places a man could hide on Oahu: the nooks and crannies of Chinatown where no one ever asks questions. The tin-roofed fishing shacks of Sand Island. The concrete alleys of Waikiki. Somewhere, in some secret place, Charlie Decker was quietly mourning for a dead woman.

They rose to leave and a question suddenly came to her mind. "Lieutenant," she asked. "What about Ellen O'Brien?"

Pokie, who was gathering a pile of papers into a folder, glanced up. "What about her?"

"Does she have some connection to all this?"

Pokie looked down one last time at Charlie Decker's photo. Then he shut the folder. "No," he answered. "No connection at all."

"BUT THERE *HAS* TO BE a connection!" Kate blurted as they walked out of the station into the midmorning heat. "Some piece of evidence he hasn't found—"

"Or won't tell us about," finished David.

She frowned at him. "Why wouldn't he? I thought you two were friends."

"I deserted the trenches, remember?"

"You make police work sound like jungle warfare."

"For some cops, the job *is* a war. A holy war. Pokie's got a wife and four kids. But you'd never know it, looking at all the hours he puts in."

"So you do think he's a good cop?"

David shrugged. "He's a plough horse. Solid but not brilliant. I've seen him screw up on occasion. He could be wrong this time, too. But right now I have to agree with him. I don't see how Ellen O'Brien fits into this case."

"But you heard what he said! Decker was a corpsman. Assistant to the ship's surgeon—"

"Decker's profile doesn't fit the pattern, Kate. A psycho who works like Jack the Ripper doesn't bother with drug vials and EKGs. That takes a totally different kind of mind."

She stared down the street in frustration. "The trouble is, I can't see any way to prove Ellen *was* murdered. I can't even be sure it's possible."

David paused on the sidewalk. "Okay." He sighed. "So we can't prove anything. But let's think about the logistics."

"You mean of murder?"

He nodded. "Let's take a man like Decker. An outsider. Someone who knows a little about medicine. And surgery. Tell me, step by step. How would he go about getting into the hospital and killing a patient?"

"I suppose he'd have to . . . to . . ." Her gaze wandered up the street. She frowned as her eyes focused on a paperboy, waving the morning edition to passing cars. "Today's Sunday," she said suddenly.

"So?"

"Ellen was admitted on a Sunday. I remember being in her room, talking to her. It was eight o'clock on a Sunday night." She glanced feverishly at her watch. "That's in ten hours. We could go through the steps. . . ."

"Wait a minute. You've lost me. What, exactly, are we doing in ten hours?"

She turned to him. Softly she said, "Murder."

THE VISITOR PARKING LOT was nearly empty when David swung his BMW into the hospital driveway at ten o'clock that night. He parked in a stall near the lobby entrance, turned off the engine and looked at Kate. "This won't prove a thing. You know that, don't you?"

"I want to see if it's possible."

"Possibilities don't hold up in court."

"I don't care how it plays in court, David. As long as *I* know it's possible."

She glanced out at the distant red Emergency sign, glowing like a beacon in the darkness. An ambulance was parked at the loading dock. On a nearby bench, the driver sat idly smoking a cigarette and listening to the crackle of his dispatch radio.

A Sunday night, quiet as usual. Visiting hours were over. And in their rooms, patients would already be settling into the blissful sleep of the drugged.

David's face gleamed faintly in the shadows. "Okay." He sighed, shoving open his door. "Let's do it."

The lobby doors were locked. They walked in the E.R. entrance, through a waiting room where a baby screamed in the lap of its glassy-eyed mother, where an old man coughed noisily into a handkerchief and a teenage boy clutched an ice bag to his swollen face. The triage nurse was talking on the telephone; they walked right past her and headed for the elevators.

"We're in, just like that?" David asked.

"The E.R. nurse knows me."

"But she hardly looked at you."

"That's because she was too busy ogling *you*," Kate said dryly.

"Boy, have you got a wild imagination." He paused, glancing around the empty lobby. "Where's Security? Isn't there a guard around?"

"He's probably making rounds."

"You mean there's only one?"

"Hospitals are really pretty boring places, you know," she replied and punched the elevator button. "Besides, it's Sunday."

They rose up to the fourth floor and stepped off into the antiseptic-white corridor. Freshly waxed linoleum gleamed under bright lights. A row of gurneys sat lined up against the wall, as though awaiting a deluge of the wounded. Kate pointed to the double doors marked No Admittance.

"The O.R.'s through there."

"Can we get in?"

She took a few experimental steps forward. The doors automatically slid open. "No problem."

Inside, only a single dim light shone over the reception area. A cup, half filled with lukewarm coffee, sat abandoned on the front desk awaiting its owner's return. Kate pointed to a huge wallboard where the next day's surgery schedule was posted.

"All tomorrow's cases are listed right there," she explained. "One glance will tell you which O.R. the patient will be in, the procedure, the names of the surgeon and anesthesiologist."

"Where was Ellen?"

"The room's right around the corner."

She led him down an unlit hall and opened the door to O.R. 5. Through the shadows they saw the faint gleam of stainless steel. She flicked on the wall switch; the sudden flood of light was almost painful.

"The anesthesia cart's over there."

He went over to the cart and pulled open one of the steel drawers. Tiny glass vials tinkled in their compartments. "Are these drugs always left unlocked?"

"They're worthless on the street. No one would bother to steal any of those. As for the narcotics—" she pointed to a wall cabinet "—we keep them locked in there."

His gaze slowly moved around the room. "So this is where you work. Very impressive. Looks like a set for a sci-fi movie."

She grinned. "Funny. I've always felt right at home in here." She circled the room, affectionately patting the equipment as she moved. "I think it's because I'm the daughter of a tinkerer. Gadgets don't scare me. I actually like playing with all these buttons and dials. But I suppose some people do find it all pretty intimidating."

"And you've never been intimidated?"

She turned and found he was staring at her. Something about his gaze, about the intensity of those blue eyes, made her fall very still. "Not by the O.R.," she said softly.

It was so quiet she could almost hear her own heartbeat thudding in that stark chamber. For a long time they stared at each other, as though separated by some wide, unbreachable chasm. Then, abruptly, he shifted his attention to the anesthesia cart.

"How long would it take to tamper with one of these drug vials?" he asked. She had to admire his control. At least he could still speak; she was having trouble finding her own voice.

"He'd—he'd have to empty out the succinylcholine vials. It would probably take less than a minute."

"As easy as that?"

"As easy as that." Her gaze shifted reluctantly to the operating table. "They're so helpless, our patients. We have absolute control over their lives. I never saw it that way before. It's really rather frightening."

"So murder in the O.R. isn't that difficult."

"No," she conceded. "I guess it isn't."

"What about switching the EKG? How would our killer do that?"

"He'd have to get hold of the patient's chart. And they're all kept on the wards."

"That sounds tricky. The wards are crawling with nurses."

"True. But even in this day and age, nurses are still a little intimidated by a white coat. I bet if we put you in uniform, you'd be able to breeze your way right into the nurses' station, no questions asked."

He cocked his head. "Want to try it?"

"You mean right now?"

"Sure. Find me a white coat. I've always wanted to play doctor."

It took only a minute to locate a stray coat hanging in the surgeons' locker room. She knew it was Guy Santini's, just by the coffee stains on the front. The size 46 label only confirmed it.

"I didn't know King Kong was on your staff," David grunted, thrusting his arms into the huge sleeves. He buttoned up and stood straight. "What do you think? Are they going to fall down laughing?"

Stepping back, she gave him a critical look. The coat sagged on his shoulders. One side of the collar was turned up. But the truth was, he looked absolutely irresistible. And perversely untouchable. She smoothed down his collar. Just that brief contact, that brushing of her fingers against his neck, seemed to flood her whole arm with warmth.

"You'll do," she said.

"I look that bad?" He glanced down at the coffee stains. "I feel like a slob."

She laughed. "The owner of that particular coat *is* a slob. So don't worry about it. You'll fit right in." As they walked to the elevators, she added, "Just remember to think *doctor*. Get into the right mind-set. You know—brilliant, dedicated, compassionate."

"Don't forget *modest*."

She gave him a slap on the back. "Go get'em, Dr. Kildare."

He stepped into the elevator. "Look, don't vanish on me, okay? If they get suspicious, I'll need you to back me up."

"I'll be waiting in the O.R. Oh, David . . . one last bit of advice."

"What's that?"

"Don't commit malpractice, Doctor. You might have to sue yourself."

He let out a groan as the doors snapped shut between them. The elevator whined faintly as it descended to the third floor. Then there was silence.

It was a simple test. Even if David was stopped by Security, it would take only a word from Kate to set him free. Nothing could possibly go wrong. But as she headed up the hallway, her uneasiness grew.

Back in O.R. 5, she settled into her usual seat near the head of the table and thought of all the hours she'd spent anchored to this one spot. A very small world. A very safe world.

The sound of a door slapping shut made her glance up. Why was David back so soon? Had there been trouble? She hopped off the stool and pushed into the corridor. There she halted.

Just down the hall, a faint crack of light shone through the door to O.R. 7. She listened for a moment and heard the rattle of cabinets, the squeal of a drawer sliding open.

Someone was rummaging through the supplies. A nurse? Or someone else—someone who didn't belong?

She glanced toward the far end of the corridor—her only route of escape. The reception desk lay around that corner.

If she could just get safely past O.R. 7, she could slip out and call Security. She had to decide now; whoever was going through O.R. 7 might proceed to the other rooms. If she didn't move now, she'd be trapped.

Noiselessly she headed down the hall. The slam of a cabinet told her she wouldn't make it. O.R. 7's door suddenly swung open. Panicked, she reeled backward to see Dr. Clarence Avery freeze in the doorway. Something slid out of his hand and the sound of shattering glass seemed to reverberate endlessly in the hall. She took one look at his bloodlessly white face, and her fear instantly turned to concern. For a terrifying moment she thought he'd keel over right then and there of a heart attack.

"Dr.—Dr. Chesne," he stammered weakly. "I—I didn't expect— I mean, I..." Slowly he stared down at his feet; that's when she noticed, through the shadows, the sparkle of glass lying on the floor. He shook his head helplessly. "What...what a mess I've made...."

"It's not that bad," she responded quickly. "Here, I'll help you clean it up."

She flicked on the corridor lights. He didn't move. He just stood there, blinking in the sudden glare. She had never seen him look so old, so frail; the white hair seemed to tremble on his head. She grabbed a handful of paper towels from the scrub sink dispenser and offered him a few sheets, but he still didn't move. So she crouched at his feet and began gathering up the broken glass. He was wearing one blue sock and one white sock. As she reached for one of the shards, she noticed a label was still affixed.

"It's for my dog," he said weakly.

"Excuse me?"

"The potassium chloride. It's for my dog. She's very sick."

Kate looked up at him blankly. "I'm sorry" was all she could think of saying.

He lowered his head. "She needs to be put to sleep. All morning, she's been whimpering. I can't stand listening to it anymore. And she's old, you know. Over ninety in dog years. But it—it seems cruel, taking her to the vet for that. A total stranger. It would terrify her."

Kate rose to her feet. Avery just stood there, clutching the paper towels as if not quite sure what to do with them.

"I'm sure the vet would be gentle," she replied. "You don't have to do it yourself."

"But it's so much better if I do, don't you think? If I'm the one to tell her goodbye?"

She nodded. Then she turned to the anesthesia cart and took out a vial of potassium chloride. "Here—" She offered quietly, placing it in his hand. "This should be enough, don't you think?"

He nodded. "She's not a very... big dog." He let out a shaky breath and turned to leave. Then he stopped and looked back at her. "I've always liked you, Kate. You're the only one who never seemed to be laughing behind my back. Or dropping hints that I'm too old, that I ought to retire." He sighed and shook his head. "But maybe they're right, after all." As he turned to leave, she heard him say, "I'll do what I can at your hearing."

His footsteps creaked off into the corridor. As the sound faded away, her gaze settled on the bits of broken glass in the trash can. The label KCL stared up at her. Potassium chloride, she thought with a frown. When pushed intravenously, it was a deadly poison, resulting in sudden cardiac arrest. And it occurred to her that the same poison that would kill a dog could just as easily be used to kill a human being.

THE CLERK ON ward 3B was hunched at her desk, clutching a paperback book. On the cover, a half-naked couple grappled beneath the blazing scarlet title: *His Wanton Bride*. She flipped a page. Her eyes widened. She didn't even notice David walk by. Only when he was standing right beside her in the nurses' station did she bother to glance up. Instantly flushing, she slapped down the book.

"Oh! Can I help you, Doctor... uh..."

"Smith," finished David and flashed her such a dazzling smile that she sank like melted jelly into her chair. *Wow*, he thought as he gazed into a pair of rapturous violet eyes. *This white coat really does the trick.* "I need to see one of your charts," he said.

"Which one?" she asked breathlessly.

"Room...er..." He glanced over at the chart rack. "Eight."

"A or B?"

"B."

"Mrs. Loomis?"

"Yes, that's the name. Loomis."

She seemed to float out of her chair. Swaying over to the chart rack, she struck a pose of slinky indifference. It took her an inordinately long time to locate Room 8B's chart, despite the fact it was staring her right in the face. David glanced down at the book cover and suddenly felt like laughing.

"Here it is," she chirped, holding it out to him in both hands, like some sort of sacred offering.

"Why, thank you, Ms...."

"Mann. Janet. Miss."

"Yes." He cleared his throat. Then, turning, he fled to a chair as far away as possible from Miss Janet Mann. He could almost hear her sigh of disappointment as she turned to answer a ringing telephone.

"Oh, all right." She sighed. "I'll bring them down right now." She grabbed a handful of red-stoppered blood tubes from the pickup tray and hurried out, leaving David alone in the station.

So that's all there is to it, he thought, flipping open the metal chart cover. The unfortunate Mrs. Loomis in room 8B was obviously a complicated case, judging by the thickness of her record and the interminable list of doctors on her case. Not only did she have a surgeon and anesthesiologist, there were numerous consultation notes by an internist, psychiatrist, dermatologist and gynecologist. He was reminded of the old saying about too many cooks. Like the proverbial broth, this poor lady didn't have a chance.

A nurse walked past, wheeling a medication cart. Another nurse slipped in for a moment to answer the ringing telephone then hurried out again. Neither woman paid him the slightest attention.

He flipped to the EKG, which was filed at the back of the chart. It would take maybe ten seconds to remove that one page and replace it with another. And with so many doctors passing through the ward—six for Mrs. Loomis alone— no one would notice a thing.

Murder, he decided, couldn't be easier. All it took was a white coat.

Chapter Nine

"I guess you proved your point tonight," said David as he set two glasses of hot milk on the kitchen table. "About murder in the O.R."

"No, we didn't." Kate looked down bleakly at the steaming glass. "We didn't prove a thing, David. Except that the chief of anesthesia's got a sick dog." She sighed. "Poor old Avery. I must have scared the wits out of him."

"Sounds like you scared the wits out of each other. By the way, does he have a dog?"

"He wouldn't lie to me."

"I'm just asking. I don't know the man." He took a sip of milk and it left a faint white mustache on his stubbled lip. He seemed dark and out of place in his gleaming kitchen. A faint beard shadowed his jaw, and his shirt, which had started out so crisp this morning, was now mapped with wrinkles. He'd undone his top button and she felt a peculiar sense of weightlessness as she caught a glimpse of dark gold hair matting his chest.

She looked down fiercely at her milk. "I'm pretty sure he does have a dog," she continued. "In fact, I remember seeing a picture on his desk."

"He keeps a picture of a dog on his desk?"

"It's of his wife, really. She's holding this sort of brownish terrier. She was really very beautiful."

"I take it you mean his wife."

"Yes. She had a stroke a few months ago. It devastated that poor man, to put her in a nursing home. He's been shuffling through his duties ever since." Mournfully she took a sip. "I bet he couldn't do it."

"Do what?"

"Kill his dog. Some people are incapable of hurting a fly."

"While others are perfectly capable of murder."

She looked at him. "You still think it *was* murder?"

He didn't answer for a moment, and his silence frightened her. Was her only ally slipping away? "I don't know what I think." He sighed. "So far I've been going on instinct, not facts. And that won't hold up in a courtroom."

"Or a committee hearing," she added morosely.

"Your hearing's on Tuesday?"

"And I still haven't the faintest idea what to tell them."

"Can't you get a delay? I'll cancel my appointments tomorrow. Maybe we can pull together some evidence."

"I've already asked for a delay. It was turned down. Anyway, there doesn't seem to *be* any evidence. All we have is a pair of murders, with no obvious connection to Ellen's death."

He sat back, frowning at the table. "What if the police are barking up the wrong tree? What if Charlie Decker's just a wild card?"

"They found his fingerprints, David. And I saw him there."

"But you didn't actually see him kill anyone."

"No. But who else had a motive?"

"Let's think about this for a minute." Idly, David reached for the saltshaker and set it in the center of the table. "We know Henry Tanaka was a very busy man. And I'm not talking about his practice. He was having an affair—" David moved the pepper shaker next to the salt "—probably with Ann Richter."

"Okay. But where does Ellen fit in?"

"That's the million-dollar question." He reached over and tapped the sugar jar. "Where does Ellen O'Brien fit in?"

Kate frowned. "A love triangle?"

"Possible. But a man doesn't have to stop at one mistress. He could've had a dozen. And they each in turn could have had jealous lovers."

"Triangles within triangles? This sounds wilder by the minute. All this romping around in bedrooms! Doctors having affairs left and right! I just can't picture it."

"It happens. And not just in hospitals."

"Law offices too, hmm?"

"I'm not saying *I've* done it. But we're all human."

She couldn't help smiling. "It's funny. When we first met, I didn't think of you as being particularly human."

"No?"

"You were a threat. The enemy. Just another damn lawyer."

"Oh. Scum of the earth, you mean."

"You did play the part well."

He winced. "Thanks a lot."

"But it's not that way anymore," she said quickly. "I can't think of you as just another lawyer. Not since . . ."

Her voice faded as their eyes suddenly locked.

"Not since I kissed you," he finished softly.

Warmth flooded her cheeks. Abruptly she rose to her feet and carried the glass to the sink, all the time aware of his gaze on her back. "It's all gotten so complicated," she commented with a sigh.

"What? The fact I'm human?"

"The fact we're *both* human," she blurted out. Even without looking at him, she could sense the attraction, the electricity, crackling between them.

She washed the glass. Twice. Then, calmly, deliberately, she sat back down at the table. He was watching her, a wry look of amusement on his face.

"I'll be the first to admit it," he said, his eyes twinkling. "It *is* a hell of an inconvenience, being human. A slave to all those pesky biological urges."

Biological urges. What a hopelessly pale description of the hormonal storm now raging inside her. Avoiding his gaze, she focused on the saltshaker, sitting at the center of the table. She thought suddenly of Henry Tanaka. Of triangles within triangles. Had all those deaths been a consequence of nothing more than lust and jealousy gone berserk?

"You're right," she agreed, thoughtfully touching the salt-shaker. "Being human leads to all sorts of complications. Even murder."

She sensed his tension before he even spoke a word. His gaze fell on the table and all at once he went completely still. "I can't believe we didn't think of it."

"Of what?" she asked.

He shoved his empty glass toward the sugar jar. It gave the diagram a fourth corner. "We're not dealing with a triangle. It's a *square.*"

There was a pause. "Your grasp of geometry is really quite amazing," she said politely.

"What if Tanaka *did* have a second girlfriend—Ellen O'Brien?"

"That's our old triangle."

"But we've left someone out. Someone very important." He tapped the empty milk glass.

Kate frowned at the four objects on the table. "My God," she whispered. "Mrs. Tanaka."

"Exactly."

"I never even thought of his wife."

He looked up. "Maybe it's time we did."

THE JAPANESE WOMAN who opened the clinic door was wearing fire-engine-red lipstick and face powder that was several shades too pale for her complexion. She looked like a fugitive from a geisha house. "Then you're not with the police?" she asked.

"Not exactly," replied David. "But we do have a few questions—"

"I'm not talking to any more reporters." She started to shut the door.

"We're not reporters, Mrs. Tanaka. I'm an attorney. And this is Dr. Kate Chesne."

"Well, what do you want, then?"

"We're trying to get information about another murder. It's related to your husband's death."

Sudden interest flickered in the woman's eyes. "You're talking about that nurse, aren't you? That Richter woman."

"Yes."

"What do you know about her?"

"We'll be glad to tell you everything we know. If you'll just let us come in."

She hesitated, curiosity and caution waging a battle in her eyes. Curiosity won. She opened the door and gestured for them to come into the waiting room. She was tall for a Japanese; taller, even, than Kate. She was wearing a simple blue dress and high heels and gold seashell earrings. Her hair was so black it might have looked artificial had there not been the single white strand tracing her right temple. Mari Tanaka was a remarkably beautiful woman.

"You'll have to excuse the mess," she apologized, pausing in the impeccably neat waiting room. "But there's been so much confusion. So many things to take care of." She gazed around at the deserted couches, as though wondering where all the patients had gone. Magazines were still arrayed on the coffee table and a box of children's toys sat in the corner, waiting to be played with. The only hint that tragedy had struck this office was the sympathy card and a vase of white lilies, sent by a grieving patient. Through a glass partition in front of the reception desk, two women could be seen in the adjoining office, surrounded by stacks of files.

"There are so many patients to be referred," said Mrs. Tanaka with a sigh. "And all those outstanding bills. I had no idea things would be so chaotic. I always let Henry take care of everything. And now that he's gone . . ." She sank tiredly onto the couch. "I take it you know about my husband and that—that woman."

David nodded. "Did you?"

"Yes. I mean, I didn't know her name. But I knew there had to be someone. Funny, isn't it? How they say the wife is always the last to know." She gazed at the two women behind the glass partition. "I'm sure *they* knew about her. And people at the hospital, they must have known, as well. I was the only one who didn't. The *stupid* wife." She looked up. "You said you'd tell me about this woman. Ann Richter. What do you know about her?"

"I worked with her," Kate began.

"Did you?" Mrs. Tanaka shifted her gaze to Kate. "I never even met her. What was she like? Was she pretty?"

Kate hesitated, knowing instinctively that the other woman was only searching for more information with which to torture herself. Mari Tanaka seemed consumed by some bizarre need for self-punishment. "Ann was... attractive, I suppose," she said.

"Intelligent?"

Kate nodded. "She was a good nurse."

"So was I." Mrs. Tanaka bit her lip and looked away. "She was a blonde, I hear. Henry liked blondes. Isn't that ironic? He liked the one thing I couldn't be." She glanced at David with sudden feminine hostility. "And I suppose *you* like Oriental women."

"A beautiful woman is a beautiful woman," he replied, unruffled. "I don't discriminate."

She blinked back a veil of tears. "Henry did."

"Have there been other women?" Kate asked gently.

"I suppose." She shrugged. "He was a man, wasn't he?"

"Did you ever hear the name Ellen O'Brien?"

"Did she have some... connection with my husband?"

"We were hoping you could tell us."

Mrs. Tanaka shook her head. "He never mentioned any names. But then, I never asked any questions."

Kate frowned. "Why not?"

"I didn't want him to lie to me." Somehow, by the way she said it, it made perfect sense.

"Have the police told you there's a suspect?" David asked.

"You mean Charles Decker?" Mrs. Tanaka's gaze shifted back to David. "Sergeant Brophy came to see me yesterday afternoon. He showed me the man's photograph."

"Did you recognize the face?"

"I never saw the man, Mr. Ransom. I didn't even know his name. All I knew was that my husband was attacked by some psychotic five years ago. And that the stupid police let the man go the very next day."

"But your husband refused to press charges," said David.

"He what?"

"That's why Decker was released so quickly. It seems your husband wanted the matter dropped."

"He never told me that."

"What did he tell you?"

"Almost nothing. But there were lots of things we never talked about. That's how we managed to stay together all these years. By not talking about certain things. It was almost an agreement. He didn't ask how I spent the money. I didn't ask about his women."

"Then you don't know anything more about Decker?"

"No. But maybe Peggy can help you."

"Peggy?"

She nodded toward the office. "Our receptionist. She was here when it happened."

Peggy was a blond, fortyish Amazon wearing white stretch pants. Though invited to sit, she preferred to stand. Or maybe she simply preferred not to occupy the same couch as Mari Tanaka.

"Remember the man?" Peggy repeated. "I'll never forget him. I was cleaning up one of the exam rooms when I heard all this yelling. I came right out and that psychotic was here, in the waiting room. He had his hands around Henry's—the doctor's—neck and he kept screaming at him."

"You mean cursing him?"

"No, not cursing. He said something like 'What did you do with her?'"

"Those were his words? You're sure?"

"Pretty sure."

"And who was this 'her' he was referring to? One of the patients?"

"Yes. And the doctor felt just awful about that case. She was such a nice woman, and to have both her and the baby die. Well . . ."

"What was her name?"

"Jenny . . . Let me think. Jenny something. Brook. I think that was it. Jennifer Brook."

"What did you do after you saw the doctor being attacked?"

"Well, I pulled the man away, of course. What do you think I did? He was holding on tight, but I got him off. Women aren't completely helpless, you know."

"Yes, I'm quite aware of that."

"Anyway, he sort of collapsed then."

"The doctor?"

"No, the man. He crumpled in this little heap over there, by the coffee table and he just sat there, crying. He was still there when the police arrived. A few days later, we heard he'd shot himself. In the mouth." She paused and stared at the floor, as though seeing some ghostlike remnant of the man, still sitting there. "It's weird, but I couldn't help feeling sorry for him. He was crying like a baby. I think even Henry felt sorry...."

"Mrs. Tanaka?" The other clerk poked her head into the waiting room. "You have a phone call. It's your accountant. I'll transfer it to the back office."

Mrs. Tanaka rose. "There's really nothing more we can tell you," she said. "And we do have to get back to work." She shot Peggy a meaningful glance. Then, with only the barest nod of goodbye, she walked sleekly out of the waiting room.

"Two weeks' notice," Peggy muttered sullenly. "That's what she gave us. And then she expects us to get the whole damn office in order. No wonder Henry didn't want that witch hanging around." She turned to go back to her desk.

"Peggy?" asked Kate. "Just one more question, if you don't mind. When your patients die, how long do you keep the medical records?"

"Five years. Longer if it's an obstetrical death. You know, in case some malpractice suit gets filed."

"Then you still have Jenny Brook's chart?"

"I'm sure we do." She went into the office and pulled open the filing cabinet. She went through the B drawer twice. Then she checked the J's. In frustration, she slammed the drawer closed. "I can't understand it. It should be here."

David and Kate glanced at each other. "It's missing?" said Kate.

"Well, it's not here. And I'm very careful about these things. Let me tell you, I do not run a sloppy office." She turned and glared at the other clerk as though expecting a dissenting opinion. There was none.

"What are you saying?" said David. "That someone's removed it?"

"He must have," replied Peggy. "But I can't see why he would. It's barely been five years."

"Why *who* would?"

Peggy looked at him as if he was dim-witted. "Dr. Tanaka, of course."

"JENNIFER BROOK," said the hospital records clerk in a flat voice as she typed the name into the computer. "Is that with or without an *e* at the end?"

"I don't know," answered Kate.

"Middle initial?"

"I don't know."

"Date of birth?"

Kate and David looked at each other. "We don't know," replied Kate.

The clerk turned and peered at them over her horn-rimmed glasses. "I don't suppose you'd know the medical-record number?" she asked in a weary monotone.

They shook their heads.

"That's what I was afraid of." The clerk swiveled back to her terminal and punched in another command. After a few seconds, two names appeared on the screen, a Brooke and a Brook, both with the first name Jennifer. "Is it one of these?" she questioned.

A glance at the dates of birth told them one was fifty-seven years old, the other fifteen.

"No," said Kate.

"It figures." The clerk sighed and cleared the screen. "Dr. Chesne," she continued with excruciating patience, "why, exactly, do you need this particular record?"

"It's a research project," Kate said. "Dr. Jones and I—"

"Dr. Jones?" The clerk looked at David. "I don't remember a Dr. Jones on our staff."

Kate said quickly, "He's with the University—"

"Of Arizona," David finished with a smile.

"It's all been cleared through Avery's office. It's a paper on maternal death and—"

"Death?" The clerk blinked. "You mean this patient is deceased?"

"Yes."

"Well, no wonder. We keep those files in a totally different place." From her tone, their other file room might have been on Mars. She rose reluctantly from her chair. "This will take a while. You'll have to wait." Turning, she headed at a snail's pace toward a back door and vanished into what was no doubt the room for deceased persons' files.

"Why do I get the feeling we'll never see her again?" muttered David.

Kate sagged weakly against the counter. "Just be glad she didn't ask for your credentials. I could get in big trouble for this, you know. Showing hospital records to the enemy."

"Who, me?"

"You're a lawyer, aren't you?"

"I'm just poor old Dr. Jones from Arizona." He turned and glanced around the room. At a corner table, a doctor was yawning as he turned a page. An obviously bored clerk wheeled a cart up the aisle, collecting charts and slapping them onto an already precarious stack. "Lively place," he remarked. "When does the dancing start?"

They both turned at the sound of footsteps. The clerk with the horn-rimmed glasses reappeared, empty-handed.

"The chart's not there," she announced.

Kate and David stared at her in stunned silence.

"What do you mean, it's not there?" asked Kate.

"It should be. But it's not."

"Was it released from the hospital?" David snapped.

The clerk looked aridly over her glasses. "We don't release originals, Dr. Jones. People always lose them."

"Oh. Well, of course."

The clerk sank down in front of the computer and typed in a command. "See? There's the listing. It's supposed to be in the file room. All I can say is it must've been misplaced." She added, under her breath, "Which means we'll probably never see it again." She was about to clear the screen when David stopped her.

"Wait. What's that notation there?" he asked, pointing to a cryptic code.

"That's a chart copy request."

"You mean someone requested a copy?"

"Yes," the clerk sighed wearily. "That is what it means, Doctor."

"Who asked for it?"

She shifted the cursor and punched another button. A name and address appeared magically on the screen. "Joseph Kahanu, Attorney at Law, Alakea Street. Date of request: March 2."

David frowned. "That's only a month ago."

"Yes, Doctor, I do believe it is."

"An attorney. Why the hell would he be interested in a death that happened five years ago?"

The clerk turned and looked at him dryly over her horn-rimmed glasses. "You tell me."

THE PAINT IN THE HALL was chipping and thousands of footsteps had worn a path down the center of the threadbare carpet. Outside the office hung a sign:

Joseph Kahanu, Attorney at Law
Specialist in Divorce, Child Custody, Wills, Accidents, Insurance, Drunk Driving, and Personal Injury

"Great address," whispered David. "Rats must outnumber the clients." He knocked on the door.

It was answered by a huge Hawaiian man dressed in an ill-fitting suit. "You're David Ransom?" he asked gruffly.

David nodded. "And this is Dr. Chesne."

The man's silent gaze shifted for a moment to Kate's face. Then he stepped aside and gestured sullenly toward a pair of rickety chairs. "Yeah, come in."

The office was suffocating. A table fan creaked back and forth, churning the heat. A half-open window, opaque with dirt, looked out over an alley. In one glance, Kate recognized all the signs of a struggling law practice: the ancient type-writer, the cardboard boxes stuffed with client files, the second-hand furniture. There was scarcely enough room for the lone desk. Kahanu looked unbearably hot in his suit jacket; he'd probably pulled it on at the last minute, just for the benefit of his visitors.

"I haven't called the police yet," said Kahanu, settling into an unreliable-looking swivel chair.

"Why not?" asked David.

"I don't know how you run *your* practice, but I make it a point not to squeal on my clients."

"You're aware Decker's wanted for murder."

Kahanu shook his head. "It's a mistake."

"Did Decker tell you that?"

"I haven't been able to reach him."

"Maybe it's time the police found him for you."

"Look," Kahanu shot back. "We both know I'm not in your league, Ransom. I hear you got some big-shot office over on Bishop Street. Couple of dozen lapdog associates. Probably spend your weekends on the golf course, cozying up to some judge or other. Me?" He waved around at his office and laughed. "I got just a few clients. Most times they don't even remember to pay me. But they're my clients. And I don't like to go against 'em."

"You know two people have been murdered."

"They got no proof he did it."

"The police say they do. They say Charlie Decker's a dangerous man. A sick man. He needs help."

"That what they call a jail cell these days? Help?" Disgusted, he fished out a handkerchief and mopped his brow, as though buying time to think. "Guess I got no choice now," he muttered. "One way or the other, police'll be banging on my door." Slowly he folded the handkerchief and tucked it back in his pocket. Then, reaching into his drawer, he pulled out a folder and tossed it on the battered desk. "There's the copy you asked for. Seems you're not the only who one wants it."

David frowned as he reached for the folder. "Has someone else asked for it?"

"No. But someone broke into my office."

David looked up sharply. "When?"

"Last week. Tore apart all my files. Didn't steal anything, and I even had fifty bucks in the cash box. I couldn't figure it out at the time. But this morning, after you told me about those missing records, I got to thinking. Wondering if that file's what he was after."

"But he didn't get it."

"The night he broke in, I had the papers at home."

"Is this your only copy?"

"No. I ran off a few just now. Just to be safe."

"May I take a look?" Kate asked.

David hesitated, then handed her the chart. "You're the doctor. Go ahead."

She stared for a moment at the name on the cover: Jennifer Brook. Then, flipping it open, she began to read.

Recorded on the first few pages was a routine obstetrical admission. The patient, a healthy twenty-eight-year-old woman at thirty-six weeks of pregnancy, had entered Mid Pac Hospital in the early stages of labor. The initial history and physical exam, performed by Dr. Tanaka, were unremarkable. The fetal heart tones were normal, as were all the blood tests. Kate turned to the delivery-room record.

Here things began to go wrong. Terribly wrong. The nurse's painstakingly neat handwriting broadened into a frantic scrawl. The entries became terse, erratic. A young woman's death was distilled down to a few coldly clinical phrases.

Generalized seizures... No response to Valium and Dilantin... Stat page to E.R. for assistance... Respirations now irregular... Respirations ceased... No pulse... Cardiac massage started... Fetal heart tones audible but slowing... Still no pulse... Dr. Vaughn from E.R. to assist with stat C-section...
Live infant...

The record became a short series of blotted-out sentences, totally unreadable.

On the next page was the last entry, written in a calm hand.

Resuscitation stopped. Patient pronounced dead at 01:30.

"She died of a cerebral hemorrhage," Kahanu said. "She was only twenty-eight."

"And the baby?" Kate asked.

"A girl. She died an hour after the mother."

"Kate," David murmured, nudging her arm. "Look at the bottom of the page. The names of the personnel in attendance."

Kate's gaze dropped to the three names. As she took them in one by one, her hands went icy.

> Henry Tanaka, M.D.
> Ann Richter, RN
> Ellen O'Brien, RN

"They left out a name," Kate pointed out. She looked up. "There was a Dr. Vaughn, from the E.R. He might be able to tell us—"

"He can't," said Kahanu. "You see, Dr. Vaughn had an accident a short time after Jennifer Brook died. His car was hit head-on."

"You mean he's dead?"

Kahanu nodded. "They're all dead."

The chart slid from her frozen fingers onto the desk. There was something dangerous about this document, something evil. She stared down, unwilling to touch it, for fear the contagion would rub off.

Kahanu turned his troubled gaze to the window. "Four weeks ago Charlie Decker came to my office. Who knows why he chose me? Maybe I was convenient. Maybe he couldn't afford anyone else. He wanted a legal opinion about a possible malpractice suit."

"On this case?" said David. "But Jenny Brook died five years ago. And Decker wasn't even a relative. You know as well as I do the lawsuit would've been tossed right out."

"He paid for my services, Mr. Ransom. In cash."

In cash. Those were magic words for a lawyer who was barely surviving.

"I did what he asked. I subpoenaed the chart for him. I contacted the doctor and the two nurses who'd cared for Jenny Brook. But they never answered my letters."

"They didn't live long enough," explained David. "Decker got to them first."

"Why should he?"

"Vengeance. They killed the woman he loved. So he killed them."

"My client didn't kill anyone."

"Your client had the motive, Kahanu. And you provided him with their names and addresses."

"You've never met Decker. I have. And he's not a violent man."

"You'd be surprised how ordinary a killer can seem. I used to face them in court—"

"And I *defend* them! I take on the scum no one else'll touch. I *know* a killer when I see one. There's something different about them, about their eyes. Something's missing. I don't know what it is. A soul, maybe. I tell you, Charlie Decker wasn't like that."

Kate leaned forward. "What was he like, Mr. Kahanu?" she asked quietly.

The Hawaiian paused, his gaze wandering out the dirty window to the alley below. "He was—he was real...ordinary. Not tall, but not too short, either. Mostly skin and bones, like he wasn't eating right. I felt sorry for him. He looked like a man who's had his insides kicked out. He didn't say much. But he wrote things down for me. I think it hurt him to use his voice. He's got something wrong with his throat and he couldn't talk much louder than a whisper. He was sitting right there in that chair where you are now, Dr. Chesne. Said he didn't have much money. Then he took out his wallet and counted out these twenty-dollar bills, one at a time. I could see, just by the way he handled them, real slow and careful, that it was everything he had." Kahanu shook his head. "I still don't see why he even bothered, you know? The woman's dead. The baby's dead. All this digging around in the past, it won't bring'em back."

"Do you know where to find him?" asked David.

"He has a P.O. box," said Kahanu. "I already checked. He hasn't picked up his mail in three days."

"Do you have his address? Phone number?"

"Never gave me one. Look, I don't know where he is. I'll leave it to the police to find him. That's their job, isn't it?" He pushed away from the desk. "That's all I know. If you want anything else, you'll have to get it from Decker."

"Who happens to be missing," said David.

To which Kahanu added darkly: "Or dead."

Chapter Ten

In his forty-eight years as cemetery groundskeeper, Ben Hoomalu had seen his share of peculiar happenings. His friends liked to say it was because he was tramping around dead people all day, but in fact it wasn't the dead who caused all the mischief but the living: the randy teenagers groping in the darkness among the gravestones; the widow scrawling obscenities on her husband's nice new marble tombstone; the old man caught trying to bury his beloved poodle next to his beloved wife. Strange goings-on—that's what a fellow saw around cemeteries.

And now here was that car, back again.

Every day for the past week Ben had seen the same gray Ford with the darkly tinted windows drive through the gates. Sometimes it'd show up early in the morning, other times late in the afternoon. It would park over by the Arch of Eternal Comfort and just sit there for an hour or two. The driver never got out; that was odd, too. If a person came all this way to visit a loved one, wouldn't you think he'd at least get out and take a look at the grave?

There was no figuring out some folks.

Ben picked up the hedge clippers and started trimming the hibiscus bush. He liked hearing the clack, clack of the blades in the afternoon stillness. He looked up as a beat-up old Chevy drove through the gate and parked. A spindly man emerged from the car and waved at Ben. Smiling, Ben waved back. The man was carrying a bunch of daisies as he headed toward the woman's grave. Ben paused and watched the man go about his ritual. First, he gathered up the wilted flowers left behind on his previous visit and meticulously collected all the dead leaves and twigs. Then, after laying his new offering beside the stone, he settled reverentially on the grass. Ben knew the man would sit there a long time; he always did. Every visit was exactly the same. That was part of the comfort.

By the time the man got up to leave, Ben had finished with the hibiscus and was working on the bougainvillea. He watched the man walk slowly back to the car and felt a twinge of sadness as the old Chevy wound along the road toward the cemetery gates. He didn't even know the man's name; he only knew that whoever lay buried in that grave was still very much loved. He dropped his hedge clippers and wandered over to where the fresh daisies lay bundled together in a pink ribbon. There was still a dent in the grass where the man had knelt.

The purr of another car starting up caught his attention and he saw the gray Ford pull away from the curb and slowly follow the Chevy out the cemetery gates.

And what did *that* mean? Funny goings-on, all right.

He looked down at the name on the stone: Jennifer Brook, 28 years old. Already a dead leaf had blown onto the grave and now lay trembling in the wind. He shook his head.

Such a young woman. Such a shame.

"YOU GOT A HAM ON RYE, hold the mayo, and a call on line four," said Sergeant Brophy, dropping a brown bag on the desk.

Pokie, faced with the choice between a sandwich and a blinking telephone, reached for the sandwich. After all, a man had to set his priorities, and he figured a growling stomach ranked somewhere near the top of anyone's priority list. He nodded at the phone. "Who's calling?"

"Ransom."

"Not again."

"He's demanding we open a file on the O'Brien case."

"Why the hell's he keep bugging us about that case, anyway?"

"I think he's got a thing for that—that—" Brophy's face suddenly screwed up as he teetered on the brink of a sneeze and he whipped out a handkerchief just in time to muffle the explosion "—doctor lady. You know. Hearts 'n' flowers."

"Davy?" Pokie laughed out a clump of ham sandwich. "Men like Davy don't go for hearts 'n' flowers. Think they're too damn smart for all that romantic crap."

"No man's that smart," Brophy said glumly.

There was a knock on the door and a uniformed officer poked his head into the office. "Lieutenant? You got a summons from on high."

"Chief?"

"He's stuck with an office full of reporters. They're askin' about that missing Sasaki girl. Wants ya up there like ten minutes ago."

Pokie looked down regretfully at his sandwich. Unfortunately, on that cosmic list of priorities, a summons from the chief ranked somewhere on a par with breathing. Sighing, he left the sandwich on his desk and pulled on his jacket.

"What about Ransom?" reminded Brophy, nodding at the blinking telephone.

"Tell him I'll call him back."

"When?"

"Next year," Pokie grunted as he headed for the door. He added under his breath, "If he's lucky."

DAVID MUTTERED AN OATH as he slid into the driver's seat and slammed the car door. "We just got the brush-off."

Kate stared at him. "But they've seen Jenny Brook's file. They've talked to Kahanu—"

"They say there's not enough evidence to open a murder investigation. As far as they're concerned, Ellen O'Brien died of malpractice. End of subject."

"Then we're on our own."

"Wrong. We're pulling out." Suddenly agitated, he started the engine and drove away from the curb. "Things are getting too dangerous."

"They've been dangerous from the start. Why are you getting cold feet now?"

"Okay, I admit it. Up till now I wasn't sure I believed you—"

"You thought I was *lying*?"

"There was always this—this nagging doubt in the back of my mind. But now we're hearing about stolen hospital charts. People breaking into lawyer's offices. There's something weird going on here, Kate. This isn't the work of a raging psychopath. It's too reasoned. Too methodical." He frowned at the road ahead. "And it all has to do with Jenny Brook. There's something dangerous about her hospital chart, something our killer wants to keep hidden."

"But we've gone over that thing a dozen times, David! It's just a medical record."

"Then we're overlooking something. And I'm counting on Charlie Decker to tell us what it is. I say we sit tight and wait for the police to find him."

Charlie Decker, she thought. Her doom or her salvation? She stared out at the late-afternoon traffic and tried to remember his face. Up till now, the image had been jelled in fear; every time she'd thought of his face in the mirror, she'd felt an automatic surge of terror. Now she tried to ignore the sweat forming on her palms, the racing of her pulse. She forced herself to think of that face with its tired, hollow eyes. Killer's eyes? She didn't know anymore. She looked down at Jenny Brook's chart, lying on her lap. Did it contain some vital clue to Decker's madness?

"I'll corner Pokie tomorrow," said David, weaving impatiently through traffic. "See if I can't change his mind about the O'Brien case."

"And if you can't convince him?"

"I'm very convincing."

"He'll want more evidence."

"Then let *him* find it. I think we've gone as far as we can on this. It's time for us to back off."

"I can't, David. I have a career at stake—"

"What about your life?"

"My career is my life."

"There's one helluva big difference."

She turned away. "I can't really expect you to understand. It's not your fight."

But he did understand. And it worried him, that note of stubbornness in her voice. She reminded him of one of those ancient warriors who'd rather fall on their swords than accept defeat.

"You're wrong," he told her. "About it not being my fight."

"You don't have anything at stake."

"Don't forget I pulled out of the case—a potentially lucrative case, I might add."

"Oh. Well, I'm sorry I cost you such a nice fee."

"You think I care about the money? I don't give a damn about the money. It's my reputation I put on the line. And all because I happened to believe that crazy story of yours. Murder on the operating table! I'm going to look like a fool if it can't be proved. So don't tell me I have nothing to lose!" By now he was yelling. He couldn't help it. She could accuse him of any number of things and he wouldn't bat an eye. But accusing him of not giving a damn was something he couldn't stand.

Gripping the steering wheel, he forced his gaze back to the road. "The worst part is," he muttered, "I'm a lousy liar. And I think the O'Briens can tell."

"You mean you didn't tell them the truth?"

"That I think their daughter was murdered? Hell, no. I took the easy way out. I told them I had a conflict of interest. A nice, noncommittal excuse. I figured they couldn't get too upset since I'm referring the case to a good firm."

"You're doing *what*?" She stared at him.

"I was their attorney, Kate. I have to protect their interests."

"Naturally."

"This hasn't been easy, you know," he went on. "I don't like to shortchange my clients. Any of them. They're dealing with enough tragedy in their lives. The least I can do is see they get a decent shot at justice. It bothers the hell out of me when I can't deliver what I promise. You understand that, don't you?"

"Yes. I understand perfectly well."

He knew by the hurt tone of her voice that she really didn't. And that annoyed him because he thought she should understand.

She sat motionless as he pulled into the driveway. He parked the car and turned off the engine but she made no move to get out. They lingered there in the shadowy heat of the garage as the silence between them stretched into minutes. When she finally spoke again, it was in the flat tones of a stranger.

"I've put you in a compromising position, haven't I?"

His answer was a curt nod.

"I'm sorry."

"Look, forget about it, okay?" He got out and opened her door. She was still sitting there, rigid as a statue. "Well?" he asked. "Are you coming inside?"

"Only to pack."

He felt an odd little thump of dismay in his chest, which he tried to ignore. "You're leaving?"

"I appreciate what you've done for me," she answered tightly. "You went out on a limb and you didn't have to. Maybe, at the start, we needed each other. But it's obvious this…arrangement is no longer in your best interests. Or mine, for that matter."

"I see," he said, though he didn't. In fact he thought she was acting childishly. "And just where do you plan to go?"

"I'll stay with friends."

"Oh, great. Spread the danger to them."

"Then I'll check into a hotel."

"Your purse was stolen, remember? You don't have any money, credit cards." He paused for dramatic effect. "No nothing."

"Not at the moment, but—"

"Or are you planning to ask me for a loan?"

"I don't need your help," she snapped. "I've never needed any man's help!"

He briefly considered the old-fashioned method of brute force, but knowing her sense of pride, he didn't think it would work. So he simply retorted, "Suit yourself," and stalked off to the house.

While she was packing, he paced back and forth in the kitchen, trying to ignore his growing sense of uneasiness. He grabbed a carton of milk out of the refrigerator and took a gulp straight from the container. *I should order her to stay,* he thought. *Yes, that's exactly what I should do.* He shoved the milk back in the refrigerator, slammed the door and stormed toward her bedroom.

But just as he got there, he pulled himself up short. Bad idea. He knew exactly how she'd react if he started shouting out orders. You just didn't push a woman like Kate Chesne around. Not if you were smart.

He hulked in the doorway and watched as she folded a dress and tucked it neatly into a suitcase. The fading daylight was glimmering behind her in the window. She swept back a stray lock of hair and a lead weight seemed to lodge in his throat as he glimpsed the bruised cheek. It reminded him how vulnerable she really was. Despite her pride and her so-called independence, she was really just a woman. And like any woman, she could be hurt.

She noticed him in the doorway and she paused, nightgown in hand. "I'm almost finished," she said, matter-of-factly tossing the nightgown on top of the other clothes. He couldn't help glancing twice at the mound of peach-colored silk. He felt that lead weight drop into his belly. "Have you called a cab yet?" she asked, turning back to the dresser.

"No, I haven't."

"Well, I shouldn't be a minute. Could you call one now?"

"I'm not going to."

She turned and frowned at him. "What?"

"I said I'm not going to call a cab."

His announcement seemed to leave her momentarily stunned. "Fine," she said calmly. "Then I'll call one myself." She started for the door. But as she walked past him, he caught her by the arm.

"Kate, don't." He pulled her around to face him. "I think you should stay."

"Why?"

"Because it's not safe out there."

"The world's never been safe. I've managed."

"Oh, yeah. What a tough broad you are. And what happens when Decker catches up?"

She yanked her arm away. "Don't you have better things to worry about?"

"Like what?"

"Your sense of ethics? After all, I wouldn't want to ruin your precious reputation."

"I can take care of my own reputation, thank you."

She threw her head back and glared straight up at him. "Then maybe it's time I took better care of mine!"

They were standing so close he could almost feel the heat mounting in waves between them. What happened next was as unexpected as a case of spontaneous combustion. Their gazes locked. Her eyes suddenly went wide with surprise. And need. Despite all her false bravado, he could see it brimming there in those deep, green pools.

"What the hell," he growled, his voice rough with desire. "I think both our reputations are already shot."

And then he gave in to the impulse that had been battering at his willpower all day. He hauled her close into his arms and kissed her. It was a long and savagely hungry kiss. She gave a weak murmur of protest, just before she sagged backward against the doorway. Almost immediately he felt her respond, her body molding itself against his. It was a perfect fit. Absolutely perfect. Her arms twined around his neck and as he urged her lips apart with his, the kiss became desperately urgent. Her moan sent a sweet agony of desire knifing through to his belly.

The same sweet fire was now engulfing Kate. She felt him fumbling for the buttons of her dress but his fingers seemed as clumsy as a teenager's exploring the unfamiliar territory of a woman's body. With a groan of frustration, he tugged the dress off her shoulders; it seemed to fall in slow motion, hissing down her hips to the floor. The lace bra magically melted away and his hand closed around her breast, branding her flesh with his fingers. Under his pleasuring stroke, her nipple hardened instantly and they both knew that this time there would be no retreat; only surrender.

Already she was groping at his shirt, her breath coming in hot, frantic little whimpers as she tried to work the buttons free.

Damn. Damn. Now they were both yanking at the shirt. Together they stripped it off his shoulders and she immediately sought his chest, burying her fingers in the bristling gold hairs.

By the time they'd stumbled down the hall and into the evening glow of his bedroom, his shoes and socks were tossed to the four corners of the room, his pants were unzipped and his arousal was plainly evident.

The bed creaked in protest as he fell on top of her, his hands trapping her face beneath his. There were no preludes, no formalities. They couldn't wait. With his mouth covering hers and his hands buried in her hair, he thrust into her, so deeply that she cried out against his lips.

He froze, his whole body suddenly tense. "Did I hurt you?" he whispered.

"No...oh, no...."

It took only one look at her face to tell him it wasn't pain that had made her cry out, but pleasure—in him, in what he was doing to her. She tried to move; he held her still, his face taut as he struggled for control. Somehow, she'd always known he would claim her. Even when the voice of common sense had told her it was impossible, she'd known he would be the one.

She couldn't wait. She was moving in spite of him, matching agony for agony.

He let her take him to the very brink and then, when he knew it was inevitable, he surrendered himself to the fall. In a frenzy he took control and plunged them both over the cliff.

The drop was dizzying.

The landing left them weak and exhausted. An eternity passed, filled with the sounds of their breathing. Sweat trickled over his back and onto her naked belly. Outside, the waves roared against the seawall.

"Now I know what it's like to be devoured," she whispered as the glow of sunset faded in the window.

"Is that what I did?"

She sighed. "Completely."

He chuckled and his mouth glided warmly to her earlobe. "No, I think there's still something here to eat."

She closed her eyes, surrendering to the lovely ripples of pleasure his mouth inspired. "I never dreamed you'd be like this."

"Like what?"

"So...consuming."

"Just what did you expect?"

"Ice." She laughed. "Was I ever wrong!"

He took a strand of her hair and watched it drift like a cloud of silk through his fingers. "I guess I can seem pretty icy. It runs in my family. My father's side, anyway. Stern old New England stock. It must've been terrifying to face him in court."

"He was a lawyer, too?"

"Circuit-court judge. He died four years ago. Keeled over on the bench, right in the middle of sentencing. Just the way he would've wanted to go." He smiled. "Run-'em-in Ransom, they used to call him."

"Oh. The law-and-order type?"

"Absolutely. Unlike my mother, who thrives on anarchy."

She giggled. "It must have been an explosive combination."

"Oh, it was." He stroked his finger across her lips. "Almost as explosive as we are. I never did figure out their relationship. It didn't make sense to me. But you could almost see the chemistry working between them. The sparks. That's what I remember about my parents, all those sparks, flying around the house."

"So they were happy?"

"Oh, yeah. Exhausted, maybe. Frustrated, a lot. But they were definitely happy."

Twilight glowed dimly through the window. In silent awe, he ran his hand along the peaks and valleys of her body, a slow and leisurely exploration that left her skin tingling. "You're beautiful," he whispered. "I never thought..."

"What?"

"That I'd end up in bed with a lawyer-hating doctor. Talk about strange bedfellows."

She laughed softly. "And I feel like a mouse cozying up to the cat."

"Does that mean you're still afraid of me?"

"A little. A lot."

"Why?"

"I can't quite get over the feeling you're the enemy."

"If I'm the enemy," he said, his lips grazing her ear, "then I think one of us has just surrendered."

"Is this all you ever think about, counselor?"

"Since I met you, it is."

"And before you met me?"

"Life was very, very dull."

"I find that hard to believe."

"I'm not saying I've been celibate. But I'm a careful man. Maybe too careful. I find it hard to...get close to people."

"You seem to be doing a pretty good job tonight."

"I mean, emotionally close. It's just the way I am. Too many things can go wrong and I'm not very good at dealing with them."

By the evening glow, she studied his face hovering just above hers. "What did go wrong with your marriage, David?"

"Oh. My marriage." He rolled over on his back and sighed. "Nothing, really. Nothing I can put my finger on. I guess that just goes to show you what an insensitive clod I am. Linda used to complain I was lousy at expressing my feelings. That I was cold, just like my father. I told her that was a lot of bull. Now I think she was right."

"And I think it's just an act of yours. An icy mask you like to hide behind." She rolled onto her side, to look at him. "People show affection in different ways."

"Since when did you go into psychiatry?"

"Since I got involved with a very complex man."

Gently he tucked a strand of hair behind her ear. His gaze lingered on her cheek. "That bruise of yours is already fading. Every time I see it I get angry."

"You told me once it turned you on."

"What it really does is make me feel protective. Must be some ancient male instinct. From the days when we had to keep the other cavemen from roughing up our personal property."

"Oh, my. We're talking *that* ancient, are we?"

"As ancient as—" his hand slid possessively down the curve of her hip "—this."

"I'm not so sure 'protective' is what you're feeling right now," she murmured.

"You're right. It's not." He laughed and gave her an affectionate pat on the rump. "What I'm feeling is starved—for food. Why don't we heat up some of Mrs. Feldman's spaghetti sauce. Open a bottle of wine. And then..." He drew her toward him and his skin seemed to sear right into hers.

"And then?" she whispered.

"And then..." His lips lingered maddeningly close. "I'll do to you what lawyers have been doing to doctors for decades."

"David!" she squealed.

"Hey, just kidding!" He threw his arms up in self-defense as she swung at him. "But I think you get the general idea." He pulled her out of bed and into his arms. "Come on. And stop looking so luscious, or we'll never get out of the room. They'll find us sprawled on the bed, starved to death."

She gave him a slow, naughty look. "Oh," she murmured, "but what a way to go."

IT WAS THE SOUND of the waves slapping the seawall that finally tugged Kate awake. Drowsily she reached out for David but her hand met only an empty pillow, warmed by the morning sun. She opened her eyes and felt a sharp sense of abandonment when she discovered that she was alone in the wide, rumpled bed.

"David?" she called out. There was no answer. The house was achingly silent.

She swung her legs around and sat up on the side of the bed. Naked and dazed, she peered slowly around the sunlit room and felt the color rise in her cheeks as the night's events came back to her. The bottle of wine. The wicked whispers. The hopelessly twisted sheets. She noticed that the clothes they'd both tossed aside so recklessly had all been picked up from the floor. His pants were hanging on the closet door; her bra and underwear were now draped neatly across a chair. It made her flush even hotter to think of him gathering up all her intimate apparel. Giggling, she hugged the sheets and found they still bore his scent. But where was he?

"David?"

She rose and went into the bathroom; it was empty. A damp towel hung on the rack. Next she wandered out into the living room and marveled at the morning sun, slanting in gloriously through the windows. The empty wine bottle was still sitting on the coffee table, mute evidence of the night's intoxication. She still felt intoxicated. She poked her head into the kitchen; he wasn't there, either. Back in the living room, she paused in that brilliant flood of sunlight and called out his name. The whole house seemed to echo with loneliness.

Her sense of desolation grew as she headed back up the hall, searching, opening doors, peeking into rooms. She had the strange feeling that she was exploring an abandoned house, that this wasn't the home of a living, breathing human being, but a shell, a cave. An inexplicable impulse sent her to his closet where she stood and touched each one of those forbidding suits hanging inside. It brought him no closer to her. Back in the hallway, she opened the door to a book-lined office. The furniture was oak, the lamps brass, and everything was as neat as a pin. A room without a soul.

Kate moved down the hall, to the very last room. She was prying, she knew it. But she missed him and she longed for some palpable clue to his personality. As she opened the door, stale air puffed out, carrying the smell of a space shut away too long from the rest of the world. She saw it was a bedroom. A child's room.

A mobile of prisms trembled near the window, scattering tiny rainbows around the room. She stood there, transfixed, watching the lights dance across the wallpaper with its blue Swedish horses, across the sadly gaping toy shelves, across the tiny bed with the flowered coverlet. Almost against her will, she felt herself moving forward, as though some small, invisible hand were tugging her inside. Then, just as suddenly, the hand was gone and she was alone, so alone, in a room that ached with emptiness.

For a long time she stood there among the dancing rainbows, ashamed that she had disturbed the sanctity of this room. At last she wandered over to the dresser where a stack of books lay awaiting their owner's return. She opened one of the covers and stared at the name on the inside flap. Noah Ransom.

"I'm sorry," she whispered, tears stinging her eyes. "I'm sorry...."

She turned and fled the room, closing the door behind her.

Back in the kitchen, she huddled over a cup of coffee and read and reread the terse note she'd finally discovered, along with a set of keys, on the white-tiled counter.

Catching a ride with Glickman. The car's yours today. See you tonight.

Hardly a lover's note, she thought. No little words of endearment, not even a signature. It was cold and matter-of-fact, just like this kitchen, just like everything else about this house. So that was David. Man of ice, master of a soulless house. They had just shared a night of passionate lovemaking. She'd been swept off her feet. He left impersonal little notes on the kitchen counter.

She had to marvel at how he'd compartmentalized his life. He had walled off his emotions into nice, neat spaces, the way he'd walled off his son's room. But she couldn't do that. Already she missed him. Maybe she even loved him. It was crazy and illogical; and she wasn't used to doing crazy, illogical things.

Suddenly annoyed at herself, she stood up and furiously rinsed her coffee cup in the sink. Dammit, she had more important things to worry about. Her committee hearing was this afternoon; her career hung in the balance. It was a stupid time to be fretting over a man.

She turned and picked up Jenny Brook's hospital chart, which had been lying on the breakfast table. This sad, mysterious document. Slowly she flipped through it, wondering what could possibly be so dangerous about a few pages of medical notes. But something terrible had happened the night Jenny Brook gave birth—something that had reached like a claw through time to destroy every name mentioned on these pages. Mother and child. Doctors and nurses. They were all dead. Only Charlie Decker knew why. And he was a puzzle in himself, a puzzle with pieces that didn't fit.

A maniac, the police had called him. A monster who slashed throats.

A harmless man, Kahanu had said. A lost soul with his insides kicked out.

A man with two faces.

She closed the chart and found herself staring at the back cover. A chart with two sides.

A man with two faces.

She sat up straight, suddenly comprehending. Of course. Jekyll and Hyde.

"THE MULTIPLE PERSONALITY is a rare phenomenon. But it's well described in psychiatric literature." Susan Santini swiveled around and reached for a book from the shelf behind her. Turning back to her desk, she perused the index for the relevant pages. Her red hair, usually so unruly, was tied back in a neat little knot. On the wall behind her hung an impressive collection of medical and psychiatric degrees, testimony to the fact Susan Santini was more than just Guy's wife; she was also a professional in her own right, and a well-respected one.

"Here it is," she said, leaning forward. " 'From Eve to Sybil. A collection of case histories.' It's really a fascinating topic."

"Have you had any cases in your practice?" asked Kate.

"Wish I had. Oh, I thought I had one, when I was working with the courts. But that creep turned out to be just a great actor trying to beat a murder rap. I tell you, he could go from Caspar Milquetoast to Hulk Hogan in the blink of an eye. What a performance!"

"It is possible, though? For a man to have two completely different personalities?"

"The human psyche is made up of so many clashing parts. Call it id versus ego, impulse versus control. Look at violence, for example. Most of us manage to bury our savage tendencies. But some people can't. Who knows why? Childhood abuse? Some abnormality in brain chemistry? Whatever the reason, these people are walking time bombs. Push them too far and they lose all control. The scary part is, they're all around us. But we don't recognize them until something inside them, some inner dam, bursts. And then the violent side shows itself."

"Do you think Charlie Decker could be one of these walking time bombs?"

Susan leaned back in her leather chair and considered the possibility. "That's a hard question, Kate. You say he came from a broken home. And he was arrested for assault and battery five years ago. But there's no lifelong pattern of violence. And the one time he used a gun, he turned it on himself." She looked doubtful. "I suppose, if he had some precipitating stress, some crisis . . ."

"He did."

"You mean this?" Susan gestured to the copy of Jenny Brook's medical chart.

"The death of his fiancée. The police think it triggered some sort of homicidal rage. That he's been killing the people he thought were responsible."

"It sounds weird, but the most compelling reason for violence does seem to be love. Think of all those crimes of passion. All those jealous spouses. Spurned lovers."

"Love and violence," said Kate. "Two sides of the same coin."

"Exactly." Susan handed the medical record back to Kate. "But I'm just speculating. I'd have to talk to this man Decker before I can pass judgment. Are the police getting close?"

"I don't know. They won't tell me a thing. A lot of this information I had to dig up myself."

"You're kidding. Isn't it their job?"

Kate sighed. "That's the problem. For them it's nothing but a job, another file to be closed."

The intercom buzzed. "Dr. Santini?" said the receptionist. "Your three-o'clock appointment's waiting."

Kate glanced at her watch. "Oh, I'm sorry. I've been keeping you from your patients."

"You know I'm always glad to help out." Susan rose and walked with her to the door. There she touched Kate's arm. "This place you're staying—you're absolutely sure it's safe?"

Kate turned and saw the worry in Susan's eyes. "I think so. Why?"

Susan hesitated. "I hate to frighten you, but I think you ought to know. If you're correct, if Decker is a multiple personality, then you're dealing with a very unstable mind. Someone totally unpredictable. In the blink of an eye, he could change from a man to a monster. So, please, be very, very careful."

Kate's throat went dry. "You—you really think he's that dangerous?"

Susan nodded. "Extremely dangerous."

Chapter Eleven

It looked like a firing squad and she was the one who'd been handed the blindfold.

She was sitting before a long conference table. Arranged in a grim row in front of her were six men and a woman, all physicians, none of them smiling. Though he'd promised to attend, Dr. Clarence Avery, the chief of anesthesia, was not present. The one friendly face in the entire room was Guy Santini's, but he'd been called only as a witness. He was sitting off to the side and he looked every bit as nervous as she felt.

The committee members asked their questions politely but doggedly. They responded to her answers with impassive stares. Though the room was air-conditioned, her cheeks were on fire.

"And you personally examined the EKG, Dr. Chesne?"

"Yes, Dr. Newhouse."

"And then you filed it in the chart."

"That's correct."

"Did you show the tracing to any other physician?"

"No, sir."

"Not even to Dr. Santini?"

She glanced at Guy, who was hunched down in his chair, staring off unhappily. "Screening the EKG was my responsibility, not Dr. Santini's," she said evenly. "He trusted my judgment."

How many times do I have to repeat this story? she asked herself wearily. *How many times do I have to answer the same damn questions?*

"Dr. Santini? Any comment?"

Guy looked up reluctantly. "What Dr. Chesne says is true. I trusted her judgment." He paused, then added emphatically, "I still trust her judgment."

Thank you, Guy, she thought. Their eyes met and he gave her a faint smile.

"Let's return to the events during surgery, Dr. Chesne," continued Dr. Newhouse. "You say you performed routine induction with IV Pentothal...."

The nightmare was relived. Ellen O'Brien's death was dissected as thoroughly as a cadaver on the autopsy table.

When the questions were over, she was allowed a final statement. She delivered it in a quiet voice. "I know my story sounds bizarre. I also know I can't prove any of it—at least, not yet. But I know this much: I gave Ellen O'Brien the very best care I could. The record shows I made a mistake, a terrible one. And my patient died. But did I kill her? I don't think so. I really don't think so...." Her voice trailed off. There was nothing else to say. So she simply murmured, "Thank you." And then she left the room.

It took them twenty minutes to reach a decision. She was called back to her chair. As her gaze moved along the table, she noticed with distinct uneasiness that two new faces had joined the group. George Bettencourt and the hospital attorney were sitting at one end of the table. Bettencourt looked coldly satisfied. She knew, before a word was even spoken, what the decision would be.

Dr. Newhouse, the committee chairman, delivered the verdict. "We know your recall of the case is at odds with the record, Dr. Chesne. But I'm afraid the record is what we must go on. And the record shows, unquestionably, that your care of patient Ellen O'Brien was substandard." Kate winced at the last word, as though the worst insult imaginable had just been hurled at her. Dr. Newhouse sighed and removed his glasses—a tired gesture that seemed to carry all the weight of the world. "You're new to the staff, Dr. Chesne. You've been with us for less than a year. This sort of...mishap, after so short a time on the staff, concerns us very much. We regret this. We really do. But based on what we've heard, we're forced to refer the case to the Disciplinary Committee. They'll decide what action to take in regards to your position here at Mid Pac. Until then—'' he glanced at Bettencourt ''—we have no objection to the measures already taken by the hospital administration regarding your suspension.''

So it's over, she thought. *I was stupid to hope for anything else.*

They allowed her a chance to respond but she'd lost her voice; it was all she could manage to remain calm and dry-eyed in front of these seven people who'd just torn her life apart.

As the committee filed out, she remained in her chair, unable to move or even to raise her head. "I'm sorry, Kate," Guy said softly. He lingered beside her for a moment, as though hunting for something else to say. Then he, too, drifted out of the room.

Her name was called twice before she finally looked up to see Bettencourt and the attorney standing in front of her.

"We think it's time to talk, Dr. Chesne," announced the attorney.

She frowned at them in bewilderment. "Talk? About what?"

"A settlement."

Her back stiffened. "Isn't this a little premature?"

"If anything, it's too late."

"I don't understand."

"A reporter was in my office a few hours ago. It appears the whole case is out in the open. Obviously the O'Briens took their story to the newspapers. I'm afraid you'll be tried—and convicted—in print."

"But the case was filed only last week."

"We have to get this out of the public eye. Now. And the best way to do it is a very fast, very quiet settlement. All we need is your agreement. I plan to start negotiations at around half a million, though we fully expect they'll push for more."

Half a million dollars, she thought. It struck her as obscene, placing a monetary value on a human life. "No," she said.

The attorney blinked. "Excuse me?"

"The evidence is still coming in. By the time this goes to trial, I'm sure I'll be able to prove—"

"It won't go to trial. This case *will* be settled, Doctor. With or without your permission."

Her mouth tightened. "Then I'll pay for my own attorney. One who'll represent me and not the hospital."

The two men glanced at each other. When the attorney spoke again, his tone was distinctly unpleasant. "I don't think you fully understand what it means to go to trial. Dr. Santini will, in all probability, be dropped from the case. Which means *you* will be the principal defendant. *You'll* be the one sweating on that stand. And it'll be *your* name in the newspapers. I know their attorney, David Ransom. I've seen him rip a defendant to shreds in the courtroom. Believe me, you don't want to go through that."

"Mr. Ransom is no longer on the case," she said.

"What?"

"He's withdrawn."

He snorted. "Where on earth did you hear that rumor?"

"He told me."

"Are you saying you talked to him?"

Not to mention went to bed with him, she reflected, flushing. "It happened last week. I went to his office. I told him about the EKGs—"

"Dear God." The attorney turned and threw his pencil in his briefcase. "Well, that's it, folks. We're in big trouble."

"Why?"

"He'll use that crazy story of yours to push for a higher settlement."

"But he believed me! That's why he's withdrawing—"

"He couldn't possibly believe you. I know the man."

I know him too! she wanted to yell.

But there was no point; she'd never be able to convince them. So she simply shook her head. "I won't settle."

The attorney snapped his briefcase shut and turned in frustration to Bettencourt. "George?"

Kate shifted her attention to the chief administrator. Bettencourt was watching her with an utterly smooth expression. No hostility. No anger. Just that quintessential poker player's gaze.

"I'm concerned about your future, Dr. Chesne," he said.

So am I, she felt like snapping back.

"There's a good chance, unfortunately, that the Disciplinary Committee will view your case harshly. If so, they'll probably recommend you be terminated. And that would be a shame, having that on your record. It would make it almost impossible for you to find another job. Anywhere." He paused, to let his words sink in. "That's why I'm offering you this alternative, Doctor. I think it's far preferable to an out-and-out firing."

She stared down at the sheet of paper he was holding out to her. It was a typed resignation, already dated, with a blank space awaiting her signature.

"That's all that'd appear in your file. A resignation. There'd be no damning conclusions from the Disciplinary Committee. No record of termination. Even with this lawsuit, you could probably find another job, though not in this town." He took out a pen and held it out to her. "Why don't you sign it? It really is for the best."

She kept staring at the paper. The whole process was so neat, so efficient. Here was this ready-made document. All it needed was her signature. Her capitulation.

"We're waiting, Dr. Chesne," challenged Bettencourt. "Sign it."

She rose to her feet. She took the resignation sheet. Looking him straight in the eye, she ripped the paper in half. "There's my resignation," she declared. Then she turned and walked out the door.

Only as she stalked away past the administrative suite did it occur to her what she'd just done. She'd burned her bridges. There was no going back now; her only course was to slog it out to the very end.

Halfway down the hall, her footsteps slowed and finally stopped. She wanted to cry but couldn't. She stood there, staring down the corridor, watching the last secretary straggle away toward the elevators. It was five-fifteen and only a janitor remained at the far end of the hall, listlessly shoving a vacuum cleaner across the carpet. He rounded the corner and the sound of the machine faded away, leaving only a heavy stillness. Farther down the hall, a light was shining through the open door of Clarence Avery's office. It didn't surprise her that he was still at work; he often stayed late. But she wondered why he hadn't attended the hearing as he'd promised. Now, more than ever, she needed his support.

She went to the office. Glancing inside, she was disappointed to find only his secretary, tidying up papers on the desk.

The woman glanced up. "Oh. Dr. Chesne."

"Is Dr. Avery still in the hospital?" Kate asked.

"Haven't you heard?"

"Heard what?"

The secretary looked down sadly at the photograph on the desk. "His wife died last night, at the nursing home. He hasn't been in the hospital all day."

Kate felt herself sag against the doorway. "His . . . wife?"

"Yes. It was all rather unexpected. A heart attack, they think, but— Are you all right?"

"What?"

"Are you all right? You don't look well."

"No, I'm—I'm fine." Kate backed into the hall. "I'm fine," she repeated, walking in a daze toward the elevators. As she rode down to the lobby, a memory came back to her, an image of shattered glass sparkling at the feet of Clarence Avery.

She needs to be put to sleep. . . . It's so much better if I do it, if I'm there to say goodbye. Don't you think?

The elevator doors hissed open. The instant she stepped out into the bright lights of the lobby, a sudden impulse seized her, the need to flee, to find safety. To find David. She walked outside into the parking lot and the urge became compelling. She couldn't wait; she had to see him now. If she hurried, she might catch him at his office.

Just the thought of seeing his face filled her with such irrational longing that she began to run. She ran all the way to the car.

Her route took her into the very heart of downtown. Late-afternoon sunlight slanted in through the picket shadows of steel-and-glass high rises. Rush-hour traffic clogged the streets; she felt like a fish struggling upstream. With every minute that passed, her hunger to see him grew. And with it grew a panic that she would be too late, that she'd find his office empty, his door locked. At that moment, as she fought through the traffic, it seemed that nothing in her life had ever been as important as reaching the safety of his arms.

Please be there, she prayed. *Please be there....*

"AN EXPLANATION, Mr. Ransom. That's all I'm asking for. A week ago you said our chances of winning were excellent. Now you've withdrawn from the case. I want to know why."

David gazed uneasily into Mary O'Brien's silver-gray eyes and wondered how to answer her. He wasn't about to tell her the truth—that he was having an affair with the opposition. But he did owe her some sort of explanation and he knew, from the look in her eye, that it had better be a good one.

He heard the agitated creaking of wood and leather and he glanced in irritation at Phil Glickman, who was squirming nervously in his chair. David shot him a warning look to cool it. If that was possible. Glickman already knew the truth. And damned if he didn't look ready to blurt it all out.

Mary O'Brien was still waiting.

David's answer was evasive but not entirely dishonest. "As I said earlier, Mrs. O'Brien, I've discovered a conflict of interest."

"I don't understand what that means," Mary O'Brien said impatiently. "This conflict of interest. Are you telling me you work for the hospital?"

"Not exactly."

"Then what does it mean?"

"It's...confidential. I really can't discuss it." Smoothly changing the subject, he continued, "I'm referring your case to Sullivan and March. It's an excellent firm. They'll be happy to take it from here, assuming you have no objections."

"You haven't answered my question." She leaned forward, her eyes glinting, her bony hands bunched tightly on his desk. Claws of vengeance, he thought.

"I'm sorry, Mrs. O'Brien. I just can't serve your needs objectively. I have no choice but to withdraw."

It was a very different parting from the last visit. A cold and businesslike handshake, a nod of the head. Then he and Glickman escorted her out of his office.

"I expect there'll be no delays because of this," she said.

"There shouldn't be. All the groundwork's been laid." He frowned as he saw the frantic expression of his secretary at the far end of the hall.

"You still think they'll try to settle?"

"It's impossible to second-guess...." He paused, distracted. His secretary now looked absolutely panicked.

"You told us before they'd want to settle."

"Hmm? Oh." Suddenly anxious to get rid of her, he guided her purposefully toward the reception room. "Look, don't worry about it, Mrs. O'Brien," he practically snapped out. "I can almost guarantee the other side's discussing a settlement right—" His feet froze in their tracks. He felt as though he were mired in concrete and would never move again.

Kate was standing in front of him. Slowly, her disbelieving gaze shifted to Mary O'Brien.

"Oh, my God," Glickman groaned.

It was a tableau taken straight out of some soap opera: the shocked parties, all staring at one another.

"I can explain everything," David blurted out.

"I doubt it," retorted Mary O'Brien.

Wordlessly Kate spun around and walked out of the suite. The slam of the door shook David out of his paralysis. Just before he rushed out into the hall he heard Mary O'Brien's outraged voice say: "Conflict of interest? Now I know what he meant by *interest*!"

Kate was stepping into an elevator.

He scrambled after her but before he could yank her out, the door snapped shut between them. "Dammit!" he yelled, slamming his fist against the wall.

The next elevator took forever to arrive. All the way down, twenty floors, he paced back and forth like a caged animal, muttering oaths he hadn't used in years. By the time he emerged on the ground floor, Kate was nowhere to be seen.

He ran out of the building and down the steps to the sidewalk. Scanning the street, he spotted, half a block away, a bus idling near the curb. Kate was walking toward it.

Shoving frantically through a knot of pedestrians, he managed to grab her arm and haul her back as she was about to step aboard the bus.

"Let me go!" she snapped.

"Where the hell do you think you're going?"

"Oh, sorry. I almost forgot!" Thrusting her hand in her skirt pocket, she pulled out his car keys and practically threw them at him. "I wouldn't want to be accused of stealing your precious BMW!"

She looked around in frustration as the bus roared off without her. Yanking her arm free, she stormed away. He was right behind her.

"Just give me a chance to explain."

"What did you tell your client, David? That she'll get her settlement now that you've got the dumb doctor eating out of your hand?"

"What happened between you and me has nothing to do with the case."

"It has everything to do with the case! You were hoping all along I'd settle."

"I only asked you to think about it."

"Ha!" She whirled on him. "Is this something they teach you in law school? When all else fails, get the opposition into bed?"

That was the last straw. He grabbed her arm and practically dragged her off the sidewalk and into a nearby pub. Inside, he plunged straight through the boisterous crowd that had gathered around the bar and hauled her through the swirling cigarette smoke to an empty booth at the back. There he plopped her down unceremoniously onto the wooden bench. Sliding into the seat across from her, he shot her a look that said she was damn well going to hear him out.

"First of all—" he started.

"Good evening," said a cheery voice.

"Now what?" he barked at the startled waitress who'd arrived to take their order.

The woman seemed to shrink back into her forest-green costume. "Did you . . . uh, want anything—"

"Just bring us a couple of beers," he snapped.

"Of course, sir." With a pitying look at Kate, the waitress turned ruffled skirts and fled.

For a solid minute, David and Kate stared at each other with unveiled hostility. Then David let out a sigh and clawed his fingers through his already unruly hair. "Okay," he said. "Let's try it again."

"Where do we start? Before or after your client popped out of your office?"

"Did anyone ever tell you you've got a lousy sense of timing?"

"Oh, you're wrong there, mister. My sense of timing happens to be just dandy. What did I hear you say to her? 'Don't worry, there's a settlement in the works'?"

"I was trying to get her out of my office!"

"So how did she react to your straddling both sides of the lawsuit?"

"I wasn't—" he looked pained "—straddling."

"Working for her and going to bed with me? I'd call that straddling."

"For an intelligent woman, you seem to have a little trouble comprehending one little fact: I'm off the case. Permanently. And voluntarily. Mary O'Brien came to my office demanding to know why I withdrew."

"Did you—did you tell her about us?"

"You think I'm nuts? You think I'd come out and announce I had a roll in the hay with the opposition?"

His words hit her like a slap across her face. Was that all it had meant to him? She'd imagined their lovemaking meant far more than just the simple clash of hormones. A joining of souls, perhaps. But for David, the affair had only meant complications. An angry client, a forced withdrawal from a case. And now the humiliation of having to confess an illicit romance. That he'd tried so hard to conceal their affair gave it all a lurid glow. People only hid what they were ashamed of.

"A weekend fling," she said. "Is that what I was?"

"I didn't mean it that way!"

"Well, don't worry about it, David," she assured him with regal composure as she rose to her feet. "I won't embarrass you any more. This is one skeleton who'll gladly step back into the closet."

"*Sit down.*" It was nothing more than a low growl but it held enough threat to make her pause. "Please," he added. Then, in a whisper, he said it again. "Please."

Slowly, she sat back down.

They fell silent as the waitress returned and set down their beers. Only when they were alone again did David say, quietly, "You're not just a fling, Kate. And as for the O'Briens, it's none of their business what I do on my weekends. Or weekdays." He shook his head in amazement. "You know, I've withdrawn from other cases, but it was always for perfectly logical reasons. Reasons I could defend without getting red in the face. This time, though . . ." He let out a brittle laugh. "At my age, getting red in the face isn't supposed to happen anymore."

Kate stared down at her glass. She hated beer. She hated arguing. Most of all, she hated this chasm between them. "If I jumped to conclusions," she admitted grudgingly, "I'm sorry. I guess I never did trust lawyers."

He grunted. "Then we're even. I never did trust doctors."

"So we're an unlikely pair. What else is new?"

They suffered through another one of those terrible loaded silences.

"We really don't know each other very well, do we?" she finally said.

"Except in bed. Which isn't the best place to get acquainted." He paused. "Though we certainly tried."

She looked up and saw an odd little tilt to his mouth, the beginnings of a smile. A lock of hair had slipped down over his brow. His shirt collar gaped open and his tie had been yanked into a limp version of a hangman's noose. She'd never seen him look so wrenchingly attractive.

"Are you going to get in trouble, David? What if the O'Briens complain to the state bar?" she asked softly.

He shrugged. "I'm not worried. Hell, the worst they can do is disbar me. Throw me in jail. Maybe send me to the electric chair."

"David."

"Oh, you're right, I forgot. Hawaii doesn't have an electric chair." He noticed she wasn't laughing. "Okay, so it's a lousy joke." He lifted his mug and was about to take a gulp of beer when he focused on her morose expression. "Oh, I completely forgot. What happened at your hearing?"

"There were no surprises."

"It went against you?"

"To say the least." Miserable, she stared down at the table. "They said my work was substandard. I guess that's a polite way of calling me a lousy doctor."

His silence, more than anything he could have said, told her how much the news disturbed him. With a sense of wonder she watched his hand close gently around hers.

"It's funny," she remarked with an ironic laugh. "I never planned on being anything but a doctor. Now that I'm losing my job, I see how poorly qualified I am for anything else. I can't type. I can't take dictation. For God's sake, I can't even *cook.*"

"Uh-oh. Now that's a serious deficiency. You may have to beg on street corners."

It was another lousy joke, but this time she managed a smile. A meager one. "Promise to drop a few quarters in my hat?"

"I'll do better than that. I'll buy you dinner."

She shook her head. "Thanks. But I'm not hungry."

"Better take me up on the offer," he urged, squeezing her hand. "You never know where you next meal's coming from."

She lifted her head and their gazes met across the table. The eyes she'd once thought so icy now held all the warmth of a summer's day. "All I want is to go home with you, David. I want you to hold me. And not necessarily in that order."

Slowly he moved around the table and slid next to her. Then he pulled her into his arms and held her long and close. It was what she needed, this silent embrace, not of a lover but a friend.

They both stiffened at the sound of the waitress clearing her throat. "I don't believe this woman's timing," David muttered as he pulled away.

"Anything else?" asked the waitress.

"Yes," David replied, smiling politely through clenched teeth. "*If* you don't mind."

"What's that, sir?"

"A little privacy."

KATE LET HIM TALK her into dinner. A full stomach and a few glasses of wine left her flushed and giddy as they walked the dark streets to the parking garage. The lamps spilled a hazy glow across their faces. She clung to his arm and felt like singing, like laughing.

She was going home with David.

She slid onto the leather seat of the BMW and the familiar feeling of security wrapped around her like a blanket. She was in a capsule where no one, nothing, could hurt her. The feeling lasted all the way down the Pali Highway, clung to her as they slipped into the tunnel through the Koolau Mountains, kept her warm on the steep and winding road down the other side of the ridge.

It shattered when David glanced in the rearview mirror and swore softly.

She glanced sideways and saw the faint glow of a car's headlights reflected on his face. "David?"

He didn't answer. She felt the rising hum of the engine as they accelerated.

"David, is something wrong?"

"That car. Behind us."

"What?"

He frowned at the mirror. "I think we're being followed."

Chapter Twelve

Kate whipped her head around and stared at the pair of head-lights twinkling in the distance. "Are you sure?"

"I only noticed because it has a dead left parking light. I know it pulled out behind us when we left the garage. It's been on our tail ever since. All the way down the mountain."

"That doesn't mean he's following us!"

"Let's try a little experiment." He took his foot off the gas pedal.

She went rigid in alarm. "Why are you slowing down?"

"To see what he does."

As her heart accelerated wildly, Kate felt the BMW drift down to forty-five, then forty. Below the speed limit. She waited for the headlights to overtake them but they seemed to hang in the distance, as though some invisible force kept the cars apart.

"Smart guy," said David. "He's staying just far enough behind so I can't read his license."

"There's a turnoff! Oh, please, let's take it!"

He veered off the highway and shot onto a two-lane road cut through dense jungle. Vine-smothered trees whipped past, their overhanging branches splattering the windshield with water. She twisted around and saw, through the backdrop of jungle, the same pair of headlights, twinkling in the darkness. Phantom lights that refused to vanish.

"It's him," she whispered. She couldn't bring herself to say the name, as if, just by uttering it, she would unleash some terrible force.

"I should have known," he muttered. "Dammit, I should've known!"

"What?"

"He was watching the hospital. That's the only way he could've followed you—"

He must have been right behind me, she thought, suddenly sick with the realization of what could have happened. *And I never even knew he was there.*

"I'm going to lose him. Hold on."

She was thrown sideways by the violent lurch of the car. It was all she could do to hang on for dear life. The situation was out of her hands; this show was entirely David's.

Houses leaped past, a succession of brightly lit windows punctuated by the silhouettes of trees and shrubbery. The BMW weaved like a slalom skier through the darkness, rounding corners at a speed that made her claw the dashboard in terror.

Without warning, he swerved into a driveway. The seat belt sliced into her chest as they jerked to a sudden standstill in a pitch-dark garage. Instantly, David cut off the engine. The next thing she knew, he was pulling her down into his arms. There she lay, wedged between the gearshift and David's chest, listening, waiting. She could feel his heart hammering against her, could hear his harsh, uneven breaths. At least he was still able to breathe; she scarcely dared to.

With mounting terror, she watched a flicker of light slowly grow brighter and brighter in the rearview mirror. From the road came the faint growl of an engine. David's arms tensed around her. Already he had shifted his weight and now lay on top of her, shielding her body with his. For an eternity she lay crushed in his embrace, listening, waiting, as the sound of the engine faded away. Only when there was total silence did they finally creep up and peer through the rear window.

The road was dark. The car had vanished.

"What now?" she whispered.

"We get the hell out of here. While we still can." He turned the key; the engine's purr seemed deafening. With his headlights killed, he let the car creep slowly out of the garage.

As they wound their way out of the neighborhood, she kept glancing back, searching for the twin lights dancing beyond the trees. Only when they'd reached the highway did she allow herself a breath of relief. But to her alarm, David turned the car back toward Honolulu.

"Where are we going?"

"We can't go home. Not now."

"But we've lost him!"

"If he followed you from the hospital, then he trailed you straight to my office. To me. Unfortunately, I'm in the phone book. Address and all."

She sank back in shock and struggled to absorb this latest blow. They entered the Pali Tunnel. The succession of lights passing overhead was wildly disorienting, flash after flash that shocked her eyes.

Where do I go now? she wondered. *How long before he finds me? Will I have time to run? Time to scream?* She shuddered as they emerged from the tunnel and were plunged into sudden darkness.

"It's my last resort," David said. "But it's the only place I can think of. You won't be alone. And you'll be perfectly safe." He paused and added with an odd note of humor, "Just don't drink the coffee."

She turned and stared at him in bewilderment. "Where are we going?"

His answer had a distinctly apologetic ring. "My mother's."

THE TINY GRAY-HAIRED woman who opened the door was wearing a ratty bathrobe and pink bunny slippers. For a moment she stood there, blinking like a surprised mouse at the unexpected visitors. Then she clapped her hands and squeaked: "My goodness, David! How nice you've come for a visit! Oh, but this is naughty of you, not to call. You've caught us in our pajamas, like two ol—"

"You're gorgeous, Gracie," cut in David as he tugged Kate into the house. Quickly he locked and bolted the door. Then, glancing out the curtained window, he demanded, "Is Mother awake?"

"Why, yes, she's ... uh ..." Gracie gestured vaguely at the foyer.

From another room, a querulous voice called out: "For heaven's sake, get rid of whoever it is and get in here! It's your turn! And you'd better come up with something good. I just got a triple word score!"

"She's beating me again." Gracie sighed mournfully.

"Then she's in a good mood?"

"I wouldn't know. I've never seen her in one."

"Get ready," David muttered to Kate as he guided her across the foyer. "Mother?" he called out pleasantly. *Too* pleasantly.

In a mauve and mahogany living room, a regal woman with blue-gray hair was sitting with her back turned to them. Her wrapped foot was propped up on a crushed velvet ottoman. On the tea table beside her lay a Scrabble board, crisscrossed with tiles. "I don't believe it," she announced to the wall. "It must be an auditory hallucination." She turned and squinted at him. "Why, my son has actually come for a visit! Is the world at an end?"

"Nice to see you, too, Mother," he responded dryly. He took a deep breath, like a man gathering up the nerve to yank out his own teeth. "We need your help."

The woman's eyes, as glitteringly sharp as crystals, suddenly focused on Kate. Then she noticed David's arm, which was wrapped protectively around Kate's shoulder. Slowly, knowingly, she smiled. With a grateful glance at the heavens she murmured fervently: "Glory hallelujah!"

"YOU NEVER TELL ME anything, David," Jinx Ransom complained as she sat with her son in the fern-infested kitchen an hour later.

They were huddled over cups of cocoa, a ritual they hadn't shared since he was a boy. *How little it takes to be transported back to childhood,* he reflected. One sip of chocolate, one disapproving look from his mother, and the pangs of filial guilt returned. Good old Jinx; she really knew how to make a guy feel young again. In fact, she made him feel about six years old.

"Here you have a woman in your life," said Jinx, "and you hide her from me. As if you're ashamed of her. Or ashamed of me. Or maybe you're ashamed of us both."

"There's nothing to talk about. I haven't known her that long."

"You're just ashamed to admit you're human, aren't you?"

"Don't psychoanalyze me, Mother."

"I'm the one who diapered you. I'm the one who watched you skin your knees. I even saw you break your arm on that blasted skateboard. You almost never cried, David. You still don't cry. I don't think you can. It's some gene you inherited from your father. The Plymouth Rock curse. Oh, the emotions are in there somewhere, but you're not about to let them show. Even when Noah died—"

"I don't want to talk about Noah."

"You see? The boy's been gone eight years now and you still can't hear his name without getting all tight in the face."

"Get to the point, Mother."

"Kate."

"What about her?"

"You were holding her hand."

He shrugged. "She has a very nice hand."

"Have you gone to bed with her yet?"

David sputtered hot chocolate all over the table. "Mother!"

"Well it's nothing to be ashamed of. People do it all the time. It's what nature intended, though I sometimes think you imagine yourself immune to the whole blasted process. But tonight, I saw that look in your eye."

Swatting away a stray fern, he went to the sink for a paper towel and began dabbing the cocoa from his shirt.

"Am I right?" asked Jinx.

"Looks like I'll need a clean shirt for tomorrow," he muttered. "This one's shot."

"Use one of your father's shirts. So am I right?"

He looked up. "About what, Mother?" he asked blankly.

She raised her arm and made a throttling motion at the heavens. "I knew it was a mistake to have only one child!"

Upstairs there was a loud thud. David glanced up at the ceiling. "What the hell is Gracie doing up there, anyway?"

"Digging up some clothes for Kate."

David shuddered. Knowing Gracie's incomparable taste in clothes, Kate would come down swathed from head to toe in some nauseating shade of pink. With bunny slippers to match. The truth was, he didn't give a damn what she was wearing, if only she'd hurry downstairs. They'd been apart only fifteen minutes and already he missed her. It annoyed him, all these inconvenient emotions churning around inside him. It made him feel weak and helpless and all too...human.

He turned eagerly at hearing a creak on the stairs and saw it was only Gracie.

"Is that hot chocolate, Jinx?" Gracie demanded. "You know the milk upsets your stomach. You really should have tea instead."

"I don't want tea."

"Yes, you do."

"No, I don't."

"Where's Kate?" David called out bleakly.

"Oh, she's coming," said Gracie. "She's up in your room, looking at your old model airplanes." Giggling, she confided to Jinx, "I told her they were proof that David was once a child."

"He was never a child," grumbled Jinx. "He sprang from the womb a fully mature adult. Though smaller, of course. Perhaps he'll do it backward. Perhaps he'll get younger as the years go by. We'll see him loosen up and become a real child."

"Like you, Mother?"

Gracie put on the teakettle and sighed happily. "It's so nice to have company, isn't it?" She glanced around, startled, as the phone rang. "My goodness, it's after ten. Who on earth—"

David shot to his feet. "I'll get it." He grabbed the receiver and barked out: "Hello?"

Pokie's voice boomed triumphantly across the wires. "Have I got news for you."

"You've tracked down that car?"

"Forget the car. We got the man."

"Decker?"

"I'll need Dr. Chesne down here to identify him. Half an hour, okay?"

David glanced up to see Kate standing in the kitchen doorway. Her eyes were filled with questions. Grinning, he snapped her a victorious thumbs-up sign. "We'll be right over," he told Pokie. "Where you holding him? Downtown station?"

There was a pause. "No, not the station."

"Where, then?"

"The morgue."

"HOPE YOU HAVE strong stomachs." The medical examiner, a grotesquely chirpy woman named M.J., pulled open the stainless-steel drawer. It glided out noiselessly. Kate cringed against David as M.J. casually reached in and unzipped the plastic shroud.

Under the harsh morgue lights, the corpse's face looked artificial. This wasn't a man; it was some sort of waxen image, a mockery of life.

"Some yachtie found him this evening, floating facedown in the harbor," explained Pokie.

Kate felt David's arm tighten around her waist as she forced herself to study the dead man's bloated features. Distorted as he was, the open eyes were recognizable. Even in death they seemed haunted.

Nodding, Kate whispered, "That's him."

Pokie grinned, a response that struck her as surreal in that nightmarish room. "Bingo," he grunted.

M.J. ran her gloved hand over the dead man's scalp. "Feels like we got a depressed skull fracture here...." She whisked off the shroud, revealing the naked torso. "Looks like he's been in the water quite a while."

Suddenly nauseated, Kate turned and buried her face against David's shoulder. The scent of his after-shave muted the stench of formalin.

"For God's sake, M.J.," David muttered. "Cover him up, will you?"

M.J. zipped up the shroud and slid the drawer closed. "You've lost the old ironclad stomach, hey, Davy boy? If I remember right, you used to shrug off a lot worse."

"I don't hang around stiffs the way I used to." He guided Kate away from the body drawers. "Come on. Let's get the hell out of here."

The medical examiner's office was a purposefully cheerful room, complete with hanging plants and old movie posters, a bizarre setting for the gruesome business at hand. Pokie poured coffee from the automatic brewer and handed two cups to David and Kate. Then, sighing with satisfaction, he settled into a chair across from them. "So that's how it wraps up," he said. "No trial. No hassles. Just a convenient corpse. Too bad justice ain't always this easy."

Kate stared down at her coffee. "How did he die, Lieutenant?" she whispered.

Pokie shrugged. "Happens now and then. Get some guy who's had a little too much to drink. Falls off a pier, bashes his head on the rocks. Hell, we find floaters all the time. Boat bums, mostly." He glanced at M.J. "What do you think?"

"Can't rule out anything yet," mumbled M.J. She was hunched at her desk and wolfing down a late supper. A meatloaf sandwich dripping with ketchup, Kate noted, her stomach threatening to turn inside out. "When a body's been in the water that long, anatomy gets distorted. I'll tell you after the autopsy."

"Just how long was he in the water?" asked David.

"A day. More or less."

"A *day*?" He looked at Pokie. "Then who the hell was following us tonight?"

Pokie grinned. "You just got yourself an active imagination."

"I'm telling you, there was a car!"

"Lot of cars out on the road. Lot of headlights look the same."

"Well, it sure wasn't my guy in the drawer," said M.J., crumpling up her sandwich wrappings. She chomped enthusiastically into a bright red apple. "Far as I know, dead men don't drive."

"When are you going to know the cause of death?" David snapped.

"Still need skull X rays. I'll open him up tonight, check the lungs for water. That'll tell us if he drowned." She took another bite of apple. "But that's *after* I finish my dinner. In the meantime—" swiveling around, she grabbed a cardboard box from a shelf and tossed it down on the desk "—his personal effects."

Methodically she took out the items, each one sealed in its own plastic bag. "Plastic comb, black, pocket-size...cigarettes, Winston, half empty...matchbook, unlabeled...man's wallet, brown vinyl, containing fourteen dollars...various ID cards..." She reached in for the last item. "And these." The set of keys clattered on the desk. Attached was a plastic tag with gaudy red lettering: The Victory Hotel.

Kate picked up the key ring. "The Victory Hotel," she murmured. "Is that where he was living?"

Pokie nodded. "We checked it out. What a dive. Rats crawling all over the place. We know he was there Saturday night. But that's the last time he was seen. Alive, anyway."

Slowly Kate lay the keys down and stared at the mockingly bright lettering. She thought about the face in the mirror, about the torment in those eyes. And as she gazed at the sad and meager pile of belongings, an unexpected wave of sorrow welled up in her, sorrow for a man's shattered dreams. *Who were you, Charlie Decker?* she wondered. *Madman? Murderer?* Here were the bits and pieces of his life, and they were all so ordinary.

Pokie gave her a grin. "Well, it's over, Doc. Our man's dead. Looks like you can go home."

She glanced at David, but he was staring off in another direction. "Yes," she said in a weary voice. "Now I can go home."

WHO WERE YOU, Charlie Decker?

That refrain played over and over in her head as she sat in the darkness of David's car and watched the streetlights flash by. *Who were you?* She thought of all the ways he'd suffered, all the pain he'd felt, that man without a voice. Like everyone else, he'd been a victim.

And now he was a convenient corpse.

"It's too easy, David," she said softly.

He glanced at her through the gloom of the car. "What is?"

"The way it's all turned out. Too simple, too neat..." She stared off into the darkness, remembering the reflection of Charlie Decker's face in the mirror. "My God. I saw it in his eyes," she whispered. "It was right there, staring at me, only I was too panicked to recognize it."

"What?"

"The fear. He was terrified. He must have known something, something awful. And it killed him. Just like it killed the others...."

"You're saying he was a victim? Then why did he threaten you? Why did he make that call to the cottage?"

"Maybe it wasn't a threat...." She looked up with sudden comprehension. "Maybe he was warning me. About someone else."

"But the evidence—"

"What evidence? A few fingerprints on a doorknob? A corpse with a psychiatric record?"

"And a witness. You saw him in Ann's apartment."

"What if he was the real witness? A man in the wrong place at the wrong time." She watched their headlights slash the darkness. "Four people, David. And the only thing that linked them together was a dead woman. If I only knew why Jenny Brook was so important."

"Unfortunately, dead men don't talk."

Maybe they do. "The Victory Hotel," she said suddenly. "Where is it?"

"Kate, the man's dead. The answers died with him. Let's just forget it."

"But there's still a chance—"

"You heard Pokie. The case is closed."

"Not for me, it isn't."

"Oh, for God's sake, Kate! Don't turn this into an obsession!" Gripping the steering wheel, he forced out an agitated breath. When he spoke again, his voice was quiet. "Look, I know how much it means to you, clearing your name. But in the long run, it may not be worth the fight. If vindication's what you're after, I'm afraid you won't get it. Not in the courtroom, anyway.''

"You can't be sure what a jury will think."

"Second-guessing juries is part of my job. I've made a good living, cashing in on doctors' mistakes. And I've done it in a town where a lot of lawyers can barely pay their rent. I'm not any smarter than the other guy, I just pick my cases well. And when I do, I'm not afraid to get down and get dirty. By the time I'm finished, the defendant's scarred for life.''

"Lovely profession you're in."

"I'm telling you this because I don't want it to happen to you. That's why I think you should settle out of court. Let the matter die quietly. Discreetly. Before your name gets dragged through the mud."

"Is that how they do it in the prosecutor's office? 'Plead guilty and we'll make you a *deal*'?"

"There's nothing wrong with a settlement."

"Would you settle? If you were me?"

There was a long pause. "Yes. I would."

"Then we must be very different." Stubbornly she gazed ahead at the highway. "Because I can't let this die. Not without a fight.''

"Then you're going to lose." It was more than an opinion; it was a pronouncement, as final as the thud of a judge's gavel in the courtroom.

"And I suppose lawyers don't take on losing battles, do they?"

"Not this lawyer."

"Funny. Doctors take them on all the time. Try arguing with a stroke. Or cancer. We don't make bargains with the enemy.''

"And that's exactly how I make my living," he retorted. "On the arrogance of doctors!"

It was a vicious blow; he regretted it the instant he said it. But she was headed for trouble, and he had to stop her before she got hurt. Still, he hadn't expected such brutal words to pop out. It was one more reminder of how high the barriers were between them.

They drove the rest of the way in silence. A cloud of gloom filled the space of the car. They both seemed to sense that things were coming to an end; he guessed it had been inevitable from the start. Already he could feel her pulling away.

Back at his house, they drifted toward the bedroom like a pair of strangers. When she pulled down her suitcase and started to pack, he said simply, "Leave it for the morning," and shoved it back in the closet. That was all. He couldn't bring himself to say he wanted her to stay, needed her to stay. He just shut the closet door.

Then he turned to her. Slowly he removed his jacket and tossed it on the chair. He went to her, took her face in his hands and kissed her. Her lips felt chilled. He took her in his arms and held her, warmed her.

They made love, of course. One last time. He was there and she was there and the bed was there. Love among the ruins. No, not love. Desire. Need. Something entirely different, all-consuming yet wholly unsatisfying.

And afterward he lay beside her in the darkness, listening to her breathing. She slept deeply, the unarousable slumber of exhaustion. He should be sleeping, too. But he couldn't. He was too busy thinking about all the reasons he shouldn't fall in love.

He didn't like being in love. It left him far too vulnerable. Since Noah's death, he'd avoided feeling much of anything. At times he'd felt like a robot. He'd functioned on automatic pilot, breathing and eating out of necessity, smiling only when it was expected. When Linda finally left him, he'd hardly noticed; their divorce was a mere drop in an ocean of pain. He guessed he'd loved her, but it wasn't the same total, unconditional love he'd felt for his son. For David, love was quantified by how much he suffered by its loss.

And now here was this woman, lying beside him. He studied the dark pool of her hair against the pillow, the glow of her face. He tried to think of the last time there'd been a woman in his bed. It had been a long time ago, a blonde.

But he couldn't even dredge up her name. That's how little she'd meant to him.

But Kate? He'd remember her name, all right. He'd remember this moment, the way she slept, curled up like a tired kitten, the way her very presence seemed to warm the darkness. He'd remember.

He rose from the bed and wandered into the hall. Some strange yearning pulled him toward Noah's room. He went inside and stood for a moment, bathed in the window's moonlight. For so long he'd avoided this room. He'd hated the sight of that unoccupied bed. He'd always remembered how it used to be, tiptoeing in to watch his son sleep. Noah, by some strange instinct, always seemed to choose that moment to awaken. And in the darkness, they'd murmur their ritual conversation.

Is that you, Daddy?

Yes, Noah, it's me. Go back to sleep.

Hug first. Please.

Good night. Don't let the bedbugs bite.

David sat down on the bed, listening to the echoes of the past, remembering how much it had hurt to love.

At last he went back to Kate's bed, crawled in beside her and fell asleep.

He woke up before dawn. In the shower he purposefully washed off all traces of their lovemaking. He felt renewed. He dressed for work, donning each item of clothing as if it was a piece of armor to shield him from the world. Alone in the kitchen, he had a cup of coffee.

Now that Decker was dead, there was no reason for Kate to stay. David had done his moral duty; he'd played the white knight and kept her safe. It had been clear from the start that none of this was for keeps. He'd never led her on. His conscience was clear. Now it was time for her to go home; and they both knew it. Perhaps her leaving was all for the better. A few days, a few weeks apart, might give him a saner perspective. Maybe he'd decide this was all a case of temporary, hormonal madness.

Or maybe he was only kidding himself.

He worried about all the things that could happen to her if she kept on digging into Charlie Decker's past. He also knew she would keep on digging. Last night he hadn't told her the truth: that he thought she was right, that there was more to this case than a madman's vengeance. Four people were dead; he didn't want her to be the fifth.

He got up and rinsed his cup. Then he went back to the bedroom. There he sat at the foot of the bed—a safe distance—and watched her sleep. Such a beautiful, stubborn, maddeningly independent woman. He used to think he liked independent women. Now he wasn't so sure. He almost wished Decker was still alive, just so Kate would go on needing him. How incredibly selfish.

Then he decided she did still need him. They'd shared two nights of passion. For that he owed her one last favor.

He nudged her gently. "Kate?"

Slowly she opened her eyes and looked at him. Those sleepy green eyes. He wanted so badly to kiss her but decided it was better if he didn't.

"The Victory Hotel," he said. "Do you still want to go?"

Chapter Thirteen

Mrs. Tubbs, the manager of the Victory Hotel, was a toadlike woman with two pale slits for eyes. Despite the heat, she was wearing a ratty gray sweater over her flowered dress. Through a hole in her sock poked an enormously swollen big toe. "Charlie?" she asked, cautiously peering at David and Kate through her half-open door. "Yeah, he lived here."

In the room behind her, a TV game show blared and a man yelled, "You retard! I coulda guessed that one!"

The woman turned and yelled: "Ebbie! Turn that thing down! Can't you see I'm talkin' to someone?" She looked back at David and Kate. "Charlie don't live here no more. Got hisself killed. Po-lice already come by."

"If it's all right, we'd like to see his room," said Kate.

"What for?"

"We're looking for information."

"You from the po-lice?"

"No, but—"

"Can't let you up there without a warrant. Po-lice give me too much trouble already. Gettin' everyone in the building all nervous. 'Sides, I got orders. No one goes up." Her tone implied that someone very high, perhaps even God Himself, had issued those orders. To emphasize the point, she started to close the door. She looked outraged when David stopped it with a well-placed hand.

"Seems to me you could use a new sweater, Mrs. Tubbs," David remarked quietly.

The door swung open a fraction of an inch. Mrs. Tubbs's pale eyes peered at him through the crack. "I could use a lot of new things," she grunted. From the apartment came a man's loud and enthusiastic burp. "New husband, mostly."

"Afraid I can't help you there."

"No one can, 'cept maybe the good Lord."

"Who works His magic in unexpected ways." David's smile was dazzling; Mrs. Tubbs stared, waiting for the proffered miracle to occur.

David produced it in the form of two twenty-dollar bills, which he slipped discreetly into her fat hands.

She looked down at the money. "Hotel owner'll kill me if he finds out."

"He won't."

"Don't pay me nearly enough to manage this here trash heap. Plus I'm s'posed to pay off the city inspector." David slipped her another twenty. "But you ain't no inspector, right?" She wadded up the bills and stuffed them into the dark and bottomless recess of her bosom. "No inspector I seen ever come dressed like you." Shuffling out into the hall, she closed the door on Ebbie and the TV. In her stockinged feet, she led David and Kate toward the staircase. It was a climb of only one flight, but for her each step seemed to be agony. By the time she reached the top, she was wheezing like an accordion. A brown carpet—or had it once been mustard yellow?—stretched out into the dim hallway. She stopped before room 203 and fumbled for the keys.

"Charlie was here 'bout a month," she gasped out, a few words at a time. "Real quiet. Caused no...no trouble, not like some...some of them others...."

At the other end of the hall, a door suddenly opened and two small faces peered out.

"Charlie come back?" the little girl called.

"I already told you," Mrs. Tubbs said. "Charlie gone and left for good."

"But when's he comin' back?"

"You kids deaf or somethin'? How come you ain't in school?"

"Gabe's sick," explained the girl. As if to confirm the fact, little Gabe swiped his hand across his snotty nose.

"Where's your ma?"

The girl shrugged. "Out workin'."

"Yeah. Leaves you two brats here to burn down the place." The children shook their heads solemnly. "She took away our matches," replied Gabe.

Mrs. Tubbs got the door unlocked. "There y'are," she said and pushed it open.

As the room swung into view, something small and brown rustled across the floor and into the shadows. The mingled odors of cigarette smoke and grease hung in the gloom. Pinpoints of light glittered through a tattered curtain. Mrs. Tubbs went over and shoved the curtain aside. Sunshine splashed in through the grimy window.

"Go 'head, have a look 'round," she said, planting herself in a corner. "But don't take nothin'."

It was easy to see why a visit by the city inspector might cause her alarm. A baited rattrap, temporarily unoccupied, lay poised near a trash can. A single light bulb hung from the ceiling, its wires nakedly exposed. On a one-burner hot plate sat a frying pan coated with a thick layer of congealed fat. Except for the one window, there was no ventilation and any cooking would have made the air swirl with grease.

Kate's gaze took in the miserable surroundings: the rumpled bed, the ashtray overflowing with cigarette butts, the card table littered with loose scraps of paper. She frowned at one of the pages, covered with scribblings.

Eight was great
Nine was fine,
And now you're ten years old.
Happy Birthday, Jocelyn,
The best will yet unfold!

"Who's Jocelyn?" she asked.

"That brat in 210. Mother's never around to watch 'em. Always out workin'. Or so she calls it. Kids just 'bout burned the place down last month. Woulda throwed 'em all out, 'cept they always pay me in cash.''

"Just how much is the rent?" David asked.

"Four hundred bucks."

"You've got to be kidding."

"Hey, we got us a good location. Close to the bus lines. Free water 'n 'lectricity." At that instant, a cockroach chose to scuttle across the floor. "And we take pets."

Kate looked up from the pile of papers. "What was he like, Mrs. Tubbs?"

"Charlie?" She shrugged. "What's to say? Kept to hisself. Never made no noise. Never blasted the radio like some of these no-accounts. Never complained 'bout nothin' far as I remember. Hell, we hardly knew he was here. Yeah, a real good tenant."

By those standards, the ideal tenant would have been a corpse.

Mrs. Tubbs settled into a chair and watched as they searched the room. Their inspection revealed a few wrinkled shirts hanging in the closet, a dozen cans of Campbell's soup neatly stacked in the cabinet under the sink, some laundered socks and men's underwear in the dresser drawer. It was a meager collection of belongings; they held few clues to the personality of their owner.

At last Kate wandered to the window and looked down at a glass-littered street. Beyond a chain-link fence there was a condemned building with walls that sagged outward, as though a giant had stepped on it. A grim view of the world, this panorama of broken bottles and abandoned cars and drunks lolling on the sidewalk. This was a dead end, the sort of place you landed when you could fall no farther.

No, that wasn't quite right. There was one place lower you could fall: the grave.

"Kate?" said David. He'd been rummaging in the nightstand. "Prescription pills," he said, holding up a bottle. "Haldol, prescribed by Dr. Nemechek. State hospital."

"That's his psychiatrist."

"And look. I also found this." He held out a small, framed photograph.

The instant Kate saw the face, she knew who the woman was. She took the picture and studied it by the window's light. It was only a snapshot in time, a single image captured on a sheet of photographic paper, but the young woman who'd smiled into the camera's lens had the glow of eternity in her eyes. They were rich brown eyes, full of laughter, narrowed slightly in the sunlight. Behind her, a brassy sky met the turquoise blue of the sea. A strand of dark hair had blown across her face and clung almost wistfully to the curve of her cheek. She was wearing a simple white bathing suit; and though she'd struck a purposely sexy pose, kneeling there in the sand, there was a sweet gawkiness about her, like a child playing grown-up in her mother's clothes.

Kate slipped the photo out of its frame. The edges were tattered, lovingly worn by years of handling. On the other side was a handwritten message: "Till you come back to me. Jenny."

"Jenny," Kate said softly.

For a long time she stood there, staring at those words, written by a woman long since dead. She thought about the emptiness of this room, about the soup cans, so carefully stacked, about the pile of socks and underwear in the drawer. Charlie Decker had owned so very little. The one possession he'd guarded through the years, the one thing he'd treasured, had been this fading photograph of a woman with eternity in her eyes. It was hard to believe that such a glow could ever be extinguished, even in the depths of a grave.

She turned to Mrs. Tubbs. "What will happen to his things? Now that he's dead?"

"Guess I'll have to sell it all off," replied Mrs. Tubbs. "Owed me a week's rent. Gotta get it somehow. Though there ain't much of value in here. 'Cept maybe what you're holding."

Kate looked down at the smiling face of Jenny Brook. "Yes. She's beautiful, isn't she?"

"Naw, I don't mean the picture."

Kate frowned. "What?"

"The frame." Mrs. Tubbs went to the window and snapped the curtain closed. "It's silver."

JOCELYN AND HER BROTHER were hanging like monkeys on the chain-link fence. As David and Kate came out of the Victory Hotel, the children dropped to the ground and watched expectantly as though something extraordinary was about to happen. The girl—if she was indeed ten—was small for her age. Toothpick legs stuck out from under her baggy dress. Her bare feet were filthy. The little boy, about six and equally filthy, held a clump of his sister's skirt in his fist.

"He's dead, isn't he?" Jocelyn blurted out. Seeing Kate's sad nod, the girl slouched back against the fence and addressed one of the smudges on her bodice. "You see, I knew it. Stupid grown-ups. Don't ever tell us the truth, any of 'em."

"What did they tell you about Charlie?" asked Kate.

"They just said he went away. But he never even gave me my present."

"For your birthday?"

Jocelyn stared down at her nonexistent breasts. "I'm ten."

"And I'm seven," her brother said automatically, as if it was called for in the script.

"You and Charlie must have been good friends," David remarked.

The girl looked up, and seeing his smile—a smile that could melt the heart of any woman, much less that of a ten-year-old—immediately blushed. Looking back down, she coyly traced one brown toe along a crack in the sidewalk. "Charlie didn't have any friends. I don't, either. 'Cept Gabe here, but he's just my brother."

Little Gabe smiled and rubbed his slimy nose on his sister's dress.

"Did anyone else know Charlie very well?" David asked. "I mean, besides you."

Jocelyn chewed her lip thoughtfully. "Well . . . you could try over at Maloney's. Up the street."

"Who's Maloney?"

"Oh, he's nobody."

"If he's nobody, then how does he know Charlie?"

"He's not a him. He's a place. I mean, *it's* a place."

"Oh, of course," said David, looking down into Jocelyn's dazzled eyes. "How stupid of me."

"WHAT'RE YOU KIDS doing in here again? Go on. Get out before I lose my license!"

Jocelyn and Gabe skipped through the air-conditioned gloom, past the cocktail tables and up to the bar. They clambered onto two counter stools. "Some people here to see you, Sam," announced Jocelyn.

"There's a sign out there says you gotta be twenty-one to come in here. You kids twenty-one yet?"

"I'm seven," answered Gabe. "Can I have an olive?"

Grumbling, the bartender dipped his soapy hand in a glass jar and plopped half a dozen green olives on the counter. "Okay, now get going before someone sees you in—" His head jerked up as he noticed David and Kate approaching through the shadows. From his wary look, it was obvious Maloney's was seldom frequented by such well-heeled clientele. He blurted out: "It's not my doing! These brats come runnin' in off the street. I was just gonna throw 'em out."

"They're not liquor inspectors," said Jocelyn with obvious disdain as she popped an olive in her mouth.

Apparently everyone in this part of town lived in fear of some dreaded inspector or another.

"We need information," said David. "About one of your customers. Charlie Decker."

Sam took a long and careful look at David's clothes, and his train of thought was clearly mirrored in his eyes. *Nice suit. Silk tie. Yessir, all very expensive.* "He's dead," the bartender grunted.

"We know that."

"I don't speak ill of the dead." There was a long, significant pause. "You gonna order something?"

David sighed and finally settled onto a bar stool. "Okay. Two beers."

"That's all?"

"And two pineapple juices," added Jocelyn.

"That'll be twelve bucks."

"Cheap drinks," said David, sliding a twenty-dollar bill across the counter.

"Plus tax."

The children dumped the remaining olives in their drinks and began slurping down the juice.

"Tell us about Charlie," Kate prodded.

"Well, he used to sit right over there." Sam nodded at a dark corner table.

David and Kate leaned forward, waiting for the next pearl of information. Silence. "And?" prompted David.

"So that's where he sat."

"Doing what?"

"Drinking. Whiskey, mostly. He liked it neat. Then sometimes, I'd make him up a Sour Sam. That's if the mood hit him for somethin' different. That's my invention, the Sour Sam. Yeah, he'd drink one of those 'bout once a week. But mostly it was whiskey. Neat."

There was another silence. The talking machine had run out of money and needed a refill.

"I'll try a Sour Sam," said Kate.

"Don't you want your beer?"

"You can have it."

"Thanks. But I never touch the stuff." He turned his attention to mixing up a bizarre concoction of gin, club soda, and the juice of half a lemon, which undoubtedly accounted for the drink's name.

"Five bucks," he announced, passing it to Kate. "So how do you like it?"

She took a sip and gasped. "Interesting."

"Yeah, that's what everyone tells me."

"We were talking about Charlie," David reminded him.

"Oh, yeah, Charlie." The talking machine was back in order. "Let's see, he came around just 'bout every night. Think he liked the company, though he couldn't talk much, what with that bad throat of his. He'd sit there and drink, oh, one or two."

"Whiskeys. Neat," David supplied.

"Yeah, that's right. Real moderate, you know. Never got out-and-out drunk. He was a regular for 'bout a month. Then, few days ago, he stopped comin'. Too bad, you know? Hate to lose a steady one like that."

"You have any idea why he stopped?"

"They say police were looking for him. Word was out he killed some people."

"What do you think?"

"Charlie?" Sam laughed. "Not a chance."

Jocelyn handed Sam her empty glass. "Can I have another pineapple juice?"

Sam poured out two more pineapple juices and slid them over to the kids. "Eight bucks." He looked at David, who resignedly reached for his wallet.

"You forgot the olives," said Gabe.

"Those are free." The man wasn't entirely heartless.

"Did Charlie ever mention the name Jenny Brook?" Kate asked.

"Like I said, he never talked much. Yeah, ol' Charlie, he'd just sit over at that table and write those ol' poems. He'd scribble and scribble for hours just to get one right. Then he'd get mad and toss it. There'd be all these wadded-up papers on the floor whenever he left."

Kate shook her head in wonder. "I never imagined he'd be a poet."

"Everyone's a poet these days. That Charlie, though, he was real serious about it. That last day he was here, didn't have no money to pay for his drink. So he tears out one of his poems and gives it to me. Says it'll be worth somethin' some day. Ha! I'm such a sucker." He picked up a dirty rag and began to give the counter an almost sensuous rubdown.

"Do you still have the poem?" asked Kate.

"That's it, tacked over on the wall there."

The cheap, lined paper hung by a few strips of Scotch tape. By the dim light of the bar, the words were barely readable.

This is what I told them:
That healing lies not in forgetfulness
But in remembrance
Of you.
The smell of the sea on your skin.
The small and perfect footprints you leave in the sand.
In remembrance there are no endings.
And so you lie there, now and always, by the sea.

You open your eyes. You touch me.
The sun is in your fingertips.
And I am healed.
I am healed.

"So," said Sam, "think it's any good?"
"Gotta be," said Jocelyn. "If Charlie wrote it."
Sam shrugged. "Don't mean nothin'."

"SEEMS LIKE WE'VE HIT a dead end," David commented as they walked out into the blinding sunshine.

He might as well have said it of their relationship. He was standing with his hands thrust deep in his pockets as he gazed down the street at a drunk slouched in a doorway. Shattered glass sparkled in the gutter. Across the street, lurid red letters spelled out the title *Victorian Secrets* on an X-rated movie marquee.

If only he'd give her a smile, a look, anything to indicate that things weren't drawing to a close between them. But he didn't. He just kept his hands in his pockets. And she knew, without him saying a word, that more than Charlie Decker had died.

They passed an alley, scattering shards of broken beer bottles as they walked.

"So many loose ends," she remarked. "I don't see how the police can close the case."

"When it comes to police work, there are always loose ends, nagging doubts."

"It's sad, isn't it?" She gazed back at the Victory Hotel. "When a man dies and he leaves nothing behind. No trace of who or what he was."

"You could say the same about all of us. Unless we write great books or put up buildings, what's left of us after we're gone? Nothing."

"Only children."

For a moment he was silent. Then he said, "That's if we're lucky."

"We do know one thing about him," she concluded softly. "He loved her. Jenny." Staring down at the cracked sidewalk, she thought of the face in the photograph. An unforgettable woman. Even five years after her death, Jenny Brook's magic had somehow affected the lives of four people: the one who had loved her and the three who'd watched her die. She was the one tragic thread weaving through the tapestry of their deaths.

What would it be like, she wondered, to be loved as fiercely as Jenny had been? What enchantment had she possessed? *Whatever it was, I certainly don't have it.*

She said, without conviction, "It'll be good to get home again."

"Will it?"

"I'm used to being on my own."

He shrugged. "So am I."

They'd both retreated to their separate emotional corners. So little time left, she thought with a sense of desolation. And here they were, mouthing words like a pair of strangers. This morning, she'd awakened to find him showered and shaved and dressed in his most forbidding suit. Over breakfast they'd discussed everything but the subject that was uppermost in her mind. He could have made the first move. The whole time she was packing, he'd had the chance to ask her to stay. And she would have.

But he didn't say a thing.

Thank God she'd always been so good at holding on to her dignity. Never any tears, any hysterics. Even Eric had said as much. You've always been so sensible about things, he'd told her as he'd walked out the door.

Well, she'd be sensible this time, too.

The drive was far too short. Glancing at his profile she remembered the day they'd met. An eternity ago. He looked just as forbidding, just as untouchable.

They pulled up at her house. He carried her suitcase briskly up the walkway; he had the stride of a man in a hurry.

"Would you like to come in for a cup of coffee?" she asked, already knowing what his answer would be.

"I can't. Not right now. But I'll call you."

Famous last words. She understood perfectly, of course. It was all part of the ritual.

He cast a furtive glance at his watch. *Time to move on,* she reflected. *For both of us.*

Automatically she thrust the key in the lock and gave the door a shove. It swung open. As the room came into view, she halted on the threshold, unable to believe what she was seeing.

Dear God, she thought. *Why is this happening? Why now?*

She felt David's steadying hand close around her arm as she swayed backward in horror. The room swam, just for an instant, and then her eyes refocused on the opposite wall.

On the flowered wallpaper the letters "MYOB" had been spray painted in bloodred. And below them was the hollow-eyed figure of a skull and crossbones.

Chapter Fourteen

"No dice, Davy. The case is closed."

Pokie Ah Ching splashed coffee from his foam cup as he weaved through the crammed police station, past the desk sergeant arguing into the phone, past clerks hurrying back and forth with files, past a foul-smelling drunk shouting epithets at two weary-looking officers. Through it all, he moved as serenely as a battleship gliding through stormy waters.

"Don't you see, it was a warning!"

"Probably left by Charlie Decker."

"Kate's neighbor checked the house Tuesday morning. That message was left sometime later, when Decker was already dead."

"So it's a kid's prank."

"Yeah? Why would some kid write MYOB? Mind your own business?"

"You understand kids? I don't. Hell, I can't even figure out my own kids." Pokie headed into his office and scooted around to his chair. "Like I said, Davy, I'm busy."

David leaned across the desk. "Last night I told you we were followed. You said it was all in my head."

"I still say so."

"Then Decker turns up in the morgue. A nice, convenient little accident."

"I'm starting to smell a conspiracy theory."

"Your sense of smell is amazing."

Pokie set his cup down, slopping coffee on his papers. "Okay." He sighed. "You got one minute to tell me your theory. Then I'm throwing you out."

David grabbed a chair and sat down. "Four deaths. Tanaka. Richter. Decker. And Ellen O'Brien—"

"Death on the operating table isn't in my jurisdiction."

"But murder is. There's a hidden player in this game, Pokie. Someone who's managed to get rid of four people in a matter of two weeks. Someone smart and quiet and medically sophisticated. And very, very scared."

"Of what?"

"Kate Chesne. Maybe Kate's been asking too many questions. Maybe she knows something and just doesn't realize it. She's made our killer nervous. Nervous enough to scrawl warnings all over that wall."

"Unseen player, huh? I suppose you already got me a list of suspects."

"Starting with the chief of anesthesia. You check out that story on his wife yet?"

"She died Tuesday night in the nursing home. Natural causes."

"Oh, sure. The night after he walks off with a bunch of lethal drugs, she kicks the bucket."

"Coincidence."

"The man lives alone. There's no one to track his comings and goings—"

"I can just see the old geezer now." Pokie laughed. "Geriatric Jack the Ripper."

"It doesn't take much strength to slit someone's throat."

"But what's the old guy's motive, huh? Why would he go after members of his own staff?"

David let out a frustrated sigh. "I don't know," he admitted. "But it's got something to do with Jenny Brook."

Ever since he'd laid eyes on her photograph, he'd been unable to get the woman out of his mind. Something about her death, about the cold details recorded in her medical chart kept coming back to him, like a piece of music being played over and over in his head.

Uncontrollable seizures.

An infant girl, born alive.

Mother and child, two soft sparks of humanity, extinguished in the glare of the operating room.

Why, after five years, did their deaths threaten Kate Chesne?

There was a knock on the door. Sergeant Brophy, red-eyed and sniffling, dropped some papers on Pokie's desk. "Here's that report you been waiting for. Oh, and we got us another sighting of that Sasaki girl."

Pokie snorted. "Again? What does that make it? Forty-three?"

"Forty-four. This one's at Burger King."

"Geez. Why do they always spot 'em at fast-food chains?"

"Maybe she's sittin' there with Jimmy Hoffa and—and—" Brophy sneezed. "Elvis." He blew his nose three times. They were great loud honks that, in the wild, could have attracted geese. "Allergies," he said, as if that was a far more acceptable excuse than the common cold. He aimed a spiteful glance out the window at his nemesis: a mango tree, seething with blossoms. "Too many damn trees around here," he muttered, retreating from the office.

Pokie laughed. "Brophy's idea of paradise is an air-conditioned concrete box." Reaching for the report, he sighed. "That's it, Davy. I got work to do."

"You going to reopen the case?"

"I'll think about it."

"What about Avery? If I were you, I'd—"

"I said I'll think about it." He flipped open the report, a rude gesture that said the meeting was definitely over.

David saw he might as well bang his head against a brick wall. He rose to leave. He was almost to the door when Pokie suddenly snapped out: "Hold it, Davy."

David halted, startled by the sharpness of Pokie's voice. "What?"

"Where's Kate right now?"

"I took her to my mother's. I didn't want to leave her alone."

"Then she is in a safe place."

"If you can call being around my mother safe. Why?"

Pokie waved the report he was holding. "This just came in from M.J.'s office. It's the autopsy on Decker. He didn't drown."

"What?" David moved over to the desk and snatched up the report. His gaze shot straight to the conclusions.

Skull X rays show compression fracture, probably caused by lethal blow to the head. Cause of death: epidural hematoma.

Pokie sank back wearily and spat out an epithet. "The man was dead hours before he hit the water."

"VENGEANCE?" said Jinx Ransom, biting neatly into a freshly baked gingersnap. "It's a perfectly reasonable motive for murder. If, that is, one accepts there is such a thing as a reasonable motive for murder."

She and Kate were sitting on the back porch, overlooking the cemetery. It was a windless afternoon. Nothing moved—not the leaves on the trees, not the low-lying clouds, not even the air, which hung listless over the valley. The only creature stirring was Gracie, who shuffled out of the kitchen with a tray of rattling coffee cups and teaspoons. Pausing outside, Gracie cocked her head up at the sky.

"It's going to rain," she announced with absolute confidence.

"Charlie Decker was a poet," said Kate. "He loved children. Even more important, children loved him. Don't you think they'd know? They'd sense it if he was dangerous?"

"Nonsense. Children are as stupid as all the rest of us. And as for his being a mild-mannered poet, that doesn't mean a thing. He had five years to brood about his loss. That's certainly long enough to turn an obsession into violence."

"But the people who knew him all agree he wasn't a violent man."

"We're all violent. Especially when it concerns the ones we love. They're intimately connected, love and hate."

"That's a pretty grim view of human nature."

"But a realistic one. My husband was a circuit-court judge. My son was once a prosecutor. Oh, I've heard all their stories and believe me, reality's much grimmer than we could ever imagine."

Kate gazed out at the gently sloping lawn, at the flat bronze plaques marching out like footsteps across the grass. "Why did David leave the prosecutor's office?"

"Hasn't he told you?"

"He said something about slave wages. But I get the feeling money doesn't really mean much to him."

"Money doesn't mean diddly squat to David," Gracie interjected. She was looking down at a broken gingersnap, as if she wasn't quite sure whether to eat it or toss it to the birds.

"Then why did he leave?"

Jinx gave her one of those crystal-blue looks. "You were a surprise to me, Kate. It's rare enough for David to bring any woman to meet me. And then, when I heard you were a doctor...Well." She shook her head in amazement.

"David doesn't like doctors much," Gracie explained helpfully.

"It's a bit more than just dislike, dear."

"You're right," agreed Gracie after a few seconds' thought. "I suppose *loathe* is a better word."

Jinx reached for her cane and stood up. "Come, Kate," she beckoned. "There's something I think you should see."

It was a slow and solemn walk, through the feathery gap in the mock orange hedge, to a shady spot beneath the monkeypod tree. Insects drifted like motes in the windless air. At their feet, a small bunch of flowers lay wilting on a grave.

Noah Ransom
Seven years old.

"My grandson," said Jinx.

A leaf fluttered down from the tree and lay trembling on the grass.

"It must have been terrible for David," Kate murmured. "To lose his only child."

"Terrible for anyone. But especially for David." Jinx nudged the leaf aside with her cane. "Let me tell you about my son. He's very much like his father in one way: he doesn't love easily. He's like a miser, holding on to some priceless hoard of gold. But then, when he does release it, he gives it all and that's it. There's no turning back. That's why it was so hard on him, losing Noah. That boy was the most precious thing in his life and he still can't accept the fact he's gone. Maybe that's why he has so much trouble with you." She turned to Kate. "Do you know how the boy died?"

"He said it was a case of meningitis."

"Bacterial meningitis. Curable illness, right?"

"If it's caught early enough."

"*If.* That's the word that haunts David." She looked down sadly at the wilted flowers. "He was out of town—some convention in Chicago—when Noah got sick. At first, Linda didn't think much of it. You know how kids are, always coming down with colds. But the boy's fever wouldn't go away. And then Noah said he had a headache. His usual pediatrician was on vacation so Linda took the boy to another doctor, in the same building. For two hours they sat in the waiting room. After all that, the doctor spent only five minutes with Noah. And then he sent him home."

Kate stared down at the grave, knowing, fearing, what would come next.

"Linda called the doctor three times that night. She must have known something was wrong. But all she got from him was a scolding. He told her she was just an anxious mother. That she ought to know better than to turn a cold into a crisis. When she finally brought Noah into Emergency, he was delirious. He just kept mumbling, asking for his Daddy. The hospital doctors did what they could, but..." Jinx gave a little shrug. "It wasn't easy for either of them. Linda blamed herself. And David...he just withdrew. He shrank into his tight little shell and refused to come out, even for her. I'm not surprised she left him." Jinx looked off, toward the house. "It came out later, about the doctor. That he was an alcoholic. That he'd lost his license in California. That's when David turned it into his personal crusade. Oh, he ruined the man, all right. He did a very thorough job of it. But it took over his life, wrecked his marriage. That's when he left the prosecutor's office. He's made a lot of money since then, destroying doctors. But the money's not why he does it. Somewhere, in the back of his mind, he'll always be crucifying that one doctor. The one who killed Noah.''

That's why we never had a chance, Kate thought. *I was always the enemy. The one he wanted to destroy.*

Jinx wandered slowly back to the house. For a long time, Kate stood alone in the shadow of the old tree, thinking about Noah Ransom, seven years old. About how powerful a force it was, this love for a child; as cruelly obsessive as anything between a man and a woman. Could she ever compete with the memory of a son? Or ever escape the blame for his death?

All these years, David had held on to that pain. He'd used it as some mystical source of power to fight the same battle over and over again. The way Charlie Decker had used his pain to sustain him through five long years in a mental hospital.

Five years in a hospital.

She frowned, suddenly remembering the bottle of pills in Decker's nightstand. Haldol. Pills for psychotics. Was he, in fact, crazy?

Turning, she looked back at the porch and saw it was empty. Jinx and Gracie had gone into the house. The air was so heavy she could feel it weighing oppressively on her shoulders. A storm on the way, she thought.

If she left now, she might make it to the state hospital before the rain started.

DR. NEMECHEK was a thin, slouching man with tired eyes and a puckered mouth. His shirt was rumpled and his white coat hung in folds on his frail shoulders. He looked like a man who'd slept all night in his clothes.

They walked together on the hospital grounds. All around them, white-gowned patients wandered aimlessly like dandelion fluffs drifting about the lawn. Every so often, Dr. Nemechek would stop to pat a shoulder or murmur a few words of greeting. *How are you, Mrs. Solti? Just fine, Doctor. Why didn't you come to group therapy? Oh, it's my old trouble, you know. All those mealyworms in my feet. I see. I see. Well, good afternoon, Mrs. Solti. Good afternoon, Doctor.*

Dr. Nemechek paused on the grass and gazed around sadly at his kingdom of shattered minds. "Charlie Decker never belonged here," he remarked. "I told them from the beginning that he wasn't criminally insane. But the court had their so-called expert from the mainland. So he was committed." He shook his head. "That's the trouble with courts. All they look at is their evidence, whatever that means. I look at the man."

"And what did you see when you looked at Charlie?"

"He was withdrawn. Very depressed. At times, maybe, delusional."

"Then he was insane."

"But not criminally so." Nemechek turned to her as if he wanted to be absolutely certain she understood his point. "Insanity can be dangerous. Or it can be nothing more than a gentle affliction. A merciful shield against pain. That's what it was for Charlie: a shield. His delusion kept him alive. That's why I never tried to tamper with it. I felt that if I ever took away that shield, it would kill him."

"The police say he was a murderer."

"Ridiculous."

"Why?"

"He was a perfectly benign creature. He'd go out of his way to avoid stepping on a cricket."

"Maybe killing people was easier."

Nemechek gave a dismissive wave. "He had no reason to kill anyone."

"What about Jenny Brook? Wasn't she his reason?"

"Charlie's delusion wasn't about Jenny. He'd accepted her death as inevitable."

Kate frowned. "Then what was his delusion?"

"It was about their child. It was something one of the doctors told him, about the baby being born alive. Only Charlie got it twisted around in his head. That was his obsession, this missing daughter of his. Every August, he'd hold a little birthday celebration. He'd tell us, 'My girl's five years old today.' He wanted to find her. Wanted to raise her like a little princess, give her dresses and dolls and all the things girls are supposed to like. But I knew he'd never really try to find her. He was terrified of learning the truth: that the baby really was dead.''

A sprinkling of rain made them both glance up at the sky. Wind was gusting the clouds and on the lawn, nurses hurried about, coaxing patients out of the coming storm.

"Is there any possibility he was right?" she asked. "That the girl's still alive?"

"Not a chance." A curtain of drizzle had drifted between them, blotting out his gray face. "The baby's dead, Dr. Chesne. For the last five years, the only place that child existed was in Charlie Decker's mind."

THE BABY'S DEAD.

As Kate drove the mist-shrouded highway back to Jinx's house, Dr. Nemechek's words kept repeating in her head.

The baby's dead. The only place that child existed was in Charlie Decker's mind.

If the girl had lived, what would she be like now? Kate wondered. Would she have her father's dark hair? Would she have her mother's glow of eternity in her five-year-old eyes?

The face of Jenny Brook took shape in her mind, an impish smile framed by the blue sky of a summer day. At that instant, fog puffed across the road and Kate strained to see through the mist. As she did, the image of Jenny Brook wavered, dissolved; in its place was another face, a small one, framed by ironwood trees. There was a break in the clouds; suddenly, the mist vanished from the road. And as the sunlight broke through, so did the revelation. She almost slammed on the brakes.

Why the hell didn't I see it before?

Jenny Brook's child was still alive.

And he was five years old.

"WHERE THE HELL is she?" muttered David, slamming the telephone down. "Nemechek says she left the state hospital at five. She should be home by now." He glanced irritably across his desk at Phil Glickman, who was poking a pair of chopsticks into a carton of chow mein.

"You know," Glickman mumbled as he expertly shuttled noodles into his mouth, "this case gets more confusing every time I hear about it. You start off with a simple act of malpractice and you end up with murder. In plural. Where's it gonna lead next?"

"I wish I knew." David sighed. Swiveling around toward the window, he tried to ignore the tempting smells of Glickman's take-out supper. Outside, the clouds were darkening to a gunmetal gray. It reminded him of just how late it was. Ordinarily, he'd be packing up his briefcase for home. But he'd needed a chance to think, and this was where his mind seemed to work best—right here at this window.

"What a way to commit murder, slashing someone's throat," Glickman said. "I mean, think of all that blood! Takes a lot of nerve."

"Or desperation."

"And it can't be that easy. You'd have to get up pretty close to slice that neck artery." He slashed a chopstick through the air. "There are so many easier ways to do the job."

"Sounds like you've put some thought into the matter."

"Don't we all? Everyone has some dark fantasy. Cornering your wife's lover in the alley. Getting back at the punk who mugged you. We can all think of someone we'd really like to put away. And it can't be that hard, you know? Murder. If a guy's smart, he does it with subtlety." He slurped up a mouthful of noodles. "Poison, for instance. Something that kills fast and can't be traced. Now there's the perfect murder."

"Except for one thing."

"What's that?"

"Where's the satisfaction if your victim doesn't suffer?"

"A problem," Glickman conceded. "So you make 'em suffer through terror. Warnings. Threats."

David shifted uneasily, remembering the bloodred skull on Kate's wall. Through narrowed eyes, he watched the clouds hanging low on the horizon. With every passing minute, his sense of impending disaster grew stronger.

He rose to his feet and began throwing papers into his briefcase. It was useless, hanging around here; he could worry just as effectively at his mother's house.

"You know, there's one thing about this case that still bothers me," remarked Glickman, gulping the last of his supper.

"What's that?"

"That EKG. Tanaka and Richter were killed in just about the bloodiest way possible. Why should the murderer go out of his way to make Ellen O'Brien's death look like a heart attack?"

"The one thing I learned in the prosecutor's office," said David, snapping his briefcase shut, "is that murder doesn't have to make sense."

"Well, it seems to me our killer went to a lot of trouble just to shift the blame to Kate Chesne."

David was already at the door when he suddenly halted. "What did you say?"

"That he went to a lot of trouble to pin the blame—"

"No, the word you used was *shift*. He *shifted* the blame!"

"Maybe I did. So?"

"So who gets sued when a patient dies unexpectedly on the operating table?"

"The blame's usually shared by. . ." Glickman stopped. "Oh, my God. Why the hell didn't I think of that before?"

David was already reaching for the telephone. As he dialed the police, he cursed himself for being so blind. The killer had been there all along. Watching. Waiting. He must have known that Kate was hunting for answers, and that she was getting close. Now he was scared. Scared enough to scrawl a warning on Kate's wall. Scared enough to tail a car down a dark highway.

Maybe even scared enough to kill one more time.

IT WAS FIVE-THIRTY and most of the clerks in Medical Records had gone for the day. The lone clerk who remained grudgingly took Kate's request slip and went to the computer terminal to call up the chart location. As the data appeared, she frowned.

"This patient's deceased," she noted, pointing to the screen.

"I know," said Kate, wearily remembering the last time she'd tried to retrieve a chart from the Deceased Persons' room.

"So it's in the inactive files."

"I understand that. Could you please get me the chart?"

"It may take a while to track it down. Why don't you come back tomorrow?"

Kate resisted the urge to reach over and grab the clerk by her frilly dress. "I need the chart *now*." She felt like adding: *It's a matter of life and death.*

The clerk looked at her watch and tapped her pencil on the desk. With agonizing slowness, she rose to her feet and vanished into the file room.

Fifteen minutes passed before she returned with the record. Kate retreated to a corner table and stared down at the name on the cover: Brook, Baby Girl.

The child had never even had a name.

The chart contained pitifully few pages, only the hospital face sheet, death certificate, and a scrawled summary of the infant's short existence. Death had been pronounced August 17 at 2:00 a.m., an hour after birth. The cause of death was cerebral anoxia: the tiny brain had been starved of oxygen. The death certificate was signed by Dr. Henry Tanaka.

Kate next turned her attention to the copy of Jenny Brook's chart, which she'd brought with her. She'd read these pages so many times before; now she studied it line by line, pondering the significance of each sentence.

"...28-year-old female, G1P0, 36 weeks' gestation, admitted via E.R. in early labor..."

A routine report, she thought. There were no surprises, no warnings of the disaster to come. But at the bottom of the first page she stopped, her gaze focusing on a single statement: "Because of maternal family history of spina bifida, amniocentesis was performed at eighteen weeks of pregnancy and revealed no abnormalities."

Amniocentesis. Early in her pregnancy, fluid had been withdrawn from Jenny Brook's womb for analysis. This would have identified any fetal malformations. It also would have identified the baby's sex.

The amniocentesis report was not included in the hospital chart. That didn't surprise her; the report had probably been filed away in Jenny Brook's outpatient record.

Which had conveniently vanished from Dr. Tanaka's office, she realized with a start.

Kate closed the chart. Suddenly feverish, she rose and returned to the file clerk. "I need another record," she said.

"Not another deceased patient, I hope."

"No, this one's still alive."

"Name?"

"William Santini."

It took only a minute for the clerk to find it. When Kate finally held it in her hands, she was almost afraid to open it, afraid to see what she already knew lay inside. She stood there beside the clerk's desk, wondering if she really wanted to know.

She opened the cover.

A copy of the birth certificate stared up at her.

Name: William Santini.
Date of Birth: August 17
Time: 03:00.

August 17, the same day. But not quite the same time. Exactly one hour after Baby Girl Brook had left the world, William Santini had entered it.

Two infants; one living, one dead. Had there ever been a better motive for murder?

"Don't tell me you still have charts to finish," remarked a shockingly familiar voice.

Kate's head whipped around. Guy Santini had just walked in the door. She slapped the chart closed but instantly realized the name was scrawled in bold black ink across the cover. In a panic, she hugged the chart to her chest as an automatic smile congealed on her face.

"I'm just...cleaning up some last paperwork." She swallowed and managed to add, conversationally, "You're here late."

"Stranded again. Car's back in the shop so Susan's picking me up." He glanced across the counter, searching for the clerk, who'd temporarily vanished. "Where's the help around here, anyway?"

"She was, uh, here just a minute ago," said Kate, inching toward the exit.

"I guess you heard the news. About Avery's wife. A blessing, really, considering her—" He looked at her and she froze, just two feet from the door.

He frowned. "Is something wrong?"

"No. I've just— Look, I've really got to go." She turned and was about to flee out the door when the file clerk yelled: "Dr. Chesne!"

"What?" Kate spun around to see the woman peering at her reproachfully from behind a shelf.

"The chart. You can't take it out of the department."

Kate looked down at the folder she was still holding to her chest and frantically debated her next move. She didn't dare return the chart while Guy was standing right beside the counter; he'd see the name. But she couldn't stand here like a half-wit, either.

They were both frowning at her, waiting for her to say something.

"Look, if you're not finished with it, I can hold it right here," the clerk offered, moving to the counter.

"No. I mean..."

Guy laughed. "What's in that thing, anyway? State secrets?"

Kate realized she was clutching the chart as though terrified it would be forcibly pried from her grasp. With her heart hammering, she willed her feet to move forward. Her hand was barely steady as she placed the chart facedown on the counter. "I'm not finished with it."

"Then I'll hold it for you." The clerk reached over and for one terrifying second seemed poised to expose the patient's name. Instead she merely scooped up the request list that Guy had just laid on the counter. "Why don't you sit down, Dr. Santini?" she suggested. "I'll bring your records over to you." Then she turned and vanished into the file room.

Time to get the hell out of here, thought Kate.

It took all her self-control not to bolt out the door. She felt Guy's eyes on her back as she moved slowly and deliberately toward the exit. Only when she'd actually made it into the hall, only when she heard the door thud shut behind her, did the impact of what she'd discovered hit her full force. Guy Santini was her colleague. Her friend.

He was also a murderer. And she was the only one who knew.

GUY STARED AT THE DOOR through which Kate had just retreated. He'd known Kate Chesne for almost a year now and he'd never seen her so jittery. Puzzled, he turned and headed to the corner table to wait. It was his favorite spot, this little nook; it gave him a sense of privacy in this vast, impersonal room. Someone else obviously favored it, as well. There were two charts still lying there, waiting to be refiled. He grabbed a chair and was about to nudge the folders aside when his gaze suddenly froze on the top cover. He felt his legs give away. Slowly he sank into the chair and stared at the name.

Brook, Baby Girl. Deceased.

Dear God, he thought. *It can't be the same Brook.*

He flipped it open and hunted for the mother's name on the death certificate. What he saw sent panic knifing through him.

Mother: Brook, Jennifer.

The same woman. The same baby. He had to think; he had to stay calm. Yes, he would stay calm. There was nothing to worry about. No one could connect him to Jenny

Brook or the child. The four people involved with that tragedy of five years ago were now dead. There was no reason for anyone to be curious.

Or was there?

He shot to his feet and hurried back to the counter. The chart that Kate had so reluctantly parted with was still lying there, face down. He flipped it over. His own son's name stared up at him.

Kate Chesne knew. She *had* to know. And she had to be stopped.

"Here you are," said the file clerk, emerging from the shelves with an armload of charts. "I think I've got all—" She halted in amazement. "Where are you going? Dr. Santini!"

Guy didn't answer; he was too busy running out the door.

THE HOSPITAL LOBBY was reassuringly bright when Kate stepped off the elevator. A few visitors still lingered by the lobby doors, staring out at the storm. A security guard lounged at the information desk, chatting with a pretty volunteer. Kate hurried over to the public telephones. An out-of-order sign was taped to the first phone; a man was feeding a quarter into the other. She planted herself right behind him and waited. Wind rattled the lobby windows; outside, the parking lot was obscured by a heavy curtain of rain. She prayed that Lieutenant Ah Ching would be at his desk.

But at that moment it wasn't Ah Ching's voice she longed to hear most of all; it was David's.

The man was still talking on the phone. Glancing around, she was alarmed to see the security guard had vanished. The volunteer was already closing down the information desk. The place was emptying out too fast. She didn't want to be left alone—not here, not with what she knew.

She fled the hospital and headed out into the downpour.

She'd parked Jinx's car at the far end of the lot. The storm had become a fierce, tropical battering of wind and rain. By the time she'd dashed across to the car, her clothes were soaked. It took a few seconds to fumble through the

unfamiliar set of keys, another few seconds to unlock the
door. She was so intent on escaping the storm that she
scarcely noticed the shadow moving toward her through the
gloom. Just as she slid onto the driver's seat, the shadow
closed in. A hand seized her arm.

She stared up to see Guy Santini towering over her.

Chapter Fifteen

"Move over," he said.

"Guy, my arm—"

"I said move over."

Desperate, she glanced around for some passerby who might hear her screams. But the lot was deserted and the only sound was the thudding of rain on the car's roof.

Escape was impossible. Guy was blocking the driver's exit and she'd never be able to scramble out the passenger door in time.

Before she could even plan her next move, Guy shoved her aside and slid onto the driver's seat. The door slammed shut. Through the window, the gray light of evening cast a watery glow on his face.

"Your keys, Kate," he demanded.

The keys had dropped beside her on the seat; she made no move to retrieve them.

"Give me the damn keys!" He suddenly spotted them in the dim light. Snatching them up, he shoved the key into the ignition. The second he did, she lashed out. Like a trapped animal, she clawed at his face but at the last instant, some inner revulsion at the viciousness of her attack made her hesitate. It was only a split second, but it was enough time for him to react.

Flinching aside, he seized her wrist and wrenched her sideways so hard she was thrown back against the seat.

"If I have to," he said in a deadly quiet voice, "I swear I'll break your arm." He threw the gear in reverse and the car jerked backward. Then, hitting the gas, he spun the car out of the parking lot and into the street.

"Where are you taking me?" she asked.

"Somewhere. Anywhere. I'm going to talk and you're going to listen."

"About—about what?"

"You know what the hell about!"

Her chin snapped up expectantly as they approached an intersection. If she could throw herself out—

But he'd already anticipated her move. Seizing her arm, he yanked her toward him and sped through the intersection just as the signal turned red.

That was the last stoplight before the freeway. The car accelerated. She watched in despair as the speedometer climbed to sixty. She'd missed her chance. If she tried to leap out now, she'd almost certainly break her neck.

He knew as well as she did that she'd never be so reckless. He released her arm. "It was none of your business, Kate," he said, his eyes shifting back to the road. "You had no right to pry. No right at all."

"Ellen was my patient—*our* patient—"

"That doesn't mean you can tear my life apart!"

"What about her life? And Ann's? They're dead, Guy!"

"And the past died with them! I say let it stay dead."

"My God, I thought I knew you. I thought we were friends—"

"I have to protect my son. And Susan. You think I'd stand back and let them be destroyed?"

"They'd never take the boy away from you! Not after five years! The courts are bound to give you custody—"

"You think all I'm worried about is custody? Oh, we'd keep William all right. There's no judge on earth who'd be able to take him away from me! Who'd hand him over to some lunatic like Decker! No. It's Susan I'm thinking of."

The highway was slick with rain, the road treacherous. Both his hands were fully occupied on the steering wheel. If she lunged at him now, the car would surely spin out of control, killing them both. She had to wait for another time, another chance to escape.

"I don't understand," she persisted, scanning the road ahead for a stalled car, a traffic jam, anything to slow them down. "What do you mean, it's Susan you're worried about?"

"She doesn't know." At Kate's incredulous look, he nodded. "She thinks William is hers."

"How can she not know?"

"I've kept it from her. For five years, it's been my little secret. She was under anesthesia when our baby was born. It was a nightmare, all that rush, all that panic to do an emergency C-section. That was our third baby, Kate. Our last chance. And she was born dead...." He paused and cleared his throat; when he spoke again, his voice was still thick with pain. "I didn't know what to do. What to tell Susan. There she was, sleeping. So peaceful, so happy. And there I was, holding our dead baby girl."

"You took Jenny Brook's baby as your own."

He hastily scraped the back of his hand across his face. "It was—it was an act of God. Can't you see that? *An act of God.* That's how it seemed to me at the time. The woman had just died. And there was her baby boy, this absolutely *perfect* baby boy, crying in the next room. No one to hold him. Or love him. No one knew a thing about the child's father. There didn't seem to be any relatives, anyone who cared. And there was Susan, already starting to wake up. Can't you understand? It would have killed her to find out. God *gave* us that boy! It was as if—as if He had planned it that way. We all felt it. Ann. Ellen. Only Tanaka—"

"He didn't agree?"

"Not at first. I argued with him. I practically begged him. It was only when Susan opened her eyes and asked for her baby that he finally gave in. So Ellen brought the boy to the room. She put him in Susan's arms. And my Susan—she just looked at him and then she—she started to cry...." Guy wiped his sleeve across his face. "That's when we knew we'd done the right thing."

Yes, Kate could see the perfection of that moment. A decision as wise as Solomon's. What better proof of its rightness than the sight of a newborn baby curled up in his mother's arms?

But that same decision had led to the murder of four people.

Soon it would be five.

The car suddenly slowed; with a new burst of hope, she looked up. Traffic was growing heavier. Far ahead lay the Pali tunnel, curtained off by rain. She knew there was an emergency telephone somewhere near the entrance. If he would just slow down a little more, if she could shove the car door open, she might be able to fling herself out before he could stop her.

The chance never came. Instead of heading into the tunnel, Guy veered off onto a thickly wooded side road and roared past a sign labeled: Pali Lookout. The last stop, she thought. Set on a cliff high above the valley, this was the overhang where suicidal lovers sealed their pacts, where ancient warriors once were flung to their deaths. It was the perfect spot for murder.

A last flood of desperation made her claw for the door. Before she could get it open, he yanked her back. She turned and flew at him with both fists. Guy struggled to fight her off and lost control of the wheel. The car swerved off the road. By the erratic beams of their headlights, she caught glimpses of trees looming ahead. Branches thudded against the windshield but she was beyond caring whether they crashed; her only goal was escape.

It was Guy's overwhelming strength that decided the battle. He threw all his weight into shoving her back. Then, cursing, he grabbed the wheel and spun it wildly to the left. The right fender scraped trees as the car veered back onto the road. Kate, sprawled against the seat, could only watch in defeat as they weaved up the last hundred yards to the lookout.

Guy stopped the car and killed the engine. For a long time he sat in silence, as though summoning up the courage to get the job done. Outside, the rain had slowed to a drizzle and beyond the cliff's edge, mist swirled past, shrouding the fatal plunge from view.

"That was a damned crazy stunt you pulled," he said quietly. "Why the hell did you do it?"

Slowly she bowed her head; she felt a profound sense of weariness. Of inevitability. "Because you're going to kill me," she whispered. "The way you killed the others."

"I'm going to *what*?"

She looked up, searching his eyes for some trace of remorse. If only she could reach inside him and drag out some last scrap of humanity! "Was it easy?" she asked softly. "Cutting Ann's throat? Watching her bleed to death?"

"You mean— You really think I— Dear God!" He dropped his head in his hands. Suddenly he began to laugh. It was soft at first, then it grew louder and wilder until his whole body was racked by what sounded more like sobs than laughter. He didn't notice the new set of headlights, flickering like a beacon through the mist. She glanced around and saw that another car had wandered up the road. This was her chance to throw open the door, to run for help. But she didn't. In that instant she knew that Guy had never really meant to hurt her. That he was incapable of murder.

Without warning, he shoved his door open and stumbled out into the fog. At the edge of the lookout, he halted, his head and shoulders bowed as if in prayer.

Kate got out of the car and followed him. She didn't say a thing. She simply reached out and touched his arm. She could almost feel the pain, the confusion, coursing through his body.

"Then you didn't kill them," she said.

He looked up and slowly took in a deep breath of air. "I'd do almost anything to keep my son. But murder?" He shook his head. "No. God, no. Oh, I thought about killing Decker. Who would have missed him? He was nothing, just a—a scrap of human garbage. And it seemed like such an easy way out. Maybe the only way out. He wouldn't give up. He kept hounding people for answers. Demanding to know where the baby was."

"How did he know the baby was alive?"

"There was another doctor in the delivery room that night—"

"You mean Dr. Vaughn?"

"Decker talked to him. Learned just enough."

"And then Vaughn died in a car accident."

Guy nodded. "I thought it'd all be okay, then. I thought it was over. But then Decker got out of the state hospital. Sooner or later, someone would've talked. Tanaka was ready to. And Ann was scared out of her mind. I gave her some money, to leave the islands. But she never made it. Decker got to her first."

"That doesn't make sense, Guy. Why would he kill the only people who could give him the answers?"

"He was psychotic."

"Even psychotics have some sort of logic."

"He must have done it. There was no one else who—"

From somewhere in the mist came the hard click of metal. Kate and Guy froze as footsteps rapped slowly across the pavement. Out of the gathering darkness, a figure emerged, like vapor taking on substance until it stood before them. Even in the somber light of dusk, Susan Santini's red hair seemed to sparkle with fire. But it was the dull gray of the gun that held Kate's gaze.

"Move out of the way, Guy," Susan ordered softly.

Guy was too stunned to move or speak; he could only stare mutely at his wife.

"It was you," Kate murmured in astonishment. "All the time *you* were the one. Not Decker."

Slowly, Susan turned her unfocused gaze on Kate. Through the veil of mist drifting between them, her face was as vague and formless as a ghost's. "You don't understand, do you? But you've never had a baby, Kate. You've never been afraid of someone hurting it or taking it away. That's all a mother ever thinks about. Worries about. It's all *I* ever worried about."

A low groan escaped Guy's throat. "My God, Susan. Do you understand what you've done?"

"You wouldn't do it. So I had to. All those years, I never knew about William. You should have told me, Guy. You should have told me. I had to hear it from Tanaka."

"You killed four people, Susan!"

"Not four. Only three. I didn't kill Ellen." Susan looked at Kate. "She did."

Kate stared at her. "What do you mean?"

"That wasn't succinylcholine in the vial. It was potassium chloride. You gave Ellen a lethal dose." Her gaze shifted back to her husband. "I didn't want you to be blamed, darling. I couldn't stand to see you hurt, the way you were hurt by the last lawsuit. So I changed the EKG. I put *her* initials on it."

"And I got the blame," finished Kate.

Nodding, Susan raised the gun. "Yes, Kate. You got the blame. I'm sorry. Now please, Guy. Move away. It has to be done, for William's sake."

"No, Susan."

She frowned at him in disbelief. "They'll take him away from me. Don't you see? They'll take my baby away."

"I won't let them. I promise."

Susan shook her head. "It's too late, Guy. I've killed the others. She's the only one who knows."

"But *I* know!" Guy blurted out. "Are you going to kill me, too?"

"You won't tell. You're my husband."

"Susan, give me the gun." Guy moved slowly forward, his hand held out to her. His voice dropped, became gentle, intimate. "Please, darling. Nothing will happen. I'll take care of everything. Just give it to me."

She retreated a step and almost lost her balance on the uneven terrain. Guy froze as the barrel of the gun swayed for an instant in his direction.

"You're not going to hurt me, Susan."

"Please, Guy. . ."

He took a step forward. "Are you?"

"I love you," she moaned.

"Then give me the gun. Yes, darling. Give it to me. . . ."

The distance between them slowly evaporated. Guy's hand stretched out to her, coaxing her with the promise of warmth and safety. She stared at it with longing, as though knowing in some deep part of her mind that it was forever beyond her reach. The gun was only inches from Guy's fingers and still she didn't move; she was paralyzed by the inevitability of defeat.

Guy, at last sensing he had won, quickly closed the gap between them. Seizing the gun by the barrel, he tried to tug it from her hands.

But she didn't surrender it. At that instant, something inside her, some last spark of resistance, seemed to flare up and she tried to wrench it back.

"Let go!" she screamed.

"Give it to me," Guy demanded, wrestling for control of the weapon. "Susan, give it to me!"

The gun's blast seemed to trap them in freeze-frame. They stared at each other in astonishment, neither of them willing to believe what had just happened. Then Guy stumbled backward, clutching his leg.

"*No!*" Susan's wail rose up and drifted, ghostlike, through the mist. Slowly she turned toward Kate. The glow of desperation was in her eyes. And she was still clutching the gun.

That's when Kate ran. Blindly, desperately, into the mist. She heard a pistol shot. A bullet whistled past and thudded into the dirt near her feet. There was no time to get her bearings, to circle back toward the road. She just kept running and prayed that the fog would shroud her from Susan.

The ground suddenly rose upward. Through fingers of mist, she saw the sheer face of the ridge, sparsely stubbled with brush. She spun around and realized instantly that the way back to the main road was blocked by Susan's approach. Her only escape route lay to the left, down the crumbling remains of the old Pali road. It was the original cliff pass. The road had long ago been abandoned to the elements. She had no idea how far it would take her; parts of it, she knew, had collapsed down the sheer slope.

The sound of footsteps closing in left her no choice. She scrambled over a low concrete wall and at once found herself sliding helplessly down a muddy bank. Clawing at branches and vines, she managed to break her fall until she landed, scratched and breathless, on a slab of pavement. The old Pali road.

Somewhere above, hidden among the clouds, bushes rustled. "There's nowhere to run, Kate!" Susan's disembodied voice seemed to come from everywhere at once. "The old road doesn't go very far. One wrong step and you'll be over the cliff. So you'd better be careful...."

Careful... careful... The shouted warning echoed off the ridge and shattered into terrifying fragments of sound. The rustling of bushes moved closer. Susan was closing in. She was taking her time, advancing slowly, steadily. Her victim was trapped. And she knew it.

But trapped wasn't the same as helpless.

Kate leaped to her feet and began to run. The old road was full of cracks and potholes. In places it had crumbled away entirely and young trees poked through, their roots rippling the asphalt. She strained to see through the fog but could make out no more than a few feet ahead. Darkness was falling fast; it would cut off the last of her visibility. But it would also be a cloak in which to hide.

But where could she hide? On her right, the ridge loomed steeply upward; on her left, the pavement broke off sharply at the cliff's edge. She had no choice; she had to keep running.

She stumbled over a loose boulder and sprawled onto the brutal asphalt. At once she was back on her feet, mindless of the pain searing her knees. Even as she ran, she forced herself to think ahead. Would there be a barrier at the road's end? Or would there simply be a straight drop to oblivion? In either case, there'd be no escape. There would only be a bullet, and then a plunge over the cliff. How long would it be before they found her body?

A gust of wind swept the road. For an instant, the mist cleared. She saw looming to her right the face of the ridge, covered by dense brush. Halfway up, almost hidden by the overgrowth, was the mouth of a cave. If she could reach it, if she could scramble up those bushes before Susan passed this way, she could hide until help arrived. If it arrived.

She threaded her way into the shrubbery and began clambering up the mountainside. Rain had muddied the slope; she had to claw for roots and branches to pull herself up. All the time, there was the danger of dislodging a boulder, of sending it thundering to the road. The crash would certainly alert Susan. And here she'd be, poised like a fly on the wall. One well-placed bullet would end it all.

The sound of footsteps made her freeze. Susan was approaching. Desperately, Kate hugged the mountain, willing herself to blend into the bushes.

The footsteps slowed, stopped. At that instant, the wind nudged the clouds against the ridge, draping Kate in silvery mist. The footsteps moved on, slowly clipping across the pavement. Only when the sound had faded did Kate dare continue her climb.

By the time she reached the cave's mouth, her hands had cramped into claws. In took her last ounce of strength to drag herself up into the muddy hollow. There she collapsed, fighting to catch her breath. Dampness trickled from the tree roots above and dripped onto her face. She heard, deep in the shadows, the rustle of movement and something scuttled across her arm. A beetle. She didn't have the energy to brush it off. Exhausted and shivering, she curled up like a tired puppy in the mud. The wind rose, sweeping the clouds from the pass. Already the mist was fading. If she could just hold out until nightfall. That was the most she could hope for: darkness.

Closing her eyes, she focused on a mental image of David. If only he could hear her silent plea for help. But he couldn't help her. No one could. She wondered how he'd react to her death. Would he feel any grief? Or would he simply shrug it off as a tragic end to a fading love affair? That was what hurt most— the thought of his indifference.

She cradled her face in her arms, and warm tears mingled with the icy water on her cheeks. She'd never felt so alone, so abandoned. Suddenly it didn't matter whether she lived or died; only that someone cared.

But I'm the only one who really cares.

A desperate new strength stirred inside her. Slowly she unfolded her limbs and looked out at the thin wisps of fog drifting past the cave. And she felt a new sense of fury that her life might be stolen from her and that the man she loved wasn't even here to help.

If I want to be saved, I have to do it myself.

It was the footsteps, moving slowly back along the road, that told her darkness would come too late to save her. Through the tangle of branches fringing the cave mouth, she saw against the sky's fading light the velvety green of a distant ridge. The mist had vanished; so had her invisibility.

"You're up there, aren't you?" Susan's voice floated up from the road, a sound so chilling Kate trembled. "I almost missed it. But there's one unfortunate thing about caves. Something I'm sure you've realized by now. They're dead ends."

Rocks rattled down the slope and slammed onto the road, their impact echoing like gunshot. *She's climbing the ridge*, Kate thought frantically. *She's coming for me....*

Her only escape route was back out through the cave mouth. Right into Susan's line of fire.

A twig snapped and more rocks slithered down the mountain. Susan was closing in. Kate had no choice left; either she bolted now or she'd be trapped like a rat.

Swiftly she groped around in the mud and came up with a fist-size rock. It wasn't much against a gun, but it was all she had. Cautiously, she eased her head out. To her horror, she saw that Susan was already halfway up the slope.

Their eyes met. In that instant, each recognized the other's desperation. One was fighting for her life, the other for her child. There could be no compromise, no surrender, except in death.

Susan took aim; the barrel swung up toward her prey's head.

Kate hurled the rock.

It skimmed the bushes and thudded against Susan's shoulder. Crying out, Susan slid a few feet down the mountainside before she managed to grab hold of a branch. There she clung for a moment, stunned.

Kate scrambled out of the cave and began clawing her way up the ridge. Even as she pulled herself up, branch by branch, some rational part of her brain was screaming that the ascent was impossible, that the cliff face was too steep, the bushes too straggly to support her weight. But her arms and legs seemed to move on their own, guided not by logic but by the instinct to survive. Her sleeves were shredded by thorns and her hands and arms were already scraped raw but she was too numbed by terror to feel pain.

A bullet ricocheted off a boulder. Kate cringed as shattered rock and earth spat out and stung her face. Susan's aim was wide; she couldn't cling to the mountain and shoot accurately at the same time.

Kate looked up to find herself staring at an overhanging rock, laced with vines. Was she strong enough to drag herself over the top? Would the vines hold her weight? The surface was impossibly steep and she was so tired, so very tired....

Another shot rang out; the bullet came so close she could feel it whistle past her cheek. Kate frantically grabbed a vine and began to drag herself up the rock face. Her shoes slid uselessly downward, then found a toe hold. She shimmied up a few precious inches, then a few more, her knees scraping the harsh volcanic boulder. High above, clouds raced across the sky, taunting her with the promise of freedom. How many bullets were left?

It only takes one....

Every inch became an agony. Her muscles screamed for rest. Even if a bullet found its mark, she doubted she'd feel the pain.

When at last she cleared the overhang, she was too exhausted to feel any sense of triumph. She hauled herself over the top and rolled onto a narrow ledge. It was nothing more than a flat boulder, turned slick with rain and lichen, but no bed had ever felt so wonderful. If only she could lie here forever. If she could close her eyes and sleep! But there was no time to rest, no time to allow the agony to ease from her body; Susan was right behind her.

She staggered to her feet, her legs trembling with exhaustion, her body buffeted by the whistling wind. One of her shoes had dropped off during the climb and with every step, thorns bit into her bare foot. But here the ascent was easier and she had only a few yards to go until she reached the top of the ridge.

She never made it.

A final gunshot rang out. What she felt wasn't pain, but surprise. There was the dull punch of the bullet slamming into her shoulder. The sky spun above her. For a moment she swayed, as unsteady as a reed in the wind. Then she felt herself fall backward. She was rolling, over and over, tumbling toward oblivion.

It was a halekoa bush—one of those tough stubborn weeds that clamp their roots deep into Hawaiian soil—that saved her life. It snagged her by the legs, slowing her fall just enough to keep her from plunging over the edge of the boulder. As she lay there, fighting to make sense of where she was, she became aware of a strange shrieking in the distance; to her confused brain, it sounded like an infant's wail, and it grew steadily louder.

The hallucination dragged her into consciousness. Groggily she opened her eyes to the dull monochrome of a cloudy sky. The infant's cry suddenly turned into the rhythmic wail of police sirens. The sound of help. Of salvation.

Then, across her field of vision, a shadow moved. She struggled to make out the figure standing over her. Against the sky's fading light, Susan Santini's face was nothing more than a black cutout with wind-lashed hair.

Susan said nothing as she slowly pointed her gun at Kate's head. For a moment she stood there, her skirt flapping in the wind, the pistol clutched in both hands. A gust whipped the narrow ledge, making her sway uneasily on the slippery rock.

The siren's cry suddenly cut off; men's shouts rose up from the valley.

Kate struggled to sit up. The barrel was staring her in the face. She managed to say, quietly, "There's no reason to kill me now, Susan. Is there?"

"You know about William."

"So will they." Kate nodded feebly toward the distant voices, which were already moving closer.

"They won't. Not unless you tell them."

"How do you know I haven't?"

The gun wavered. "No!" Susan cried, her voice tinged with the first trace of panic. "You couldn't have told them! You weren't certain—"

"You need help, Susan. I'll see you get it. All the help you need."

The barrel still hovered at her head. It would take only a twitch of the finger, the clap of the pistol hammer, to make Kate's whole world disintegrate. She gazed up into that black circle, wondering if she would feel the bullet. How strange, that she could face her own death with such calmness. She had fought to stay alive and she had lost. Now all she could do was wait for the end.

Then, through the wind's scream, she heard a voice calling her name. *Another hallucination,* she thought. *It must be....*

But there it was again: David's voice, shouting her name, over and over.

Suddenly she wanted to live! She wanted to tell him all the things she'd been too proud to say. That life was too precious to waste on hurts of the past. That if he just gave her the chance, she could help him forget all the pain he'd ever suffered.

"Please, Susan," she whispered. "Put it down."

Susan shifted but her hands were still gripping the pistol. She seemed to be listening to the voices, moving closer along the old Pali road.

"Can't you see?" cried Kate. "If you kill me, you'll destroy your only chance of keeping your son!"

Her words seemed to drain all the strength from Susan's arms. Slowly, almost imperceptibly, she let the gun drop. For a moment she stood motionless, her head bent in a silent gesture of mourning. Then she turned and gazed over the ledge, at the road far below. "It's too late now," she said in a voice so soft it was almost drowned in the wind. "I've already lost him."

A chorus of shouts from below told them they'd been spotted.

Susan, her hair whipping like flames, stared down at the gathering of men. "It's better this way," she insisted. "He'll have only good memories of me. That's the way childhood should be, you know. Only good memories..."

Perhaps it was a sudden gust that threw Susan off balance; Kate could never be certain. All she knew was that one instant Susan was poised on the edge of the rock and then, in the next instant, she was gone.

She fell soundlessly, without uttering a cry.

It was Kate who sobbed. She collapsed back against the cold and unforgiving bed of stone. As the world spun around her she cried, silently, for the woman who had just died, and for the four others who had lost their lives. So many deaths, so much suffering. And all in the name of love.

Chapter Sixteen

David was the first to reach her.

He found her seventy-five feet up the mountainside, unconscious and shivering on a bloodstained boulder. What he did next had nothing to do with logic; it was pure panic. He ripped off his jacket and threw it over her body, only one thought in his mind. *You can't die. I won't let you. Do you hear me, Kate? You can't die!*

He cradled her in his arms and as the warmth of her blood seeped through his shirt, he said her name over and over, as though he could somehow keep her soul from drifting forever beyond his reach. He scarcely heard the shouts of the rescue workers or the ambulance sirens; his attention was focused on the rhythm of her breathing and the beating of her heart against his chest.

She was so cold, so still. If only he could give her his warmth. He had made just such a wish once before, when his only child had lain dying in his arms. *Not this time,* he prayed, pulling her tightly against him. *Don't take her from me, too. . . .*

That plea rang over and over in his head as they carried her down the mountain. The descent ended in mass confusion as ambulance workers crowded in to help. David was shunted to the sidelines, a helpless observer of a battle he wasn't trained to fight.

He watched the ambulance scream off into the darkness. He imagined the emergency room, the lights, the people in white. He couldn't bear to think of Kate, lying helplessly in all that chaos. But that's where she would be soon. It was her only chance.

A hand clapped him gently on the shoulder. "You okay, Davy?" Pokie asked.

"Yeah." He sighed deeply. "Yeah."

"She'll be all right. I got a crystal ball on these things." He turned at the sound of a sneeze.

Sergeant Brophy approached, his face half-buried in a handkerchief. "They've brought the body up," said Brophy. "Got tangled up in all that—that—" he blew his nose "—shrubbery. Broken neck. Wanna take a look before it goes to the morgue?"

"Never mind," Pokie grunted. "I'll take your word for it." As they walked to the car, he asked, "How did Dr. Santini handle the news?"

"That's the weird thing," replied Brophy. "When I told him about his wife, he sort of acted like—well, he'd expected it."

Pokie frowned at the covered body of Susan Santini, now being loaded into the ambulance. He sighed. "Maybe he did. Maybe he knew all along what was happening. But he didn't want to admit it. Even to himself."

Brophy opened the car door. "Where to, Lieutenant?"

"The hospital. And move it." Pokie nodded toward David. "This man's got some serious waiting to do."

IT WAS FOUR HOURS before David was allowed to see her. Four hours of pacing the fourth-floor waiting room. Four hours of walking back and forth past the same *National Enquirer* headline on the coffee table: Woman's Head Joined To Baboon's Body.

There was only one other person in the room, a mule-faced man who slouched beneath a No Smoking sign, puffing desperately on a cigarette. He stubbed out the butt and reached for another. "Getting late," the man commented. That was the extent of their conversation. Two words, uttered in a monotone. The man never said who he was waiting for. He never spoke of fear. It was there, plain in his eyes.

At eleven o'clock, the mule-faced man was called into the recovery room and David was left alone. He stood at the window, listening to the wail of an approaching ambulance. For the hundredth time, he looked at his watch. She'd been in surgery three hours. How long did it take to remove a bullet? Had something gone wrong?

At midnight, a nurse at last poked her head into the room. "Are you Mr. Ransom?"

He spun around, his heart instantly racing. "Yes!"

"I thought you'd want to know. Dr. Chesne's out of surgery."

"Then . . . She's all right?"

"Everything went just fine."

He let out a breath so heavy its release left him floating. *Thank you,* he thought. *Thank you.*

"If you'd like to go home, we'll call you when she—"

"I have to see her."

"She's still unconscious."

"I have to see her."

"I'm sorry, but we only allow immediate family into..." Her voice trailed off as she saw the dangerous look in his eyes. She cleared her throat. "Five minutes, Mr. Ransom. That's all. You understand?"

Oh, he understood, all right. And he didn't give a damn. He pushed past her, through the recovery-room doors.

He found her lying on the last gurney, her small, pale form drowning in bright lights and plastic tubes. There was only a limp white curtain separating her from the next patient. David hovered at the foot of her stretcher, afraid to move close, afraid to touch her for fear he might break one of those fragile limbs. He was reminded of a princess in a glass bell, lying in some deep forest: untouchable, unreachable. A cardiac monitor chirped overhead, marking the rhythm of her heart. Beautiful music. Good and strong and steady. Kate's heart. He stood there, immobile, as the nurses fussed with tubes, adjusted IV fluids and oxygen. A doctor came to examine Kate's lungs. David felt useless. He was like a great big boulder in everyone's path. He knew he should leave and let them do their job, but something kept him rooted to his spot. One of the nurses pointed to her watch and said sternly, "We really can't work around you. You'll have to leave now."

But he didn't. He wouldn't. Not until he knew everything would be all right.

"SHE'S WAKING UP."

The light of a dozen suns seemed to burn through her closed eyelids. She heard voices, vaguely familiar, murmuring in the void above her. Slowly, painfully, she opened her eyes.

What she saw first was the light, brilliant and inescapable, glaring down at her. Bit by bit, she made out the smiling face of a woman, someone she knew from some dim and distant past, though she couldn't quite remember why. She focused on the name tag: Julie Sanders, RN. Julie. Now she remembered.

"Can you hear me, Dr. Chesne?" Julie asked.

Kate made a feeble attempt to nod.

"You're in the recovery room. Are you in pain?"

Kate didn't know. Her senses were returning one by one, and pain had yet to reawaken. It took her a moment to register all the signals her brain was receiving. She felt the hiss of oxygen in her nostrils and heard the soft beep of a cardiac monitor somewhere over the bed. But pain? No. She felt only a terrible sense of emptiness. And exhaustion. She wanted to sleep....

More faces had gathered around the bed. Another nurse, a stethoscope draped around her neck. Dr. Tam, dour as always. And then she heard a voice, calling softly to her.

"Kate?"

She turned. Framed against the glare of lights, David's face was blackly haggard. In wonder, she reached up to touch him but found that her wrist was hopelessly tangled in what seemed like a multitude of plastic tubes. Too weak to struggle, she let her hand drop back to the bed.

That's when he took it. Gently, as if he were afraid he might break her.

"You're all right," he whispered, pressing his lips to her palm. "Thank God you're all right...."

"I don't remember...."

"You've been in surgery." He gave her a small, tense smile. "Three hours. It seemed like forever. But the bullet's out."

She remembered, then. The wind. The ridge. And Susan, quietly slipping away like a phantom. "She's dead?"

He nodded. "There was nothing anyone could do."

"And Guy?"

"He won't be able to walk for a while. I don't know how he made it to that phone. But he did."

For a moment she lay in silence, thinking of Guy, whose life was now as shattered as his leg. "He saved my life. And now he's lost everything...."

"Not everything. He still has his son."

Yes, she thought. *William will always be Guy's son.* Not by blood, but by something much stronger: by love. Out of all this tragedy, at least one thing would remain intact and good.

"Mr. Ransom, you really will have to leave," insisted Dr. Tam.

David nodded. Then he bent over and dutifully gave Kate a gruff and awkward kiss. If he had told her he loved her, if he had said anything at all, she might have found some joy in that dry touch of lips. But too quickly his hand melted away from hers.

Things seemed to move in a blur. Dr. Tam began asking questions she was too dazed to answer. The nurses bustled around her bed, changing IV bottles, disconnecting wires, tucking in sheets. She was given a pain shot. Within minutes, she felt herself sliding irresistibly toward sleep.

As they moved her out of the recovery room, she fought to stay awake. There was something important she had to say to David, something that couldn't wait. But there were so many people around and she lost track of his voice in the confusing buzz of conversation. She felt a burst of panic that this was her last chance to tell him she loved him. But even to the very edge of consciousness, some last wretched scrap of pride kept her silent. And so, in silence, she let herself be dragged once again into darkness.

DAVID STAYED in her hospital room until almost dawn. He sat by her bed, holding her hand, brushing the hair off her face. Every so often he would say her name, half hoping she would awaken. But whatever pain shot they'd given her was industrial strength; she scarcely stirred all night. If only once she'd called for him in her sleep, if she'd said even the first syllable of his name, it would have been enough. He would have known she needed him and then he would have told her he needed her. It wasn't the sort of thing a man could just come out and say to anyone. At least, *he* couldn't. In truth, he was worse off than poor mute Charlie Decker. At least Decker could express himself in a few lines of wretched poetry.

It was a long drive home.

As soon as he walked in the door, he called the hospital to check on her condition. "Stable." That was all they'd say but it was enough. He called a florist and ordered flowers delivered to Kate's room. Roses. Since he couldn't think of a message, he told the clerk to simply write "David." He fixed himself some coffee and toast and ate like a starved man, which he was, since he'd missed supper the night before. Then, dirty, unshaven, exhausted, he went into the living room and threw himself on the couch.

He thought about all the reasons he couldn't be in love. He'd carved out a nice, comfortable existence for himself. He looked around at the polished floor, the curtains, the books lined up in the glass cabinet. Then it struck him how sterile it all was. This wasn't the home of a living, breathing man. It was a shell, the way he was a shell.

What the hell, he thought. She probably wouldn't want him anyway. Their affair had been rooted in need. She'd been terrified and he, conveniently, had been there. Soon she'd be back on her feet, her career on track. You couldn't keep a woman like Kate down for long.

He admired her and he wanted her. But did he love her? He hoped not.

Because he, better than anyone else, knew that love was nothing more than a setup for grief.

DR. CLARENCE AVERY stood awkwardly in the doorway of Kate's hospital room and asked if he could come in. He was carrying a half dozen hideously tinted green carnations, which he waved at her as though he had no idea what one did with flowers. Tinted green ones, anyway. The stems were still wrapped in supermarket cellophane, price tag and all.

"These are for you," he said, just in case she wasn't quite certain about that point. "I hope... I hope you're not allergic to carnations. Or anything."

"I'm not. Thank you, Dr. Avery."

"It's nothing, really. I just..." His gaze wandered to the dozen long-stemmed red roses set in a porcelain vase on the nightstand. "Oh. But I see you've already gotten flowers. Roses." Sadly, he looked down at his green carnations the way one might study a dead animal.

"I prefer carnations," she replied. "Could you put them in water for me? I think I saw a vase under the sink."

"Certainly." He took the flowers over to the sink and as he bent down, she saw that, as usual, his pants were wrinkled and his socks didn't match. The carnations looked somehow touching, flopping about in the huge, watery vase. What mattered most was that they'd been delivered in person, which was more than could be said about the roses.

They had arrived while she was still sleeping. The card said simply, "David." He hadn't called or visited. She thought maybe he'd decided this was the time to make the break. All morning she'd alternated between wanting to tear the flowers to bits and wanting to gather them up and hug them. Now that was an apt analogy—hugging thorns to one's breast.

"Here," she said. "Put the carnations right next to me. Where I can smell them." She brusquely shoved the roses aside, an act that made her wince. The surgical incision had left her with dozens of stitches and it had taken a hefty dose of narcotics just to dull the pain. Carefully she eased back against the pillows.

Pleased that his offering was given such a place of honor, Dr. Avery took a moment of silence to admire the limp blossoms. Then he cleared his throat. "Dr. Chesne," he began, "I should tell you this isn't just a—a social visit."

"It's not?"

"No. It has to do with your position here at Mid Pac."

"Then there's been a decision," she said quietly.

"With all the new evidence that's come out, well..." He gave a little shrug. "I suppose I should have taken your side earlier. I'm sorry I didn't. I suppose I was... I'm just sorry." Shuffling, he looked down at his ink-stained lab coat. "I don't know why I've held on to this blasted chairmanship. It's never given me anything but ulcers. Anyway, I'm here to tell you we're offering you your old job back. There'll be nothing on your record. Just a notation that a lawsuit was filed against you and later dropped. Which it will be. At least, that's what I'm told."

"My old job," she murmured. "I don't know." Sighing, she turned and looked out the window. "I'm not even sure I want it back. You know, Dr. Avery, I've been thinking. About other places."

"You mean another hospital?"

"Another town." She smiled at him. "It's not so surprising, is it? I've had a lot of time to think these last few days. I've been wondering if I don't belong somewhere else. Away from all this—this ocean." *Away from David.*

"Oh, dear."

"You'll find a replacement. There must be hundreds of doctors begging to come to paradise."

"No, it's not that. I'm just surprised. After all the work Mr. Ransom put into this, I thought certainly you'd—"

"Mr. Ransom? What do you mean?"

"All those calls he made. To every member of the hospital board."

A parting gesture, she thought. *At least I should be grateful for that.*

"It was quite a turnaround, I must say. A plaintiff's attorney asking—demanding—we reinstate a doctor! But this morning, when he presented the police evidence and we heard Dr. Santini's statement, well, it took the board a full five minutes to make a decision." He frowned. "Mr. Ransom gave us the idea you wanted your job back."

"Maybe I did once," she replied, staring at the roses and wondering why she felt no sense of triumph. "But things change. Don't they?"

"I suppose they do." Avery cleared his throat and shuffled a little more. "Your job is there if you want it. And we'll certainly be needing you on staff. Especially with my retirement coming up."

She looked up in surprise. "You're retiring?"

"I'm sixty-four, you know. That's getting along. I've never seen much of the country. Never had the time. My wife and I, we used to talk about traveling after my retirement. Barb would've wanted me to enjoy myself. Don't you think?"

Kate smiled. "I'm sure she would have."

"Anyway..." He shot another glance at the drooping carnations. "They are rather pretty, aren't they?" He walked out of the room, chuckling. "Yes. Yes, much better than roses, I think. Much better."

Kate turned once again to the flowers. Red roses. Green carnations. What an absurd combination. Just like her and David.

IT WAS RAINING HARD when David came to see her late that afternoon. She was sitting alone in the solarium, gazing through the watery window at the courtyard below. The nurse had just washed and brushed her hair and it was drying as usual into those frizzy, little-girl waves she'd always hated. She didn't hear him as he walked into the room. Only when he said her name did she turn and see him standing there, his hair damp and windblown, his suit beaded with rain. He looked tired. Almost as tired as she felt. She wanted him to pull her close, to take her in his arms, but he didn't. He simply bent over and gave her an automatic kiss on the forehead and then he straightened again.

"Out of bed, I see. You must be feeling better," he remarked.

She managed a wan smile. "I guess I never was one for lying around all day."

"Oh. I brought you these." Almost as an afterthought, he handed her a small foil-wrapped box of chocolates. "I wasn't sure they'd let you eat anything yet. Maybe later."

She looked down at the box resting in her lap. "Thank you," she murmured. "And thank you for the roses." Then she turned and stared out at the rain.

There was a long silence, as if both of them had run out of things to say. The rain slid down the solarium windows, casting a watery rainbow of light on her folded hands.

"I just spoke with Avery," he finally said. "I hear you're getting your old job back."

"Yes. He told me. I guess that's something else I have to thank you for."

"What's that?"

"My job. Avery said you made a lot of phone calls."

"Just a few. Nothing, really." He took a deep breath and continued with forced cheerfulness, "So. You should be back at work in the O.R. in no time. With a big raise in pay, I hope. It must feel pretty good."

"I'm not sure I'm taking it—the job."

"What? Why on earth wouldn't you?"

She shrugged. "You know, I've been thinking about other possibilities. Other places."

"You mean besides Mid Pac?"

"I mean . . . besides Hawaii." He didn't say a thing, so she added, "There's really nothing keeping me here."

There was another long silence. Softly he said, "Isn't there?"

She didn't answer. He watched her, sitting so quiet, so still in her chair. And he knew he could wait around till doomsday and there she'd still be. *A fine pair we are,* he thought in disgust. They were two so-called intelligent people, and they couldn't hunt up a single word between them.

"Dr. Chesne?" A nurse appeared in the doorway. "Are you ready to go back to your room?"

"Yes," Kate answered. "I think I'd like to sleep."

"You do look tired." The nurse glanced at David. "Maybe it's time you left, sir."

"No," said David, suddenly drawing himself to his full height.

"Excuse me?"

"I'm not going to leave. Not yet." He looked long and hard at Kate. "Not until I've finished making a fool of myself. So could you leave us alone?"

"But, sir—"

"Please."

The nurse hesitated. Then, sensing that something momentous was looming in the balance, she retreated from the solarium.

Kate was watching him, her green eyes filled with uncertainty. And maybe fear. He reached down and gently touched her face.

"Tell me again what you just said," he murmured. "That you have nothing to keep you here."

"I don't. What I mean is—"

"Now tell me the real reason you want to leave."

She was silent. But he saw the answer in her eyes, those soft and needy eyes. What he read there made him suddenly shake his head in wonder. "My God," he muttered. "You're a bigger coward than I am."

"A coward?"

"That's right. So am I." He turned away and with his hands in his pockets began to wander restlessly around the room. "I didn't plan to say this. Not yet, anyway. But here you're talking about leaving. And it seems I don't have much of a choice." He stopped and looked out the window. Outside, the world had gone silvery. "Okay." He sighed. "Since you're not going to say it, I guess I will. It's not easy for me. It's never been easy. After Noah died, I thought I'd taught myself not to feel. I've managed it up till now. Then I met you and..." He shook his head and laughed. "God, I wish I had one of Charlie Decker's poems handy. Maybe I could quote a few lines. Anything to sound halfway intelligible. Poor old Charlie had that much over me: his eloquence. For that I envy him." He looked at her and a half smile was on his lips. "I still haven't said it, have I? But you get the general idea."

"Coward," she whispered.

Laughing, he went to her and tilted her face up to his. "All right, then. I love you. I love your stubbornness and your pride. And your independence. I didn't want to. I thought I was going along just fine on my own. But now that it's happened, I can't imagine ever not loving you." He pulled away, offering her a chance to retreat.

She didn't. She remained perfectly still. Her throat seemed to have swollen shut. She was still clutching the little box of candy, trying to convince herself it was real. That he was real.

"It won't be easy, you know," he said.

"What won't?"

"Living with me. There'll be days you'll want to wring my neck or scream at me, anything to make me say 'I love you.' But just because I don't say it doesn't mean I don't feel it. Because I do." He let out a long sigh. "So. I guess that's about it. I hope you were listening. Because I'm not sure I could come up with a repeat performance. And damned if this time I forgot to bring my tape recorder."

"I've been listening," she replied softly.

"And?" he asked, not daring to let his gaze leave her face. "Do I hear the verdict? Or is the jury still out?"

"The jury," she whispered, "is in a state of shock. And badly in need of mouth-to-mouth—"

If resuscitation was what he'd intended, his kiss did quite the opposite. He lowered his face to hers and she felt the room spin. Every muscle of her neck seemed to go limp at once and her head sagged back against the chair.

"Now, fellow coward," he murmured, his lips hovering close to hers. "Your turn."

"I love you," she said weakly.

"That's the verdict I was hoping for."

She thought he would kiss her again but he suddenly pulled away and frowned. "You're looking awfully pale. I think I should call the nurse. Maybe a little oxygen—"

She reached up and wound her arms around his neck. "Who needs oxygen?" she whispered, just before his mouth settled warmly on hers.

Epilogue

There was a brand-new baby visiting the house, a fact made apparent by the indignant squalls coming from the upstairs bedroom.

Jinx poked her head through the doorway. "What in heaven's name is the matter with Emma now?"

Gracie, her mouth clamped around a pale pink safety pin, looked up helplessly from the screaming infant. "It's all so new to me, Jinx. I'm afraid I've lost my touch."

"Your touch? When were you ever around babies?"

"Oh, you're right." Gracie sighed, tugging the pin out of her mouth. "I suppose I never did have the touch, did I? That explains why I'm doing such a shoddy job of it."

"Now, dear. Babies take practice, that's all. It's like the piano. All those scales, up and down, every day."

Gracie shook her head. "The piano's much easier." Resignedly, she stuffed the safety pin back between her lips. "And look at these impossible diapers! I just don't see how anyone could poke a pin through all that paper and plastic."

Jinx burst out in hoots of laughter, so loud that Gracie turned bright red with indignation. "And exactly what did I say that was so funny?" Gracie demanded.

"Darling, haven't you figured it out?" Jinx reached out and peeled open the adhesive flap. "You don't use pins. That's the whole *point* of disposable diapers." She looked down in astonishment as baby Emma suddenly let out a lusty howl.

"You see?" sniffed Gracie. "She didn't like your pun, either."

A LEAF DRIFTED DOWN from the monkeypod tree and settled beside the fresh gathering of daisies. Chips of sunlight dappled the grass and danced on David's fair hair. How many times had he grieved alone in the shade of this tree? How many times had he stood in silent communion with his son? All the other visits seemed to blend together in a gray and dismal remembrance of mourning.

But today he was smiling. And in his mind, he could hear the smile in Noah's voice, as well.

Is that you, Daddy?

Yes, Noah. It's me. You have a sister.

I've always wanted a sister.

She sucks the same two fingers you did....

Does she?

And she always smiles when I walk in her room.

So did I. Remember?

Yes, I remember.

And you'll never forget, will you, Daddy? Promise me, you'll never forget.

No, I'll never forget. I swear to you, Noah, I will never, ever forget....

David turned and through his tears he saw Kate, standing a few feet away. No words were needed between them. Only a look. And an outstretched hand.

Together they walked away from that sad little patch of grass. As they emerged from the shade of the tree, David suddenly stopped and pulled her into his arms.

She touched his face. He felt the warmth of the sun in her fingertips. And he was healed.

He was healed.

What Dr. Anne Eldridge doesn't need:

☑ *A sexy male housekeeper with a private agenda.*

AN UNEXPECTED MAN

Jacqueline Diamond

For Ari

Chapter One

The cesarean section had gone well. After her patient was wheeled out to the recovery room, Anne stopped by the nursery to check on her newest arrival.

The tiny red creature, given a clean bill of health by the pediatrician, lay wailing lustily while a nurse cooed soothingly.

Anne rubbed the back of her hand wearily across her forehead. For a moment, she couldn't even remember whether it was a boy or a girl. Oh, yes, a girl, although she'd scarcely had time to check as she lifted it from its mother's womb. It was a little girl, with a big head, who hadn't wanted to arrive in the world the usual way. Maybe that's where the term headstrong had come from.

She smiled to herself. She'd have to tell that one to her partner, John Hernandez. He'd been accusing her of losing her sense of humor lately.

Stretching her cramped shoulders, Anne made her way to the telephone at the nursing station and called her receptionist to check for messages.

There was nothing urgent, Ellie said, just a few routine matters that Meg, the nurse-practitioner, had been able to handle.

"And don't forget you have to be home by six." Ellie was only twenty-five, but she had a motherly air that managed to make Anne feel like a child sometimes, especially when she was tired. In addition, they'd become good friends outside the office, so Ellie wasn't shy about teasing. "I know you usually forget about anything that isn't work related."

Absentmindedly, Anne fingered the name bar attached to her white coat, the one that said Anne Eldridge M.D. and had thrilled her so much the first time she wore it, which felt like eons ago but was really less than eight years. "Actually, I was thinking of coming back to the office to pick up some of the new journals; I'm a little behind in my reading. Refresh my memory; what's going on at six o'clock?"

"Four would-be housekeepers will be descending on the Eldridge residence. If you're not there, who knows what they might do?" Ellie chuckled. She'd been in a good mood for the last few months, ever since she got over her morning sickness. It sometimes seemed to Anne that everybody in the world was pregnant. Everyone except Anne, of course.

Now she groaned. The last thing she felt like doing tonight was talking with a bunch of matronly women about their references as live-in housekeepers.

But duty called, and whenever it did, Anne Eldridge could be counted on to snap to attention. "I'll be there," she promised, and hung up.

Oh, Ada, how could you do this to me? she wondered as she trudged out to the doctors' parking lot and shrugged off her coat to reveal the crisp, no-wrinkle sheath dress underneath.

Her Oldsmobile—a model chosen for its reliability and practicality—seemed to know its own way home from Irvine Doctors Medical Center. The air conditioner purred quietly, blotting out the warmth of a Southern California June day.

Actually, it was all the fault of the state lottery, Anne reflected as she drove.

Her longtime housekeeper, Ada Allen, had been an avid player. Last month, she'd finally hit pay dirt—twenty-five thousand dollars—and announced she was moving to Northern California to be with her daughter and grandchildren.

Was it possible to find another woman so efficient, so self-contained, so unirritating at the end of a hard day?

Turning onto one of the wide, straight boulevards of the planned city of Irvine, Anne mentally reviewed the course of her day. It was Wednesday, she reminded herself; halfway through the week.

She'd been on call the previous night and had delivered a baby at 5:00 a.m. There hadn't been time to go home before making her rounds and then reporting to the office for the usual prenatal checkups and Pap smears. After a lunchtime meeting of the hospital's perinatal committee, she'd performed two D & Cs and then the C-section.

Anne's partner, John Hernandez, was a perinatalogist, specializing in complicated pregnancies. Although Anne chiefly handled the less difficult cases, she often found herself filling in for him on C-sections and other surgeries. In truth, she admitted to herself, it gave her a sense of achievement when she was able to save a baby who, without careful monitoring and care, might have been lost. But it was hard, intense work, leaving her drained at the end of a long day.

No wonder Anne's shoulders ached and her feet felt swollen, even in her sensible flat shoes, and all she wanted was a bath and to be able to go to bed early.

Anne experienced only a trace of her usual surge of pride as she turned into the road she lived on, with its elegant and costly two-story houses, all tidily landscaped.

She'd come a long way from the dreamy-eyed girl she'd been as an undergraduate at UCLA, when she'd toyed with the idea of becoming an actress and working side by side with the handsome, single-minded actor whom she'd nearly married. But on days like today, Anne wondered if maybe she hadn't come a little too far, if she might not have been happier if she'd found time along the way for a husband and a child, like that squalling bit of humanity back at the hospital.

Oh, nonsense. It was just her puffy feet talking.

It was only five-thirty. Well, at least she'd have time to catch her breath before confronting a roomful of would-be housekeepers.

THE TRAFFIC WAS GETTING heavy by the time Jason Brant piloted his restored 1964 Mustang convertible through Newport Beach on the way to Irvine. He'd made a leisurely journey down the coast from Santa Monica, enjoying the smell of the salt breeze, the sight of bronzing bodies strewn about the sand

and the cheerful shouts of teenagers as they darted across the road to the funky shops on the other side.

But now he was headed away from the coast, and the landscape was changing.

What must once have been scenic coastal bluffs and fields of orange groves were now covered with condominiums and houses of cookie-cutter similarity. Everything looked as if it had been lifted bodily from an architect's rendering, even the wandering paseos that were supposed to be an improvement on old-fashioned sidewalks but instead looked contrived, at least to Jason.

He smiled and shook his head. Still the young renegade even at thirty-five, he scolded himself. How could his editor have thought otherwise? The man just didn't understand that political significance began at home. Literally.

Actually, Jason knew, he ought to be angry. His publisher had no business refusing to give him an advance until his latest book was completed. By all rights he ought to take the book elsewhere, but he liked his editor, and the company's printing was top quality, which was important with photography.

Besides, having to conserve his funds had given him a splendid idea, one that dovetailed neatly with his plans for the new book.

What had finally decided him was the ad. "Housekeeper to Irvine physician. Live-in. Refs. reqd." He'd have to fudge on the references, but he'd gotten the impression that the doctor was single, when he spoke to the secretary, and he figured the guy would probably be relieved to have another man around, instead of some motherly woman who'd turn up her nose at overnight female guests or smoky, early-hours poker parties.

Or whatever games rich doctors in Irvine played these days.

Jason grinned ruefully. He'd have to watch himself. He still retained his hungry-days prejudices against rich folks, even though he wouldn't mind qualifying for that description himself. But, despite the warm reception of his first book, *The Private Life of a Revolutionary*, photography wasn't a field in which one was likely to make a fortune. That was all right with Jason. He was glad just to be able to make a living doing what he loved best.

It had been the greatest challenge of his life, spending three months at a training camp for revolutionaries in the Middle East. Jill had claimed she understood why he had to do it; only afterward, looking back, could he clearly see how unhappy she'd been with his long absence. He couldn't really blame her for leading such a wild life in New York, even though her spending sprees had nearly cleaned out their savings account.

Then there'd been *The Private Life of a Politician*. That time, Jill had gone with him on the campaign trail with a congressman, a low-key bigot whose hypocrisies Jason had managed to portray with his camera, even without the man's realizing it. Jill had enjoyed that trip, mainly because of all the parties and occasions for showing off her elegant wardrobe. She'd changed, he realized then, from the idealistic girl he'd met in college.

Maybe that was when their marriage had begun to come unglued. Or perhaps it was afterward, when Jason had begun to feel it was time to settle down, buy a house, think about starting a family. Jill wasn't ready for that, she said. He'd offered to compromise, but she'd decided it was time to strike out for herself and had gone to live with friends in New York. He didn't fight the divorce; sometimes people just drifted apart, he told himself, although the failure hurt.

The truth was, he decided as he turned onto a small residential street, that despite his spirit of adventure, he'd been the one who tried to make a home wherever they were. If it hadn't been for Jason, there never would have been a dinner cooked or laundry done or any of those other things wives were supposed to be so good at.

No wonder he felt qualified to apply for a job as a housekeeper.

Jason double-checked the address as he pulled up in front of a two-story house that looked very much like all the others on the street. Yep, this was perfect.

It was a long way from the slums of Tijuana, or even the rundown areas of Santa Ana, to this bastion of upper-middle-class achievement—a route that probably half or more of the maids had traveled. It was a contrast he meant to capture with the set of camera lenses that lay hidden in his trunk.

Underneath the upper-middle-class luxury of Orange County, Jason knew, lay deprivation and fear for some. In order to earn enough to support their families, maids often had to leave their children with relatives and live in their employer's house. Fearful of losing their job, they often worked long hours for low wages. Perhaps such conditions weren't unusual in the rest of the world, but it angered Jason to find such misery in his own country, amidst wealth. The conservative residents of Orange County talked a lot about their patriotism and their ideals, but they didn't always live up to their rhetoric. He supposed he wanted to hold up a mirror to the employers even more than he wanted to expose the situation to the general public.

Jason checked his watch. Five past six. Well, that wasn't bad timing, considering the leisurely course he'd taken. He strolled up the walk and pressed the doorbell.

A grey-haired, thin-faced woman answered. "Yes?"

"I have an appointment with Dr. Eldridge. About the housekeeping job."

The woman looked puzzled but stepped aside to let him enter. "We're supposed to wait in the living room. The doctor asked me to answer the door." From her aggrieved tone of voice, it sounded as if answering the door had been a great deal of trouble.

Jason felt a momentary pang of guilt as he entered the house and followed the woman. He certainly didn't want to deprive someone of a job she needed badly. On the other hand, this woman already looked defeated.

As Jason stepped into the living room, he made a mental note of the plush carpet, the high-beamed ceiling and oversize fireplace and the costly, subdued furnishings with coordinated paintings, undoubtedly selected by an interior designer.

This confirmed his mental picture of Dr. Eldridge as a middle-aged man who was probably divorced and who spent most of his spare time at the racquet club, or chasing women, but who also worked sixty to eighty hours a week to rake in the money. Not someone who spent much time making a house a home.

Which suited Jason just fine.

The doctor had thoughtfully set out some magazines—*Discover*, the science magazine, and *National Geographic*. He wondered if the guy ever bothered to read them himself.

Two other women, in addition to the one who'd opened the door, were staring at him curiously from where they sat on the couch. He pretended not to notice their scrutiny.

Jason had just settled down with a copy of *Discover* when an inner door opened and a plump woman stepped out, nodding obsequiously. Behind her was an attractive woman whom he guessed to be in her mid-thirties.

So the doctor was married, after all. He swallowed hard against his disappointment. That meant he probably wouldn't have a chance at the job.

The younger woman glanced at him in surprise. "Can I help you?"

He explained why he was there.

"I see." The woman frowned and tapped her foot lightly on the carpet. "Well—all right. You'll have to be last to be interviewed, though. The others have been waiting."

"Fair enough." He grinned. She didn't grin back.

Jason watched as she turned to summon one of the other applicants. Mrs. Eldridge was tall and capable looking—qualities he appreciated after Jill's flightiness—with a trim figure and dark-blond hair pulled back into a bun.

All in all, she was a damn good-looking woman. Yet the plainness with which she was dressed and the starchy way she moved hinted that she was largely unaware of her own allure.

No doubt Dr. Eldridge didn't pay much attention to his wife. Idly, Jason wondered if they had children. He wouldn't mind that; he liked kids, and he'd enjoy looking after them, as long as they weren't spoiled brats. With this woman for a mother, he had a feeling they wouldn't be.

Patiently, with the magazine in hand, he sat back to wait his turn.

EVEN A DOSE of Extra-Strength Tylenol wasn't doing much for Anne's headache as she questioned the last of the three women in the tight confines of her home office. The man, of course, was out of the question for the job, but since Ellie had arranged for him to drive all the way out here, Anne knew she had to give him the courtesy of an interview.

"I don't do windows or move furniture, anything heavy like that." The thin-faced applicant, sitting ramrod straight in her chair, reminded Anne of the farmer's wife in the painting *American Gothic*. "And I must have my weekends off."

Anne tapped the erasered end of the pencil against the woman's résumé. "Naturally, you would have two days off per week, but my former housekeeper occasionally rearranged her schedule when I was entertaining...."

"I have other commitments." The woman glanced down at the disorder of bills and circulars on Anne's desk, her nostrils flaring slightly.

"Now, about cooking..."

"My day begins at eight and ends at five, like anybody else's." The applicant stared Anne straight in the eye. "I believe in sticking to schedules."

"I see." Anne groaned inwardly. The first candidate had lacked references, spoke little English and didn't appear to know much about housekeeping. The second lady chatted on and on endlessly, a habit that would drive Anne crazy within a matter of days, and also had revealed a number of personal details about her previous employer. The last thing Anne needed was to have her private life discussed all over the neighborhood. She'd sent both women home with her thanks and a promise to call them within a few days. If she got really desperate she might have to hire one of them, although she certainly hoped not.

But this woman was intolerable. Anne would be glad to give a housekeeper extra time off during the day just so there was a hot meal waiting when she got home from work. What she really needed, she told herself wryly, was a wife.

"Well, thank you." Anne stood up, bringing the interview to an end. "I'll be notifying everyone within a few days."

"I'd like to know by Friday, if you don't mind." The woman collected her purse.

"Very well." Anne wondered what it was this woman did on weekends that was so inflexible. Her imagination conjured up a murderer son who required weekend visits in prison, or a ring for which this woman smuggled in drugs from Mexico....

She certainly was tired to think of such nonsense, she scolded herself as she showed the woman out.

Anne took a moment to reapply lipstick, then chuckled at her own vanity. True, the man—Jason Brant was his name—was well-groomed and rather nice looking, but she was interviewing him as a prospective employee, not as a boyfriend.

The résumé he'd mailed to Ellie was rather scant, and under references he'd put merely: "On request." Her instinct was to dismiss him quickly, but she suspected a well-to-do physician would be a likely target for a discrimination suit if the man didn't feel he'd been given a fair hearing.

Fine. She'd question him, just as she'd done with the others. And then she'd ask Ellie to put the ad back in the paper.

Chapter Two

The office seemed to shrink to even tinier proportions than usual as the man relaxed in the chair opposite Anne, his long legs stretching so close to hers that they nearly touched.

"Have you worked as a housekeeper before?" She couldn't help noticing the intelligent glimmer in his dark-brown eyes, a hint of humor and of something deeper that intrigued her. And then there was the softly mussed but well-cut brown hair that looked as if he'd just gotten out of bed, as if someone ought to run her fingers through it....

Anne was surprised by her own thoughts.

"Only unofficially." His calm self-confidence made her feel as if he, not she, were conducting the interview.

"Unofficially?"

From an expensive leather portfolio, he produced several letters. Curious, Anne inspected them. One was from a lawyer, attesting that he'd eaten Jason's cooking on a number of occasions and found it excellent. Another was from a woman named Jill Brant, attesting to Jason's skills as a housecleaner and launderer.

"Is Jill Brant a relative of yours?" She handed the letters back to him.

"My ex-wife." He spoke easily, amusement quirking the corners of his mouth.

Anne started to choke and ended up coughing. "You brought a recommendation from your ex-wife?"

"Who knows my housekeeping skills better than she does?" Jason spread his hands expansively. He had nice hands, Anne noted from the corner of her eye—slightly roughened, as if he knew the meaning of real work, but well kept and clean under the nails.

She blushed, hoping he hadn't noticed her inspection and half-aware that she was focusing on the peripheral portions of his anatomy to keep her gaze from the lean rugged length of him. There was something unsettling about the man. Why did she keep getting the feeling that there was more to him than appeared on the résumé?

"Why do you want to work as a housekeeper? Don't you have some other occupation? I mean, it is a bit unusual for a man to seek a job like this, particularly when he has no previous experience." She was pleased by the professional, clipped tone of her voice. All business.

"Well, I have done some professional photography, but my divorce pretty well cleaned me out financially." The strong bone structure of his face and slightly pronounced jaw were offset by the velvety softness of his eyes, she noted before dragging her attention back to his words. "I thought this would be a secure setting, doing work I enjoy, while I indulge in taking the kind of photographs that interest me."

"I see." It was out of the question, of course, but how was she going to tell him that?

Before she could find the words, Jason took the initiative. "Tell me more about you and Dr. Eldridge, about your lifestyle. Do you have children?"

"I beg your pardon?" She gaped at him for a moment.

It was his turn to look confused. "Excuse me. I just assumed you were Mrs. Eldridge...."

Anne felt the heat rising to her cheeks. "My friends call me doctor."

He ducked his head, a gesture she found appealingly boyish. "And I thought I was the most liberated male in Southern California. My apologies, doctor. Somehow I was picturing a man."

At least he'd brought the subject of gender out in the open, she reflected. "And I was picturing a woman."

"For the job?"

"As you can imagine, a single woman like me would find it awkward to have a man around the house." Anne took a deep breath. She wished he wouldn't stare at her so intently, as if he were regarding her in a new light, as if...as if he'd become aware of her as a woman. An unmarried woman. "Besides the way it might look to others, there are questions of privacy."

Instead of taking the hint and agreeing with her, Jason shook his head. "I'm sure you have some living quarters set aside for the housekeeper in a place this big."

She admitted there was a bedroom and bath off the kitchen, while her own quarters were upstairs. "Nevertheless, I'm naturally in the habit of wandering around in my bathrobe." She cut off the words abruptly. Why on earth was she disclosing such personal details to this total stranger?

"On the other hand, you might want to consider the advantages." He leaned forward, his eyes catching hers and locking them in an intimate way. "The added security of having a man on the premises, for example."

"I have an excellent burglar-alarm system." *Besides, what am I going to do for protection when the most dangerous man around is already living here?*

"And there must be times when furniture needs to be moved or there's other heavy work that most women couldn't handle."

"I've never denied that men could be useful for their brawn." Anne smiled to take the edge off her words. "But my gardener comes once a week, and he handles any heavy work for a few extra dollars."

"Then there's my cooking." The man certainly didn't give up easily! "You're probably used to rather plain fare from your housekeeper—meat loaf, or maybe enchiladas. Well?"

Reluctantly, Anne nodded. Ada's repertoire had extended only as far as frying chicken and broiling steaks.

"Cooking's always been a hobby of mine. French, Italian, Chinese—you name it." From the glow on his face, Jason was obviously enjoying this match of wits. "Let me tell you about my fettucine. I have my own pasta-machine, and I use heavy cream, lots of butter..."

"Cholesterol," Anne pointed out.

"Doctors never pay any attention to their diets. Everybody knows that." He leaned back, as if he'd won his point, which, in fact, he had. Anne thought ruefully of her own hasty lunches at the hospital cafeteria, usually involving overcooked green beans, a gravy-laden entree and Jell-O for dessert.

"Well..."

Unexpectedly, he sprang to his feet. "Like right now. You haven't eaten dinner yet, have you?"

"No," she admitted, reluctantly following him out of the office and down the hall to the kitchen. "I was thinking of sending out for pizza."

Jason's long legs cut across the expanse of off-white tile and he swung open the door of the side-by-side refrigerator-freezer. Fortunately, Ada had gone grocery shopping before she left on Monday, and it was well-stocked.

"You'll need to use up some of these vegetables before they wilt." Jason began removing packages from the shelves and laying them on the counter. "Got an apron?"

Anne pointed wordlessly to a towel rack at one side, and Jason equipped himself with a black apron trimmed in red and white. She knew she ought to stop him, but darn it, she was hungry. Maybe she could hire him for an interim period, a week or so, until she found a permanent housekeeper. "I suppose I could take you on temporarily...."

"I'll tell you what." He began unwrapping a package of Swiss steak. "We'll have a trial period of one month. If at the end of that time either of us is dissatisfied, we'll call it quits and no hard feelings. What do you say, doc?"

She chuckled inwardly at his use of the nickname, which managed to sound both respectful and irreverent at the same time. "Well, a month might be a bit long."

"Now, you have to be fair about this." Wielding a heavy knife that resembled a miniature hatchet, he began chopping the steak into narrow strips. "I'll be giving up my apartment in Santa Monica, so naturally I'd need to stay at least a month. But I'm willing to gamble that you'll keep me on permanently, once you get used to me."

With a sigh, Anne sank down into a chair at the kitchen table, watching the whirlwind of energy with which he chopped everything up and located the appropriate seasonings, from teriyaki sauce to fresh garlic.

She was too tired to throw him out of here and too hungry to resist the mouth-watering smells arising from the stove. A few weeks. What could go wrong in so short a time?

"Well, all right," she said. "But only for a month."

AFTER SO MANY YEARS spent traveling, Jason had reduced his possessions to the bare minimum—which included the pasta maker and a cappuccino machine that wheezed and groaned like a calliope but made delicious coffee.

He managed to stuff most of his possessions into his car and make it down to Irvine by Thursday afternoon. Anne—or should he call her Dr. Eldridge?—had informed him she'd be gone until late that night, lecturing to a nursing class, so he could move in at his leisure. She'd given him a key and the combination to the burglar alarm; trusting woman, he reflected.

As he turned the car away from the coast and into the pre-digested city of Irvine, Jason felt doubts begin to nag at him, doubts that he'd shoved aside last night in his elation at having landed this job.

The fact was, he was coming here under false pretenses. In much the same way that he'd exposed that politician for the hypocrite he really was, Jason intended to show this wealthy community its own darker side. Through his photographs, the public would see the harsh private lives of the servants who kept the rich people in comfort and ease.

He didn't like the feeling that he was double-crossing Anne.

She certainly wasn't like any other woman he'd ever met before—any more than she was like the imaginary middle-aged Dr. Eldridge who played racquetball and chased young women.

There was a fundamental honesty about her that appealed to him. And a sense of humor. And a wariness in those green eyes that made him want to win her over, to make her laugh and trust him.

So how could he violate that trust?

On the other hand, perhaps he was underestimating her, Jason told himself as he paused for a traffic light, one part of his mind noting that it must have cost the city well over a hundred thousand dollars just to install the computer-controlled lights and pressure plates at a single intersection.

Anne might make a lot of money, but he didn't get the impression she was obsessed by it. In fact, judging by her practical and not particularly stylish clothes and her long working hours, he suspected she got little enjoyment from her high income.

Perhaps she would understand, even sympathize with his project. But he couldn't tell her about it, not yet. She would never accept him as a housekeeper if she knew he was really there for another purpose. And he wanted the experience, wanted to know firsthand how it felt to launder and mop and dust day after day, wanted a common ground on which to meet the cleaning ladies in the neighborhood.

Pulling up in front of the house, Jason began unloading the car.

He certainly did like this kitchen, he reflected as he passed through it on the way to his cheerful bedroom, which looked out on a tiny manicured lawn and a bed of marigolds and pansies. The kitchen was huge and well designed, perfect for gourmet cooking; he'd long dreamed of having a facility such as this, with butcher-block counters, double ovens and a gleaming array of copper pots and pans.

His thoughts returned to Anne. Apparently she didn't cook, but Jason knew better than to equate domesticity with femininity.

What kind of a love life did she have? Obviously, no man had awakened the woman within her; he'd seen that at a glance. Yet there was enough sensuality left over, even unconsciously, to intrigue him. How would she look with her hair down, and a glittery dress revealing that splendid form, and a touch of the right eye shadow to bring out the green in her eyes?

Stowing his camera bags under the bed, he went out for another load and tried to get his thoughts back onto a more mundane level.

In all fairness, he admitted to himself as he carted in two suitcases of clothing, this elegant life-style had a certain appeal. He could get used to living in a fine house with five bedrooms and four bathrooms—Anne had given him a tour of the premises last night—as well as a video recorder, compact-disc player and two color televisions, including one in his own quarters.

It's only for a few months, he told himself firmly. But there was no rule that said he couldn't enjoy himself in the meantime, was there?

Anne had assured him he wouldn't need to start work until Friday, and as far as he could see, everything was spick-and-span. Still, out of curiosity, Jason inspected the laundry room, which was connected by a chute with Anne's upstairs bedroom, and noticed a pile of delicate lingerie in rainbow pastels, peach and soft blue and aqua. Now, who would have suspected something such as that underneath that businesslike dress?

Grinning, Jason turned away. His new employer clearly had forgotten about this aspect of her privacy, and he certainly wasn't going to remind her.

He could go back to Santa Monica for a last load, but that would mean getting stuck in rush-hour traffic. No, he had the apartment through the weekend, and he could live without the remaining odds and ends for a day or so.

Deciding instead to enjoy the rest of the day, Jason changed into his swim trunks and walked out through sliding glass doors onto the redwood deck, its corners anchored by wooden half barrels spilling out flowering geraniums.

Spreading a towel on a chaise lounge, he was preparing to sun himself when he heard a yapping noise from the house next door and glanced over.

"You get back in there!" snapped a woman's voice with a slight Hispanic accent as a screen door slapped shut.

Jason swung to his feet and walked over to the low dividing wall to take a look.

Standing on the rear deck was a large-boned, dark-haired woman carrying a bucket and mop. Dancing about her feet was a second mop, which on closer inspection revealed itself to be an indefinable species of dog.

"Need some help?" Jason called.

The woman shot him a look full of frustration. "He's always under my feet. And try to catch him? Not me. I'm too old."

Jason vaulted over the wall and strode across the lawn to scoop up the eager ball of fur, which promptly licked his cheek.

"Thanks." The woman opened the door. "Just toss him in." Jason obeyed, and she managed to close the screen just in time to stop the dog from bounding out. He sat inside, peering out through the mesh, and yapped once, with a wistful note that made Jason wish he could let the dog out again.

The maid was wringing her mop. "You just move in next door?"

"I'm the new housekeeper," Jason said.

The woman straightened and regarded him dubiously, from his bare feet to his swim trunks to his uncovered chest. "Oh?"

"My name's Jason." He stuck out his hand and she shook it with her own, which was still damp from the mop.

"Rosa." She cocked her head. "Are you really the housekeeper?"

"That's right." He leaned against the wooden railing that ran around the deck. "Actually, I don't start work until tomorrow. Dr. Eldridge was kind enough to let me move in a day early."

Rosa frowned at her mop. "This is one of those new things? A man cleans house for a woman?" At his nod, she reflected for a moment and then said, "You want to come inside for some coffee?"

He accepted with pleasure and soon found himself sitting in a kitchen much like Anne's, except that it had been decorated with an unfortunate taste for cheap knickknacks and cartoon-covered curtains.

Rosa, he quickly gathered, was too Americanized to be an appropriate subject for his book. Her English was excellent, which meant she'd been in the United States most of her life, and he drew her out enough to learn that she had several grown children who held down responsible jobs.

But Rosa knew every other maid for blocks around and could tell him who was newly arrived from Mexico or Central America, who had children not living with them, and anything else he wanted to know. She was a gold mine of information.

It was too soon to admit his real purpose in being here, but an hour later, as he bid Rosa a reluctant farewell, Jason had a real feeling of accomplishment. With the help of his new friend, he should be able to find the right subject without difficulty.

Not bad for his first day in Irvine, he reflected as he jumped back over the fence and went to collect his towel.

It was too late now for sunbathing, he noticed with regret. But if he scheduled his chores well, he ought to have time for some tanning tomorrow before Anne arrived home for dinner.

Feeling quite pleased with himself, Jason went inside.

FRIDAY WAS ONE of those days Anne wished would end almost before it began. One of her first patients was an unwed teenager who cried when her pregnancy test came up positive, and Anne spent nearly an hour comforting her and talking. Finally she referred the girl to a service that offered free counseling and adoption referrals.

As a result, Anne was late for all her other morning appointments. The patients were annoyed, and her own usual even temper began to fray by noon.

Then one of her maternity patients developed complications, and Anne had to perform an emergency cesarean. The baby and mother, fortunately, were both healthy—probably in better shape than the doctor, she told herself wearily.

By six o'clock she was exhausted, hungry and crabby.

Anne had barely seen Jason the day before, merely calling out a good-night as she fetched a snack of milk and graham crackers to carry up to her room. Now, walking into the house, she was pleased to be greeted by the familiar lemon scent of cleansers and to see that the carpets had been vacuumed.

Maybe she hadn't made such a big mistake after all.

Her partner, John, had taken the whole situation as a lark when their receptionist told him about it yesterday, and at the hospital the other doctors had given Anne quite a bit of joshing about her new kept man. More and more she'd questioned the wisdom of her decision, but now, sniffing the aroma of ham and baked apples, she decided she could have done worse.

Heading for the kitchen, she stopped in the doorway, shocked.

Her first impression was that Jason was wearing nothing underneath his apron. On second glance, she realized that he had on a rather skimpy pair of tan bathing trunks that hid almost none of his lean body. From where she stood, Anne had an unobscured view of the dark fur on his legs, the play of muscles across his back and, in between, a very tight and nicely shaped derriere that twitched appealingly as he moved.

Oh, good heavens. She wasn't used to thinking about men this way. And Jason was—well, he lived here, for heaven's sake!

"I—" She cleared her throat as she sought a way to make a joke out of her embarrassment. "I don't know why I bothered to study anatomy. You're a complete lesson in yourself." Anne set her briefcase down on a chair.

"Actually—" Jason finished grating cheese and popped a leftover crumb into his mouth "—I was sunbathing and the time sort of got away from me. I meant to put some clothes on before you got here."

"Oh, don't get dressed on my account." Anne waved her hand airily, half of her mind wondering at her own light-hearted approach and the other half feeling as if she'd fallen down the rabbit hole and the whole world had turned topsy-turvy. "I'll just wander on upstairs and scrape off the day's grime."

"Dinner should be ready in fifteen minutes."

"Great."

When she came down again, Anne was relieved to see that Jason had changed into jeans and a formfitting navy sweat shirt that made him look like an athlete. She wondered at her own reaction. She hardly ever noticed how men were built—but then, baggy white coats didn't do much for a man's shape, and that was mostly what she saw.

The truth was, she acknowledged silently, that she wouldn't have been particularly stirred by Jason's looks if he were an airhead. But his efficiency around the house had already impressed her, not to mention his incredible cooking. And when she'd glanced into his room his morning, she'd noticed some striking photographs on the wall, scenes whose settings varied from everyday life in small-town America to the Middle East, shot with a keen eye for lighting and detail. When asked, Jason had modestly admitted shooting them and then quickly changed the subject.

Now, she saw, he'd set the table with a small vase of freshly picked flowers and a bottle of wine. "That's a nice touch," she said.

"I didn't know if you were in the habit of eating with the help, but since we're both hungry..."

"No, no, perfectly all right." She pulled out one of the rattan-backed chairs at the kitchen table. "Ada preferred to snack rather than eat full meals, but actually, I don't mind the company."

They didn't say much for a while, digging into the ham, baked apples, cheese-covered potatoes and salad. Anne wondered if her body might revolt against eating so much healthy food at one sitting.

As her hunger waned, her attention returned to Jason. Unselfconscious as a cat, he savored his food, apparently having worked up quite an appetite on her patio. At least, she assumed that's where he'd added to his tan, which was a degree or so darker than it had been on Wednesday.

Quickly, Anne dug into the remnants of her apple. Her train of thought was entirely too dangerous. Now, wasn't there something she'd meant to ask him, before she'd caught sight of his nearly nude body in the kitchen?

"Oh." She set down her fork. "I have a favor to ask."

"Shoot." He sipped at his wine.

"Normally, Saturday and Sunday will be your days off, but I hoped you wouldn't mind taking off Sunday and Monday this week. I've invited a dinner guest for tomorrow night, and I'd really appreciate it if you could cook. Of course, you're free to go out for the evening afterward."

Jason studied her with interest. "I wouldn't dream of it. Suppose you need a chaperon?"

Anne glared at him. "I hardly think that's likely."

"All the same, I did point out the advantages of having a male protector on the premises." He smiled lazily. "Don't worry. I'll fade right into the background. Your friend will hardly notice I'm around.

It was probably best to ignore his teasing tone. "I thought perhaps we could have something French. You did say that was one of your specialties."

"Leave it to me."

Irrationally, she found herself feeling embarrassed. What would Jason think of the rather pedantic Horace Swann, M.D., gastroenterologist cum laude and ad nauseam? Her own opinion was that Horace was not only balding and rotund but rather boring. Furthermore, his endless pontificating on intestinal disorders had a depressing effect on the appetite.

Still, he'd escorted her to a county-medical-association function, and she felt obligated to repay the courtesy. Besides, Horace might not be the most exciting date in the world, but he was better than sitting home watching TV.

Not that Anne didn't have other men she went out with occasionally. But not as many as she would have liked. First of all, she didn't meet very many unattached men; second, many of the ones she did meet preferred scatterbrained and doting women half their age; and third, her field of choice was rather narrow. How many men were there whom she could consider an equal? She'd discovered long ago that most men were intimidated by a woman doctor unless they, too, had advanced degrees and high earning power; that narrowed her selection of dates considerably.

"By the way..." Jason cleared away the dishes and poured them each another glass of wine. "No criticism intended, but I've been wondering how it is you grew up without learning to cook. Unless I'm mistaken about that?"

Anne shook her head. "I can make a few things, but nothing fancy. My mother was a tyrant in the kitchen. She still is, actually; when I visit my parents in Denver, she won't let me near a stove."

"Probably a wise woman."

"No doubt." Why did his comment bother her? Anne had never particularly wanted to be domestic. "Actually, I was pretty good at opening cans and heating the contents when I was in college.''

"Stanford?" he guessed.

"Just plain old UCLA." This man must imagine she came from a rich family, Anne realized. "My father's a retired army officer and my mother teaches high-school English."

"Tell me how you came to be a doctor. Were you one of those little girls who listen to their dolls with a stethoscope?" His eyes seemed to shine at her across the table, or maybe, Anne reflected, she'd drunk too much wine.

"Actually, I started out wanting to be an actress."

Under his gentle prodding, she poured out the story of her college days and of Ken, a professional actor whom she'd met when she was nineteen. At first, she'd been thrilled by the idea of joint careers, of becoming another onstage couple like Jessica Tandy and Hume Cronyn.

That summer, she'd agreed to stay for a month with Ken at his Hollywood apartment. It was a rude awakening. His days were spent going out on fruitless auditions, trying to reach his agent by phone and rehearsing an unpaid role at a hole-in-the-wall theater. Anne quickly realized that she came in a distant second to his career.

Furthermore, by the time she'd wiped out her second colony of cockroaches in his run-down flat and helped Ken mail out the third bunch of photographs to producers who would probably throw them in the trash, she'd realized that the acting life was not for her.

Temporarily at a loss, Anne went home to Denver, where she volunteered to work at a women's health-care center. It was during those remaining summer months that she realized what she really wanted to do with her life.

"There's nothing more rewarding than helping other people." Anne rested her chin on the palm of her hand, gazing dreamily across the table at the quietly attentive Jason. "And obstetrics and gynecology is particularly satisfying because so often I see results right away, which rarely happens if you're, say, treating cancer or managing a patient's diabetes. Sometimes when I can correct an infertility problem or catch an abnormal Pap smear in time to prevent cancer, I feel like I've been given a gift, to hold lives in my hands and help pat them back into shape.''

"That's a lovely image." His voice was deep and thoughtful.

"Unfortunately, sometimes things get so hectic I don't have time to think about the significance of what I'm doing." Roused from her reverie, Anne pushed back her chair and carried her dishes to the counter. "But I'm not complaining."

"Dessert?" Jason stretched as he stood up. "There's ice cream in the freezer." He walked toward her and reached around, rescuing her glass from the rim of the sink, where she'd accidentally set it. "I hope you're more cautious when you perform surgery."

"It's—a matter of concentration." Anne's breath came more quickly as his arm brushed her shoulder. Their bodies were only inches apart, his hip nearly touching hers through the simple sun dress she'd thrown on.

"I see." He paused, his mouth close to her lips, as if he were about to kiss her. "Is it really? I mean, a matter of concentration?" The boyish confusion only added to her sense of a growing intimacy between them.

"I think I'd better pass on dessert." Anne forced herself to step back. "Thanks anyway."

"My pleasure." He was still regarding her with a curious expression, almost of surprise. Or perhaps it was speculation.

"I—I usually sleep late on Saturdays, and then I have an appointment at the hairdresser's." The words poured out, creating an invisible fence around her. "I'll be on call in the afternoon, and I'll probably be catching up on my reading, so you're free to do whatever you like, as long as it isn't noisy." She suddenly realized that he hadn't asked if it was all right to bring dates over. Did he have a girlfriend? Why should she care whether he did? "Horace should be here around seven...."

"Horace?" Jason grinned unexpectedly. "That's really his name?"

"It runs in his family. For three generations." As he'd told Anne in great detail, she remembered. "You might need to do some extra shopping. I'll leave out grocery money." Resisting the urge to back up cautiously, she added a quick good-night and turned to go.

"Don't worry." Jason hadn't moved from his position beside the sink. "If you need any help getting ready tomorrow night, with zippers or anything, just let me know."

"Sure." Furious with herself for her own inexplicable panic, Anne fled out of the kitchen and up to the safety of her bedroom.

Why had she ever thought it was a good idea to hire Jason Brant, regardless of how well he cooked? He was entirely too disturbing, too masculine and too cocky.

And not her sort of man at all, Anne reminded herself. She'd always gone for the steadier sort, ever since she discovered how unhappy she would have been if she'd married Ken. Jason had something of the same zest for life, the same sense of daring—he ought to make a good friend and employee, she decided firmly. And that was all.

Chapter Three

Saturday was, on the surface, a quiet day. As she had planned, Anne slept late, got her hair trimmed and spent the afternoon reading medical journals.

Or rather, she spent the afternoon staring at the open pages of a magazine.

Her ears were following every movement Jason made. She knew when he went out to sunbathe, when he chatted with someone across the back fence, when he came in to change clothes and when he left to go to the supermarket.

After he returned, his soft whistling in the kitchen didn't annoy her the way whistling usually did. It had a Huckleberry Finn lightheartedness that reminded Anne of finding violets in the spring when she was a girl, and of squishing mud between her toes as she stood on the creek bed, fishing with her father.

Wait a minute. She'd never gone fishing with her father. They hadn't lived anywhere near any creeks that she could recall. And her parents would never have let her go barefoot in the mud.

This man was definitely having a strange effect on her.

There must be something to the old saying that opposites attract, Anne told herself, forcing her attention back to the printed page. No doubt it was the novelty of Jason Brant that fascinated her.

Like hell it was.

She was almost relieved when the telephone rang. She could use a nice, minor problem right now, a patient who needed to be checked at the hospital, something to get her out of the house.

But the answering service connected her with a maternity patient who had developed a sore throat, and all Anne had to do was telephone a prescription to the woman's pharmacist.

She should have known better. In obstetrics, emergencies happened only at two o'clock in the morning or on Christmas Day.

The hands on Anne's watch inched toward five-thirty. Too impatient to sit still any longer, she went upstairs to change for her date.

Originally, she had intended to wear a simple navy shirtwaist with pearls, but that hardly seemed festive enough to accompany what she presumed would be an elaborate French dinner. Besides, although she wasn't particularly crazy about Horace Swann, she felt an inexplicable reluctance to let Jason know that.

Instead, Anne decided on a dress she'd bought for her parents' thirty-fifth anniversary party, a flattering emerald crepe with a deeply slashed V-neck that was set off by a rhinestone-studded belt and matching shoes.

The intense color required complementary makeup, of course, so Anne dug through her cosmetics drawer to find the little-used palette of green eye shadows. Bright scarlet lipstick, a dab of blusher and eyebrow pencil—she sat back to regard herself. Satisfied, she brushed out her hair and fixed it in a sophisticated French twist, fastened with a jeweled comb.

Horace wasn't going to know what hit him, she thought as she pirouetted in front of the mirror. That was, assuming Horace would notice anything not shaped like an intestine.

It was still only six-thirty, but Anne decided her duties as hostess required that she go downstairs to make sure everything was in order.

Jason had straightened up the living room and put away her journals, she noted as she walked past toward the kitchen. And, spotting a vase filled with daisies, she had to admire his thoughtfulness in picking those up this afternoon.

Why didn't she ever think of things like that? Anne wondered as she headed down the hall. Unlike most women, she sometimes felt she'd been born without an ounce of romance in her soul. Even as a teenager, she'd never hung around the perfume counters trying on scents the way other girls did or bought hairstyling magazines and tried setting her hair different ways.

For some reason, the observation left her feeling vaguely dissatisfied, as if she'd slipped up somewhere. Anne shook away the thought and poked her head into the kitchen.

Attired in a discreet pair of slacks and a polo shirt, Jason was chopping shallots on the cutting board. Set out on the counter was an impressive array of spices, white wine, vegetables and chicken.

"You seem to have everything under control." Anne hovered a few feet away. "Is there anything else you need?"

Jason looked up. "Yes. You could sit down and keep me company." His gaze moved slowly across her face and down to the dress, lingered for a moment on the soft swell of cleavage revealed by the neckline, and proceeded down her stocking-smooth legs. "You look terrific. This Horace must be someone special."

"He's one of the most prominent gastroenterologists in Orange County." As she sat down, Anne realized that her answer must not have been what he expected, but what else could she honestly say? "What are you fixing?"

"Chicken in wine sauce with glazed carrots and new potatoes, followed by chocolate mousse. I hope that's all right. You seemed to be willing to leave the menu up to me." He spoke over his shoulder while continuing to chop the onions deftly.

"Sounds terrific."

Silence stretched between them, broken only by the chunk-chunk of the knife against the wooden board. There was something appealingly offbeat about the sight of such a well-constructed male form clad in a black apron, attending to domestic duties, Anne mused. Somehow Jason managed to imbue every movement with intense masculinity; in fact, he appeared to have taken charge of the kitchen like a captain ruling a pirate ship. No potato would dare to emerge half-cooked beneath his command; no butter would have the nerve to blacken and burn.

The irony of his position struck her again. Jason just didn't seem like the type to be satisfied with a low-paying, dead-end job as a housekeeper.

On the other hand, Anne had known professionals who chose to work at a routine occupation for a while in order to concentrate on some creative project. Jason had mentioned something about taking pictures, she recalled.

"Tell me about your photography." She crossed her long legs, being careful not to snag her stockings with the rhinestone-covered shoes.

Jason stopped cutting the onions. For a moment, Anne thought she'd said something to startle him, but then she saw that he had finished his task and was transferring the shallots to a plate.

"Well, I've always been fascinated by how much people reveal of their inner personalities in the way they look and move and dress." His back still toward her, he began unwrapping a package of chicken. "I like to take pictures of people at their ordinary tasks and see how much I can reveal of what lies beneath—of their thoughts and fears and hopes. Not to mention vices."

"That sounds challenging." Anne wasn't sure it was possible to show so much with a still camera, but she was impressed by Jason's concept. "You said you did some professional photography?"

"Oh, from time to time." Expertly, he skinned the chicken and began removing it from the bone. "Actually, my ex-wife and I did some traveling, and I took photos wherever we went."

"I see." She supposed he must have sold scenic shots to travel magazines. That couldn't have paid very well, but he obviously wasn't unduly concerned with accumulating material possessions, a quality that was rare among the people Anne had met these last few years. It brought back, with a twinge of nostalgia, the dedication of her theater friends during the early years at college. "I take it housekeeping isn't something you plan to do permanently."

"Well, no." What expressive shoulders he had, Anne couldn't help noticing as Jason opened another package of chicken. What power he conveyed, even in such simple chores.... She bit her lip and returned to the subject under discussion. "Do you want to pursue photography full-time?"

"Eventually, yes."

She wished he would talk about himself more freely. Anne hesitated, not wanting to pry, but finally said, "Did you grow up around here?"

"Boston. My mother was ill a lot, so I learned to help out around the house." Jason removed the chicken to a pan and began scrubbing the cutting board.

The doorbell rang. Anne glanced at her watch and saw that it was seven o'clock on the nose. With a sigh, she went to greet Horace Swann, M.D.

STIRRING UP WHIPPED CREAM for the chocolate mousse, Jason kept his ears tuned to the desultory conversation emanating from the dining room.

What on earth did Anne see in a man like Horace? The bald head and paunch could be overlooked; in fact, Jason told himself, he would have admired Anne if he'd thought she loved a man despite his lack of good looks.

But even taking into account Jason's ignorance of medical minutiae, it had become apparent within the first half hour that Anne's dinner guest was a crashing bore.

To make matters worse, from Jason's perspective, the man hardly appeared to notice what he was eating, shoveling the food into his mouth between descriptions of his latest medical research. For the first time, Jason understood how chefs in restaurants felt when their best meals were sent back by some picky eater who wanted the steak burned and the potatoes fried in deep fat.

It was possible that Anne had merely accepted a date with the man from politeness, of course. But that didn't explain the stunning dress she'd put on or the carefully applied makeup.

Jason jabbed viciously at the whipped cream. Love might be blind, but he couldn't allow Anne to waste her time on a fool like Horace.

Spooning the cream onto the mousse, he carried the two dishes out into the dining room.

Anne smiled up at him. In the indirect light from the chandelier, he thought her eyes had taken on an animated sparkle. Could that be a result of the ramblings of her pompous windbag of a date? Surely not, but Jason wasn't going to take that chance. He was not only her housekeeper but her protector, after all.

"Dr. Swann." Jason stood respectfully behind one of the straight-back chairs. "I hope I'm not interrupting?"

"Oh, no, no." The rotund physician waved a hand expansively.

"Actually, I had sort of a personal question to ask you." He saw Anne's eyebrow arch upward but ignored it. "You see, colitis runs in my family, and I've wondered if I might have inherited it."

Immediately, Swann began questioning him about symptoms clearly unfit for dinner-table discussion. Jason answered gravely, noticing with some regret that Anne had barely touched her dessert. He felt more than a twinge of embarrassment at having raised such an indelicate topic, but it was right in line with what the gastroenterologist had been prating about all evening.

"As a matter of fact, I'm involved in some research on hereditary aspects of colitis." Swann waved Jason into a chair. "Tell me about your family...."

Silently asking his mother's forgiveness, Jason described her problems with colitis in detail, feeling Anne's outraged glare boring into him all the while. Well, it was for her own good, he reminded himself.

"Why don't we adjourn to the living room?" Anne stood up and led the way. Jason hesitated, but Horace caught his arm and pulled him along.

Once in the living room, the gastroenterologist whipped out a note pad and began taking down Jason's comments, continuing to probe with questions for the next half hour. By then, Anne was having a hard time stifling her yawns, and Horace took his leave. He pumped Jason's hand, thanked him for a splendid evening, said a cursory farewell to Anne and bustled off into the night.

Well, Jason thought as he turned to face Anne's wrath, things *had* gone a bit farther than he'd expected, but his ploy had worked, hadn't it?

"Very nice," she said.

Jason waited.

"Is this free with your housekeeping services, or do you charge extra for entertaining my dates?" Clearly she didn't realize that her folded arms merely emphasized the womanly swell of her breasts, or that the way her chin was tipped upward made her mouth look deliciously kissable.

On the other hand, he told himself, if he gave in to temptation, he was likely to find himself out on the sidewalk in the wake of the good Dr. Swann.

"I'm really sorry." He tried to inject into his voice the appropriate degree of contriteness. "It was a matter that had been on my mind, you see, and he did seem interested, but I didn't expect to monopolize his attention." That was true enough, he told himself, so why did he feel a twinge of guilt?

He hadn't meant to hurt her by driving away a man who was worthy of her. But Horace Swann clearly wasn't.

He couldn't imagine that tubby blowhard taking the willowy Anne in his arms, murmuring soft phrases into her well-shaped ears or pressing his lips to hers. Not for one second could he visualize that man nuzzling her slender neck, or tracing the sweet valley between her breasts with his tongue, or...

Oh, Lord. What was he thinking?

Suddenly Jason realized that Anne wasn't glaring at him anymore. Her mouth was twitching in an odd way, and it struck him that she was trying hard not to giggle.

"All's well that ends well?" he prompted.

She burst out with a chuckle. "He is ridiculous, isn't he? Oh, Jason! But you have to promise never to do anything like this again, or I simply can't keep you around."

He lifted his right hand as if taking an oath. "I will never again mention my mother's colitis at the dinner table."

"That isn't what I meant!"

"Or in the living room."

"Jason!" She clutched her sides, tried to give him a dirty look and went off into gales of laughter. "Horace had no idea you were putting him on! He was so earnest! He'll probably present a paper about you at the next convention!''

''Are you on call tomorrow?'' he asked suddenly.

''Not until evening.''

''How would you like to drive up to Santa Monica with me?'' Now that the idea had struck him, it was obvious he and Anne were meant to spend the day together. ''I've got to pick up a last load of stuff at my apartment. It's right on the beach, so if you want to bring a bathing suit, we could go for a dip.''

Anne hesitated. ''Actually, I didn't make much progress on my reading today, and I was planning to use tomorrow to catch up.''

''Don't you think a break would do you good?'' Jason could see she was about to argue, so he hurried on. ''You need to be fresh to concentrate on your cases, you know. I'd say a little R and R was in order.''

He could see the duty-bound physician in Anne warring with the lively young woman. Finally, she said, ''Well, maybe just for a few hours . . .''

''Now go and get some sleep.'' He headed for the dining room before she could change her mind. ''Leave the cleaning up to me. Breakfast is at nine.''

''Jason.'' Standing there in the hallway with her eyes wide in the dim light, she looked like a little girl.

''Mmm-hmm?''

''Thanks.'' Anne's mouth stretched upward at the corners. ''Tonight really was awfully dull until you came in.''

He gave her a mock bow. ''I aim to please, *madame*.'' Feeling a growing impulse to stride across the intervening space and sweep her into his arms, he forced himself to turn and hurry away.

This was becoming a dangerous assignment, Jason told himself as he cleared the dishes from the dining table. He'd never expected his rich physician to turn out to be a vulnerable and infinitely desirable woman.

Well, they were both adults, he reminded himself, fitting the plates into the dishwasher. Neither of them was going to get carried away. They could enjoy their mutual attraction as a harmless flirtation, and maybe in the process Anne would come to accept the feminine self she evidently preferred to lock away.

He was doing her a favor, actually. By the time Jason was through rescuing Anne from herself, she'd be ready for a real love affair with some appropriately well-established doctor or lawyer who had a whole lot more to offer than Horace Swann, M.D.

Yes, he was only doing this for Anne's own good, Jason mused as he cleaned the counters and sink. And in the meantime, of course, he would serve as her mentor, guiding and protecting the butterfly Anne as she emerged from the cocoon in which she'd hidden for so long.

If the thought of her finding happiness in another man's arms wrenched at his heart in an inexplicable way, well, that was probably the way a parent felt when a child grew up and left home, Jason told himself. It certainly couldn't mean any more than that.

Chapter Four

Jason couldn't have conjured up better weather on Sunday if he'd tried. It was a postcard-perfect Southern California day, without even the morning fog that usually descends in June. The Los Angeles–Orange County basin stretched to the San Bernardino Mountains, which, although usually lost in haze, now were sharply visible, with snow still clinging to the highest peaks.

As the Mustang paced out of Irvine with the top down, a mild breeze ruffled Anne's dark-blond hair. She looked young and adventuresome; it was hard to picture her as a no-nonsense doctor in a white coat. What a complicated woman she was, Jason reflected, remembering how sternly she'd interviewed him for the housekeeping job and then how meekly she'd succumbed when he cooked what appeared to be the first decent meal that she'd eaten in days.

The many sides of Anne intrigued Jason—her underplayed femininity, her intelligence and the dedication it must have taken to become a doctor. He knew some men might be put off by having to measure up to such a highly competent woman, but he'd never felt he had to compete with anyone.

If he had, he decided as they turned onto Pacific Coast Highway, he probably wouldn't create the kind of books he did. There were certainly more prestigious jobs for a photojournalist, not to mention ones that paid a hell of a lot better.

At the beginning of his career, he'd free-lanced for the Associated Press in Europe and had been offered a full-time job based in Paris. He'd turned it down. A photographer for a wire service worked at a dead run, flying to a war zone one day, an athletic competition the next and an economic summit the day after. That wasn't the way Jason wanted to live his life. He wanted to get inside things, to capture on film the essence of people's inner selves.

But today, he was happy just to be driving along the coastal highway with Anne at his side.

They'd left Newport Beach and were heading north through the funkier regions of Huntington Beach. As he paused at a crosswalk for a trio of teenage surfers, Jason glanced sideways at Anne.

She was smiling, watching the youngsters' horseplay as they sauntered across the highway. As he started up the car again, Jason noted the way her eyes traveled to the window of a shop where hand-crocheted sweaters and brightly printed shirts were stretched on wires. From the intensity of her examination, one might conclude that Anne was a visitor from a foreign land who had never seen a beach boutique before.

What went on inside her mind? Jason wondered as they rolled northward. Surely she hadn't always buried herself in her work; when she was younger, she must have spent some time just having fun. Where had that part of her gone? Wherever it was, he intended to find it and bring it out again.

THE TANG OF SALT AIR and the play of sunlight on her cheeks reminded Anne of her college days. Unknowingly, her thoughts paralleled Jason's. When had she stopped going to the beach on impulse? What had happened to the friends who used to call on the spur of the moment to suggest going out for a pizza and beer or taking in a new movie?

I guess we just grew up and drifted apart. The thought saddened her, and she fought to banish it. Today was an island in time, a minivacation that she sorely needed, and she wasn't going to muddy it up with painful nostalgia.

Anne welcomed the distraction as Jason turned off the highway, and then she realized they hadn't reached Santa Monica yet.

To her questioning look, he said, "One of my favorite used-book stores is here in Long Beach. I though you might want to pick up something obscure. Like how to deliver a baby brontosaurus."

Laughter welled up in Anne's throat. "I wouldn't mind digging into an antique medical text—not quite that old, though. Maybe something with leeches and elixir of crushed jewels."

"Sounds terrific." Jason shook his head. "I suppose medicine used to be rather barbaric, didn't it?"

Anne told him about a museum she'd visited in Toronto that displayed wooden forceps and other instruments formerly used in obstetrics. "Some of them look as if they'd be better suited to torturing women than to helping them," she said. "Wood can't even be sterilized."

"Well, I can't promise you'll find a gem of medical history, but there's something about dust and mold that makes dull old books seem fascinating." Jason pulled the car to a halt in front of a rather shabby-looking store fronted by a dusty plate-glass window.

Inside, Anne found, the store rambled from one room to the next, turning out to be much larger than it had appeared at first. Together, she and Jason prowled through the stacks, from time to time selecting a volume and reading aloud from it. Deliberately seeking something far removed from her everyday life, Anne finally selected *The Life and Times of Beau Brummell*.

Jason turned up a few minutes later with a collection of bawdy limericks. "I thought I'd improve my mind by reading poetry," he told the clerk, straight-faced. The man merely nodded as he rang up the sale on an old-fashioned cash register.

For about the dozenth time, Anne found herself wanting to laugh out loud. What was it about Jason that made her spirits feel lighter than they had in a long time?

Or maybe it wasn't Jason at all, just her own natural buoyancy breaking through, she told herself as she paid the huge sum of two dollars for her book. She should have realized that she needed a break from her hard-driving routine.

Still, Anne had to admit as she glanced sideways at Jason, having someone to share her amusement added considerably to the enjoyment.

Back at the car, she tucked the book into her beach bag and settled into the passenger seat. "You seem to know this area rather well. Have you lived in Southern California for long?"

"No." Jason headed back toward the highway. "I make a habit of exploring whatever place I happen to be in, including Southern California. It's amazing how much you can learn from combing the newspapers and guidebooks and then going out and poking around. A newcomer can discover more about an area in a few months than most longtime residents ever know."

"Were you referring to anyone in particular?" Anne murmured, beginning to regret how little exploring she'd done over the past few years.

Jason ducked his head. "Actually, that wasn't meant as a dig. But if the pedal appliance fits..."

"Pedal appliance?"

"Well, I don't know the medical term for shoe, but I figured that was close." He grinned and sped away from a signal light.

Oddly enough, his teasing made Anne suddenly uncomfortable. She'd almost forgotten she was a doctor out for a spin with her own housekeeper. The medical reference, even though in jest, brought her back to reality.

How was a person supposed to behave under the circumstances, anyway? she asked herself, and realized there weren't any guidelines. Emily Post never had to deal with this one, she decided.

She fell silent, watching the beach towns roll by. It struck Anne that whenever she'd driven north, she'd always taken the freeway, not the rambling old Coast Highway. It wasn't the sort of road you took when you were in a hurry. And she always seemed to be in a hurry.

By the time they reached Santa Monica, she felt as if she'd traveled through another world, one where time moved at a slower pace than usual. She'd forgotten there were so many children in sunsuits and teenagers in bikinis, so many mom-

and-pop coffee shops and daredevil skateboarders and senior citizens on bicycles.

She was jolted from her thoughts as the car stopped alongside a garage in a neat whitewashed alley. A sign on the garage said Park Here and You'll Never See Your Car Again.

"It's okay." Jason opened his door and came around to help her out. "The garage is mine. For the rest of today, anyway."

Anne stretched as she emerged, sniffing the salt air and looking up, her attention drawn by the mewing of seagulls overhead. "I'm surprised you're willing to give it up for Irvine."

"The beach isn't going anywhere." Jason led the way up a narrow outdoor staircase. "If you decide to fire me next month, I can always come back."

Anne bit her lip. She wished that, just for today, she wasn't Jason's employer. Wielding authority was something she did every day at the office and the hospital. Right now, she wanted to be free of all that.

Jason opened the door to the apartment, which sat atop the garage. Anne hesitated for a moment as her eyes adjusted to the dim light.

It was a furnished apartment, impersonal looking now with Jason's own decorations stripped away. The couch was a nondescript brown, the walls a serviceable off-white and the tan carpet an outdated shag.

"The color scheme isn't much, but it hides the sand." Jason opened the curtains, and clear late-morning light flooded in. "Want to change in the bedroom?"

Anne agreed and hurried into the other room. She felt awkward as she pulled off her jeans and blouse and put on the one-piece blue maillot she'd bought two years ago and rarely worn. Dressing in Jason's bedroom made her feel vulnerable somehow, almost as if he could see her.

She returned to find he'd stripped off his own clothes down to rakishly slim gray trunks beneath. As when she'd seen him similarly clad in her own kitchen, Anne was struck by how comfortable Jason seemed with his own body, no more self-conscious than if he were wearing a three-piece suit. Or maybe less so.

"You don't get out in the sun much, do you?" He quirked an eyebrow as he regarded her, and Anne realized how pale she must look beside his bronzed body.

"The lights in the delivery rooms are pretty bright," she shot back. "I'll have to see about getting some adjustments so I can work on my tan while I work on my patients."

"They'd probably appreciate it." He gathered up some towels and a cooler and escorted her out the door, leaving it unlocked. "Why not put in tanning lights? It might take their minds off their labor pains."

"Only a man would think so." Anne led the way down the stairs.

"I have to admit, having babies is one area I don't know much about." Was that a wistful note in his voice? Or was it merely sarcasm?

"Let's get back to suntans." Anne's thong sandals, dug up from the back of her closet, flip-flopped against the pavement as she and Jason turned toward the beach. "Don't you know they're bad for your skin?"

"No worse than eating take-out food," Jason said as they emerged from between two houses onto the sidewalk that ran along the beach.

The Pacific Ocean stretched in front of them, Catalina Island jutting in the distance like a magical retreat. Small waves rippled placidly to shore, and the beach was dotted with bodies, gaily colored towels and squealing children.

Jason found a stretch of sand where they could have a measure of privacy—at least, there wasn't anyone breathing down their necks, Anne reflected. The nearest sunbathers were a young couple lying a few dozen feet away and smooching recklessly on a blanket.

"Ah, youth." Jason spread out their towels and set the cooler to one side. "Want something to drink? I'd offer you a beer, but alcohol is off limits on the beach."

Anne was about to point out that it wasn't a good idea to consume alcohol in direct sunlight anyway, since it could make you more vulnerable to sunburn, but she stopped herself. *Let's forget you're a doctor for the time being, okay?* "I'll take anything low-cal."

They settled down with their soft drinks and began tanning in earnest. Lying there with her eyes closed, Anne found herself tuning in to her other senses. She listened to the beach sounds of voices, surf and gulls and inhaled the smells of the ocean and of sunscreen lotion.

Gradually, she became more aware of Jason's nearness. His leg touched her calf lightly; perhaps he wasn't even aware of it. She could hear his deep breathing and smell the muskiness of the sun against his skin.

Restlessly, she sat up and squinted into the sun.

"Had enough?" Jason sat up beside her. "After all, you've been relaxing for at least ten minutes. We wouldn't want to overdo this. Maybe we could come back next week and try for fifteen."

Anne resisted the urge to throw sand at him. "Smart aleck."

"Am I wrong?"

She couldn't admit that her real motive had been to put a little distance between the two of them. "It's just that I find lying here motionless rather boring. How do you stand it?"

"I think profound thoughts." His eyes glowed amber in the sunlight, and Anne noticed that there was a dimple in his right cheek that flashed whenever he smiled.

"Maybe that's my problem. I have a shallow mind." She took another sip of her cola and found that it had gone flat and warm. Nevertheless, the heat had made her thirsty, and she drank it.

"Want to take a dip in the ocean, or would you find that boring, too?" Without waiting for an answer he stood up, and Anne jumped to her feet, glad for the diversion.

They raced down to the water. It felt surprisingly warm against Anne's ankles as she waded.

As soon as they reached knee depth, Jason dived in and began swimming away from shore with long, sure strokes. Anne continued out to waist depth and lowered herself till the waves tickled her neck, letting the water soothe her body as she watched Jason arc around and swim back toward her.

He belonged here, a free spirit in a place of unfettered souls, she thought. While she—well, she liked to visit the beach area, but the Anne of the old days had gone forever.

"A penny for your thoughts." Jason bobbed up beside her.

"Oh—" Anne shrugged "—I was feeling old and staid."

She looked anything but that, he observed silently. Anne had let her hair down today and it glowed golden against her bare shoulders. Oddly enough, the rather modest swimsuit merely emphasized the long slim line and gentle curves of her body.

"Hardly." He stifled the urge to tell her how lovely she looked; he sensed that compliments would only make Anne uncomfortable. "As a matter of fact, I'd like to take your picture."

"Oh, no, please!" She splashed back onto the beach, then stared in dismay as sand clung to her damp ankles.

"I'll make you a deal. I'll fetch your sandals if you'll let me take a few shots."

Anne considered for a moment. "All right."

He loped over to the towel, scarcely noticing the sand that stuck to his own legs, and brought her shoes back as promised. "You can relax for a minute. I've got to check the light."

"Don't make a big production out of this." Flopping onto the towels, she squirmed a bit—or perhaps it was his imagination—as Jason took the camera from the cooler and adjusted the lens aperture and speed.

Gazing at her through the camera, he recognized the difficulty of his task—to capture her inner womanliness, when the very presence of a camera made her even more tense than usual.

"Why don't you tell me something about yourself," he suggested as he angled around. "Where did you grow up?"

"A lot of places." Anne pushed back a strand of damp hair. "My dad was in the military, so we moved frequently."

"That must have been hard on you." Already, he could see the stiffness easing out of her muscles.

"In some ways." She leaned forward, hugging her knees. "My sister Lori and I got very close, because it was hard to make other friends. And we really valued our extended family, too—we have annual reunions, so that gave us a bit of stability, seeing the same faces every year no matter where we were living."

"Did you go overseas?" She'd almost forgotten about the camera; Jason took a shot and held his breath, hoping the click of the lens wouldn't destroy Anne's thoughtful mood. It had no effect, he noted with relief.

"Yes—Germany, for a while." A faraway look drifted across her face. What was she remembering—some special man, or perhaps a castle on the Rhine? Jason captured the moment on film. "We ended up in Colorado when I was a teenager, and then I came out here to college." Anne stretched with an instinctive grace.

"And then you met your actor friend," Jason prompted.

"Oh, yes." Anne tilted her head to one side. For some reason, recounting her life to Jason was helping her to see how the pieces fit together. "I suppose a part of me wanted excitement—maybe all young people do—and that's part of what Ken represented for me.

"Until you ran into the cockroaches." Jason would have made a good psychologist, she reflected; his voice had just the right impersonal but inviting tone, skillfully drawing forth her memories.

"Oh, I could put up with poverty if I had to—not that I like it." Anne sifted a handful of sand into a small pile. "It was the instability that got to me. So many years of pulling up roots, tearing friendships apart until I stopped bothering to start new ones—well, that made me realize what I really wanted. A home, a community, someplace where I belonged."

"Do you ever regret going into medicine?" He certainly was taking a lot of pictures, she noted, but it was his film and he could waste it if he wanted.

"For about five minutes at a time, mostly when I'm really tired and never want to see a white coat again." She smiled lazily. "But no more than that."

Jason lowered the camera. "You're a terrific model, when you're not thinking about it."

Anne shook her head so her hair fell across one cheek, half-hiding her face. "Just don't ever show me the photographs. Hey! Turnabout's fair play." She reached across and grabbed the camera. "Got any film left?"

"It's a roll of thirty-six—there should be about a dozen shots to go." He didn't seem to mind as she fiddled with the instrument until she got the hang of it. Anne had owned a thirty-five-millimeter camera herself, and this one wasn't too different from the one she'd lost at last summer's family reunion.

"Now, you're the expert on models, so show me how it's done." She peered through the lens. It was easy to see that the man was spectacularly photogenic, with his strong bone structure, lively eyes and well-toned muscles.

Jason lounged back on the towels and grinned. "Shoot away."

Anne clicked the lens. "It's your turn to tell me about yourself."

"Some other time." He seized a handful of sand and tossed it up in the air. "Something about the beach brings out the kid in me." He jumped to his feet. "Follow me!"

Startled, Anne trailed after Jason as he raced down to the strip of wet sand near the waterline and began mounding up what was obviously the foundation for a castle.

Delighted, Anne captured on film the building of what she had to admit was an expert construction, complete with turrets and tiny windows. But the real sight was Jason himself, beaming with enthusiasm as he created his fantasy world.

Soon a circle of children gathered, and Jason put them to work where they would do the least damage. He had a knack for dealing with them, Anne observed. Without talking down, Jason managed to reach the kids at their own level, as if he knew instinctively that one little girl wanted to fetch sand for him in her new red bucket, while an older boy yearned to construct his own tower.

It was almost a relief when the camera refused to advance any farther. Returning it to the cooler, Anne joined the castle-construction crew, shoring up a crumbling wall.

Kneeling in the sand, she scarcely noticed how it clung to her legs. The grittiness that had bothered her when she emerged from the water didn't matter anymore. *After all, no one's going to ask you to scrub yourself for the operating room.*

Finally the castle was complete. Anne was surprised to find they'd attracted quite a crowd.

"It's all yours," Jason told the children. "At least, until the tide comes in."

Anne sighed. "I hate to think that it's only temporary."

"The best thing is just to walk away and not look back."
Jason took her arm and drew her to the towels, which they
gathered up. "Hungry?"

"Starved." Anne gazed longingly toward a nearby taco
stand. "I suppose fast food is out of the question?"

"I make exceptions for special occasions." Jason led the way,
and soon they were stuffing themselves on junk food.

Finishing up the last of her diet soft drink, Anne wrinkled
her nose. "I'm beginning to feel like I burned a little."

"You're turning red," Jason admitted. "I should have
thought about that earlier. Let's go in."

Side by side, they sauntered back to the apartment, where he
produced a large bottle of moisturizing lotion. "Let me." He
guided her to a seat on the couch. "You can't reach your own
back, you know."

Anne sank down and closed her eyes. The couch creaked as
Jason sat beside her, his hands strong and cool as they stroked
the lotion into her back with a circular motion. She winced as
he slid her straps down onto her arms. "I must look like a 'before' ad for Coppertone."

"Something like that." Jason dropped a cold dab of lotion
onto her shoulder. It felt wonderful. "You're going to hate me
in the morning."

"I hate to think what Ellie will say—she's my receptionist."
He was massaging her neck, making her forget about Ellie and
the sunburn, about everything but the way his touch shivered
down her spine.

"Tell her you were playing tennis with Dr. Intestine. She'll
understand." Jason's deep chuckle echoed through Anne's
nervous system.

The rich smell of sun rose from both their bodies, mingling
in Anne's senses like a rare perfume. She could feel the heat of
Jason's body radiating against hers, and his knee brushed sensually against her thigh.

The swimsuit felt clammy on her body, and she found herself wanting to strip it off. The air would be cold, but Jason was
here, still warm from the sun....

Slowly he turned her to face him. Anne didn't open her eyes,
engulfed in sensations she'd never known before. This feeling

wasn't sexual so much as earthy and natural. Skin belonged against skin, not against stretch fibers. Legs ought to entangle with each other, lips ought to touch....

Then his lips did touch hers, very gently. Anne's mouth opened of its own accord. His hands caressed her forearms, and her palms pressed lightly against his chest, feeling the texture of thick hair over broad muscles.

The kiss deepened. Anne's arms twined around his neck and she stretched instinctively, the motion thrusting her breasts forward. Jason's hand at her waist drew her closer.

Anne had felt passion before, or what she'd thought was passion, but not this welling up of desire from deep within, as if she'd discovered a new part of herself.

What's wrong with you? This is Jason. You hardly know him. The unwelcome thought came from a part of her mind that Anne was beginning to dislike intensely. It ruptured the mood, and her eyes flew open.

"I . . ." She didn't know what to say.

Jason released her slowly. "Consider it a natural extension of our day at the beach." Anne was grateful that he refrained from making any disparaging remarks about her inhibitions. Instead, he gave her a wry smile. "I guess we both got carried away."

She stood up and found that her knees were definitely wobbly. "I'll go change. Then we'd better be getting back. I'm on call in a couple of hours." Without waiting for a reply, she darted into the bedroom.

They were both subdued on the drive home. Anne wished she could read Jason's mind. Had their embrace been as special to him as it had to her, or was she merely one in a string of interchangeable women whom he'd held?

She wished they had mutual acquaintances so she could find out more about him. The only thing she knew was that he'd been married once and was still apparently on friendly terms with his ex-wife. But he didn't lack experience when it came to applying lotion to a woman's back. Had he intended their kiss to happen?

His face, as he drove, told her nothing. He looked comfortable, as always. He seemed like the kind of man whom a woman would remain friends with, whether she'd been married to him or not.

Friends. That was good enough, Anne decided firmly. Today she'd let herself go—well, she'd needed a break, hadn't she? That didn't mean she was going to turn into a beach bunny. Surely Jason realized as well as she did that their kiss could never be repeated. They were too different, despite the undeniable physical attraction.

When confronted with a confusing situation, Anne had learned that the best tactic was to analyze things rationally and decide on a course of action. As they whirred home—on the freeway, this time—she did exactly that.

Clearly, she told herself, her own overwork had made her vulnerable to Jason's easygoing charm. She needed to allow herself more time off and spend some of it with attractive men. No doubt her response to his touch was the result of overly restrained impulses....

Boy, do I sound clinical. It's a good thing Jason can't hear what I'm thinking; he'd get a good laugh out of it.

All the same, there was truth in what she'd concluded, Anne mused as they turned off the freeway in Irvine. She'd have to make a point of expanding her love life to include men more appealing than Horace Swann, M.D.

That way, Jason wouldn't dominate her thoughts the way he was doing now. That way, her arms wouldn't ache to hold him again, and her lips wouldn't tingle at the thought of renewing their kiss.

Solutions were easy when you approached a problem sensibly, Anne reflected.

Like hell they were.

Chapter Five

On Monday, Jason developed and printed the roll of film in his bathroom, which he'd turned into a temporary darkroom. Watching the images emerge was, as always, a moment touched with magic. He stared down at the pictures, wishing he could make out more of the details in the red light.

As soon as it was safe, he switched on the overhead light and lifted an eight-by-ten print out of the pan. Anne gazed up at him, her eyes focused somewhere in the distance—or perhaps on a time long past.

Jason examined print after print. As he'd hoped, the camera had caught a range of expressions that together formed a portrait of the woman he was coming to know better than any woman since his divorce.

After the breakup with Jill, Jason had been lonely and had sought out the company of women. But although he'd enjoyed some pleasant relationships, none had really satisfied him.

Finally the intensity of his yearning had abated, and he'd begun to revel in having his freedom again. Now he could consider future projects without worrying about their effect on someone else. He could travel as much as he wanted, cultivate new acquaintances and not have to worry about how much money he had in the bank, beyond what was needed for his immediate expenses.

He'd thought he was finished with wanting any kind of entanglement. So why was he standing here like a star-struck adolescent, gazing at pictures of Anne and wondering what memories had been floating through her mind when he photographed her?

Jason fished out the last prints, the ones of him building a sand castle. He noted with interest some aspects he hadn't caught at the time: a boy frowning in concentration as he scalloped the edges of a tower, a mother's glowing face as she watched her children play....

Children. That was the reason Jason had wanted to settle down with Jill, to give up his traveling for a few years. Intellectually, he could understand why she'd refused. Children were a big responsibility and a long-term one—and although Jason had never meant to force Jill into any stereotyped roles, he knew that women often found their own interests sidelined when they had little ones to raise. And she'd never wanted a family the way he did.

But emotionally, Jason couldn't see how anyone wouldn't want a couple of those little munchkins toddling along at your side, forcing you to view life through new eyes. It would be well worth making some sacrifices.

How did Anne feel, delivering babies day after day and not having any of her own? Was she so obsessed with her career that everything else took second place?

It was too bad she'd been behind the camera during the sand castle building, Jason reflected as he cleaned up the trays of chemicals. He would have liked to see the expression on her face as she watched the children.

Washing his hands to get rid of the pungent smell of the photo chemicals, he stepped out into the bright light of the kitchen. Monday was grocery-shopping day, according to the schedule Ada had left behind, and he didn't want to slight his housekeeping duties.

Still, it gave him a funny feeling, picking up the envelope of money Anne had left on the counter. Taking a paycheck was one thing; accepting her money, even though it was for expenses, made him feel like a kept man.

Well, what's wrong with that? Jason paused as he tore the grocery list off its pad and folded it into his shirt pocket. He supposed he wouldn't mind, if it was anyone but Anne.

In some ways, he wished he could go back and start over, not as her employee but as, well, a friend and equal. But then, how would he have met her? And what pretext would he have for coming over here day after day, seeing her wander down to breakfast with her hair freshly washed and not yet dried, or watching her stand at the counter fixing a midnight snack, wearing a pair of panda slippers that were especially endearing for being so completely out of character?

No, he couldn't have gotten to know her any other way, so there was no use hassling about it, Jason told himself. What he really needed to do was to get on with his photo project; the sooner he completed it, the sooner he could level with Anne.

Going out the back door, he vaulted over the fence to the house next door and tapped on the rear screen. After a moment, Rosa appeared.

"I was going to the supermarket and wondered if you'd like a ride." Seeing her hesitation, Jason added, "Actually, I don't know my way around the store very well yet. I thought maybe you could give me a few tips."

Rosa nodded. "Okay. You know, you ought to get the newspaper on Thursdays. That's when they advertise the grocery specials. Wait a minute, I'll bring the ad."

A short time later, as they drove to the store through the cool morning fog, Rosa pointed out a sale on corned beef and cabbage and an unusually low price on strawberries.

"Thanks." Jason really meant it; he did love food and cooking, and the strawberries in particular appealed to him. He could imagine Anne's face as she trudged in from another of her long days. The sight of fresh berries with whipped cream would chase away her weariness....

Oh, Lord, I sound like a television commercial! Next I'll be prattling on about ring around the collar.

The supermarket, like everything else in Irvine, looked discreet, expensive and up-to-the-minute. Tucked into a landscaped shopping center, it came complete with its own bakery, a fresh-fish counter and a bountiful display of cheeses.

Jason and Rosa pushed shopping carts side by side, chatting as they strolled. He'd been here before, to buy food for Anne's dinner date with Horace, but that had been a quick expedition with specific targets. Today there were detergents to choose and a hundred other decisions to make.

It would have helped if he'd drawn up a meal plan for the week, Jason concluded. Well, live and learn.

They were almost finished when Rosa clucked her tongue sharply, drawing Jason's attention to a young Hispanic woman standing beside a cart and looking thoroughly bewildered as she gazed at the brightly lit aisles and stacks of promotional merchandise.

"A lost soul." Rosa heaved a sigh. "She'll probably panic in a minute and run out of here, and there goes her job."

"Why don't we help her?" Jason turned his cart around. "We left the frozen food till last, so nothing's going to melt."

Rosa frowned. "Why are you so concerned? You might get fired, too, if you spend so much time at the supermarket."

"Dr. Eldridge won't know the difference, and neither will your folks." Jason had learned last week that Rosa kept house for a pair of lawyers who worked even longer hours than Anne.

Rosa shrugged. "Okay, I don't mind. You wait here so we don't scare her."

Jason watched as Rosa approached the girl and said a few words in Spanish. The response mirrored on the girl's face at first was fear, then doubt, then relief. Rosa gestured him over.

"Her name is Juanita and she doesn't believe you're a housekeeper, too," Rosa said. Jason turned to the girl and saw a shy smile lighting up her face.

He'd brushed up on his Spanish before undertaking this project, and, begging her pardon for his occasionally fractured verbs, he explained that he liked to take photographs and had chosen the job because it allowed him a lot of free time.

Then he and Rosa read over the list Juanita's employer had written in English and walked through the store with her, pointing out items on the shelves. Fortunately, there weren't many shoppers at that time of day and the aisles were wide, so they were able to manage as a threesome.

Afterward, they paid for their groceries and headed home. Juanita had driven in her employer's car, a large sedan that clearly frightened her, and she admitted she didn't have a driver's license.

"I'm surprised her boss didn't check," Jason muttered.

Rosa clucked. "In Southern California, people take it for granted. You can see, Juanita speaks only a few words of English, but the woman just assumed she could read the list. People don't realize what it's like when you come from another country."

They decided to have Rosa drive Juanita home, while Jason followed in her car. Since Juanita's employer was at the house, Rosa sneaked away unseen with a promise that she and Jason would return the next afternoon, when they could answer more questions for Juanita.

"She's very lonely. You should have heard her talk when we were in the car!" Rosa folded her arms in front of her as she rode back to Anne's house. "She's only been in this country a few months and she was lucky to get this job. Her husband is a migrant worker, and she has two little children who stay with her sister in Santa Ana."

Jason crossed his fingers on the steering wheel. Juanita sounded as though she might be the subject he was looking for. That didn't necessarily mean she'd be willing for him to photograph her, though. And it bothered him to think that, in a way, he'd be taking advantage of her plight for his own purposes, just as her employer was doing.

Well, that was a concern every journalist and photographer had to deal with, he reflected—that you were exploiting the very people you sought to help.

Anyway, this was no time to lose himself in moral perplexities. As they pulled up in front of the house, he realized the hot June sun had finally burned away the last of the fog. Frozen broccoli and ice cream wait for no man.

THE HOSPITAL CAFETERIA was crowded at noon. Anne debated about skipping lunch but didn't want to take a chance on getting light-headed in the middle of the afternoon.

Standing in line holding her tray, she thought back to yesterday's outing with Jason. Not that she had any problem remembering it—her nose and shoulders smarted from sunburn.

But she didn't mind. In fact, the discomfort was almost welcome. It made her feel that the day wasn't entirely past and that she hadn't completely gone back to being the workhorse she'd become in the last few years.

More than a few years, she reflected ruefully. There'd been medical school, internship, residency, a fellowship at a hospital and then her partnership with John Hernandez—always a reason to work weekends and evenings, to turn down dates and grab a sandwich while she tried to keep up with the latest medical literature.

She'd never paused to ask herself when it was going to end—or, at least, when it was going to slow down a little. Even now that she was becoming established, Anne felt guilty about taking any time for herself.

She studied a neurologist who was ahead of her in line, a man she'd known for several years. He wasn't much older than she was, but his gray pallor reminded her of her own before yesterday, and he had bags under his eyes.

How come we don't play golf on Wednesdays the way doctors are supposed to? she asked herself. Oh, perhaps some physicians worked so hard because they wanted to make as much money as possible, but she suspected most of them were as stuck on a treadmill as she was.

The problem now was how to get off it without sacrificing her work—and without spending too much time in the dangerously alluring presence of Jason Brant.

Finally reaching the salads, Anne picked out one sprinkled with shrimps and slices of hard-boiled egg. That wasn't enough to hold her all afternoon, she decided, and added a plate of overcooked green beans and mashed potatoes to her tray.

I sure hope Jason never finds out about this. He might start making me come home for lunch.

Unfortunately, she conceded silently, the idea had a lot of appeal. For the first time in ages, she felt as if she actually had a home instead of merely an expensive, empty house.

Rebelliously, Anne took a glass of Cherry Coke. She would have added a slice of apple pie, but better judgment prevailed.

Besides, she might want to wear her swimsuit again this summer.

After paying the cashier, Anne stared around the room, looking for a vacant table. Failing to see one, she searched for an empty chair. Mentally, she eliminated several tables occupied by nonhospital staff—probably relatives of patients—and a long table at which half a dozen nurses were chattering. She wasn't concerned about the unwritten snobbery that separated doctors from nurses, but she knew her presence would make the other women feel restrained.

At that moment, she spotted a couple of hospital volunteers getting up from a table, and she started toward it. Unfortunately, someone else had made the same observation, and he and Anne arrived at the table at the same time.

"I don't mind sharing if you don't." The darkly handsome face and rakish smile belonged to Aldous Raney, M.D., a plastic surgeon with a reputation for playing the field among the nurses.

Anne had been introduced to him once, but they'd never exchanged more than a few words. Now she sank into a chair and said, "Of course not. Please join me."

"Looks like you had a good time this weekend." Aldous was clearly referring to her bright-red nose and cheeks. He flashed white teeth and a dimple at her. "Not used to the beach, eh?"

He himself sported a rich tan. Although many plastic surgeons did excellent rehabilitation work with victims of accidents and birth defects, Aldous was better known for his nose bobs and tummy tucks. As one of the nurses had commented in Anne's presence, he specialized in reconstruction of the rich.

"I suppose I overdid it." How could anyone prepare green beans that had so little flavor? Anne wondered as she ate. And the mashed potatoes would have made the state of Idaho blush with shame.

"So tell me, doctor, what are your hobbies, since you're clearly not accustomed to the great outdoors?" Aldous consumed his meat loaf with flair, holding the fork in his left hand European-style.

"My idea of a really wild Saturday night is to have three patients in labor at the same time." Anne sipped her drink and nearly choked as the bubbles went up her nose. Being with Aldous made her feel adolescent and awkward.

Somehow she managed not to sneeze, cough or tip over the rest of her Coke, but it wasn't easy. Still, she reminded herself, she was almost thirty-four, and she could certainly handle Aldous Raney.

"Sounds like you need some help livening things up." The way Aldous fixed his gaze on Anne conveyed the impression that she was the only other person in the room.

Embarrassed, she wondered what the nurses must think about this little tête-à-tête, then decided it didn't matter. She could handle him, couldn't she? "That sounds like an offer."

"As a matter of fact, it is. I've noticed you for a long time, but you're a hard woman to get near. You always seem to be loping through the halls at a dead run." He sipped his coffee without taking his eyes from her face.

"I guess sunbathing isn't the only thing I overdo." Anne smiled apologetically. "I've been known to run into lab technicians in the corridor without even seeing them."

"How does Saturday night sound?" He certainly didn't beat around the bush.

"I'm on call. How about Friday?" Never let it be said that she lacked boldness, Anne mused.

"Great. I know a little French restaurant in Hollywood, and then we could hit the nightclubs. Or perhaps you'd rather dine at my place? I barbecue a mean steak."

So much for boldness, Anne reflected; she was already having second thoughts at the prospect of being alone with Aldous. *Maybe before I tackled the big time I should have practiced on someone with a little more panache than Horace Swann.*

Without thinking, she blurted out, "Why don't you come over to my place for dinner?"

"Great!" From the masterful way Aldous was working his dimple, she gathered that he expected something special for dessert. "I'll be there about seven."

Anne provided the address and watched with misgivings as Aldous departed, leaving his tray behind despite the signs that urged Please Bus Your Own Dishes.

She wondered what Jason was going to think about this.

"I CAN'T BELIEVE you're actually working for Dr. Eldridge!"
Deanie Parker's voice rose to a near squeal over the telephone
line.

Jason lifted his ear a little from the receiver. He'd forgotten
how enthusiastic—and loud—his cousin could be. "It's just a
way to make some money while I work on my next book. Of
course, I haven't told her anything about what I really do...."

"No problem! I won't say a word!" Deanie sounded as if she
might be jumping up and down with excitement—an alarming
thought, since she was eight months pregnant.

Jason had had dinner with his cousin and her husband, Tom,
at their house in Newport Beach about six months ago, catching up on old times. Deanie had just learned at the time that she
was pregnant and had talked of little else.

It was only this morning, as he was doing the laundry—
Tuesday's main chore, according to Ada's schedule—that he
remembered her mentioning a Dr. Eldridge. Sure enough, when
he'd called a few minutes ago, she'd confirmed that Anne was
her doctor.

He'd hoped Deanie knew Anne well enough to fill him in
about her background and social circle. In his work as a photojournalist, Jason had learned the value of questioning a third
party, and for some reason he found himself wanting to learn
all he could about Anne; but his cousin, as it turned out, knew
Anne only as the doctor who saw her briefly once a month for
prenatal checkups.

Fortunately, Deanie was, as usual, too preoccupied with her
own concerns to ask any probing questions about what kind of
work he was doing for Anne. She took at face value Jason's
remark that he was "just doing some odds and ends around the
house," which was understandable, since he had worked as a
handyman during the summers when he was in college.

Deanie had a heart of gold, but she just wasn't the type you
wanted to confide your deepest secrets to, Jason reflected as his
cousin chattered on.

"I mean—the reason I think it's so terrific about you working for Dr. Eldridge—well, you know Tom's company sends
him overseas?" Deanie didn't seem to be making much sense,
but Jason made appropriate noises of agreement. "Well, he's

in Germany right now and I'm afraid he won't get back in time for the delivery.''

''That's too bad.''

''So I thought maybe you could photograph it, so at least he could see how it went. I mean, since you're working for Dr. Eldridge, that makes it easy, doesn't it? She knows you, so she'll have to say yes, won't she?''

''I think it would be better if you asked her. After all, you're the patient.'' The idea of photographing a birth appealed to Jason strongly. True, it could be a bit embarrassing when the woman was his own cousin, but Deanie obviously wasn't disturbed by the prospect of having him see her in such intimate circumstances. Childbirth was a miracle, after all, not a time for misplaced prudery.

''Sure! I mean, even if Tom does get back, he'd be too busy helping me to take pictures, wouldn't he?''

''I don't think the doctor will want a roomful of people watching when you give birth, but I'm willing to go along with whatever she approves.'' Inwardly, Jason winced. He didn't think Anne was going to like this, but once Deanie got hold of an idea, she never let go.

''Okay! Thanks a lot, Jase.''

For the rest of the morning, he was busy with the laundry and ironing. Bored with removing creases from blouses and sheets, he flicked on the TV set that Ada had kept near the ironing board and watched a soap opera. It was hard to follow the half dozen plot twists, so Jason tried to make up a story built around the commercials. He came up with something about a rustic family in a log cabin serving powdered lemonade to a jolly green giant, who then staggered through a group of dancing teenagers to buy life insurance from Snoopy.

After he finished folding away the last pillowcase, Jason went next door to pick up Rosa as they'd planned.

''Juanita called and said it's okay to come over.'' Rosa settled into the passenger seat of his car. ''Her lady's gone to the gardening club.''

''Gardening?'' Jason couldn't suppress a skeptical grin. ''In these tiny yards? There isn't room for more than a tub of pansies on the patio.''

Rosa shrugged. "Maybe she grows orchids in the bathroom. You never know."

The house where Juanita lived was the largest model in the development, with five bedrooms, and the family that lived there had three teenagers, Jason learned when they arrived. He didn't envy Juanita the job of keeping up with the work.

When they arrived, Juanita was clearly nervous. "Maybe they'll fire me if they learn my friends come here," she explained in Spanish.

"But you live here," Jason pointed out. "Surely you can have a few visitors."

"I don't know. I don't want to ask them." Juanita ushered Jason and Rosa into the utility room, where they sat at a small, scarred table. "It's not that I'm complaining. I was lucky to get the job."

When Jason ventured to ask about her salary, Juanita named a very low figure. Jason tried not to show his dismay. He could understand how her employers might not want her to have visitors in the house and might overestimate Juanita's grasp of English and of American customs, but how could they pay her so little? She was making less than minimum wage and working far more than forty hours a week.

But then, she needed the job so badly she wouldn't dare complain, he reflected angrily.

"Why don't I answer your questions about the house?" Rosa suggested, indicating the computerized washing machine for a start.

Juanita jumped as a car drove by on the street. "Maybe the children will come home from school early. You'd better go."

"But—" Jason started to protest and then cut himself off. The last thing he wanted was to make Juanita any more frightened than she already was. "All right. Maybe we can come back another time."

"Maybe I'll come to your house." Juanita got directions from Rosa.

"When will you come?" the other woman asked.

"Whenever I get a chance. I don't know. I'm supposed to be here all the time, except Sundays." Juanita looked relieved but also rather forlorn as her two guests departed.

As they drove home, Jason said, "Maybe she's exaggerating things in her own mind. Do you really think her employers are such slave drivers?"

"It wouldn't surprise me." Rosa glared out through the windshield. "Last night I talked to my friend who works down the block and she said those people have a bad reputation. They fired the last maid because she had to take a few weeks off to go back to Mexico and take care of her sick mother. And she'd worked for them more than a year."

When he got home, Jason started grating cheese for the lasagna he was making tonight. Anne hadn't gotten home on Monday until nearly ten o'clock and had gone straight to bed, and he was sure she hadn't eaten properly all day. At least tonight she'd be well fed.

You'd think I was her mother! But somebody's got to look after her.

Jason thought about Juanita and about the network of neighborhood domestic workers with whom Rosa kept in touch. In the text that would accompany his photographs, he wanted to make the point that a housing tract was a small world unto itself, with as much intrigue, joy and sorrow in its own way as the larger world.

He finished his advance preparations for dinner by midafternoon and sat down to make some phone calls. He'd already done preliminary research for his book by gathering statistics about domestic workers, but now he wanted some more personalized information.

A woman at a Hispanic-rights group was more than happy to oblige. She knew of families that hired Latino day laborers and cleaning ladies and then intentionally fired them on flimsy pretexts to avoid paying them.

Afterward, as he stirred the sauce for the lasagna, Jason felt his anger begin to subside. In reality, he knew, such abuses were the exception. Rosa, for example, had told him she was happy with her employers, and Anne certainly wasn't exploitive.

Was he being fair in this book? Would a brief disclaimer be enough, or would he be leaving the untrue impression that Irvine was a hotbed of Simon Legrees?

The front door clicked open and Jason heard Anne's familiar footstep in the entrance hall. It surprised him how quickly he'd come to know her habits and even her customary noises—the absentminded way she talked to herself when she was concentrating on a task, the scuff of her shoes when she was tired, the two quick breaths she took as she inhaled the fragrance of good cooking.

"Lasagna?" She leaned wearily in the kitchen doorway. "I'm impressed. And today's laundry day, too. Or did you work out a new schedule?"

Jason laid one hand over his heart. "And abandon Ada's brilliant scheme of things? Never."

It was amazing that a man so masculine could look so good in a kitchen, Anne reflected. Or maybe it was just his talent at the stove that was overwhelming her resistance.

Something red caught her eye, and she looked more closely at the colander sitting on the counter. "Strawberries!"

"With homemade whipped cream." Jason began layering lasagna noodles into a pan. "Now this has to bake for a while. Cocktails and antipasti will be served on the patio in fifteen minutes, so why don't you freshen up?"

Anne nodded and hurried upstairs. Despite the air conditioning in her office and car, the June heat made her tailored suit and white coat nearly unbearable.

Her thoughts returned to the hospital and to her conversation at lunch. Maybe it hadn't been wise to invite Aldous here on Friday, in light of the way Jason had handled Horace.

Or maybe I'm just feeling guilty about letting another man invade Jason's domain.

Jason's domain! Anne shook her head furiously as she slipped on a short-sleeved blouse and a white skirt. He was becoming altogether too cocky. And then there was that phone call she'd received a few hours ago. . . .

It was hard to confront a man who so graciously brought her a daiquiri and an antipasti tray on the patio, but Anne forced herself to look him straight in the eye. "About Deanie Parker . . ."

"Oh." A sheepish look crossed Jason's face as he sat beside her at the white wrought-iron table. "She gets a little carried away. I agreed to oblige her, but only if it's okay with you."

Anne fought down the urge to refuse this further encroachment of his, this progression from her private to her professional sphere. After all, she did try to accommodate her patients whenever possible, and Deanie had the same rights as anyone else.

Swallowing a gulp of daiquiri, Anne forced herself to say in a calm voice, "My concern is that you not interfere in any way with Deanie's medical needs. Sometimes complications crop up...."

"If that happens, I'll get the hell out of there." Jason wasn't joking this time. His dark eyes bored into Anne's. "Give me credit for a little common sense."

She nodded. "I told Deanie it would be all right, if her husband can't be there. If he's in town, though, I'd rather not have a third party present. Every additional person increases the risk of infection, and frankly, you'd be in the way of the nurses."

"I understand."

Maybe she'd misjudged him. This was probably Deanie's idea entirely. Just because he'd taken over her house before she quite realized what was happening, that was no reason to think Jason wanted to take over the rest of her life, Anne told herself sternly.

"By the way, I'm expecting a dinner guest on Friday." She nibbled at a black olive. "You can take the evening off as soon as dinner is served—I'll clean up. You can use your own judgment as to the menu."

Jason's face was expressionless. "If you tell me a little about your guest, it would help me choose something appropriate."

What would you say if I told you he's the hospital playboy? "I think he has rather cosmopolitan tastes."

Jason nodded gravely. "I can handle that. What time?"

She told him.

"No problem. And I promise to keep my mother's colitis to myself." Before she could respond, Jason vanished into the house to see to the lasagna.

Chapter Six

After vacuuming and dusting on Thursday as per Ada's schedule, Jason flipped through Anne's collection of cookbooks. He enjoyed experimenting with new recipes and could usually tell by reading them whether they'd turn out well. Of course, he wouldn't want to risk giving Anne any unpleasant surprises tomorrow night. Better to stick with one of his old favorites, pork strips stir-fried with peanuts and seasoned with rosemary.

Thoughtfully he drew up a grocery list. They were running low on milk and eggs, as well....

Good Lord. I'm starting to take this housekeeping business seriously! Maybe I should consider it as something to fall back on between books.

But there weren't likely to be many employers like Anne.

Jason lifted his head sharply as he heard noises next door. Women's voices were speaking rapidly in Spanish, one of them near hysteria.

He stuck the shopping list in his pocket and went over the fence, his usual route.

In answer to his rapping, Rosa flung open the back door. "It's Juanita. You heard her wailing all the way over at your house?"

"What's the matter?" His throat tightened. Housekeeping might be a mere diversion for Jason, but Juanita needed her job badly.

Rosa let him inside. At the kitchen table, the younger woman sat sobbing into a tissue.

"Her lady yelled at her for using the wrong kind of bleach with the towels. She ruined a couple of them and she's afraid she's going to be fired if she makes a mistake like that again." Rosa poured three cups from the coffee maker and set them on the table. "I'm trying to convince her to let me come over and show her what to do with all that equipment. They didn't even have flush toilets in her hometown, so how would she know how to use all this fancy stuff?"

It was the longest speech he'd ever heard Rosa make, and Jason couldn't help but be impressed by her concern.

He turned to Juanita and said in halting Spanish, "If no one's at home, why not let us help?"

She stared down into her coffee. "I'm afraid...."

"You see?" Rosa glared at the younger woman in disgust. "She's scared of her own shadow."

There had to be some approach that would work. "Even if your boss saw us, maybe she would think it was funny, meeting a male housekeeper."

Juanita brushed aside a tear. "You weren't joking? That's really what you do?"

"I'm a good cook, too." At least she'd stopped crying; that was a positive sign.

"You aren't ashamed, to do a woman's work?"

"Why? Am I going to turn into a woman if I put on an apron?"

Juanita smiled. "Of course not."

Gradually, Jason drew her out by talking about his own trials and tribulations with housework, including the mess he'd made changing a vacuum-cleaner bag. Rosa helped when his Spanish fell short, and Juanita seemed to enjoy his account.

Finally she agreed to let them both come over and help her out.

He drove them the three blocks to Juanita's house. She went in alone first, to make sure no one else was home, and then invited them in.

Surely her employers couldn't really be such ogres, Jason reflected as he gazed around at the immaculate, tastefully decorated home. But it grated on him to know that they spent so much money on their possessions and yet grossly underpaid their housekeeper.

It took Rosa half an hour to explain to Juanita the intricacies of American laundry and of the computerized washing machine, which, to Jason, was far more elaborate than it needed to be.

Next they tackled the microwave oven, the food processor, the dishwasher and a number of lesser appliances. As time passed, Juanita looked less and less confused, but she jumped every time a car drove by on the street.

Finally, she relaxed enough to fix some coffee and invite them into her small room off the kitchen, where Jason and Rosa sat on the bed while Juanita perched on a small chair.

Under Jason's gentle questioning, she began to talk about her life back in Mexico and her family. Her husband was a farm worker who had to travel to wherever there was planting or a harvest, she explained. Right now he was up in the Salinas area.

Mostly, Juanita admitted, she missed her children, who were two and four years old. They stayed in Santa Ana, about fifteen miles away, with her sister's family, and she was able to see them only on Sundays.

Jason looked around the room. On the wall over the bed was a cross; on the opposite wall hung an inexpensive print of the Madonna. "You don't have any photographs of your children?"

"My sister used to have a camera but one of her children broke it," Juanita said.

"I could take some." Not wanting to trick her, Jason explained about his book and that he wanted to take pictures of her at work, as well. "Of course I wouldn't use your name or show anything that would identify your employers."

"Why do you want to do this?" Rosa asked. "What good will it do?"

It was a fair question. "I'm not sure. Sometimes I think it's important just to show that a situation exists. Maybe someone will pass legislation or organize a union. Maybe some families who exploit women like Juanita will feel guilty and pay them better. Maybe nothing will happen. I can't make any promises."

The women nodded, and Jason was glad he'd answered honestly. Rosa and Juanita might not be very sophisticated in academic terms, but he suspected they could spot a phony a mile away.

"I would like pictures of my children. I will let you take the other photographs, too, if you want. You and Rosa are my friends." Juanita fingered the hem of her embroidered skirt. "Maybe you can show me some of your books."

They set a tentative date for the next morning. Juanita would leave the shade in her room up if it was all right for Jason to come in; if someone else was home, she'd pull the shade down.

"I feel like a character in a spy novel," Jason admitted as he drove Rosa home.

"If someone catches you, you can always say the pictures of her at work are for her children, so they can see what she does," Rosa suggested.

"That's a terrific idea. Thanks."

His plans for the book were working out even better than expected. Jason wished he didn't still have a nagging sense of guilt at the way he was deceiving Anne. He would tell her the truth as soon as he dared risk getting kicked out of her house.

"THE GRAPEVINE SAYS you've got a date with Dr. Raney." It was nearly five and the telephones had finally stopped ringing, giving Ellie a chance to chat with Anne for the first time that day.

"A person certainly can't keep any secrets around here." Anne handed her receptionist a patient's records to file. Her feet ached and her stomach was growling, a reminder that she'd skipped lunch.

"You watch out, Anne." It was John Hernandez, Anne's partner. "Aldous has a terrible reputation and a big mouth to go with it."

"Well, I plan to stuff it full of food, and that's about all I plan to do." Anne really liked her partner, as well as respecting his professional abilities. She wished they could talk more often, but mostly they saw each other for only a few moments a day, like now.

She peered past the reception desk into the waiting room. Two women were leafing through magazines. "Do I have any more appointments?"

Ellie shook her head. "No. One's for Dr. Hernandez and one's having an ultrasound."

In addition to Ellie and a nurse-practitioner, the office employed a part-time ultrasound technician who came in on Tuesdays and Thursdays. Sometimes Anne wondered how doctors had managed without that invaluable tool for diagnosing a wide range of problems.

"Don't change the subject." John broke into her thoughts. "I hope you plan to keep that male housekeeper of yours around to make Aldous behave himself."

"Maybe I should hire a Pinkerton guard. And maybe you should take care of your patient."

John grumbled good-naturedly and moved away.

Although her office duties were over for the day, Anne planned to spend the next hour catching up on medical literature in her office. Science was making rapid advancements in every field, but particularly in obstetrics.

About half an hour later, she heard Ellie moving about, using one of the bathrooms, which she had to do frequently since she'd gotten pregnant. A moment later, the receptionist tapped timidly at Anne's door.

She looked up and was shocked to see that Ellie's face had turned a pasty white. "What's the matter?"

"I'm bleeding." Ellie's voice shook. "I mean—not real heavily but—this hasn't happen to me before."

Anne sprang to her feet. "Has it stopped?"

"I think so."

"Any contractions?"

"No."

"Let's go find out what the problem is. Has the technician left yet?" Anne led the way to the ultrasound room, with Ellie trailing behind.

"I think she's still cleaning up."

Within a few minutes, Ellie was lying on an examining table and Anne and the technician were scrutinizing images on the monitor. The baby, a healthy size for its thirty-two weeks, was moving around and looked fine. There was no sign of a placental abruption, a dangerous condition in which the placenta separated from the uterus before birth and threatened the baby's oxygen supply.

However, the placenta had clearly attached low in the uterus, not quite touching the cervix. That made it vulnerable to bleeding.

After explaining the situation to Ellie, Anne said, "I want you to have your husband come and pick you up. Then I want you to go home and stay in bed through the weekend. Give me a call Sunday night and we'll decide whether you're well enough to come to work on Monday, okay?"

Ellie nodded, looking relieved.

"And I want you to call me immediately if there's any more bleeding or if you feel any contractions."

Ellie's husband, Dennis, arrived twenty minutes later, his face creased with worry. He looked relieved to see his wife smiling, although a bit shakily.

"Try not to worry too much," Anne tried to reassure her friend and co-worker. "It's probably nothing. And you're already at thirty-two weeks, so the baby would most likely be fine if it was born now anyway."

But they both knew that a premature infant would require weeks of hospital care and could suffer from lung immaturity.

That was the problem when medical workers got pregnant—they knew too much, Anne reflected as Ellie departed on the arm of her solicitous husband.

Concerned as she was for Ellie, Anne couldn't repress a twinge of envy. What would it be like to be expecting a child and to have a husband who loved you the way Ellie's husband obviously loved her?

Unexpectedly, Anne caught a mental image of Jason leaning toward her, his eyes alight with tenderness, his hand reaching out to stroke the curve of her belly where their child was growing. What a good father he would make, building sand castles with a toddler, teaching a youngster how to cook....

I must be working too hard, like everybody says. My brain's getting addled.

Wearily, she closed up the office and went home.

Anne noticed something amiss as soon as she walked through the door, but it took her a moment to pinpoint what it was. She didn't smell anything cooking.

"Jason?" She walked into the kitchen.

He was putting groceries away. "Just got back. Things took a little longer than I planned today."

It wouldn't be reasonable to expect him to have dinner ready the instant she got home. For one thing, Anne acknowledged silently, he couldn't have known exactly what time she'd arrive, but she felt disappointed all the same. It wasn't because she was starving, although that was certainly part of it; but the delicious smells of cooking had become a welcome part of her daily homecoming.

"There are probably some TV dinners in the freezer...."

Jason's uplifted hand cut her off. "Nonsense. It's my responsibility to provide dinner. Now look here." He opened a drawer and pulled out a slip of paper.

Leaning against the counter, Anne regarded him warily.

"I bought the newspaper today to clip the food coupons, and I discovered an ad for a new restaurant." Jason read to her from the piece of paper. "Two barbecue-rib dinners for the price of one—seven ninety-five—including corn on the cob and baked beans.' That's a special for four days only."

Anne shook her head. "I don't think..."

She might as well have been talking to the toaster for all the notice Jason paid. "I went over the grocery list and deleted the stuff I would have bought for tonight's meal, and, along with what I saved by using coupons, I come up with a grand total of twelve dollars and seventy-five cents. Now, I figure that's enough to cover dinner, a glass of wine apiece and a reasonable tip. So, are you going to wear your white coat or would you prefer to change?"

He wasn't leaving her much of a choice, and Anne was too tired to care. Besides, in a peculiar way, what he said made sense. If he'd saved the cost of a restaurant meal out of the grocery money, why not?

Upstairs, as she was changing into slacks and a knit top, the humor of the situation struck her. Jason was acting like an old-fashioned housewife saving nickels in the cookie jar. And she herself felt like an old-fashioned husband, coming home grumpy from the office.

But when she descended the staircase and saw Jason's lean figure silhouetted in the entranceway, he didn't look anything like an old-fashioned housewife. He looked like a very desirable man, and a rather mysterious one, with his face shadowed against the fading daylight.

Who was he really? When she'd asked at the beach about his past, he'd avoided answering, and the only thing she really knew was that his mother had suffered from colitis. Come to think of it, she really didn't know much about what he'd done or where he'd been.

Involuntarily, Anne shivered. During the past week, she'd come to feel comfortable with Jason and to trust him. Yet now she recalled her initial misgivings when she'd seen his résumé.

True, there'd been a reference from a lawyer, but she hadn't even bothered to check whether the man really existed. Anyone could print up letterheads....

The hunger pangs must be addling my senses. What do I think he is, a hit man for the Mafia?

"You know," she said, trying to keep her tone casual as they walked out to the car, "you still haven't told me much about your background."

"If you really want to know, I promise to bore you to death with it over dinner." He held the door for her.

The restaurant looked like a modern version of the Hanging Gardens of Babylon. Inside, plants trailed down from a row of window boxes near ceiling height. Most of the walls and roof were made of glass, revealing the fading pink remains of the sunset against a darkening sky.

"Very scenic," Anne observed as they followed a waitress to their seats.

Jason held her chair, then addressed the waitress. "We won't need a menu—we're having the special." He turned to Anne. "Unless you'd like something else?"

"Oh, no. I wouldn't think of it."

When their glasses of rosé wine had been set in front of them, Jason began, "I promised you my life story, more or less."

"Mmm-hmm." The wine had a pleasant fruity tang.

"I'm from Boston originally."

"You don't have an accent."

"I never did, really—I don't know why. Everyone else in my family has one." His eyes narrowed, remembering. "My dad's an auto mechanic—owns his own shop—and my mother was a secretary. But she was sick a lot when I was young, and being the oldest of five kids, I did a lot of cooking and cleaning."

"Five kids?"

"Three girls and one other boy. They all still live back in Massachusetts. I'm the one who wandered."

"I used to wish I had more than just one sister." Anne rested her chin on the heel of her hand. "And that my family would stay in one place for more than a year at a time."

"And I used to wish I could fly off to some exotic place. My favorite books were *Treasure Island* and *Robinson Crusoe.*"

"Did you ever get to travel to places like that?"

"Yes, I did." She hoped he would elaborate, but he merely sipped at his wine for a moment. "That's why I'm still rattling around like a loose wheel at the age of thirty-five. But it was worth it."

Had his wife gotten tired of all that wandering? Anne wondered. Was that why the marriage had broken up? But it was too personal a question to ask.

"You said you were interested in photography. Were you taking travel pictures?"

"Something like that."

Their dinners arrived, and Jason felt as if he'd been saved by the bell. He didn't mind telling Anne about his life—in fact, he wished he could be even more open with her—but it was too soon.

Too soon because of your project? Or because you don't want to risk losing her? The thought startled him. He would have to mull that one over later, when her green eyes weren't focused so intently on his face.

The ribs were tasty but messy. Anne dug in with gusto and didn't seem to mind when she wound up with barbecue sauce on her chin.

Sometimes she could be frustratingly prim and proper, and at other times, like now, a lively, uninhibited side of her shone through. Jason cherished these glimpses of what he considered to be the real Anne, the girl she must have been all those years ago when she battled cockroaches in Hollywood and dreamed of becoming an actress.

"After we finish this, we ought to go jump in the nearest swimming pool." He rinsed his hands in a fingerbowl the waitress had provided.

Anne wiped her chin with the napkin. "Actually, I'm more in the mood for a walk."

Through the broad windows of the restaurant, Jason could see a full moon rising. The night looked clear and inviting.

"I know just the place." He paid the check and helped her up. "One of my discoveries."

"No concrete, I hope?" Anne led the way out of the restaurant. "I feel like getting some exercise, but my feet may give out."

"No concrete. I promise."

He drove up the coast to Newport Beach. Anne didn't appear to be paying much attention to their route; she was gazing through the windshield at the stars.

What was the man like whom she was having over for dinner tomorrow night? Did he mean anything to her? Jason doubted it. There had been no excited ring to her voice when she told him to expect a guest for dinner.

Besides, although Anne would probably rather perform surgery on herself than admit it, the chemistry between her and Jason was too strong to yield to some other, newer attraction.

Chemistry. Maybe that was the wrong word. It was used so often to describe mere sexual attraction, and what he felt for Anne was much more than that.

She intrigued him, true; in many ways they were opposites, and opposites were supposed to attract. But he suspected that at a deeper level they were very much alike.

Still, he might be wrong. He'd misjudged Jill, or perhaps he'd misjudged his own needs within a marriage. He hadn't realized, when the two of them decided to elope on the spur of the moment after graduation, how important having children would become to him later.

His reflections ended as they reached their destination, a quiet side road, where he pulled over onto a dirt shoulder.

"Where are we?" Anne blinked as if she'd just awakened.

To their left across the road stretched a row of standard-issue ranch-style houses. But off to the right, there was merely open space.

"Come on and I'll show you."

Getting out of the car, he sniffed the salt air and listened for a moment to the hushed calls of night birds. Anne joined him, her expression puzzled.

"It feels as if we're out in the wilderness."

"In a sense, we are." He took her arm and led her down a dirt path between tall wild grasses. The air around them even felt different from that in the manicured suburbs; there was an untamed, adventuresome quality to it that he relished.

"The Back Bay!" Her eyes lit up with excitement. "All the years I've lived here I've meant to come down and explore, but I never have."

The Back Bay—whose official name was Upper Newport Bay—was a wildlife preserve despite efforts over the years to turn it into yet another Southern California marina. Silently, Jason thanked the environmentalists who'd fought to save one of the last remaining saltwater estuaries along the West Coast.

A haven for migrating birds, it also was home to many species of fish and small animals, he knew from having taken a tour here one Sunday. Set down into a natural bowl, its serenity shut out the clatter and clutter of nearby housing developments.

They walked for a while without speaking, stepping carefully along the raw pathway. The bay spread before them, scarcely rippling in the moonlight. Its primeval calmness touched them both with magic.

"At times like this I wish I were a poet." Jason helped Anne navigate a treacherous rut in the path. "There's something almost metaphoric about this place."

"Metaphoric?"

"As if it meant something beyond itself. A last wild spot remaining in a tamed land."

Unexpectedly, Anne felt tears prickle in her eyes. Jason might as well have been describing himself. She sensed the restlessness within him, the wanderlust that could never be stilled. This man who had turned her suburban dwelling into a home would never be happy living there permanently; he was too much like her father, eager to see what lay beyond the horizon.

But then, she'd never expected Jason to stay with her permanently, had she?

It must be the moonlight that's making me maudlin. She swallowed hard, glad for the darkness that hid her expression.

They stopped at the edge of a low cliff, looking down over the water. Far off, Anne could hear the murmur of cars across the bay bridge on Pacific Coast Highway. Beyond lay Lower Newport Bay, which over the decades had been dredged and turned into a major pleasure-boat harbor.

That wasn't so bad, either, she reflected. She'd gone sailing with friends once on the bay and had been entranced by the row upon row of tethered boats of all sizes.

Although the day had been hot, the air was turning chilly now, and Anne shivered. Jason slipped his arm around her, and Anne relaxed into the warmth.

Her head rested against his shoulder and she could feel the pulsing of his heart even through the soft fabric of his jacket.

How strange it was that they'd come to be here, that they'd met at all, she mused.

It felt like the most natural thing in the world when he turned her toward him and his lips grazed her forehead, then touched the tip of her nose and moved down to her mouth.

For a moment Anne couldn't breathe. The reality of Jason blotted out everything else around them. She wanted to stroke his cheek, to explore the contours of his bones and the sinuousness of his muscles beneath the jacket.

Slowly she responded to his kiss, her tongue flicking lightly against his teeth. Jason's mouth opened wider and his arms tightened around her waist.

Her entire body responded, silvery sensations flickering through her. How good it would feel to entwine her legs with his, to run her hands along his back, to nuzzle the soft shock of hair on his forehead. . . .

Reluctantly, Anne drew back. *Too dangerous.* "We'd better go."

A glimmer of moonlight touched Jason's eyes as he nodded slowly.

They walked back to the car together, not touching, but Anne felt as if her entire body were being caressed. She'd never responded to a man this way before. What was it about Jason that affected her so strangely?

At home, alone in her room upstairs, she undressed in front of the mirror, wondering how she looked to him and what he thought of her.

She tried not to think about how she would feel when, like a wild bird, he took wing from his temporary perch and resumed his migrations through the world.

Chapter Seven

Juanita's face filled with wonder as she gently polished an antique vase and traced the intricate figure of a Greek goddess. The morning light, filtering through lacy curtains, emphasized her broad cheekbones and dark eyes as she studied the beautiful vase, giving an ethereal, timeless air to the photograph Jason was taking.

Friday morning had been a time of revelation to him. The house where she worked might be a symbol of materialism and exploitation to Jason, but to Juanita—now that her initial fears were fading—it was a storehouse of wonders and, in a way, a promise of what she might achieve someday here in America.

"You should see the village where I grew up," she observed half an hour later as he took pictures of her mopping the redwood deck, with a hot tub in the background. "The streets are dirt. The houses are made of adobe; sometimes a man gets drunk on Saturday night and puts his fist right through a wall."

"I'd like to see it." Jason was coming to realize he would have to visit Mexico in order to complete his book. "Would it be all right if I went to see your parents and told them I was your friend?"

"Of course." She gave him the name of the village and the province. "They would be so glad to meet someone from America who knows me."

"And I'd be delighted to meet them."

She also agreed that a week from Sunday would be a good day to photograph the children.

Afterward, over a cup of coffee, he produced copies of both of his books and autographed them for Juanita. They were sitting in Juanita's small room, drinking from two chipped cups that obviously didn't belong to her employers.

She leafed through *The Private Life of a Revolutionary*, examining the pictures of a dusty Middle Eastern training camp, the grim-faced young men and women in fatigues, the piles of weapons. "Why are they so angry? Why do they want to make war?"

Jason wished he could find the words to explain in Spanish. Or maybe the problem wasn't words; it was that he himself found it hard to understand why mankind seemed so intent on blowing itself up.

"Sometimes when people suffer, they learn to hate." She nodded in understanding at his words. "We have a saying in English—two wrongs don't make a right. But some people don't believe that."

"We suffer, too, where I come from, but there is also much joy."

"I'm sure there is." He checked his watch. "I'd better be going. Your lady is due back soon from her gardening club, isn't she?"

"Yes. Thank you for coming. You and Rosa have helped me very much. And I look forward to having pictures of my children."

There was always more to a story once you got involved with it than you'd expected, Jason mused as he strolled the three blocks back to Anne's house. In his study of the politician, he'd been intrigued by the man's wife, a real old-fashioned Southern lady who epitomized the image of an iron fist in a velvet glove.

Now, working on this story, the vague ideas he'd had of an oppressed woman had given way, bit by bit, to a portrait of a real, three-dimensional person. Juanita was intelligent and sensitive. In addition, he sensed an undercurrent of strength in her; it was a trait that reminded him of Anne.

Well, he'd better not forget that he had a job to do, in addition to taking pictures of Juanita.

Friday was, according to Ada's schedule, the day for scrubbing the bathrooms and kitchen. Ignoring her supply of plastic gloves, Jason went to work with a whistle, running through his favorite tunes by Rodgers and Hammerstein.

Within an hour, both his musicality and his skin were fading fast. Reluctantly, he pulled on a pair of the gloves—fortunately, Ada had had large hands for a woman—and resumed work with renewed respect for the term "dishpan hands."

By three o'clock his back ached, and he soaked in a bath for half an hour before beginning preparations for Anne's dinner date.

He'd decided to make sauteed pork strips with peanuts, saffron rice and a *niçoise* salad, served with a Chablis from his favorite small winery, Glen Ellen. Then, for dessert, there would be a rich crème caramel.

This guy had better be worth all the trouble.

SEVERAL OF THE NURSES in the obstetrics-gynecology wing shot knowing looks at Anne. Damn the hospital grapevine, and damn Aldous's big mouth.

She was beginning to wish she'd never accepted his invitation. Did he really think she'd believed that old line about him wanting to get to know her better?

Really, she'd much rather just slump home in her usual Friday-night fog and let Jason perk her up with a tasty meal and his easygoing comradeship.

Well, she couldn't back out of it now. Besides, it would be interesting to find out what Aldous really had in mind and how he operated. Maybe he'd surprise her, Anne told herself without much conviction as she drove home. Maybe he'd actually prove to be an interesting, likable fellow.

Coming in the front door, she could smell something delicious in the air—was that saffron and rosemary?—and hear Jason moving about in the kitchen, stirring something in a pan and whistling under his breath.

She tried to identify the song and then wished she hadn't. It was "People Will Say We're in Love" from *Oklahoma!* Was that a satiric reference to her date or a comment on last night? Her stomach fluttered in midair, remembering the taste of his lips on hers.

Nonsense. He's probably not even aware of what song he's whistling.

She went upstairs to get ready.

Anne's instinct was to put on the highest-necked, longest-sleeved dress in the closet. But she refused to make herself look like a stereotypical prim old maid. No, she would wear a floating lavender crepe dress with a somewhat daring scoop neck.

When she came downstairs, Jason was whistling "I Cain't Say No."

Smart aleck, she commented silently.

It was a quarter past seven when the doorbell rang. Standing outside, Aldous sported a smooth grin and a dozen roses wrapped in green paper, the kind vendors sold at freeway off-ramps.

"They're beautiful." Anne sniffed the flowers as she took them, but there was no fragrance. "I'll put them in a vase."

She rattled around in her china cabinet before realizing that Jason must have already put some flowers in her favorite vase. Sure enough, she spotted it on the mantel in the living room, full of yellow and purple tulips.

How did he know that's the vase I like best?

Finally the roses were ensconced in another vase on the coffee table, and Aldous was reclining on the couch, guzzling Anne's Scotch.

"Boy, did I have a rough time today!" He proceeded to regale her—rather amusingly, she had to admit—with the story of his run-ins at the hospital. It was only half an hour later, as Jason announced dinner, that she realized Aldous hadn't once asked how *her* day had gone.

Not that she particularly wanted to tell him.

The food was delicious, but Anne scarcely tasted it. Aldous apparently believed food was the perfect vehicle for lovemaking. He fed her morsels from his plate—a tactic that disgusted her, but she was at a loss for a way to refuse without insulting him—and pursed his lips at her as he downed an anchovy from his salad.

Behind her, Anne heard Jason cough discreetly as he brought out a second bottle of wine. Subtle as the signal was, Anne knew Jason well enough to deduce from one cough that he found Aldous's posturing every bit as repulsive as she did.

Well, she wasn't going to admit it, not in front of Jason. Resolutely, Anne smiled at her guest.

His eyes gleamed wolflike in the light from the chandelier.

Oh, good heavens.

When Jason served the crème caramel and a bottle of brandy to go with it, she feared for a moment that he was going to spill something on Aldous. When she could do so unobserved, she shot Jason what she hoped was a quelling look.

He blinked in pretended innocence. But at least he didn't spill anything.

Finally, Aldous had romanced the last of the dessert and suggested they retreat to the living room. Restraining an impulse to pitch him out on the seat of his too-tight slacks, Anne agreed, if only to show Jason that she knew what she was doing.

But did she?

Aldous cut off her attempts to sink into an armchair by seizing her arm and guiding her to the couch, where he slid down beside her with his leg touching hers.

So much for subtlety.

"There's something I've been wanting to tell you," Aldous murmured in her ear.

"There is?"

"Yes. You know, as a plastic surgeon, I am an expert in bone structure."

That wasn't what she'd expected to hear. "I'm aware of that."

"But I've never seen a face like yours." He ran his fingers along the line of her jaw and tipped her face toward his. "Such classic perfection."

Such classic garbage!

Anne was about to pull away when she heard footsteps approaching through the dining room.

"Don't mind me." Jason knelt by the fireplace and lowered an armful of firewood to the hearth with a clatter. "I just thought you two might enjoy a nice fire."

"In June?" Aldous snapped. "It must have been eighty degrees out today."

"But it gets cold at night." Jason wedged a log into the fireplace and began stuffing kindling around it.

Anne glared at him. "Thank you, Jason, but we can do without the fire."

"Oh, well—if you insist." With a shrug, he stood up, brushed his hands off noisily and ambled away.

"Are you sure hiring a male housekeeper was such a good idea?" Aldous looked distinctly displeased at the interruption.

"It's just an experiment—for a month."

It didn't take Aldous long to get back to his attempted seduction. "You know, some men would be intimidated by you. But I like liberated women."

"You do?"

"I could see at once that you don't believe in old-fashioned inhibitions, that you take what you want when you see it. I'm the same way."

"Oh?" Anne was curious to hear what came next, but she didn't get the chance.

Jason bustled into the room carrying a plate of chocolate-covered wafers. "I thought you folks might like some after-dinner mints."

An inarticulate noise issued from Aldous's lips.

"No, we would not." Anne's tone was crisp.

"I'll leave them, in case you get hungry." Jason set the plate on the coffee table. "Boy, I really made a mess with that kindling, didn't I?" He pulled a small brush from beside the fireplace and began sweeping up the shavings. "Just pretend I'm not here."

"Out!" Anne's temper snapped. "And don't come back! Even if the house burns down!"

Jason shrugged. "Anything you say, Dr. Eldridge." He finished a last bit of sweeping and departed.

"The man is insufferable." Aldous shifted uncomfortably on the couch. "How can anyone feel the least bit romantic with him around?"

"Exactly." Anne seized the opportunity to pull away. "I should never have suggested we have dinner here. But it was a lovely evening, wasn't it?"

Aldous ignored the hint for him to depart. "I'm glad you got rid of him. Now, at last, we're alone."

Before Anne could think of an appropriate rejoinder, she found herself seized in Aldous's arms as he rained kisses on her neck, heading lower and lower toward the cleavage revealed by her low-cut dress.

"Hey, wait a minute!" She braced herself against him. "Just cut that out!"

"You've been giving me signals all night." Aldous pressed her down onto the couch. "It's not unusual for a woman to get cold feet. Let me show you how wonderful lovemaking can be. You need a real man to arouse the woman in you."

"I need—" Before she could get the words out, his lips closed over hers.

Anne found herself struggling in earnest. She couldn't believe Aldous actually meant to assault her, but obviously his idea of a romantic evening and hers were not even in the same universe.

All she could get out was a series of unintelligible grunts as she fought to free herself.

What was it they taught you in self-defense class? Grab his little finger and bend it backward until it breaks. No, that was when someone was choking you. Knee him in the groin—that was it! But how was she supposed to do that when her legs were pinned underneath him?

Then, suddenly, Aldous's unwelcome weight lifted off her. Anne gasped for breath and then saw with amazement what had happened.

Jason had a lock-grip on Aldous's throat and was marching the plastic surgeon across the living room toward the front door. Aldous's protests were stifled by the firm grasp across his throat, and Anne felt a moment of intense satisfaction at seeing the tables turned.

Somehow Jason managed to open the door without losing his

grip on Aldous and tossed the gasping physician out onto the doorstep.

Without a word, Jason slammed the door. He turned to face Anne. "Are you all right?"

Embarrassed, she nodded. "I—he really jumped me. I wasn't expecting that."

"Neither was I." Jason came to sit beside her. "Frankly, I thought his technique would be a bit smoother than that. But those noises you were making didn't sound like you were having a good time."

Relief washed over her as she leaned against Jason's sturdy shoulder. He smelled fresh and good, of spicy after-shave lotion and a hint of saffron.

"Where did you learn to do that? You handled Aldous like a real commando."

Jason coughed. "I, uh, included a little military training in my travels. Just to see what it was like."

"Thank goodness."

He slipped an arm around her waist. How different it felt from Aldous's selfish gropings, Anne reflected as she heard a car start on the street and listened to Aldous drive away. This would be one encounter he wouldn't gab about to his pals at the hospital.

For a time, Jason sat there holding her, comfortingly. He seemed to sense that Anne didn't want to be fondled or kissed, not so soon after Aldous's attack.

The phone rang.

"Are you on call?" he asked.

She shook her head. "But I'd better get it. You never know." Reluctantly, he released her, and she went to get the phone.

It was Ellie. "I know you're not on call but—I've started having contractions." Her voice sounded shaky. "They're about fifteen minutes apart."

"I'll meet you at the hospital. Come right in through the emergency room and have them take you up to Labor and Delivery. I'll call to let them know you're coming."

The crisp commands seemed to relieve Ellie. "Thanks. I—we'll be there in a few minutes."

Anne hung up and quickly explained the situation to Jason. "Do you want me to drive you?"

"No." She managed a weak smile. "I can handle it." But it felt good, knowing Jason was there if she needed him.

There was no more time that night to think about Jason or about her close encounter with Aldous Raney.

Ellie's contractions were only ten minutes apart by the time Anne examined her. She had already instructed the nurses by phone to start giving Ellie medication intravenously. The question now was whether it would take effect before her labor progressed too far to be stopped.

It wasn't the first time Anne had dealt with premature labor, but never before had she been dealing with someone she felt close to. Of course, she cared about all her patients—but she knew Ellie's hopes and dreams for this child, and that made the danger all the more real to her.

While Ellie's husband held his wife's hand, Anne made arrangements for a staff neonatalogist—a specialist in dealing with newborn babies—to stand by in case he was needed. There was no time to test for the baby's lung maturity, so they would have to assume it might need extra care.

When she went back to check on Ellie, Anne saw the relief on her friend's face at once.

"They're slowing down."

Anne checked the printout on the monitor, which showed both the baby's heartbeat and the mother's contractions. Sure enough, the contractions were spacing out, coming about twenty minutes apart and slowing down.

"The baby looks fine." Anne smiled for the first time in hours. "The heartbeat's strong and reactive—it speeds up during the contractions, which means he's getting plenty of oxygen."

Under other circumstances, Anne would have gone home now and let the nurses keep in touch by phone, but instead she waited until the contractions had stopped.

It was close to four o'clock in the morning when she took her leave. "I'll have them transfer you over to a semiprivate room in a couple of hours," she told Ellie. "I think you'd better stay in the hospital for a few days."

Her friend nodded. "Thank you."

The exhaustion didn't hit until Anne was halfway home. Then, all at once, she found herself yearning to sleep for a month.

Yet, despite the weariness, she felt a sense of satisfaction, too. At this stage in a pregnancy, every day inside the mother meant the baby had a stronger chance of surviving in good health. Maybe Ellie would go full-term, or maybe she'd deliver early, but if they gained a few weeks or even a few days, that could make a tremendous difference.

This is what I studied so hard for. This is why I gave up weekends at the beach and going to the movies with my friends.

It was worth it.

At the same time, as she staggered out of the car and up the front walk, Anne was glad she wasn't coming home to an empty house. Even though he was probably sound asleep, Jason was there.

Trying to make as little noise as possible, she fit her key into the lock and opened the door. A lamp glowed in the living room, and she went in to turn it off. That was when she saw Jason asleep on the couch, where he'd obviously been trying to wait up for her.

Anne smiled. How young he appeared in repose, his face unlined, his dark eyelashes pressed against his cheek. She could imagine how he must have looked as a young boy—rather angelic, but no doubt with a devilish glint in his eyes.

Perhaps he sensed her presence even in his sleep, for at that moment he woke up. "What time is it?"

She checked her watch. "Almost four-thirty."

"You must be wiped out." He sat up.

"I'm okay. You should have seen me when I was an intern—once I worked for forty-eight hours straight. This is nothing by comparison."

But she hadn't been thirty-three years old then, either, had she? Anne thought as she tried to make her weary muscles carry her toward the stairs. Instead, she staggered and had to grab onto a chair for support.

Jason caught her arm. "First of all, you need some nourishment. I prescribe hot chocolate with real milk, none of that instant stuff." How could he be so wide awake at a time like this? "You're not due anywhere first thing in the morning, are you?"

"Not on Saturday."

"Good." He escorted her into the kitchen, where Anne collapsed into a chair while Jason bustled around at the stove.

"You would have made someone a good mother."

An unreadable expression crossed his face—almost regret, she thought, but was too dazed to try to figure it out.

The hot chocolate tasted wonderful, but by the time she finished Anne was nodding over the table.

"Time for bed." Jason helped her up.

It wasn't until they'd reached the bedroom that it occurred to Anne she ought to shoo him away. She tried to find the words, but nothing came out.

Calmly, he retrieved one of her nightgowns from the closet.

"You—you shouldn't . . ."

"Hey. You're talking to the man who does your laundry every week, remember? I washed this, ironed it and hung it up. Let's just say that putting it on you is merely an extension of my duties."

In her befuddled state, what Jason was saying almost made sense.

Vaguely, Anne was aware of her outer clothing being removed and the gown being slipped over her head. She thought about protesting and dismissed the idea as far too strenuous.

A rustling noise told her Jason was turning down the bedcovers, and then Anne found herself being lifted into bed.

Her body ached all over, but it was a pleasant ache as she relaxed against the sheets. Strong hands moved over her back, finding the tense muscles and soothing them into submission. His sturdy, probing fingers took on a life of their own; Anne yielded with a sigh.

A stray wisp of hair was brushed away from her cheek, and someone touched a kiss to her temple. She was a child again, trusting and dreamy.

The mattress sagged beside her, and she felt a warm breath across her neck. Then the massage resumed, moving from her shoulders down her spine to the small of her back.

Gradually the movements slowed. Anne slept, and Jason slept beside her.

Chapter Eight

Anne came awake all at once, a habit she'd picked up during years of responding to medical emergencies. Sunny morning light flooded the bedroom, and someone was snoring quietly beside her.

Oh, my God.

She rolled over slowly. Despite her alertness, last night had blurred in her memory. She knew where she was, but not who this was.

Aldous? It couldn't be....

Then she nearly laughed. Of course, it was Jason, his head thrown back on the pillow, his well-shaped nose pointing skyward and a faint but unmistakable snore emanating from his nasal passages.

Anne's mirth died quickly. They hadn't made love, had they? Surely she would remember. But he was here beside her, and she was wearing a nightgown.

He, however, was still clad in the slacks and shirt he'd worn the night before. It was hardly likely he would have put them back on after making love to her.

She ought to be relieved. So why did she feel a pinch of disappointment?

Quietly, Anne slipped out of bed. In the bathroom, she changed into jeans and a blouse, then tiptoed downstairs. Trying not to bang the pots, she began fixing cheese omelets and bacon, with fresh-brewed coffee. Activity always helped to clear her head, and right now she needed to think.

As she popped the bacon into the microwave oven and the cheese into the food processor for grating, Anne tried to assess what was troubling her.

Without realizing it, she'd grown closer to Jason than she ever had to a man before—even to Ken back in her college days. Jason belonged here, in Anne's house.

But he didn't belong in her life. Like Ken, he appealed to the wild side of her, the part of herself that she'd left behind when she went to medical school. Sure, for a while Anne might be happy living in a more carefree way, throwing aside the routine that sometimes chafed at her, traveling with Jason and spending long lazy days at the beach.

But not permanently. And she couldn't see him living here permanently, either. There was a restlessness about Jason beneath the deceptively domesticated exterior. He was only playing at being a housekeeper until he saved up enough money to take off again.

And how would she feel when he did?

Anne turned, the omelet pan in her hand, as Jason sauntered in. "A heavenly smell wafted upward and roused me from the arms of Morpheus. And to think, I didn't believe you could cook."

"Only when necessary to avoid starvation." Anne transferred the food onto plates she'd warmed in the oven. "Or when I owe somebody a favor. Thanks for waiting up for me last night, Jason."

"My pleasure." He poured two cups of coffee.

"But..."

He cocked an eyebrow at her.

"This isn't working."

"What isn't?"

"Our experiment. Having you as my housekeeper." Anne took a deep breath as she sat beside him at the breakfast table. "Things have gotten out of hand."

He was silent for a moment. Anne would have given a month's income to be able to read his mind.

Finally the stillness became unbearable, and she blundered on. "It's... too intimate, living in the same house, seeing each other constantly. I'm asking you to leave as soon as you can find another place to stay. I'll pay you for the whole month; that was our deal.''

Jason continued to stare down at his black coffee.

"You do understand, don't you?" Darn him, why didn't he say something!

"I suppose I do." He spoke slowly, his face more serious than she'd ever seen it before. "But I think we could work this out."

"I don't."

They finished their breakfast without another word. Jason collected the dishes, and Anne sat at the table feeling as though she'd just lost her best friend.

Glumly, she put in a call to the hospital. Chatting with Ellie cheered her up a little; her friend was feeling much better and was even talking about coming back to work on Monday, but Anne wouldn't hear of it. When Ellie was well enough to leave the hospital, she was going home on strict bed rest for at least two weeks.

The rest of the day dragged by. Jason gathered up his swimsuit and took off for the beach before noon, but his presence continued to fill the house. Everywhere Anne looked, she saw some reminder—the tulips blossoming in her favorite vase, a rumpled cushion where he'd fallen asleep on the couch, a recipe for spaghetti *alla carbonara* set out on the kitchen counter in readiness for tonight.

The house took on an empty, hollow feel, like a model home in a new development. Anne tried to read a medical journal, but she found the articles intensely boring and finally switched on a television documentary about wild geese, which turned out to be a sure cure for insomnia.

Although she was on call, the phone rang only twice, and both times it was a patient with questions that didn't require any immediate action. Just when Anne could have used a good emergency to keep her mind off Jason!

He returned about four o'clock, his bronze skin smelling of suntan lotion but his expression still sober. After a brief hello, he retreated to his room, and a moment later Anne heard his shower running.

That night, she went out to a movie by herself. It was a light comedy, and several times during it she noted that Jason would have enjoyed a particular line, or she wondered what he would have said about a character's actions.

When she came back, he was sitting in the living room with his feet up, watching an old Cary Grant movie on TV with a big bowl of popcorn at his side. It would have been a lot more fun spending the evening here than going out, Anne thought, and to her disgust found herself wanting to cry.

It would be a good thing after all when he left, she told herself as she went upstairs. She was acting like a lovesick teenager.

WHY WAS IT BOTHERING him so much?

Of course, it would be inconvenient, having to move out so soon. And of course he'd miss Anne's companionship—but they could stay friends, couldn't they?

Staring at the comics on Sunday morning without really seeing them, Jason listened to the sounds of Anne getting dressed upstairs. He would have recognized her noises anywhere—the way she scuffed her panda slippers across the floor, her habit of leaving the water running while she brushed her teeth, the scrape of hangers as she considered and rejected several outfits before deciding what to wear.

He would tell her today why he'd really come to work here. There wasn't much more she could do than to throw him out, and she was already doing that.

Upstairs, Anne finally decided on a pair of white cotton slacks and a red-and-blue-print blouse. Not that it mattered what she wore; she was just going to be sitting home reading her journals and perhaps skimming the newspaper. But Jason would be living here for only a few more days, and it did seem reasonable for her to dress up a little.

The phone rang. Since she wasn't on call, Anne's first thought was that something had gone wrong with Ellie.

She grabbed the phone off the night table. "Yes?"

"Anne? Am I interrupting something?" The connection was as clear as if the call came from next door, but Anne immediately recognized her sister's voice, all the way from Oregon.

"Oh—no, Lori. I thought it might be some bad news about one of my patients."

They chatted for a moment as Lori caught Anne up on the doings of her husband and two sons. Then there was a brief but awkward pause, and Anne knew her sister was about to ask for a favor.

Lori never intended to get into a fix, but she always had, even when they were children. She just couldn't seem to plan ahead, to weigh the consequences of her actions, and as a result she frequently bit off more than she could chew. Anne, the well-organized one, usually ended up stepping into the breach. In fact, she sometimes reflected, maybe that's why she'd become so well organized, because one of them had to be.

So she wasn't surprised when her sister said, "Actually, I have a request to make."

"Oh?" Anne pretended innocence.

"I, uh, I have kind of a problem."

"Gee, Lori, I hope it isn't anything serious." She knew perfectly well that it wasn't, or Lori would have gotten to the point immediately.

"No, no, but . . ." A child shouted in the background, and Anne could hear Lori turn away from the phone to make peace between her youngsters. "Sorry about that."

"I always enjoy hearing my nephews' voices, even when they're fighting." Anne sat down on the bed, wishing she could see the boys. They must have grown a lot since last summer.

"It's . . . well, you know I'm hosting the family reunion this year." Lori plunged ahead. "Anne, I just can't do it. We're adding a playroom onto the back of the house and the contractor is way behind schedule. Jeb and Sammy both had chicken pox, so the carpenter had to wait, and then it rained. . . . The house is a mess and the reunion's only three weeks away. I'll never make it!"

Anne groaned aloud. This *was* serious! Since childhood, she'd looked forward every year to these annual gatherings, the one stable event in their peripatetic existence. Now that she was grown, it remained important, a chance to see her extended family and to watch the children grow.

"Everyone looks forward to it. You knew what was involved when you took it on."

"Yes, but..." Lori's voice quavered. "Oh, Anne, I know I'm always asking you to get me out of scrapes, but I'll never do it again, I promise! I can't ask Mom and Dad, not after Dad's ulcer attack last month. If you can't host it, I'll have to cancel."

"You wouldn't!" It would mean not only a severe disappointment to Anne but an even greater one to her parents and some of the older members of the family.

Furthermore, their branch of the family hadn't hosted the reunion in several years. Even if one of the cousins took on the project at the last minute, it wouldn't be fair—and Anne knew that her own embarrassment would dampen the fun of attending.

"Anne, there's no way we can have the house ready in three weeks! Please, please, please. If you say yes, I'll call everyone myself, today, and make the arrangements. I'll even mail out little maps so people can find you! The only thing you'll have to do is actually host the event. Your house is big enough, and it always looks perfect...."

I'll have to keep Jason until then. I wouldn't be able to manage by myself.

He would do a splendid job. Anne could picture him, whipping up mammoth breakfasts for the whole gang, swapping jokes with the kids....

"Well, I don't suppose I have much choice." There was no point in letting Lori get off too easily; one of these days, she'd have to learn her lesson. "But it's really inconvenient."

"I know! Oh, Anne, thank you!" Lori renewed her promise to call everyone, and finally they said goodbye.

Well, she should have expected it, Anne told herself as she hung up. But she'd thought that this time, finally, Lori would come through.

Still, her sister was delightful, and she could be wonderful in a pinch. Once, when Anne had come down with the flu during medical school, Lori had moved into her apartment for a week to ply her with chicken soup and aspirin while Anne studied for exams.

Her spirits surprisingly light, Anne went downstairs to tell Jason.

He was sprawled on the sofa reading the comics, looking as comfortable and unselfconscious as a cat. When she entered the room, he glanced up and they both spoke at once.

"Anne, there's something—"

"Jason, I've got a—"

They both stopped.

"You go ahead," Anne said.

"No, you."

She took a deep breath and explained about Lori and the family reunion. "There's no way I can manage it myself. Would you consider staying on for another three weeks?"

He nodded. "Sure. I'm not the one who wanted to leave. How many people can we expect?"

"Usually about thirty. Most of them stay in hotels or in their motor homes. But my parents and Lori's family will be staying here—that's six people altogether. We usually eat buffet-style, with everybody bringing something. Thank goodness for kitchens in motor homes!" As she spoke, Anne dropped into an armchair. How easy it was to work things out with Jason; even Ada would have squawked about taking on such a chore on short notice.

"Nothing I can't handle." He appeared to be doing some mental calculations. "You'll have to give me a list of how many meals we'll be having and when everyone will be hitting town."

"Sure." It wouldn't hurt to have him stay the extra few weeks; in fact, now that Anne thought about it, it made perfect sense. He'd have more time to find another place to live, and she'd have time to locate another housekeeper. "What were you going to say?"

"I beg your pardon?" His eyes had a faraway expression, as if he were already planning the menus.

"When I came into the room, you started to say something."

"Oh." He looked down at his hands. "Have you ever noticed how newsprint turns your fingers black? You'd think modern technology could come up with a better kind of ink."

"Is that what you were going to say?"

"Actually, no." He tossed the comics aside. "Mmm—are you busy next Sunday?"

She reflected for a moment. "I don't think so."

"Maybe you could come with me to Santa Ana." He told her that he'd offered to take photographs of some children for their mother, a live-in housekeeper whom he'd met at the supermarket. "They don't live all that far away, but it's a different world from Irvine. I thought you might be interested in coming along."

"Well—sure." Anne's curiosity was aroused. It was certainly generous of Jason to do the mother a favor, but she sensed there was more to it than that. "Are you taking on some special project? Some kind of charitable work?"

"This isn't charity." The sharpness of his tone surprised her. "Juanita wouldn't accept charity unless she was desperate. These people may be poor, but they have their pride."

"That wasn't what I meant. It was the way you sounded, as if you were on some kind of mission. When I hired you, you said you wanted to pursue your own photography interests. Is this part of it?"

"In a way." He jumped up. "I'm going to get a cup of coffee. Want some?"

"Sure." Now what was he being so secretive about? But she didn't have a right to pry, Anne told herself. Jason was entitled to his private life, one that didn't include her. After all, he would only be working here for three more weeks.

THE APARTMENT BUILDING in Santa Ana had obviously seen better days. A ramshackle one-story structure, it had peeling paint, a dirt yard pierced only by a few bedraggled weeds and walls defaced by graffiti.

Anne inhaled the cooking smells of chilli powder and hot peppers as she slid out of Jason's car. A dirty-faced little girl ran past her, not more than three years old but playing with the other children without adult supervision.

And there certainly were a lot of children. The yard was full of them, kids of all ages, most with lovely dark hair and olive skin but also some with blond hair and blue eyes. Despite the shabbiness of their clothing, they looked as if they were having a good time as they shrieked and sprayed each other with a hose.

Juanita had insisted on coming down earlier in the day by bus so she could go to church with her family. Now, Anne and Jason threaded their way along a cracked walkway littered with toys as they searched for the right apartment.

Most of the numbers had crumbled away, and finally Jason had to knock on an apartment door to ask directions.

The woman who answered couldn't have been more than Anne's age, but habitual weariness had creased the skin around her eyes and mouth. She carried a baby on one hip and in the apartment behind her Anne could hear a toddler banging on pots and pans.

I wonder what she does about medical care?

The thought troubled Anne as they thanked the woman for her help and proceeded on to Juanita's sister's flat. A lot of women right here in Southern California never got medical care, Anne knew; they gave birth at home, with an unlicensed midwife in attendance. Minor problems went untreated and often became serious as a result.

The number of low-cost health clinics had shrunk in recent years. For a long while she'd been meaning to do something to help, but she'd never been able to find the time. But she would. One of these days.

When they reached the right apartment, Juanita answered the door. Anne liked her at once. There was a calm strength about Juanita that was extremely appealing, as well as an aura of happiness at being with her children.

The two youngsters, Carlos and Lourdes, were neatly clad in their Sunday best, with shining clean faces brimming with curiosity. Jason immediately scooped them up, one on each knee, and sat on the worn sofa joking with them.

"This is my sister." Juanita spoke in English as much as she could, and Anne guessed that the woman was trying to improve her skills. She was grateful, since her own Spanish was limited to the few phrases needed to tell a laboring woman when to push and when not to.

The sister, Maria, had a distracted air, and it was easy to see why. Three young children dashed about, and, Juanita informed them, Maria's two older ones were playing outside.

"Seven children in one apartment?" Anne glanced down the corridor and could see there were only two bedrooms and one bathroom.

"And her husband and his brother." Juanita shrugged. "What can we do?"

Anne turned to Jason and saw that his expression was grim. She shared his dismay.

Maria offered them something to drink, but they declined, not wanting to impose. Anne had to suppress her instinct to run out to buy the family a couple of bags of groceries. Jason was right—these people had pride. But there had to be something she could do to help.

The apartment was dark even though there was bright sunlight outside, so Jason suggested they walk to a nearby park to take the pictures, and Juanita agreed.

Her children proved to be well behaved, especially considering they were only two and four years old. They clung to their mother's hand and kept quiet as they walked, but their big eyes stared around with fascination.

The park was only two blocks away, but Anne guessed from the children's delight that they didn't get to visit it often.

The park was well tended, with thick grass and luxurious cypress trees. On the far side, some booths had been erected and decorated with balloons and banners. From the number of people gathering there, Anne surmised a local carnival was in progress.

"Let's take them to the playground." Jason pointed the way to an area far from the booths. "I'd like to shoot them in action, without a lot of people around."

The two were shy at first, but with their mother's encouragement they tentatively began exploring the jungle gym and then the slide. Soon the air filled with their laughter.

Anne studied Jason as he moved intently from one position to another, taking photographs of the children and their mother. Clearly he'd closed off awareness of everything but what he was seeing through the lens.

He certainly had talent; she knew that from the pictures on his wall and from the shots he'd taken at the beach. She'd never been photogenic, so it had amazed her to see how much of her inner self was revealed in those prints.

If he wanted to, she was sure Jason could make a good living as a studio photographer, but it was easy to understand that he'd get bored shooting weddings and graduation pictures. Or perhaps he could work for a newspaper. But apparently he'd rather have the freedom to choose his own subjects, even if it meant working as a housekeeper to cover his expenses.

You had to admire him for that, Anne reflected as she sat on a bench to watch.

Jason didn't appear to be in any hurry, nor did he seem concerned about how much film he was using as he shot roll after roll.

Soon Juanita and the youngsters had all but forgotten he was there. Watching the joy in the other woman's face as she played with her children, Anne couldn't help envying her. Juanita was rich in her own way, even if she only got to enjoy it one day a week.

Finally the children began to tire, and Juanita scooped little Lourdes up in her arms. "You go to the carnival," she commanded Jason. "It will show you something of our life here, not just crowded apartments."

It surprised Anne that Juanita would be so concerned about Jason's impressions, but she supposed she'd feel the same way in Juanita's place.

Jason agreed, and they said goodbye to the mother and children.

"They're really delightful." Anne strolled beside Jason across the grass. Ahead, a mariachi band began to play its cheerfully enticing music. "I'd like to do something to help, but I don't want to seem like I'm playing Lady Bountiful. You were right; I can see that Juanita wouldn't take charity."

"What she needs is a job that pays enough for her to have her own apartment or that provides live-in arrangements for the children." Jason seemed to be speaking to himself as much as to her. "And her husband is a migrant farm worker, so it would be nice if he could stay with them, too, when he's in town."

At the moment, Anne hadn't a clue where to find such a job, but she tucked the idea away in the back of her mind.

The carnival, they soon found, made up in exuberance what it lacked in grandeur. Around them, young couples and large families shopped for food and souvenirs at unimposing booths and danced to the music of the band. The bright colors of clothing added to the festivity of balloons and banners.

Unobtrusively, Jason began taking photographs. Some included Anne, but most focused on the events around them. She could see that he zeroed in on faces: a youngster's, smeared with ice cream; an old woman's, creased by a Mona Lisa smile; a young man's as he gazed lovingly at his wife. Through close-ups, she could tell, he was capturing the spirit of the festival.

Finally Jason tucked his camera away in his shoulder bag and caught Anne's arm. "Wanna dance, lady?"

"I'm not sure I know the steps."

"Neither do I, but I'll bet we can fake it."

At first, Anne felt stiffly self-conscious amid the whirling crowd of uninhibited merrymakers. But Jason had the knack of blending in wherever he was; he hooted and cheered, clapped and kicked up a storm with the best of them, and Anne's laughter quickly dissolved her restraint.

Breathlessly, she caught Jason's arm and let him swing her around. Energy welled up in her, and she threw her head back, joining in the general noisemaking.

Jason caught Anne's waist and swung her off her feet, around and around.

Her green eyes sparkled in the sunlight, and her dark-blond hair had come loose from its bun and floated around her shoulders. He'd never seen her let go this freely, and he never wanted the afternoon to end.

When the band finished, she leaned against him, catching her breath. Jason felt as if he held a wild creature in his arms, one that had begun to trust him at long last.

Afterward, they munched on tacos and wandered through the crowd. Anne tried on a straw sombrero, pulling it low over her eyes. "Hi, amigo." She faked a low voice. "You want to come and cook at my cantina? I hear you make a mean enchilada."

"Try this." Jason selected a green-and-gold woven serape and tossed it over Anne's shoulder. "Not your usual style, but the colors look vibrant on you."

"You think so?" Anne took off the sombrero and examined the serape. "It looks nice and warm for evening walks along the Back Bay."

Jason handed a bill to the booth owner. "My treat."

"I wouldn't hear of it!" Anne started to reach for her purse.

"Consider it a souvenir of the day."

"Yes, but..." She hesitated. "Jason, I don't feel right somehow."

"Because I work for you?" He accepted his change and waved away the offer of a paper bag to wrap the purchase in. "My money's still as good as the next man's."

"I didn't mean that." Anne pressed her cheek against the soft wool of the serape. "Thanks, Jason. I really like it."

The crowd was beginning to disperse, and the two of them headed back toward the car.

Anne certainly needed a man who was worthy of her, not some jerk like the two doctors she'd brought home for dinner, Jason mused as he watched the play of sunlight and leaf shadows across Anne's face.

She needed someone who would bring out the spirited woman inside her, someone who would put her needs on a par with his own, someone whose life meshed with hers....

What she needed was someone like him.

Jason had to fight the impulse to stop dead. How could he have failed to see it before? He didn't want to bring out Anne's sensuous inner self and then hand her over to another man. He wanted her for himself.

And he was going to get her. But it was a task that called for tremendous delicacy, skill and gentleness.

And he had only three weeks to do it.

Chapter Nine

Juanita's problem remained in Anne's thoughts for the next few days, but she didn't come up with any brilliant solutions. She was also troubled by her memory of the other woman they'd seen in the complex, haggard looking as she answered the door to give directions.

Anne had read enough articles and attended enough lectures to know that babies were dying or becoming ill unnecessarily here in Orange County, one of the wealthiest places in the world. And women were going without proper medical treatment. Anne wanted to help.

Her partner, John Hernandez, had always taken an interest in the needs of the community, so she asked him for suggestions.

He paused in the hallway of their office, brushing a lock of graying hair off his forehead.

"Well—" John stared off into space, in the general direction of the temporary receptionist filling in for Ellie "—I did hear something about a new clinic opening in Santa Ana. If you like, I could check into it."

"I'd really appreciate it." Anne pulled a folder from its wall holder to check the medical records of her next patient. "It may be hard to find the time, but I promise our practice won't suffer."

"Don't worry. I only gave up volunteering myself until I put my kids through college. We'll make the time—it's important."

What a good man, she reflected as she read over the chart. Like Jason. Caring about others was high on both their lists of priorities.

Her thoughts were interrupted by the receptionist. "Dr. Eldridge? It's the hospital. One of your patients is in labor. Deanie Parker."

"Fine. Pull her records for me, will you?" As she went in to see the waiting patient, Anne mulled over the name. Deanie Parker. Deanie Parker. Which one was she? Why did her name ring a bell?

A few minutes later, pausing for a red light on her way to the hospital, Anne finished reading over Deanie's records and was still puzzled. Her pregnancy had been uncomplicated, so there was no reason for her to stick in Anne's memory.

It wasn't until Anne arrived in Labor and Delivery and saw Jason waiting, scrubbed and wearing a blue gown and mask, that she remembered.

Deanie was his cousin. And he was planning to photograph the birth.

Well, Anne had given her consent, hadn't she? But it was unnerving to see him in her professional setting, in this other part of her life.

She gave him a curt nod. "You'd better wait out here. Does Deanie have a coach?"

"Not as far as I know. She's kind of scatterbrained. I doubt if she took classes."

"I'll get one of the nurses to stay with her."

Unfortunately, as it turned out, Deanie lived up to Jason's description of her. She hadn't participated in childbirth classes, so she was unprepared to deal with the waves of pain. One of the nurses had to sit with her and conduct on-the-spot training, teaching Deanie breathing patterns to cope with the contractions.

Fortunately, nurses in Labor and Delivery tended to be very patient and sympathetic, Anne reflected. She'd often been impressed with how calmly they dealt with their patients during the difficult transition stage.

Deanie was close to that phase of labor, but it was progressing slowly, in part because this was her first child. After checking the patient and the monitors and making sure everything was normal, Anne went out to get a cup of coffee at the nurses' station.

"How's it going?" Jason was putting film in his camera, leaning against the counter. The secretary eyed him with considerable interest, Anne noted.

"She's coming along." Anne poured the coffee into a Styrofoam cup. "It would have helped if she'd been prepared."

As if to validate Anne's words, a moan emanated from Deanie's room. Anne turned to one of the nurses. "How long has Mrs. Parker been in labor?"

"About twelve hours."

"Twelve hours!" Jason stared at her in shock. "Deanie's been going through this for twelve hours?"

"I'm sure it wasn't this intense in the beginning." Anne had seen dozens of women—or was it hundreds by now?—go through labor. Suddenly it struck her that someday she might experience it herself.

What would it be like for Anne? Would she be one of the lucky ones who had a relatively easy time of it, or would complications set in? Well, she'd deal with that when the time came, she supposed. It was too bad a medical degree didn't make you any more immune to pain than anyone else.

"Yes, but—shouldn't you do something? I mean, give her something to kill the pain?" Jason's whole body radiated tension, as if he were identifying with his cousin, which he probably was.

"Not until the end, or the labor will stop. And we don't want to give any more anesthetic than necessary, for the baby's sake." Anne drained her cup. "Jason, twelve hours isn't long. Some women go through this for twenty or thirty hours."

As another moan sounded from the room, he shook his head in disbelief. "How do they bear it?"

"Most of them at least have practiced breathing techniques and have someone to coach them. But I'm sure it's never easy."

"You don't just let it go on and on? That can't be good for the baby, either."

"Of course not. If the labor doesn't progress normally, we have to do a cesarean section. But we'd rather not. Surgery has certain risks, too." She had to smile at his anxiety. "If you're this upset about your cousin, I can't imagine what you'll be like when it's your own baby."

The expression that crossed his face was so complex Anne wished she could photograph it and study it at length. Wonder; alarm; yearning; or was she reading all that in? Maybe it was just plain fright at the prospect of settling down someday.

"I'll tell you one thing—the first thing I'd do is read every book I could find on the subject, so I'd know what to expect." He scratched the back of his neck. "The TV shows make it look like a glorious experience. I should have known better."

A nurse came to tell Anne that Deanie was fully dilated. After that, things happened fast. The patient, moaning all the way, was wheeled into the delivery room, while Jason adjusted the settings on his camera.

Anne watched to be sure Deanie hadn't changed her mind about having the birth photographed, but the young woman didn't even seem to notice Jason's presence.

After confirming that Deanie was ready, Anne instructed her to push. The moans grew more frequent, and a nurse whose hand Deanie was holding winced in pain.

Although she'd delivered many babies, Anne never lost her wonder at the miracle. There was nothing else in life that could match the thrill of pulling a tiny baby into the world, watching its little face scrunch up and its mouth open and hearing the resounding wail that brought air into its lungs.

Quickly, a nurse took the baby boy and began suctioning his mouth to clear away the mucus. Within minutes, the infant was swaddled and placed in his mother's arms.

"Oh, my God." Deanie, her face bathed in sweat, stared in amazement at the perfect little features. "I mean, it's really a baby, isn't it? He's really mine?"

Keeping her in the center of his viewfinder, Jason snapped the shutter. He knew he'd caught that moment of intimacy, of bonding between mother and child. He would never forget the look of joy on Deanie's face, so swiftly replacing the discomfort of moments before.

I can't imagine what you'll be like when it's your own baby. He couldn't get Anne's words out of his head.

It would tear his heart out to see the woman he loved go through any pain. To see Anne suffering that way, to hear her cry out. But now he could picture what she'd look like afterward, how exhilarated she'd feel and how incredibly miraculous the whole experience would seem in retrospect.

He couldn't wait.

Jason's eyes met Anne's, and he saw that she was smiling. But she couldn't possibly guess what he was thinking. If she did, she'd probably run right out of here this minute, toss his possessions out of her house and bolt the door, family reunion or no family reunion.

He turned to Deanie. "Have you got a name picked out?"

"Alexander James Parker." She didn't even hesitate.

Anne glanced up at the clock overhead, and Jason realized it was after 6:00 p.m. "Congratulations, Mrs. Parker."

A few minutes later, they met outside in the hallway. A hint of weariness showed at the corners of Anne's eyes. "What would you like for dinner?" Jason asked. "Tacos? Burgers? Pizza?"

"Pizza, with lots of cheese and mushrooms and pepperoni."

"Done. I'll meet you at the old homestead."

He ordered ahead, calling from a nearby bank of pay phones. Next to him, a young man was eagerly pouring quarters into the phone, calling relative after relative to announce, "It's a girl!"

Jason felt a squeeze in the vicinity of his heart as he strode out to the parking structure. Would it ever be him at the phones?

Until now, he'd thought of children rather vaguely, in terms of the youngsters at the beach and other kids he saw on the street. The reality of what it would mean to have a baby had never come home before. Now, driving to the pizza parlor, he mulled over the sight of Deanie's son emerging into the light and letting out that life-giving squall. He could still see his cousin cradling the infant in her arms.

As he parked at the pizza parlor, Jason noticed a discount mart next door. Impulsively, he went inside, making his way to the baby department.

What a lot of equipment it took for such a tiny person! There were strollers and high chairs, playpens and bassinets, and rack after rack of clothes, crib sheets, bibs, bottles and quite a few things he'd never even heard of before—receiving blankets, nursing pads, activity centers.

Finally he selected a musical crib mobile, along with a book on infant care, since he suspected Deanie wasn't prepared in that department, either.

The purchases tucked under his arm, Jason picked up the pizza and headed home.

He found Anne in the living room, a scrapbook spread in front of her. When he came in, she lifted dreamy eyes that widened as she inhaled the rich aroma of pizza.

"What are you doing?" He couldn't help smiling at the picture she made, reclining on the carpet with her head resting against the armchair. There was something young and vulnerable about her and very, very sensuous.

"Looking at pictures of my nephews when they were little." Anne flipped the scrapbook shut. "Would you believe my sister delivered both her kids at home? My reputation would have been ruined if anyone had found out! Lori's as scatterbrained as Deanie. But fortunately everything turned out okay. And the pictures are great—kind of fuzzy, but the wonder shines through."

"That's one scene it would be hard not to photograph well." Jason was reluctant to risk breaking the mood by leaving the room, but he was also near starvation, so he went into the kitchen to fetch plates and tall glasses of iced tea.

They ate sitting on the rug in the living room, thumbing through family photo albums. Anne turned out to be quite a packrat. She'd amassed pictures going all the way back to her great-grandparents, along with dozens of shots of herself and Lori as children.

"I'm surprised you pried these away from your parents." Jason finished off his second slice of pizza.

"Actually, it wasn't hard. The last time my parents moved, they decided on a small apartment, and my mother was delighted to give me her boxes of photographs. She pointed out that I certainly had room for them." Anne paused in the middle of reaching for her iced tea. "I suppose it is rather strange that I bought such a big house just for one person, isn't it?"

"Not at all." Jason stretched out his long legs. "You were giving yourself what you always wanted as a child."

She turned to look at him. "How come you figure out things like that? You're really perceptive."

He couldn't resist teasing her. "Oh, some of us manage to figure out a few things even though we don't have advanced degrees."

"That wasn't what I meant." She punched his arm playfully. "To tell you the truth, I've met psychiatrists who didn't have as much insight as you do; at least, not in everyday life."

"I'll send you my bill in the morning."

"Do you take Monopoly money?"

"I can see what you think my brilliant perceptions are worth." He decided four pieces of pizza really were enough, although the remaining two slices were staring up at him enticingly.

"You know, it works both ways." Anne reclined next to him on the carpet. "By traveling around the world, you've been filling in what you needed in childhood, too."

He reached over and casually traced a finger along the curve of her jaw. "Since I've grown up, I've been giving myself a lot of things I missed as a child."

"Are we talking about childhood or adolescence?" But she didn't push his hand away.

He decided the wisest course was to overlook her remark. "I certainly saw a different side of you today."

"Oh?"

"Anne in action. Anne the doctor. Of course, you were rather stiff and stern the day you interviewed me, but I'd never seen you with nurses leaping at your command."

"I try not to make them leap. It's tough on their feet, and they work hard enough as it is."

Jason gave her a gentle poke in the side. "You know what I mean. It's one thing for me to be aware, intellectually, that you're a professional; it's something else to see you actually in charge of a delivery room, pulling that baby out of Deanie."

"Does it bother you?" She rolled over to face him, her expression serious.

"Bother me?"

"To see me in charge of things. It makes some men really uncomfortable. I made the mistake a few years ago of dating one of my fellow residents. Then one night we were both on duty at the same time. The next day he muttered something about how much he respected my professionalism, and that was the end of our relationship."

"What a donkey." Jason teased a strand of her hair down from its topknot. "Frankly, I find competence in a woman highly appealing."

"Kind of a turn-on?"

"You might say." He hadn't meant to caress her, but his hand couldn't resist the inviting curve of her cheek. "You were exciting in the delivery room, Anne."

She ducked her head. "Isn't that carrying things a bit far?"

"I like people when they're most themselves, when there aren't a lot of conventions and anxieties blocking their emotions. And you weren't holding anything back when you looked at that baby. It's nothing to be embarrassed about."

His comments and the way he was stroking her combined to arouse Anne in a way she'd never experienced before. It wasn't exactly sexual; it was far more complex and far deeper.

She wanted to lie here forever next to Jason, to let their words drift into murmurs, to let their bodies slide closer and closer until there was no distance between them at all. It felt safe being with him, as if she need never fear that anything she did would offend or displease him, not as long as she was honest and open.

Her entire body tingled. She was keenly aware of the coolness of the room and of the tangy spice smell of Jason's skin.

Gradually, her arms found their way around Jason's neck, and their bodies touched, hip against hip, her breasts grazing his chest. Anne nestled her nose against his throat, closing her eyes, at peace.

Languorously, his lips found hers. The touch of his mouth was whisper light and tantalizing. Anne pressed closer, wanting to experience him more fully. Her tongue explored the edges of his teeth, then the firmness inside his mouth, and gradually he responded.

Strong arms encircled her. Every movement of his muscles resounded through her sensibilities, so keenly was she tuned to his being.

His lips found the corners of her mouth, then the tip of her nose, then the delicate contours of her temples. His warm breath sighed against her skin deliciously.

With one hand, Anne traced the shape of his shoulder blade, probing around it to find and release a small knot in the muscle. Then she explored the vertebrae of his spine, one by one.

He in turn massaged the small of her back, his touch sending quivers along her hip bones and into her core. Some long-frozen pond inside Anne turned liquid.

By mutual understanding, their mouths met again, more fiercely this time, and his grip on her tightened. The shape of his body seemed to imprint itself against hers, and Anne pressed closer, wanting to eliminate even the faintest hint of space between them.

The phone rang.

"Ignore it," Jason murmured.

Anne started to agree, then pulled away. "Oh, hell. I'm on call."

The answering service relayed a message that another patient had been admitted to the hospital in the early stages of labor. It would be several hours before Anne would be needed, but she'd have to keep checking in by phone.

As she hung up, she shook away the last remnants of the daze that had come over her in Jason's arms. She must have been crazy. Plain old crazy. There was no denying the chemistry between them, but that wasn't enough.

You can't make the same mistake again, the way you did with Ken. You're not nineteen anymore.

Slowly, Anne walked back to the living room. "I'm going upstairs before we both do something stupid."

Jason was sitting on the carpet, calmly finishing up the last of the pizza. "This tastes pretty good cold."

"Did you hear me?"

"Yes." He licked his fingers. "I'm not going to get into an argument, Anne. I knew perfectly well that once we were interrupted, your intellect was going to start working again and sound off all the alarms."

She waited, expecting him to say more, but he just sat there looking infuriatingly smug, as if he knew her better than she knew herself.

The possibility that he might be right was something she didn't want to deal with. And she didn't want to consider how he might be planning to circumvent her intellect, since he obviously had rejected the direct approach.

"Well—I'll see you in the morning." She started toward the stairs.

"Sleep well."

But she didn't, not for more than an hour, while she listened to the sounds of Jason moving around downstairs: the shower running, the refrigerator door opening and closing, the TV muttering. She knew he was probably watching another old movie—he loved the films of the thirties and forties and Rodgers and Hammerstein musicals—and wondered if it was one she'd seen.

So many of them had bittersweet endings. Well, that was life, wasn't it? she thought, and finally fell asleep.

THE NEXT DAY Anne decided to give Ellie a break from hospital food and had a catered lunch brought in from a nearby Chinese restaurant.

The other bed in the semiprivate room was vacant, so they had the luxury of talking freely as they consumed Mongolian beef and *moo shu* pork.

The contractions had stopped, and Ellie was already planning how she'd manage once she got home, since she would be allowed to get up only to go to the bathroom.

"Dennis can fix breakfast and leave a cold lunch for me in the refrigerator," she itemized, sitting up in bed and eating on the freestanding tray table that Anne had swung into position. "My mother's already offered to bring dinner over several times a week, and Dennis can pick up takeout food the other nights. My sister's offered to loan me her cleaning lady. Say, I could get used to this!''

Anne chuckled. ''Don't get too spoiled. Babies have a way of turning households upside-down.''

''I won't mind.'' Ellie settled back against the pillows. ''Oh, Anne, do you really think the baby's going to be all right?''

''Of course it is.'' Anne handed her a fortune cookie. ''Here's everything you ever wanted to know about your future. Read it to me.''

Ellie broke it open and unfolded the slip of paper. ''It says, 'You are headed in the right direction.' ''

''What did I tell you?''

''Go on. Read me yours.''

Anne retrieved her own fortune. '' 'The other person in your life is the right one for you.' ''

''What other person?'' Ellie perked up. There was nothing she loved better than gossip. ''Not Dr. Raney!''

Anne laughed and told her how Jason had thrown him out of the house. ''I don't think he'll be coming back.''

''I can't wait to meet Jason. He sounds more like a jealous husband than a housekeeper.''

Her remarks caught Anne off guard, and she swallowed her tea the wrong way. The fit of coughing did nothing to throw Ellie off the scent.

''There's something going on between you two, isn't there? Come on, you can't fool me.''

Anne shifted uncomfortably in the straight chair at Ellie's bedside. She glanced at the open door to make sure none of the nurses was close enough to overhear. ''It's more of a brother-sister thing.''

''Uh-huh.'' Ellie sounded totally unconvinced.

''No, really.'' Anne pressed on, talking more to herself than to her friend. ''Although I'll admit, having him around has helped me realize a few things.''

''Like what?''

''How much I want children, for instance.'' Anne saw Ellie's expression soften. ''There hasn't really been time to think about it until now, or maybe I haven't wanted to. But now I've sort of gotten used to having another person in the house, and that got me thinking about what it would be like to have a family. And then yesterday..." She described how Jason had photographed his cousin's delivery.

"You sound like a changed woman." Ellie sipped at her tea. "Up to now, all you've talked about were what conferences you planned to attend and what new techniques you'd learned. Suddenly, I'm hearing about men, and now it's babies. I'd say you were ready for a new phase in your life."

"Thanks, Confucius." Anne ducked her head, not wanting Ellie to see the heat rising to her cheeks. "I didn't realize I'd been so fixated on my work before. I must have been a real bore."

"Not at all. I find your dedication inspiring. In fact, when the baby's older, I've been thinking of going back to school and getting a nursing degree so I could work in obstetrics." Ellie hurried on before Anne could respond. "But don't think I'm going to change the subject. What you need is a husband, and if you'd like any help..."

Anne smiled. Ellie loved helping people out and solving their problems. "No, thanks. I'd prefer to find my own man."

"Maybe you already have."

She shook her head firmly. "Absolutely not. I need stability, and he's, well, a free spirit."

"Sounds like just what you need."

"You're impossible."

"I do my best." Ellie stacked the empty Chinese-food cartons neatly to one side. "Honestly, I've never seen you look as happy as you have since you hired that man. He's the best medicine you ever took."

At Ellie's words, Anne's thoughts flew to the special times she'd shared with Jason: that day at the beach, their walk in the Back Bay at twilight, the festival in the park. She *had* felt more energetic than usual these last few weeks, hadn't she?

But her own practical side intruded. "Ellie, I'm not about to pick up and travel around the world with him. That's no way to raise children."

"Maybe he wouldn't expect you to travel all the time. You could work something out." Ellie tended to believe there was a solution to any problem. If only she were right!

"Even so, he doesn't earn enough to let me take a few years off or even for me to work part-time. And I don't want my children to grow up in day-care centers. I know some mothers have no choice about going back to work, but I think it's best if kids can stay home with a parent for the first few years." Anne wished she didn't sound as if she were delivering a lecture. No doubt Jason would say it was her intellect speaking.

"Well, I haven't met Jason, so I can't say for sure he's the right man for you." Ellie's eyelids were beginning to drift down, but she fought to stay awake. "Dennis has a good friend I think you might like. . . ."

"No, thanks. Now I'm going to let you get some sleep." Anne stood up. "You'll need it after the baby comes, believe me."

But the conversation wouldn't stop resounding through her mind. Talking with Ellie had crystallized some thoughts that had been troubling Anne for the last few weeks. Driving back to her office, she decided it was time to consider the situation objectively.

She was thirty-three years old. Even if she met Mr. Right now, it would be a year or so before they'd be ready to get married and have a baby. By then she'd be at least thirty-five. And since she'd really like to have two children . . .

There was no time to waste.

The problem wasn't meeting men; Anne met quite a few in her line of work. And she knew that when she bothered to take the time with her hair and makeup, she could be reasonably attractive.

But her last two dates had been disasters, and her attraction to Jason proved how easily she could be led astray. How was she going to zero in on the right man so she didn't waste any more time?

As usual when confronting a problem, Anne proceeded to analyze it. She'd always felt that getting one's priorities organized was half the battle.

She needed a list of criteria, something she could check off mentally to eliminate men who simply weren't right for her. Well, that ought to be easy.

First of all, he had to be dependable and settled, financially as well as emotionally. That eliminated Jason.

He had to be honest and fair-minded, someone she could respect. That eliminated Aldous Raney.

And of course he should be someone she found attractive. So much for Horace Swann.

Furthermore, he would have to want children and be a good father.

That seemed like a reasonable list, Anne decided as she pulled into her reserved parking space. She had the feeling there was something missing, something she'd overlooked, but she was sure it would come to mind sooner or later. In the meantime, at least she'd reached a starting point.

Chapter Ten

During the next few days, Anne made a point of keeping busy and out of the house. In only a couple of weeks Jason would be gone, and she didn't trust herself to spend too much time with him in the interim.

Unfortunately, crowding her schedule with seminars and consultations did little to ease the sense of emptiness inside Anne. Grabbing a quick dinner in the hospital cafeteria, the way she used to do, now struck her as a lonely way to cap off the day. And on Sunday afternoon, lecturing to a group of nurses on new developments in obstetrics, she had to chase away the mental image of Jason sprawled on the living-room carpet reading the comics, and the strong desire to be lying there next to him.

When she came home late that evening, he merely whistled his way around her, inquiring politely about her lecture without a hint of possessiveness. But she knew him well enough to be sure that his disinterest was a sham. What was he up to?

Jason could see that he had her puzzled. Frankly, he reflected as he fixed her a late-night snack of graham crackers and milk, he was a little puzzled himself. He knew what he wanted to accomplish, but he was still figuring out exactly what tactics to use.

Anne's long absences from the house didn't surprise him. Each time her emotional inner self broke through, he'd observed during their time together, it was followed by a period of denial and intellectualizing. That was the way Anne was, and he loved her in spite of it.

Patience, Jason sighed to himself as he handed the tray to Anne at the foot of the steps and watched her vanish into her sanctum upstairs. He'd learned patience as a photographer, waiting for the right light, the right moment. But it never came easily.

Still, her busy schedule had given him time to work on his book undisturbed. He'd taken more photographs of Juanita and gone through hundreds of negatives selecting the ones to print for his publisher. In addition, he'd printed up several dozen for Juanita herself.

The one step remaining was a trip to Juanita's village in Mexico. Actually, the timing with Anne had worked out well; he'd have to be leaving here soon anyway, even if she hadn't fired him.

But he planned on coming back.

And this time things would be on a different footing, Jason mused as he wiped crumbs off the kitchen counter and switched off the lights. When he returned, he'd tell her the truth. She'd probably be angry, but gradually she would come to see that he was a more responsible man than he'd seemed, that he was someone she could rely on when it came to raising a family.

And he intended to be the one she raised a family with. Whether she liked the idea or not.

ANNE CHOSE A SEAT near the front of the hospital auditorium. She was tired from a long day's work and didn't feel like craning her neck to see over the heads of the rest of the audience.

Under other circumstances, she probably would have skipped the talk on "Legal Aspects of Medical Care" and gone straight home to take a hot bath. But she suspected that if she did, Jason would be waiting outside the bathroom door, probably with a towel draped over one arm and a tray of perfumed soaps in his hand.

The irreverent image made her smile.

At that moment, she glanced up and saw a man smiling back at her, apparently thinking she'd meant to be friendly.

Well, what was wrong with that? He wasn't bad looking—not as tall or distinctive as Jason, but he had well-groomed brown hair touched with gray, and pleasant crinkles around the eyes.

She'd never seen the man before. Surreptitiously, Anne took in his expensive tailored suit and general air of confidence. He was chatting with the hospital director, so he must be someone important.

The guest speaker! Quickly Anne glanced down at the flier she was holding. Mitch Hamilton, attorney at law. According to the photocopied information sheet, he was a prominent civil lawyer who had represented several doctors in malpractice cases.

She peeked at his left hand. No ring.

Glancing up, she felt herself flush with embarrassment. He'd seen her examining his ring finger. But he looked pleasantly amused rather than scornful, and she answered with a playful shrug.

Flirting with a man across a room was something Anne hadn't done since her college days, and she hoped she wasn't being awkward. What complicated everything was that she didn't feel entirely sincere. She kept mentally comparing the man to Jason and finding him less intriguing, more ordinary.

But from what she could see so far, he was right in line with her list of criteria.

The lecture turned out to be well organized and informative, but afterward Anne didn't remember a thing Mitch Hamilton had said. She was too busy wondering if she should stick around and find an excuse to talk to him or if she was simply going to make a fool of herself.

As it turned out, once the question-and-answer session was over and the attorney stepped down, he saved Anne the trouble by coming over to her.

"Dr. Eldridge." He'd apparently managed to read her name badge. "I believe I know your partner, John Hernandez."

Anne perked up. "How do you know John?" Any friend of her partner's was likely to be worth knowing.

"We've been involved in some fund raising together." He didn't specify for what cause. "You know, obstetrics is a particularly vulnerable field for lawsuits. I understand some doctors have entirely stopped delivering babies."

"There's a lot that can go wrong," Anne agreed. "Of course, since we deal with many high-risk cases, we practice very aggressive medicine. And we keep our patients fully informed of what we're doing and why."

She had the feeling neither of them really cared about this conversation. It was just a ploy to introduce themselves. That would be all right, but where were the sparks that should be flying between them?

Forget sparks. They aren't on the list.

They chatted for a few more minutes, during which time she learned that he was amicably divorced but had no children, that he liked to play tennis and was a connoisseur of fine wines.

The only thing that struck her as a bit odd was that his former wife had been a nurse. Was he particularly attracted to women in the medical field? Perhaps it was because that was his area of specialization and he enjoyed having a knowledgeable wife; she couldn't fault him for that.

Unlike Aldous, Mitch showed a reasonable interest in Anne's activities, too, although she found herself rattling off facts rather than divulging her feelings. Well, the hospital auditorium was hardly a place conducive to heart-to-heart revelations.

When they'd finished with the amenities, Mitch asked her to dinner Saturday night, and Anne agreed. She was relieved when he suggested an elegant restaurant in Newport Beach; after her last two dates, she had no intention of inviting Mitch home for a meal.

For some reason, Anne found it hard to tell Jason that she wouldn't be home for dinner Saturday night and why. Over the next few days, she found herself reviewing her phrasing and imagining his responses.

Anne, breezily: "Oh, by the way, I'm going out for dinner Saturday night."

Jason: "Great, I'll come too."

Anne: "I've got a date."

Jason: "After the last two you've brought home, I'd say you need a bodyguard."

Better to take a different tack.

Anne, distantly: "*I'm going out for dinner Saturday night, so you can have the evening off.*"

Jason: "*Fine. Maybe I'll try one of the local restaurants. Where are you eating?*"

No. She'd have to put her foot down.

Anne, sternly: "*I have a dinner date Saturday night and I don't want you interfering.*"

Jason: "*I wouldn't dream of it. I'll just watch quietly.*"

In the end, Anne said nothing until Saturday morning, when she noticed Jason's fettucine recipe set out in its plastic holder. She couldn't let him go to all the trouble of fixing it and then discover she wouldn't be there.

Anne found him in the dining room, cheerfully polishing her best silver. "Jason, about tonight, I'm—"

"Going out to dinner?" He buffed a serving spoon to a bright shine. "Okay. I was planning to wander around the swap meet this afternoon, and flea markets always wear me out. I could use a break from cooking."

Lack of interest was one response she hadn't anticipated. "Well, good." Anne waited for him to say something further, but he merely turned his attention to a salad fork.

Going back to her bedroom, she felt rather deflated. Perhaps she'd misjudged Jason's possessiveness toward her.

Laying several dresses out on the bed, she wondered why she couldn't work up much enthusiasm for selecting an outfit for tonight. Mitch did seem to have the qualities she was seeking, although it was too soon to know how he felt about children.

Well, there was no hurry in deciding what to wear. It wasn't even noon yet. She had plenty of time to do something relaxing today—like pay the bills that had piled up on her desk.

It was her own fault for keeping so busy, Anne admonished herself as she trudged downstairs to her office.

A few minutes later, she heard Jason whistling "Oh, What a Beautiful Mornin'" as he went out the door. Was he meeting someone or going alone? It was none of her business, of course. But it would be fun, wandering through the swap meet, picking through tables of everything from junk to antiques.

The afternoon dragged by. Anne actually found herself with a free day, and she didn't know what to do. If Jason had been home, they could have played Scrabble, or gone for a walk, or just talked.

Anne called the hospital and made sure Ellie had been discharged as scheduled. Yes, the nurse told her, Ellie's husband had picked her up that morning. It was easy to picture him escorting her solicitously out to the car, tucking her into the front seat, gazing at her lovingly....

I'll have to get her a gift, Anne decided. There was still time to run out to the bookstore today.

But as she was getting ready to go, the phone rang.

"Anne? Mitch."

Her first thought was, *he's canceling the date. Oh, terrific.*

"Hi. What's up?" She was pleased at the casual sound of her voice, although she was ready to strangle the man if he disappointed her.

"Listen, I've been playing tennis this afternoon and I hurt my back." He uttered a convincing groan. "I really hate to postpone our date, but I'm not going to be able to sit up straight for a couple of days, so I don't think I can handle a restaurant."

Anne thought rapidly. Jason was gone for the afternoon and didn't want to cook, so he'd probably eat out. Maybe things had worked out better than she could have hoped.

"I'll tell you what," she said. "If you can handle reclining on my couch, I could cook dinner for us. I've got a lap tray you can use."

"If it wouldn't be too much trouble." He sounded relieved. "That's really kind of you. I'd like that."

Anne felt rather pleased with herself as she hung up.

She decided to use Jason's fettucine recipe, since the ingredients were already on hand. Although she felt somewhat as if she were stealing something of his, she reminded herself that it was her money that had paid for the groceries.

By six o'clock, half an hour before Mitch was to arrive, Anne was dressed and had covered herself with one of Ada's oversize aprons. Carefully, she put water on to boil and measured butter into a large pan.

The phone rang. Surely Mitch wouldn't change his mind at this late hour....

It was Ellie. "I wanted to let you know that I'm home and I feel fine. Are you sure I can't get up? Some of our friends from church are having a barbecue, and I promise I'll stay on the chaise longue...."

"Bed rest means bed rest!" Anne delivered a quick lecture on the need to stay flat.

Ellie conceded gracefully. "I just thought I'd ask."

"I'll come and visit you as soon as I get a chance. Meanwhile, if I catch you misbehaving, it's back to the hospital!"

As she hung up, Anne smelled something burning. Oh, no! She'd left the pan on the burner!

The butter was hopelessly scorched, and the pan was going to need a tough scouring. Jason would kill her, Anne reflected miserably as she ran water onto the mess. And here she was with a kitchen full of smoke and Mitch scheduled to arrive any minute.

What would he think if she sent out for pizza? Somehow, she couldn't picture Mitch digging into pepperoni and cheese with gusto.

It was with mixed emotions that she heard a key turn in the back-door lock and someone whistling "Some Enchanted Evening."

She wondered briefly if Jason chose his tunes sarcastically. But then, how could he know she was still home?

He lifted an eyebrow as he came in. "I thought you were going out. Mmm. What a wonderful smell. But you're supposed to char-broil things outside on the grill, Anne, not in the kitchen."

"Cute. Very cute." She glared at him. "As you can see, I'm not much of a cook." She explained about Mitch's back. "Don't worry, I'm not going to ask you to work tonight. I'll run out for Chinese food or something."

Jason lowered a canvas tote bag to the floor, and Anne heard something clank. He must have picked up some interesting stuff at the swap meet. "I've got to eat anyway, so I'll cook enough for three. And don't worry. I don't plan on interfering with your date, unless he jumps you like the last one."

"Thanks. You're a good sport." The doorbell rang. "And just in time. I owe you a favor for this, Jason!" She disappeared out the kitchen door.

Wearily, Jason stretched his sore muscles and pushed the tote bag out of the way. He couldn't even muster much pleasure at the thought of his purchase, a lightweight folding tripod. Shopping at the flea market would have been more fun with some interesting companionship. Like Anne's.

Well, he'd volunteered to cook, so he'd better get on with it.

As he pulled out a clean pan and began to melt butter, Jason listened to voices in the other room. He couldn't help hoping this Mitch would turn out to be as big a loser as the other two men.

Unfortunately, that wasn't true.

Jason had to admit, after delivering plates of fettucine and salad, that the man seemed reasonably presentable. Not bad looking, polite and even affable, considering the pain he must be in as he reclined on the sofa.

It would be just like Anne to let her intellect talk her into marrying the guy simply because he wasn't a jerk. Even though, of course, her heart belonged to Jason.

The problem was that she didn't know that. Or wouldn't admit it.

The best Jason could do, he decided, was to make sure she and Mitch didn't have a chance to get too well acquainted that evening.

After considering various alternatives, he settled on the tender-loving-care approach. No use trying the fireplace bit again; Anne would have a fit the moment she saw him approaching with an armful of firewood.

Instead, Jason dug out a heating pad that Ada had left behind in her closet. He filled it with warm water, making sure it wasn't too hot; you didn't want to burn a lawyer, not with the way liability suits were going these days, he reflected mockingly.

He ignored Anne's wary glance as he entered and offered the heating pad.

"Hey, that looks terrific." Mitch sat up straighter so the pad could be slipped behind his back.

"Nothing hurts like a back injury." Jason made a point of fluffing up the cushions that supported Mitch. "Can I get you anything else? Some aspirin?"

"Well, yes, if you don't mind." The guy settled back with a murmur of relief.

"Right." Avoiding Anne's glare, Jason vanished into the bathroom and found a bottle of aspirin, then poked through the medicine cabinet. What else could he use to distract the man? Did he dare suggest a massage? Well, what the hell.

To his surprise—and Anne's disgust—Mitch agreed immediately, after Jason explained that he'd once studied massage with an expert from Sweden, which was not entirely untrue. He omitted mentioning that she'd been a Swedish actress whom he'd dated briefly and that the massages had been preludes to more intimate encounters.

Anne sat back, her arms folded stiffly, as Jason administered the massage. He quirked an eyebrow at her, as if to ask whether she'd like to do the honors herself, but she ignored him.

He knew she was angry. But he was saving her from herself, after all.

"Boy, that's terrific," Mitch said as Jason finished. "My ex-wife was a nurse, and she could give a great back rub, too. That's one of the things I missed most after the divorce."

Jason refrained from asking what the other things were and, instead, stayed on the subject of Mitch's back. "Has it bothered you before?"

"Oh, quite a bit." The attorney relaxed against the heating pad. "But you know what really bothers me? My feet. You can't imagine how sore they get. I have a terrible time finding shoes that fit. My wife used to buy those foam innersoles and cut them specially."

Jason didn't dare glance at Anne. "I guess it helps to marry a nurse."

"It sure does." The man appeared to have forgotten where he was and whom he was talking to. "I can't tell you how nice it is to come home after a hard day in court and have a hot bath waiting...."

Jason let him ramble on for a while before excusing himself to go and clean up the kitchen. He had a feeling Mitch had cooked his own goose with Anne.

Sure enough, it wasn't more than ten minutes later that he heard the front door closing and light footsteps approaching. Quickly Jason poured some detergent into the burned pan and began scouring it mightily.

Anne stood watching him for a full minute without saying anything. Finally Jason couldn't stand the suspense.

"Well? Are you going to kill me?" He looked up and was startled to see her smiling.

"No, you goofball." Anne was somewhat surprised herself. She'd been angry at first at the way Jason was interfering, but gradually she'd become more and more annoyed with Mitch for allowing it. Then, as she realized what a hypochrondriac Mitch was, she'd found herself fighting back a chuckle at Jason's masterful performance. "I did wonder if it was a coincidence that he seemed attracted to women in the medical profession."

"Can you blame him?" Jason set the pan aside to soak overnight. "What man wouldn't want to come home to a hot bath and a woman who cut foam innersoles for his aching feet? She probably rubbed his corns with baby oil, too, and applied leeches to his throbbing back...."

Laughter burst from Anne. She didn't know why she felt so lighthearted. After all, Mitch had seemed like the perfect man for her, and she ought to be severely disappointed. "You rascal."

"I was only trying to help." Despite his earnest expression, Jason couldn't suppress a chuckle. "You don't mind that I used some of your perfumed oil for the massage? The man must smell like a flower shop."

"Thanks a lot!"

"Hey, don't take that the wrong way. What smells good on a woman doesn't necessarily sit right on a man."

Standing here laughing with Jason, Anne felt right and natural and completely at home. She didn't want to question that feeling just now. "We didn't even get to dessert."

"What did you have in mind?"

"Chocolate mousse will do."

Jason peered into the freezer. "How about vanilla ice cream topped with Grand Marnier and fresh cherries?"

"Sold."

They sat across from each other at the kitchen table, spooning up the delicious sundae. Despite her elegant silk dress, Anne curled her legs up, hooking her feet on the chair supports. She felt like a 1950s bobby-soxer on a soda date.

Every time she dared look at Jason, he would say something like, "Gee, my feet hurt, Anne. Would you mind...?" and they'd both be off in gales of laughter.

It was only after they'd finished, as she was getting ready to go upstairs, that Anne felt serious again. "Why do you suppose I have such lousy luck with men?"

"Because you're picking the wrong ones." Jason downed the last of the cherries.

"And where do I find the right ones?"

"Try the kitchen."

Her heart thudded loudly in her throat. He was bringing it out in the open, the attraction they felt for each other. "Jason..."

"Wait a minute." He leaned forward, elbows on the table. "Anne, you crazy woman, do you think I don't know what's going on in your head? You've intellectualized this whole thing, sorted it out and analyzed it and decided you need a particular type of man, and I don't fit the description."

"It's not that simple." Wasn't it? She ignored the question as soon as it popped up. "I know myself, despite what you think. I know what I need."

"And I'm not it?"

"In some ways, you probably are. But this wouldn't be the first time I'd be leading myself astray...."

"Forget what happened in college." He swung to his feet and advanced toward her, his eyes hungry and demanding. Anne's knees threatened to buckle, and she leaned against the door frame. Her mind told her to run away, and her heart told her to fall into his arms.

Then Jason reached her, and her heart won the skirmish. Strong arms encircled her and drew her close, and his lips claimed her with kisses that started on her mouth and blazed down her throat.

Her blood turning to liquid silver, Anne melted into his embrace. Her fingers found the buttons to his shirt and opened them, then pressed into the thick mat of hair on his chest.

His breathing quickened, matching hers, as his thumbs stroked upward from her waist, brushing the edges of her breasts. Anne felt herself come alive in a new way, as if she'd just been born into an unexplored world of flame and brightness and incredible desire.

A radiance enveloped her as she yielded to him, sought him, caressed him and felt his answering caresses draw passion from its hiding place in her soul.

"I'll never let you go," Jason murmured. "Anne, can't you see that we belong together?"

His words broke through the spell he'd woven. Anne's mind kicked into gear again. Belong together? That was just the problem. For tonight, for a few weeks or even months, she and Jason could blaze together like a shooting star, but they would never belong together. They were too different, in their goals, their life-styles—even their passions.

Wrenchingly, she pulled back. "No. No, Jason, I'm sorry. It was wrong to...to let this happen tonight, between us. I should never..."

"Would you cut that out?" Anger flared across his face. "This has nothing to do with what you 'should' do. Damn it, Anne...!"

"I'm going upstairs before we both say something we'll regret." She wished her words didn't sound so prissy and trite, but she had to get away from him somehow, before she gave in to the fire still raging through her body. "Good night, Jason."

His hands clenched into fists as he watched her go. A few minutes ago, he'd broken through that protective armor she always wore, and then it had snapped shut again. Damn it! Jason glared at the dirty ice-cream bowls, as if they were somehow to blame.

Well, he wasn't going to throw them, so he might as well rinse them. He carried the dishes to the sink, working off his fury on the dinnerware.

Gradually, as his frustration cooled, Jason had to admit that he was partly at fault. If he told Anne the truth about himself, that he wasn't just a happy-go-lucky wanderer but a serious photographer, surely she could see that they did suit each other, that they could work out their differences.

He thought about going upstairs after her. But this wasn't the time, not while they were both upset. It was important that he explain things to her calmly and at length, that he be able to soothe her resentment at having been deceived and bring her to see that he, as much as she, had been caught off guard by the love blossoming between them.

Tomorrow was Sunday, an easygoing day and the perfect time to have a heart-to-heart talk. His mind made up, Jason went to bed in good spirits.

ANNE HAD TROUBLE FALLING ASLEEP until the early hours of the morning, and as a result she slept until nearly noon. Waking to see the sunlight streaming through the window, she groaned to herself.

By now, Jason would be ensconced in the living room. It would be difficult to avoid another confrontation.

At least she wasn't on call today. Maybe she could sneak out of the house and have breakfast somewhere else.

The muscles in her neck and back ached as Anne crawled out of bed, and she knew she must have been tensing them in her sleep. She could use one of Jason's massages right now....

No. She wouldn't even think about it.

Groggily, she washed up and slipped on slacks and a blouse. Then, feeling like Daniel venturing into the lion's den, she went downstairs.

A quick glance into the living room showed her newspapers strewn about, but no Jason. From the kitchen wafted the whistled notes of "Oklahoma!"

Feeling like a thief, Anne scurried out the front door, scarcely daring to breathe until she was in her car and had taken off.

Well, great. Now she was in exile from her own house.

But only until she could sort out her thoughts, she reminded herself. Still, she had to go somewhere, so Anne headed for the

Fashion Island shopping center. There was a good bookstore where she could find something to help Ellie pass the time.

Jason. What was it that made her forget all her careful reasoning when he took her into his arms? And how was she going to steel herself against him?

Anne hadn't reached any momentous conclusions by the time she arrived at the bookstore. Well, after she bought Ellie a gift, she'd have breakfast at some coffee shop and mull over the whole mess thoroughly.

The bookstore was bright and modern, with eye-catching displays of the latest releases. Anne browsed through the bestsellers, wishing she had time to read some of them herself.

Ellie liked travel books, Anne recalled. Nearby was a selection of oversize photography books, and she wandered over to it.

A pictorial of Ireland looked interesting, but there wasn't enough reading material to keep Ellie occupied. Anne took her time, sorting through the books carefully. Perhaps she should be more practical and get something on child care instead....

As she turned away, Anne glimpsed a book out of the corner of her eye, something about a politician on the campaign trail.

It wasn't the sort of book she had in mind, and yet it drew her. After taking a closer look, she realized why.

The author's name was Jason Brant.

Now, there was a coincidence. She smiled, wondering if she should buy it for Jason, or if it would bother him to learn that there was another, more successful photographer with the same name.

Curious, she leafed through the book. The photographs were striking, and the accompanying text looked intriguing.

Then she stopped, aghast. One of the photographs was all too familiar. A print of it hung on the wall in Jason's room.

Her throat tightening, Anne flipped to the back. There on the inside flap of the cover was a photograph of Jason.

With a numb feeling of betrayal, she read the brief summary of his life. A former wire-service photographer in Europe... author of a previous book...

And what was his current project? The private life of a California obstetrician?

Moving in a fog, Anne picked out a child-care book for Ellie and took it to the register along with Jason's book.

And then she went home, to face the man whom she'd trusted and who had been playing her for a fool.

Chapter Eleven

A light turned red ahead of her, and Anne slammed on the brakes. She'd been so preoccupied with her anger that she hadn't been paying attention and could easily have had an accident.

I've got to calm down before I see him.

Impulsively she headed for Ellie's house a few blocks from the beach in nearby Corona del Mar.

For a moment after the car halted, Anne sat there unmoving, inhaling the salty breeze and wondering whether to tell Ellie what she'd discovered. No, the wound was too fresh to share with anyone. But the visit would give her time to collect herself.

The child-care book in hand, Anne went inside.

She was pleased to find Ellie, as per instructions, tucked in bed. The remains of a lunch sat on a tray atop the bedside table.

"See? I've only been up to go to the bathroom. Honest, doc!" Her friend grinned at her.

Anne managed a smile. "Glad to see it. Here's something to help while away the hours."

Ellie examined the book with delight as Anne pulled up a chair. "Hey, this looks terrific. I've bought quite a few books, but I don't have this one."

"It, um, seemed to have a lot of practical tips and also some good pointers on child development." Actually, Anne wasn't quite sure what had led her to select that book; she'd been too upset about Jason to pay much attention. "So—everything's going along smoothly with your housekeeping arrangement?"

"Mmm-hmm." Ellie studied her, head cocked to one side. "Okay, out with it."

"Out with what?"

"You've got something on your mind. Come on, fess up. You know I can read expressions—it's my speciality." Hands folded in her lap, Ellie wore an air of patient waiting.

I should have known better than to come here. Anne searched for a credible explanation. "Well, I'm concerned about a Hispanic woman who works down the street from me. She has to be away from her children...."

The story of Juanita spilled out, bringing an expression of concern from Ellie.

"So what she needs is a job where her children could live with her," Anne concluded. "I wish I could hire her myself, but..."

"You wouldn't want to fire Jason," Ellie finished for her with a wink.

Swallowing hard, Anne nodded vaguely. "Besides, I don't have enough room."

"I can't imagine having to live apart from your children." Ellie tapped her fingers against the quilt. "You know, I think I'll ask around in our church. There might be someone who needs a maid—it's a large congregation. The minister will be visiting me this week, and I could talk to him."

"Would you? I'd appreciate it." Anne decided to depart before her friend's all-too-keen intuition impaled her again. "Give me a call if you find anything. And stay in bed!"

"I promise."

It would certainly be nice if Ellie could come up with a solution for Juanita, Anne reflected as she drove home. But neither Ellie nor anyone else could come up with a solution for Anne.

Jason. How could he have done this? He'd used her, plain and simple. She didn't yet know why. Surely he didn't plan to publish those photographs he'd taken of her at the beach? Heat stung Anne's cheeks as she recalled how open she'd been with him.

When she came through the front door, Jason was lying amid the newspaper sections, reading the entertainment pages. A look of surprise flashed across his face as he saw her.

"I thought you were still asleep upstairs."

Wordlessly, she held out the copy of his book.

Jason frowned. "Where did you get that?"

She ignored the question. "What an interesting book. Can you imagine, the author has the same name you do. And he looks like you, too."

Damn it. Jason had to fight down the impulse to take her in his arms. That was obviously the last thing she wanted. "I intended to tell you about it today."

"Oh, sure."

"It's the truth. I've been trying to figure out how to explain things for quite some time. I'll admit, I've been something of a coward." His words were inadequate; he could see that from the pain in her eyes. Lord, he'd never meant to hurt her! "Anne..."

"Would you mind telling me exactly what you're doing here?" Her whole body quivered with anger. "You can skip the apologies. Just get to the point."

"I'm working on a book about housekeepers. Exploited ones, like Juanita. That's how I got involved with her, why I was taking pictures of her kids." There was a lot more he wanted to say, but Anne cut him off.

"And am I one of the exploiting employers? Is that the idea? You can show me frisking about the beach, having a good time while—"

"Those pictures weren't for my book!" Outraged, he strode across the room and gripped her arms. "Anne, how could you even think that? My working for you was just a way to make contacts. And I really did need the money. Books of photography don't exactly earn millions, you know."

"I want you out of here!" She knew she was losing her grip on her emotions, that the tears were going to stream out any second.

"I'm not going to leave you in the lurch, with your family coming next week." He kept his tone level, trying to calm her. Thank heaven for the reunion; it would give him time to reason with her, time for her to calm down and listen to him rationally.

"Don't bother, Jason. I'll hire someone, get a caterer—I don't care." She took a step backward, fists clenched.

"Maybe you could send out for pizza." He did his best to sound bland and helpful. "Or bring in Chinese food. Your aunts and uncles and cousins could all sit around digging into little white cartons with chopsticks. That would be a family reunion to remember, wouldn't it?"

Anne would have been all right if it weren't for Great-aunt Myra.

As Jason spoke, she could picture Great-aunt Myra's thin face twisting as she confronted a pair of chopsticks and a carton of cashew chicken. Great-aunt Myra was outraged by finding anything foreign on her plate. Served a taco at a picnic once, she had wrinkled her nose, regarded it as if it were a roach caught sneaking into her house and pushed the plate away with a snort of disgust.

At the image of Great-aunt Myra eating takeout Chinese food, Anne felt the corners of her mouth start to twitch. Darn it, she wasn't going to let Jason see her smile!

She turned away sharply. "Very well. But the day after the reunion—out!" Without waiting for a response, Anne mounted the stairs to her room.

Safely inside, she realized that she hadn't eaten breakfast yet. But it would be too humiliating to go down again now, after her dramatic exit.

Then she heard the front door shut and the sound of Jason's car starting on the street.

Where was he going? In spite of herself, Anne hurried to the window in time to glimpse the Mustang disappearing around a corner.

She knew he hadn't gone for good; for one thing, there hadn't been time to pack. And she ought to be glad that he'd gone out and left her some privacy.

The trouble was that she loved him.

The realization hit Anne hard. For a moment, she couldn't breathe. It was true. In spite of everything, she'd fallen in love with Jason, so much that it hurt to see him drive away without a word, even though she herself had ordered him out. So much that she wanted to know where he was going for consolation and when he would be back and what he was thinking.

A hard lump formed in her chest as she went downstairs to the kitchen. Getting over Jason was going to take all her strength. But it had to be done.

She had one more week to enjoy his madcap smile and the teasing sound of his voice. And then, Anne told herself, she would never see him again.

Chapter Twelve

Deanie Parker's house looked as though a tornado had blown through it, Jason observed as he stepped inside. Although it was afternoon, his cousin still wore her bathrobe, and he'd never seen her hair in such a mess.

From a back bedroom came the persistent, angry wailing of a baby.

It didn't take a genius to figure out that Deanie hadn't slept much last night. And, as she blearily informed Jason, her husband was still overseas, so Deanie was trying to cope with a colicky infant alone.

"I had no idea it would be like this." She led the way back to the nursery. "In all the TV shows, the babies coo and smile, and the mothers look radiant."

The tiny face of Alexander James Parker was scrunched into a mask of indignation as he shrieked, pausing only briefly to suck in air before launching into another tirade.

Maybe it was because he hadn't been kept awake all night, but Jason found himself intrigued rather than dismayed. For one thing, it was a relief to deal with a straightforward problem rather than replaying the scene with Anne one more time, trying to figure out what he might have said to get through to her.

"I've fed him, diapered him, rocked him—I just can't take any more." Tears streaked down Deanie's face. "I'm not cut out to be a mother, Jason. I don't know what to do with him."

He assessed the situation quickly. "You need a few hours of uninterrupted sleep. Go on, Deanie. I'll make sure Alexander doesn't take the house apart."

She looked dubious but finally went off to bed.

Left alone with the baby, Jason began to doubt his own sanity. He'd changed a few diapers for friends' babies over the years, but that hardly made him an expert in child care.

Gingerly, he reached down to pick up the squalling infant. Alexander's cries intensified. Oh, great. At this rate, poor Deanie would never get to sleep.

More firmly, Jason lifted the baby, supporting the little head. "Now look here," he said. "We've got to get this figured out, okay?"

The baby paused, perhaps at the sound of an unfamiliar voice. Then his face started to wrinkle again, preparing for another round of wails.

"Oh, no, you don't!" Jason scooted through the house, clutching the wriggling child. "Uh—how about a rattle?" He found one in the living room, but Alexander ignored it and began screaming full tilt.

He'd have to take the baby outside to give Deanie some peace, Jason concluded. And, he discovered, the rocking motion as he walked seemed to calm Alexander, at least briefly.

For the next hour, Jason walked around the block, talking to the baby all the while and cringing when fresh cries burst forth. But gradually they diminished until the tiny head rested against Jason's chest and the little eyes closed.

Strolling back to Deanie's house, Jason gazed down at the now angelic face. Tenderness and wonder tugged at his heart. How trusting the little guy was, and how vulnerable.

Raising a child wasn't going to be easy, Jason reflected as he sat down on the front-porch steps, cuddling Alexander. He could imagine how tired Anne would be after a long night of breast-feeding and soothing a baby. But then he would take over and let her go to bed for a long snooze.

Well, maybe it wouldn't always be so idyllic. But gazing down at the baby, Jason knew for certain that it would be worth it.

He was going to win Anne back. There wasn't much time left, but somehow he was going to break through that intellectual barrier she'd raised around herself and introduce her to her own heart.

JASON DIDN'T COME HOME until Sunday night, and Anne was too proud to ask where he'd been. Besides, she told herself sternly, it was none of her business.

There was some kind of stain on his shoulder, she noted as she walked past him that evening to fetch herself some graham crackers from the kitchen. And he smelled of something familiar....

Baby powder.

She smiled to herself. He must have gone to visit his cousin. It was just like Jason to plunge right in and play with the baby and not to care if he ended up with a stain on his shirt.

It was hard, staying away from him all evening and then hurrying off to work on Monday morning without a word. There was so little time left before he would be gone forever. But Anne had to be honest about her own weakness. If she gave in now, she might never be able to bring herself to send him away.

Monday night, going over medical charts in her office after John and the staff had left, Anne was surprised when the phone rang. Who would call on her private line at this hour?

It was Ellie. "I called your house and Jason said you were still at work. Listen, I've got good news! My minister has some elderly cousins who've been looking for a live-in housekeeper, and they've got an apartment over their garage. I just called them...."

The couple was willing to hire Juanita right away, based on Anne's recommendation. The wife had recently broken a hip, and she and her husband needed a housekeeper urgently.

"I already told Jason about it," Ellie added. "You know, he's very interesting. We talked for quite a while. You ought to hold on to him."

"I'll be the judge of that." Anne immediately regretted her sharp tone. "Look, Ellie, I really appreciate what you've done for Juanita."

"I'm just glad I could help."

By the time Anne got home, Jason had already informed Juanita and called the new employers to make arrangements for her to move in Wednesday evening. "I offered to provide transportation."

"We'd better use my car." Anne dropped her purse on a table in the front hall. "It's got a bigger trunk."

"Good idea." There was something tender in the way Jason was looking at her. "Anne, I didn't expect you to solve Juanita's problem. Rosa and I had been talking to people around the neighborhood, hoping to come up with something. It was really kind of you."

Maybe it was her weariness, but Anne resented the implication. "Just because I live in a nice house doesn't mean I don't care about other people!"

"I never thought that."

"Didn't you?" She looked directly into his eyes for the first time since Saturday night. "Tell me the truth, Jason. When you began this project, when you took this job, didn't you expect me and everyone else who lives around here to be insensitive and selfish?"

He was about to argue when he remembered his thoughts that first day, imagining a male Dr. Eldridge who spent his time raking in money and running around with women. "I suppose I did have some prejudices, Anne."

"Well, that's quite an admission." His words had deflated her anger, but she didn't want to let him get too close. "Score one for the citizens of Irvine."

"Anne, I can't blame you for getting the wrong idea about me." He wasn't about to let this opportunity slide by. "I know I got off on the wrong foot with you."

She lifted a hand in warning. "I don't want to talk about it, Jason. It's been a long day and I'm in no mood for an argument."

Jason took a deep breath to stop himself from pressing her further. Were there any words, no matter how carefully selected, that could make Anne see the truth, that they loved each other and belonged together?

There were only a few days left until the reunion, and yet to pressure her would only backfire. "Okay. Go and get comfortable and I'll get your graham crackers and milk ready."

He could see the tension ebbing from her shoulders and neck. "Thanks, Jason."

But I'm not giving up. He watched until she was out of sight upstairs before heading for the kitchen. He'd have to give matters a rest for the time being.

On Tuesday, Anne worked late again—intentionally, Jason knew—so he had no chance to talk to her until dinner on Wednesday, for which he prepared one of his specialties, lamb chops flambé.

Anne hardly spoke until they reached dessert, which was homemade apple pie. Then she said, "By the way, I figured Juanita didn't have much in the way of furniture or kitchen equipment, so I made a few phone calls. Several people I know said they'd be glad to help."

"Have some whipped cream." Jason handed her the bowl and watched as she plopped a spoonful onto her pie.

"My partner's loaning us his pickup—that's what I drove home in, in case you hadn't noticed." He hadn't. "You can take Juanita and her kids tonight, and I'll drive around and pick up the equipment."

Jason had to think fast. It was important to get Juanita's family settled, but he didn't want to be apart from Anne. There was only a day and a half left until her relatives began to arrive.

"You can't lift furniture yourself." He kept his tone matter-of-fact. "Hold on a minute." Before she could object, he dashed out the door, leaped over the fence and went to confer with Rosa. She gladly agreed to drive Juanita and her children in Jason's car.

He returned and told Anne about the arrangement. "So I'm free to provide manual labor. Okay?"

For a moment, as she stared at him without speaking, his heart sank. Then she shrugged. "Sure. I suppose it makes sense."

Dinner over, they set out in the pickup. As Anne drove through the fading daylight, Jason observed her from the corner of his eye. She looked tired, and he felt a pang of guilt. If it weren't for him, Anne wouldn't have made such a point of working late this week.

If only he had another month! They needed a chance to cool off and spend some relaxing time together. One more day at the beach, perhaps. He'd even settle for an evening spent tossing out another unsuitable boyfriend.

The first house they arrived at was only a few shades this side of a mansion, on a cliff overlooking Newport Harbor. The owners had set out a refrigerator and a box of dishes in the driveway.

Jason reached down to the floor of the truck for his camera.

"You're going to take pictures?" Anne frowned. "I'm not sure..."

"Look." He slung the camera over his shoulder and came around to help her down. "Obviously, I had some stereotypes about the rich people of Irvine. Well, it's only fair to show their generous side, too, don't you think?"

She nodded slowly. "I suppose it is."

During the next two hours, they collected a convertible sofa, twin beds, an assortment of pots and pans, towels and flatware and even several framed reproductions of Van Gogh paintings.

"I'm impressed," Jason admitted as they headed through the twilight to the address Ellie had given them. "Your friends aren't even getting a tax deduction."

"They were delighted to help." Anne had relinquished the wheel and was curled sleepily in the passenger seat. With her hair falling across one cheek, she looked remarkably childlike. "Jason, just because people settle down and buy comfortable homes doesn't mean they're Scrooges."

"I didn't think that. Well, not exactly." The last thing he wanted was an argument, especially when she was in such a mellow mood. "I suppose the problem here is the system. The maids like Juanita don't have anyone to go to bat for them, and they need the work so badly they'll take almost anything."

"So you're not really attacking the employers?"

"I suppose not." He had intended to, he conceded silently, but he was certainly getting a different perspective on things.

"Of course, some people are exploitive. But mostly the Hispanic immigrants here are victims of economics." He started to explain about his plans to go to Mexico and visit Juanita's family, but they'd reached their destination, a charming California bungalow in a middle-class neighborhood of Costa Mesa, one of the towns bordering Irvine.

The two children came out running ahead of their mother. "Jason! Jason!"

Juanita followed, smiling. "So many things. All for us?"

"You can thank Anne and her friends." Jason began unloading the truck. "Where do we put them?"

It took another hour to drag everything up the stairs to the apartment above the garage. Then Jason and Anne paid their respects to Juanita's new employers: a hearty white-haired man and his wife, who welcomed them warmly from her wheelchair. With their permission, Jason took photographs for his book, using the soft illumination of the porch light.

Watching the happiness shining on the two deeply etched faces, Anne felt a pang of envy. She was sure it would be obvious even in a photograph that the lives of these two people had intertwined over the years, like morning-glory vines on a picket fence.

And if anyone could capture that inner joy with a camera, she knew it was Jason.

In spite of herself, Anne looked forward to seeing his book when it came out. She wished she could compare the final product to the way Jason had envisioned it initially. After the pictures he'd taken tonight, she suspected his outlook had undergone considerable revision.

Her attention snapped back to the present as Jason put his camera away and Juanita wheeled their hostess into the house.

"We were so glad to find Juanita," the husband explained as he walked them to the truck. "I don't mind helping my wife around the house, but she knows how much I love playing golf, and she gets upset when I stay home all the time. She's crazy about kids, too. Our grandchildren live in Oregon, so we don't get to see them as much as we'd like, and Juanita's pair are real cute."

Waving goodbye as they pulled away, Anne felt a squeeze in her heart. This was what she wanted in her own life—an old-fashioned marriage, an old-fashioned home. But to have that, she needed an old-fashioned man, not a muckraking, world-wandering photographer.

The truck rattled down a slope and turned onto Coast Highway, headed for Irvine.

Jason began to speak as if addressing himself. "Now, there are two schools of thought on the subject of graham crackers."

"I beg your pardon?"

"There are those who maintain that they're basically a form of cracker and therefore not unhealthful, perhaps even virtuous."

"A virtuous graham cracker?" She wasn't sure what he was getting at, but weariness had made her so light-headed that it didn't seem to matter.

"On the other hand, some people assert that the graham cracker is merely a cookie in disguise and that its sole merit is that it is usually consumed with milk."

"Are you out of graham crackers?" she guessed. "Is that why you're telling me this?"

"I was merely trying to ascertain your point of view." Jason steered around a slow-moving van. "Because if you happen to believe that a graham cracker is a cookie at heart, then you might be willing to consider hitting a cookie boutique on the way home."

Anne could almost taste the richness of a thick, gooey chocolate-chip cookie. "Twist my arm."

But it was after nine o'clock, and they soon discovered that cookie boutiques didn't keep late hours.

Now that their appetites had been whetted, finding those rich cookies became an irresistible challenge. By ten o'clock, they had covered half a dozen neighboring towns, only to be taunted by the sight of luscious nut-studded cookies locked away behind glass.

"There's one last place I want to try." Jason guided the truck through an intersection.

"I'm afraid to ask. Do we need another tank of gas first?"

"I promise, it's not far." Sure enough, a minute later he pulled into the parking lot of a supermarket. "Coming in?"

The store had its own bakery, Anne was surprised to find. And then she realized that she hadn't been inside a supermarket in months. She was impressed by the array of coffee cakes and homemade pies, although the bakery itself was closed now.

On the counter stood a glass-covered rack of the thickest, richest-looking chocolate-chip cookies Anne had ever seen.

"Those aren't chips, they're chunks," she murmured.

"Would I steer you wrong?" Jason lifted the glass covering and transferred a dozen cookies into a white paper bag.

"That's a lot of cookies." Anne stared at them, feeling like a child at Christmas. "On the other hand, are you sure you took enough?"

He added six more.

They were hardly through the quick-check stand when Jason fished a cookie out of the bag and wolfed it down.

"Hey!" Anne grabbed playfully at the bag. "That's cheating! You have to wait until we get home."

"Who says?" He began munching on a second cookie before handing her the bag.

"Well, you could be arrested for driving under the influence of cookies."

"I'll take it slow. They'll never suspect."

She couldn't resist. Anne chomped down one. It was entirely worth the effort they'd expended to find them.

At home, they scarcely paused to pour two glasses of milk before attacking the remaining cookies. Anne had never felt so happily piggish. After the long hours she'd worked all week and the physical labor of helping load and unload the truck today, the treat seemed like a fair reward.

"I ought to find a recipe for these." Jason gestured at her with half a cookie. "They're not all the same, did you notice? This one has macadamia nuts."

"If you can make cookies like this, I'll follow you anywhere."

"Is that a promise?"

She felt light spirited and reckless. "Yes, but only as long as the chocolate chips last."

"I'll take my chances." He reached across the table and flicked a crumb from her lips. Instinctively, Anne nibbled at his finger. "Still hungry, eh?" He picked up the last cookie and waved it in front of her tauntingly. "What's it worth to you?"

"May I remind you who your employer is?"

"Ah, but I'm a short-timer, remember?" Jason dangled the cookie above his mouth. "Say bye-bye to the chocolate chips."

"Don't you dare!" Anne lunged at him, nearly knocking over the table in the process.

Jason leaped up from his chair and dashed into the living room, with Anne in hot pursuit. She caught him near the fireplace and wrestled him down onto the carpet, finally catching the edge of the cookie and breaking it free.

With one swift motion, he pinned her to the rug. Her breath coming rapidly, Anne found herself suddenly, intensely aware of his body pressed against hers, their legs tangled together and her hip nestled against his waist.

In that instant of immobility, he snatched the cookie back and brushed it across her mouth. Anne took a bite, and then his lips closed over hers and the sweetness of the cookie blended into the sweetness of his kiss.

She hardly dared breathe. After all her protestations, all her rational reasons for sending him away, she could no longer deny that at least for this moment she wanted him.

His fingers fanned her hair out on the carpet, stroking it from the scalp. Anne closed her eyes, feeling him massage her temples and the bridge of her nose, until he leaned down to kiss her again.

Jason. She knew his scent, the masculine tang spiced now with chocolate; but she'd never known his body this way, never traced it before with such loving hands. Slowly she explored the strong line of his cheekbones, the curve in his collarbone and the broad power of his shoulders.

Velvet kisses traced her throat and made a V on her chest. She offered no protest when he slipped off her blouse and caressed the soft swell of her breasts.

"Anne." He spoke her name as if it were a jeweled thing, bright and timeless. "My love."

She couldn't say the word aloud, but it echoed through her mind. Love. Love. She loved him.

They didn't need a fire on the hearth as their last reservations melted away. Anne shed her clothing with a sense of relief, of becoming at last the self who had been locked away for so long.

Tonight, time lost its meaning as Jason caressed her, pausing to gaze into her eyes, then unexpectedly finding some sensuous curve of flesh to arouse, from the arch of her foot to the back of her earlobe.

Mind fused with body for the first time in Anne's life. She relished the gentle friction of her bare skin against his and took pleasure in stroking him until his moans mingled with hers.

Long before the act of union, they were united. Over the past few weeks, without her realizing it, Jason had become a part of Anne. Now, floating her hair across his stomach tantalizingly, she had a sense of coming home.

But when he drew his hands to the most private regions of her being and roused her expertly, the waves of desire caught Anne unaware. There was no gentleness in this, but a raging fire she'd never guessed lay hidden within her.

Eagerly, Anne caught his shoulders, but Jason would not be hurried. Deliberately, he brought her again and again to the edge of an inferno.

And then he plunged them into it. Gasping, Anne clung to him, writhing with him through the flames. Jason. Her arms would never let him go, her body never survive without this joyful thrusting.

They blazed together, hotter and hotter, until a tide of pleasure washed over them, momentarily heightening the flames and then soothing them away, leaving behind a quiet pool of contentment.

Sleepily, she felt herself lifted and carried up the stairs. *I ought to walk. I'm too heavy for him to lift. He shouldn't . . .* But the sensible voice within her muttered away into silence. For one night, it had lost its grip on Anne.

Chapter Thirteen

The alarm clock woke Anne much too early, to hazy morning sunlight. Outside, birds hooted, chirruped and babbled. She had never noticed before how loud they were or how insistent in their varied calls.

Beside her, Jason stirred, groaned and went back to sleep. The sheet was thrown at an angle across his chest, baring his shoulders. Anne fought back the urge to run her hand over his skin and caress him into wakefulness.

She had to go to work.

For the first time, Anne found herself strongly resenting the demands of her job. There were rounds to make at the hospital, nurses waiting for prescriptions, patients restless to be visited and examined; and then the waiting room at the office would fill up with women needing her attention.

This one day, Anne wanted to keep all her attention here at home. For a rebellious moment, she thought of calling in sick.

Instantly, her rational mind filled with the consequences. Ellie's substitute would have to try to reach all the patients by phone; John would have to rearrange his plans to make her hospital visits....

She couldn't be that selfish. Damn it.

Regretfully, Anne rolled out of bed. Jason uttered a vague *whumphing* noise and went back to sleep.

Maybe he had the right idea. Take life as it came, and to hell with responsibility.

Almost by instinct, Anne went through her morning ritual of showering, dressing and eating breakfast. She felt as if she were pretending to be someone else, another Anne from another world.

Her daze filtered away slowly during the drive to the hospital. It vanished entirely when she reached the obstetrical ward and learned that Ellie had been admitted, in labor and already four centimeters dilated, too far to be stopped.

Panic knotted Anne's throat for a moment, and she had to force herself to breathe calmly. Ellie's pregnancy was in its thirty-sixth week; a week later, and it would have been considered full term. There was no reason the baby shouldn't be just fine.

For the rest of the day, Anne went through her duties with half her mind attuned to the continuing reports from labor and delivery. Ellie's labor was progressing normally; monitors indicated the baby was receiving plenty of oxygen. But she couldn't shake the feeling something would go wrong.

Maybe it was because of Ellie's previous episode of bleeding, followed by premature labor. But such things weren't uncommon with a low-lying placenta, and ninety-five percent of the time everything turned out okay.

It was the remaining five percent that had Anne worried.

She had just finished a routine examination in her office when one of the nurses called to say that Ellie was dilating rapidly and would soon be in transition, the stage just before delivery.

"I'll be right there." Calling to John—who'd been warned in advance—to take over the rest of her patients, Anne raced for her car.

She arrived to find Ellie's husband, Dennis, pacing worriedly in the corridor. "She's started bleeding," he blurted out as soon as he saw Anne. "Is that normal?"

Without a word, Anne rushed into the room. Yes, Ellie was bleeding—a lot. "We're going to do an emergency C-section," she called to the nurses. It took all her self-control to sound calm as she turned to her friend, whose hair was matted with perspiration and whose eyes widened with fear. "Don't worry. Everything's going to be all right."

But was it?

A placental abruption was one of the complications of pregnancy that doctors feared most. More than three weeks ago, the ultrasound had shown that the placenta was still in place. And the bleeding could mean other things, but Anne wasn't about to take any chances.

Within minutes, an anesthesiologist was preparing Ellie for surgery. A neonatalogist and a team of nurses were summoned to take care of the baby in case it had trouble breathing when it arrived.

The next hour was the tensest of Anne's life. She'd worked on emergency cases before, but never had it been a friend. Damn it, she should have referred Ellie's case to John or to another colleague. It was too difficult emotionally to take life-or-death responsibility for the child of someone who meant so much to her.

Well, it was too late to worry about that now.

Anxious moments ticked by as she made the incision. The doctor assisting her said little, seeming to pick up Anne's spring-coiled intensity.

For one terrifying instant, as she lifted the baby girl from its mother's womb, Anne thought it wasn't going to start breathing. And then that life-giving cry burst through the operating room, and the tension wheezed out of her like air from a balloon.

The placenta was still adhering to the wall of the uterus by a patch. Had Anne been less concerned, had she waited even a few more minutes to operate, the baby might have been lost.

Instead, Ellie had a healthy little girl who weighed in at five pounds four ounces, a good size for a preemie. She'd probably be able to go home from the hospital when Ellie did.

Afterward, congratulating Dennis and watching the infant being wheeled to the nursery, where she would be observed closely for the next few hours, Anne realized for the first time that it was almost seven o'clock in the evening and she was bone tired.

Jason would be worried. No, he'd probably called the office already and found out where she was.

As she washed up, Anne realized that she hadn't thought about him for hours. Already their night together seemed like a dream, like someone else's dream.

What if I'd called in sick this morning, as I wanted to?

The possibility sent a chill shuddering through her.

Driving home, Anne faced a grim truth. There was another person who lived inside her, a younger, wilder Anne who was ready to throw everything aside for love. But that wasn't the person she'd become, the person she had to live with for the rest of her days.

This morning, she'd gotten everything backward. The stranger hadn't been Anne Eldridge, M.D., it had been Anne, Jason's lover.

Under other circumstances, perhaps the two could have merged. If only she'd fallen in love with a man who fit in with the life she had to lead!

But Jason... She respected his talent and his role as an outsider and critic of society. But travel and risk taking were vital to his career. It would be as unfair to expect him to give up his work as for him to demand that she abandon the trust her patients had placed in her.

Painful as it was, Anne at least felt on familiar ground as her intellect returned to its accustomed place, ruling over her emotions.

She'd read enough about marriages to know that love rarely survived the daily toll of conflicts between two fundamentally incompatible people. And there had probably never been two souls more different than she and Jason.

Even if he agreed to stay here in Irvine, there was the problem of children. She didn't want them raised by a housekeeper or a day-care center. It might be possible for her to work part-time for a while, but Jason would have to give up the work he loved and accept some spirit-grinding job as a studio photographer to support them. Eventually, he'd come to hate it—and her.

Marriage would destroy the love between them. The result would be two miserable adults and, eventually, children growing up in a broken home.

The time to stop things was now, before they went any farther, Anne told herself firmly. Their night together would remain a moment of bliss stolen from the locked treasury of her heart.

She tried to ignore the knife twisting in her chest. Anne knew she would be doing the right thing, to send him away after this weekend.

IT TOOK ALL of Jason's self-control not to slam shut the door to his room as he headed into the bathroom-turned-darkroom.

Blast Anne's intellectual rubbish! He'd known there would be repercussions, recriminations, uncertainties after last night. But this cold dismissal of him was infuriating!

She'd had her speech all rehearsed the moment she came through the door, before he could even greet her with a glass of sherry and the tempting hors d'oeuvres he'd prepared.

What nonsense! Career conflicts, finances, children. Those things could be worked out. Those things meant nothing compared to the love blazing between the two of them. Why couldn't she see it?

As usual, his words had bounced off her like play darts against armor. The impulse to sweep her into his arms and force out the passionate side of her had been restrained only by the conviction that such tactics would backfire. In the end, he would have to win her brain as well as her heart, and Anne's intellect was a formidable enemy.

As usual when he was upset, Jason found relief in the absorbing magic of printing photographs. Images blossomed up at him from the tray of chemicals: Juanita moving into her new home; the elderly couple with their arms around each other; the pickup truck filling with donated furniture and supplies.

As he calmed down, Jason began to assess the situation rationally.

There were two phases left to complete his book: traveling to Mexico and putting the finishing touches on the text. Then he'd need to deliver the manuscript and prints to his publisher. Of course, they could be mailed, but Jason felt safer presenting the entire precious package in person.

He didn't want to leave Anne, but there was no time to bring her to her senses. The relatives would start arriving tomorrow, and he suspected there wouldn't be a quiet moment all weekend. And then he was under orders to leave, unless she changed her mind. Which wasn't likely to happen, in view of the mood she was in tonight.

Maybe some time apart would be good for them. It might finally give her stubborn brain a chance to work itself around to the truth, that they belonged together.

And there was something else nagging at him, Jason conceded as he finished his printing and turned on the overhead light.

Money had never been important to him before, except to have enough to pay his current expenses. But now he wanted to become a family man. He didn't mind sharing the earning power with his wife, and he wasn't chauvinistic enough to insist that he had to earn more than she did.

But there was a matter of pride here. He wanted this book to do well. He wanted to show Anne that he wasn't the ne'er-do-well drifter he might have seemed at first.

He would need to concentrate on making this book the best it could possibly be. For that, he'd need some time alone, holed up somewhere—perhaps in New York, near his publisher—to concentrate on selecting the right pictures from the stacks that he'd taken and making sure the text was the most evocative he could create.

So for the time being, he had no choice but to go along with Anne's edict that he leave.

But he would be coming back. Whether it took weeks or even months, he would be coming back to Anne.

Chapter Fourteen

The Eldridges didn't so much arrive at Anne's house as they invaded, swarming into the neighborhood in a bevy of vehicles that ranged from the elegant to the barely operating.

At first it seemed to Jason that there must be Eldridges from every state in the union. He noted the long-jawed accent of Oklahoma, the lively tang of Tennessee, the nasal enthusiasm of New York.... And children! They ranged from a three-week-old infant, to supercilious preteens, all the way up to a young man about to enter Stanford.

Without realizing it, he now saw that he had envisioned dozens of people very much like Anne: self-controlled, highly educated, with a sense of fun bubbling beneath the surface but usually kept in check.

Instead, he found that family occupations ranged from farming to pharmaceuticals, that there was a prim Great-aunt Myra and a bluff joke-cracking Uncle Gary who used to be a rodeo rider; that, in short, most of them were nothing like Anne.

It was all he could do to suppress the temptation to photograph them. What a rich assortment of portraits they would make, from the bright eyes of the baby to Uncle Gary's weathered face! But he knew that if he so much as removed a lens cap where she could see him, Anne would take drastic steps. And he didn't want to spoil the reunion by finding out exactly what those drastic steps would be. Still, he might manage to sneak in a few shots here and there.

As the babble of the first day subsided, Jason began to sort out the players. Loving Anne as he did, he wanted to get to know the people most important to her.

Matters were simplified by the fact that only her immediate family was actually staying at the house. After the last plate of ham and baked beans had been cleared away—he'd decided to keep the fare simple—and the last game of Uno had been played, the uncles and aunts and cousins retired to their hotels and motor homes. Only Anne's parents and her sister's family were left behind.

From his careful observations that day, Jason knew that Anne's father, Sutter Eldridge, was the center around which the others revolved. So he wasn't surprised when the older man, whose straight back and proud bearing bore testimony to his military experience, cornered Jason in the kitchen.

"My daughter says you're her housekeeper." Sutter poured himself a glass of milk, regarded it with distaste and then downed it in a gulp. "Now, exactly how does that work?"

Jason had no intention of beating around the bush. "Sir, I'm in love with your daughter and I intend to marry her."

Even Sutter hadn't been prepared for that much directness. He nearly choked on his milk but recovered quickly. "And what does Anne say about this?"

"In a word, 'No.'" Jason went on to explain how he'd come to work here and why Anne was throwing him out as of Monday. "But I'll be back."

Sutter wasn't a man to belabor a point. Apparently satisfied that Jason was neither a bum nor an opportunist, he changed the subject. "Tell me about this photographic work of yours."

After showing polite interest in the book about the politician, Sutter perked up when Jason described the paramilitary camp he'd visited in the Middle East. An hour later, they were firmly ensconced at the kitchen table, Jason on his second beer and Sutter on this third glass of milk.

From the living room they could hear the soft voices of the three Eldridge women, but not what they were talking about. An occasional giggle wafted from upstairs as Lori's husband, Bob, read their sons a bedtime story.

"Damn stuff," Sutter observed as he regarded his milk. "Take it from me, son, never get ulcers. So tell me, what's your next project?"

"I haven't quite decided." Jason leaned back in his chair. "There are several ideas I've been toying with."

"Such as?"

"One of these days I'd like to photograph the private lives of three factory workers." Sutter was proving to be a splendid audience, and Jason allowed his imagination free rein as he described how he'd like to examine one worker in Japan, one in the United States and another in the U.S.S.R. "It would tell us more about our values and economic systems than all the doctoral dissertations ever written."

"I'll drink to that."

A rustling noise in the doorway made Jason look up. Anne was leaning there, a slight frown puckering her forehead. How long had she been listening?

"Either of you want to make a fourth for bridge?" Neither her tone nor her expression revealed anything.

"Sure, I'm game." Sutter scraped his chair back. "You're a fine young man, Jason. Good luck with all your projects."

It was hard to keep a straight face, but he managed. "Thank you, sir."

Well, at least he had her father's blessing, Jason reflected as he went to work on his menu for tomorrow.

SATURDAY'S HIGHLIGHT was a picnic in a nearby park. The weather was perfect, everyone's spirits were high.... So why did Anne feel restless, she wondered as she spread a checkered tablecloth across a wooden picnic table.

She took a deep breath and willed herself to relax. Gradually some of the tautness eased from her shoulders and back, but a reservoir of it remained.

There was no reason in the world not to share everyone else's good cheer. She'd called Ellie this morning, even though John was officially in charge this weekend, and had been delighted to learn that mother and baby were both doing well. Nothing to worry about on that score.

And no one in the family seemed upset by the last-minute change of location. Even Great-aunt Myra had cocked a knowing eye at Anne last night and said, "I didn't expect we'd actually end up at Lori's house. The age of miracles is long past."

As others began loading up the table with buckets of fried chicken, corn on the cob and potato salad, Anne's attention turned to Jason.

Having worked since early morning to coordinate the feast, he was taking a few well-deserved hours off. But instead of heading for the beach, he'd chosen to stay with her family. At the moment he was trotting toward the playground, each hand clasped by one of her nephews, with a handful of other children swarming around them.

There was something about Jason that drew children like a magnet, Anne admitted to herself with a touch of envy. He knew just how to wiggle his fingers at a baby and tickle a toddler, how to address a high-school student with suitable dignity and, a moment later, one-up a preteen with lines like "What tells jokes and changes colors? A stand-up chameleon!"

"He's some guy." Lori finished setting out napkins and came to stand beside Anne. They didn't plan to eat for another half hour, until the children had raced off some of their energy, and the other adults were drifting over to the inviting shade of benches around a manicured duck pond. "Are you sure he's just the housekeeper?"

Thinking of the night Jason had spent in her arms, Anne blushed guiltily and ducked her head so her sister wouldn't see. "He'd like to be more than that, but it just wouldn't work."

"If you say so." Lori plopped onto the bench. "Hey, thanks a lot for stepping in for me this weekend. You saved my life."

"Lori, you've got to start planning ahead." Relieved to change the subject, Anne delivered a short but pointed lecture about the need for responsibility.

"You're absolutely right." Lori met her gaze squarely. "Bob and I both tend to leap before we look. But you know what, Anne? People can be happy even when they're not perfect."

"Exactly what does that mean?"

"You're always so hard on yourself." Lori's freckled face wore an unaccustomedly serious expression. "You expect so much. Anne, I know that Bob and I have had a lot of ups and downs. Maybe you remember that minimarket we invested in that went broke. And then he hurt his back skiing right after we bought our house and I had to go to work while the kids were still small. But things have worked out."

"You and I have always been very different, Lori." Anne closed her eyes, letting the sun warm her face.

"What I'm trying to say..." Her sister paused, searching for words. "Anne, it's not in spite of the foul-ups that we've been happy. In a way, they've actually strengthened our marriage. We've had to pull together, make adjustments."

"I wouldn't argue with that." With her eyes shut, Anne was intensely aware of the shouts of laughter emanating from the playground, of Jason's deep bass counterpointing the sweet sopranos of the children. "But, Lori, you and Bob are fundamentally compatible. You have the same values. What you both wanted most was a home and children."

"Don't you?"

It wasn't like Lori to be so probing. Anne opened her eyes reluctantly and turned to face her sister. "What are you getting at?"

"I can't help notice certain, well, vibrations between you and Jason.

"And you're trying to save me from myself?"

"Just because I goof up when it comes to practical things doesn't mean I'm completely lacking in sense. Anne, sometimes I think you're so organized you haven't left room for love."

Lori's words hit much too close to home. But her sister couldn't possibly understand what Anne's life was like. "I know what I'm doing. Trust me."

The younger woman sighed. "You're so self-assured. I've always kind of envied you, Anne. But...well, I guess I've said enough."

Touched by the remorse in her sister's voice, Anne cupped her hand over Lori's. "I appreciate your concern. Believe me, I've gone over those same thoughts more than once. But I know myself, and I have to choose what's right for me. Now, I'm starving. How about you?''

Without waiting for an answer, Anne rang the large dinner bell, and they were promptly inundated with hungry relatives.

The rest of the day sailed by smoothly. Part of the family made an outing to Disneyland, while the others assaulted a nearby beach. Jason was kept busy preparing dinner, to Anne's relief, and that evening he played poker with Bob and some of the other young men.

If she could only get through the rest of the weekend without finding herself alone with him. . . .

That hope dwindled the next morning. Used to getting up early during the week, Anne woke at six-thirty and an hour later abandoned hope of falling asleep again, even though visitors weren't expected until ten.

Making her way downstairs, she heard her nephews playing quietly in their room. Despite Lori's scatterbrained approach to life, she'd raised two contented, well-behaved little boys, Anne had to admit.

It was in the front hall that Anne ran into Jason. Wearing a light jacket against the coolness of the morning, he had one hand on the front doorknob when he spotted her.

"I'm going out for doughnuts." He grinned engagingly. "Can I talk you into coming? Otherwise, I might not get enough chocolate ones. Or is it peanuts you like?"

"Chocolate with peanuts on top." Suddenly Anne was starving. And she knew the doughnuts tasted best right at the bakery. The prospect of waiting here for a half hour or so until he returned was pure agony. "I suppose you might need help carrying them. . . .''

He held the door for her.

Already regretting her impulsiveness, Anne headed down the sidewalk. How was she going to get out of this one? It was too much to hope that Jason wouldn't take advantage of the opportunity.

Rescue arrived in the form of a taxi pulling up in front of her house. As Anne watched, mystified, Great-aunt Myra paid the driver and climbed out.

"Thought I'd leave the hotel early and get a head start on the rest of the family," she informed Anne and Jason as she came up the walk. "Figured you could use some help with breakfast."

"How thoughtful." Anne took her great-aunt's arm. "As a matter of fact, we're going out for doughnuts, and we'd love to have you come and help pick the varieties."

"Well." Great-aunt Myra regarded the two of them sharply. She might be eighty-six years old but there was nothing wrong with her powers of perception. "I wouldn't want to be in the way."

"Not in the least," Anne said heartily, and Jason was forced to agree.

On the way to the doughnut shop, Anne pointed out places of interest to distract Great-aunt Myra. Unfortunately, there weren't many, so the conversation finally died away.

"The two of you getting married?" the older woman inquired out of the blue.

Anne coughed. "I beg your pardon?"

"Getting married? With the two of you living together, a person can't be blamed for wondering."

"You don't understand." She refused to meet Jason's eyes. "Jason works for me. He's my housekeeper. He has his own quarters downstairs."

"I can see that." Great-aunt Myra's voice conveyed barely restrained impatience. "And I can see a great deal more than that. So can anyone else who's got eyes."

Only their arrival at the doughnut shop saved Anne from trying to answer the unanswerable.

Among the three of them, they made a large selection of fragrant doughnuts—maple covered and cream filled and sugarcoated and chocolate and frosted with multicolored sprinkles.

Jason consulted his watch and turned to Great-aunt Myra. "We've got another hour before people start arriving. Now, I personally think doughnuts taste best when they're fresh, don't you? And I'm sure Anne would agree."

"The tea here is probably that terrible instant stuff," the older woman observed. "However, I suppose that can be tolerated."

And so the three of them sat at a booth and consumed far more doughnuts than Anne was willing to count. As they ate, Jason regaled Great-aunt Myra with tales of his housekeeping mishaps, and she responded with an openness Anne had never seen in her great-aunt before.

"My fiancé sent me a beautiful sweater from England during the Great War," Myra recalled. "The softest wool you ever saw, and a fine shade of lavender. Well, first time I wore it, wouldn't you know I spilled something on it. So I got out my washboard and I soaked that thing in the hottest water I could find, and then I scrubbed it and scrubbed it. By the time I was done, there wasn't enough left to use as a postage stamp."

"That must have broken your heart," Anne sympathized.

Her great-aunt impaled her with a look. "Broken my heart? I should say not. What broke my heart was when my fiancé was killed in action six months later. Oh, I had my share of suitors later on, but none of them was good enough for me. Damn fool I was."

This speech left Anne too startled to reply.

"People ought to take love where they find it, wouldn't you say?" Jason, of course, never ran short of words.

"I would indeed." The older woman stared straight at Anne. "Some people have too much pride for their own good."

"I think we'd better be getting back." Anne stood up, brushing away the crumbs that had evaded her skimpy paper napkin.

Without a word, Jason rose and offered each lady an arm. The three of them remained silent on the trip back, but the air vibrated with Great-aunt Myra's final words.

It isn't pride, Anne told herself, wondering why the remark stung. *It's common sense.*

Is it possible a person can have too much of that for their own good, too?

She was grateful for the hullabaloo that greeted their arrival. Her nephews, Jeb and Sammy, came running out to help carry in the doughnuts, and for the rest of the day there was no more need to be alone with Jason—or with Great-aunt Myra.

That evening, Anne had arranged a special treat: she'd chartered a yacht. Since it came with its own crew, including a cook, Jason was free to mingle on the deck with the rest of the family, and a group of children quickly gathered around him.

"Now, that's a sloop." Jason pointed to the boats in New-port Harbor as the yacht glided past. "And that one with the colorful sails is a catamaran."

"Why's it called that?" one of the girls asked. "Does it have something to do with cats?"

"Nope." Jason hoisted her up so she could see better. "It's because there are two separate hulls. Originally, a catamaran was made by lashing two logs together. The name comes from the Tamil language that's spoken in the country of Sri Lanka, in Asia. *Kattu* means to tie and *maram* means tree."

"Wow." The little girl's eyes widened. "Have you been to that place?"

Even before Jason nodded, Anne knew the answer. Of course he had, she reflected with a pang. And if he hadn't, it was probably on his list of places to visit next.

She thought back to the conversation she'd overheard be-tween Jason and her father. So Jason's next project was going to involve traveling to Japan and Russia. Terrific. And what was she supposed to do while he spent his days photographing factory workers?

A crew member called out that dinner was served, and she wandered in, feeling lost and apart even as she stood elbow to elbow with her laughing relatives.

The swordfish was superbly prepared; Jason freely admit-ted he couldn't do better. But Anne hardly tasted it. She was too busy trying not to look at him as he amused Jeb and Sammy with stories of the exotic foods he'd eaten in China and India.

After dinner, one of the crew members appeared on deck with a guitar and launched a sing-along.

Anne's first thought was, *doesn't the salt air warp the gui-tar?* And her second was, *maybe I really have forgotten how to have fun. The condition of his guitar is none of my business.* The reunion was almost over, and she was letting her own anxieties spoil it. Shaking away her mantle of worry, Anne joined the circle of relatives singing "If I Had a Hammer."

Then her spine tingled like a tuning fork. Not far behind her, someone was whistling the melody. Jason. Nobody could whistle like that but Jason.

And then he was standing by her side, his arm linked through hers as the group finished mangling the melody and began dismantling "Lemon Tree."

She could feel the heat of his body in the cool night air. Every sensory detail of their night together rushed back into Anne's veins like an infusion of wine. Weakly she leaned against Jason, and his arm encircled her waist.

To one side, Great-aunt Myra was smiling.

All too soon, the yacht returned to the dock, and the family trooped off reluctantly. Children yawned and drooped in their parents' arms as goodbyes were said.

Except for Anne's immediate family, she wouldn't see the others for a full year. Hugging Great-aunt Myra, she wondered how much longer the feisty older lady would be around, and she was grateful she'd had a chance to get to know her better—in spite of the unwelcome advice.

Jeb and Sammy rode home with Anne and Jason. At the house, after a late-night snack of doughnuts that Jason had managed to secrete that morning, the family trooped up to bed.

But sleep didn't come easily for Anne. Trained by her years as an intern and resident, she usually dropped off immediately. But tonight, staring out the window at a mariner's sky brilliant with stars, she couldn't stop thinking about the fact that she would be saying goodbye tomorrow to more than her family.

Jason. There was no more reason to keep him around—except for that near-fatal temptation she was determined to resist.

It was hard to imagine the house without him. No more whistling when she came down in the morning; no more cooking smells when she arrived home at night; no more newspapers scattered around the living room; no more having someone here to talk things over with at the end of the day; no more strong arms clasping her. . . .

Restlessly, Anne got out of bed and began to pace. A floorboard squeaked beneath the carpet. Darn, he'd hear her downstairs; besides, she knew her father had ears like a fox.

Drawing a flannel robe around her and sticking her feet into the panda slippers, Anne made her way quietly downstairs. Through the side door by her office, she padded out onto the patio.

The night was quiet. Far off, Anne could hear the occasional murmur of a passing car, and somewhere a bird mumbled in its sleep. There was no wind.

Love. When she was younger, she used to dream of finding it, magically, perhaps at a glittering ball, or accidentally, while browsing through a bookstore. Always the handsome stranger and she would recognize the truth at first sight; obstacles would melt away before them, and after that . . . well, she'd never worried about what came next.

Smiling to herself, Anne thought back to the day Jason had first come to this house. She'd been startled to see him sitting in the living room with the other applicants. An attractive man, she'd noticed immediately, but unsuitable for the job, of course.

Of course.

How had he talked her into hiring him? Looking back, it was hard to remember. Vaguely, she recalled that he'd taken over the kitchen and that she'd been dying of hunger. Even then, he'd known instinctively how to bypass her defenses.

When had she fallen in love with him? Maybe it had been when he routed Horace Swann with those ridiculous questions about his mother's colitis. Or when he tossed Aldous Raney bodily out the door. Or when he showed Mitch Hamilton up for the hypochondriac he was.

Or had she fallen in love that night when they walked by the Back Bay and she realized the freshness Jason brought to her everyday world?

It was impossible to say. More likely she'd fallen a little bit at a time, day by day, living here with Jason. He was charming, admirable and caring, she admitted. If there had been no question of having to plan a future, of taking care of children, of conflict with Anne's own needs and goals . . .

"Can't sleep?" It didn't surprise her to find Jason standing in front of the sliding glass doors that led out from the kitchen. He'd probably known instinctively that she was here.

"Overexcited, I guess." Anne sat on one of the patio chairs. "I'd been looking forward to the reunion for so long, it's hard to believe it's over."

Jason sat across from her, leaning across the wrought-iron table. "Anne, I have to say this...."

"Please don't."

"You don't know what I was going to say."

"I think I do."

The silence of the night sifted between them. Anne caught a whiff of poignant sweetness from the neighbors' lemon tree. Jason, sitting there regarding her, seemed to fill the whole world.

"I'm going away," he said.

Anne caught her breath sharply. She'd expected him to argue. Deep inside, she realized with sudden and painful insight, she'd expected a fairy godmother to wave a magic wand and somehow resolve the differences so that Jason could stay. But it wasn't going to happen.

"I...I know." Surely he could hear how breathless she was, how stunned.

"There are a lot of things I want to tell you, but maybe it's better if I don't." He looked away. "We had fun tonight, didn't we?"

"Yes." She ached to lean across and smooth the sadness from his face. "This whole weekend went beautifully. Thank you, Jason." The words sounded stiff and distant, not at all what she meant, but she didn't know how to explain without letting him know how much she yearned to keep him here forever.

"I kept thinking you would change your mind." He inhaled deeply. "I love you, Anne."

She hadn't expected her own tears, so sudden and overwhelming. Could he see them in the darkness? If she sat here for one more instant, she'd lose the will to resist. With a low moan, Anne wrenched herself away from the table and ran down the path to the side door.

Jason didn't try to follow her. He was too angry to confront her now; angry not with the Anne he loved but with that damn interfering brain of hers, the one that told her things that simply weren't true.

Several times this weekend, he'd thought she might waver. He'd noticed the heart-to-heart talk with Lori; and then there'd been Great-aunt Myra's pointed remarks; and it had been obvious tonight on the boat that everyone in the family thought the two of them belonged together. They'd been accepted as a unit, by everyone except Anne.

Yes, it was best that he go away tomorrow and finish his book. But he'd wanted to discuss his absence with her, to assure her that he'd be coming back.

Chapter Fifteen

"Here's the information you wanted." John Hernandez handed Anne a jiffy-printed brochure with the name of a clinic on it. "They just opened in Santa Ana and they're desperately in need of doctors to volunteer a few hours a week."

She stared at him blankly. This morning, saying goodbye to her parents and sister and trying to avoid Jason's eyes as they ate breakfast, she'd scarcely thought about work.

Arriving at the office had been a bit of a shock to her nervous system. Everything looked smaller than she'd remembered, more confining. It had been hard to concentrate on her cases, and now...

"Oh. Right. I'm sorry, John." She tucked the brochure into her pocket. "I'm kind of distracted this morning."

"I noticed. Must have been a busy weekend with the family. Everything go okay?"

"Terrific." Forcing herself to smile, she turned to go about her work.

An hour later, at lunchtime, Anne drew the brochure out of her pocket as she consumed a sandwich in her office. The clinic, it said, had been started by a coalition of nonprofit community groups concerned about the lack of adequate medical care for the poor.

Several doctors, dentists and nurses were listed on the brochure as having agreed to donate services. But there was no obstetrician, Anne noticed immediately.

This was exactly what she needed to take her mind off Jason. And, at the same time, she could fulfill one of her goals in pursuing a medical career—to help women who really needed it.

As the afternoon went by, Anne resolutely pushed the thought of Jason's departure from her mind. Instead, she called the clinic and set up an appointment for later in the week to meet with the director. The woman who answered her call sounded excited when she learned of Anne's credentials.

"We can really use your help. There was a girl in here today—nineteen years old and pregnant, and she doesn't know where to turn for medical help. We get them all the time. They're afraid to venture out of the area, and they're confused by paperwork, so they don't even get what treatment's available. The director will be thrilled when he hears."

As soon as she hung up, Anne got a call from the hospital about a patient ready to deliver, and she was busy for the rest of the afternoon. By six o'clock she was bone weary and ready to go home.

Pulling up in front of the house, she felt her spirits lift automatically. Coming home was always something to look forward to. What would Jason be cooking tonight?

As soon as she opened the door and sniffed the air in vain, the realization hit her.

He was gone. He'd really left.

Anne stiffened. It was what she'd wanted, wasn't it?

No, but it was the right thing. Regardless of what anyone else thinks.

Still, her first impulse was to turn right around and march out the door, away from this cold and empty house that echoed with his memory. She could go out and get a pizza. No; pizza was one of Jason's favorite foods, and she'd think of him with every bite. How about chicken? Or Mexican food? Or Chinese?

If she left this house now, she might never find the nerve to come back again.

Rationally, Anne knew she wasn't just going to walk away from her house. But she didn't see how she could face coming back to it again tonight. No, she'd better stay right here and raid the refrigerator. There were, she knew, plenty of leftovers from the weekend.

Almost too tired to propel herself forward, she forced herself into the kitchen, the room which most reverberated with Jason's absence. And stopped in the doorway, shocked.

The entire wall adjacent to his room was covered with a mosaic of photographs.

Slowly, as if in a dream, Anne walked along the wall, retracing the weeks she and Jason had spent together. Here was that precious day at the beach—the sand castle, her introspective mood, Jason's high spirits. And there were Juanita and her children at the playground, one of the youngsters laughing as he swooped down the slide into his mother's arms.

And of course the fiesta afterward, with its gaiety and wealth of interesting faces. Oh, and moving day— Anne stood for a long time gazing at the picture of Juanita's new employers, their arms around each other, their eyes reflecting a serenity she might never know.

The last photographs were a surprise. Jason must have returned alone to the Back Bay to capture its spirit: the wildness contrasting with the silhouette of houses in the background; the balletic movements of a flock of migrating birds settling onto the water; the enchanting play of light over the high grasses. She could almost see movement in the still photographs.

Then there was the family reunion. Anne had to smile at the man's audacity. Somehow he'd managed to snap pictures of Jeb's and Sammy's dirt-smeared faces at the picnic; where had he hidden the camera when she was around? He'd even composed a portrait of Great-aunt Myra sitting on Anne's patio, drinking a cup of tea and staring straight at the lens with her chin lifted authoritatively. Anne could almost hear the old lady saying what a fool she'd been more than half a century ago and how Anne shouldn't make the same mistake.

Was it a mistake?

Damn it, she should feel more confident! Anne pulled herself away, going to the refrigerator to dig out some leftover chicken and potato salad.

She wasn't going to take the mosaic down. That would be admitting it hurt too much for her even to look at it. No, she'd leave the pictures up until they lost their power over her, until her memories of Jason mellowed and she no longer felt this throbbing ache inside.

Why had Jason printed these photographs and left them for her? Anne wondered as she fixed herself a glass of iced tea. Since he was gone now, he couldn't have meant them to win her over.

Yet it wasn't like him to mock her, either. Perhaps he'd meant them as a sentimental farewell, a last reminder of what she'd thrown away. Or perhaps he'd intended them as a gift, guessing how much these memories would mean to her.

As she sat alone at the table, staring at the photographs, it occurred to Anne for the first time that she didn't know where Jason had gone.

Her heart sped up and for a minute she felt as if she couldn't breathe properly. Had he gone back to Santa Monica to find another apartment at the beach? Or was he flying abroad even now, perhaps to Japan to start his new book? Even if she wanted to, there was no way to reach him. Unless he chose to contact her, she had no way of finding Jason every again. Or—

Deanie Parker! The likelihood that he would stay in touch with his cousin comforted Anne far more than she wanted to admit. Of course, she had no intention of inquiring after him— well, not right away. In six months or so, she might ask Deanie casually how Jason was doing. Surely that would be only natural.

She wished she knew where he was right now. She wished she could hear him whistling, eavesdrop on his conversations, watch as he focused his camera on a new subject.

Blast it, she wouldn't go on torturing herself! Resolutely, Anne headed out to the video store so she'd have something to watch that might to distract her.

And if she happened to pick *Oklahoma!* and hum along with the melodies, what did that have to do with Jason?

"WE'D LIKE TO MOVE your publication date up a month." The editor's voice bristled with static over the long-distance line to Mexico.

Jason cupped his hand over his ear to hear better. The only telephone in Juanita's hometown was located in the general store, and it was anything but quiet. A heavyset woman was bargaining loudly for a length of cloth, and just outside the open door two dogs circled each other in the dust, growling threats.

"You'd like to what?" Jason knew he couldn't have heard correctly. On his last two books, publication had been delayed several months each time. Works of photography didn't have the highest priority on a publisher's list, he'd learned.

"We're real excited about this one." The voice was tinny but the words were quite clear. Jason had heard right, after all. "Several of us have looked at the preliminary material you sent. This contrast between a wealthy Southern California community and the poor people who do the dirty work, well, our promotions people think we can book you on some talk shows. And you know what that does for sales."

Jason wondered what Anne would think if she saw him glibly chatting away on a talk show. She'd probably feel exploited all over again. But he did want this book to be a success.

"We need the rest of the material as soon as possible," his editor continued. "When will you be finished there?"

"I was planning to head back to Mexico City tomorrow and catch a flight out." Jason tried to ignore the shrieks of two barefoot children as they raced up to the counter to buy candy. "But I intended to stop over in California for a few days."

He'd been gone for two weeks. Although he'd been busy meeting Juanita's family and photographing them, his thoughts had never been far from Anne. Did she miss him? Was she even now contemplating a doomed marriage to some fool like Horace Swann, merely because it seemed to make sense? What had she thought of the wall of pictures he'd left behind?

"You can go to California later. We need the rest of those pictures and the text, pronto!"

It occurred to Jason that his editor had a lot of nerve, particularly after refusing to give him an advance because the project "wasn't commercial." But there was nothing to be gained by arguing. After all, this book might be the only way to prove to Anne that he wasn't as flighty as she believed.

With a sigh that must have been audible all the way to New York, Jason said, "All right. I'll see you day after tomorrow."

Anne would just have to wait.

RELAXING ON A CHAISE LONGUE on Ellie's patio, Anne sipped a glass of beer and watched two couples play a good-natured, fumbling game of badminton. A card game was under way a short distance from Anne, and several of the other guests were taking a dip in the hot tub.

In a shaded stroller, Ellie's baby lay dozing, waking occasionally with a loud groan to protest her digestive upsets. Or just plain old gas, if you wanted to be frank about it, Anne thought with a smile. Fortunately, the little girl wasn't a screamer, just a groaner.

"Having a good time?" Ellie plopped into a chair. She'd recovered amazingly well from her C-section and would be going back to work soon.

"Thanks for inviting me. Your parties are always fun. And that chicken on the barbecue smells terrific."

Her friend regarded her knowingly. "You've lost some weight, haven't you?

"Oh, a few pounds, maybe."

"Not eating so well since Jason left?" It was the first time Ellie had mentioned the subject in weeks. "Aren't you going to hire another housekeeper?"

Anne shrugged. "I've been using a cleaning service. It seems to work out well enough." *How could I let someone else live in Jason's room and cook in his kitchen?*

"Heard anything from him?"

"No."

Ellie looked as if she wanted to say more, but her husband, Dennis, came by to ask for some help fixing drinks, and she followed him into the house.

About a dozen people had been invited today. Anne watched through half-closed eyes, pretending to sunbathe as she observed the card game.

Ellie had invited several unattached men and one other single woman, probably to avoid making it look like the point of the party was to pair Anne off. But Anne had a suspicion that had been a primary motive.

One of the men seated at the table had light-brown hair like Jason's, but his eyes lacked the dark fire she was used to, she noted as he dealt the cards. He looked, well, pleasantly bland. He worked with Dennis at a computer firm, she recalled. You certainly couldn't imagine him suggesting a romantic twilight stroll in the Back Bay.

The other fellow, a redhead, struck her as a bit more energetic as he slapped a card down on the table. But maybe too much so. He didn't have Jason's sensitivity; she could see that.

The baby's groans intensified into the beginnings of a wail. Ellie was still indoors, so Anne hurried over and picked up the child.

An angelic smile was her reward, followed by a loud burp. Ah, innocence.

Well, there would be plenty of time to find another man and have her own babies, Anne told herself as she rocked the infant in her arms. Surely it wouldn't be long until she found someone who appealed to her.

Just as soon as she stopped comparing every man she met to Jason . . .

"I ALMOST DIDN'T recognize you." Jason stood up and pulled out a chair for Jill. She looked smart in her designer suit, with matched Gucci bag and shoes. The restaurant she'd chosen was the perfect setting for her—sleek and hushed despite the crowd at lunch. The predominant sound was the clink of expensive crystal glasses.

"You haven't changed—maybe a few gray hairs." Even her smile was more premeditated than it used to be. Suddenly Jason wondered if he'd ever known his ex-wife at all.

They filled the minutes with chitchat as they studied their menus. She chose the seafood salad; he preferred to try the shrimp crepes, which were outrageously overpriced. But he could afford it, with the hefty advance his publisher had finally coughed up.

He'd decided to look Jill up on a whim. No, it was more than that. For a few years, the two of them had shared their lives.

Since the divorce, they'd all but lost contact. Now that he loved someone else, he'd felt the need to see her again, although he wasn't quite sure why.

"Tell me about your new book." It was hard to tell if she was really interested, but Jason dutifully described the premise. Jill nodded slowly as she listened. "I was right. You haven't changed. Still the same old crusader."

"You sound as if you're not sure whether that's good or bad."

She shrugged and sipped the white wine the waiter had set in front of her. "It's okay, I guess. Someone's got to improve the world; heaven knows, it could use it."

"So tell me what you're up to."

She rested her chin on the palm of her hand. Jill was still an attractive woman, Jason noted, and yet he felt no more drawn to her than to a stranger on the street. In a way, she *was* a stranger. He tried to picture the girl he'd met in college, with her long hair and high-flying ideals, but he couldn't see her in this woman sitting across from him.

"First of all, I'm getting married." Jill waited expectantly for his response, and Jason didn't let her down.

"Married? I'm glad for you! Must be a special guy." His enthusiasm came from the heart.

"Ralph's the manager of a major hotel and he's due for a promotion in the chain." Jill went on to sing the praises of her fiancé. She herself had become a designer of linens and had met Ralph when she was hired to create a new line for his hotel.

"Sounds like you two are really on the way up."

Jill paused as the waiter delivered their orders; then she replied, "That's right, we are. The president of the company likes my work, and they may be hiring me to design for them exclusively. Ralph and I could travel together to visit the various hotels. You'd love it, Jason! They've got establishments in Paris, Tokyo, Cairo—all the best places!"

All the best places. Jason hoped she didn't see the irony in his smile as he thought of Juanita's hometown in Mexico. That certainly wouldn't qualify as one of the best places on Jill's list, and yet there'd been a closeness and warmth among the people that came from years of struggling together and sharing joys as well as sorrows.

"It doesn't sound like you're planning on having children." He knew it was none of his business, but he couldn't restrain his curiosity.

"Children? You've got to be kidding!" Jill stared at him over a forkful of salad. "What would I want children for?"

"Some people think they're cute."

"Cute? Dirty diapers and breast-feeding in the middle of the night? Oh, come on!" She was genuinely horrified.

"They're not for everyone," he conceded. "I'm glad you're living the kind of life you've always wanted."

"So am I." She grinned, and for a moment he glimpsed a trace of that younger, more carefree Jill who he'd once thought shared his ideals. "And I hope you find the kind of happiness Ralph and I have."

"Thanks." He didn't feel like telling her about Anne. He knew Jill would approve, but for the wrong reasons—because Anne was successful in a prestigious job, not because she was strong and caring.

Walking back to his hotel after lunch, Jason caught sight of his reflection in a store window. Almost defiantly, he'd chosen to wear jeans today, with a polo shirt and a tweed jacket that he'd removed as soon as he stepped out of the restaurant into the heat of the August day.

Yes, he looked much as he always had. You couldn't see gray hairs in a window reflection, he noted with a half smile.

But Jill was wrong when she said he hadn't changed. He had. Traveling to exotic places and trying to show the world its own face through his photographs still appealed to him. But he was ready for a new phase in his life.

Raising children meant staying in one place for a while and spending time with them. But then, wasn't a home really the entire world in microcosm? Surely there were plenty of insights for a photojournalist in any corner of the world, including the manicured comfort of Irvine.

Jason's step faltered. The need for a transition in his life-style had seemed so obvious to him that he hadn't thought about how he must look to Anne.

Maybe her resistance to him wasn't entirely pigheaded. If she thought he intended to combine having a family with hopping around the globe...

An image of her came to him, standing in the doorway of the kitchen as she had so often. This time she was regarding him and her father with an unreadable expression.

What had he been talking about right before he noticed her? Oh, yes, about wanting to photograph factory workers in three different countries. But that could wait, of course.

Only she hadn't understood that. Maybe because Jason hadn't told her. Oh, damn his own shortsightedness!

At that moment, he would have given anything to sprout wings and fly to California to be with Anne. But he was still finishing revisions on his text, which would take another week at least. And some things simply couldn't be explained over the phone.

Jason's steps dragged the rest of the way to the hotel.

ANNE WIPED BEADS of sweat off her forehead. The one thing she hadn't given much thought to before volunteering was that of course the clinic couldn't afford air conditioning. And today was a real early-September Southern California roaster.

Stretching her shoulders to ease a cramp in her back, she finished jotting down notes in the folder in front of her. The girl who had been Anne's last patient of the day was only seventeen and pregnant for the second time. Amazingly, she'd known almost nothing about the human reproductive cycle and how to avoid getting pregnant.

In the weeks since Anne had begun spending one afternoon a week here, word had spread among women in the area and she'd found herself with as many patients as she could handle. Some had neglected infections; others needed information almost as much as they needed medical care.

We're the richest country in the world, and still people fall between the cracks, she reflected as she stepped out into the now empty waiting room. It was five o'clock, and Anne realized for the first time that she hadn't eaten lunch.

Well, she'd pick up a hamburger on the way home. But the prospect didn't have much appeal. Somehow Anne lacked an appetite these days; maybe it was the heat.

"You're doing a terrific job." The receptionist was a woman in her forties who Anne knew had volunteered to work in this oven even though she could have spent her days at an expensive country club. "One of the women told me she was going to come back next week and bring her two daughters. She's afraid they might get pregnant and she figured they'd listen to you."

Anne leaned wearily against the edge of the desk. "Isn't it ironic? Half the women I know can't seem to get pregnant, and the other half can't seem to avoid it."

"That's life." The receptionist regarded her sympathetically. "You look like you could use a nice relaxing weekend."

"Oh—it's Friday, isn't it?" Anne hoped she didn't sound as confused as she felt. The weeks had lost their shape recently, with nothing to look forward to. "I'm not on call until Sunday. Maybe I'll do something exciting—like sleep late."

"Have fun." The receptionist was getting ready to lock up, so Anne said good-night and departed.

She didn't want to go home yet, to that empty house with the mosaic of photographs waiting for her if she ventured into the kitchen. Well, Anne had been meaning to stop by to see how Juanita was getting along with her new employers. Ellie had relayed glowing reports, but Anne wanted to see for herself.

As she pulled up in front of the cozy bungalow, it occurred to her that the family might be at dinner. Then she saw Juanita's children playing with tricycles in the side yard.

Anne's light tap at the door brought Juanita. "Dr. Eldridge! Please, come in."

"I hope I'm not intruding." She looked around, but the homey living room was unoccupied.

"No—they went to their daughter's house for dinner, and we ate already. If you're hungry, I could cook for you."

Juanita's English had improved greatly, Anne noted as she said, "No, but thank you. I just wanted to see how you were doing."

They sat out on the back porch, enjoying a refreshing breeze and drinking iced tea as Juanita told Anne how much happier her children were now. In the dusk, Anne watched the two little bodies fling themselves about joyfully, shouting and giggling and then turning to their mother for reassurance every few minutes.

Best of all, Juanita added, Ellie's congregation was trying to find a permanent gardening job for her husband. That way he, too, would be able to live here instead of traveling to farms across the state.

In the comfortable silence that fell between them, Anne found herself remembering summer evenings of her childhood—the soft twilight, the sharpened chirps of insects, the sense of security.

Juanita caught her off guard by saying, "How is Jason? When is he coming back?"

Taking a deep breath, Anne said, "I don't know, Juanita. I haven't heard from him. And I doubt if he's going to be coming back."

"He will." The other woman nodded confidently. "He loves you."

It was impossible to explain how she felt to Juanita, Anne reflected. Maybe that was because she wasn't entirely clear how she felt herself.

"Sometimes love isn't enough."

A puzzled frown marked Juanita's confusion. "Yes, but you have enough money. He doesn't have to go away to work."

"Yes, he does, but not because of the money." Anne shifted, suddenly uncomfortable despite the deep cushion on her willow rocking chair. "You know he takes photographs around the world."

It was clear from Juanita's face that she didn't understand why two people who loved each other would allow anything to come in their way, except such dire poverty as had forced her and her husband temporarily apart.

I suppose, from her point of view, we must look like fools, Anne reflected ruefully. *And maybe we are.* Finally, giving in to the hunger pangs that had reasserted themselves, she said goodbye to Juanita and the children and headed for Irvine.

On the way, Anne stopped at a drive-in hamburger joint and picked up dinner. It smelled . . . well . . . edible, anyway, she decided as she drove on.

Maybe it was time to remove the photographs from the kitchen. By leaving them up these past few months, she'd proved her point that they held no particular power over her.

If only there were someone there to know she had proved her point.

Suddenly Anne began to laugh. How ridiculous she would look to anyone who came in and discovered that she was taunting herself with those photographs! She hadn't been indifferent to them at all. Why, she'd hardly been able to force herself into the kitchen. Last night she'd gone out for ice cream rather than run the gauntlet of memories in order to fetch her usual graham crackers and milk.

Oh, Jason, what have I done?

The laughter warped into tears, but Anne fought them back. She'd made her decision and she was going to live with it.

And yet, as she did every evening, Anne found herself half-hoping when she turned the corner onto her street that she'd see Jason's car parked in front of the house.

There was nothing by the curb.

She pulled to a stop and cut the motor. Home. Only this wasn't home; it had reverted to being just a house.

Enough self-pity, she commanded herself sternly, and marched up to the front door with the hamburger sack in her hand.

But her imagination wouldn't leave her alone. As soon as she stepped inside, Anne fancied she smelled something cooking. Fettucine. Cheese and cream and a hint of nutmeg . . .

She must be light-headed with hunger, because she believed she heard, coming from the direction of the kitchen, the whistled strains of "People Will Say We're in Love."

Someone emerged—a tall figure stood silhouetted against the bright kitchen lights. He was built just like Jason.

"Hi." That was his voice, too, rich and warm and, well, just right.

"I—I already bought dinner." It was a dumb thing to say, Anne noted with one part of her mind, after she hadn't seen Jason for months.

He strode across the hallway and lifted the sack from her hand. "You call this dinner? Doctor, you're in dire need of help."

And then strong arms surrounded her, and it finally came home to Anne that he was really here. But it was all an illusion just the same, because he wasn't going to stay.

Chapter Sixteen

"Anne." Jason whispered her name into her hair. "Oh, God, you smell wonderful—just like medicine."

She started to giggle. And she couldn't stop. Hoots of laughter welled up, and she leaned against him weakly. "We're—we're terrific, aren't we? I—I talk about hamburgers, and you make stupid jokes."

"You've lost weight." He ran his hands along her sides. "About ten pounds, I'd say, and I can see why. The refrigerator was almost empty, and your graham crackers had gone stale."

"The photographs . . ."

"I didn't mean to scare you into starving to death!" Jason held her away from him, his eyes focusing deep into hers. "Why did you leave them up?"

That was a question Anne didn't want to think about. "Oh—just lazy, I guess." Quickly she changed the subject. "Where's your car?"

"It's still at Deanie's. I took a cab from the airport. I figured if you saw my car in front of the house, you might drive off into the night and never return."

"Oh, Jason . . ."

"Is that your stomach rumbling, or has World War III started? Maybe we ought to continue this conversation after dinner."

Hovering between laughter and tears, Anne agreed.

The kitchen smelled like home again. The track lights overhead were no longer harsh and glaring; the white Formica counters had lost their Saharalike bleakness; the refrigerator no longer loomed at one side like a hungry giant poised to devour the unwary. The air radiated rich cooking smells and a welcoming, indefinable quality that transcended the five senses.

It struck Anne that the photographs on the wall no longer threatened to overwhelm her. They were just pictures, after all.

"I was afraid you might have hired another housekeeper and I'd be forced to bribe her into taking the evening off." Jason dished his sumptuous fettucine onto Anne's best plates. "Or, if it was a man, I'd have to throw him out."

"How could I hire anyone to take your place?" Anne couldn't stop the words from pouring out. "Oh, Jason, it's been horrible! But . . ."

"Save the buts until after dinner, all right?"

"All right."

Questions bubbled up in her. Where had he been? Why had he come back? What did he want from her?

Across the table, Jason watched Anne as she wolfed down her food. It looked as if she hadn't eaten a bite in the months since he'd left. If he'd had any idea she was starving herself, he would have come back sooner, deadline or no deadline.

He wished he knew how to begin. Perhaps he should tell her about his book—that the publisher was launching a major advertising campaign, that a book club had shown interest and that there was even talk of basing a television movie on the theme.

Or it might be better to plunge ahead, to get right to the heart of the matter. *No, I don't plan to be an absentee husband and father. No, I don't expect you to follow me from one hotel room to another.*

Anne was avoiding his eyes as she attacked a marinated artichoke heart in her salad. Or maybe she was so devastated by hunger that she could think of nothing else. At the very least, she ought to hire him back as her cook, Jason mused.

But he knew her lack of appetite hadn't been due to a lack of food. Anne could perfectly well afford to have her dinner catered every night if she wanted. It was his own fault, for putting these photographs here to haunt her. He'd hoped that she would finally confront her own heart, but instead she'd abandoned her kitchen.

Did that mean his quest was hopeless?

"Let's go for a walk," he said when their plates were finally bare.

"A walk?"

"Down the street and back. It's beautiful out tonight, you know—lots of stars just making their appearance, and it's cool."

Puzzled, Anne agreed.

As soon as they stepped outside, she saw that he was right. With its arid climate, Southern California cooled off the instant the sun went down. The temperature must have dropped by at least fifteen degrees since that afternoon, she discovered as the evening air washed over her face and shoulders.

In the fading light, the entire world had mellowed to sepia tones. Children were indoors now, eating dinner or watching television; the only creature Anne saw stirring was a lone cat that twitched its tail as it observed them, then stalked regally away.

Jason linked his arm with hers and guided her along the sidewalk. Trying to see her neighborhood through his eyes, Anne noticed how similar all the houses were. When she'd moved here, she'd found the area appealingly modern and well constructed, but to him . . .

"I guess you must find this place boring," she said.

"Boring?" He raised an eyebrow in mock amazement. "Why, Anne—don't you know the people who live in that house?" He indicated one of the homes, almost indistinguishable from the rest.

"No. Why?"

"They're jewel thieves. Notice the stained-glass design in the upstairs window. Those aren't nuggets of red glass; they're stolen rubies. That's how they hide them."

She smiled. "You'd make a terrific father." *If you could stay in one place long enough.* "Kids love stories like that."

"You think I'm making this up?" He waved at another house. "Those people have orgies in the basement. Have you heard of the Hellfire Club?"

"Never have."

"Used to exist in England a few centuries ago. Some of the lords and ladies in the Age of Reason figured they'd taunt the old notions of religion. They used to meet in an old underground salt quarry and commit hanky-panky."

"Commit hanky-panky?"

"Sound like fun?"

Anne had trouble catching her breath. She'd been so busy with her thoughts this past hour that she'd managed to ignore the signals her body was sending her. Now they rushed in on her all at once.

Jason. How his eyes glowed in the gathering darkness as he looked at her; how perfectly his lean body fitted against hers as he slipped an arm around her waist; how tantalizing his skin felt when his cheek brushed her temple.

She didn't care about the future. Right now he was here, and that was all that mattered.

"How—how do you commit hanky-panky?" she whispered, knowing it was an invitation.

"You start with the lips." He demonstrated, the kiss intensifying until shivers ran through Anne. She didn't care in the least that they were standing in the middle of the sidewalk, where anyone could see them.

"Hair," she murmured.

"What?"

"Hair. Don't forget about hair." Her fingers stroked his head, fluffing the soft brown hair, feeling the heat from his scalp meet the cool evening air.

"Ears." His tongue found her lobe, then traced the curves and inlets above it. Her knees weakening, Anne sagged against him, giving in to the tickling, tantalizing sensation.

But she had no intention of being a passive partner. This was her Jason, the man she loved and had waited for even without knowing it. They might have only a few days or weeks together—or maybe only tonight—before he jetted off to some new destination, but she meant to make the most of it.

"Throat." As she said the word, she leaned forward to nuzzle the pulse point at his collar. There was something warm and vulnerable about the way he closed his eyes and lifted his chin to give her access. Anne's tongue sought the contours of his throat, and she tingled with pleasure at the groan that welled up in him.

"Shoulders." His hands explored, kneaded, caressed. Until that moment, shoulders had never struck Anne as a particularly sensual part of the body, but he was teaching her otherwise.

"Hands." She brought his up to her lips, kissing the lightly callused palms, tasting the knuckles and fingertips. She could hear Jason's breath coming faster and faster. . . .

"Bed," he said.

"Bed?"

"If we go any farther, we could be arrested."

Damn propriety. Damn the neighbors. Damn what people would say. Still, it *was* getting cold. "Bed," she agreed.

It was outrageous how many obstacles had been erected by unfeeling engineers and architects. Stretches of sidewalk, a front door, a flight of stairs. Why couldn't people just fly over them, the way they seemed to in movies?

Finally, finally, they were alone in the bedroom. Yet Jason didn't appear to be in a hurry. After tossing his jacket across the back of a chair, he walked slowly around the room, running his hands across the furniture and pausing by the window to stare down at the patio.

"I was afraid you'd never let me come up here again." He swung around to face her. "Anne, we need to talk."

"Not now." She didn't want to hear about his next project in Japan, or Russia, or the far side of the moon. She didn't want to think about what came next and how much it was going to hurt. This one night belonged to her.

When he didn't respond, Anne crossed the room and unbuttoned his shirt with calm authority. Still Jason remained silent and motionless.

"I believe this comes next," she said, and stepped out of her dress.

"Anne, are you sure . . . ?"

"Are you chickening out?"

"Of course not."

"Well, I think we got as far as shoulders and hands. Your turn."

At first, as the silver light of the rising moon flowed through the window and touched Jason's face with a strange new expression, Anne feared he might pull away. Then he said quietly, "You know what comes next."

Gently, his fingers explored the swell of her breasts, teasing the nipples into erectness. Anne let her eyes fall shut, losing herself in pure bliss.

Jason gathered her into his arms and lifted her onto the bed. As if the moon had invaded her soul and infiltrated its light through her veins, Anne found herself touched with magic.

Every move Jason made was a solemn pact between them—his lips against her stomach, his fingers stroking her thighs, his cheek brushing her soft center. . . .

Promises made by moonlight lasted only until dawn. But Anne no longer cared.

Like a woman in a dream, she felt her mind merge with her body, so that there was no thought left but Jason. Every breath he drew echoed through her nerve endings. She wanted to touch him everywhere and to be touched by him.

As they explored, tasted, probed, stroked each other, it might have been for the first time. And perhaps for the last. But it was worth it, Anne knew.

This woman inside her, the one she had feared for so long, had become her mistress tonight. And finally Anne knew why women down the ages had thrown common sense to the wind and loved madly, wildly and endlessly.

She met kiss with kiss, caress with caress. They played across each other like currents in the ocean, merging and parting and merging again. It was impossible to tell where he ended and she began.

Waves of passion engulfed her. The moon called to the tides in her blood, and she responded without restraint.

Jason seemed to sense the change in her. Several times he paused to look at Anne in wonder. Each time, she assaulted him again with her silken body, driving conscious thought from his mind as it had been driven from hers.

As their bodies merged, they became one person and at the same time an entire universe. Flames played across the ocean beneath a fiery moon, and Anne cried out with joy.

Jason joined them again and again, sometimes almost roughly, and then with infinite tenderness. New and unsuspected hungers danced and raged through Anne as the two of them were swept up together, higher and higher, until they touched the moon and the world turned silver.

And then there was nothing but the counterpoint of their breathing and the last glorious rays fading over the ocean like the final notes of a symphony.

How could she ask any more of life than this, Anne wondered vaguely as she drifted into sleep. Her last awareness was of a sheet being pulled softly over her.

ANNE AWOKE with the odd sense of having been on a long trip to a strange land. Was she really still here in her familiar bedroom, outwardly unchanged since the day before?

She turned and saw that Jason's half of the bed was empty.

Despite the sharp pang of sorrow, Anne told herself that it was only natural he should have gone. It was useless to try to hold back the moon or the tide, or to tie Jason down to the dull routines of everyday life.

On the other hand, bacon had never been known to cook itself, and she could definitely smell bacon. Wasn't it just like Jason to cook for her before he left?

Anne showered quickly and threw on a jade-green sun dress that matched the color of her eyes. In every movement, she noted how new and fresh her body felt. Had she always had so many nerve endings, such sensitive skin, such a yearning to be touched?

Even the scents of Jason's cooking as she descended to the kitchen seemed somehow different from in her previous life, from the life known by that half-asleep woman who called herself Anne Eldridge, M.D.

Anne slipped up behind Jason at the stove and wrapped him in her arms, pressing her cheek against his back.

"Good morning." He grinned over his shoulder. "Thought I'd get a head start on fattening you up."

"Don't worry. The photographs don't frighten me anymore."

"Oh? Well, I plan to replace them with new ones, so don't speak too soon."

She drifted over to the table. "Are you going to send them to me?"

"Come again?"

"The pictures. From Japan or wherever you're going next."

Jason laid the strips of bacon on paper towels. "Actually, I've got something really difficult in mind."

How could he look so incredibly appealing wearing one of Ada's old aprons, Anne wondered. "What's that?"

"Well, have you ever heard of anyone photographing their own wedding?"

She stared at him blankly. "You're getting married?"

"Well, aren't we?"

"I—I'm not sure I see the point." She tried to choose her words carefully. "Jason, I do love you, but . . ."

He lifted the frying pan with teasing menace. "I'm getting awfully tired of your buts."

"That's because you never let me finish."

"Okay." He cracked half a dozen eggs into the pan, swirled in milk, salt and grated cheddar and set it on the burner. "You have until this is done—a couple of minutes. Make the most of it."

Why wasn't he taking her seriously? Anne inhaled deeply and poured out her thoughts. "Love isn't enough to make a marriage work. We're both old enough to know that."

"Granted." He stirred the eggs.

"I can't live the way you do. Oh, maybe for a while I'd enjoy traveling around, not having any roots, but then what? That's no way to raise children. And my medical training—I've started volunteering at a clinic for poor women. Jason, they need me. I don't have the right to throw all that away."

"I don't remember anyone asking you to." He added a dash of pepper to the pan.

"So what are you going to do? Leave me here while you roam the world? Or maybe get a job in some studio, taking high-school-graduation photos? How long would it be before you came to hate me?"

Jason transferred the eggs onto two plates, added the bacon and set them on the table. "Would you pour the coffee, please? It's already made."

Anne glared at him. "Did you hear what I said?"

"Yes, but I don't argue well on an empty stomach."

The man was impossible. And outrageous. And right. She was starving, too.

Anne poured the coffee and tackled both her food and her topic at the same time. "Well? Exactly what did you have in mind for our future?"

"We could try sausage for breakfast some mornings. Or maybe kippers. Have you ever had them? They're a kind of salty fish, I think. The English seem to like them." Jason stirred sugar into his coffee with a liberal hand.

"Jason!"

He heaved a deep mock sigh. "A man can't even eat his breakfast in peace. All right, Anne."

Her heart shivered upward toward her throat. Even though she'd been pushing for an answer, Anne suddenly wasn't sure she wanted to hear it.

"You've made a lot of assumptions." There was no teasing in his voice this time. "First of all, I'm not as poor as you think. I won't go out on a limb and say this book will make me wealthy, but I don't need to take a studio job."

Anne clasped her hands together under the table to stop herself from trembling. "That's—that's not really the problem. I'm not so much concerned about finances . . ."

"Wait." He cocked an eyebrow at her warningly. "You wanted to hear this, so don't interrupt."

She sipped her coffee and waited.

"You overheard me talking about a project I wanted to do on three continents. Well, there's no urgency about doing it now. Maybe I'll never do it. Or maybe we'll have to be apart for one or two months each year. Other couples manage."

A hundred responses rattled through her mind, but this time Anne shoved them aside. Jason didn't sound the way she'd expected, rash and even a bit flip. He'd obviously thought the subject through, and a glimmer of hope pierced her soul for the first time.

"I want children as much as you do," he went on. "You've probably noticed how much I love kids. Neither one of us wants them raised in hotel rooms or spending most of their lives in day-care. I can't promise a perfect solution. A lot of the time I can stay home with them; sometimes you can; and sometimes they may have to be with a sitter. Other families work it out, and we can, too."

He'd answered two of Anne's concerns but there was one major one left. "I'm glad your new book is earning more than you expected. But, Jason, I know you. Your life is all tied up with that camera. How long will it be before you can't stand being idle anymore, before you need to start a new project? Your work is as much a part of you as mine is for me."

Her gaze drifted, as it had so often these past few months, to the wall of photographs. The composition, the lighting, the printing were highly professional, of course, but there was something more.

Jason's own personality and insight shone through the work. Somehow, through the impersonal medium of a camera, he'd infused his subjects with his own heart. To take that away would be to diminish him, and that was something Anne would never do.

He reached across the table and touched her chin, turning her head until they faced each other.

"Oh, Anne. You're afraid I'll be unhappy, is that it?"

Wordlessly, she nodded.

He yearned to scoop her into his arms and kiss away the misery in her eyes. But this time, finally, he had to win Anne's intellect as well as her love, and so he went on talking.

"I've been reflecting on that myself. And as I said, there will probably be times when I'll need to go away for a while. But there's a lot to be found right here. In fact, there's one project I've been giving a lot of thought to, and my publisher feels it would be popular."

"Migrant farm workers?" Anne guessed. "Or smuggling—oh, Jason, you're not going to do anything dangerous, are you?"

"I was thinking more along the lines of—*The Private Life of a Baby*."

"A . . . baby?" The word caught in her throat. And then a teasing smile lit up her eyes. "Jason, are you trying to tell me you're pregnant?"

A joke was the last thing he'd expected from Anne at this point, and Jason stared at her in confusion for a moment before chuckling. "I wish I were. Then you'd have to do the honorable thing and marry me."

"I certainly believe in honor."

"Well, what do you think?"

She took another sip of coffee, not seeming to notice that it was cold by now. "You appear to have considered all the angles."

"There's just one left."

"What's that?"

"You, Anne." He reached for her hand under the table. "Are you going to hide out in that damn intellect of yours, or are you finally going to do the sensible thing and throw caution to the wind?"

She regarded him gravely. "I think I'll do the sensible thing."

There probably wasn't another woman in the world who would have accepted a marriage proposal with those words, Jason thought happily. But then, there wasn't another woman in the world he wanted to marry, either.

Chapter Seventeen

"I knew it! I knew it!"

Even over the phone, Anne could visualize the expression on her sister's face: pure glee. "If you say 'I told you so,' I'll never speak to you again."

"You'll have to. I'm going to be one of your bridesmaids, aren't I?"

"Of course. I mean, I guess so. To tell you the truth, I hadn't even thought about what kind of wedding we're going to have." Anne balanced the receiver on her shoulder and looked across the kitchen at Jason, who was leaning on the counter wearing a smug expression, as if he were a cat and she were a pitcher of cream.

"Now you sound more like yourself," Lori teased. "Anne, you can't just throw something together in the hospital cafeteria. Weddings take planning."

Anne groaned. "I can't ask Mom to come out for a few weeks to make the arrangements, not with Dad's ulcer flaring up, and I just don't have time. Oh, well. I'll think of something."

"When's it going to be?"

"The middle of October." A vision of the last wedding she'd attended—Ellie's—flashed through Anne's mind. The little church had been beautiful, and so had the reception; she simply hadn't thought about how much work must have gone into it. Let's see, there'd been flowers and champagne and musicians and that long ivory dress and food....

"Well, put Jason on!" Lori's impatient voice broke into Anne's contemplation. "I want to congratulate my new brother-in-law-to-be."

Anne handed the phone to Jason, half-listening to the exchange of good wishes as her thoughts flicked back to earlier this morning, when they'd called her parents. Her mother's quiet joy had radiated over the phone lines. The puzzling thing had been her father's reaction: he'd merely said, "It's about time. When we went on maneuvers in my day, we didn't take two months to do it."

Now, watching Jason grin as he chatted with Lori, it struck Anne that he must have told her father during the reunion that he intended to marry her. What nerve! But then, chutzpah was one of Jason's most endearing qualities.

A minute later, after they'd both said goodbye to Lori and Bob, Anne and Jason sat back down to restore themselves with a second round of scrambled eggs and bacon.

"Lori couldn't stop talking about the wedding," Jason observed, eyeing Anne over a cup of coffee. "Do you think we can still get reservations for Westminster Cathedral? I doubt she'll be satisfied with anything less."

Anne groaned. "Let's elope."

"Right." Chuckling, he flipped two more slices of rye bread into the toaster.

"No, seriously, Jason." Breakfast sat like a lump in her stomach. "I don't have time to plan a wedding. We could drive up to Lake Tahoe and have a combination wedding and honeymoon. Then maybe we could plan some kind of reception when we get back."

Jason stared at her in mock horror. "No way, Anne." She couldn't help noticing how wonderful he looked this morning, the angles of his face softened after a night of lovemaking, his eyes bright with happiness. Like her own. "I want everybody in the world to know we're getting married. This is important, and it deserves the honor of a real ceremony."

It hadn't taken them long to have their first disagreement—about ten hours into the engagement, she figured. Oh, well, she hadn't expected their temperamental differences to disappear, had she?

Then Anne had a stroke of brilliance. She knew exactly how to make him agree to elope! "Fine. We can have as big and fancy a wedding as you like, on one condition."

"Oh?"

"You do the whole thing." She gestured with her fork. "Find the location, hire the caterer—the whole shot. I'll help address invitations and buy myself a suit and decide on something for Ellie and Lori to wear if they want to be my bridesmaids. And that's all." Anne sat back triumphantly.

Jason didn't say anything for several minutes. Then he muttered, "I guess they put out books on how to do this sort of thing, don't they?"

It was Anne's turn to be thunderstruck. "You mean you'd actually consider it?"

"Why not? I'm between projects at the moment." He shrugged. "I'm good at planning things; that's what makes me such a terrific housekeeper."

"I don't believe it."

"You don't think a man can put on a wedding?"

"Well, of course, but—"

"Don't worry, I'll consult you on the major decisions." Obviously, his mind was already racing ahead. "Maybe a garden setting—October's a beautiful month for a wedding." Suddenly he snapped back to the present. "Now, about the honeymoon. Lake Tahoe is out. We can go there anytime."

Anne sighed. She really did want some time alone with Jason. But it would take a lot of work to clear her calendar. She could arrange for her partner to cover emergencies while she was gone, but she hated to dump all her regular office visits on him. She'd have to schedule as many of her prenatal checkups as possible before the wedding. And then there was her volunteer work at the clinic....

"All right, I'll concede that point," she said. "I think I can manage to get free for a week. How about Hawaii?"

From the shocked look on his face, you'd think she'd suggested they spend a weekend in Tijuana. "Hawaii? For a week? Anne, a honeymoon is supposed to be the experience of a lifetime. People around here run over to Hawaii for a week every time the airlines offer a discount special."

She had a sinking feeling. "What did you have in mind?"

"There's only one place romantic enough for a honeymoon: Paris. And we'll need three weeks at least. Preferably a month."

"A month!" Anne couldn't remember the last time she'd had a month off. During medical school, probably. "That's impossible."

"What if you got sick? You'd take a month off then, wouldn't you?"

He had a point, but she refused to give in. "Sure, but I'm not sick."

"Yes, you are. In the head. Anne, why don't you bring a few patients along so you'll feel at home? Maybe you could get guest privileges to practice at a hospital in Paris."

She had to laugh. "Okay, Jason. You win, but only if..."

"I know. I have to make the arrangements." He reached over and took out the two slices of toast, which had popped up several minutes ago. "No problem."

As she buttered her toast, Anne began to see the advantages of going to Paris. She'd never taken time to travel and had always wanted to. "While you're picking up a book on weddings, would you get a guidebook, too?"

"Okay." He stretched out, propping his feet up on one of the empty chairs. "I'm glad we finally agree on something."

"Mmm." Anne rested her chin on her palm. "We'll have to plan our time carefully so we can see everything. I mean, of course there are the obvious things like the Louvre and the Eiffel Tower, but I'd like to visit Versailles and the Bois de Boulogne, and I'm sure there are a lot of smaller museums...."

"Hold it!" Jason straightened up. "I'm not opposed to sight-seeing, but let's not overdo it. I had in mind some late nights in the clubs on the Left Bank, sleeping late, then lounging around at a sidewalk café for a few hours watching the world go by."

Anne bit off her arguments. "It looks like we're both going to have to give a little."

"That sounds fair to me."

They clasped hands across the breakfast table, letting the crumbs fall where they would. "We might even have a good time," Anne said, and they both laughed.

THE WOMAN with the upswept gray hairdo handed Jason a plate of sample hors d'oeuvres—Swedish meatballs, little sausages, stuffed mushrooms and barbecued chicken wings. "Of course, you'll want to bring your fiancée in before you make your selection."

Jason nibbled at the tasty if not particularly original offerings. This was the third caterer he'd visited today. "That won't be necessary."

The woman cleared her throat. "I'm sure she'll want to approve the menu. Or perhaps the bride's mother could do it?"

"The bride's mother is in Denver. I'm afraid I'm all there is. Couldn't you pretend I'm wearing a dress?" Jason knew he was bordering on rudeness, but he'd received the same reception everywhere.

Florists, photographers—he'd conceded that he couldn't shoot his own wedding—and bakeries had all asked, with varying degrees of subtlety, when the bride-to-be would accompany him to make the final selection.

They seemed united in believing either that he was incapable of making such decisions or that she'd end up countermanding his orders.

"Well, really." The gray-haired woman looked affronted. "Certainly you can place the order if you like. It's only that it's customary for the bride to review the menu."

"My bride couldn't care less what she eats as long as it doesn't talk back to her," Jason assured the woman. "Now, what do you have in the way of caviar?"

Half an hour later, driving back to Irvine, he had to admit Anne had been right about one thing: planning a wedding was a major undertaking.

He'd never realized there was so much involved. The first time he got married, Jill had made all the arrangements. Looking back, Jason couldn't remember much except that everything was white, which he'd considered rather boring. This time, he'd chosen a color scheme of gray and magenta, which he was beginning to regret. He'd had to drive all over Orange County to find paper plates and napkins in those colors.

There'd been the need to line up a minister—fortunately, Ellie's pastor turned out to be a sympathetic spirit—and a location. There, Jason had gotten lucky. Anne's partner, John, owned a beautiful old house on a quarter-acre lot in Santa Ana and, as his wedding present, had offered the use of his garden.

Then he'd had to find a printer for the invitations and line up musicians and coerce Anne into touring jewelry stores with him. Fortunately, once she was actually confronted with a trayful of gold and diamonds she'd forgotten her impatience, and they'd spent several hours selecting a sparkling pair of his-and-hers rings.

Yes, things were finally coming together, but there was a lot left to do.

Jason pulled up in front of the house and had nearly reached the front steps when he heard the phone ringing. Hurriedly, he let himself into the house and grabbed the phone in the hallway.

"Hello?"

"Jason? This is Anne's great-aunt Myra." The voice might be a bit thin and dry, but it crackled with energy. "I just talked to Janine—Anne's mother—and I can tell she needs her mind put at rest about the wedding."

"Everything's fine."

"I don't doubt it for a minute, but a helping hand never hurt. A friend of mine is driving over your way—" Myra lived in Palm Springs, as he recalled, about two hours from Irvine "—and if you don't mind, I thought I'd ride along."

"We'd love to have you," he said, and meant it. "I don't know if Janine told you, but Anne's too busy, so I'm planning the wedding myself."

"Yes, and a good thing, too, because if it were up to Anne we'd be cutting the wedding cake with scalpels." Obviously, the concept of a man handling a wedding didn't faze Great-aunt Myra. "I'll see you day after tomorrow then, around four."

As he hung up, Jason realized he was going to be glad of the help. And he was looking forward to seeing the feisty old lady again, too.

But before she got here, there was one more point he needed to resolve with Anne. And he wanted to tackle it tonight, so they'd have plenty of time to work it out before Myra arrived.

Anne looked harried but happy when she arrived home from work at six. Jason waited until they were both pleasantly stuffed on roast chicken and then escorted her into the living room, with glasses of white wine to relax them.

"How's it going?" Anne curled up on the couch, tucking her feet under her. She looked younger and softer than she used to, despite her heavy work load, and her green eyes glowed. For a moment, Jason was tempted to forget about the business at hand and take Anne into his arms, but he forced himself to postpone that pleasure.

"Great." He told her about the menu he'd chosen, featuring caviar, lobster and pâté, and about Myra's upcoming visit. "Now, there's one more decision we have to make."

"What's that?"

"The ceremony itself." Jason hesitated, not sure how best to continue.

Anne waved a hand airily. "Oh, the usual will be fine—love, honor and cherish."

"Yes, but I want a two-part ceremony. Before the minister actually marries us, I think we should say a few words ourselves."

She wrinkled her nose. "You mean recite poetry and sprinkle each other with flower petals? I thought that went out with the Sixties."

Jason laughed. "I wouldn't dare suggest you recite poetry, Anne. Listen, maybe I'd better explain my philosophy about weddings."

She took a sip of wine. "I didn't know you had one."

"Neither did I. It's come on me suddenly over the past week." He reached back absentmindedly and rubbed his neck. It had gotten stiff during all the driving he'd done looking for magenta-and-gray paper goods. "You know what normally happens when you go to a wedding? Usually you know either the bride or the groom well but you have no idea how they met or what kind of relationship they have."

"So?"

"Then you stare at their backs while the minister conducts the ceremony, and then down the aisle they go, and you shake their hands in the receiving line and eat some cake and go home. And you don't know anything more about them than you did when you came in."

She regarded him dubiously. "What are you suggesting?"

"I think the people we invite are special, and we want them to feel after the ceremony that they've really participated with us, that they understand why we're getting married and what it means to us."

Skepticism was a mild word for the expression on her face. "And how do you propose to accomplish that?"

"I think we should tell them."

The sound of fingers tapping on the oak end table was the first response, followed by, "You've got to be kidding!"

"Why?"

Anne glared at him. "Jason, I'm not going to stand up there and tell everybody about our private life."

"I don't mean the gory details. But don't you think they'd be interested to know how we resolved our differences and what kind of marriage we plan to have?"

"Of course they would!" Irritably, she brushed a lock of hair out of her eyes. "People are always curious about one another. But that's the sort of thing I'd expect to discuss with my mother or sister in private—not tell the whole world!"

"Hold on a minute." He tried to keep his voice calm. "Obviously, we'll have to decide which details to leave in and which to leave out. I just want us to agree in principle that we'll make some sort of statement beforehand." Then he threw in his ace. "You said we could have any kind of ceremony I wanted as long as I did the work. Isn't that right?"

"Well, yes, but I didn't mean we could say our vows while jumping out of airplanes or snorkeling in the ocean! I meant within reasonable limits."

Jason didn't answer right away. It was hard to handle Anne when she was upset. He supposed he could go along with a conventional ceremony, but...

A new thought occurred to him. "You know why I picked gray and magenta for our colors?"

"Because you like them, I assume." She wasn't going to give an inch.

"Yes, but also because my first wedding was white. Entirely, totally, boringly white."

"I haven't bugged you about the colors, have I?"

"And our ceremony was so ordinary I don't remember a bit of it. I don't even remember saying 'I do,' although I'm sure I must have. Anne, this is different. Our marriage is something special, and our life together will be, too, and I want our ceremony to reflect that."

"Oh." She bit her lower lip reflectively. "You know, that's a sweet thing to say. I certainly don't want this wedding to be like your first one, either."

"I thought we might start by describing how we met," he said. "It's kind of funny, when you think about it."

"Yes, I guess it was. Are you going to tell them how you stole my heart with your fettucine?"

He knew better than to show by so much as a grin that he knew he'd won.

THERE WERE a number of things about this household and this wedding that would have been unthinkable in Myra's day. Back then, the bride-to-be certainly didn't sleep with her future husband or, if she did, they made sure nobody knew about it. And she spent her time stitching up her trousseau, not stitching up patients, unless she'd gone off to play Florence Nightingale in the Great War.

However, those things didn't bother a person anywhere near as much as the dress.

You couldn't even call it a dress. Anne had bought herself a suit, the kind a bride might take on her honeymoon, but she was planning to wear it to the ceremony itself.

It was an attractive suit, in the soft shade of gray that Jason had picked as one of the wedding colors. But Anne needed a proper gown, and Myra felt she owed it to her niece Janine, Anne's mother, to make sure the bride got one.

Now, how was she to accomplish that?

Jason was a sterling young man, but he was no help in this department. When Myra broached the subject, he merely chuckled and said, "I'm just glad she's not planning to wear a surgical gown."

The only person who might be able to help was that nice young Ellie, Anne's matron of honor. She'd been over almost every night, for one thing or another, trying in vain to talk Anne into being the guest of honor at a shower, making sure Anne got Lori's measurements for her bridesmaid's dress, helping prepare invitations and so on.

There wasn't much more than a week left before the wedding. Why, Janine and Sutter would be arriving in a few days! Something had to be done quickly about the gown, and Myra seized the first opportunity.

Anne and Ellie had been planning to go shopping that Saturday morning to pick out Ellie's and Lori's dresses, but wouldn't you know it, Anne got called in to the hospital. So Myra volunteered to go along instead.

As soon as she got into the car with Ellie, Myra said, "About Anne's dress."

And Ellie said, "I was thinking the same thing."

They smiled at each other.

"The truth is, I've been nagging her to go shopping with me for weeks, and she kept putting it off," Ellie said. "I think she suspects I wanted her to try on gowns."

"She wears a size nine. I looked through her closet," Myra replied.

"I've got a list of shops." Ellie was obviously a kindred spirit. "But I don't want to wear you out."

"The only thing that would wear me out is having to watch my grand-niece get married in a plain old suit."

The first shop didn't have much, but the second had an excellent selection and a most cooperative manager. Ellie quickly picked matching pink dresses for the bridesmaids—Jason had approved the color in advance—and Myra impulsively selected a dignified outfit for herself, with a small gauzy cape that gave her shoulders a filled-out look.

After making their purchases, they explained the situation to the owner, who agreed to let them take several gowns home for Anne to try on when they offered to leave a large deposit.

"I hope she doesn't kill us," said Ellie as the two drove away.

Myra wasn't worried. Her grand-niece was a mighty stubborn young woman, but she *was* a woman. How would she be able to resist these wonderful creations of lace and satin when they were laid right in front of her?

THIS WAS ONE TIME Anne hadn't really minded having her Saturday interrupted by work. Not that she objected to looking at dresses with Ellie. The problem was, the wedding was becoming all-consuming to everyone around her. Jason, Myra and even Ellie talked of little else—except at the office, where Ellie kept a discreet silence on the subject.

The phone seemed to ring a dozen times an evening with RSVPs, and the dining-room table was covered with gifts sent by friends and relatives who couldn't attend.

So far, except for writing thank-you notes, Anne had kept her resolve to stay out of it. But it hadn't been easy. She would hear snippets of conversation that aroused her curiosity. Had Jason ordered the pineapple cake or the one with layers of chocolate and raspberry? How was he going to arrange the platform for the ceremony? And what kind of music had he decided on?

One slip and she'd be a goner. Anne simply couldn't do things halfway; she knew herself too well. She had to stay aloof or she'd cave in altogether, and going shopping with Ellie might have weakened her resolve.

It was midafternoon by the time she got home. The house was quiet. By the middle of the week, her parents would be arriving, and then Lori's family. Anne looked forward to seeing them, but it was nice to have a moment's peace and quiet, too.

She reclined on the couch and leafed through a travel brochure. Paris! She was glad they hadn't decided on Hawaii, even though she wanted to go there someday, too. But as Jason said, it would be easy to fly to the islands for a week, whereas they might not go to Europe again for years.

Women's voice floated in from outside, and Anne hurried to the door in time to hold it while Ellie staggered in under a load of clothing bags. Myra followed right behind.

"You two look as though you bought out the store." Anne relieved Ellie of several bags. "What's going on?"

She didn't miss the smile that passed between the two women. "We couldn't resist," Ellie answered. "We brought home a couple of gowns for you to try on."

Anne might have known they were up to something! "I already bought my suit. Really, what's the sense in buying a dress I'll only wear once?"

"This is not the time to be practical." Myra shepherded them up the stairs. "The least you can do is try the gowns on before you send them back."

Anne didn't want to be rude to her great-aunt. "Well, okay, but don't get your hopes up."

Seizing the opportunity, Ellie hurried ahead to Anne's bedroom and hung the dresses in the closet. "Come on! There's no telling when Jason will be home, and you don't want him to see you trying on your dress before the wedding, do you?"

"Why not?" Anne asked as she kicked off her shoes.

The other two women stared at her in disbelief.

"Sometimes I wonder if you were raised on another planet." Myra shook her head.

"Oh—it's traditional, isn't it?" Anne slipped out of the slacks and blouse she'd worn to the hospital. "But it's traditional for the woman to plan the wedding, too."

"That's different," Ellie said. "I mean, it's not bad luck for the man to plan the wedding, probably because nobody ever thought it would happen."

"Well, let's get on with this."

"Try this one first." Ellie lifted a white gown out of its bag. It was a simple, elegant style with a high neck and a V-shaped yoke.

Anne slid it over her head, grateful for her friend's help in zipping up the back. Then she stepped in front of the mirror.

The dress fit, but the color was too stark against Anne's pale skin and dark-blond hair. "It makes me look washed-out." She turned so the other two women could see.

"I was afraid of that," said Myra. "But don't worry, we have others."

"Even Princess Diana wore ivory," Ellie added as she lifted down another dress.

This one was a rich cream color that flattered Anne's coloring. Trimmed with lots of lace and ribbon, it had puffed sleeves and a Cinderella dreaminess to it.

"Now, that's more like it." Myra folded her arms as if daring Anne to disagree.

Yes, it was beautiful, Anne had to admit. When she was eighteen years old, she'd dreamed about someday picking a wedding dress like this.

That was precisely the problem. The gown was lovely, and she looked fresh and bridelike in it, but she didn't feel like herself. She felt as if she were masquerading as the girl she'd been fifteen years ago.

"There's nothing wrong with the dress, but I can't get married in it." Reluctantly, Anne faced her great-aunt. "I feel as if I'm wearing a costume. Look, I appreciate all the effort you went to, but I'm too old for this sort of dress."

Myra regarded her combatively for a moment and then apparently thought better of it. "You do have a point, I suppose."

"That's why we brought this one." Ellie lifted down a third clothes bag. "Actually, your great-aunt had her doubts, but I persuaded her that it fit in with Jason's color scheme, so we should at least give it a chance."

The dress must have been intended for a bridesmaid. There couldn't be another bride on earth, even in California, who would choose to wear that shocking shade of magenta.

"It certainly is—bright." Anne regarded the gown doubtfully.

"Well, put it on!" Ellie unzipped the ivory dress, and soon the change was made.

Anne studied herself in the mirror. She never would have chosen this color, even for a street dress, yet it highlighted the rose tones of her skin and made her eyes look brighter than usual. The fabric itself was a very rich, soft silk, cut in clean, classic lines without any ribbons or lace.

"I suppose I wouldn't have to worry about getting hit by a bus," she murmured. "You could see this thing for blocks."

"Light your way home at night," Myra agreed.

"It looks terrific," said Ellie.

Reluctantly, Anne had to agree with her. It was a smashing dress. Why, she'd even be able to wear it again, perhaps on her honeymoon; didn't people dress up for the evening in Paris?

The more she looked at the dress, the more she couldn't bear the idea of returning it to the store. How could she let someone else own this gown that had so obviously been made with Anne in mind?

"Okay, I'm sold." She fingered a fold of the silk. "I'll take it."

Ellie clapped her hands in excitement. "I'm so glad! With the gray tuxedo Jason's planning to wear, you'll look fabulous!"

All Myra could say was "I hope Janine doesn't kill me."

ON TUESDAY NIGHT, Anne's parents arrived, followed the next day by Lori, Bob and the boys. The house throbbed with laughter and giggles and shared confidences. It was impossible not to pick up the spirit of excitement.

Jason's parents arrived on Wednesday. At the airport there was a moment of awkwardness as they stepped off the ramp from the plane, and then Jason's mother caught Anne's hands and said, "I'm so glad he's finally going to settle down. You're wonderful for him; I can tell from his letters."

Jason's brother, Ed, who was single, flew in Thursday morning to be the best man. The trip from Boston was too expensive for Jason's sisters to make, but they sent their love and good wishes.

Delighted though she was to see everyone, Anne couldn't help feeling a bit dazed. When she and Jason decided to get married, it had been a private moment. She hadn't thought about how many other people would be affected. The realization that her marriage was part of a web of relationships that went back for generations and involved people thousands of miles away was a bit daunting.

The night before the wedding, while Jason and the other men were downstairs fighting to conquer the world in a game of Risk and most of the women were playing bridge, Anne's mother came up to her bedroom and sat on the bed, just as she used to do in Anne's high-school days.

"Before I was married, my mother gave me a heart-to-heart talk about the facts of life," Janine observed wryly. "In view of your occupation, I'm sure you know more about that than I do."

Anne finished removing her makeup at the vanity table and turned around. "Oh, Mom, it's the sentiment that counts."

"Then you won't mind if I give you a few words of advice." Janine took a deep breath. "Anne, I can't help wondering if you really know what it means, getting married. You seem so, well, preoccupied with your work, as if you've kept yourself aloof from everything."

"Mom, it's the wedding I've stayed out of, not the marriage!" Anne protested.

"Yes, but I never saw such a calm bride before. You don't seem to have the least bit of jitters."

"Why should I? Jason and I love each other, and we're old enough to know what we want out of life."

Her mother searched for the right words. "I know, but you sound so—intellectual about it! Anne, this is an emotional time. You should be at least a little scared of the big commitment you're making. I know you and Jason love each other, and I'm sure you'll be happy together, but...." She paused. "I'm not entirely sure what I want to say. Just that I don't think you've really come to terms with what it means to get married."

Anne smiled. "Oh, Mom, you always were the sensitive one in the family, and I've always just clomped ahead. But I've done all right, haven't I?"

"I only want you to be happy." Janine's eyes sparkled with tears. "I hope you will be, Anne."

She hurried across the room and they hugged each other.

I will be happy, Anne thought. *With Jason, how could I help it?*

ON SATURDAY MORNING, Jason went out to pick up the wedding cake and to make sure the chairs and platform were set up properly at John's house. The wedding wasn't until three o'clock in the afternoon, but there was a lot to do.

Anne awoke at nine, feeling a touch nervous, but she quickly forgot her concerns in the bustling household. She even cooked breakfast, in Jason's absence, and found herself reassuring everyone around her that the wedding would come off fine.

Maybe her mother had a point. In a way, Anne felt as if she were going to someone else's wedding, even though she and Jason had walked through the ceremony Thursday night with the wedding party and the minister. And she and Jason had spent hours preparing what they were going to say. And they'd gone down to the county registrar's office to get their marriage license earlier in the week. Still, she felt as if they were rehearsing for a play, not a wedding.

It's just the way I am, Anne told herself as she popped another pound of bacon into the microwave oven for latecomers and covered it with a paper towel to prevent splattering. *I'm not the excitable type.*

"Aunt Anne, are you going to have a baby?" Jeb asked as he and Sammy raced in and grabbed biscuits off a plate.

"I hope so, one of these days," she said absently. "Why?"

Jeb shrugged. Then Sammy poked him, and Jeb said, "Well, this boy at school, his sister's getting married, and she's stagnant."

"I think you mean pregnant." Anne looked up, embarrassed, as Great-aunt Myra came into the kitchen.

"Who's pregnant?" Myra regarded her sharply.

"Jeb's friend's sister," Anne said. "He wondered if I was. But I'm not."

"At least you're doing something the old-fashioned way." Myra helped herself to a plate of scrambled eggs from the sideboard.

The phone rang. "I'll get it!" Jeb and Sammy shouted at the same time and nearly collided in their rush to answer it.

Anne lifted the phone off its cradle before her nephews could attack it.

"Dr. Eldridge?" It was the receptionist from the clinic where she volunteered. "I know you're getting married today, but we've got a problem."

Immediately, Anne tuned out the noisy scene around her. "What's wrong?"

"You remember Anita Nuñez? Well, she's in labor and she refuses to go to the hospital unless you'll be there. I offered to drive her, but she won't get in the car."

Anne glanced at the clock and saw it was ten-thirty. She didn't need to be at John's until one. "How far apart are the pains?"

"Twenty minutes, but they seem to be speeding up."

She calculated quickly. "You'll have to bring her down to Irvine. Can you do that?"

"Sure."

"I'll meet you at the hospital."

Anita Nuñez was a heavyset young woman who had previously delivered a stillborn baby at a hospital and blamed the doctor. Anne doubted that he was at fault, but she certainly didn't want Anita giving birth at home and possibly losing another baby.

She explained the situation to Great-aunt Myra. "Please tell everyone not to worry. I'll be at John's house in plenty of time."

"Bring the lady along. Maybe you could deliver her baby during the ceremony. I doubt anyone would be surprised, knowing you," Myra said.

Anne chuckled. "Okay, okay, but this really is an emergency. Ask Lori to pack my makeup and curling iron, would you? Thanks!"

And she was gone, leaving Great-aunt Myra to try to explain to the others why the bride had gone to work on her wedding day.

Chapter Eighteen

With John's and Ed's help, Jason spent about an hour arranging the chairs and setting up the platform and speaker system. Fortunately, the weather had turned out beautiful, sunny with a hint of crispness, and John's yard was the perfect setting. Tall hibiscus bushes blocked any view of neighboring houses, and the lawn was a velvety green that testified to professional gardening.

About noon, Jason reviewed his checklist. He already had the plates and eating utensils on hand. The cake was safe in the kitchen, and he'd picked up his tuxedo yesterday.

It was hard to believe everything was going so smoothly.

As he strolled across the yard, straightening the alignment of a chair here and there, he couldn't help smiling to himself at the story Ellie had told about Anne's dress.

He couldn't wait to see what it looked like. Even more, he couldn't wait to see Anne, radiant as a bride.

If he had any quibble about the past few weeks, it was that he and Anne hadn't had nearly enough time together. For one thing, there always seemed to be someone else around—Great-aunt Myra tried to be discreet, but she *was* their houseguest. And Ellie, much as he liked her, had a way of getting underfoot.

Also, Anne had kept busy at work, and Jason suspected he knew why. Just as she'd caved in about the dress, she would have thrown herself into the wedding preparations if she'd spent much time discussing them. So she'd stayed away.

He missed her, but he didn't really mind. After all, he was going to have Anne to himself for the next month, in one of the most romantic cities in the world. They would make up for lost time and then some.

Jason swung around and regarded the small platform, reflecting that it looked awfully bare. Surely he'd had something else in mind. . . .

The flowers!

Sheer panic shot through Jason. He'd gone through half a dozen florist shops, had settled on the one he wanted and the type of arrangement—but he'd forgotten to call back and place the order!

With a groan, he let his mind race over the possibilities. He could run out and select something himself, but then he wouldn't be here to make sure the caterer and other tradespeople got set up properly.

Ellie had enough on her hands, taking care of the dresses. And he couldn't count on Ed to make an appropriate selection. What his brother knew about flowers could be stuck in a buttonhole.

Maybe Deanie and her husband . . . but they had the baby to hassle with. Surely there must be someone he could ask who wouldn't be too inconvenienced.

Rosa! She'd been bursting with curiosity over the details of the wedding, as imparted by Jason across the backyard fence, and was planning to bring Juanita. There was still time for her to run by a florist shop.

He raced into the house and dialed her number, hoping she hadn't left early for any reason. Luckily, she was still there, and Jason explained the situation and asked her to pick out two large vases or baskets of flowers.

"Pink flowers, or a deep rose color, something that will fit in with the color scheme. I'll pay you back when you get here, if that's okay. Can you do it?"

"No problem," said Rosa. "I was hoping you'd let me help. I'll get Juanita to help me make the selection. We'll be there as soon as we can."

Hanging up the phone, Jason exhaled with relief. He knew he was going to get kidded about the oversight; but as long as the flowers arrived on time, he didn't mind.

His first inkling of trouble didn't come until one o'clock, when Ellie drove up in her car with Lori. Jason glanced down the street, expecting to see Anne's car right behind, but there was no sign of it.

"She had to go deliver a baby," were the first words Ellie said as she got out of the car.

"A baby?" Jason stared at her in disbelief. "She's not on call today."

Quickly, Ellie explained about the woman from the clinic. "According to Myra, she swore she'd be here on time."

Jason refused to give in to negative thinking. "Then I'm sure she will be. Why don't you go upstairs and get ready? Clear the decks so you can help her when she shows up."

"Right." Ellie pulled some garment bags out of the back seat. "Dennis will be bringing the rest of the family in our van."

"Great." Jason stood there staring down the street for a moment after Ellie and Lori disappeared into the house, willing Anne to appear.

A car turned onto the block. Could it be . . . no, that was Rosa's car, not Anne's. As they pulled up, he stepped forward and held the passenger door for Juanita.

"You wouldn't believe what happened!" Rosa came around to open the hatchback. "We went to two shops and they were nearly cleaned out! They said there's a lot of weddings this weekend. So look what we got!"

The back of the car was bursting with roses—not tame, odorless florist roses but vibrant blooms in a riot of colors that filled the air with their fragrance.

"My employers are out of town and they told me to cut all the flowers I wanted," Juanita explained.

"It's the best we could do." Rosa spread her hands apologetically. "I'm sorry there weren't enough pink ones."

"That's okay. It's my own fault." At this point, Jason was a lot less worried about the flowers than about the bride. "Let's go and see what kind of vases we can scare up."

With the help of John's wife, two large Chinese vases were soon set up in front of the platform, adding a festive note to the surroundings. They might not fit into the color scheme, Jason decided, but the roses were much prettier than a formal arrangement, and they certainly smelled a lot better.

The house began filling up. The caterer and her assistants bustled about the kitchen, the musicians tuned their instruments, and the photographer looked perplexed at the announcement that the bride was not there yet.

"I'll put in a call to the hospital," John said. A few minutes later, he came back. "She's in the delivery room now. It shouldn't be much longer."

Jason glanced at his watch. It was five minutes after two.

Early guests began to arrive. Ellie volunteered to make sure they signed the guest book, while the musicians launched into a selection of melodies from Rodgers and Hammerstein, as Jason had requested.

The Hernandez yard took on the look of a garden party. More guests showed up, arranging their gaily wrapped presents on the gift table. The minister, looking suitably official in a black suit, chatted with Ellie as she greeted the guests, most of whom she knew.

By two-fifteen, Jason was really worried. He knew Anne wouldn't purposely be late to her own wedding, but the welfare of a patient came first. In a way, he had to agree with her. And yet, he couldn't help thinking that if she'd been as involved with this event as he had, she would somehow have managed to be here by now.

He could tell that some of her relatives were thinking the same thing. The guests, of course, had no idea what was going on.

The hands of his watch inched toward two-thirty. Where the hell was Anne?

THE DELIVERY HAD BEEN a difficult one, compounded by the patient's fear of losing this baby, too. Her tension had increased her pain and made it harder for the baby to come out.

But he *had* come out, a strong, lusty little boy who yelled his head off, peed on a nurse and quieted immediately when placed in his mother's arms.

Wearily, Anne congratulated the woman and made her way out of the delivery room. Then, for the first time in hours, she glanced at a clock. It was almost two-thirty.

Two-thirty! She was supposed to get married in half an hour!

Anne washed up in record time and sprinted for her car. It was ten minutes to three when she reached John's house and to her dismay discovered she had to park two blocks away. Who'd ever heard of a bride who couldn't find a place to park at her own wedding?

She ran the two blocks, ignoring the startled gasps of last-minute guests as they spotted her, and dashed into the house.

To his credit, Jason refrained from saying, "It's about time." Instead, he said, "Lori's got the curling iron ready upstairs. Did the delivery go all right?"

"Fine." Anne loved him for asking, but she didn't have time to say that now. Instead, she sprinted up the stairs.

The next few minutes sped by in a blur. Ellie and Lori would have received a gold medal if preparing the bride were an Olympic event. Lori curled Anne's hair while Ellie applied makeup, and then they both helped her into the dress.

By a quarter past three, she was ready to go. The finishing touch was her bouquet of lace and ribbons. She'd decided she preferred its old-fashioned elegance to having a conventional bouquet of flowers; and, as Lori had pointed out, this way the bridesmaids could keep their versions as mementos.

"Don't worry," Ellie said. "Weddings never start on time anyway."

Then her sister and her best friend hurried out to take their places in the procession.

Anne stood in the front hall, trying to get her bearings. The house felt empty, except for the clinking noises coming from the kitchen. In the morning's haste, she'd forgotten where she was supposed to await her cue. Or what her cue was. Or what she and Jason were supposed to say. Or...

"Scared?" Sutter Eldridge strolled to his daughter's side.

"I—I guess so," Anne admitted. "Oh, Dad, I'm glad you're here. I can't remember anything."

"As long as you don't forget how to say 'I do,' you'll be fine."

Anne clung to her father's arm. What was wrong with her? Her body simply wasn't functioning properly. Her ankles nearly buckled and her knees wobbled as her father guided her out the side door to a shaded area where, she now remembered, they were supposed to await their musical signal. Her heart was thudding much too fast, probably approaching tachycardia, and as for her brain, well, she might as well donate it to science, since she obviously would never be able to use it again.

Calm down, girl. Focus on your surroundings. That ought to help.

From here she couldn't see the guests, but she could hear them. Their chatter had an expectant quality to it. And the music—it was a medley from *The Sound of Music*. Didn't that mean something?

The players began a slow version of "Maria," as in the wedding scene of the movie, and Anne remembered that this was Lori's and Ellie's cue. She tried to imagine them walking down the aisle as they had Thursday night but this time wearing their floating pink dresses. What came next? Was Jason already waiting by the platform? Had he forgotten his part, too?

Then the music swelled into a stately rendition of "Climb Every Mountain," and Sutter Eldridge stepped forward with Anne on his arm.

They moved out from the shady nook and suddenly she could see everyone, rows and rows of people turning to look at her, smiling and nodding to each other. She knew almost everyone, and yet at this moment she couldn't have coughed up a single name, not even her own mother's.

Marriage. How many millions of brides had gone forward as she was doing now, into an unknown future? As well as she knew Jason, Anne realized with a start that she had no idea what lay in store for them. Marriage meant a whole lifetime—children, and growing old together, and facing the unexpected. There were sure to be some difficult times; would she and Jason weather them? This was a huge commitment they were making. It was like stepping out blindfolded, not knowing how much light and how much darkness lay ahead or whether she was really ready for it.

For one panic-stricken moment, Anne wanted to flee. Then she saw Jason.

He was standing next to his brother, to the minister's left, but she scarcely noticed anyone else. Only Jason, and the glow of pure love in his eyes. The panic faded into nothingness, and a bubble of joy rose in Anne, so powerful she thought she would float the rest of the way up the aisle.

Of course the future was a blank. No one knew what lay ahead, whether they got married or not. But one thing she did know: that she and Jason could overcome any obstacles.

UNTIL THE MOMENT when he saw Anne move toward him on her father's arm, Jason's head had been buzzing with details. Did the flowers look okay? Would the public-address system work properly? Did Ed have the rings?

Seeing Anne jolted him back to himself. Jason's first thought was, *that dress certainly is bright!* His second was, *God, she's beautiful.*

Anne glanced up and her eyes met his. He'd never seen her look quite so—ecstatic. And he suspected he looked equally blissful as he watched her mount the steps.

Sutter handed his daughter to Jason with a wink that the guests couldn't see, then went to join his wife in the front row.

As they'd planned, Jason and Anne joined hands and stepped up to the microphone.

"Before we take our vows, we wanted to tell you something about us—how we met and fell in love and why we decided to get married," Jason said. "We want you all to feel that you know us and are part of this special occasion with us."

He glanced at Anne and she smiled at him reassuringly. "I guess you could say it's a bit surprising we ever got together," Jason went on. "The first time I met Anne, I thought she was already married."

"And I thought he was the strangest-looking housekeeper I'd ever seen," she added.

The words flowed easily as they ran over the key moments in their relationship: the discovery that they loved each other; his realization that he hadn't told her he didn't plan to be a jet-set father; and even how she'd agreed to have a big wedding only if Jason would plan it himself.

"So if you don't like the food, you know who to blame," he said, and heard several people chuckle. It was a warm sound, and he knew he and Anne had accomplished what they intended: strengthening the bond between themselves and their friends and family, sharing their happiness.

Then they turned to the minister and the ceremony began. It seemed to Jason to go much too fast. Before he knew it, the rings had been exchanged and the vows said, and he was kissing his bride.

They were married. Really and truly married.

To the tune of "Oh, What a Beautiful Mornin'," they strolled back down the aisle together. Jason had to fight off the impulse to skip, and he suspected Anne did, too.

They'd decided against a formal receiving line, and he was glad. Within minutes, the scene turned into a rollicking party, with good food, champagne and dancing. Anne's nephews were galloping about the lawn with shouts of delight, and Rosa and Juanita chatted merrily with Mrs. Hernandez. Even Great-aunt Myra got a little tipsy, and Jason could have sworn there was a flirtatious look in her eye as she danced with the best man.

ANNE HATED TO LEAVE. She'd never expected to enjoy the reception this much. Looking back, she realized she'd thought of it as something to endure; instead, this had turned out to be one of the most enchanting afternoons of her life. They'd gone through all the rituals she'd always thought were corny—cutting the cake and posing for photographs and tossing her bouquet, which had been caught by John's eldest daughter. And she'd loved every minute of it.

But it was getting late, and they had a plane to catch that evening.

Reluctantly, she began saying goodbye to everyone who meant so much to her. True, she was going away for only a month, but when she came back she would be changed, perhaps in subtle ways, but definitely not the old pigheaded Anne Eldridge.

Now that she'd discovered what marriage really meant, she wasn't going to waste her time disagreeing over petty details. If Jason wanted them to wallpaper the house in bright orange, or plant Venus-flytraps in the backyard, or take up snorkeling, that was fine with her.

"Don't worry about the wedding presents and locking up the house. We'll take care of everything," her mother promised, and gave her daughter a big hug. "Oh, Anne, I'm so glad for you."

"You know what?" Anne blinked back an unexpected film of moisture from her eyes. "You were right. I *didn't* realize what I was getting into. But I do now, Mom."

"It was a beautiful ceremony." Her father slipped his arm around Anne's waist. "Frankly, I wondered what on earth you two were going to say, but, well, I'm glad you did it."

"I feel as if I understand you better now," her mother admitted.

Jason's parents, too, were beaming as they said their farewells. "Welcome to the family." His mother touched Anne's dress admiringly. "That color's a bit shocking, but it looks wonderful on you."

The last word, as usual, came from Great-aunt Myra. "Don't sit around your hotel room writing postcards. And, Jason, don't let Anne get near a hospital, even if she breaks her leg."

Then Jason escorted Anne to the limousine he'd hired to whisk them home for their luggage and on to the airport.

"We cut that a bit close, didn't we?" Anne had retrieved her wristwatch and saw it was getting late. She would barely have time to change into her suit.

"Oh, I'd say we've got about half an hour to spare." Jason began whistling "I Cain't Say No," which immediately made Anne suspicious.

"Just what did you have in mind?" Surely he didn't intend to start their marriage with a hurried fling in the bedroom! Although, having spent the past few hours noticing how handsome he looked in his gray tuxedo, Anne decided she wouldn't mind stripping it off him.

"I think there's a cookie boutique on our way."

"A what?"

"You heard me."

Anne stared at him in consternation. "Yes, but—aren't you full of wedding cake?"

"There's always room for cookies."

"I don't believe it!" She sank back against the seat. "Our wedding day, and he wants to go to a cookie boutique!"

"Look at it this way," Jason said. "They probably don't even have chocolate-chip cookies in Paris. Don't you want to stock up?"

"We'll probably miss our flight!" Anne glared at him. "Of all the crazy ideas . . ."

"I don't think it's crazy." He rolled down the interior window and told the chauffeur where to stop.

"If you think I'm going into a cookie boutique in my wedding dress . . ." And then Anne started to laugh.

"What's so funny?"

"Me!" She leaned over and rubbed her cheek against Jason's shoulder. "An hour ago I was resolving not to argue over little things. And here I am, as stubborn as ever."

"I'll say."

"You don't have to agree with me!"

The limousine pulled into a parking lot, passed a group of teenagers licking ice-cream cones, paused at a supermarket for a procession of casually dressed shoppers pushing grocery baskets and then halted in front of the cookie shop.

Anne peeked out the window. As she'd suspected, everyone in the parking lot was staring at the limousine.

The driver came around and opened her door. As Anne stepped out, she found Jason at her side, looking quite at home in his tuxedo.

"Shall we?" He offered his arm.

"Indeed we shall." Anne knew her face was probably as bright red as her dress, but she held her head high as they swept into the store.

After all, Jason might be right. Suppose they *didn't* have chocolate-chip cookies in Paris?

Epilogue

"Why do you think she's crying?"

In the lamplight, Anne regarded Jason with red-rimmed eyes. Cradled in her arms, two-month-old Beth was howling with scarcely a pause for breath, her little round face screwed into a mask of misery.

Jason glanced at the clock. Oh, Lord, almost four o'clock, and Beth had been crying on and off since midnight. He huddled deeper into his bathrobe against the chilly November night.

"I suppose you fed her?"

Anne nodded impatiently. "And I tried the pacifier, but she spit it out. And I burped her, and I played her music box."

"Did you try sitting her up in the infant seat? That calms her down sometimes." Jason couldn't suppress a yawn. Two months without a single night of uninterrupted sleep. He wondered if he and Anne should take turns spending the night at a motel.

"I tried it. Besides, that was last week. This week, she screams at the sight of the thing." Anne's eyelids began to droop, and Jason immediately felt guilty. At least he didn't have to sit there for an hour and feed Beth twice a night.

"We could bring her into bed with us. . . ."

"If she's still screaming in my arms, why should she stop just because she's in our bed?"

That made sense. "I suppose if I pointed out that you're the doctor and you ought to know what to do, I might be in danger of my life?"

Anne didn't have to reply. Her fierce glare was enough of an answer.

"Wait a minute." Stifling a yawn, Jason searched his memory. Unfortunately, his brain didn't function very well at four o'clock in the morning. "I seem to recall there's something else that works."

"Not playing the radio. That was only good the first few days, when she missed the hospital nursery." Anne looked down in dismay at the still-yowling baby. "And to think, she looks like a perfect angel when she's sleeping. Oh, Jason, I know this isn't her fault, it's just her immature digestive system, but..."

"Walking," he said.

"I beg your pardon?"

"The motion of walking. And maybe some fresh air. That *might* work." Jason stretched, feeling the muscles knotting up in his back as he contemplated a future as sleepless as the immediate past. "How well do you like our neighbors?"

"I hardly know them."

"Thank goodness," he said.

Ten minutes later, with clothes thrown on hastily and hair still tangled from lying sleepless in bed, Jason and Anne let themselves out the door. Beth had subsided to whining with an occasional screech, but she looked as though she was working her way back up to a full-fledged tantrum.

Jason shifted the baby's weight so she lay securely in his arms, and they set out along the sidewalk. Sure enough, wails cut through the night, and he sped up his pace. Maybe if he went fast enough, they'd be out of sight before the neighbors were thoroughly awakened.

"I feel like a criminal," Anne admitted as she lengthened her stride to match his. "Could we be arrested for disturbing the peace or something?"

"It certainly isn't child abuse," Jason muttered. "More like parent abuse."

They walked faster. Beth took a deep breath, groaned loudly and fell silent.

Jason's ears continued to ring for several seconds. He realized that his entire body was tensed, waiting for the howls to resume. But his daughter lay yawning in his arms, trying her best to stay awake but losing the battle.

"Amazing." Anne jammed her hands into her sweater pockets as she paced beside him. "Where did you learn that trick?"

"Deanie's kid." Jason smiled. His little cousin Alexander was two years old now and a bright, inquisitive boy.

"I hear he swallowed half the contents of his parents' medicine cabinet and had to be rushed to the hosptial," Anne said. "Fortunately, he threw most of it up on his own."

"How on earth did he get into the medicine cabinet?"

"He pulled out the drawers in the bathroom counter and made stairs out of them."

That won't happen to us, Jason told himself as they turned a corner. His steps slowed for a moment and Beth began to whimper, so he sped up again.

He would put a latch on every conceivable cabinet and drawer in the house. There would be gates at the top and bottom of the stairs, and he'd lock his photographic chemicals so well even a commando force couldn't break them out.

There was only one thing wrong—he'd been sure he could outmaneuver a crying baby, too. Only it hadn't worked out that way, had it?

Jason forced himself to stop worrying and pay attention to his surroundings. How beautiful the night was, crisp and full of stars. Maybe there was something to be said for staying up until four in the morning.

Beside him, Anne stumbled with weariness. He'd forgotten that, while he could sleep late, she had to be at the hospital first thing.

As soon as they were sure Beth was sound asleep, they staggered home. Laying her gently in the bassinet and observing the sweep of dark lashes against the chubby cheek, Jason thought, *our little girl.*

Beside him, Anne shrugged off her sweater. "I'm going to bed."

"I'll be with you in a minute."

He tucked the crocheted blanket over Beth's little body—the blanket had been handmade by Anne's mother—and stood there for a moment watching her breathe.

It seemed like only yesterday they'd come back from Paris. Anne had fallen in love with its broad boulevards and the tang of excitement in the air. Jason had never seen her look more alive—and he'd never been happier.

Adjusting to marriage had been occasionally frustrating but exhilarating nevertheless. And then had come Anne's pregnancy. She'd gone through all the symptoms, from morning sickness to swollen feet. "Now I know why my patients grumble so much," she'd told him one night as he massaged her aching arches.

Jason had done his best to make things easy for her. There'd been plenty of time to keep up with the housework and cooking—he'd become rather possessive of the kitchen and rarely allowed her to cook even when she offered to. And he'd begun a short-term project, a photo essay for a prestigious magazine about the foster-grandparents program at a nearby retirement home.

Anne's medical knowledge hadn't made her delivery any easier. Despite Jason's attempts to assist with her breathing exercises, she'd moaned in a most un-Anne-like manner. And then out came Beth, beautiful, crying, red-faced Beth. Their daughter.

That night, as Anne slept, Jason went to the nursery and held the baby. Almost instantly, he'd felt a special bond with the little girl.

The first few weeks at home had been confusing, exhausting and delightful. And then Beth had figured out how to scream.

Jason had stripped the library of child-care books, and every one of them said the same thing: nobody really knew why babies cried, and all you could do was hang on until the magic age of three months, when the crying stopped. Although, one book added darkly, some babies had colic for a few months longer.

"Jason?" He looked up to see Anne in her nightgown. "Aren't you coming to bed? I miss you."

"Right away." But he stood there for a minute, just looking at Anne. God, she was beautiful. Every woman in the world ought to have exactly that rebellious lick of hair sticking up where she'd lain on it wrong and that hint of dark circles under the eyes and that forgotten cloth diaper pinned to her shoulder and those laugh lines touching her mouth.

"Let's go," said Jason, and took his wife to bed.